THE TREASURE OF DEAD MAN'S CHEST

by Roger L. Johnson

Commander, U.S. Navy (Ret.)

iPicturebooks

Habent Sua Fata Libeli

iPicturebooks
1230 Park Avenue, 9a
New York, New York 10128
Tel: 212-427-7139 • Fax: 212-860-8852
bricktower@aol.com • www.BrickTowerPress.com

Library of Congress Cataloging-in-Publication Data

Johnson, Roger L.
The Treasure of Dead Man's Chest, The Sequel to Treasure Island

ISBN-13: 978-1-87696-328-6, Trade Paper

Library of Congress Control Number: 2010934200
Fiction/Suspense, Adult/General
Historical/Adventure, Pirates

First iBooks ebook Edition

July 2010

Dedication

I dedicate this work to my soul mate, Elizabeth. She has been a dear mother to our children and a faithful for forty-four years. I thank her for her unending love, patience, and support while I wrote this novel.

Acknowledgement

I thank Bruce T. Paddock for his expert help in editing and fine-tuning this; my first novel.

Cover art courtesy of the Library of Congress:

Vue d'optique showing naval battle during Revolutionary War between John Paul Jones of the Bonhomme Richard and Capt. Richard Pearson of the British naval vessel Serapis, Sept. 22, 1779.

Preface

They say that the salt content of seawater is identical to that of our blood. Maybe that explains why so many of us are drawn to the sea and the wonderful stories it has spawned over the centuries. One of those stories fascinated most of us as children and still holds a special place in our hearts. If you share my love for adventure, then perhaps, like me, you've wondered after that classic threesome; the lice-infested maroon Ben Gunn, the courageous Bristol lad Jim Hawkins, and that most famous of all pirates, the softhearted cutthroat Long John Silver. Did they really? And if they did, what happened to them after their legendary eighteenth-century adventure? I believe I found the answer to those questions during the summer of 1982, when I chanced upon the hand-written transcript of a 1777 Royal Navy Admiralty Court of Inquiry that dealt with the attack and near-sinking of HMS Wasp, a fourth-rate British man-of-war, near Andros Island in the Bahamas. There were dozens of similar investigations made by the Royal Navy, but none with the significance of the questioning of Lieutenant Desmond R. Roberts.

I was in London that summer to attend a NATO-sponsored leadership symposium for command-grade military officers. Since I had arrived early at Whitehall, three days before the first session, I had the entire weekend to collect gifts and keepsakes for my wife and three children. My elder son had asked that I do some research for a term paper he was writing, so a few minutes before one in the afternoon, on Friday, I signed into the search room of the House of Lords Record Office in the southern section of old London.

My son's term paper was on relations between the United States and England following World War I, and he had become frustrated with the lack of information in our local libraries. My search for the raw material he needed began with the Parliamentary proceedings of December, 1918, the month following the allied and central powers' signing of the armistice.

The transcript of Lieutenant Roberts's testimony measured seventy pages and was misfiled between the February and March, 1919, Parliamentary records. The cover page was embossed with the Royal Navy seal, and it was dated 5 April, 1777. The knot in the thin blue ribbon that bound the neat stack of parchment was crushed in such a way that it was very probable that the transcript had not been disturbed since its writing. Naturally I became curious, but it was not until the fifth page that I began to realize what I had discovered. In his defense, Lieutenant Roberts had requested that a seaman's ballad be entered into evidence. The name of the song was, "Fifteen Men on the Dead Man's Chest."

In the few hours available to me before the search room closed, I managed to read the entire document, and make notes of the major events it described. The chief witness in the case was one Desmond R. Roberts, a lieutenant and mid-grade officer on the ill-fated man-of-war HMS Wasp. Although many of his fellow crewmembers survived the assault, Lieutenant Roberts was the only man able to identify the pirate captain who had attacked his warship.

What was most amazing about the document was that in a short section near the beginning, Lieutenant Roberts described a series of events that matched in nearly every detail a pirate story I had read as a child. The transcript also provided a concise record of a great American naval hero's movements during a hitherto unknown twenty months of his life, and explained how he overcame several tremendous obstacles to obtain one of the very first Colonial Navy commissions. The man was John Paul Jones, a Scotsman and fugitive from King George III.

After comparing the dates, places, and events Lieutenant Roberts had described, I became convinced that he was the very Jim Hawkins of Robert Louis Stevenson's novel Treasure Island. This conclusion, however, was not based entirely upon the transcript. In my subsequent research, I discovered that retired Commander Desmond R. Roberts had married one Christiana Osbourne of Edinburgh, Scotland, the same town where Francis Osbourne was born nearly a hundred years later. It was a common practice for women to keep journals, and then pass them on to their daughters. In 1880, while Robert Louis Stevenson was in San Francisco, California, he met and married Francis Osbourne. I believe Francis inherited Christiana's journals, and Robert used them as the inspiration for his classic pirate novel, just as I have used the Admiralty's transcript for this present novel.

As I checked out of the search room that Friday evening, I told the Clerk of the Records, a Mr. Cobb, about the misfiled transcript and asked if I might borrow it for the weekend, promising to return it the following Monday after my first NATO session. He told me that if it were up to him, he would be glad to oblige, but, "the '67 Public Records Act only allows for the reading of these older documents, not their removal or copying." He did, however, agree to hold the transcript aside for me. But when I returned Monday afternoon, there was only a note from the clerk informing me that the transcript had been "collected by two gentlemen from the Admiralty."

I can only speculate as to why the transcript was taken. It may have been the Royal Navy's desire to keep a certain questionable incident aboard the Wasp from becoming public. According to Lieutenant Roberts's testimony, two weeks prior to the attack on his ship, one of the midshipmen lost his life during some horseplay with several of his mates. The ship's captain singled out two of the ensigns who had been hazing the cadet and accused them of murder. After a quicker-than-normal court martial, they were hanged. Not only did this action violate Admiralty law, but there was compelling evidence in Lieutenant Roberts's testimony that the captain had had a personal vendetta against the two, not to mention several of the other officers.

I have not seen the transcript since that Friday afternoon in London, and my letters of inquiry continue to elicit the same response: "The document you cite in your letter of 29 January, 1983, is not available at this office, nor is there any record of it having been held by the Royal Navy at any time."

Unless I have been duped by a cleverly conceived hoax—and I sincerely doubt that I have—I present to you what I believe is the entire story of Long John Silver, and the only true account of John Paul Jones's movements during those missing twenty months; and this from the Royal Navy Lieutenant who was kidnapped and forced to watch the destruction of his ship, and then to walk the decks of the treasure ship where he later learned the complete tale from three of the pirates who manned it during its final voyage.

I have included, from notes and memory, a portion of the Admiralty transcript as my first and last chapters. While the historical personages were identified in the transcript, the names of Mr. Stevenson's characters do not appear. I have, of course, changed their names as appropriate in my story so that they coincide with the characters in the novel Treasure Island, as well as in A.D. Howden Smith's prequel to that tale, Porto Bello Gold.

It is a complicated story of piracy, politics, greed, and lost love; and of how one man was able to manipulate the lives of hundreds of patriots and pirates in his attempt to attain a King's ransom in buried treasure. You may notice, as I did, that Lieutenant Roberts's testimony describes a great number of coincidences. This disturbed me until I realized that the world was much smaller back in 1775, just prior to the American Revolution. Merchants knew every other merchant of stature, just as statesmen and sea captains knew their important counterparts. Stories of the famous and infamous spread throughout the world as quickly as the winds pushed a brigantine to a far shore or a horse galloped across the countryside.

As you set your sails and cast off your last line for this complicated armchair adventure, my hope is that you sail before fair winds and following seas. If I have stretched or compressed the truth slightly, I beg your indulgence. I was only in possession of the transcript for a very short time. Besides, without a certain degree of journalistic elasticity, my story would simply be a dry expansion of Desmond Roberts's testimony.

I leave you with your battle cry:

THE ARMCHAIR PIRATE
The meeker the man, the more pirate he be,
Snug in his armchair, far from the sea.
He has all the fun and none of the woes,
Masters the ladies and scuttles his foes.
His armchair's his ship and reclined his position,
As he cheats the hangman, hellfire, and perdition.

Roger L. Johnson
Commander, US Navy (retired)

Prologue

The Royal Navy Admiralty Board of Inquiry; called together at the direction of the First Lord of the Admiralty, John Montagu, Fourth Earl of Sandwich, for the purpose of investigating the attack and near-sinking of His Majesty's Ship, the Man-of-War Frigate Wasp, and the death of its Commanding Officer, Commander Alexander Stevens; the Ship's Surgeon, Lieutenant Benjamin Cooper; seven of the ship's officers and forty-three crew members, on or about 13 June, in the year of our Lord 1775 near Andros Island in the West Indian Colonies.

Members of this Board of Inquiry are Commodore Henry Stewart, Commander James Reynolds, Commander Abraham Arnold, Lieutenant Christopher James, and I, Commodore Anton Fairchild as Chairman.

Testifying before this Board of Inquiry is Lieutenant James Andrew Hawkins, R.N., who recently returned to the Royal Navy following a period of imprisonment for eighteen months in the Colony of Georgia.

Following, is the complete transcript of the hearing begun on 3 April 1777 at the Admiralty Offices in London, Whitehall, England. Proceedings recorded by Benjamin Hewett, Yeoman First Class, R.N.

Fairchild: Lieutenant Hawkins, before these hearings begin, I wish to inform you that you are not yet charged with any specific crime against the King of England, his subjects, the Royal Navy, nor against any officer or seaman of your last assignment, the H.M.S. Wasp. The purpose of today's questioning is to determine the details leading to the attack upon your ship by the Dutch merchantman Silver Cloud. The survivors of H.M.S. Wasp have already told this board what they witnessed that day, but they were unable to testify to several issues, including the identity of the captain of the attacking ship, to what port he sailed after the attack, and finally, the verification of your Executive Officer's claim that certain dispatches received shortly before the attack were false and possibly influenced the fate of H.M.S. Wasp.

Because of the highly sensitive nature of the matters to be discussed at these hearings, the Board is pleased that you have agreed not to be represented by a Public Solicitor. You are however, cautioned that if the Board deems it necessary to stop the hearings in order to prefer formal charges against you, that you immediately seek legal counsel at that time. Do you still wish to continue this hearing without a Solicitor present?

Hawkins: Yes I do, sir.

Fairchild: Very well. Please approach the bench and surrender your sword. According to the previous testimony of several of your fellow officers, and especially the Executive Officer and Lieutenant Junior Grade Montgomery Mason, you were the only member of the inspection party to meet with and speak to the captain of the Silver Cloud. Therefore, keeping in mind the above previous testimony of your shipmates, I will begin the questioning by asking you to describe the exact circumstances surrounding the attack on H.M.S. Wasp on 13 June 1775.

Hawkins: Well, sir, begging the Board's indulgence, I'm not certain if that's the right place to begin.

Stewart: You did see the Wasp attacked, didn't you, Lieutenant Hawkins?

Hawkins: Yes I did, sir. I was in the Silver Cloud's main cabin, standing next to the pirate captain and his two mates. I saw the whole thing.

Stewart: Then why the uncertainty?

Hawkins: Because there's so much more to it than simply the attack.

Arnold: So much more?

Hawkins: Well, for one thing, sir, the Silver Cloud was not a Dutch merchantman, as the others have told you.

Stewart: Oh? And just what was she?

Hawkins: She was a disguised twenty-gun Colonial frigate.

Stewart: That can't be! (To the board) According to our records, the first Colonial Navy fighting ships, thirteen of them as I remember, were not built until early last year as a result of their Act of 13 December 1775.

Fairchild: Commodore Stewart is correct, Lieutenant Hawkins. There were no Colonial frigates in existence at the time the Wasp was attacked.

Hawkins: The Silver Cloud was built in '74 in Charles Town, sir, at the Forrestal Shipping Company. Several last minute modifications suited her to her secret mission a year later.

Fairchild: Secret mission? (to James) Why wasn't I informed of this at yesterday's briefing?

James: I had no idea, sir, until last evening—after the hearings closed. The report from Lloyd's came by courier and there's no record in their registry of a ship by that name.

Fairchild: (to Stewart) Then perhaps we should back our sails for a moment and allow Lieutenant Hawkins to tell his story from the beginning.

Stewart: (to Fairchild) If you wish, sir. (to Hawkins) Go ahead, Mister Hawkins. Tell us about the "much more" you spoke of a moment ago.

Hawkins: Well, for one thing, there was Captain Silver.

James: (to Fairchild) That's the pirate mentioned at last week's hearing.

Fairchild: (to James) Yes, I remember. (to Hawkins) Didn't he have something to do with a treasure several years back—Flint's Fist, I believe it was called?

Hawkins: No, sir. That's the name the Walrus's men called the treasure map. And yes, John Silver was very much involved. When I was twelve years old, helping my Mother run the "Admiral Benbow" inn on the road to Bristol, I came into possession of John Flint's map showing the location of several treasures buried on a small island. A good friend of my recently departed father, a Doctor Livesy, led a voyage to recover Flint's share of the treasure in '64. The one-legged pirate, Long John Silver, signed on as ship's cook and fooled us into hiring the rest of his pirates as our crew. None of us suspected anything of course, not until I overheard his mutinous plans as we were nearing Spyglass.

Fairchild: Spyglass?

Hawkins: It's called by several names; Spyglass, the Rendezvous, Treasure Island and Flint's Island, sir.

Fairchild: This treasure—tell us more about it, Mister Hawkins.

Hawkins: The seafaring man I got the treasure map from—a Captain Billy Bones—explained it to me. Flint had been burying treasures on Spyglass for several years before he and his crew buried the 700,000 pounds in gold, silver bars and jewels from a Spanish treasure ship. Captain Bones sang a seaman's ballad at the inn every day for several months before he died. I wrote the words down. (Lt. Hawkins hands paper to Commodore Fairchild) None of us realized it at the time, but the second verse of this seaman's ballad tells of a greater portion of the original treasure—the portion John Flint had never touched.

Fairchild: Yeoman Hewett, enter this in the record. (to the Board) We'll take a ten-minute recess while the Yeoman finishes.

DEAD MAN'S CHEST

Through winds of treachery a bloody tale's told,
Of Captain Rip Rap and Porto Bello Gold.
How he left Flint an' Silver on Spyglass to wait,
While he took Saint Trinidad's pieces of eight.

Buckets of blood were spilled in the hold,
Flint accused Rip Rap, "The treasure ye've stol'd.
Ye took it to the Island called Dead Man's Chest,
Where ye laid it by fer half a scores rest."

Flint killed Rip Rap an' on Spyglass did hide,
O'er half a million where six men died.
Bones took the map an' to Bristol did run,
An' left Flint's bones to bleach in the sun.

A curse on the jewels, the pearls and the gold,
A curse on the pirates what's honor was sold.
A curse on the Yorkm'n what refuses to tell,
Of the treasure laid by—may he rot in hell.

(Chorus)

Fifteen men on the Dead Man's Chest,
Yo-ho-ho, and a bottle of rum.
Drink and the devil had done for the rest,
Yo-ho-ho, and a bottle of rum.

Fairchild: So you and this Captain Silver retrieved the entire 700,000 pounds worth of treasure from Spyglass?

Hawkins: All but the silver bars, sir. And as I found out during my brief time on the Silver Cloud, there was also a small chest of jewels hidden in the same cave.

Fairchild: Captain Bones's ballad tells quite a story, Mister Hawkins. Can you tell us more about the other portion of the treasure?

Hawkins: Well, sir, as I was saying, in '54, Flint buried his share of the treasure on his private island, and Captain Murray buried the rest—around 800,000 pounds worth—with the help of four friends, on the Dead Man's Chest.

Arnold: Dead Man's Chest?

Hawkins: It's actually Buck Island, sir. It's a desolate piece of dirt just off the north coast of Saint Croix, near Christiansted.

Fairchild: This Captain Murray. Would he happen to be the Captain Rip Rap of your ballad?

Hawkins: Yes, sir. Next to Long John Silver, Andrew Murray was perhaps the world's greatest manipulator. As I found out from Captain Silver and his two mates on the Silver Cloud, Murray and his consort, Colonel O'Donnell were Jacobites and hoped to use their part of the treasure to help finance Bonnie Prince Charlie's return to the throne. O'Donnell used his position and influence with Spain to ascertain when the Santissima Trinidad would sail, and sent word by sloop so Captain Murray could effect his intercept and attack.

Arnold: How ironic. If the reports we've received concerning the cannons are true, it would mean the treasure would have ended up being used against the Hanovers rather than in defense of them.

Fairchild: This pirate—Long John Silver—what happened to him back in '64, after your voyage to Flint's Island?

Hawkins: He escaped, sir. The maroon we rescued from Spyglass—Ben Gunn was his name—let Silver go while the rest of us were off the ship. It wasn't until after the Wasp was attacked in '75 and I was taken prisoner by Captain Silver that I learned the whole story. Silver was always one who enjoyed bragging, and he and the other two spent many evenings aboard the treasure ship discussing their adventures.

Arnold: Who were those "other two"?

Hawkins: An orphan from Tortuga named Henry Morgan and the bastard son of John Flint—Joshua Smoot.

Arnold: Correct me if I'm wrong, Lieutenant, but is this Board to assume that everything you know about the incident with the Wasp came from these three pirates?

Hawkins: Most of it—yes. The rest comes from several loyalists in the Colonies who are acquainted with...

Fairchild: (interrupts Hawkins and addresses Arnold) We can discuss those two later, Mister Arnold. (to Hawkins) For the sake of a sequential record of the events leading up to the attack, please get back to this Captain Silver and his escape.

Hawkins: Well, sir, as I was saying, after we loaded what we could of Flint's treasure, Captain Smollet became concerned that the three pirates who had escaped into the jungles of Spyglass might attempt another attack, so we left the silver bars behind and sailed from that place to the nearest port where John Silver could be tried and executed. Except for the maroon—Benjamin Gunn, who was left on board to guard John Silver—we all went ashore to purchase provisions and hire a new crew to help us sail the Hispaniola back to England. The officers met the Captain of an English man-of-war and went aboard his ship for several hours to report our recent misfortunes on Spyglass. By the time we got back to the Hispaniola, John Silver had taken one of the ship's boats and was long gone. I had a strong notion he would try something like that, because he kept telling me we'd meet again someday. I believed him, sir.

Fairchild: You believed him, even though you knew him to be a mutinous cutthroat and liar.

Hawkins: Yes, I did. You see, every time Captain Silver confided something special, he would drop the language of the bilges and speak the King's English as properly as you and me. When he was with the other pirates, his language...

Fairchild: Get back to his escape, Lieutenant Hawkins.

Hawkins: Well sir, according to Long John Silver...

Chapter 1

"Damn yer hands, Ben!" The water cask crashed into the small boat next to the old pirate's foot. He cocked his head back and raised a fist. "That one came close to goin' clean through me planks, ya sun-addled maroon!"

"Forgive me!" Up on the deck of the ship, Ben Gunn held tight on the rope. He was as strong as a monkey of equal size, but the years alone on Spyglass without the benefit of cheese and flour had reduced his bulk to less than eighty pounds.

John Silver pried at the cask's lashings. "Belay! Slack the damn line, Ben, so's I can set the cursed thing free!" Silver's leathery fingers twisted at the large iron hook, but even though black grease coated its rust, Ben's continued tension on the halyard kept the hook set firmly in the knotted hemp.

"Are ya daft, man?" Silver gave up on the hook to see why Ben had failed to slack the line. Thirty feet above the water and twirling in the evening sky like a marionette caught in a gale hung Ben Gunn, snatched up to within three feet of the pulley, rising and falling with the gentle swells that lapped against the old ship. The water cask outweighed the poor maroon by fifty pounds.

"Pray don't be unhookin' me yet, Cap'n Silver!" The old man clung to the halyard for dear life. "Not 'till I can shinny down to the rail!"

John Silver gave a hearty laugh. "I don't want'a be tellin' you yer business, Ben, but if it were me, I'd throw a couple turns about that rail fer the next load. That's unless ya don't mind bein' hauled up again and pulled clean through that block!"

Ben slid down the hoisting line toward the rail. With each of the poor maroon's spins about the untwisting hemp, Silver laughed louder and louder, until tears were streaming down his sunburned cheeks.

"That's near the best show I've seen in years, Ben Gunn!" He wiped his eyes dry with a sleeve. "But time's a slippin', an' my speedy escape'll prove far more precious to me throat than the good this laughter does me innards."

Silver's wooden sea chest was the next-to-last load. It contained the bag of gold coin he'd liberated from the ship's lazarette during the night.

John Silver raised his voice with his usual scolding tone. "Don't be forgettin' me crutch!" Ben finally hooked the rail with a foot and pulled himself back to the deck. "It's layin' next to the hatch cover where me victual basket be restin'!"

"Aye, Cap'n Silver!" With the hook finally released from the water cask, Ben retrieved the object of his consternation and snagged the bindings Silver had tied to his sea chest. As ordered, Ben pushed the pirate captain's trusty length of mahogany under the barrel hitch and then took the recommended wrap about the rail. With a grunt and several kicks, John Silver's chest was set free in the air above the waiting pirate. Like the water casks before it, the chest began to spin in the humid air as the hemp untwisted under the strain.

"Easy there!" Silver held up his hands in defense and watched as his trusted crutch begin slipping from its lashings. With each rotation of the chest, the sharpened metal spur thumped the weathered side of the old Hispaniola, until a dozen horizontal lines were scribed at equal intervals from the deck to just above the water line.

With the skill of a jousting knight, Silver thrusted and parried until he finally caught the twirling stick and eased this most precious load over his boat.

"Steady there, mate, an' give me some slack!" Silver grabbed the overfilled chest and guided it down into the boat just as gently as he would assist a fat woman into a church pew in August.

"Oof!" Silver pushed the rectangular chest up next to the mast step amidships, snug between the two water casks. He turned and studied the shoreline and the dock at Puerta Plata for any sign of the returning crew. All was quiet.

John Silver whispered to himself. "If Cap'n Smollet lays 'is 'ands on me hide, I'll be swingin' from that same yard what me goods been hoisted from, an' before week's end, I'd wager." It was taking the old maroon far too long to make his knots, so Silver set to urging him with a new string of threats.

"An' I lay it wouldn't go too good for you neither, Ben Gunn, to be discovered with yer prisoner at the water line, with you bein' on watch o'er him, an' all!"

With a kick from the old maroon's bony foot, the pirate captain's victual basket swung out over the water and began its unsure descent. Silver reached up to stop it from crashing into the ship's side, and then eased it down just aft of the water casks and sea chest.

"Master Silver!" Ben loosed the old pirate's hawser and threw it down into the small craft. "Would ya be tellin' old Ben once more why I be lettin' ya loose?" His memory was shorter than it used to be. As he waited for Silver's answer, he pulled a crawling tick from his chest. "When the good cap'n returns, he'll be askin' me where ye be, on account as he were of a mind to hang ya, says he. Cap'n Smollet won't be takin' kindly to you bein' gone, says I."

"Why, you tell 'im the God's truth, Ben, 'cause that's what it be!" Silver set his oars into their locks one at a time. "You tell 'im it's to preserve their bloody lives! You tell 'im that, Ben Gunn!" Silver shook his head in wonder at how the old man had been able to survive alone on Spyglass for so many years. "Curse me fer a lubber if I wouldn't be slittin' their throats one by one if I be left onboard fer 'alf a fortnight. Why, in no time at all, there'd be only you, me, and the ship's boy, Jimmy Hawkins, to sail this 'ere ship and that treasure back to Bristol!"

Silver shoved with his crutch and waved to his old friend. Then he spat in his palms and adjusted his oars for their first sweep toward freedom. On the deck above him, the once-again abandoned maroon scratched his throat, trying to remember his story for Captain Smollet.

"That be the truth, Ben Gunn!" John Silver pulled toward the Hispaniola's bow. "An' knowin' Cap'n Smollet as I do, he'll be relieved to not have one such as me tangled in his riggin' no more!" Silver lifted his hat high in the evening sky and called out one last time to his mate. "Farewell, Ben Gunn. Our wakes'll cross again some day, you can lay to that!"

After several strong pulls, Silver feathered the oars and twisted about for one last look for his captors. There was no movement on the docks or aboard the man-of-war. The light breeze that tickled the dark waters of Puerta Plata Bay brought a rich mixture of smells to the pirate's nostrils—mostly the stench of low tide and the rotting pilings, but also the pungent odors of freshly cooked meals and the perfumes of the ladies—a delight John Silver had been without for much too long.

Satisfied that his escape had gone undetected, Silver turned back to resume his pull northward. As he set his oars for another bight, something in the dark waters toward shore caught his eye. A single, slate-gray fin fully eighteen inches tall sliced through the dark water, distorting the reflection of the town and dark hills behind it. Silver watched with interest as the shark circled in a wide arc toward the stern of his small craft. At ten feet it slowed its speed, and then it stopped next to the larboard oar.

"Well, well. Could it be you?" It had been nearly forty years since the pirate's severed leg had been thrown to the sharks. He reached up and tipped his hat to the predator. Then, as if the creature recognized the human as an equal, it nudged his oar with its snout, much the same as a pet dog would give an encouraging push on its master's musket during the hunt. With the salute properly returned, the great shark gave a single thrust of its mighty tail and turned about to resume its tireless search for food.

Two hours later and five miles beyond the last gun emplacements of the Spanish town, Silver began to look for a place to beach his small craft for the night.

Should make Tortuga tomorrow, if I get an easterly. He came about and pulled to the mouth of a small stream. A twenty-yard stretch of white sand and low-hanging palms would serve him well for the night.

Daybreak found the old pirate pulling his way northwestward just outside the surf line and half a mile from where he had made landfall the night before. The wind was calm, but at four bells—ten o'clock—a gentle breeze began to blow from his starboard. Pleased with his good fortune, he raised the small lateen sail and trimmed it for a starboard reach. The canvas bellied and filled with the pressure of the wind. It was a welcome relief for his blistered hands and sore back to let the wind finally do his work.

By noon and six hours at sea, the nagging soreness in his lower back had turned to resentment. The ever-present ghost pains in his missing left foot acted like a rudder to his thought processes, steering his mind back to that first time at sea.

He was no more than a lad, a powder monkey on the Queen Ann's Revenge under the unpredictable and bloodthirsty Captain Teach. Old Teach—or Blackbeard, as most of his victims called him—chose young John Silver to stay topside that day during a beam engagement with an Indian pirate named Yamar Booheesh—one of the ablest foes with which the old scoundrel had traded hot iron. Drummond claimed it was for luck that he kept at least one of the powder monkeys at his side during battle. The two ships had traded broadsides for several minutes when a ball crashed through the starboard rail of the quarterdeck. There was an explosion of splinters and screams that sent the nine-year-old John Silver spinning through the air like a rag doll without its oats. When he landed next to the lee rail, his left leg was severed above the knee.

Silver mumbled. "Good luck, me backside!" A shift in the wind brought the sail across at him, and the boom gave him a vicious smack on the left temple. He gave the rough piece of wood an angry push and corrected both his course and his trim.

He raised a fist and called across the sea at Blackbeard's ghost. "Wasn't much luck for Ezra Pew neither!" Ezra Pew was a few years senior to Silver and had earned himself a place at the starboard guns. Moments after Silver's leg had been thrown to the sharks, Pew poked his head out through the gun port to swab his cannon of unspent powder. He caught a face full of fire that blinded him for the rest of his natural life—until his untimely death at the Admiral Benbow Inn. "Blinded the poor wretch, it did. But blind as he be, I never seen a man steer a ship straighter nor bring a prize to port quicker than he. Just like a merchant with a bonus ridin' on an early arrival."

Silver surveyed the surrounding islands, turned his craft slightly to windward and trimmed his sail to remove the luff. He reached down and massaged the tender nerves at the end of the mutilated stump.

The sun passed its zenith and his stomach gave out an insubordinate groan, reminding him that it was past his feeding time. He tore a palm-sized piece of hard bread from a moldy loaf that lay in the victual basket and dipped its corner in the sea.

"A cook!" He chewed the softened bread. "That's all they'll allow a cripple like me to be!" A shadow skipped across the water cask and danced lightly up the sail to meet its author at the masthead—a brown gull intent on a share of the pirate's meal. John Silver liked animals, and the bird seemed to know it, for no sooner had Silver begun to hum his favorite sea chantey than the gull glided to a light-footed landing on his lee gunwale, just beyond his reach.

"Welcome aboard, me little lady! Does ye wish a ride west to Tortuga with old Long John Silver?" The gull acknowledged his question with a tilt of its head and a twitch of its wings. It surveyed the contents of the boat. "Be ye hungry, me lass?" He pulled a small scrap from his lunch and carefully laid it atop the basket.

The bird studied the morsel for a moment while she mustered her courage. When she was finally satisfied this human posed no threat, she hopped over the water cask, across Silver's sea chest and onto the victual basket, dispatching the offered bread in one bite.

"Does ya have it in ya to give yer host a thank you?" Silver's words had a scolding tone. "Well, what say ye?"

The gull tilted her head slightly at the human for a second time and let go a load of lime on the woven lid of the basket. Before Silver could prevent it, the excrement had run through the wicker and onto the contents within.

"Damn yer feathers!" Silver swung a backhand at the gull, catching her with a direct hit to her tail as she took wing.

"A curse out o' Egypt on ya, ye ungrateful daughter of a tavern hag!" He raised a fist at the fleeing begger. "You'll be back, I'll lay to that! And when ya touch down next time, it'll be me crutch to yer back, just like the turncoat, John Mary!"

Silver sailed on toward his destination for several more hours, brooding over the treasure of the Santissima Trinidad. His fingers tightened on the tiller and he yelled at the sky. "By all what's holy and unholy, I'll have that treasure some day or I be not Long John Silver!"

His fertile mind went back to the several plans that scampered about in his head. Perhaps I'll sail to New York and strike a bargain directly with the Yorkman. After all, it were me who helped him, his woman and them other two escape at Savannah. Maybe he'll draw me a map fer debt's sake. The old pirate slapped himself on the cheek. "Damn yer thoughts, John Silver. Ye're startin' ta sound as addled as Ben Gunn!"

***

The pickpockets of Bristol reasoned that if a man's neck would be stretched for a farthing, it might as well stretch for a whole purse full of gold. Driven to crime by starvation or the abuses of the law, many in the Caribbean likewise figured they might as well take a whole ship as a man's purse. Thusly, new names were added to "the account" of the Brotherhood of the Coast every day. In the 1600s, for the pirates of French and English extraction, the small island of Tortuga suited this new trade well. Not only were its hills abundant with streams, fruit and game, it was situated at the eastern gate of the most heavily traveled waterway between the Spanish Main and Europe, the Windward Passage.

Warehouses to store the pirate's swag and taverns to fulfill the lusts of their hearts sprang up on Tortuga like weeds. But now, in mid-June, 1764, as Long John Silver skirted its northern coast around Devil's Rock and into what was commonly called Buccaneer's Cove, there remained only the memory of this once-busy haven of rest.

"Where to land?" He made a quick survey of the cove. The old wooden pier where Blackbeard's crew had docked their boats was now a broken and scattered skeleton, with its bones sticking up as if it were trying to crawl from a watery grave. Silver chose a spot at mid-beach and steered for it, unaware of the battle that was about to unfold a short distance beyond, halfway to the tree line.

The rotted hulk of an old ship's boat lay at the high-water mark, half-filled with sand. Fifteen yards further up the beach lay a pile of dry palm fronds from which a large red and green crab began to creep forward into the hot afternoon sun. It turned its periscope eyes right and then left to scan the beach for its enemies—the three dogs that lived in the burned-out storehouses a hundred yards inland. They must be busy elsewhere! It crept forward a few more inches, then stopped for a moment to test the winds for scent. Much further and it would be committed to the mad dash for the safety of the water and the spiny coral that provided its room and board.

Nothing stirred. No enemy in sight…except for the two motionless emerald-green eyes of the young pirate, Henry Morgan, peering over the gunwale of the small sand-filled vessel. The lad's windswept orange hair danced from his scalp like the fires of hell themselves.

Patiently, the nine-year-old orphan watched his nemesis—Captain Claw, as he had named the creature—creep onto the deck of his imaginary ship, the Cobra. Inch by inch, the sea-devil scuttled forward in its characteristic sideways gait, until it stood next to the boy's mainmast, just three feet from Henry's hiding place. Suddenly, there was an explosion of curses and long orange hair. The cutlass-wielding buccaneer flew through the air to a perfect landing between the crab and the water's edge.

"Aha!" The lad's voice was low and mean—pirate-like. "At last we meet face to face, you bilge-sucking scum!" The surprised crab rose on its legs and spun to meet this unexpected foe, both claws held high and snapping in defiance.

"Ya thought yer broadside killed me, didn't ya?" Henry smacked the sand to the crab's left side with his cutlass—a carved mandrake root—blocking its escape. "And then ya sneaks aboard the Cobra to steal me treasure? Well…fer that ye'll pay dearly, Cap'n Claw!"

The panic-stricken crab swayed right and left for a moment and then made a dash for the boat. The boy was too quick. Again the boy's cutlass jabbed into its path. Bending low over his armored enemy, the lad took a deep breath and mustered all the bravado he possessed. "This time, by the gods, yer gonna stand an' fight!"

The crab quickly recognized its fate—that flight was no longer an option. With its large claws waving back and forth to meet each cruel thrust of its tormentor's weapon, the crab had now been forced to join this grizzly dance of death. Three pristine gulls stood on a section of the old pier watching the scene with detached interest—their wings twitching now and then in anticipation of a fine meal, should the battle follow its normal course.

"Raise that ugly claw to me once more and it'll be yer last, you barnacle-covered son-of-a-scab! I'll split ya starboard from larboard with me cutlass and send ya to torment yer father, the devil!"

Henry pinned his enemy to the hot sand with a bare foot, reached down and grabbed the extended right claw in his hand. With a quick twist, he wrenched it from the socket. Then, holding the claw and his mandrake root high, he threw back his head in triumph. "Ha! Ha! Ha! Morgan triumphs again!"

"Ahoy there!" The stem of John Silver's boat scraped over some sunken debris near the water's edge, and the boom of his sail pressed against his starboard shoulder.

Henry twisted about at the new voice.

"I say, lad! Ye wouldn't be of a mind to be helpin' an old landlubber ashore from his misery aboard this 'ere water craft, would ya? There be a sixpence ta sweeten' yer labors!"

The boy dropped his arms for a moment to watch the old man take the last sweep with his oars, which drove him onto the sand. "Make it a full shillin', Govn'r, an' I'll be carryin' yer sea chest up the beach to yonder inn, I will!" With Henry's foot off its back, the crab seized the moment to break into its best sideways gallop toward the security of the bay, its balance thrown off slightly by the missing claw.

"A shilling it be, lad!" Silver loosed his main sheet to luff his sail.

The boy started to run toward Silver's boat, but stopped for just a moment when he passed the escaping crab. With a snap of the wrist, the lad gave the hapless crab a single crack to its shell with the play cutlass. The crab stopped, cracked starboard from larboard, and bringing the three gulls diving to the sand to pick clean the newly exposed innards.

At water's edge, Henry grabbed the old pirate's hawser and tied it to a rusty, half-buried anchor.

"Aye!" The lad waded out to Silver's oarlock and studied the old man's belongings with a scavenger's eye. "Fer a silver shilling I be a right fine servant, Govn'r!"

John Silver reached out and touched the lad's red hair, causing the boy to jerk away. "Sorry, lad. I was just admirin' the color of yer hair."

"Cap'n Smoot says I'll make one o' the best powder monkeys he's got! Tells me 'cause of that—my red hair—that I'll have me own cutlass an' brace o' pistols before I be passin' puberty, whatever that is!"

Silver gave the boy one of his squint-eyed looks. "So, who might that be—Joshua Smoot?"

"He's a famous pirate! He was by here a fortnight past—tolt me I could join his crew after he finishes 'is business at Cuba. Somethin' 'bout freein' all the slaves and indentureds."

"A pirate, huh?" Silver pulled his dirk from its scabbard and touched it to the boy's stomach. "Tell me, lad. Do ya have the kidney ta gut a man fer his purse?"

Henry looked down at the blade. "Aye, an' I'd wear 'is ears 'bout me neck fer a right fine trophy too, I would!"

"And how are ye called, lad?"

"Morgan!" The boy thrust the mandrake root high in the air. "Henry Morgan's the name, Govn'r! An' it be common knowledge 'ere on Tortuga that I be the great-great-grandson of Sir Henry Morgan, the grandest pirate to ever sink a Spanish galleon or sack a city on the Main!"

As with most orphans on the tiny island, young Henry had assumed the surname of his favorite hero. There were other orphans named for Henry Avery, William Kidd, Calico Jack Rackham and several other legends of the Caribbean.

"Well, son of Henry Morgan, this old landlubber be missin' his larboard leg, so he'll be needin' a strong lad's help from his craft." Silver threw his crutch to the dry sand, sending the three ravenous gulls to the air for a brief moment and giving their dinner one last chance to drag its broken carcass to the water's edge. It never made it.

"Since I tolt ya my name, Govn'r, might ya be tellin' me yer's?"

Silver thought for a moment and then smiled. "I'm a wanted man—a highwayman it is—so I don't tell nobody my name."

Henry gave the old man a scowl.

"But since you're to be a pirate soon, I think I can trust you to keep my secret." Silver looked about the bay for a name. Since he didn't see anything promising, he thought of the scriptures. He leaned over and whispered, as if they were being watched. "Pottersfield…Judas Pottersfield."

"Might it be…Captain Pottersfield?"

"So ye've heard of me, have ya? Army Captain Pottersfield!"

Henry hadn't, but wanted in the worst way to please the old man. "Aye, but..."

"Famous in three colonies, I am!"

"What were it that took off yer leg, Cap'n?"

Silver gave the stump a rub. "When I were fightin' Indians in Florida with the Spaniards—a paid mercenary at the time—I were captured and tortured. The damn savages were gonna eat me, and started with me left leg."

The lad's eyes were as wide as doubloons. He whispered the words in reverence. "Did ya kill any of 'em—the ones what ate ya?"

"Aye—every one of the savages—with my leg still in their bellies." Silver slid his backside up and over the rail, and stepped down into the water. He hadn't stood for hours and had to hold onto the gunwale for a moment to gain his balance. "Tell me, Son-of-Morgan, where might a worn-out traveler be findin' a soft bunk, a bath and some landlubber's cookin'?"

"There be only one place left, Cap'n." Henry turned and pointed across the beach. "That be the Musket's Muzzle yonder."

The two-story brick structure stood alone among a growth of coconut palms. Its roof was shingled with Spanish tiles, and the ivy was so thick on its red brick walls that only the windows and doors showed through. The buildings to either side had long since been burned out or ravaged for their building materials.

"Innkeeper Smeeks hasn't been servin' much rum, what with the Walrus bein' gone so long, an' not many other ships makin' port since. But there's sure to be another ship pullin' in any day now, says Keeper Smeeks."

"The Walrus, ye say? That wouldn't be John Flint's old ship, would it?"

"Aye Cap'n, it be the very same ship what's been plyin' these 'ere waters fer close to two decades."

John Silver reached out and pulled Henry under his armpit for a temporary crutch. Amongst a chorus of grunts and curses from both of them, the old pirate gained the dry sand and retrieved his crutch.

Relieved to be free of the smelly old man, the boy backed toward the boat and brushed his long hair from his eyes. "Do ya know anybody on the Walrus?" The boy waded back to the oarlock and began wrestling the heavy sea chest toward the rail. With a string of obscenities that would make any seaman proud, he pulled it up onto the gunwale, turned and slid it onto his back.

"No...not a one of 'em." Silver chuckled as he watched the lad stomp and weave his way up the beach under the chest's crushing weight. Silver hopped to the porch alongside him and paused while the lad turned about and let the chest slip to the weathered planks.

"The Musket's Muzzle, Govn'r." Henry stood up and rubbed the pain from his lower back. "Standin' where she did when me namesake learnt his trade. Fer another shilling, I'll tell ya the whole history."

Silver gave a dismissive wave of his hand and hopped to the door for a look at the public room. "Can a landlubber book passage to King's Town in this place?"

Henry turned about and pointed at Silver's boat. "Aye, but if ya be bookin' passage fer Jamaica, what will ya be doin' with that worn out ship's boat yonder?"

Silver knew exactly what the lad had in mind. "Well, me hatin' the sea like I do, I hadn't thought much about it. Maybe I can find someone to purchase her."

"That piece of flotsam?" Henry had a fistful of coins saved up, but hardly enough to buy a fine craft like her. "Only a fool'd pay good money for such a hulk!"

"Aye." Silver gave an agreeing chuckle. "With the little I know of boats, I'd say she's 'bout ready to sink. Maybe some lad'll steal her durin' the night and save me the trouble o' hagglin' fer her price."

"Aye!" Henry surveyed the fine craft. "Hagglin' o'r a ship's boat be nothin' but a waste o' time fer a fine Indian fighter like you, Cap'n." The boy was thrilled with his good fortune. Captain Claw was finally dead, and with this new boat, he was no longer a landlubber. Soon as Cap'n Pottersfield's gone to his room, the boat goes 'round the point into Morgan's cove, it does! An' then she gets her new name. He reached down and fingered the chisel that hung like a dirk at his belt. The Cobra, cut with me own hand!

Silver turned about for another look inside the tavern. With the old man's attention diverted, Henry's admiration for his new vessel gave way to curiosity over the unusually heavy sea chest. The lock was of a common type—easily picked by the most dim-witted of the island's orphans. With a quick glance to make sure the captain was occupied elsewhere, Henry raised the lid and surveyed the contents. His eyes settled on the bag of gold coins.

Before he could pull away, Silver's stumped leg pushed down on the lid of the chest, capturing Henry's left arm at the elbow.

"So!" The pressure on the lid let up for a moment, allowing Henry to slide his arm free. But before he could duck out of the way, Silver's backhand caught him on the left side of his head, spinning him through the air to the hot sand next to the steps. He lay senseless for a moment—plenty of time for the old pirate to step off the porch and grab the lad by the long hair at the nape of his neck.

"So!" Silver whispered in the lad's bloody ear. "Little Henry Morgan wants a look-see in me chest, does 'e?" Silver gave a twist of his wrist, turning the little face about until the two were nose to nose.

It's been claimed that some people are so mean that they can put a curse on you with just a look. According to one story, John Silver's evil stare had gone beyond curses, actually fracturing a fine lady's china teapot from a distance of six spans. This was one of those looks. On top of it was the old seaman's foul breath and flecks of saliva that showered the boy's face.

"Aye, ye can look, Henry, but it'll be yer last!" The back edge of Silver's knife blade was now at the boy's throat.

"Oh Lordy!" Henry was certain his next words would be spent explaining his sins to Lucifer. "No sir, Cap'n Pottersfield! Henry Morgan 'as no business lookin' in no honest highwayman's personal belongin's, he don't!" With that, Silver threw the lad backwards to the sand.

Silver pointed back at the chest. "You've a burden to carry inside, if I recollect!"

Thankful for this second chance at living, Henry scrambled up onto the porch, hefted the chest onto his back and followed the strange one-legged man into the Muzzle and over to the innkeeper.

"A room for one, overlookin' the bay." Silver scrawled the false name in the desk ledger. Then he turned back to the waiting lad. "By the powers, boy, I trust ye've learned a lesson this 'ere day, 'bout which business that nose of yer's can be thrust into."

"Aye, Cap'n, an' I be obliged fer the lesson too." Henry caught the tossed shilling and backed out of the tavern to the safety of the beach.

**

A week later, the merchantman Belgium Hawk sailed into King's Town, past an anchored second-rate British man-o'-war, and tied up at the western end of the dock. John Silver was the first ashore, and he quickly made his way to the door of the Whore's Breath—one of many public houses on the waterfront. If a man wanted to make contacts or gain information, a busy tavern was his best choice. Silver dragged his sea chest into the public room by its arm-length lanyard and found himself a table near the galley that had a good view of the entrance. He ordered a pint of ale.

"Aye, she's Dutch all right." The seaman at the next table spoke with apparent authority to the others. He looked about the tavern and spotted John Silver. "You, there! You came in on her. Where's she bound for?"

Silver sat his tankard down and wiped the ale from his upper lip. "She sails for Cartagena within a fortnight, an' the master were tellin' me just this mornin' he'll be lookin' to replace a dozen of 'is crew 'afore she ships out." This last piece of information put the group into a lively discussion, leaving the old pirate to his own contemplations and the refreshing drink.

John Silver tilted his head back to drain his third tankard. He was beginning to feel the numbing effects of the cheap brew and humming a sailor's ballad when a large man stepped into the doorway. The newcomer was tall—over nineteen hands—with a military look about him. Silver lowered his head and studied the bottom of the ale-stained container while the man walked to the center of the pub and looked about.

"Barkeep!" After a moment, a little man in an apron scuttled from the kitchen. He reminded Silver of Henry Morgan's crab.

The little man gave his waist towel a nervous twist. "Here, Mister Noble!"

"Have you seen that son of mine?"

"No sir, Mister Noble. The lad hasn't been hereabouts fer nigh onto two days now. I'd check up at the boat yards if I were you, sir."

"Ah, yes, the yards!" The man made a quick survey of the men sitting about the tavern. It was the same collection of flotsam and jetsam—nobody he recognized. "If you see him talking to any of the men from that Dutchman out there, you get word to me right away, you hear?"

"As you please, sir." The little man gave another twist to his towel. "Has the lad run off again?"

"No, he hasn't." Noble's gaze stopped on the older man in the corner with the sea chest beside him. "But I can't be too careful with that man-of-war anchored off the point. It never fails. When the Jack Tars finally leave, no fewer than a dozen young boys are missing." He turned to leave.

John Silver raised his head slightly and addressed the sailors at the next table, as if to continue a previous conversation. "Aye mateys!" Silver sang out in a nasal twang. "An' speakin' o' the ridiculous, I once heard of a man bein' named after a galley's stovepipe, I did." Everyone in the room heard and understood the insult.

"That'll cost you!" Noble turned and walking to the table. Before any of the sailors knew what happened, the tall man had driven his thin-bladed knife into the table between Silver's thumb and forefinger.

Without looking up or pulling back his hand, Silver gave a cryptic warning. "I hear tell a man can come up with leprosy from stickin' another man with a gift knife, 'specially when the giver's the one what gets stuck."

"John Silver?" Noble sat down across from his antagonist. "Is that you?"

Silver raised his head slowly and gave Noble one of his famous sideways looks. "Greetings, Charlie. Are ya glad to see me?"

"Well you old son-of-a-gun!"

"Son-of-a-gun, is it?" Silver barked back like a bull sea lion backed against a cliff. "An' I suppose you were conceived betwixt the satin sheets o' some fancy palace?"

"Well it wasn't on the gun deck of a British man-of-war like you!"

Silver gave a toothy smile. "At least I knew who me mum were, bless 'er sweet departed soul, which be twice what you know o' yer pedigree."

"I may not know who my parents were, but I'd wager a week's receipts they were better stock than yours!" To the other eight customers of the Whore's Breath, these two middle-aged men sounded as if they would draw weapons at any moment.

"And since we're talking of names, it's pure blasphemy to be named for the thirty pieces of silver old man Taylor paid for you—it being the same price the traitor Judas was paid for betraying our Lord and Savior."

"Blasphemy or not, you can fetch me up daft, Charles, if we weren't cut from the same bolt o' cloth." Silver gave a throaty laugh. "Only difference bein' that they used shears for you an' fer me they ripped it with their bare hands. And just because our adopted father—or should I say owner—taught you the King's English an' I've the tongue of some fouled scupper, it don't make me yer lesser."

By now, the other patron's hands were on their weapons.

"Your tongue was your own decision, John Silver, and has nothing to do with either your wasted birthright."

"Speakin' o' birthrights, Charlie, only time'll tell what happens to yours."

"My birthright?" The younger man sat back. "And just what's that supposed to mean?"

"Nothing, Charlie. Nothing at all." Silver signalled for two more tankards of ale. "There be too much water through that scupper to be worth our sweat."

"Tell me, John." Charles twisted his knife from the table and pushed it into its sheath. "Did you bring back Flint's treasure, as you promised you would?"

"Belay!" Silver looked about the tavern, then pulled his stepbrother close and sighted between his finger and thumb. "No, but I came this close."

"Really? That close?" Charles leaned back and broke into a broad grin. "What happened this time? I thought nothing could get in the way when Long John Silver puts his mind to a thing."

Silver continued at a whisper. "Charles, sit close so's we can trade wind without bein' overheard. And fer God's sake, stop callin' me by my actual name in public. I'm a wanted man." He paused for a moment to survey the room again. His evil-eyed stare sent every man back to his own conversation. "As fer the treasure, well, it be a long story."

"A long story. You failed, didn't you?"

Silver's jaw tightened until Charles could hear his older brother's teeth grind.   "And I suppose you'll be wanting your old job back."

"No, Charles, I've decided I'm not cut out to run a warehouse no more."

"That doesn't leave you many choices, then, especially at your advanced age. How do you intend to fill your belly and keep clothes on your back if you won't work?"

"I've a little money, and I've discovered I can run a tavern at a fair profit."

"A little money? How much is a little money?"

"I still got the eight hundred pounds o'screw hid away fer this larboard leg, an'—"

"Screw?"

"You know, Charlie. Like what Lloyd's pays you when one of your ships is lost."

"Ah...insurance money." Charles gave his older brother a squint. "And just when and where did you learn to run a tavern?"

"I did it fer several months in Bristol while I was waitin' for Billy Bones to show hi'self. Worked my way up and ended up inheriting the place. Found out I'm right good at it, too."

"Hmmm." Charles sat back and stroked his chin.

"What is it, little brother?"

"There's a recently widowed woman running the Man-O'-War Tavern down at the west end of the docks...close to my warehouses."

"Nathan Bridger died?"

"You knew him?"

"Aye, and if I remember right, the little woman's quite a looker, too." Silver reached across and grabbed the younger man by the forearm. "Think she'd consider a partnership?"

"Wouldn't hurt to ask. I would expect she's even looking for a new husband."

"Well, then, what are we waiting for?" Silver pushed himself up onto his crutch, grabbed the lanyard to his sea chest, and began hopping toward the door. "Let's go have a talk with the widow Bridger!"

Once outside, Silver gave his younger brother a backhanded thump to the arm. "Tell me, Charlie, what have you been up to since I been gone? Still workin' for old man Taylor?"

"No, I'm not."

"Oh?"

"Taylor died and I'm now the owner of Noble Shipping."

"So, the old man finally got 'is due? My pitty fer the Devil."

"Take care, John. He was good to us."

"Good to you, ya mean."

"He was better to you than you deserved, John Silver, what with all your running off to sea and stealing his things." Charles realized the conversation was leading nowhere but to a fight, so selected a diversion. "Tell me more about you being a wanted man. I thought the King's men were always after you."

"Yeah, but not like this. If they catch me this time, I'll swing fer sure. I be needin' a place to hide out and an incognito."

"An incognito, eh?" Charles stepped back and looked at his brother from head to foot. "I'd start by growing a beard and doing something about that missing leg of yours."

Silver looked down at where his left leg should have been. "A beard's easy, but growin' a new leg's gonna be a little difficult."

"I've a very talented sawyer in my employ who could fashion you a right smart wooden leg—one that articulates."

"Articulates?"

"That means it bends at the knee. I saw one on a British officer several weeks back, and he allowed me to inspect the mechanism."

"I know what the word means, little brother. I just don't understand how or why you'd want to put a joint in a peg leg. The thing'd never hold me up."

"If you don't want to try it, my man'll carve you a real fancy peg leg and cover it in silver."

"Let me think on it while we walk." Silver gave the sea chest a pull. "First I wanta see this widow an' her tavern."

A few minutes later, the two stood under the bowsprit that jutted from above the double doors of the tavern. Silver leaned his weight against the cold stones and turned to his brother.

"I'll take the one that articulates." Silver turned and looked through a pane of colored glass into the busy tavern.

"A good choice."

"Aye. It'll help hide me past from anyone lookin' fer the one-legged pirate named Long John Silver."

Chapter 2

In late November, 1773, a young Scottish sea captain ran through a rainsquall toward a whitewashed brick building at the western end of King Street in Scarborough, Tobago. A lightning bolt shattered a tree a hundred yards away, prompting him to take temporary refuge in a doorway. He was a short man by the day's standards, with a sharp, wedge-shaped nose and high cheekbones. His jaw line was reminiscent of a Viking's, with a strong, deeply cleft chin. And even though he was possibly facing a trial and prison term, his expression was eager and resolute.

He wiped the rain from his intelligent brow, gave his head a shake and looked through the rain toward his destination. The sign above the door read, SCARBOROUGH JUSTICE OF THE PEACE: MAGISTRATE MARCUS CUTTER.

He ran from the doorway, across the cobblestones and into the foyer of the small building. The door crashed shut behind him, the sound bringing the justice up from his supper with a start.

"May I help you?" Justice Cutter was a thin, tall man in his mid-fifties. He stepped into the office while pulling his table linen from his collar.

"Yes you may!" The young ship's captain threw back his cape, pulled his pistol from his sash and drew his sword. "My name is John Paul, and a short time ago I was forced to kill a man aboard my ship, the merchantman Betsy."

The justice stepped back from the counter. His frightened wife stood in the doorway to the dining room with a hand to her mouth. His breathing became labored as he stared at the two weapons. "I've no argument with you, good sir. I know no man aboard the Betsy, and I hold no personal malice against you."

"But you are Marcus Cutter, the justice in Scarborough?"

"I am sir, but please…"

"Then I've found the right man after all." The captain looked down at his weapons and realized his mistake. "There was a mutiny aboard my ship this afternoon, and I was forced to kill the ringleader of the group— a half-breed named Jack Fry. I've come to report the incident and surrender myself." John lay the sword and pistol on the counter.

The tall man's color began to return. He wiped the sweat from his throat and gave his wife a reassuring look. He walked forward to the counter. "There'll be no need for your arrest, sir, leastwise not until I've investigated the matter."

"And in the meantime?"

"You may return to your ship, with the provision that you'll not leave Scarborough until this matter has been thoroughly investigated. You understand there will have to be a hearing."

"Thank you, sir." John gave the magistrate a curt nod. "When you need me, I'll be aboard my ship, or at my partner's warehouse at Raney's dock."

"Would you be the partner of Archibald Stewart?"

"Yes, I would. Do you know of me?"

"It's a small island, Captain Paul. I know something about every white man on Tobago, and most of the slaves and natives as well."

"Then I'll await your call." The young Scotsman turned and walked to the door.

"You may take this with you, Captain." The justice held up John's sword. "If I can trust you to remain in Scarborough, I'm sure I can trust you to keep your sword."

The rain had stopped by the time John stepped from the office and onto the wet cobbles. He slid the long blade of his sword into its scabbard, looked about at the row of whitewashed homes and then set off at a brisk pace toward the bay.

"John Paul!" It was a familiar voice. "Hold up a minute!" The speaker kissed a young woman goodbye and then trotted nimbly across the wet street to John. "When did you get back into port, John, and what's your hurry?"

William Young had been the first man in the West Indian colonies, other than Arthur Stewart, to befriend the Scotsman. As lieutenant governor, he was the highest-ranking British official on the island. John slowed his pace until the other man could catch up and match strides with him.

"I got here three days ago. My hurry is because I must return to the Betsy as quickly as possible." John stopped and gave William a long look. "I must confess it's good to see a friendly face for a change."

"A friendly face? You talk as if something were amiss." The lieutenant governor was a tall man of thirty-five, with premature gray above his ears. Like most of John's friends, he towered over the short Scotsman. He motioned toward the bay. "There's some sort of trouble I have to look into down at the docks. We can talk on the way."

John lengthened his stride to keep up with his friend. "I'm in serious trouble myself."

"Does it have anything to do with that sword?"

John nodded. "Yes, it does."

"I figured as much, the way you're never without it. Do you want to talk about it?"

John stopped in the street and faced his friend. If he could tell anybody, it was William. "There was a mutiny aboard my ship this afternoon, and I had to kill the new ship's cook."

"Then it's your ship I was summoned to!"

"You already heard?"

William gave John a concerned look. "That wouldn't be the half-breed, Jack Fry, by any unfortunate chance?"

"You know the man?"

William gave a slow shake of his head. "Everybody in Scarborough knows that troublemaker. He's been like a bad case of the gout since he was a pup. I'm surprised he wasn't killed before this."

"Then Magistrate Cutter should find my actions fully justified?"

"Not necessarily."

"Your tone worries me, William."

"Fry may have been a chronic problem for the Crown, but among the natives he's some sort of local hero." They resumed their walk, but much more slowly this time. "I assume you were forced to kill him?"

"My first officer signed the bloody troublemaker on for the sail back to Cork not three hours after we docked. First thing he did was to whip the rest of the crew into a flap about their pay."

"Sedition, eh?"

"Yes."

"Did he attack you?"

"Of course he did! You don't think I'd kill a man in cold blood, do you?"

"What did Magistrate Cutter say?"

"He released me to my own keeping, but told me that I was not to leave port."

"Hmmm." William considered. "He's not thinking of trying you here in Tobago, is he?"

"I assume so, if it goes that far. He told me there'd have to be an investigation and hearing." John gave his friend a long look. "Why? What's the matter with that?"

William stopped. "John, what I'm about to tell you is as your friend and not as the lieutenant governor of Tobago." William took a long breath and looked back up the street toward the magistrate's house. "You'll have to flee Scarborough. If Fry's relatives don't kill you before the hearing, there's a great probability that you'll be convicted and hanged by a jury made up of his friends. Good Lord, man, why did it have to be Jack Fry?"

I'm a ship's captain. I killed a hired seaman. That makes it an Admiralty case. I'll stand before the Admiralty"

William shook his head.

"What's the matter, William?"

"There's revolution in the air, John, and that's drawn nearly every naval officer to the American colonies. Any court that Magistrate Cutter convenes here in Scarborough will be a court made up of Jack Fry's friends. You have to get off the island."

"Off the island? That's a wonderful piece of advice!" John searched the branches above him as if an answer to his predicament hid somewhere in the Spanish moss. "I don't have any money with me, William, and what's more, I'm on foot. If what you say is true, I can't even risk returning to the Betsy." John looked at his friend for several moments. "So, what would you suggest?"

"Well, before we do anything else, let's get you off this public road."

Soon William had ushered his young friend back up the street, into his house and through the hallway to the kitchen. His wife, Margaret, was helping the maid clear the supper dishes from the table. The two young women gave a start when William stepped into the room.

"William!" Margaret dropped a teacup and saucer. They shattered on the floor. "What are you doing back so soon?"

"I ran into an old friend."

"But I thought you were needed at the docks—something about a killing."

"Something more important has come up." William pulled John from the hallway. "Margaret, this is...Michael Stevens, a friend to whom I owe a great debt."

"Pleased to make your acquaintance, Mister Stevens." Margaret gave William a questioning look as she wiped her hands dry. "Would you like some tea?"

"Dear, I need to speak with Mister Stevens alone. Do you mind?"

"Of course not." She set a pot of water on the stove and woofied up the fire. "This stove will need more wood anyway." Margaret gave the maid a gentle push toward the back door. "I'll be back in a few minutes, if that's not too soon."

William gave her a smile. "Five minutes."

Margaret and the maid turned and walked through the kitchen.

"You have a lovely wife, William. I hope I can find a woman as nice as she some day."

"Thank you, but let's keep our voices down. I don't want her to know what's going on here."

"Is that why you lied about my name?"

"I don't believe she would inform on you intentionally." William pulled a small traveling bag from a closet and set it on the dining room table. "But the less she knows about you, the less she can tell her father, should the subject come up."

"Her father?"

"Her maiden name is Cutter."

"Your wife is the magistrate's daughter?"

William nodded. "John, you must take my horse and ride to the other end of the island. A postal packet should arrive in Charlottesville in a day or two. It will take you as far as Jamaica. There should be enough naval officers in King's Town to convene a proper hearing. That may be your only chance of living through this affair."

William left the kitchen with the traveling bag. When he returned several minutes later, the bag was full. "Everything you'll need—several changes of undergarments, toiletries and such—is in this bag," William set it next to the table and opened a small metal box. "I'm lending you fifty pounds. When you arrive at Charlottesville, leave my mare with the innkeeper at the Milk n' Honey tavern. He'll get her back to me." William hesitated. "Do you have a weapon?"

"I have my sword and..." John searched his belt. "I left my pistol at the magistrate's house!"

"I know you're handy with that blade, John, but I'm afraid it won't be enough." William turned and left the kitchen once more. A moment later, he was back with a polished cherrywood box. "You can have this fowling pistol."

"But..."

"Don't worry." William set the money inside the box, which he then pushed into the bag. "I've three others just like it. Seems every time I'm reappointed, somebody gives me another one."

"My partners have all my money. I'll send them a letter and have them settle with you."

"Don't bother yourself, John. We're both Christian men." He handed John the duffle. "Consider all this as an opportunity to stretch my soul a bit."

William escorted John out the back door and across the yard to the stables. Margaret and the maid passed them with their basket of firewood.

Margaret looked at the traveling bag suspiciously. "Is something the matter, William?"

"No, dear. I'm lending Mister Stevens one of the horses. He needs to ride to Plymouth."

She gave William a long look and then walked into the house with the maid at her heels. Once inside, she stood at the window and watched William saddle the mare and then send John on his way. "Emily, I'm going to my parents home for a few minutes."

***

John's mind was reeling. It was a little over two hours from the time his sword had pierced Jack Fry's heart, and here he was on horseback, fleeing for his very life.

He arrived in the small seaport of Charlottesville just before dawn on the 21st of November, 1773. Because of the early hour, John left William's mare in the Milk n' Honey stable with a note attached to the saddle. The twenty-five-ton topsail schooner Falmouth Packet had just finished taking on its cargo when John reached the dock.

"Ahoy there! Captain of the Falmouth Packet!" John stepped to the dock's edge. "Ahoy! Have you room for a passenger?"

"Not for a paying passenger, we don't!" The gruff voice came from within the bowels of the small craft.

John looked about the deck for the owner of the voice.

The master climbed from the companionway and looked to the dock. "But if you're willing to work, you can go with us as far as you'd like."

"Aye! Working passage will do!"

"But so you know where that is before you commit yourself, young man, we'll be stopping at all of the islands to pick up and drop off the mail. That will be Bridge Town on Barbados, Saint Vincent, Saint Lucia, Martinique, and so on. Then San Juan, Santo Domingo, and finally King's Town."

"King's Town will be just fine!" John stepped to the plank, pleased to hear that William had been correct. "May I come aboard?"

At a wave of the master's hand, John stepped across the gangway.

The Falmouth Packet was a typical interisland schooner with a "sharp" hull and a single mast and square topsail aloft. A cutlass-like bowsprit nearly as long as her hull enabled the agile craft to carry an enormous jib and fore staysail, giving her an edge over the brigantine and most of the larger schooners favored by the pirates. A single swivel gun, which could be moved to any of several stations along her rails, was all the protection she carried. With the signing of his clearance papers, the master ordered the sails unfurled and the lines singled up. In a moment, the spry craft was loose from the dock and reaching into Man-o'-War Bay.

"My name is James Jones." The master pushed the tiller to windward while he looked at John. "How shall we hail you, young man?"

"My name is John Paul, and I'm a captain out of London, most recently. My ship, the..." John fell silent, realizing he'd probably told the older man too much already.

"Your ship?"

"My ship is laying up for repairs at Scarborough for a few weeks, so I fancied a leave to the northern islands." It would do no good to tell the truth, especially to a British master carrying the King's mail. "Do you have an estimate to Jamaica?"

"If all goes well, we should tie up at the place early in the second week of November."

This was great news for the young sea captain. The packet's speed would get him to King's Town ahead of any warrant for his arrest, despite all the stops she would make en route. And then, with any luck, he could obtain passage to the colonies in America within a week of arrival. William was right. An Admiralty court far removed from the incident was always the best choice.

John looked about the deck. "Why no cannons, sir? Aren't you afraid of pirates?"

"Oh, I'm afraid of them, Captain Paul, but as long as we have winds, we can outrun nearly anything afloat. That is, anything up to twice our waterline. But you're correct to be concerned. These are lean times for the few pirates still working these waters. They might think we're carrying more than mail." He called out for the men to trim the topsail. "There's one other group I'm very wary of, however, even though they seldom come this far south."

"And who would that be?"

"American privateers. There are hundreds of them prowling the trading routes of the Atlantic and down as far as Cuba and Hispaniola, looking for anything with a British flag on it. There's a chance that we could run up against one as we near Jamaica. If it comes to that, Mister Paul, I could use your help on that swivel gun."

"I have a brother in Fredericksburg. He's told me about the privateers, but not how they operate."

"They're pirates with a license."

"Do they kill the crews and passengers of the ships they take?"

The master gave John a flat look. "Are you a coward, Captain Paul?"

"I'm a realist, sir. A swivel gun will only provoke violence."

The master called to one of his men. "Grady! Report aft!" The master turned back to John. "Seaman Grady will show you where you can stow your gear. We're short on bunks, but we've some extra blankets you can use for a mattress."

"It will do." John noticed movement on the pier. Two soldiers stood on the dock with their mounts several yards behind them. One of them was pointing at the small ship while the other was waving his arms above his head. John wondered after the two and noticed a puff of smoke from the hand of the one that was pointing. John grabbed James and pulled him down to the deck just as a lead ball whistled overhead. It punched a clean hole through the mainsail just beyond their heads. A second later, the report reached the small ship.

"What the hell?" James stood up and looked at the hole in the sail. "They were terribly lucky to hit so close at this range." He turned to the shore. The two soldiers were still waving their arms. "They've done that before—fired a weapon to hail me back to the dock for another mailbag or passenger—but this is the first time they've tried to hit me!"

"You think they were shooting at you?"

James gave John a questioning look. "You knew they'd shoot at us, didn't you?"

John opened his mouth to answer, but James cut him off. "That ball was meant for you!"

"I'm..."

"Speak straight with me, Captain Paul, or I'll turn about and deliver you into their hands."

John looked aft at the two soldiers. "My ship is the merchantman Betsy. I was forced to kill a mutineer yesterday afternoon in Scarborough. I have to get to King's Town where I can be heard before a proper Admiralty Court of Inquiry."

"This man you killed. Might he be someone I know?"

"It's unlikely. He was a native half-breed—a prodigious brute of three times my strength."

"Not Jack Fry."

"You knew him also?"

"Everybody in the Antillies knows Jack Fry." James gave the two soldiers another look and turned back to John. "Good Lord, man. You'd have done better shooting Magistrate Cutter."

"If you take me back, I'll be executed."

James looked to the pier. The corner of his mouth curled up slightly. "If they fire again, you have my permission to use the swivel gun."

John smiled at the older man.

"You know, of course, that you just went deep in my debt."

"And grateful to be there, sir."

It took the small craft two days to reach Bridge Town. After the routine of unloading the cargo and taking on the outgoing mail, water, and victuals for the crew, the Falmouth Packet was at sea again. For the next week she would make a new port each day. John had quickly adapted to the small ship's routine and was at the helm the morning of the third day.

Just before four bells—ten o'clock—a seaman approached the Scotsman. "Mister Paul?"

"What's the matter, Kirkland?"

"Excuse me, sir, but Master Jones hasn't come from his cabin yet. He wasn't looking too well last night when he retired, and I'm worried for him."

"Is his fever worse?"

"Don't know, sir. He didn't show for his mid watch last night, an' he never touched his supper, neither. The other men an' me would be obliged if you'd be lookin' in on him for us."

"Of course I will. Fetch me a pitcher of fresh water and some towels." The young Scotsman turned the helm over to one of the other men and made his way down the short ladder to the cabin door. He listened for a moment but could hear nothing.

"Captain?" There was no answer. He tapped three times. "Captain Jones, are you awake?" There was still no answer, just the quiet hiss of the sea slipping along the weathered hull and the creaking of hemp against the spars aloft.

"Is he about, sir?" It was Kirkland with the basin of water and towels the Scotsman had requested.

Without answering the young seaman, John Paul pushed open the narrow cabin door. The distinct odor of malaria filled his nostrils, causing him to recoil a step.

"Kirkland, is there any quinine in the medical chest?"

"I believe so, sir, but flog me if I could tell ya which bottle its in. Master Jones be the only man aboard what's able to read."

"Bring the chest, and be quick about it." As the seaman rushed to do the Scotsman's bidding, John carried the water and towels into the dark cabin. With the only light coming from the hatchway behind him, he could barely make out the tormented figure of the ship's master. He lay twisted in his sweat-soaked blankets—the stench of his illness almost more than John could bear.

"James?"

The master jerked awake with a cry. "Who is it?"

"It's me, John Paul. I'm bringing some medications for your fever. Do you think you can sit up in your chair while I change your blankets and swab you clean?"

James pushed himself up on an elbow and looked about the cabin, confused. "Are we still at sea?" The voice that ventured from his parched throat was no more than a harsh whisper.

"Don't talk." John poured a large glass of cool water and squeezed two limes into it. From his waistcoat pocket he pulled half a dozen red cherries he had picked on Barbados. He laid them on the small table, then helped his shivering friend to the chair and offered the glass.

"Drink this. And when you're able, I want you to eat all of these berries. They prevent scurvy, and I suspect they'll help with your fever also."

"Thank you, my young friend." James sipped the limewater. "Yes. That tastes good."

While James chewed the cherries, John stripped the bunk and threw the foul bedding to the waiting seaman. Turning back to James, he stripped the man naked and began to swab his feverish skin.

"My sister lives on Guadeloupe with her husband." James took another sip of the refreshing water. "We have to make port there anyway, so I'll go ashore and stay with them until I get well."

"But what about the ship and the crew?" John knew the warrant was close in their wake. "You could be laid up for several weeks."

"I know." James put one of the berries in his mouth and chewed it. He turned to face the Scotsman. "There's mail aboard that must reach King's Town as quickly as possible, and the next postal packet won't be by for two weeks." He reached out and took John's arm. "I know it's a lot to ask of you, but would you be willing to take the Falmouth to King's Town for me?"

"The Postal Service would allow that?"

"The mail is their only concern, not who delivers it."

It was perfect—exactly what John needed: a ship of his own that would take him to the colonies. He feigned uncertainty. "I would, but how—"

"It would be simple, Captain Paul. All you'd have to do is sign as I do—J. Jones—on the entrance and clearance papers at the stops between here and King's Town. Once there, you could leave my ship with the port authority until I'm well enough to come for her." James took another sip of the water. "Remember those soldiers at Charlottesville?"

"I know, James." John nodded. "I am in your debt."

***

The late fall of 1773 was nine and a half years after Long John Silver had returned to his birthplace as a fugitive from the King. Within three months of that return, the aging pirate had met, courted and proposed to Betty Bridger, the widowed owner of the Man-O'-War Tavern. Taking the name of Jack Bridger, John Silver and his bride changed the name of the tavern to Silver Jack's—a decision born more of pride than of good sense. As promised, his brother, Charles, had commissioned one of his carpenters to fashion an articulated leg for the old pirate. As hoped, it gave the old pirate the look of a full man.

John Silver stood at the edge of the dock amongst a flurry of white and brown seagulls. With each handful of waste came renewed squaks from the diving scavengers competing for the choisest morsels. After so many years performing the afternoon ritual, he knew every bird by name and nature.

Far to the south and still out of sight of the townsfolk, the Falmouth Packet rounded the point for her starboard reach into the King's Town harbor. Aboard the small ship, one of the seamen studied the rubble that used to be Port Royal. He secured a sheet to the starboard pinrail and then pointed to windward. "Captain Paul? What town was that, and why is it in such a state?"

John stepped to the rail. "This must be your first time to Jamaica."

"It is, sir."

"That's Port Royal, or rather, what's left of it." The young Scotsman studied the sun-bleached remains of the wasted town for several moments. Three hermits in tattered rags scuttled about the shadows of the littered streets and broken buildings with their pull carts, picking up anything that might bring the price of a loaf of bread and a tankard of ale.

"Is that where Sir Henry Morgan ruled when he was still a pirate?"

John nodded.

"It must have been a terrible battle."

John shook his head. "Wasn't a battle at all."

"Then what happened to the place?"

"Some say it was an ordinary earthquake, but others believe the Lord did this in judgment for her sins." John gave the young seaman a quick look, wondering if he was a spiritual man.

"The Lord did that?" He gave a whistle of respect. "How long ago?"

"I believe it was early summer in 1692. The sand ran out and the sea ran in. That's about one-third of the city you see there. The rest is under water. By best count, five thousand souls perished that day, as well as the town."

Sanders shook his head. "Why would anybody build a town on sand?"

"Pirates don't always think of such things. They must have figured it served their needs better than a town further up the bay, such as where they finally built King's Town. They needed a port where they could unload their swag quickly and make a run for the open sea if a man-of-war showed on the horizon."

"They should have read the Good Book, sir, before they built their town on sand."

"Aye! That they should."

After a long moment, the seaman changed the subject.

"What do you expect will happen to the Falmouth if Captain Jones doesn't come for her?"

"She'll be docked at the mail house and remain there until a new master is assigned." The question set John to thinking. "But then again, I may get a new crew and return her to Captain Jones on my way back to Tobago."

"Then you don't mind if we sign onto another ship?"

"It isn't up to me, Sanders. I'm not the real master of this ship."

"I hear tell the Americans may be putting together a navy."

"Yes, I've heard the same rumor."

Although John had called at King's Town several times in the past, this was the first time he had tied up so far toward the western end of the waterfront. He was tired and hungry, and he wanted to get away from the ship. After turning over the mail and packages to the postal authorities and paying the crew their wages, he closed up the small ship and stepped ashore.

The King's Town dock was strewn with a variety of small shops selling all manner of commodities. Most of the shops catered to the rigging and repair of the ships that brought and took the goods of Jamaica. Interspersed among these were the taverns where a seaman could quench his thirst and satisfy his animal needs. Some of their names told the stories of both the exploits and eventual demise of the local heroes and pirates they represented, such as Morgan's Revenge, Blackbeard's Treasure, and Captain Jacob's Gallows. There were also the usual names—the ones so common along the harbors of England and the new world—such as The Bucket of Blood, The Ivory Bosom, and The King's Ransom.

John stood for several minutes musing at the rigging of the miniature bowsprit that supported the cleverly decorated sign that read, "Silver Jack's Tavern."

"As likely a tavern as any." John stepped into the public room—a perfect replica of the gun deck of a frigate. It was fifteen paces long and seven paces wide, with wooden cannons, false gun ports, and all the appropriate tools and rigging lined up along the starboard and larboard walls. There were eight tables in two rows next to the cannons, and trussed-up hammocks hung from hooks in the overhead. The walls curved outward, exactly like a ship's hull, and even the ceiling curved upward as if to shed the sea water off each side to the scuppers.

John let his eyes become accustomed to the dark. The public room was empty of patrons, except for one young man in his late teens sitting near the door to the galley. Assorted charts and a Nautical Almanac lay on the table in front of him. The lad looked up at John and smiled. "That was quite a landing you made."

"Pardon?"

"We watched you dock your postal packet. It's more than evident that you've done that many times." The young man stood, extended a hand and flashed John a broad smile. "My name is David Noble."

"I'm John Paul...Jones. John took David's hand of greeting.

"Pleased to meet you, John Paul...Jones."

John didn't like this young pup mimicking him, but pretended he hadn't noticed the jibe. "May I join you?"

David swept his hands over the table. "By all means, Captain Jones, please join me." The two settled onto the benches. "As you can see, I'm in the midst of my studies, and I could certainly benefit from the advice and instruction of an experienced man of the sea." David was just seventeen years old, but tall and muscular. His hair was coal black and cut neatly about the ears. He had intelligent features, with a fine Roman nose and an almost lyrical tone when he spoke.

John looked about the table. There was the almanac, a book on basic navigation and assorted pencils and charts. "I hope somebody's helping you with this. Navigation can be a difficult subject without an experienced tutor."

"Exactly." David gave the captain an expectant grin. "I'll strike a bargain with you. I'll pay for as much food as you want to eat and as much ale as you can drink if you'll play the part of that...experienced tutor."

"Agreed!" John pulled back the chair and sat down.

Long John Silver approached their table with two fresh tankards. "Welcome to Silver Jack's!" The retired pirate set the tankards between the two young men. "I'd be Jack Bridger, the 'umble proprietor of this 'ere tavern." He looked out the window at John's ship. "That be a winsome little lass ye be master of, good sir. Will ya be takin' 'er north or back to the Antilles?"

"I haven't decided yet."

"Well, until ya makes that decision, might ya be gracin' me humble inn with at least one night o' yer presence?" John Silver had taken to this landlubber's life and it rode well on his planking. His gaunt and leathery lines from years in the "Brotherhood of the Coast" had softened remarkably with the addition of thirty pounds to his frame. In the nine years he had owned the tavern, his full head of dark brown hair had turned snowy white, and he had acquired a grandfather's mannerisms. With the addition of a full beard, he resembled Father Christmas. "An' what might yer name be, young sir?"

"I'm John Paul Jones." John stood and shook Silver's large hand. "And regarding my lodging, if your price is right, I'll take one of your rooms for two or three nights."

"I'm a shillin' below the rest, Cap'n Jones." Silver gave him a wink. "An' if ya don't believe old Jack Bridger, just you ask about."

"I'll take your word on it." John sat down. "Does the price of that room include a bath?"

"Well, not normally, but if you pay for the three nights in advance, I'll throw her in to the deal, what say?"

John nodded. "Done."

While Silver returned to the kitchen, John whispered to David. "I don't wish to be inquisitive, but what's that clicking sound when the old man walks about?"

"It's my uncle's wooden leg. My father's sawyer made it for him almost a decade ago. As I understand the thing, it uses a catch and a length of sword blade for a spring. It's the catch you're hearing. I believe it needs an adjustment."

"Your uncle?"

"Aye. He and my father were both orphans and kept their own surnames when they were purchased as children."

"Interesting." John took a deep swallow of ale and set the tankard on a corner of David's chart. "So, back to your studies. What kind of assistance were you looking for?"

"Well, except for deep-water navigation, I'm nearly ready to take a position on one of my father's ships." David brightened. "You may have heard of my father! Charles Noble, of Noble Shipping?" His British accent had a touch of the French, which gave him that familiar Jamaican accent.

"I've heard the name, but I've never met your father." John turned one of the charts about so he could see David's calculations. As he studied the young man's notes, John Silver came back with two more drinks.

"Here be some fresh spirits, good sirs!" Silver slid the two tankards onto the table. "An' just call out when them two be empty!" As he turned to leave, Silver gave David a stern look and a tilt of the head toward the Scotsman. David replied with a perturbed stare and obedient nod. Silver returned to the galley.

"I've crewed aboard many of my father's ships between the islands, and as long as I can see an island, I've never gotten lost." David pushed the almanac across the table to John. "My question, sir, is: how do you know where you are east and west in the open sea, without reference to land?"

"Well, I won't try to convince you that it's a simple matter, because it's not." John looked about the table. "You haven't a sextant, do you?"

David shook his head.

"I have one aboard the Falmouth Packet." He stood. "I'll be back in a moment."

As soon as John was out of the door, Silver hurried to David's table. He glared at the lad. "Who is he, and what's he doin' in King's Town?"

"I don't know, Uncle Silver." David was confused. "He only sat down a few minutes ago. How would I—"

Silver reached out and grabbed the lad's forearm. "What the hell 'ave I been lookin' for these past nine years?"

"Oh, that."

"Yes, that!" The old man gave David's arm another squeeze. "A lot is riding on this."

John returned a few minutes later and set a polished cherrywood case in front of David. He unlatched the hook and opened the case, revealing a gleaming new sextant. "Have you ever used one of these?" John lifted the finely crafted instrument from its green felt indentations and handed it to David.

"No, not yet."

"But it's at the heart of navigation."

David studied the polished brass scales and hinged mirrors. "I've used an old octant. And my father has a special quadrant that he keeps in a glass case above the mantle. He claims it belonged to Sir Henry Morgan when he was a pirate. He's promised to give it to me some day."

"Henry Morgan!" John was jealous.

"My father told me that he got it from one of Morgan's descendants." David could tell John was impressed. "So, tell me about longitude?"

"By knowing the day of the year and the actual angle of the sun above the horizon at noon, you have your latitude north or south of the equator."

"As I told you, I've seen that done often."

John gave David a sideways look and continued. "Longitude is a little more difficult, and this is where I use an old seaman's trick." He unrolled a large chart of the Atlantic and used their tankards to hold the corners in place. "Longitude would be much easier to find if we had better timepieces. All we would need to know is the time at Greenwich, England and compare it to the time on board when the sun's at its highest angle."

David looked up from the map. "Well, since we don't have good timepieces, what's the trick? How do you make a proper landfall?"

"The trick is to first depart on the general course toward your destination—such as the Bristol Channel. It lies at fifty-one degrees north latitude. So when your sextant says you've reached fifty-one degrees north latitude, you alter your course to due east. Continue on that latitude until your lookout sights the channel. It's called 'sailing down the latitude.'"

"Well, that's no trick." David gave the table a slap. "Everyone I ask keeps telling me some rot about the sea birds and the water temperature. They were guessing too, weren't they?"

John smiled. "Aye, navigation's a lot of guesswork."

John Silver returned to their table. "Excuse the intrusion, Captain Jones, but might I be interestin' you in a plate o' me little wife's lamb an' cabbage? She's a Scot like yerself, an' still cooks like the old people."

"Lamb and cabbage!" John looked at David.

David nodded. "Yes, I'm buying." He looked up at his uncle. "A plate for each of us."

"An' I've a score of bottles of Madeira wine on me shelf what would wash yer throat clean as a young maiden's soul, it would."

John gave the old man a smile. "I'm sure your wine's the finest in the colonies, Mister Bridger, but there's another drink I'd fancy if you stock it."

"Ha!" The old pirate put a finger to the side of his nose. "I knew ye were a man of deeper water, I did! What be yer poison?"

"Single-malt Scotch whiskey." John spoke the words as if he were saying the secret name of God Himself. "You wouldn't have any about, would you?"

"If I did, good sir, ye could 'ave the whole bottle. But the only whiskey I be havin' is diluted two times over—once by the merchant what sold it to me and once before I serve it to the regular riffraff what frequents Silver Jack's Tavern. But I'll look about me larder."

"Then it'll be two plates of lamb and cabbage." John was beginning to feel the effects of the ale. "If you can't find it, then I'll stick with the ale." John reached across and put a hand on David's forearm. "Since you're buying the ale, I'll pay for supper. Just payment for the good fellowship you've already given me this evening."

Dinner was a treat. The lamb was freshly killed, lightly seasoned with garlic and laid up beside a quarter slab of steamed cabbage. After dinner, John and David shared their backgrounds and experiences until nearly four bells. John hadn't intended to tell anybody about his recent troubles in Tobago, but regret it as he might, he—and the spirits that shared his brain—couldn't hold the words back. The late hour finally took its toll on John, so he excused himself to his room and the feathered bed that beckoned.

His shadow had no more disappeared up the stairway when John Silver seated himself across the board from his nephew. He reached out and took hold of the lad's forearm. "Choose your words well, David. What have you learned? Might your new friend be the one?" John Silver's heavy accent and salty vernacular had mysteriously vanished.

"His real name is John Paul." David winced at the constricting hand on his arm. "Jones is an assumed name to prevent the authorities from catching him. He's a fugitive from Tobago, where he killed the ringleader of a mutiny. As soon as he can get supplies and a crew together, he sails the Falmouth Packet for Fredericksburg, Virginia, where his older brother lives."

"Anything else?"

David nodded. "I don't know how serious he is, but he mentioned that he might try to get an officer's commission with the Continental Navy."

Silver's grip remained firm while he let his eyes drop slowly to the chart of the Atlantic Ocean and the American colonies. With his right index finger, he traced several invisible lines across the chart. Finally he looked up at the lad with determination.

"Go to your father and tell him I must meet with him at his home in half a glass. That'll give me time to close the tavern and do a little more thinking." Silver released David's arm and pulled a large gold watch from his pocket. The cover sprang open with a loud click. After a quick glance, he snapped the lid shut and looked up at the lad. "Go now, Davey, and do as I say!"

Chapter 3

Long John Silver pushed through the courtyard gate of the Noble estate just before five bells. Inside the house, Charles Noble stood at the mantle stuffing a clay pipe with an aromatic blend of Turkish and Cuban tobacco. He stood an inch taller than David, but he had the same Roman features as his son, except that his hair had begun to gray at the temples.

He took a sliver of wood and put it to the flames. After a few puffs, the pipe smoked smoothly. "So, what is it about this Scotsman that has your uncle so excited?"

"He thinks this might be the one." David rubbed his right forearm where the old pirate had squeezed it.

"We'll see." Charles looked about at the familiar clicking sound that announced his stepbrother's approach. He whispered, "Your uncle is obsessed, you know."

"Fetch aft the brandy, Charles Noble!" Silver gave a growl. "And I'll need a dry towel to wipe off my transom." The old pirate stopped in the library doorway and made a quick survey of the familiar room. The layer of dust on the poetry books and the single yellowed doily on the table gave mute testimony that a woman's hand hadn't touched the place in more than a decade. The knife the old pirate had stuck in the desktop several weeks before stood undisturbed. Silver walked across the room and pulled it from the wood while Charles poured him a glass of the thick liquor.

Charles handed his older brother a tea towel with a chuckle. "Fell on your arse again, I see. How long have I been telling you the mechanism in that wooden leg needed work?"

"There's nothin' wrong with the mechanism, Charles." Silver took a step to demonstrate. He swung the leg forward for the next step, giving it a stronger than usual kick, just to make sure it would lock. "See?"

Charles gave a puff on the pipe. "Well, then, if that's none of my business, get to what is! Why this important meeting?"

Silver threw the towel back to his brother and downed the brandy. Then he pulled a whetstone from his pocket. He spat on the stone and stroked the blade. "Nine years ago, when Flint's treasure slipped through these bony fingers, I swore I'd have the other part of it some day—the part Murray's grandnephew buried on Dead Man's Chest." Silver hesitated to sight down the blade, looking for irregularities along its cutting edge. "I've kept tellin' meself that there's a man out there somewhere what will bring it to me if I'm patient enough."

He leaned forward and gave the two a hard stare as his cockney twang was replaced with the finest King's English either had ever heard the old man speak. "Gentlemen, unless I'm a poor judge of character, David's new friend—this fugitive captain named John Paul Jones—is that man."

"So that is it!" Charles gave his older brother a tired look. "David told me you'd found another one."

"Another one?" Silver poured himself another glass of brandy. "What's that supposed to mean?"

Charles got a glass and filled it half full. "Well, by my count, he'll be the tenth—or does he make the eleventh?"

"It's different this time."

"That's what you claimed about the last nine! Just what makes—"

"I've changed the plan, and this man's better suited to the task than any of the rest." Silver slowed his speech for emphasis. "And this time, Charles, I'll finally have my treasure."

Charles took several puffs at his pipe. "You have a fine wife, a prosperous tavern, and all the money a man of your age needs. We both know the evil you did before you settled down and married sweet Elizabeth. You've been a faithful husband and a good man these ten years. That treasure will only bring that evil back into your life."

Silver sat down in his favorite chair and considered his brother's words for a moment. "You're correct, Charles. I do have everything a man my age needs." He hesitated while he searched his soul for the words. "But that treasure is…" He closed his eyes and fell silent, letting his memory run for a moment. He finally looked up at the two. "Maybe it's to fulfill a dream, or to remove a curse…I don't know. Or maybe it's so that the world will know that Long John Silver made it happen."

Silver took a deep breath and touched his heart with an open hand. "The treasure of Dead Man's Chest has become a legend, and I'm a part of that legend. I was there through the whole thing. I was John Flint's quartermaster. I'm the only one left." He made a fist of the hand. "Yes, Charles, I have more than a man my age deserves, but I do need that treasure."

Charles began to protest, but was stopped by his brother's upheld hand.

"Call it the soul of a pirate, if you must. I know I'm not going to live much longer. The Good Lord's given me more time than I deserve, but I'd like to go out with the knowledge that I was the one."

"But maybe it's not supposed to be found, Uncle Silver."

Silver looked to the lad. "You may be right, Davey, but nothing else will sate this hunger in my soul."

Charles took another sip of his brandy. "David told me about the young sea captain staying at your inn. What makes him different?"

"Its not just Captain Jones that's different, Charles."

"Oh?"

"It started several months ago when you traded away the Hesperus to that bastard son of John Flint."

"Joshua Smoot?" Charles considered for a moment. "You think this trouble up on the mainland might work to your advantage, don't you?"

"It was tailor-made for me, Charles." Silver pulled a piece of folded paper from his vest pocket and read down the list aloud. When he had finished, he leaned back and waited for his brother's reaction.

"All of that sounds grand, but I still don't understand why you need Captain Jones. We have the bait, we know who wants the bait, and I already know the 'Yorkman.'"

"Go on, Charles."

"Now that we have the cannons, why don't we go straight to Robert Ormerod?"

Silver's mood darkened. "Because I've already tried and failed."

"You never told us." It was David. At seventeen years, he was finally included in his father's and uncle's conversations. "When? What happened?"

"I didn't want to involve either of you, in case anything went wrong. Nobody knew except the two men I hired." Silver stared across the room as if the far wall had vanished. "I've lived a long life and—as you reminded me—I've dealt out more than my share of evil. I have missed golden opportunities and I have taken risks, seldom with regret." The old pirate shook his head from side to side. "But of everything I've ever done, I regret the affair with the Yorkman above all else—and wish the whole thing had never happened."

"Why?"

John looked across at the lad. "Three or four years back, I sent two men to offer him half the treasure for a map. When Ormerod refused the offer, my surrogates got greedy and exceeded their authority—a risk you take when you send others to do your bidding." Silver held out his glass for a refill.

Charles walked from the fireplace and filled the old pirate's glass. "It was Joshua Smoot, wasn't it?"

"Aye—he and his mate, Henry Morgan. The map they brought me was false, and cost me more than just the time it took me to sail to Dead Man's Chest."

"I remember it well." Charles took a puff at the pipe. "You aged a year in those two months."

Silver gave a laugh. "Fate works her way, though."

"Oh? What did Mistress Fate do?"

"The price for Smoot's services was that Long John Silver would provide a map showing where John Flint's body was buried."

"But you told David and me that you sewed him up in sailcloth and dumped him into the Savannah River."

John Silver gave his younger brother a toothy grin. "I got a false treasure map, but Joshua Smoot dug up some poor Papist's body and spent two weeks tormenting it."

"Does Mister Ormerod know you sent Smoot and Morgan?"

"I must assume not, Davey, since he never came to kill me."

"Why would he need to come after you?" Charles freshened Silver's brandy. "What did you do to him?"

Silver sipped the mellow drink. "It's not important now."

"If Ormerod would have killed you if he knew, then he won't be apt to draw a map for you, will he?"

"No, Charles, he won't." John Silver emptied his glass and held it out again. "I know the man well. The only way he'll ever do it is if we can appeal to something he considers a..." He searched for the words. "A higher and nobler purpose."

"And what might that be, Uncle?"

Silver gave the lad a knowing raise of his brows. "Yes, Davey, and that's where Captain Jones and the cannons fit into my plan." Silver took back the note and skimmed over it quickly. "Timing is everything. If we use them at the wrong moment, the whole plan will go up in smoke."

"The wrong moment?" David was enjoying his participation in this important discussion. "Timing?"

"Aye, and that's where you come in, Davey."

David gave his uncle a questioning stare. "Oh?"

"First, it's important that Captain Jones never learns that there's a connection between the Nobles and the inkeeper Jack Bridger."

"I don't follow you, John." Charles tamped the tobacco down in his pipe and puffed it back to life. "What difference should that make?"

"Think about it, Charles. The Yorkman, his betrothed, and I spent several weeks together on the Walrus with John Flint and his crew. He knows me, and he knows I still want that treasure."

"But if he never came to kill you, then those two you sent to get the map never told him about you or where you were."

David raised a hand. "You told us that Smoot and Morgan don't know to this day that you're Long John Silver."

Charles pointed the stem of his pipe at the old man. "I see it. Ormerod's certain to ask Captain Jones if there's a one-legged old man involved in all this."

Silver reached down and gave the wooden leg a tap with his glass. "If Captain Jones learns the true nature of this leg, he and the Yorkman might just figure it all out. If so, then Mistress Fate gets her revenge. I prefer to think that she's kinder than that." John Silver turned to David. "Back to what I was saying, lad."

"Yes?"

"If he asks, you're to tell him you've only been in Silver Jack's one other time and you consider me a friendly old tavern keeper. The name and image of the limping Jack Bridger must fade from our little captain's memory."

"It's too late."

Silver turned to his nephew. "Too late?"

"He heard the clicking and asked about it. I told him you were my uncle and that it was a wooden leg."

"Damn you!" Silver threw the knife, missing David's ear by an inch and burying itself in the wood paneling.

"I'm sorry!" David craned his neck for a look at the still-quivering blade. I didn't think—"

"It's done, John!" Charles moved between the two. "Leave the boy alone!"

David stepped from behind his father. "There's something else."

"Something else?" Silver glared back at the youth. "What?"

"I'm not so sure he wants to be a Colonial naval officer after all—or at least not as much as I...as you're hoping he does."

"What are you saying, Davey?" Silver pushed up from the chair with an angry grunt and stepped toward the lad.

"Well..." David looked to his father for support while he retreated a step. "It's just that your whole plan depends on Captain Jones, and he could change his mind once he reaches Virginia."

"Go on! Explain!"

"After he came back from his ship last night, he talked about the naval commission, but..."

"But what?"

"He told me his brother owns a very prosperous tailor shop in Fredericksburg, with a highly-placed clientele, and if things went well for him, he'd like to get himself a wife and a plantation where he could retire in 'calm contemplation and poetic ease.'"

Charles gave Silver a glance and looked back to his son. "He told you that?"

"Those were his very words, father." David turned back to his uncle. "I'm just saying it might not work out the way you've hoped."

The old pirate stepped to the fireplace and fell into deep thought. Charles and David knew to hold their tongues.

Silver looked up from the flames. "I'm getting too old to wait for this." The old man spoke as if he was reading his own obituary. "If Captain Jones chooses to follow 'The Seasons' and purchase a plantation to retire, then my dream will die with him."

"Give this up, John. The strain of it will end up killing you and making Elizabeth a widow again."

"As far as killing me, it's the treasure's that's kept me alive this long."

Charles reset his sails and took up another tack. "Your plan hasn't a prayer of working anyway, even if Captain Jones wants that commission."

"Oh? And why not?"

"Well..." Charles hesitated while he thought of an illustration his older brother might accept. "Here!" David and his uncle watched as Charles withdrew a handful of coins from his pocket. Selecting six, he laid them in a straight row on the table and then placed his pocket watch several inches beyond the last coin.

"What are you doing, Charles?"

"Come here and watch."

Silver stepped to the table. "Farthings?"

"Yes!" Charles gave the watch a tap. "Your plan is too much like playing farthings."

"That's a child's game! We're talking about the colonial rebellion, Captain Jones, Robert Ormerod, and a real Spanish treasure!"

"But the principle of the game will demonstrate." Charles put his finger on the coine furthest from the watch. "There are too many ways for this fantastic plan of yours to go wrong between today in King's Town..." He touched each of the six coins in succession. "...and some day on Dead Man's Chest."

David looked down at the table. "Would one of you explain what you're talking about?" David looked to his uncle. "What's 'farthings'?"

"It's a game I taught your father when he was just a pup." Silver twisted his knife from the wall and returned to the table. "If you had a brother, I suppose you'd know it too."

Charles pointed at the watch. "The watch represents your uncle's treasure."

"And the coins?"

"The coins are all the people and elements in his plan, with this last coin, the one nearest the watch, representing the island." Charles looked to his brother. The retired pirate nodded in agreement.

Charles looked to his son. "Try it."

"What am I supposed to do?" David looked to his father and to his uncle. "How does the game work?"

"Very simple, Davey. Put your finger on the coin that's furthest from the watch and then push at the row so the one at the far end moves across the table and touches your father's pocket watch."

"That's easy enough." David put his finger on the end coin and gave the line a confident shove. But just as John and Charles knew they would, the coins slid askew, like so many boats without rudders. The last coin was no closer to the watch than it had been before the push.

David lined up the coins a second time and pushed. He looked up at his father. "You're right, father. There are too many coins."

"That game has nothing to do with my plan, Charles, and you know it!"

"Oh?" Charles picked up the last coin, the one nearest the watch, and held it up to his older brother. "Unless you can guide Robert Ormerod in just the right direction and at just the right time, you'll never get close to that treasure. And as you so aptly pointed out, if he ever suspects he's being manipulated by the pirate Long John Silver, the whole thing falls apart." He replaced the coin in front of his son.

"Exactly!" Silver walked to the table and reached down with both hands, placing a finger on each of the coins. "But if I could control every step of the plan, then I could reach the watch every time, regardless of how many other coins there were in the line." He moved all the coins together, still in a row, across the table until the lead coin clinked against the watch.

"And how do you propose to accomplish that, my older and wiser brother?"

Silver walked behind David and placed a hand on the lad's shoulder. "You truly don't know?"

"You'd have to put somebody..." Charles suddenly realized what the old pirate was suggesting. He pointed at the door. "David! Go to the kitchen and remain there until I call you. Your uncle and I need to speak in private."

Obediently, David turned and left the room.

It's my son, isn't it? Your plan calls for my son—"

"There's no other way, Charles. Davey has to go with him."

"Absolutely not!"

"Good Lord, Charles! He's a grown man! When we were his age, you had already killed several men, and I had a price on my head. You've got to let him go sooner or later."

"But he's all I have left."

"Charles, Charles, Charles." Silver put an arm around his younger brother's shoulder. "You make me so tired when you get on that subject."

"My dead wife is more than a tiresome subject!"

"Aye! Your wife, bless her soul, and that son you're afraid to let grow up!"

"How will he grow up if he's hanged as a spy against the Crown?" Charles walked across to the fireplace and turned about. "If you're so determined to get that treasure, then go along with Captain Jones yourself. I'll not agree to letting my son—" Charles fell silent when he noticed that Silver was pointing at something. "What?"

Silver stepped to the door and jerked it open to reveal the eavesdropping lad. "Look, Charles! Davey's a spy after all, whether you like it or not."

"A spy?" David looked at his uncle and then across to his father. "What..."

"It has nothing to do with you, son!"

"Wrong!" Silver pulled David into the room and put his arm about the lad's shoulder. "It has everything to do with Davey."

"You want me to go to America with Captain Jones, don't you?"

"No he doesn't!" Charles pulled David away from the old pirate's grip. "Captain Jones can go alone. Once your uncle explains the plan to him—"

"That won't work, father."

"You can't know that!"

"But don't you see it, father? Captain Jones can't know he's part of it. I have to go with him to America as your eyes and ears. And when the time's right—"

"Your uncle already tried, so hold your breath."

David gave his father a cold look. "Captain Jones was right about you."

"Right about me? What did he say about me?"

"You don't want me to ever go to sea, do you, Father?" There was a long moment of silence.

"Let the lad grow up, Charles. We all need this."

Charles picked up a small painting of his wife and held it near his chest. After several minutes, he set the picture down and turned back to his brother.

"If I agree, I'll want several assurances."

"Anything, little brother!" Silver was ecstatic. "Anything you want!"

"He's only to be a messenger."

"Agreed!"

"You have to swear to me that he will never go with you or anybody else to Dead Man's Chest."

"Done!" The old man gave a confirmatory wave of his hand. "If he asks me to take him along, I'll refuse!"

"Swear to God!"

"I swear!"

"I'll hold you to that, John Silver!"

"Then it's back to business!" Silver gave a clap of his large hands. "For starters, Captain Jones will need provisions and a crew to help him sail to Virginia." Silver turned to David. "He's sure to ask for your help, Davey. When he does, be sure to take him to your father's main warehouse to make the arrangements. And mind you, it's essential that you've already got him to agree to let you go along—before you meet with your father."

"Yes, sir."

Silver turned to Charles. "Can you arrange—"

Charles was already nodding. "Since David is going along, I'll take care of their provisions."

"And a crew?"

"There'll be no problem getting three or four men willing to take working passage north to the colonies." Charles turned to David. "You can assure Captain Jones of that."

"And you, Charles, will need to play the part of the reluctant father."

"That'll be the easiest job I have.

David gave his uncle a questioning look. "Tell me something. How'd you know that verse was from 'The Seasons'?"

"Oxford." David's face was blank. "The university, lad!"

Charles folded his arms and leaned back against the fireplace mantle. "Go on. Tell him about Oxford."

"I was a restless lad." Silver sheathed his knife and sat back down. "My left leg had only been blown off a couple of years prior to when I caught that ship. Met a kindhearted professor on board who took me under his wing. Figured it would be quite a feather in his cap if he could take a poor, one-legged lad what can't 'ardly speak a lick, an' make a gentlem'n of 'im." Silver winked at David. "Four years of free tutoring he gave me, in exchange for all my pirate stories, most of which I had to make up on the spot. By the time I returned to King's Town in '25, I could read and write like a master. Read all of Defoe's works and half of Shakespeare's."

"Uncle Silver! Do you honestly think I would believe such a tall tale? You at Oxford University?"

"Your father doesn't. But check the record. I sat behind Sir Berrymore—that was my professor's name—when he debated the authorship of the Shakespearean plays in '24." Silver leaned forward and whispered. "It was the Seventeenth Earl of Oxford—Edward de Vere— who really wrote those plays. Used his father-in-law, Lord Burghley, for the character Polonius in Hamlet."

"It does explain your command of the King's English. But why do you talk that way—like a pirate—around your tavern?"

"Ah!" Silver slapped the wooden leg. "Long John Silver's nobody's fool." He resumed his thick cockney twang for effect. "Why, me clientele would be slippin' their hawsers an' spillin' their gold at the Bucket o' Blood or the Maiden's Breath if I be drivin' 'em off wi' the words o' some bleedin' professor. Har! Har! Har!"

A second bottle of Charles's finest brandy was emptied before the meeting ended. And at his insistence, the old pirate slept the night at the Noble mansion. John Silver was up early and pressed David into helping him back down the hill to his tavern.

***

John awoke just before first light by the squaks of two gulls fighting over a fish carcass on the roof outside his room. After a quick shave he dressed, set the sextant in its case and walked down to the tavern. The public room was empty, with the chairs still stacked atop the tables. John could hear a woman humming a Scottish tune to the cadence of rattling pans.

"Hello?" He walked toward the galley. "Are you there, Mister Bridger?"

Elizabeth Bridger stepped to the public room and pointed toward the docks with a large spoon. "He's outside feeding his other ladies, Captain Jones."

"You know me?"

"Well—I know about you. Jack was quite impressed with you, Captain." She was a short woman at five foot four inches, and pleasingly overweight. Her hair was turning gray across the forelocks.

"Thank you, Ma'am." He gave her a curt salute, turned and walked out through the front doors.

Jack Bridger, as John knew him, was standing alone at the edge of the dock. He held a two-gallon cask beneath his left arm and dug at its contents with his free hand. A dozen gray and white gulls circled overhead in the sultry dawn air, hoping to take part in this oft-acted ritual.

"Come to Silver, me little orphans, an' get yer mornin' vittles!" A handful of kitchen cuttings flew into the sky amongst the scavengers, sending them into a mad dive toward the water. "And you too, Sadie!" The oldest of the birds took flight from the forechains of a nearby bowsprit. "Unless yer gettin' too fat." A second handful flew skyward in her direction. "Catch it girl!" The aged gull folded her wings for a half-second in an unsuccessful attempt to intercept one of the larger pieces of waste.

John Silver recognized the distinctive, almost military gait of the young sea captain approaching across the weathered planks. He spoke without turning about. "Top o' the mornin' to ya, Captain Jones!"

"Good morning, Mister Bridger!" The young man walked to Silver's side and feigned interest in the gulls. "Have you seen your nephew yet this fine morning?"

Without answering, Silver turned and shot his rancid-smelling right hand toward the young captain. John stepped back two paces and transferred the sextant—Silver's intended target—to his other hand.

"No, Captain Jones. Haven't seen the lad since you an' he was tradin' wind last night in me tavern." Silver stepped toward John and pointed with his dirty hand. "My guess is he's still in bed—what with all the ale he drank last night." Silver looked right and left as if someone might overhear. He reached out and touched John's blue waistcoat in the spot where British soldiers hung their medals. "Don't be tellin' nobody, but just between you an' me, Captain, I think the lad wants to go to sea with ya."

"Ahhh!" John looked down at the spot of filth on the blue wool.

"Now look see what I went an' done, an' just when we was gettin' to know each other!" Silver pulled his filthy towel from a pocket and came at the young man. "Here! Let old Jack Bridger clean that off!"

"No thank you!" John backed away several steps. "I can clean it off when I get aboard my ship." He turned and walked quickly across to the short gangplank. Silver stomped his feet as if in pursuit, and John quickened his pace. The old pirate let out a hearty laugh.

As John approached the Falmouth Packet, the sun burst from behind a cloud, silhouetting the topsail yard with its neatly furled sail, to form a distorted crucifix in the bright morning sky. A light breeze brought with it the sweat-like smell of the warm seawater and the ever-present odor of rotting fish carcasses from under the dock.

The changing tide had upset the gangway, so John gave it a kick as he stepped aboard. Passing the binnacle, he stowed the sextant in its drawer, and then dropped through the companionway and aft to his cabin. He took up the ship's logbook and made his daily entry: "Monday, 6 December, 1773. Laid up at King's Town for provisions and a fresh crew. Mail delivered to the Postal House. J. Jones; Master." As he signed the entry, his attention was drawn to footsteps on the main deck forward.

"Hello!" It was the voice of David Noble. "Are you aboard, Captain Jones?"

"Down here, in the cabin!" He truly liked this young Jamaican and hoped what Jack Bridger had told him was true. "Come back and I'll show you about."

The young man stepped down the short ladder and stood at the small cabin's doorway. He made a quick survey of the cramped spaces—forward and aft—and stepped into the cabin.

"Good morning, David!" John closed the logbook and offered his hand.

"And good morning to you, Captain Jones. Did you sleep well?"

"I never sleep well the first night ashore." John made a side to side motion. "One gets used to the roll of a ship, and that makes the steady deck ashore quite annoying." The two young men stood looking at each other for an awkward moment. "So...are you ready for that tour?"

"Yes, by all means."

John led the way topside and forward toward the bow, but stopped beside the main hold. "The ship is empty now, but I'm hoping I can contract to take a cargo north to Virginia."

"Then you're serious about going to your brother's place in Fredericksburg?"

"Yes, I am." John knew what the lad wanted to hear, so didn't disappoint him. "If you'd agree to working passage, I'd enjoy having you come along."

"But what about provisions and the rest of your crew?" David figured to fish for a moment. "You'd need at least four others to man this ship properly."

"Last night, you mentioned that your father is a merchant." John crossed to the larboard rail and looked out at the water and the line of anchored ships. He turned back to the young Jamaican. "You don't suppose he'd need a cargo taken to Virginia?"

"I believe my father's at his main warehouse right now. If we're quick, we might be able to catch him before his first appointment."

"Would he look kindly upon an unannounced visit like that?"

"He's a patient man, and I'm his son. We wouldn't be an intrusion."

John stepped toward the gangplank and hesitated. "I appreciate this, David."

"I have a confession, Captain Jones."

"Oh?"

"I told him about you last evening, and about you possibly sailing to Virginia. He's actually expecting us."

John smiled. "Well then, let's not keep him waiting."

The walk westward along Harbor Street took only a few minutes. Ornate whitewashed homes lined the narrow cobblestone road, with the ever-present ivy clinging tenaciously to their walls. The Spanish moss added a carnival-like atmosphere to the trees, which formed a thick canopy over the road. Two dogs in Buccaneer's Park played tug-of-war at an empty sugar sack, but they retreated at the two men's approach.

David stopped next to a neat stack of fragrant timbers. "Last evening, you were saying something about a commission in the Continental Navy."

"That might have been the ale speaking, David."

David gave a laugh and continued. "I've been hearing quite a few rumors that the Americans are on the verge of a revolt."

"I've heard those same rumors. But whether or not I could get such a commission doesn't change the fact that I must get to America as quickly as possible. There's another postal packet due from Trinidad within a fortnight, and I'm certain that arrest warrant I told you about will be among her papers."

David stopped and turned to his new friend. "I'm serious about going with you, John, but I've never been away from my father. He may agree to send you with a cargo, and even find you a crew, but as far as me..." David gave John a look like a schoolboy waiting for his grades.

John smiled. "I can't give you any guarantees, David. We could become naval officers or we could end up as common sailors on a river ferry. This could be the adventure of our lives, or we could die at the attempt. But yes, I do want you to come with me, and I'll intervene with your father." John offered his right hand. "To America then, at whatever the price."

"At whatever the price!" David took John's hand and shook it vigorously. "And if we find my father in a good mood, we'll have both provisions and a crew!" David turned and broke into a run between the stacks of freshly sawn timbers and planking toward his father's warehouse, with John close behind. Just as John Silver had planned it, Charles Noble was waiting in his office.

David climbed the single flight of stairs and pushed through the office door. "Excuse me, Father. Are you busy?"

The elder Noble sat at his massive desk reading through a stack of letters. The office, which smelled of tea and pine smoke, measured approximately five paces in each direction. There were two bookcases and a Franklin stove to the left, two harsh chairs in front of the desk, and a large window to the right that looked down into the Noble Warehouse.

Charles removed his reading glasses. "No, not yet." He rubbed his eyes. "Just a few figures to put together before I meet with Mister Ericksen. I'm rather reluctant to do business with the old thief. Cheated me out of five hundred pounds last year." He looked at John. "Ah! This must be the young man you told me about last evening."

"Father, I'd like you to meet Captain John Paul Jones. Captain, this is my father, Charles Noble."

Charles stepped past his desk and offered his hand. "I'm honored to meet one of the King's postal captains. He gave a knowing chuckle. "You and your little fleet of ships are a merchant's lifeblood."

John gave the older man a quick smile. "Pleased to meet you too, sir."

Charles turned about to his stove and picked up a badly stained teapot. He turned back to John. "Could I offer you a cup of tea?"

"That would be nice, sir." John looked to David and mouthed the words, Are you going to ask him?

The merchant poured three steaming cups, and set John's on the ledge of the warehouse window. "My son was telling me that you're on your way to Virginia."

"That's true, sir. I was hoping that you might be able to help me."

"Help you with what?" Charles held a tray toward John with cream and sugar.

"I'm…" John looked through the window down onto the warehouse floor. There, lined up like dead soldiers were the thousand new cannons that the Nobles and Silver had been discussing the night before.

"He's out of money, father, and needs provisions and a crew for the passage."

"Out of money?" Charles gave David a wink while John counted the cannons. "But doesn't the Postal Service provide everything you need?"

John was too occupied with his calculations to hear him.

"Captain Jones?"

John jumped and turned back to the merchant. "Sir?"

"Did you hear anything I just told you?"

"I'm sorry, sir. I was counting your cannons." John turned back to the warehouse. "I've never seen so many new cannons in one place. How did you get them?"

"That's not your affair, Captain Jones." Charles took a sip of tea and walked to his desk. "My son tells me you need provisions and a crew to sail to Virginia. Is that true?"

"I have some money, sir, but I'm afraid it wouldn't be enough. I was hoping that you would have a cargo you'd want delivered to Savannah, Charles Town or the Chesapeake River."

"Hmm. A cargo?" Charles thought for a moment and shook his head. "There's no shortage of strong backs in King's Town, Captain Jones, but provisions are another matter. How much money do you have?"

"I have forty pounds of my own and another thirty-two in the ship's till. Will seventy-two—"

"For the trip you describe, your seventy-two pounds would purchase provisions for only three, maybe four men at most. If you could get together another, let's say..." The merchant scratched some figures on a piece of paper. He looked back to John. "If you had another fifty pounds, I think I could outfit a crew of six." He paused and looked over his glasses at the young man. "But there is another possibility."

John had turned and was looking at the cannons again.

"Captain Jones?"

John jumped, and then turned back to his host. "Yes? You were saying?"

"I was going to say that there might be another way for you to finance your trip to Virginia, provided my business deal goes well this morning. But if it doesn't work out, you'd need at least fifty pounds more."

"Fifty pounds? But I don't know where I—"

David interrupted. "I can provide the extra money you need."

Charles turned on his son. "What are you saying?" He pointed back at John. "Captain Jones may not even make it all the way to America, much less return here and be able to repay you."

"He wouldn't have to, Father."

"Why?"

"Because I've decided to go with him."

"You've what?"

"They're looking for men to become officers in the Continental Navy. Captain Jones has already agreed to take me along."

John was nearly finished with his count of the cannons, and only half aware of the argument going on behind him.

"I forbid it!" Charles glanced quickly at the sea captain and then back to his son—giving David a wink and nodding at John. "I have plans for you, and they don't include you running off to fight against your own government!"

"I'm almost eighteen years old, father, and I'm going with Captain Jones! It would be better for both of us if it was with your approval!" The two looked around at John, hoping he was enjoying their theatrics. But he was completely absorbed with the cannons. Charles stepped to the window and pulled the sash cord, closing the curtain.

John stepped back and turned to Charles. "Those are carronades from Scotland! I was born and raised not a furlong from the Carron Iron Foundry."

"I was under the impression that you desired my assistance in acquiring a crew and provisions for your trip to Virginia! Is that true or not?"

"It's true, sir!"

"Then you'll attend to the conversation at hand and disregard my cannons." He turned to David. "Being an experienced sea captain, I would like for you to have a word with my son!"

"A word with your son?" John looked to David and back to Charles. "Sir?"

"He seems to have it in his mind to go with you! If you want my assistance, Captain Jones, then you'll join me in convincing him of the folly of this decision."

"Your son is old enough to make his own decisions, Mister Noble. He's welcome to come with me to Virginia, but I'll not intervene for either of you. It's not my place to get involved in a family matter."

"Since it seems that you and he have already agreed to his going along, you're very involved. Do you intend that my son take up arms against his country?"

"My intentions are to get to Virginia as quickly as possible. If it's his or my fate to fight in America's revolt, then none of us can stop that." John looked to David. "It's up to you and your father, David."

David looked at his father. "I'm still going with him, Father."

"Damn!" Charles glared at the two youg men. "I've neither the time, nor the patience to discuss this matter further this morning. I can only hope that within the next few days you'll come to your senses and change your mind." He turned away. "I would appreciate being left alone now."

Chapter 4

Charles Noble stood in his office with his arms crossed and jaw set, scanning the dormant arsenal of slept below in his warehouse. None of the bronze and iron monsters had ever tasted gunpowder, nor had their bellies yet been filled with the hideous assortment of iron that would someday rob men of their lives and limbs. Yet he could already hear the faint roll of battle drums and the bugler's call to arms—signals that would quicken this silent, metallic army into battle. It was a good exchange, albeit somewhat felonious, that he'd made with Joshua Smoot—the Dutch merchantman with the thousand cannons secreted away in her bilge for the 40-gun Hesperus. While he had gained an arsenal with tremendous political leverage, the pirate had acquired a ship without equal in the Caribbean. But no matter! After all, business is business. Let the Lord sort the victor from the victim. There was a knock at the door. "Come!"

"You asked to see me, sir?"

"Yes, Captain Jones, I did." Charles pointed at one of the chairs. "Please have a seat."

"I'd rather stand, sir." John looked at the wall clock. "David told me this was urgent."

"My son sometimes exaggerates things." Charles pulled three rolled parchments from a map holder beside his desk and held them out to the young sea captain. "I thought you might like to have some charts of the—"

"I already have a full compliment of charts, sir. Was there something else?"

"Have my fitters completed the work as you requested?"

"Yes, sir. Everything's perfect, especially the four cannons."

"And do you have the right assortment and quantity of powder and ammunition?"

"Sir!" John was getting frustrated. Preparations for the voyage had taken nearly two weeks. Every day of those two weeks he had expected the arrest warrant to arrive from Tobago. It hadn't yet, but he didn't want to try the patience of any guardian angel he might have by staying in King's Town one minute longer than necessary. "The provisions are fine, the cannons are a blessing demanding my deepest gratitude, and David tells me the crew is aboard. There's nothing left but for me to get underway."

"You sound upset, young man."

"I don't mean to appear insubordinate, sir, but you didn't ask me back this morning just to discuss my provisions and crew. There's something else, isn't there?"

Charles moved across to his desk. "Yes there is." He walked past his observation window to a shelf set with various nautical instruments, including Sir Henry Morgan's quadrant, which David had always admired. Next to the quadrant stood a painting of a young woman.

"Pardon me, sir, but I'm in rather a hurry. I must reach the ruins at Port Royal before the tide turns." John could see that the older man would have his say, so offered a sympathetic word. "I know this is difficult for you."

"Difficult?" Charles spun around. "You don't know anything, Captain Jones!" The older man ground his teeth. "Did David tell you about about his mother."

"No sir, except that she died when he was very young."

"He's my only son and the only heir to my estate. You'll be taking him to a strange land and possibly into a war against his own people." Tears began to well in Charles' eyes. "I don't think I could bear it if David were killed also."

"Also?" John looked to the small painting of Charles' wife. "David told me that his mother died of natural causes—an illness."

"He was only five at the time—hardly knew his mother." Charles picked up the painting. "Oh Alexandria..." He turned back to John, the tears now flowing freely over his cheeks. "I killed her, Jones. I killed my beloved Alexandria."

"I don't understand, sir."

"She was already sick with the flu—weak beyond measure. It must have been the meat I brought to her, because she fell into convulsions shortly after she ate it. I called a physician, but nothing could be done for her."

"If it was food poisoning, then it was an accident. You didn't kill her."

"But don't you see? I was the one who brought it to her." He set her picture down on the desk. "If I were to lose David..."

"If you will permit me, sir, you're going to have to face the fact that David's a grown man and will do what he wants. He told me about your fear of him being abducted by pirates or pressed into service aboard one of the King's warships. Isn't it better that he goes freely to America with me?"

"Regretably, it's no longer my decision." The older man ran his fingers through his thick, graying hair. "Moments before she died, she asked me to promise to never let David go to sea. I didn't want to agree to such a thing, and I may have waited too long to answer her. I'm afraid she died before she heard my promise."

"If she didn't hear it, then I'd say you aren't bound by it."

"Whether she heard my promise or not, I still made it." Charles wiped a tear from his cheek. "I'd like to make a bargain with you, Captain Jones."

"A bargain?" John's eyes narrowed with suspicion.

"No." Charles corrected himself. "Let's call it an agreement between friends. My part of the agreement concerns those four cannons and the provisions for your ship."

"I've already paid you the forty-five pounds for the provisions, and you told me that those cannons were throwaways." John reached into his waistcoat for his purse. "You've left me with only twenty-two pounds until I reach Virginia. Surely you don't intend to take all the—"

"Put your money away, Captain Jones." Charles turned and placed a heavy purse on the desk. "What I'm proposing is that you take back the money you've already paid me in exchange for—"

"But we had an agreement. Your concern for your son's safety is justified, but I'm a man of my word."

"And that's exactly what I'm hoping to purchase from you—your word."

"Sir?" John was confused.

"David is young, and sometimes acts in a foolhardy manner. I can't begin to tell you how many times I've had to rescue the lad from the local constable or an irate father protecting his daughter's virtue. I want your word that you'll make an extra effort to watch after him."

"Go on."

"In exchange for your promise, you may have the provisions, the cannons, the extra powder you asked for, and the forty-five pounds you've already paid me." John began to speak, but Charles stopped him with an upheld hand. "We'll call it my investment in David's and your future in the Continental Navy, if they ever get around to putting one together."

"I need no bribe to stand by a friend, be he your son or another's. I'll be just as dependent upon his protection as he'll be on mine. That's what friendship is about."

"You'll not give me a lesson in friendship, young man."

"No? Then why do you insist it carries a price?" There was a long pause as the tension between the two filled the office.

"Forgive me, sir." Charles picked up the painting of his wife once again and stared at her likeness. "I underestimated you. I only wanted—"

"You only want what any father wants." John recognized the older man's repentance. "I understand."

"Then accept that money as a gift."

"I will, sir, but only as a gift." John picked up the purse and put it in his pocket.

"Good!" There was relief in the older man's voice.

"This will certainly help." John offered his benefactor his right hand. "With God's help, I'll send your son back not only as a man, but as a naval officer and war hero."

"May The Good Lord go with both of you, John Jones."

"Thank you, sir." John picked up his hat. "If there's nothing else, sir, I'll—"

"There is one more thing."

"Sir?"

"Please don't say anything to David about my fear of his going to sea. I'd rather he believe it's to get the naval commission and to establish contacts for my shipping company that I let him go. Will you do that for me?"

"I will, sir." John opened the office door. "Farewell."

"Thank you, young man, and may the Lord grant you fair winds and following seas."

The narrow streets were still wet from the rainsquall that had passed across the island just before sunrise. A Negro child chased one of the many stray cats across the street in front of John and into a tree. Fearing the well-dressed white man who approached from the Noble warehouses, she ran into a stone house and peered from the door. John gave her a smile, and in exchange the girl stuck out her tongue. John gave a laugh and returned the gesture. A moment later, he emerged from the town at the docks.

"Be gettin' underway I see!" It was the keeper of Silver Jack's. "Take my advice, Cap'n Jones. If ye come up against a red flag, pack your cannons with barstock and give 'em hell!"

"Thank you, Mister Bridger." John stopped for a moment. "And thank you for your hospitality. I'll carry fond memories of King's Town for many years because of you and your fine tavern."

"The least I could do fer a seafarin' man o' yer fine caliber." The old pirate remembered something. "An' regardin' that bottle o' Scotch whiskey I promised ya, I'll make good on it some day, by the powers!"

John gave the old man a smile, then skipped across the gangway onto his small craft. He made a quick survey of the last-minute preparations. Two men were lowering a green turtle into the hold, and the deck was stacked neatly with flour barrels, grain bags, and salted beef in new wooden boxes.

He stepped to the youngest of the four men Charles had provided. "Do you men know where Master Noble is?"

"He's below, sir, with Seamus." The young seaman pointed at the mid ship hatch.

"David!" John stepped to the opening and looked down. "Are we ready to sail?"

"Aye, Captain Jones!" David held a twelve-pound cannonball in each hand. "Matter of fact, if you hadn't come pretty soon, I'd be sending Barragan after you."

A well-tanned Irishman in his late thirties stepped into the light and looked up at John. He was a skinny man with the look of a gecko lizard. The deep lines about his squinted eyes testified to many an hour spent peering across the reflective sea.

John gave the man a quick inspection. "You must be the new man."

The Irishman wrestled a turtle onto its back and laid it next to several others in the hold. "Aye, sir, that I am. Master Noble been tellin' me an' the rest o' the crew 'bout ya sir, an' we be lookin' forward to this 'ere trip o' yers."

"Well, I hope it's everything you expect, Barragan."

Seamus gave the turtle a kick. "It were my idea to take these along fer fresh meat, seein' as how—"

"We can talk about that later." John turned his attention back to David. "Stow those cannonballs, David. The tide—we need to get underway."

A broad smile flashed across the youth's face. He tossed the iron spheres to Seamus, and then, with the agility of a cat, he leapt up the ladder and into the bright morning sun.

"Clark! Carini!" David barked the orders like a veteran. "Unfurl the mainsa'l! Etinger and Barragan, single up and stand by to cast off all lines!"

The small ship came alive to David's well-rehearsed commands. As the east wind caught the backside of the staysail to pull the little ship's bow from the dock, the last line slipped from the well-worn bollard, freeing the craft for its long voyage to America. The flying jib and square topsail soon joined their larger canvas siblings, opening like the wings of a butterfly to grab their share of the breeze coming over the green hills of Jamaica.

***

John Silver stood in the doorway of his tavern with a Royal Navy dispatch in his hand, watching his investment shrink away toward the ruins of Port Royal. A second figure stepped from the shadows of the public room and stood next to the old pirate.

"Well, Charles, from what I read in this dispatch I intercepted, our plan is working out better than I expected."

"What is it? What does it say?"

"Parliament is going to prohibit the importing of all large weapons and gunpowder to the colonies. There's a war brewing, little brother, and my plan will be right in the middle of it." He waited for the younger man's answer, but there was none. "You aren't having any regrets, are you?"

"I wouldn't call it a regret, exactly."

"Then what would you call it?"

"Doesn't it matter to you that what you're doing could determine the outcome of that war?"

"Why should it?"

"Because we're both British subjects, that's why."

"Speak for yourself, Charles. I may be British by birth, but I'm a gentleman of fortune. My breed profits regardless of who rules a country, be he a king on a throne far across the sea, a new king on this side of the ocean, or some other type of government in the American colonies. If your God purposes that America be free from the motherland, those cannons won't frustrate His will."

"As much as I hate to admit it, you're right." Charles put a shading hand to his eyes as they watched the Falmouth Packet shrink away to the south. "I just don't like using my son and his friend this way."

"Cheer up, little Brother. You'll see the good in it when they bring us that treasure." John Silver brightened. "And maybe someone will write a fifth verse to "Dead Man's Chest" in my honor."

***

The Falmouth Packet responded like a yearling colt, steering around Port Royal and into the deeper waters of the Caribbean. By midmorning the winds had freshened and shifted to the southeast, putting the starboard reach for Hispaniola and the Windward Passage well within the craft's lay line. John leaned against the windward rail and watched David ease the long tiller to lee.

"Your father had a very difficult time letting you go."

"I know." David cast a gaze across the isthmus toward the row of shops and taverns of King's Town. His father and John Silver were gone. "Why did he call you back to his office?"

John pulled the purse from his inner pocket. "He wouldn't take my money."

"I'd guessed he'd do something like that." David pulled a similar bag from his own pocket. "He gave me a hundred pounds to help us when we reached Virginia. He told me that it was part of my inheritance." David scanned the rigging and barked an order at one of the crewmen. "He tries so hard to come across like a taskmaster, but under that thin coat, my father's as soft as cream pudding."

"He told me about your mother—about the tainted meat he brought her."

"Hmm. He's told very few people about that. Every year at her birthday, and then again on their wedding anniversary, he takes her painting into his study and locks the door. I've listened to him cry for her every year for as long as I can remember." David's voice began to tremble and a cold tear spilled from his eye.

"He's quite a man, David. You're fortunate to have a father like him."

"I know. And I know how deeply my leaving hurts him."

While they spoke, one of the lines worked its way loose, allowing the topsail to rotated on its rigging and catch the wind on its front side. The little ship heeled over to lee and came to a near stop. A harsh order from David brought the crew alive to correct the problem. Within seconds, the loose brace was captured and the topsail—as they called the single square sail high atop the main mast—was secured and trimmed.

"Your father didn't see you off. Did you and he have words?"

Before David could answer, seaman Barragan approached from amidships. "By yer leave, Master Noble, but this here be my watch. You an' the Cap'n can go 'bout yer affairs, if it pleases ya."

"Thank you, Seamus." David turned the helm over to the Irishman and pointed ahead. "Hold her near shore until we pass Morant Point, and then steer for the center of the Windward Passage."

"Aye, aye, sir." Seamus put a knuckle to his forelock, man-of-war style.

The days and nights were long as Jamaica shrank behind them and Hispaniola grew in size to the east. When the natives of Hispaniola were distinguishable on the western beaches of their island, John ordered a course change for Punta Maisa on the eastern tip of Cuba. On the 19th of December, the Falmouth Packet began her run along Cuba's north coast toward Spanish Florida.

David approached his friend and captain. "Something's bothering you. What's the matter?"

"How could you tell?" John leaned forward against the stern rail and looked across the waves to the south.

"The men came to me first—bothered. You've been especially quiet for the last two days."

John turned about and faced the young Jamaican. "It's your father. I feel like a puppet on his strings."

"A puppet? I don't know what you're— "

"That first day you introduced us. As I think back, it was as if you and he were reading lines from a carefully scripted play."

David didn't answer.

"You haven't told me everything, have you?" John waited for the younger man's reply. When it didn't come, he continued. "This whole matter of getting my ship provisioned and you coming to the colonies with me...there's something going on that I don't know about, isn't there?"

"I don't know what you're talking about." A hot tingle crept up David's back to his neck. He looked into the rigging as if to study the trim of the sails.

"I'll be blunt, David. Has your father turned me into a smuggler?"

"A smuggler?" David gave a laugh, relieved that John's suspicions were so far from the truth. "That's ridiculous. Why would you think such a thing?"

"Because nothing else fits." John studied David's expression for any hint that his guess was right. "Maybe it's my suspicious nature, but it seems to me that your father agreed much too quickly to your going along."

"And that makes you think we're carrying something illegal in our hold?"

"I've thought of everything, and smuggling is the only thing that makes sense."

"Well, it's not smuggling."

"Then there is something!" John snapped back.

"What?"

"The way you answered my question. It implies there is something else—besides smuggling. What are you and he up to?"

"There's nothing. Except..."

"Aha!" John was pleased that he had broken the younger man's resolve so quickly.

"He's afraid that I was about to go to sea with one of the pirates. I've heard him and my uncle argue about it more than once."

"Your father mentioned that to me, but it still doesn't quite fit."

"If you don't want my father's help, then turn about and take me— and everything my father has given you—back to King's Town!"

John weighed his options quickly. "I guess you're right. It's just that I've never seen a man so generous with his property or so caring for his son. I can't help it, David. It just suggested..." John extended his hand to the young Jamaican. "Can you forgive my suspicions?"

"Consider it done." David accepted the older man's hand. "I'm sure I'd have reacted the same way if the situation were reversed."

***

The winter of 1773–74 was mild in comparison to several in the past. The small postal packet had run into two insignificant storms between King's Town and the east coast of Spanish Florida—a rarity during December. Their good fortune with the weather was matched by their seeming immunity to other ships they had passed along the way. Three different colonial privateers had come close, but had broken off when it was clear the Falmouth Packet carried only the King's mail.

But a sailor's luck can only hold for so long. As the ship passed three leagues seaward of Florida's Point Royal Sound, the sky turned dark, and a cold southeasterly began to whip at the rigging. The gentle swells that had lifted and pushed the small craft forward for so many days now became angry at the wind's rough touch, with whitecaps leaping from the dark waves like rabbits running before a wildfire.

David called out to the youngest crewman. "Etinger, go below and get Captain Jones!" The young Dutchman ran to the aft hatch and dropped out of sight. The seaman knocked urgently at the door. "Captain Jones!"

"Yes?"

"It's Etinger, sir! Mister Noble wants you on deck. We've another storm pressing from the sou'west, and it looks to be a bad one this time!"

"Tell Mister Noble to begin reefing the sails. I'll be there in a few minutes."

"But, Mister Noble told us..."

"I'll only be a moment."

"Aye, aye, Captain!"

By the time John had donned his foul weather gear and made his way to the deck, the raging wind had already begun to tear at the tiny ship with the ferocity of an angry lion. David had waited too long to take action, and he lacked the experience necessary to give his frightened and confused crew the proper orders to fight off this sudden attacker. It was no more than a third-rate tropical depression, but to this green crew it was a ravenous monster, intent on their destruction. It came upon them with its teeth and claws bared for a fight.

John surveyed the situation and barked out a series of orders. "David, I'll take the helm. I want you to get all hands on that topsa'l! If we don't lower the yard and furl the sail quickly, we're likely to lose it, along with the top mast!" John took the tiller under his right arm and braced himself in a wide-legged stance. The following sea was throwing the small vessel sideways with such force that the tiller lifted John from the deck and threw him against the rail.

"David!" John shouted with a hand to his injured ribs. "I want all the sails taken in and the sea anchor rigged forward. Once we have those sails down we'll put her nose to the sea and ride this thing out!"

David dropped through the forward hatch while the others went about their assigned tasks. Coordinating their efforts, the two teams lowered the mainsail and lashed it securely to its boom. The two jibs offered no immediate threat, so all hands went to work on the topsail. It lacked the buntlines found on most square sails, so the first step was to lower the yard and pivot it to spill its wind. At Seamus's signal, both the lift lines were slacked, but the larboard side refused to give way.

John saw that something was amiss. "What's the matter, Barragan?"

"It's the larboard lift, sir! It's fouled at the mast head!" The Irishman pointed at the slacked line where it was twisted about the block. "Should I go up an' loose it, Cap'n?"

"Not in this gale!" The winds had reached forty knots and were increasing a knot every minute. "We'll have to release the sheets, let it fly free and hope for the best!" He felt his ribs. They were clearly broken. "Secure the starboard lift and stand by the braces!" It was too late. Before the sheets could be untied, the topmast broke just above its housing, releasing the flying jib and allowing the topsail to hang upside-down against the main mast.

John cried against the wind. "Damn! Stand by to come about!"

By this time David had pulled the sea anchor from its bag and secured its line to the cat's head. "David, when I give the word, deploy the sea anchor to windward!"

John watched the swells rushing upon their craft from astern. Blue water had already begun breaking over the bow and into the bilges. There was no time to waste.

But before he could give the command to deploy the canvas drag, a large swell crashed against the stern, pushing the rudder flat against the transom. The force of the tiller swinging sideways lifted John off the deck and threw him headlong against the starboard rail. The little ship turned sideways in the trough, allowing the next swell to devour the quarterdeck and rip along the planking forward. Several of the crew and two of the hatch covers were thrown across the deck. When the sea washed away through the scuppers, the Falmouth Packet's deck resembled the trash-filled streets of Jamaica during a monsoon.

There was a flurry of confusion and frantic gesturing at the main mast. The fouled topsail had caught the wind and billowed like a spinnaker, pulling sideways and heeling the ship over forty-five degrees to starboard. While the sea once again began to spill across the deck, John changed his mind. Since there was no way to spill the wind from the uncontrolled sail, his only option was to turn and run with the wind.

"David! Hold that sea anchor and come aft to help me on the tiller!"

"Aye, but we can't run with the sea!" David stowed the sea anchor and began the arduous run for the stern. "We're taking water over the bow and without the hatches, the hold's beginning to fill!"

"We have no choice!"

"Can't we at least run on a quarter, so our bow doesn't dig into the swells so badly?"

"I tried that already, and it's only worse!"

David struggled against the wind and water to reach John at the helm, and together they managed to turn the little ship northward again to run with the swells.

"Barragan!" John pointed toward the hold. "Put two men on the pump!"

The storm's full force was now upon the tiny ship. With each rise of the sea and push from astern, the bowsprit cut deep into the swell ahead. John felt it first—that unmistakable heavy wallowing that meant the hold was filling.

Seamus had put Clark and Carini on the bilge pump, but water was coming over the bow and into the missing hatch covers faster than the pump could push it back. The Irishman came aft to report.

John called out before he could speak. "I know, Barragan! If we don't figure a way to lighten the bow, we'll continue to ship water till we swamp." John looked about him for some glimmer of hope. "I'm open to suggestions."

Seamus pondered the situation for a moment and then brightened. "The anchor chain, sir!"

"What about it?"

"If Master Noble can find something to cover the hatches, Etinger and I could move the chain aft!"

"Move it aft?"

"Aye! We gotta shift the load, not just lighten it! An' the anchor chain's the only thing heavy enough to make a difference!"

"How heavy do you figure?"

"A hundred, maybe a hundred an' fifty stone, sir, if we be lucky!"

"Leave Clark on the pump and the rest of you get to it. It may be our only hope."

While Barragan, Etinger and Carini went about their unorthodox task, the sea continued to flow over the bow with each swell. The water in the hold was now deep enough that the last two turtles had righted themselves, thrilled with the prospect of escape.

John and David struggled with the tiller and watched the rusty chain snake out of the forward hatch, through the crew's hands and aft across the deck.

John called forward. "Where's that thing going?"

"Into your cabin, sir! It's the only place to put it if we want to raise the bow!" The Irishman disappeared down the hatch for a moment and then reappeared. "But don't worry, Cap'n. We're putting it to starboard, away from your desk and bunk."

Slowly—almost imperceptibly at first—the bow began to ride higher and higher as more and more of the heavy links moved aft. By the time the chain locker was empty, the sailor on the pump saw the water stop rising and then begin to drop. With the chain moved, the men turned their efforts toward the last uncovered hatch. Within minutes, a spare piece of canvas had been lashed over the hole, stopping the open sea from filling the bilges.

John called to the crew. "We're going to make it!" He was bruised and battered from the thrashing the tiller had given him, and blood was running down his side under his left arm. It was painful to take a breath, but with any luck, his injuries would be limited to only one or two broken ribs. John whispered through his atheism "Thank you, Lord."

By dusk, the storm had moved beyond the Falmouth Packet to the northeast, leaving the sea as it had been before the attack. At John's order, the sea anchor was deployed, and all hands enjoyed a well-earned night of rest and recuperation. The upper main mast was broken and the topsail was badly torn, but the six-man crew had survived.

***

John slept a painful twelve hours. The tiller had left its grizzly signature on his body from head to toe.

Seamus was the first to look in on John and David. He set a tray of food on the desk and raised John's shirt where the blood had soaked through. "You've two broken ribs, Cap'n, and one of 'em has breached yer hull."

"Wonderful!" John looked up at the Irishman. "How long do ribs take to mend?"

"A month, provided ye give them a chance." He applied a dressing over the puncture wound and then wrapped John's chest with a restricting bandage. "Since we aren't going nowhere until we do some repairs, you might as well stay down here and rest a little longer."

John nodded. "Thank you. I will."

Most of the tangled lines and broken yards had been cleared by the time the afternoon sunlight shown through the open porthole and began to play across John's face. There was a heavy odor in his nostrils as he heaved into painful consciousness. Am I still bleeding? He looked down at his chest. The dressings are all in place, yet I smell fresh blood.

He turned his hands in the bright sunlight, looking at his skin color. Normal, but that smell?

On the starboard side of his small cabin, piled high against the ships planking, was the large hump of rusty anchor chain they had moved aft during the storm.

"That's what I'm smelling." He struggled up from his bunk. Without washing, he climbed the short ladder to the main deck.

David saw his captain first. "Welcome back from the dead!" The lad sat in a rope sling high above the deck where he was working to repair the masthead. "What finally woke you?"

"The sun through the porthole and the smell of that rusty chain." John shaded his eyes to get a good look at his young friend. "Hope you know what you're doing up there. Tie the wrong hitches and we'll have that yard down around our ears again with the first wind."

"Don't worry about my knots!" David gave two firm tugs on the fresh manila line and drove a marlinspike through its strands to hold it in place. "It's that torn tops'l we've to worry about. None of us has ever mended a sail before."

John's eyes were becoming accustomed to the bright afternoon sun, but he still had to peer between his hands at the men on the deck. Clark, Barragan and Carini had the large topsail spread across the deck and were stitching closed the single rip it had sustained the previous afternoon.

Seamus looked up at his captain and sucked at one of the three fresh needle wounds in his left hand. "If we can just make 'er strong enough to get us into Charles Town, we should be able to find us a real sailmaker, Cap'n."

"Do the best you can, Seamus." John walked forward. At the bow, he turned and looked again to David high atop the damaged mast. "How long before we can be underway?"

David pulled one of the lifting lines up and passed it through a double sheave block while he considered. "It'll be a couple of days, Captain! Maybe as many as three. There's a lot more damage than I thought."

"No faster?"

"What's your hurry?" David gave a jerk on one of the lifts. "Wouldn't it be better to put the ship back together the right way and get to Charles Town in one piece than risk another breakup?" David cut a piece of the old rigging away and threw it to the deck near John. "Besides, you've some bad injuries that could use the time to mend."

John touched his injured ribs. "You're right, David. Let's do the job right."

The coastal current pulled the languishing Falmouth Packet northward toward Savannah at a rate of a mile every six hours. The topgallant mast was splinted together with pieces of oars and wedged lashings, and the square topsail was lashed to the yard almost as well as before the storm. The rip was closed, but each of the three crewmen used his personal brand of stitch, making the large sail look as though it had been mended during an argument.

True to David's prediction, the ship was ready to get underway just before noon the fourth day after the storm. John was in no condition to stand his watch, so the others agreed to fill in. Hurt as John was, he insisted on remaining topside throughout most of the remaining repairs. While he paced about the deck, he remembered one additional task.

"David, before we pull in the sea anchor and get underway, I have a request.

"What is it, Captain?"

"Would you and the others move that chain from my cabin? Three nights with that smell is enough for any man."

"I've three of the men working on the pump packing. As soon as they're done, we'll get to it."

"Thank you. I guess if I had to, I could..."

He was interrupted by seaman Etinger's cry. "Sail on the horizon, sir! Starboard quarter!"

"David, would you go to the binnacle and fetch my spyglass?" A moment later, John was peering at the distant sail in hopes it would be another merchantman or a fisher. "If we're lucky, she'll pass us by like those privateers."

David studied the ship under a shading hand. "I don't like the looks of her, sir. She's too big for a fisherman and her course is wrong for a merchantman. Can you make out her colors yet?"

"I'm afraid so. It's a skull and crossed cutlasses." John handed the glass to his young friend. "They're pirates, and by their course, I'd guess they've set their lay line for us."

"Crossed cutlasses?" David steadied himself against the mainmast. "That's Jack Rackham's old flag."

"But Rackham's dead, isn't he?"

David nodded while he continued to study the approaching ship. "Hung for piracy in King's Town back in '21."

"Any idea who this might be?"

David lowered the glass and smiled. "Fortunately for us, I know that ship well."

"You do?"

"That's the fastest ship in the Atlantic. My father designed her himself, and with several important modifications."

"Modifications?"

"Her hull, for starters. She's longer than a man-o'-war, with the lines of a French racing sloop. With her forty cannons, you have the perfect pirate—the fire power of a frigate, but with superior speed."

"Back to my question. Who is she?"

"When my father owned her, she was the Hesperus, the crown jewel of his fleet. Now she's called the Tiburon."

"Who's at her helm?"

"It would be my father's good friend, Captain Joshua Smoot."

"What do you know about him?"

"I've met him several times—he comes to dinner when he's in port—and my uncle has told me about him." David looked at John. "As the story goes, Smoot's the bastard spawn of John Flint, the pirate."

"I know all about John Flint, but nothing about this man." John looked at the ship under a shading hand. "What are the chances that he'll let us go, unmolested?"

"Very good, especially when he recognizes me." There was a cheer from the Tiburon. David raised the glass and surveyed the approaching ship once more. "Oh, my God!"

"What's the matter, David? What do you see?"

"They're dropping Smoot's flag, and raising the red no-quarter flag in its place. Something's terribly wrong."

"I don't understand. Why would Smoot—"

"My father warned me of this." Panic gripped David's spine as he raised the glass and studied the coastline. He spun to John and pointed west. "We've only one chance!"

John looked to the coast and back at the approaching ship. "Cut the sea anchor and spread all the canvas she'll carry! We've a race to run, with our lives as the prize!"

***

The new Tiburon had proven herself superior against several merchantmen and one of the King's smaller men-of-war. As agreed with the merchants of Savannah, the prize ships were all sailed to Savannah, but the man-of-war was sunk and her crew set adrift in their boats.

It was just before noon that the top watch spotted the small British postal packet drifting on her sea anchor several leagues off the coast of South Carolina.

Smoot studied the small ship through his glass for a full minute.

Daniel Turner, a lad of sixteen, held a shading hand to his forehead. "Is it them, Cap'n?"

Smoot lowered his spyglass and turned to rest his backside against the rail. "Aye, and from the looks of them, they've suffered some storm damage."

"Do ya think they might be carryin' any booty?"

"It isn't booty I want, Danny."

"I know ya want David Noble fer ransom, Cap'n, but they might still be carrying something the crew can split up."

Smoot turned to his young first mate. "Once I have David Noble, I don't care what you and the others do with the ship or the rest of her crew."

Danny smiled and looked again at the floundering packet a half a league ahead. "Look at 'er, Cap'n! Why, she'll be easier to take than a maiden's favors in springtime. Ha! Ha!" He stepped to the rail and pointed with his cutlass. "She's lyin' dead in the sea—just waitin' ta be plucked like the sweet fruit she be!"

"She looks harmless enough, but don't underestimate her. According to my spies, she's been fitted with a few cannons." He handed the glass to Daniel.

The boy studied their prey. "She's a swivel gun on 'er poop, an' nothin' more! Them postal packets got sail, not cannons."

"Just the same, Danny, watch yerself. Foolhardiness accounts for there not bein' many old pirates."

Daniel looked up at their flag. "Can I run up the red flag, Cap'n?"

A moment later, the red flag replaced the skull and crossed cutlasses, and was met by the demonic cheers of the crew.

***

Captain Jones was in pain, but refused to step aside. "We've precious little time before she's within range, so let's step lively. I'll man the helm while the rest of you set all the sail she can tolerate."

The men scattered themselves about the deck in what appeared at first to be mass confusion. Halyards were hauled, and belaying pins were pulled. Several sheets to lee were released, and their counterparts to weather were hauled—all of this while Seamus yelled orders only a seaman could understand. From the midst of the confusion emerged a well-planned and executed set of tasks that had the little ship cut loose and turned about, and her main and foresail set wing-and-wing for the run downwind.

Seamus ran aft and knuckled his forelock. "A word, Cap'n?"

"Make it quick!"

"Those other three are scared, Cap'n! They never seen a real battle at sea, only the stories."

"We're all scared! What are you getting at?"

"They want to know if we have to fight. They want to know if we'd stand a better chance if we struck our colors and raised a white flag."

"You, of any of us, should know what that red flag means!"

"It means 'no quarter,' Cap'n. I seen it once before."

"They intend to kill us for our cargo. Wouldn't you rather die fighting, like a man?"

"Well..."

"I don't have time for this! Tell the others I have a plan—that we have a good chance of coming through this alive!"

"But we don't, Cap'n!" The Irishman looked aft at the Tiburon. "We're outnumbered twenty to one!"

"You know how to tell a lie, don't you?"

"Aye, but—"

"Do this for me, Barragan! A crew without hope is dead already!" John pointed forward. "I want all the small arms loaded and stacked at the rails, with plenty of ammunition. We'll also need two axes at each rail to cut grappling hooks. Now, get to your cannons!"

While the Irishman ran forward, John called to the young Italian. "Carini! As soon as you've secured those lines, break out the medical supplies and put all the irons we have on the fire. If we survive this, there's sure to be casualties."

"The irons?"

"You've cauterized a wound before, haven't you, Mario?"

Carini trotted aft and stopped several yards away from John. "No sir, not me."

"Oh, Lord!" John glanced back at the pirate ship. "I'm probably the only one who's been in battle or knows anything about battle surgery!"

After some hasty instructions, the Italian ran forward, dropped below and set to his task.

While the wounded bird fluttered toward the safety of the shore ten leagues to the west, the cruel and bloodthirsty Tiburon was closing quickly for her first kill in three days.

"What do you think, sir?" David pointed. "Can we make that inlet with this canvas, or would we stand a better chance by reaching for that other one, just outboard of the cat's head?"

"Our only hope is on a direct run, wing and wing. On that course, the Tiburon's aft sails will block her fore sails and perhaps give us the edge we need." John laid a hip to the tiller and looked aft once more at their pursuer. She was now less than three a thousand yards away. "I'd sure like to know what's inside that inlet."

"My father provided several detailed charts of this coastline. Why don't I take the helm while you go below? You need the respite, however brief."

The Scotsman was grateful he had brought the young Jamaican along, and relinquished the tiller without objection. Stepping away, he stumbled slightly from fatigue. Catching himself, he turned back to his young friend and took a long, painful breath.

"Thank you, David."

"You'd do it for me, John." David pointed. "Now, get below and find us a safe haven." John's sharp glance brought a quick response. "Captain...Sir!"

Moments later, John slumped into the chair before his table and let his tortured body rest. "Just a moment, that's all I need." He pulled a chart labeled S. CAROLINA from the tall box to his left, unrolled the parchment and searched for his landmark. While he studied the chart, he felt something wet inside his waistcoat. He reached his hand inside and brought it out bloody. He looked back to the chart. "Saint Helena Sound. That's where we'll put in! If we can just make it into the Edisto River and then into one of the smaller tributaries. It should be narrow enough that the pirates can only bring their swivel guns to bear. That'll give us a near equal advantage while we outdistance them. And with our shallow draft, we could..." John's ears began to ring and the small cabin seemed to spin about for a moment. His breathing quickened and then he fell forward onto the table unconscious.

A large dagger plunged through the Scotsman's left hand, pinning it to the oaken tabletop. Gazing up through the blur of searing pain, John Paul looked into the eyes of a lobsterback—a uniformed British soldier.

"You didn't think we'd ever catch up with you, did you, Captain Paul?" The soldier pulled a piece of rolled parchment from his sleeve and threw it in front of the Scotsman, along with a bottle of ink and a quill.

John wanted to scream, but his vocal chords were numb with pain and fear.

"I've already written out your confession—how you killed Jack Fry in cold blood." He pulled his pistol and pointed it at John's forehead. "Sign your name to it, or I'll kill you here and now!"

My sword! Where is it? John's mind cried out in a panic. His heart was racing, the sound of it becoming louder and louder until its pounding had become a deafening roar against his temples. "The pounding...stop the pounding!"

"Captain! Are you there?" David pounded again at the locked cabin door. "John, are you all right?"

The lobsterback was suddenly gone, and the dagger no longer stood in the flesh of his hand. John stared down at the chart. "Charles Town! Savannah! I've got to get to shore!" He felt his chest over his heart. "That pounding! What on earth—" Suddenly the slide bolt tore through the jam, and the door burst open in a shower of splinters. It swung back and struck the pile of anchor chain next to the Scotsman, startling him back to reality. He looked up at David in confusion and back at the chart.

"The stays'ls aren't enough! They'll be on us in ten minutes! What's taking you so long?"

"I must've lost consciousness!" He turned back to the chart and set a point of his dividers to a small river stretching inland from Saint Helena Sound. "The Edisto River! That's where we'll make our stand." He looked up at David. "Did you say they'd be on us in ten minutes?"

"Captain, we need you on deck, now!" David noticed the blood on his friend's hand. "Your ribs are bleeding again, aren't they?"

"I'm afraid Barragan was right. He told me that I'd have to take it easy or the wound would open up." John got up and pushed past his young friend. "If we survive Joshua Smoot, then my ribs will have plenty of time to heal. If we don't survive his attack, then my bleeding ribs won't matter." He turned and climbed onto the deck just as a cannonball splashed a hundred yards off the larboard bow, followed a moment later by the cannon's report from a half mile aft.

"Damn!" John looked to the men at work at the cannons. "Barragan, Etinger! Are your cannons loaded and ready?"

"Aye, Cap'n!" Seamus stood out of respect while he answered. "Both fore guns is loaded wi' grape shot an' the aft two be carryin' barstock, just as ye ordered, sir!" The Irishman welcomed the chance to trade iron with such a famous pirate as Joshua Smoot, but feared this first battle would also be his last. "Our powder be dry an' the linstocks is burnin' bright, Cap'n Jones, jest like ya showed us!"

Except for Seamus, the four crewmen were young and had no concept of what they were to experience in a few moments, and John figured it would do no good to extinguish their spirit with the truth.

He walked toward the three men. "And those muskets, are they loaded also?"

"That they be, Cap'n! An' every man jack o' us be totin' a brace o' pistols, fer the close-in fightin'!!" Seamus and the other two pulled open their shirts to expose the weapons hidden in their braces.

Carini brandished his cutlass. "And we got our cutlasses an' daggers besides!"

"I hope it doesn't come to that, Mario." John turned and looked to the pirate ship. "David! Relieve Clark at the tiller so he can man his gun with Barragan. I'll be staying forward as long as possible."

David touched his own ribs where John was bleeding. "Are you sure you're strong enough for that?"

The Scotsman was in no mood for arguing. "We've no choice, David! I need Clark forward...now!"

No sooner had Clark joined Barragan at the larboard cannons than the Tiburon made a course change. Like every student of blue water warfare, John recognized the tactic. "Watch her! It's an old ploy to make us think she's going to overshoot!" He turned to David at the helm. "When I drop my hand, I want you to throw the tiller to larboard as far as it'll go, no matter what's happening at the time!"

David seemed confused.

"Is that clear?"

David nodded. "Clear!"

"Once she's in position, she'll spill her sails and back down just enough so our gunwales meet, at which time we can expect their grappling hooks!"

The Tiburon was now nearly parallel to the little packet and closing quickly. Suddenly, there was an explosion from one of the larger ship's guns, followed by a sickening shudder along the entire length of the smaller ship's frame.

"How could they be so stupid?" John jumped up and ran aft to the starboard rail. "No!" Two jagged rows of splinters raised pivot-like on the ship's ribs where the ball had pierced the oak planking below the waterline—one of the worst hits a ship could take. Looking up at the Tiburon in defiance, John saw the first sheet released to luff the sails for her expected backing-down maneuver.

Ignoring the searing pain in his side, John ran back toward his cannons while barking orders. "Ready on both cannons!" He leaped between the two seamen, watching for the exact moment. Stand by...Stand by...Fire!"

Both starboard cannons kicked aft as their deadly loads ripped at the Tiburon's great stern. The barstock took a large chunk off the upper edge of the rudder while the second cannon's grapeshot peppered the master's cabin, breaking out most of the larboard windows.

John waved his arm and yelled aft. "Now, David! Tiller hard to larboard!" Turning about, John leaped across the deck to his larboard gun crew.

"Barragan, Clark, stand ready!" Both seamen crouched next to their pieces, linstocks held just above the touchholes. By now, the Falmouth Packet was well into its starboard turn behind the Tiburon's stern, avoiding the rest of the larger vessel's broadside. They all watched with gritted teeth while the Falmouth's bowsprit clipped the great lanthorn hanging from the larger ship's taffrail, sending it twisting as it fell end-over-end into the dark blue water.

Startled at this unexpected change in their plans, Smoot and the lad ran aft and peered down at the little ship passing under their stern. Captain Jones's eyes met Smoot's for several angry seconds. Mistaking David Noble for the captain, Daniel pulled a pistol from his sash and leveled his barrel on the Jamaican.

"Run an' twist, little girl! Danny Turner'll have you fer his prize, or send you to Davey Jones' locker in the effort!" He raised the pistol and sighted down his barrel at David. At the same time, the Scotsman's hand rested on Seamus's shoulder, waiting for the exact moment.

"Ready now...fire!"

Seamus's linstock dropped an inch and ignited the powder in the cannon's base ring. The primer flashed brightly, followed an instant later by the twelve-pounder belching forth its deadly load of grapeshot at the great ship. The crew of the Falmouth Packet would never know how effective that third shot had been, for it stopped the Tiburon's attack completely. Inside the cloud of white smoke, the spreading pellets ripped upward through the larger ship's taffrail and into her lower rigging. Daniel Turner and six feet of polished rail were now raining over the Tiburon's foredeck and sails in a grisly shower of mahogany splinters, blood, shattered bones and body parts.

Not having the time or the manpower to trim the sails for their starboard reach, the Falmouth lost much, if not all, of her headway. Before the acrid cloud of their first larboard shot had cleared, the Tiburon's great rudder began to pass the second cannon. As with

Seamus, Captain Jones held Clark by the shoulder, waiting for just the right moment.

A only took a whisper. "Now!" The second cannon barked forth its destructive barstock.

For several moments, the smoke from both cannons hung between the two ships, obscuring not only the setting sun, but the entire stern of the ominous foe that towered over the small postal ship. Then, as if a blacksmith's hut had been caught up in a tornado, oak and mahogany splinters, enormous pieces of flat iron, and bolts began to rain down onto the Falmouth's deck. John ran aft toward David for an unobstructed look at his foe. Whatever they had done, it was working, because the great ship had lost all headway, but for a slow turn to larboard.

"Larboard cannons, reload with barstock! Starboard crew, haul in the starboard sheets and trim for a larboard reach!" Captain Jones turned and shouted at David. "As soon as we're at a hundred yards, I want you to come about to a starboard beam reach! We've a hole below the starboard water line aft, and we'll sink if we don't keep her heeled over to larboard!"

John and the four seamen set about their tasks while David watched the wind to select the optimum course. As instructed, he turned back to the heading they'd been on before the Tiburon's attack. "That's good!" John called aft, looking to the Tiburon again. She was still floundering. "Hold that heading until we can assess damage and get a wet patch on that hole!"

David pushed the tiller back to midships and then looked about at the pirates. "Look, Captain!" He pointed at the other ship. "Her rudder! It's gone! We beat her!"

"Aye, we beat her, but we've no time to glory in our victory until we can get out of range and patch that hole."

Their cannons now reloaded, Seamus and Clark joined the others hauling the mainsail sheet to bring the great boom directly over the helm.

Once the ship was trimmed on the new course, John stepped to the Irishman. "Barragan, you claimed you've some carpentry experience. Is that true?"

"Aye, Cap'n! I were a planker an' caulker at—"

John didn't want to listen to the man's lengthy story. "Can you make up a canvas patch and get it in place as soon as we put some distance between us and the Tiburon?" Before Seamus could answer, a ball from one of the pirate's forward swivel guns whistled overhead.

Everyone ducked, and the ball punched through the deck. "I never done it 'afore, Cap'n, but I seen it once on that man-o'-war I were tellin' ya 'bout. Cap'n Jenkins told me he'd—"

"Do your best." John cut the Irishman off again. "We've no more than an hour before we sink." John turned back to David. "I'm going below to see where that ball went. If we're lucky, it stopped somewhere inside the ship. If not, then we'll have two holes to repair."

John descended the short ladder that led to his cabin. Water was still flowing at a steady, but greatly reduced rate, from his open cabin door and forward into the main hold, much to the pleasure of the turtles. Once inside the cabin, he immediately saw what had stopped the ball. In the center of the deck, where it had been pushed by the impact, lay the anchor chain. Setting within its rusted links was the single six-inch ball, stopped dead in its path of destruction. John made a quick assessment of the damage to the hull and returned to the companionway and up to the deck. Another one of the pirate's swivel guns fired, punching a hole in the flying jib.

"Damn!" John looked across at their attacker. "We're still in range!" John looked up at the luffing sails and aft at David. "What's—"

"Don't mind him, Clark!" It was David yelling. Something was terribly wrong. "Man the main sheet with Barragan 'til we're underway!"

It took John's eyes a moment to re-adjust to the sunlight. Two of the men were screaming and running about the deck. The mainsail sheet trailed across the deck and over the rail into the sea.

John stumbled when the ship lurched. "What happened to the mainsa'l, David?"   David pointed at the main mast. "Carini's been hit!"

John turned and looked. Propped against the mainmast with his head resting against Clark's chest lay the young Italian, his left arm torn away at the shoulder.

John stepped to the two and pointed at the mainsail. "Clark! Leave Carini and get back to your duties! We're still in range and we're taking on water!"

The kneeling seaman looked up from his dying mate and shook his head. "I'll not let Mario lay here to die fer any mainsa'l."

"Do you really want him to live?"

Clark looked up through his tears. "How can you ask that, Cap'n? We're like brothers."

John pointed forward. "Before we were attacked, Mario put several irons in the galley stove. His only hope is for you to get the irons and stop his bleeding."

While the others manned the mainsail, Clark lowered his friend to the deck and ran forward. He was back in a minute with a glowing iron in each hand. He stopped in front of John. "Help me, Cap'n. I don't know what to do."

John grabbed the irons and looked down at Carini. The blood was still pumping from the veins. "Turn him so I can see that shoulder!"

Clark pulled Carini up and turned him sideways. "Oh, God! The ball tore his whole arm off!" Tears streamed down both of Clark's cheeks as he choked the words out. "Help him, sir! Please help him!"

"Hold him steady, Edgar!" John pressed the first iron to the exposed veins, causing Carini's body to stiffen.

"You hurt him, Captain!"

"Good! It means he's still alive!" A sickening stream of blue smoke climbed quickly into the air, swirled about the mast and trailed over the lee rail. John pressed the second iron to the wound, but this time, Carini's body relaxed and the bleeding stopped. Clark looked up at his captain with a smile of gratitude.

"Ya did it, sir! Ya stopped the bleeding, just like a surgeon, ya did!"

"It wasn't me that did it." John stood and dropped the last iron to the deck in the pool of blood. It gave out a hiss. "The bleeding stopped because his heart isn't beating anymore."

Clark looked up. "Sir?"

"He's dead, Edgar. There was just too much damage." Clark eased his friend's limp body back down to the deck and looked up.

"But he was just talking to me, and—"

"There's nothing further we can do for him, but there's a lot we'd best do for ourselves!" John looked back at the pirates. "We've a ship to sail and a hole to patch before we all join Carini."

The grieving seaman rose slowly to his feet and stood over his friend's torn and lifeless body. Seamus stepped next to John. "He told me that his parents live up in Alexandria."

"We can't have him aboard that long. We'll have to bury him at sea. Can you tell his people what happened and give them his belongings?"

"I'll tell them, sir." He stepped to Clark's side. "Come on, Edgar. Cap'n Jones'll take care o' Mario. We got work to do."

At approximately a thousand yards from the floundering pirate ship, David turned the Falmouth into the wind just long enough for the crew to grab the mainsail boom and pull it over the deck, flat against the wind, bringing the small ship to a crawl. Adjusting the jib and mainsail held the wind on the starboard beam, keeping the little ship heeled over far enough to lift the hole above the water until the canvas patch was in place. Clark and Etinger, being the better swimmers, volunteered to pull the two larboard ropes under the keel to hold the lower two corners of the patch. Within an hour, the Falmouth Packet was once again underway, but no longer headed for Virginia.

"David, since we're damaged, I've decided to put in at Saint Helena Sound and anchor in the shallows for the night. If something happens to that patch, I don't want to be caught in deep water. I've checked in our hold and we don't have any planking to repair the hull."

"Think it'll hold through the night?"

"Oh, I'm sure of that, but we'll need to keep a man on the pump from now on, or at least until we make Savannah for repairs."

David shook his head. "We can't go to Savannah."

"Why not?"

"Because that's where Smoot will take the Tiburon."

"Oh?"

"He has a home on the bluff east of the town and he keeps the Tiburon in a creek a thousand yards down river—the creek that waters the rice fields. He's also in league with most of the Savannah merchants."

John walked to the hatch and called. "Barragan!"

The Irishman walked forward to the hatch and looked up at his captain. "Sir?"

"Will that patch hold for three days?"

Seamus looked aft at the man on the pump. He looked up and nodded. "I heard what Master Noble told you about Smoot and Savannah. We can make it to Charles Town easy, Cap'n."

John turned back to David. "This will be better. I know people in Charles Town, and counting the distance we'd have to pull up the Savannah River, it's only a few hours difference. Besides, there are more shipyards in Charles Town, and therefore a much better chance of a quick repair."

"The crew'll be glad to make port for a few days, and your ribs could use the time to begin knitting properly."

John walked to the larboard rail and peered at the thickly wooded coastline. "You wouldn't know there was anything wrong in America by looking at the place, would you?" He turned, leaned his backside against the rail, and put a hand to his side. The bleeding had stopped, but there was still the searing pain. "When we make Charles Town, let's poke around a little along East Bay Street. Maybe we can find out about the Navy."

***

In the afternoon of the 30th of December, 1774, Captain Jones and his crew of five sailed past the newly-built Morris Island Lighthouse and into the Charles Town harbor. The water was teeming with returning boats and merchant ships of every size and description. The Falmouth Packet sailed to the southern end of East Bay Street and anchored a hundred yards straight out from the end of Broad Street. With less than an hour of sunlight remaining, John and David rowed ashore to arrange for repairs

Seamus called to them upon their return. "What did they say, Cap'n? Is there a place where we can careen her?"

"Tipton's Dock." John pointing up the Cooper River. "They have a stretch of beach with an open spot that will take the Falmouth Packet. Can you and the others move her up there and get her hauled down for repairs without us?"

"Aye Cap'n." Seamus gave a nervous look back at the three others. "Will you and Master Noble be stayin' ashore for the night?"

John nodded while the small boat bumped against the Falmouth's hull. "I have to sign in at the Harbor Master's office and deliver the mail, and then we have some other business to conduct." John fished through the inside pocket of his waistcoat and produced a handful of silver coins. "Don't wait for us. Here's enough money to purchase the wood you'll need to patch those three planks, and some extra for you and your mates to get dinner and drinks. Get as much done tonight as you can and then take your mates into town."

Seamus took the coins and knuckled his forelock. "Aye, aye, Cap'n!"

John pushed away and David began pulling on the sweeps.

Seamus called after them. "You and Master Noble watch yerselves, now. I been here 'afore an' there's some rough characters in some o' them taverns."

John held up his sword and David opened his waistcoat to reveal the two fowling pistols. "Don't worry. We can take care of ourselves."

Like King's Town, Charles Town had its long row of taverns strewn along the docks, catering to the needs of the men who had just come up from the sea. It was neither by tradition, nor design that these public houses served as the collection point for word from the four points of the compass. It was just that way. After asking about and dropping several important names, John and David headed for the Patriot's Rest.

They took a small table at the back of the public room, near several well-dressed businessmen. The oldest of the four was very angry, so it wasn't difficult to overhear his conversation. John and David took their seats, catching the older man in mid-sentence.

"...taken about all they can, James. If the damned Parliament doesn't back off soon, they're going to be up to here in—" He broke off when the younger man on his left put a hand of caution to his arm. With a quick look about the tavern for strangers and loyalists, the older man leaned forward and continued in a quieter voice. "Word's come from the Committees of Correspondence in Virginia of some trouble in Boston Harbor in protest of this bloody tea tax. I read the letter myself and recognized the signatures of both Henry and Jefferson. Seems some 'Indians' dumped a whole shipload of monopoly-tea bricks from the Beaver into the harbor back 6th. There's a rumor that the Indian chief's name was Sam Adams." The other three roared with laughter.

"Then that explains why these local customs men locked up all of the East India Company warehouses the other day." It was a younger man in a beaver hat. "They must be afraid a group of Charles Town Indians'll dump their tea in the harbor too."

The older man raised his hand. "The government will, of course, retaliate. I have just heard from London that the port of Boston is now closed. No ships will go in or out until the tea is paid for." Shock and surprise ran through the room. "And it is now illegal to have any sort of public meeting in Boston." This provoked cries of outrage and disbelief. "There's more, gentlemen. The same letter told of a new Quartering Act, which will apply, not just to Massachusetts, but to all the colonies, including us."

The others stopped laughing. One spoke up. "The law allows soldiers to take quarters in taverns and unoccupied buildings. That's not news."

"No, it's not. But the new law expands that to include private homes." He looked at each man in turn. "This is most serious."

The others waited.

"Not only will the home owners have to take the food from their own mouths to feed the lobsterbacks, but they'll put their children on the floor so the soldiers have a comfortable bed to sleep in."

The man in the beaver hat slapped the table, causing most of the clientele to look about. "I'll be damned before any soldier's going to move into my house uninvited!" The others tried to calm him. "Mother England's sitting on her brain again, and this time she's going to get bit!"

"You can thank Lord North for that. These new laws are his doing, and he's pushing us right into war."

"You don't know how prophetic your last words are, Christopher." It was the older gentleman speaking, once again just above a whisper. "There's strong evidence that most of the members of the Marine Committee have been chosen, and that Esek Hopkins will be selected as Commander in Chief of the Continental Navy."

One of the others reached across and put a hand on the forearm of a white-haired man who had not spoken yet. "But why not you, Mister Forrestal?

"I've the name, but not the military background for it, William. No, Hopkins would be the best choice. Besides, I'm too old and broken in body for the strain."

"How soon do you think they'll be outfitting ships and selecting the men to man them?"

Forrestal leaned forward. "I'll be laying the keels for two large Dutch brigs at my yard this summer, William. I expect them to be ready to float by the following spring at the latest. Depending on the decisions made between now and then, they can become merchantmen or frigates. Then let the government deal with us however it wishes."

The younger of the five men stood, raised his tankard and his voice. "Gentlemen! A toast!" Everybody in the tavern stood. "To freedom!" Everyone drank, then retook their seats. The younger man continued. "Surely God is on the side of freedom." From all around the tavern came echoing shouts of agreement.

John and David had heard enough. A Continental Navy was more than just a rumor, and possibly within a year. They downed their drinks and left the tavern to look for the provisions they would need to continue their trip.

Chapter 5

Charles Town, the largest settlement in South Carolina, was situated on a point of land between the Ashley and Cooper rivers, six miles inland from the open Atlantic Ocean. Except for the waterfronts, the streets followed a grid pattern, and the many elegant homes and churches attesting to the affluence of the community. The surrounding countryside consisted of low farm and pasturelands, little elevated above tidewater, making the area liable to the occasional inundation from ocean storms and high tides. It was the colony's center of government and trade, and its pleasant climate made it a favorite vacation resort for the wealthy from the West Indies.

The Falmouth Packet's repairs were completed early on the morning of her third day in Charles Town. The crew stood barefooted in the rising waters of the Cooper River while John made his inspection of the hull and upper mast.

"You do fine work, Barragan." John ran a hand along the newly painting planking. "I've no doubt whatsoever that she'll be seaworthy."

Seamus flashed the others a quick glance and smile. "Thank you, sir!"

John and David waded back up to the dry sand. "I've my business with the harbor master, David. Would you oversee her launching?"

"Aye! We'll be ready to sail when you return."

By four bells, John had signed clearance papers for departure, and an hour later, the newly repaired vessel was once again underway. Upon David's orders, she spread her sails in the morning breeze and took up a starboard reach toward the partially built Fort Sullivan. Three days before, when the crippled craft had entered Charles Town harbor, a large merchantman had lain aground on the sandbar that blocked most of the entrance to the bay. Passing close by the fort, David ordered the ship slightly to windward in order to follow the seaward side of Sullivan's Island, and then into the open waters of the Atlantic. By noon on the 2nd of January, the Falmouth Packet was once again en route to the north coast of Virginia.

The crew was finishing their noon meal of fresh fruit, biscuits, and salt pork when John stepped up on deck from his cabin. He held a leather bag the size of a woman's church purse. After a quick survey of the rigging, he stepped near the main mast.

"Assemble for Captain's Mast!"

David and the remaining three crewmen jumped up and looked at the young Scotsman with puzzlement. "Captain's Mast? What on earth—"

"Seaman Clark, front and center."

The young seaman stepped forward. "What did I do now?"

"It's what you did when Carini was killed. Not only were you insubordinate, but you disobeyed a direct order to man the mains'l sheet during battle. That could have cost us the ship and the rest of your mates' lives."

"And you're gonna punish me now, a week after it happened?"

"I could have you hung for what you did, but considering your worth to the crew, you'll receive only six lashes." He pulled the cat-of-nine-tails from its bag. John looked at the sailor's crewmates. "Tie Clark to the main!"

Everybody stood their ground.

John held the cat out to David. "I want you to administer the punishment."

"Not me, Captain!" David shook his head and backed away a step. "If you insist on this insanity, then you'll have to flog Clark yourself."

"That sounds like factiousness, Mister Noble. Are you trying to incite a mutiny, or are you just ignorant of maritime law?"

"Since it's not a mutiny, then it must be my ignorance!" David stepped to Clark's side. "What Clark did was wrong. But if it had been you cut down by that cannon shot, I would have been in Clark's place—tending to my fallen friend." David shook his head and began to unbutton his shirt. "I'll not be the instrument of your misdirected revenge, and if you're so determined to punish somebody, let it be me."

Clark put a hand to David's arm and then stepped past him to the mast. "I'll take my own punishment, Mister Noble." He wrapped his arms about the mast and stared at his captain in defiance.

The wind seemed to die and the sun lost part of its brightness during those six lashes. When the cat was once again in its bag, the others helped Clark below to his rack and attended to his wounds with an application of salve.

The three-day trip from Charles Town to Virginia was without further incident, except for the two separate colonial merchantmen they observed being detained by a man-of-war near the Cape Hatteras Inlet.

On the 5th of January just before change of watch, John came from his cabin with a chart of the north Virginia coastline. "David, when I take the helm at eight bells, I want to speak to the men. I've decided where we'll dock the Falmouth."

"I'll pass the word, Mister Jones."

"You'll address me as "Captain" while we're under sail, Mister Noble."

David gave John a hard look and then answered sarcastically, mimicking his commanding tone. "Sorry...Captain."

When John took the helm at eight bells—four o'clock in the afternoon—David and the three seamen stood just aft of the main mast as ordered. The chart John had been studying lay on the deck at his feet.

"I must assume you already know, but in case you don't, we should reach the Potomac River tomorrow." He pointed to the large body of water with the tip of his sword. "As you can see, there are several small towns on the east bank of the river where we can dock. Mister Noble and I will be going to my brother's home in Fredericksburg, so we'll be landing as close to that place as possible." He looked at each of the men. "The map shows that the Rappahannock goes all the way to Fredericksburg, but there's a town on the Potomac called Dahlgren, about twenty-four miles from Fredericksburg—they have ship yards there too—where we should be able to turn the Falmouth over to another master." He waited for the men to answer. "Since there are no objections, then Dahlgren it is."

By now, the two younger seamen looked to Seamus for leadership, and let him be their spokesman when it came to matters with the captain.

"Dahlgren'll be just fine, Cap'n." He gave Clark a quick glance. "Clark an' me, we got family in Hanover Township, an' Etinger'll be goin' along with us fer a job. Dahlgren's 'bout as close as any place else, Cap'n."

"Good!" John took up the chart and rolled it back into a tube. "Take the tiller for a few minutes, Barragan."

"Aye, Cap'n."

"Mister Noble, step close so we can have a word." John slid the chart into a leather tube that already held several others.

"Yes?"

"Something's been eating at me."

David fell in step alongside his captain. "The same thing's been eating at me and the crew."

John furled his brow at the young Jamaican. "Oh?"

"Flogging Clark like that. I'd feel bad about that too."

"Is this another instance of insubordination, Mister Noble?"

"But, isn't that—"

"It has nothing to do with Clark's discipline." They stopped next to the companionway. John took a large breath and let it out with a defeated huff. "Yes...that was a mistake—waiting that long. I've learned a lesson and it will never happen again."

"We both learned lessons that day." David looked forward to where Etinger and Clark were trimming the main sheet. "As much as I objected to what you were about to do, I was out of line standing with the crew against you."

"I'm glad you recognize that, David. This has been one of life's important lessons for both of us."

David gave John a questioning look. "That isn't what you wanted to ask me, is it?"

John shook his head. "We have no prize aboard. Why would Joshua Smoot attack us like that?"

"It was to get his cannons back."

"Smoot's cannons? Do you mean the ones in your father's warehouse?"

David nodded.

"I asked your father about them, but he refused to tell me where he got them."

"I know." David shook his head. "It's not that complicated."

"We nearly got killed for those cannons, so please explain it to me."

"Late last summer, there was a Dutch merchantman on its way from Scotland to the colonies—Charles Town, I believe. Smoot figured she'd be an easy prize, so he took her when she was thirty or forty miles to sea. He was hoping for a general cargo and rich passengers, but all she carried was a minimal crew and hundreds of bolts of cloth."

"What's that have to do with your father's cannons?"

"I'm getting to that."

"Sorry. Go on."

"As I told you before the attack, Smoot had his eye on the Hesperus, so he decided to bargain with my father for her—a straight-across trade. With his contacts, my father knew he could get top dollar for the cloth, and the ship would add to his merchant fleet. He liked the Hesperus, but he also knew that the cloth would far exceed that ship's worth."

"But Smoot came to regret the deal?"

David nodded. "It was a week before my father's shipwright discovered the cannons. They were in the bilges for ballast, rather than the usual rocks. When word got back to Smoot, he was furious."

"He assumed they were still his, even though he had already traded the ship away?"

David nodded.

"And when your father refused to hand them over?"

"Pirates like to take important people for ransom." David touched his chest. "One of Smoot's spies must have discovered I was with you—aboard the Falmouth."

"Then I was right. He would have killed the rest of us, wouldn't he?"

"Yes, without a doubt."

***

Before dawn on the 6th of January, while John and David lay asleep in their cabin, Seamus steered the small sloop from the Potomac River into Machotick Creek, a small tributary several miles short of their intended landfall. Between the larboard cannons lay three canvas bags. At Seamus's signal, Clark and Etinger moved quietly to the bow with pike poles to help ease the ship onto a mud bank. Only John stirred when the slow-moving craft came to a quiet rest.

He raised himself on an elbow and looking about the small cabin. "David?" The younger man groaned and threw an arm across his eyes to block out the light from the porthole. "Did you feel that?"

"Feel what, Captain?" David looked across at John. "Is it my watch already?"

"No, I felt something." John sat up and pulled on his boots. He pulled back the curtain and looked out through the porthole. "There's a thick fog. I think we've gone aground."

David sat up and rubbed his eyes with the heels of his hands. "That's not possible."

"Get dressed and come above deck!" John stood and stomped his feet to adjust his boots. A moment later, he was gone. David could hear him calling the names of the crew and then several swear words.

John flung the door back on its hinges. "Get up! I was right! Those three your father gave us have put us aground and jumped ship!"

"Aground? Jumped ship?" David scrambled to his feet and followed John back up to the main deck.

John stood pointing to larboard. "Look! You can see where they jumped to the mud and ran into the trees!"

David looked up and down the narrow creek. "Do you have any idea where we are?"

"This is obviously not the Potomac, and there's no telling how far we've come since I came down from watch last night."

"What about Dahlgren?" David stepped to the stern and pointed. "Can we get her off the mud and sail back to the Potomac?"

"No!" John walked aft toward the companionway. "We'll take what valuables we can carry and leave the ship here."

"But..." David followed John down the short ladder. "You were going to turn her over to another captain."

"I suppose we can tell somebody about her when we reach the first settlement. Otherwise, she's the property of the first to find her."

"But won't we be in trouble with Lloyd's or somebody?"

"Not you and me!" John began throwing his things into his bag. "The log still shows James Jones as the Falmouth Packet's master, and I plan to resume using my real name from now on. Get your things together! I don't want to stay aboard any longer than we must."

Within a half-hour, the two young travelers were walking through the same trees through which their crew had so recently made their escape. By John's estimate from the ships compass and his memory of the area, they would reach a roadway within a half a day, and that would then take them south-by-southwest to Fredericksburg.

The following article appeared in the Virginia Gazette on the 25th of January, 1774:

Virginia Gazette

Williamsburg   25 January 1774   Purdie & Dixon

Some time in the early part of the month a sloop of about 100 hogsheads burthen stood in for Machotick Creek, on the Potomac, and ran aground on a mud bank a little way up the creek. Soon after, a decent well looking man and his young companion of slightly lesser years, both dressed in black, with gold laced hats, came on shore from the sloop, and calling at a gentlewoman's house in the neighbourhood, told her they were bound for Alexandria, to purchase a load of wheat, but that their hands had left them, and they wanted the loan of two horses to carry them to Leeds Town, to engage others. Being disappointed in getting the horses, they went to a planter's house a few miles distant, where they lodged all night, and went off in the morning. They stopped at a petty ordinary, where they left three ruffled shirts, a neat fouling piece in a cherry wood case, and a great coat; but the older man carried with him a pair of saddle bags, which the landlord concluded, from their weight, contained a considerable sum of money. They have not been heard from since. After the vessel had continued near a fortnight in the creek, with her sails standing, some of the gentlemen in the neighbourhood went on board; and upon searching her, found neither provisions nor water, chests, papers, nor any other effects, than one feather bed, a gold laced hat, a sailor's jacket, a pair of trousers, some cooking utensils, and two sea compasses made in Salem and four small ship's cannons. She is a long sharp-built vessel, with only a cabin, containing five berths, and hold. On her stern is painted, in white letters, Falmouth Packet; and the same words, in white Letters made of cloth, are on her pennant.

***

A two-day-old snow had turned to a muddy slush, making the last three miles to Fredericksburg both cold and difficult for the two weary travelers. John stopped to gather his bearings where the trail met a paved road. A young boy with red cheeks and a runny nose hurried past them with a load of firewood on a pull-sled. Although it was not unusual for strangers to be seen coming and going from the town, the lad gave the two a suspicious glance and quickened his pace.

"We must look a sight." John reached down and attempted to brush some mud from his stockings. It only made it worse.

"You certainly do." David ran his fingers through his hair and looked about. "How much further?"

"He lives at the corner of Prussia and Caroline Streets." John pointed to the right. "This road will take us to the railway station. It's just two streets from there." A half-hour later, the two young travelers stopped and John pointed at the house on the northeast corner of the intersection. "Unless he's moved in the last couple of years, that should be his house."

The Paul residence was a two-story home faced with three-inch lapstrake siding—boat-fashioned. It sported two chimneys, one standing above the parlor and the other from the kitchen at the back of the house. Light gray smoke curled upward from each of them. A flurry of brown and orange leaves scuttled before an icy gust, past the travelers feet and down toward the Rappahannock River. John led the way across the cobblestone boulevard to the front door.

John paused before lifting the iron knocker. "You'll like my brother. He's nothing at all like me."

David wasn't sure how to take the remark, so he simply smiled, sniffed and wiped his runny nose on his coat sleeve. "When did you see him last?"

"Late '68 or early '69." John lifted the knocker and let it fall against the heavy oak door. "I don't know about you, but if I don't get out of this cold, William won't be able to recognize me for the body parts I'll lose to the frostbite."

A very attractive young woman opened the door several inches and held it against the cold. "May I help you?"

"Uh..." John stammered. "Who are you?"

"I'm Dorothea Dandridge." She closed the door slightly. "Who are you?"

"I'm..." John looked to David and back to the beautiful creature before him. "We've come from King's Town to see William Paul. Has he moved away?"

"He still lives here, but he's with his doctor and can't receive any guests."

"His doctor? Is he ill?"

"Sir, if you're not going to give me your name or why you wish to see Mister Paul, I'm afraid you'll have to go."

"I'm his younger brother, John." He gave David a quick glance. "This is my traveling companion, David Noble."

"Why didn't you say that in the beginning?" Dorothea opened the door and ushered them into the foyer. "Wait here while I ask the doctor if he's finished." She turned and walked down the hallway.

The the two road-weary travelers unwrapped their scarves and unbuttoned their coats. David nodded toward the young woman. "Who is that?"

"Dorothea Dandridge." John gave a shrug. "I've never seen her before."

"She's very pretty."

John nodded. "Yes, she is."

Dorothea pushed through the parlor door and stood at the edge of the rug. The flickering light from the large fireplace cast a dancing patchwork of amber shadows across the parlor. Two men sat close to the warming fire—William Paul in a large wingback chair and Ezra Read on a stool at his right side, with his ear pressed to William's chest.

"Excuse me, sirs, but there are two gentlemen from King's Town to see William." She stepped closer and looked at William. "One of them claims to be your younger brother, John."

William looked up. "John's here, in Fredericksburg?" The words trailed into a wheezing cough. William was thirty-five, a full nine years older than John. He was the oldest son of John and Jean Paul of Kirkcudbright, Scotland. He stood three inches taller than his younger brother, but his chronic illness had reduced his formerly solid frame to what resembled a stack of yards and masts under rain-soaked sailcloth.

William pushed Ezra aside and started to rise from his chair, but the doctor put a hand to his shoulder and stood. "Sit where you are, William. I'll go and get them." Ezra was in his early fifties, short and stout. He rose and stepped into the hallway where John and David were shaking the last of the bad weather from their clothes.

"Gentlemen!" The doctor took John's offered hand. "I'm Doctor Read. Your brother has told me many stories about your seafaring exploits."

John looked past the doctor, expecting to see his brother follow. "Thank you, sir. I hope he didn't tell you very many lies about me."

The doctor glanced back toward the parlor and turned back to John. He whispered. "You're wondering why I'm here, aren't you?"

"What's the matter with William?"

The doctor shook David's hand. "It started with a cold a month ago, and he isn't getting over it as quickly as I'd like."

John looked past the doctor to Dorothea. "Is he well enough to receive visitors?"

"Of course I can receive visitors!" William stepped to the doorway. "Get in here, little brother, and tell me what you've been doing these last six years!" He put a kerchief to his mouth and let out a string of deep, rasping coughs. Dorothea took him by the arm and pulled him back to his chair.

"Good Lord, Brother!" John followed David and the doctor into the parlor. "What's gotten hold of you?"

William tried to answer, but could only wave a hand and choke out two or three unintelligible syllables. John gave the young woman an inquiring look, wondering who she was. She met his stare with a sympathetic—almost motherly—scowl.

William finished his coughing fit and whispered trough the kerchief. "It's just a cold. I'll be back to myself in a week or two." He settled back into the warm chair and pulled the lap blanket across his knees. "I picked it up a few weeks ago, and these two insist on treating me like an old lady."

Dorothea tucked the blanket around him. "He is an old lady!"

David stepped close to the fire, warming his hands and backside. William nodded toward him. "Who's your young friend, John?"

John stepped to David and put a hand on his shoulder. "This is my good friend and traveling companion, David Noble." John turned to his brother. "David, this is my older brother, William."

"Well, well!" William gave his brother a raise of the brow. "This is a special treat! John's never had a close friend before."

"He has one now, sir." David shook the older man's hand and returned to the warmth of the fire. There was an uneasy moment while Dorothea gave William a scolding look.

"Forgive me, dear, but with all this attention you and the doctor have been giving me, I've forgotten my manners." William struggled to his feet. "Gentlemen, this fair young lady isn't my housekeeper, as I've mistakenly allowed you to believe. Other than my tormentor, Doctor Read, she's one of the few friends I have left in this world."

Dorothea stepped forward to William. He put an arm around her shoulders. "This is Dorothea Dandridge, one of Virginia's finest young ladies, and a most capable nurse, I must add." He turned and stepped back to his chair. "Why, without her constant help these past three weeks, I would surely have succumbed to this dreadful cough."

Dorothea gave the ailing man a motherly pat on the shoulder and turned to John. "I'm very pleased to meet you, John."

John took the delicate warm fingers and held her hand for a long moment. "The pleasure is all mine...Dorothea."

"William's told me so much about you." She pulled away and turned to David. "Welcome to Virginia, Mister Noble."

William cleared his throat. "So, tell me, John, what brings you and your young friend all the way from Jamaica to Virginia, and at this time of year?"

John considered his answer, but before he could form his words, David was already speaking.

"It's the Continental Navy!" David gave John a glance. "John and I have come to seek commissions!"

William shot an accusing scowl at John. "Is that true, John?"

"Well..." John gave a sideways glance at the Jamaican.

"You were never one to get involved in politics, much less fight somebody else's battle." William coughed into the kerchief. "You're a Scotsman like me, and this war that's brewing has nothing to do with us."

A thick silence hung over the room while the four waited for John's side of the story. "My young friend tends to exaggerate. He's correct that while I was in King's Town I spoke of a colonial naval commission. I've had time to reconsider, and what I really want now is to purchase a small plantation of my own where I can live someday in leisure."

"Trade away the sea to become a dirt farmer?"

"Yes."

"That's nothing like the John Paul I remember." William threw himself into another fit of painful coughing. Dorothea crossed to the sideboard where she fetched a fresh kerchief to replace the blood-stained one he had been using.

William took the offered kerchief and whispered. "I'd love to lend you the money to buy your farm, but I'm a little low on funds right now. All I can offer you is free room and board while you raise the money you'll need."

John gave a smile. "I would be much obliged."

William brightened. "I might even know of one or two small plantations nearby that you could have for next to nothing." While William choked out the words between dry coughs, John couldn't help but notice the signal Dorothea was giving him.

"William, why don't you and the good doctor get David to tell you about their sea voyage for a few minutes while I get your brother to help me with the goose?" She looked to John. "You do know how to carve a roast goose, don't you?"

"Just lead the way, Miss Dandridge." John pulled his sword halfway from its sheath and winked at his older brother. "I've been known to carve a few geese in my day." Turning, he followed the young woman into the hallway and to the back of the house. When they reached the kitchen, he put his hand on her shoulder to stop her. "It's worse than the doctor is telling us, isn't it?"

Dorothea nodded.

He pulled back his hand. "The bloody kerchiefs. What's the matter with my brother?"

Tears had begun to well in her eyes. She sat down at the kitchen table. "I...I don't really know where to begin."

"Are you and my brother..." John seated himself across the table, but fell silent when he realized such a question might not be appropriate.

He pulled a wadded, not-so-clean kerchief from his back pocket and offered it to dry her tears. She thanked him but declined.

"There's nothing untoward between your brother and me, Mister Paul. I live in Hanover County—a half-day's journey to the west. I've been a very close friend of your brother and his wife, Helen, for several years." She paused to wipe a tear from her cheek. "Would you be offended if I spoke candidly, Mister Paul?"

"Not at all. And please call me John."

"Your brother is a very selfish man."

John nodded. "I know. He was a selfish child too."

"Then it won't surprise you that his selfishness has driven his wife away." She searched her soul for the strength to continue. "You can't imagine how painful it has been watching William while all of this..." She stopped to choke back a sob. "I've stood by him during these last several months since she left him, watching the toll the affair has taken on him, both mentally and physically."

"His illness?" John glanced back toward the hallway as his brother began to cough once more. "How long has he been this way?"

"Six or seven weeks—since mid-November. Before it's finished, I fear he'll lose more than just his wife." She lowered her head and began to sob quietly.

"Are you saying this illness may be his demise?"

"It isn't just a cough, as William claims. Doctor Read says it's consumption, and he told me this very evening that he doesn't expect William to last through the spring."

John rose to his feet, walked to the hallway door and looked back toward the parlor. The coughing had stopped for the moment. "But there must be something..." He turned back to meet the teary stare of the young woman. "A prescription, or a change of climate?"

She shook her head. "It's too late for that. I suggested it to the doctor, but he told me that any extended trip—even to King's Town—would do more harm than good."

"I saw the bottle of laudanum on the table next to his chair."

"That's only for his pain, John. The doctor has tried everything else, and nothing has worked."

He walked back to the table and sat down.

She reached across and took John's hand in an attempt to comfort his troubled spirit. He didn't pull back. His eyes ran over her peach-smooth face like a child across a spring meadow, fascinated at the way the blonde ringlets caressed her delicate throat and how her light blue eyes reminded him of raindrops on alabaster.

"Does he know?"

She was momentarily confused. "Does he know what?"

"Has he been told how bad his condition is?"

She shook her head.

"Surely he must suspect something—the blood—and with no improvement in so much time."

"No, neither Doctor Read nor I have had the courage to tell him. But I'm sure you're correct; that he suspects the worst." She paused for a moment. "I've already told my father that I'll be staying with William as long as he needs me, and he's consented. But now that you and your friend are here, I might as well—"

"Please don't leave, Miss Dandridge. William needs you. Besides, David and I wouldn't know how to care for him properly once the doctor leaves."

She considered for a moment. "I could show you how to do it—what he needs."

"Maybe I need you also."

"I don't understand."

John opened his waistcoat to expose the dried blood on his shirt. "We had a little trouble a couple of weeks ago—a most severe storm—and I'm certain that at least two of my ribs were broken by a bad swing of the tiller."

"Oh, my!" She helped him remove his coat. She eagerly unbuttoned his shirt and opened it, but stopped and pulled back her hands. "Excuse me. I forgot myself."

"It's all right." John gave a laugh and pulled his shirt loose from his trousers. "You're my nurse."

She unwrapped the bandage that Seamus had applied and looked at the wound. "This needs to be tended to."

He spread his arms, as if giving up to an attacker. "I'm in your hands."

"I'll get some hot water and towels." In a few minutes, John's wound was cleansed, dressed, and bandaged.

"Does this make a difference?" John groaned as he pushed an arm into one of the sleeves. "Will you stay on—at least until I'm well?"

"Only if you're certain I wouldn't be in the way."

"In the way!" John gave a curt laugh. "My brother needs a nurse more than he needs two extra mouths to feed."

"Very well. I'll stay." She dried her hands on her apron and looked back toward the parlor. "I think we'd best be getting back to your brother and the others. It's early yet to carve the goose, and besides,

William will be anxious to hear of your recent adventures—of which I'm certain there must be many."

When they entered the parlor, David was in the middle of the cannon battle between the Tiburon and the Falmouth Packet. "You'd have loved it! Captain Paul lowered his slow match to the touch hole and a dozen of Captain Smoot's were parcelled and blown to the four winds!" William noticed John and Dorothea in the doorway. The three men stood.

"Aha! Where have you two been for so long?" William gave John a wink. "Is that goose all carved?"

"Not yet." John gave Dorothea a nod. "Miss Dandridge checked the bird and decided it needed a little more time."

She smiled at the three men and gestured for them to take their seats. "It will be at least another fifteen minutes." She pointed toward the dining room. "If you'll excuse me, I have a table to set."

Ezra patted David's knee. "Your friend is quite the storyteller, John. I'm anxious to hear your version of the adventure, and why you left Tobago to come to America."

"How much did David tell you?"

William held up a hand to quiet the doctor. "He tells us that you had to kill one of your crewmen in Tobago. Is that true?"

"It was a mutiny." John gave David a scalding look. "The man gave me no choice."

"But why wouldn't you remain for a trial, dear brother? Surely they'd believe you over a pack of mutineers."

"Not the court I'd have faced."

"Oh?"

"An Admiralty court would have exonerated me. But without the required naval officers, the magistrate would have convened a jury of the locals, and I would never have survived."

"So, the truth of the matter is that you ran away to King's Town." William muffled a cough and looked to the doctor. "Sounds to me like the actions of a guilty man."

"That's because you don't know the natives as I do, William, and neither do you know who recommended I flee."

"And who would that be?"

"It was none other than the lieutenant governor himself."

The doctor turned in his chair. "And what were your intentions when you departed Tobago, Mister Paul?"

"My intention was to turn myself in at the nearest Admiralty office. Perhaps on Saint Vincent or one of the other smaller islands. It all depended on whether there were enough naval officers present." John shook his head. "It seems most of them are tending to the blockade of your ports."

William put a hand to the doctor's arm. "Is that all?"

"When the master of the Falmouth Packet took ill with malaria and asked that I take his ship on to Jamaica, I decided I could report my affair as easily in King's Town as anywhere else."

"Did you?"

"Did I what?

"Did you report it at King's Town?

"I didn't get a chance, what with all..."

"Ha! I thought as much." William wasn't too ill to needle his younger brother. He gave the doctor a wry smile. "And what's this that Noble tells us about you taking on the surname of 'Jones'?"

John gave David another angry stare. "I took on the surname so I could sign the port clearance papers as we made our rounds of the islands. Nothing more, nothing less."

"Nothing more, nothing less." William looked to David. "Your young friend tells us you left your ship on a mud bank in Machotick Creek. What do you intend to do with it?"

"It belongs to a Michael McClure of Cork. I was hoping to find a new master for her when we passed through Leeds Town—someone who might sail her back to Ireland."

The doctor leaned forward. "And did you...find anybody?"

"There were no takers."

The doctor thought for a moment. "I have a friend—an Irishman named Allan Cosgrove—who is looking for a ship to sail back to Ireland. Shall I ask him to speak with you?"

"By all means, provided my older brother can keep from telling the King's men about me." He gave William a hard look.

"Would I do that?" William gave John a look of childlike innocence. "I don't want you to get the idea I'm forcing you into anything, but I've a proposition for you, little brother."

"A proposition?"

"I had to close my tailor shop because of this cough. If you were inclined to open and run it for me until I'm back on my feet, say in exchange for—"

"Your silence?"

"Now, there you go!" William looked to the good doctor and the lad from Jamaica, and then back to John. "Do you think I'd—"

"Of course you would blackmail your own brother!"

"Blackmail or not, it's a wonderful offer."

"Assuming I'd agree to your proposition, how are we to split the proceeds?"

"In twain, naturally. I'd have it no other way."

"And what about David? He'll be needing an income as well." John leaned forward and pointed a finger at his older brother. "Agree to split the profit three ways, with each of us getting equal shares, and I'll do it."

William, who had planned on such an arrangement from the start, chuckled to himself. "Agreed!"

"One other thing, William, before I agree."

"What?"

John leaned forward and whispered. "Promise me you'll keep all this about the trouble in Tobago and my temporary surname from Miss Dandridge."

"Why, of course, John! Anything for my new business partner."

"Keep what from me, William?" Dorothea stood at the parlor door with a mixing spoon in her hand. The four men stood.

"Nothing important, my dear. Just...masculine talk."

She raised the spoon. "Here's a little feminine talk for you. Supper will be on the table in five minutes. If you don't wash up now, you'll go without."

While she turned to leave, William mimicked her scolding manner to the others, thinking she wouldn't see.

She stepped back to the door and raised the spoon. "Take care, William! You're not too old or too ill for a whipping."

William gave a sheepish shrug. "Oh my."

John stepped to William and reached for his arm. "Do you need help to the back porch?"

"No!" William stepped closer to the fire. "I'll be fine. You two go first. I'd rather wait here with the good doctor until the food is actually on the table."

The two young travelers walked down the hallway past the kitchen and stopped at the door to the back porch. David pushed the door open and stepped to the sink. "Your brother doesn't look at all well."

"He has consumption."

"That's bad, isn't it?"

"As bad as it can be."

"How long does he have?"

John shook his head. "I don't know."

***

After William had led them in the blessing, Dorothea uncovered the plates to reveal a symphony of flavors that surpassed their expectations. The young goose was spiced and baked to perfection, and served with plates of fresh string beans, pickled peaches that stung the palate, and honeyed yams on the side. The delicious aromas and provocative flavors made for the best meal the two seafaring men had tasted in several weeks—far better than the constant diet of turtle soup and salt pork they had eaten at sea. The hot cornbread and molasses was a special treat for David, for it was exactly as his mother had made for him when he was a child. William ate very little, but made up for it with conversation.

"So, John—who is this Joshua Smoot, and why was he after you?"

John looked to David. "How much did you tell them?"

"Only that we were attacked by the Captain Smoot at the command of the Tiburon. I didn't tell him why."

"Why?" William looked to David and back to John. "Did you somehow provoke the attack?"

John was becoming angry, but before he could do anything about it, the front door opened. An icy wind blew up the hallway, through the dining room and out past the kitchen, followed by the solid bang of the front door closing again.

Dorothy looked to William. "Are you expecting somebody else?"

William looked to the doctor and the two young men from Jamaica. "Not that I know of, unless you two brought Captain Smoot along with you."

John turned to the approaching footsteps and regretted that he had left his sword in the parlor. "We weren't followed."

All eyes were riveted on the hallway. A tall man stepped into the doorway and stopped. He took a well-worn kerchief from his pocket and blew the chill from his nose.

William twisted about in his chair. "Well, I'll be parcelled and thrown to the tax collectors! If it isn't Mister Henry!"

The new arrival surveyed the room, his eyes hesitating on John and David. "Good evening! I see that I'm late for dinner." He was a tall man at six foot—slim and strong. He had a long face, a round forehead with a high hairline, a strong Roman nose, and piercing dark eyes. He could have been a pirate or a king. He laid his saddlebags in the corner and hung his coat on a hook next to the archway.

Dorothea brought a sixth chair from the wall and pushed it up next to the doctor. She touched the newcomer's arm. "Patrick, we didn't expect you until tomorrow afternoon."

"Good evening, my dear." Patrick squeezed her had. "A slight change of plans and appointments."

Even though John had only known Dorothea for less than an hour, he felt a tinge of jealousy. He gave the statesman a suspicious look. He had heard of Patrick Henry, but only as a leading light of the revolution, not as a lover.

Patrick stepped behind William and massaged the sick man's shoulders. "And how's our loyalist patient tonight?"

William stifled a cough. "Oh, much better." Everyone knew it to be a lie except William, and even he suspected the truth.

Patrick stepped to his chair and looked across to John and David. "And might I assume that you, sir, are William's seafaring younger brother, John?" John and David looked down at their clothing.

John stood and offered his hand. "Yes, I'm John Paul, and this is my traveling companion, David Noble."

"It's the smell of the sea that betrays you, good sirs, and you'll not be rid of it until you've had a thorough bathing and one of William's tailors sews you a new set of clothes. Besides, William's spoken often of his younger brother the sea captain, and you match his description like a portrait." Patrick shook David's hand and then sat down and started to eat. "When did you arrive?"

"They've just arrived an hour ago from King's Town, and they've had some grand adventures en route." William gave David a quick glance, and looked back to Patrick.

The doctor wanted to hear more about the pirate attack. "David was just telling us about an encounter they had with pirates off the coast of South Carolina."

"Pirates, you say?" Patrick gave the two a raise of the brow. "Finally a topic William and I can discuss without the clash of rebellious writer's quill and tailor's shears."

"And I suppose the clothes-making business is too boring for you?"

Patrick was pleased that he had goaded his old friend. "Do I detect a wounded spirit?" Patrick looked to the others and gave a knowing laugh. "I don't know that I'd call it boring, but I've never heard of a person getting their blood up over a pair of new knickers."

"And what would you wear before a judge if it weren't for the fine clothes I've fashioned for you?"

"I didn't intend it as an attack, William, but since it was so well executed, I'll just let it stand." Patrick smiled and nudged William in the ribs.

Dorothea set a glass of brandy beside Patrick's plate and gave William a mother's look of reproach.

"Ah!" Patrick grabbed Dorothea around the waist and gave her a flirtaceous tickle, as it she were a tavern wench. "Thank you, my dear. My mouth's been waiting for brandy for the past three or four hours."

"Is that all your mouth's been waiting for?"

Patrick feigned shock. "Yes. But my eyes have been waiting for a smile on the sweet lips of my fiancée!" He pulled her close, but she broke away with an embarrassed look at John.

Patrick noticed John's expression. "You seem concerned about something, Captain Paul. Didn't your brother tell you about Dorothea and me?" He gave William another nudge.

William was still in a bristle from the last jab and jerked away from the friendly poke. "We didn't have time to speak of such mundane topics. As I told you, John and David have been here less than an hour, and we've done nothing but talk about their voyage." William took a sip of his brandy and wiped his mouth on his shirtsleeve.

Patrick became impatient. "Well if you're not going to tell them about me, I'll have to." The statesman turned to John and David. "I've been a close friend of your brother for the better part of five years. It is he who has graciously supplied me with most of my clothing, and at no cost, I must gratefully add. His kindness has indirectly provided a substantial part of my tuition to become a lawyer. And, but for his kindness this cold evening, I'd probably spend the night shivering with my horse in some drafty stable."

William saw his moment. "And I'm not so sure you don't deserve that bed of straw either, the way you barged in tonight without an invitation."

"Ah!" Patrick leaned across and gave William's hand a brotherly pat. "The milk of human kindness personified!"

William took a sip of his drink and pushed the conversation in a new direction. "Tell us, Patrick, what new treason have you and your little band of renegades hatched since we last spoke?"

"Why do you insist on provoking me, William? The things I'm involved in will affect you as surely as any other man in the colonies, rebel and Tory alike."

"Ooo..." William smiled. "Who's getting testy now?"

"Gentlemen!" It was the doctor. "Can we keep this civil?"

Both men sat upright in their chairs as if scolded by a stern schoolmaster.

"I'm sorry, Patrick." William gave the doctor a nod. "Watching you get worked up about this trouble with the government is about the only stimulation I've gotten since I caught this damned cold."

"Your apology is accepted, and I'm equally to blame. You have your cold and I have the colonies. Sometimes I get so caught up with all of this trouble that I lose my sense of humor."

There was a momentary lull in the conversation, so David blurted what both he and John had discussed at King's Town. "But what of the war?"

"What concern is that of yours?" Patrick wiped his mouth, stood, and walked to the fireplace mantle where three clay pipes lay in a neat row. He selected the longest one, broke off a half inch of used stem and filled it with tobacco. "You're a Jamaican. That makes you a loyalist. What do you know of our troubles?"

"Plenty!" David spoke before John could shush him. "We know about Samuel Adams dumping all of those bricks of monopoly tea up in Boston Harbor last month. We also know about the Townsend acts and the quartering of British soldiers in private residences."

"Interesting." Patrick dipped the end of a sliver of birch in the fire and then applied it to the tobacco. "Anything else?"

"We also know that Esek Hopkins will be appointed as Commander in Chief of the Continental Navy. That's why we're here—to get naval commissions."

"You know quite a bit for such a young man." Patrick puffed the pipe alive. "Do you hope these random bits of information somehow might endear the two of you to Mister Hopkins?"

David gave John an expectant nudge. "Tell him, John. Tell him that's why we came to Virginia."

"Well, John?" Patrick blew a smoke ring across at the young sea captain. "Does your young friend speak for you?"

"Not exactly."

David twisted in his chair. "But you told my father—"

"No, David. You told your father I was coming to America to join their navy."

"Then why—"

"Not now. Not here."

***

The Paul tailor shop was located up the hill on Princess Ann Street—a five minute walk from William Paul's home. Several other small shops stood to either side. The large hall upstairs was used for overflow storage by the sailmaker next door, and the room also served as a meeting place every Friday night for the Masons.

Provided with a list of William's previous employees, John and David made a personal visit to each, offering to hire them back at their previous salary. Then, using the shop's last three years of receipts, the two new proprietors circulated printed handouts to as many of William's regular customers as they could locate. Within a week, three of the four previous tailors were once again at work, and nearly all of the past clientele had returned with large orders.

Sequestered in his home, William called from his place next to the fireplace. "Dorothea!"

She stepped into the parlor and picked up William's dinner tray. "Finished already?"

"You asked me to call you at five o'clock."

"Oh my!" Dorothea set William's tray of picked-at food on the hearth and walked quickly from the room.

He called after her. "You're in love with my brother, aren't you?"

Dorothea stopped in the hallway and turned, placing her hands on her hips with her head tilted like a schoolgirl. She gave a laugh that sounded like sleighbells. "No! I'm engaged to Mr. Henry. I just enjoy meeting them when they get home."

"Of course!" William gave her a toothy grin. "Just remember. It won't set too well with either your father or your fiancé if you become too friendly with my brother."

The young woman gave a huff and spun away. A moment later, she sat in the window seat of her second story bedroom, watching for her young men to turn the corner onto their street.

Just as they had done for a month, John and David appeared from behind the large birch tree at the corner of Prussia Street. David ran across to the south side of the street and caught the ball of tailor's twine that John threw toward the railroad tracks. In a moment, the two reached the front door.

Dorothea opened the door and stepped outside. "How was your day?"

"Very good. All of our tailors are backlogged a month, and David received four more orders this afternoon." John looked past her and whispered. "How is William?"

She stepped outside and pulled the door closed. "His spirits are up, but he's eating less and less each day."

John returned her pained look. "He doesn't have very much longer, does he?"

***

William's condition worsened in mid-June, confining him to his bed. Doctor Read had done all that he could for the poor man. He left a liberal supply of laudanum and the necessary instructions for the dying man's care. It was a trying time for John, Dorothea and David to stand by helplessly while William lost more weight, along with his desire to live. It was especially difficult for Dorothea in the last weeks, having to care for the poor soul in his decimated condition. On the 28th of July, well after Ezra Read had predicted, William Paul died of advanced tuberculosis. After the burial service at Saint George's Church, Dorothea returned to her father's plantation in Hanover County, some fifteen miles to the southwest.

Throughout the summer and fall of '74, John and David were regular guests at the Dandridge estate, spending the entire second weekend of each month. Captain Nathaniel Dandridge was retired from the British Navy, and with their common love of the sea, he and John had quickly become friends—sharing all of their sea adventures. Dorothea, despite her full knowledge of the difficulty it would cause, had fallen deeply in love with John.

***

Using a secret mailing address that John could not possibly discover, David had maintained a regular correspondence with his father in King's Town. On the 24th of February, 1775, a letter arrived at the counting house of Charles Noble.

Dear Father,

I am writing to you with great concern and frustration. I now agree fully with your first estimation of Uncle Silver's plan, and not without reason. It was, as you predicted, only a pipe dream. Do you remember my telling you about the tailor shop John inherited from his brother?

Well, it's doing much better than John and I expected. So well, in fact, that he is on the verge of asking the young woman Dorothea Dandridge for her hand in marriage and purchasing a farm in the countryside. I've lost all hope that he still intends to seek a naval commission.

The only impediment to the Captain's matrimonial plans lie with her father, Nathaniel West Dandridge. It is no secret that he intends that his daughter marry the rebel Patrick Henry, but Captain Jones doesn't seem at all put off by this paternal insistence.

I'm certain my uncle has erred, Father, and I believe my continued presence in Virginia is without purpose. I wish to come home as soon as possible. Please advise.

Your humble & obedient son,
David

A thick course of raucous laughter erupted from the public room of Silver Jack's Tavern. Charles Noble stepped through the arched doorway with David's folded letter in his left hand. He scanned the dimly lit room for his older brother.

"Charles!" John Silver called from his brother's left. "So, ye've decided to take me up on me bet after all!"

Charles strode to the table where Silver had just set out a half dozen tankards of warm ale and was collecting the empties. "I'm not here for your stupid bet!"

"Now it's a stupid bet?"

"Morbid is more like it."

"The scurvy swabs'll die whether we lay a wager on their heads or not, little brother, so I don't see the harm in it."

"Aye!" It was one of the intoxicated seamen at the table. He wiped the warm foam from his beard. "An' if the King's men don't sink 'em, then the toredo worms will!"

"You'd bet on anything, wouldn't you?"

"Life be one bet after 'nother, little brother!"

Charles held up David's letter. "Well, big brother, this is one meal that has lost its flavor altogether."

"Aa, ha!" Silver recognized his nephew's handwriting and gave the seamen an apologetic shrug. "You good sirs'll hafta 'scuze me fer a glass while I have a word with Charlie here." The old pirate set the empty tankards on a nearby table, snatched the letter from Charles's hand and marched toward his private office.

Charles followed at several paces. "It's your plan and some very bad news."

"What?" Silver pushed through the office door and scanned his nephew's words. He looked around at Charles. "Since when is it bad news that a man has fallen in love with a maiden?"

"That's not what I was referring to, Brother. Read on—near the end."

A moment later, Silver found it. "The hell he has!" The old pirate crumpled the letter and threw it across the room. "What's the matter with that good-for-nothing son of yours?"

"There's nothing the matter with David. What's wrong is your plan."

"My plan was perfect. All your son had to do was keep Captain Jones on the right course. Evidently he's not capable of even the simplest of tasks."

"David's done exactly what you've demanded of him."

Silver pointed down at the letter. "That says he hasn't!"

"But all you required was that he keep us informed of Captain Jones's progress, and to tell him about the treasure when it was most appropriate." Charles picked up the letter and spread it flat. "He had no control over Captain Jones giving up his desire for the naval commission and purchasing a farm. Even if you were there in person, you couldn't have done any more."

"You're wrong, little brother." Silver pulled a piece of parchment from a stack of papers. "There's something I can still do."

"What?"

"It's time once again to intervene in our little captain's affairs—to apply a little leverage, if you will."

"But how?"

"With this!" John Silver handed his brother the parchment.

***

The estate of British Naval Captain Nathaniel Dandridge stood on forty acres of rich Virginia bottom land in the western half of Hanover County. Four ancient live oak trees stood watch over the two-story red brick home and the spacious flower and vegetable gardens.

Nathaniel was a large and powerful man in his mid-forties, with a full head of coal-black hair just beginning to show grey at the temples. His long career onboard His Majesty's men-of-war had given him that weathered and adventurous look that women say they find so attractive. He stepped from his study to the stairs and called down. "Jenny! Are you in the house?"

The housekeeper ran from the kitchen with dripping hands and looked up the stairs to her master. "Sir?"

"A man has just ridden up and will be at my porch in a moment. When he knocks, remember what I told you."

Jenny nodded. "Yes, Mister Dandridge." She turned about just as the knock came. She stepped across the foyer and pulled open the door several inches. "May I help you?"

"It is I, Jenny. Is something the matter?"

"Good morning, Captain Paul."

"Is Dorothea here?" He put a hand to the door but the maid held it in place with her foot. "What's the matter. Why won't you let me inside?"

Jenny liked John, but she feared her employer. "I would sir, but..." She looked nervously behind her.

"But what?" John pushed the door against her foot.

"Please, sir." She dropped her voice to a whisper and looked once more behind her. "I'm not supposed to let you in, sir. The captain's threatened to sell the remaining years of my indenture to another master if I do. Please go, sir, before I get in trouble."

"Go?" John stepped away from the door several paces so he could see the second story windows. "What's going on, Jenny? Why aren't you supposed to let me in?" John looked up at the windows of Dorothea's room. "Where is she?"

"She's in her room, but Captain Dandridge told me just minutes ago—" Before she could finish, Dorothea pulled the door open and gave the housekeeper a stern look.

John stepped toward Dorothea. "What's going on? Why won't Jenny allow me in the house?"

Dorothea pushed past Jenny and pointed toward the gardens. "Outside, John." She turned and looked to her father's window. "We can talk under the oak tree." She stepped past him and walked quickly across the lawn to the old tree. She stopped and turned. "I didn't expect you today."

"But I wrote! Didn't you get my letter?"

She stopped at the bench, turned and shook her head. "You haven't written for more than a month."

"But I have—every week without fail. There should have been at least two—"

She looked at the house. "Something's happened, John."

"What are you talking about? What could have happened?"

"My father's taken a dislike to you."

"A dislike? But why? What have I done?"

"I'm as baffled as you. This morning, just after that man arrived, Father told Jenny and me that you're no longer welcome in our home. I asked him why, but he refused to explain."

"That man?"

"A tall man with an accent. He carried a satchel with the seal of the Magistrate of Tobago."

John stared at the flower garden without answering her. It's finally caught up with me.

"You know who it is, don't you, John? You're in some sort of trouble, aren't you?"

John looked up at the line of windows. A man was standing behind the lace curtain. "We'll have to meet somewhere else." John turned back to Dorothea. "Perhaps at Doctor Read's home."

"What's going on John? Who is that man?"

"I was on a merchant ship—there was some trouble—a mutiny. He probably wants to question me."

Dorothea shook her head. "If my father wanted you to talk with the man from Tobago, he wouldn't have told Jenny to turn you away."

"Doctor Read has invited me for dinner tonight." John rubbed his chin in thought. "Is there somewhere nearby where we might meet tomorrow, after I speak with him?"

She considered for a moment and pointed to the east. "There's that small park just this side of the bridge."

"I know the place." John stepped close, hoping for a kiss. "Will you meet me there at noon?"

"Of course I will." She gave him the kiss and then flashed a look up at the windows. "I'll bring us something to eat."

"Good! If the doctor agrees, I'll arrange to stay with him a second night. We can ride there together after the park."

Dorothea put her arms around John's chest and pressed her cheek against his. "Father's been talking more lately about my marrying Mister Henry."

John pulled back and looked into her eyes. "He doesn't think I'm good enough for you, does he?"

"Please keep your voice down." She put a fingertip to his lips. "I don't know that for certain, but it's no secret that Patrick's been courting me since at least a year before you and David arrived in Fredericksburg."

"I'll stand toe to toe with Mister Henry any day." John looked toward the setting sun and realized the hour. "It's late. I'll have to leave now. I'll see you at the park tomorrow?"

"I'll be there, John."

He gave her a light kiss on the cheek. Within a minute, he was once again on his horse and riding away to the northeast. Dorothea watched him until he vanished beyond the bend in the road, and then returned to the house.

Jenny was busy in the kitchen, putting together the last touches for dinner. She gave Dorothea a frightened look.

Dorothea stepped to the worktable and tasted one of the cooked onions. She studied the maid while she chewed. "Captain Paul told me that he has sent a letter every week since his last visit. Have you seen them?"

"No, Miss Dotty." Jenny kept her eyes down at her work. "If they came—and I'm not saying they did—I'm sure your father would know about them."

"If I find out you had anything to do with Captain Paul's letters not reaching me, it won't be my father selling your remaining years! It'll be me, and I'll see to it that your new master is somebody dreadful!" Turning indignantly, Dorothea walked to the base of the stairs and stopped. "I'll be up in my room. Call me for dinner." She started up the stairs and then stopped a second time.

"There is one other thing, Jenny. I'll require a basket lunch for two people tomorrow morning. Have it ready by eleven-thirty."

"Yes, Ma'am." As soon as Dorothea was settled in her room, Jenny walked to the hallway and crept up the stairs. She tiptoed past Dorothea's room to Nathaniel's study.

The room was stark, much like the master's cabin on a British ship of the line. The furnishings were austere—two stuffed chairs, a small table between them, a large desk and chair—nothing more. Captain Dandridge stood with his backside against the desk reading the warrant.

His elderly guest sat in one of the chairs sipping at his second glass of brandy. He cleared his throat to get the captain's attention.

Nathaniel looked about at his visitor. "I'm sorry. You were saying?"

"I was telling you that sometimes it's the smallest things that count the most."

"Meaning what, exactly?"

"Take our mutual friend, John Paul." He sipped his brandy. "If it weren't for my wife's brother being a bachelor, the King's men would be arresting Captain Paul in Fredericksburg, rather than me coming to ask your assistance to insure his safety."

"I don't follow you, Mister Young. How could your brother-in-law's marital status have anything to do with your visit or John Paul's safety?"

"Samuel is the postmaster of Scarborough and has never been married. The only home-cooked meals he gets are when he brings my mail, which is always just before suppertime. He wasn't looking for that specific letter, but the King's men were."

Natahniel held up the warrant. "And he showed it to you first?"

The older man nodded. "So you see, Samuel's marital status did make a difference."

"But you claim that you told Paul never write to you."

"That's true, but he was ready to burst at the seams to tell me how well he was doing at his brother's tailor shop, and about you and his love for your daughter. That's why my visit here was so imperative, don't you see? It was only a matter of time before the King's men would have discovered he has a brother in Virginia. He would have been arrested and convicted of the murder of Jack Fry."

"I suppose you're correct."

"So you can see, can't you, why I had to come in person, before he wrote to me again?"

"But why not go to him in Fredericksburg?"

"That was my intention until I discovered I was being followed."

"Followed? From Tobago?"

"First, the King's men have a certain smell." The man touched the side of his nose. "We weren't aboard the Bristol Twins more than an hour before a little man began to circle me like a fly. The moment he found out I was headed for Virginia, he told me this was his destination also." There was a soft knock on the door.

Nathaniel held up a quieting hand to his visitor. "Come!"

The door pushed open. It was Jenny. "It's just me, sir." She gave the visitor a nervous look. "I..."

"What is it, Jenny?"

"He's gone, sir." She stepped into the room. "You asked that I tell you when he left. Will there be anything else?"

"Yes, Jenny, there is one other thing." Nathaniel unlocked and opened the center drawer of his desk. "I'm finished with Captain Paul's letters. See that they are included with tomorrow's mail." He handed the letters to her and turned back to his guest.

"Sir?"

"Was there something else?"

"Begging your pardon, sir, but I hope you don't require this of me again." She held up the letters. "It's not right, and Miss Dotty told me that if she finds out I had anything to do with it, she'll sell my contract to someone dreadful. I agree that Miss Dotty should marry Mister Henry, but it grieves my soul to deceive her like this."

He closed and locked the drawer on his desk. "Jenny, you've only done that which I've required of you. Unless you feel compelled to tell her, my daughter will never know you had anything to do with this matter." He took up his glass of brandy. "Concerning your contract, you needn't worry about those remaining four years. I'm your master, and I'm well pleased with your service. Was there anything else?"

"Just one more thing, sir."

"Yes?"

"Miss Dotty has asked that I prepare a basket lunch for two. I believe she's meeting Mister Paul somewhere at noon tomorrow."

"Thank you for that information, Jenny. Call us when dinner's ready."

"Yes, sir." Jenny stepped into the hallway and pulled the door closed.

"Did I hear right?" It was the visitor. "Did your housekeeper say that John Paul was just here?"

"Yes he was, but he's gone now."

"Damn! I could have told him all of this to his face, rather than relay it through you! Did you know he was coming?"

"Of course I did."

"Ah!" The visitor pointed at the door. "Those letters!"

"Yes, the letters. John Paul always writes before he pays my daughter a visit."

"What did you tell them—your housekeeper and your daughter—about Captain Paul?"

"Only that he was no longer welcome in my home." Nathaniel gave his visitor a questioning look. "Wasn't that your purpose in showing me this warrant?"

"Well...yes and no."

"Which is it? Dorothea's my daughter, and Captain Paul is a fugitive from the King, is that not so?"

"It is, but—"

"You're not making any sense, Mister Young. If this matter is important enough to bring the lieutenant governor of Tobago all the way to Virginia, why aren't you riding the additional two miles that would allow you to catch up with your friend? You could speak with him face to face."

"Not out in public—at least not while that little man is still sniffing around. Besides, I have already shown you the warrant. If John were to find out I was here, he would know it was I who showed it to you. I shouldn't like him to think I was operating behind his back. You can see that, can't you?"

"I suppose so." Nathaniel picked up the warrant. "But you didn't come all this way just to show me this. You want me to do something else for you."

"John's in immediate danger, sir, and must leave Virginia as quickly as possible. You're the only person—besides your daughter—who cares for him enough to do this for me."

"Leave Virginia…hmmm."

"With your connections, you must know of something he would be drawn to."

Nathaniel stroked his chin. "There might be a way." He picked up the parchment. "Tell me about this warrant. What really happened in Tobago?"

"Well, according to Captain Paul, he was attacked aboard his ship by one of his crewmen. The man was fomenting a mutiny over the crew's pay. John told me that the man attacked him with a belaying pin and John had to defend himself."

"And you believed John's report?"

"I didn't at first—not until he told me who it was he had to kill. The man was a good-for-nothing half-breed who had been in trouble from birth. I was surprised he hadn't been killed sooner."

"You said earlier that you'd be willing to testify before the Admiralty on Captain Paul's behalf."

"That's true—if it ever comes to that."

"Then why don't I simply inform the authorities that—"

"Because you're a man of your word, Captain Dandridge." The older man stood. "You gave me your word that if I confided in you, you'd maintain what I told you in the strictest confidence."

"Calm down, Mister Young. I was only suggesting that acquittal would be preferable to flight."

"But he wouldn't be acquitted, given the heightened level of animosity between the Americans and London. It hasn't helped his case at all that John fled Tobago, even if it was me who insisted he do it."

"Then what do you propose?"

"He mentioned in his letter that up until he fell in love with your daughter and the tailor business began doing so well, that he was considering a commission in the Continental Navy. I was counting on you and your connections—that you might know someone who could write him a letter of recommendation to Ezek Hopkins. If not, his only hope is to disappear until this unrest with Mother England is settled."

Nethaniel nodded. "Yes. I do know some people with the kind of influence you are suggesting."

As Nathaniel pondered the challenge, the taller man turned and walked across the room to refill his glass with brandy. There was a double clicking sound each time the left leg straightened for its next step.

***

After a chilly morning ride through the countryside, John reined his horse to a stop under a weeping willow and a short distance from a duck pond. He was early, for he didn't want to miss Dorothea's arrival. After a quick survey of the park, he dismounted and tied his horse to the tree. Two couples sat on their blankets watching their children play near water's edge. John walked toward them, but stopped when he heard his name called from windward.

"Captain Jones!"

John spun about to meet the cold stare of Nathaniel Dandridge. The older man held a single piece of parchment in his left hand. At his left side and partially hidden under his long coat hung a British naval officer's sword. Only the tip of the scabbard was visible next to his boot.

"Captain Dandridge!"

"It's true, isn't it?" Nathaniel stepped closer and continued to hold the paper toward John. "You have been using an alias."

"What are you talking about?"

"What is it today—John Paul or John Paul Jones?"

John's hand went instinctively to where his sword normally hung. It wasn't there. "What are you doing here?"

"I know! You were expected my daughter, weren't you?" Mister Dandridge stood a full four inches above John, and outweighed him by at least fifty pounds. The older man stepped closer.

"I've very little time, so I'll make this short. I know you're fond of Dorothea, and may even have secret plans for marriage someday." His countenance darkened. "Forget my daughter! I would never give her hand in marriage to a murderer and fugitive of the King!" He raised the document so John could see his name. It was the arrest warrant for the killing of Jack Fry, with the seal of the Admiralty at King's Town at its top. "Is that clear, Mister Paul?"

"Shouldn't we consult Dorothea about her future?"

"It isn't a matter of what Dorothea wants! I'm telling you to never see her again! If it weren't for her feelings toward you, I'd have brought the constable with me to arrest you. But I'm assuming you're a reasonable man, Mister Paul. I'll not report you in exchange for your word to never see my daughter again. Do I have it?"

John stared into the older man's eyes for half a minute, but refused to speak the words he demanded.

"You seem to have difficulty with the idea, Mister Paul, so I'll put it in the clearest terms I can." He took a long breath while he considered how to frame the ultimatum. "If you ever meet with my daughter again, or even write to her, then I'll inform the King's men of your whereabouts that very day! Is that clear enough?"

John nodded. "Does that include my meeting with her today?"

"It does." Nathaniel pulled his watch from his pocket and opened the cover. "I've seen to it that my daughter is delayed long enough to see you on your way back toward Fredericksburg."

"But—"

"But, nothing!" Nathaniel pressed his finger firmly against John's chest, pushing the smaller man back a step. "If you persist, not only will the King's men come for you, but I'll show Dorothea this warrant."

Inside, John was in a rage, but he had neither the ability nor the means to counter this attack.

"I'll take your silence as an agreement to my demands, Mister Paul. Don't show your face in Hanover County again, or you'll find yourself hanging from a gibbet."

Without a word of protest, John turned and walked to his horse. Within a minute, he was across the footbridge and swallowed up by the trees to the east.

Chapter 6

On Saturday, the 18th of March, 1775, just before lunchtime, an elderly man of slight frame and feeble countenance stood in the cutting room of the Paul tailor shop. He carried a canvas satchel on his arm and a brown felt hat in his hand. Jason Peters, the first tailor to be hired back when the shop reopened the previous year, motioned for his friend to set his things next to the cutting table.

Jason gave the man a friendly pat on the shoulder. "Mister Paul hasn't been himself this past week."

"Is he ill?"

Jason shook his head. "There's some sort of trouble. He comes in before the rest of us and stays to lock up every night. Very unlike his normal self."

"Do you think this is a bad time to solicit him for a job?"

"Not at all. He asked me to find him another tailor, and I've recommended you highly. His spirits are low, but he still needs you."

With that, he knocked lightly upon the frame of John's office door. "Yes?"

Jason stepped inside the office. "The tailor I told you about—Mister McCreedy—is here to see you, sir. Shall I show him in?"

"Yes. By all means." John folded the warrant and slipped it into his desk drawer.

McCreedy stepped into the room behind Jason.

"Come in, Mister McCreedy." John set a chair in the center of the room and motioned for the man to sit down. "I didn't realize how quickly the time had passed. Jason tells me you've been a tailor in New York for eighteen years, and there's none quicker or better at cutting and fitting."

"My friend flatters me, Mister Paul."

"Well, I've never known Jason to exaggerate, so I'll take him at his word." John looked down at the man's shoe. Excuse me, but there seems to be a bit of string caught on your shoe."

The older man looked down. "Oh no, sir. It's a fastening called a shoe 'lace.'" He bent over and grabbed the untied lace. "It's easier than a buckle in some ways, and certainly lighter." He pulled, and the right lace snapped in two. The tailor grinned ruefully. "Of course, it has its disadvantages as well."

"Don't worry about it. We have plenty of twine in the shop. I'll have Jason get—"

"No need, sir." The old man's nimble fingers spun a slipping noose in the end of the broken lace. Then, with a quick snap, he captured the short piece of string a quarter inch above the eyelet. A moment later, his shoe laces were retied.

John handed the man two short lengths of twine. "Would you do that again?" I've never seen a knot like that before."

"It's nothing new, Mister Paul, but I'm surprised that a tailor like you wouldn't have seen it before this."

"I'm a sea captain, recently turned businessman."

Mister McCreedy measured the two pieces. "Besides its practical usage mending broken shoe laces and joining thread, it makes a wonderful parlor trick."

"Show me. I like parlor tricks."

He handed one of the strings back to John. "If it's the trick you want to perform, you might prefer to use rope. Stand on your chair and hold your rope as high as you can."

John stood on the chair and held the two-foot string by the end. "Like this?"

"It works best if the rope is just an inch or two beyond your guest's reach. The challenge is to see if anybody can jump into the air and tie their rope to the dangling one." McCreedy reached up, and John adjusted the height of his string. The old man tied a quick slip knot in the end of his piece and looked up. "This happens very quickly, so watch close to what I do."

With a slight jump and a snap of the ends of his noose, the two strings were joined.

John tested the strength of the knot and then inspected it closely. "Why, that's a common sheet bend!" John looked down at the man. "Where'd you learn that?"

"It's an old tailor's trick, sir." The old man gave John a proud smile. "Its proper name is the 'short-end bend.'"

"Well, it's new to me and I'm very impressed."

"Impressed enough to offer me a job?"

John gave the old man a broad smile. "When can you start?"

"This afternoon, if that's agreable with you, sir."

John began to answer, but noticed a wagon parked in front of the shop. "Did you come to Fredericksburg alone?"

"No, sir." The old man looked to the street. "I have my wife with me."

"Have you found a place to stay yet?"

McCreedy shook his head. "I wanted to be sure I had the job first."

"I've...reconsidered, Mister McCreedy." John jumped down from the chair and stepped to his desk. "You can't start today after all."

"But, sir! You just told me—"

John held out two gold pieces. "First, you'll find a home for your wife and buy food for your table. Once you're settled, then you can start work."

The old man was shocked.

"And so that I can properly address you, what's your first name, Mister McCreedy?"

"It's Angus, sir." The old man's voice cracked while he took the coins. "May the Lord bless you for your kindness." He pressed the coins to his lips for a moment while his eyes filled with tears. "How can I ever thank you, Mister Paul?"

"By seeing to your wife, and being the tailor Jason tells me you are."

Angus turned and stepped to the door. He stopped and turned back. "I..."

John held up a hand. "Jason will show you the ropes tomorrow." With that, the older tailor excused himself, leaving John to the two pieces of twine on his desk.

Shortly after lunch, while John was occupied with his new trick, a tall visitor entered the Paul tailor shop. One of the younger tailors recognized the man as one of their older customers.

"Mister Henry!" Jason set down his scissors and took up his tape. In a moment, he had circled the statesman and taken several preliminary measurements. "It's a little worn, sir, but still quite a respectable riding coat." He continued to circle the tall man. "We've just received the latest patterns from England and could have you a new one in two days."

"I'd love a new set of clothes, Jason, but that's not why I'm here."

The tailor was crestfallen. "Then how may we help you?"

"I'm here to speak with one of your proprietors. Is Mister Paul on the premises?"

Jason pointed to the office door. "You'll find him in the back, sir. He needs a visitor." Jason walked toward the office and stopped. "Shall I announce you, sir?"

"Thank you, but it won't be necessary." Patrick pushed the door open and stepped inside. John was at his desk with his back to the door. "John?"

At the sound of his name, John looked around. "You!" John leaped up and took a step toward his sword.

"Did I come at a bad time?"

"Yes, considering!" John grasped his sword and pulled it half from its sheath.

"Considering what?"

"Did Captain Dandridge send you here to threaten me also?"

"To threaten you?" Patrick looked at the sword and retreated a step. "My God, man, I've come to offer you and Noble something few men..." He hesitated to give John a moment to cool down. "Do you remember that first evening we met? I believe it was in late January of last year?"

"Of course I do."

"Then you also remember what your traveling mate told me at the dinner table—why you had come to America." John remembered nearly every word from that most interesting evening, but gave Patrick an inquisitive look.

"Correct me if I'm wrong, but I understood that you and he came to Virginia to seek commissions in the Continental Navy, if and when it began to form."

"You're wrong, Henry." John allowed the sword to slide back into the scabbard. "I talked about it the night David and I met in King's Town, but only in passing. I'm afraid it was David's wishful thinking you heard last year, and I was only going along to patronize him. But go on. What have you come here to offer me?"

"Evidently, you have a friend—a James Smith of Kirkcudbright, Scotland—whose brother is the partner of a Mister Joseph Hewes of Edenton, North Carolina."

"Yes, that would be Robert Smith. James and I were lodge brothers in Scotland. He did mention that he had a brother in America."

"Joseph Hewes and Robert Smith own the largest shipping company in North Carolina. Both of these gentlemen were present with me and several other influential patriots at a meeting of the Committees of Correspondence three nights ago at Harrisonburg. Several very important decisions were made at that meeting."

"Decisions concerning the navy?"

Patrick nodded. "What I came here to tell you is that Mister Hewes has been appointed chairman of the Marine Commission."

John's heart flew to his throat. "Did Smith tell Hewes that he knew me?"

"I mentioned your name to Robert and he remembered that you were his brother's friend, but that was all."

"You had the chance to recommend me and didn't?"

"Calm down, Paul. It would have been highly presumptuous of me to suggest that he recommend you to Mister Hewes. But I'm fairly certain he heard our conversation concerning you and your young friend."

"But..."

"I'm prepared to write the two of you a letter of introduction to Joseph Hewes today, provided you can leave for Edenton tomorrow morning."

"Tomorrow morning? But—"

"Mister Hewes is sailing to Edenton as we speak. He will be at his shipping company for three days to attend several important meetings and catch up on business. Then he will sail back up to Boston the middle of next month. Considering the distance over land, you will miss him if you delay your departure."

"Of course I can go!" John pulled a piece of writing paper from the desk drawer, along with a bar of red sealing wax.

Patrick used the quill and ink on the desk to write out several sentences. After signing the note, he handed it to John for his approval. "You'll notice I refrained from making a direct recommendation. Mister Hewes's partner will know of you, and besides, it would be best if you were selected for your qualifications, rather than your acquaintanceships."

"But..." John looked up from the letter. "Couldn't you say something more? This only says—"

"I'm sorry, Paul. Console yourself with the knowledge that I've recommended no other men for commissions, as yet."

"Be honest with me, Henry. Tell me whether David and I have a chance."

"I'd consider your chances very good, unless there's something I'm not privy to."

The warrant for John's head lay folded on his desk. He gave it a touch and then read Patrick's letter once more. "This is better than most of the others will have, I suppose. Seal it, sir, and I'll begin packing."

A large drop of red wax was dripped onto the folded letter and impressed with the signet ring on the statesman's right forefinger. Patrick turned to leave.

"Before you go, could I prevail upon you to deliver a letter for me?"

"Of course. Who's it to?"

"Dorothea. I could be gone for months if things go our way. She'll wonder where I've gone, and I won't have time to make the side trip to her home."

"I'll be passing through there within the week, and I'd be glad to deliver it for you." A moment later, John had written two short paragraphs and sealed the letter with the same wax Patrick had used.

"Here!" John handed over the letter. "And I'd ask that you hand deliver this."

"As you wish." Patrick opened his coat and put the letter into his inside pocket.

John straightened up, trying to look as tall as he could. "Concerning the naval commission, if I succeed, I won't disappoint you or the colonies."

"If I had any doubts about that, I wouldn't have given you the introduction to Mister Hewes. You and David will do just fine."

John followed Patrick out to his horse.

Patrick put a foot in the stirrup but hesitated. He reached in and pulled out John's letter. "Considering that we're rivals for Dorothea's hand, are you sure you can trust me with this?" A palm-sized scrap of brown paper fluttered to the ground next to John's foot. The younger man picked it up and let his eyes dart over the five dozen words. He looked up at Patrick. "These are powerful words."

Patrick darkened. "They're not mine, though I wish they were."

"Oh?"

Patrick stepped away from his horse. "I'm to attend the Second Virginia Convention, which opens in Richmond on Monday. What's written on that scrap of paper has inspired the speech I will be giving."

"I'm sorry I'll miss it." John handed the note back to Patrick. "Considering those words, it certainly must be an important speech."

Patrick nodded. "Since you'll likely be in the center of the war that these words may help create, you should know more about what inspired them." Patrick looked about for eavesdroppers. "Do you mind if we return to your office?"

Once inside, John offered Patrick a cup of tea. "So, whose words are they?"

"On my way back from that meeting I told you about in Harrisonburg, I stopped for the night at Culpeper."

"I know of the place."

"I arrived just in time to witness a man in his mid-sixties being led in chains to the whipping post at the town center. The man was thrown headlong against the post and then chained up so hard that his unshod toes barely reached the ground."

"What had the old man done?"

"Now that I've had time to consider the affair in retrospect, I find it incredible the constable even consented to give the brittle old man the opportunity to speak his piece." Patrick ground his teeth. "The constable rammed a sharpened stick into the little man's stomach when he asked to be judged by his neighbors."

John winced at the picture the statesman was painting.

"Torn and bleeding from the wound in his side, the old man twisted about in his chains and choked out these words. 'Neighbors and friends. You all know me. I've baptized your children and comforted you when sickness was upon your homes. I've joined you in marriage and spoken the last words over the graves of your loved ones. You're about to behold how Mother England treats a minister of the Gospel when he does that which his Lord demands—preaching salvation of your souls by faith in the finished work of Jesus Christ—without the State Church's permission. I told yonder constable that I will never submit to taking his license—thereby turning my right to preach into a mere priviledge—in place of the demands of the Holy Spirit. It is the God of Abraham, Isaac and Jacob Who commands me to preach the Gospel of Grace, not the government." I'll not allow them to control me with a license, no matter what they may do to me! Watch carefully my brothers and sisters. Watch, and learn a lesson in liberty.'"

Patrick looked down at the scrap of paper. "And then he spoke these words. 'Is my life so dear or is my peace with the King so sweet that I should purchase them with chains and slavery? Oh no, Lord! Forbid it! I know not what course each of you will choose on the day that you hang in these same chains, but as for me, give me liberty or give me death!'" Patrick looked up at John. "You should have seen it, my young friend. That peevish little bureaucrat was so infuriated by the preacher's words that he took the cat and whipped the man to death in front of the entire town."

"He killed a minister of the Gospel?"

Patrick nodded. "I should have pulled my pistol and shot the constable on the spot."

"What's happening to England?" John shook his head. "Why would she set herself up against Almighty God like that?"

"It's her soul, my friend."

"Her soul?"

"Aye, and this incident in Culpeper proves it. She's dying, and if we're not careful, she'll drag these thirteen colonies down into her grave and pull the dirt in upon them before they can take their first breath of life."

Patrick refolded the paper. "It is all of one piece, Paul. We have no say in whether or not we will be taxed. We have no say in how we choose to worship the Lord. These last few words of a Baptist preacher, just before they took his life! Listen to the words, my young friend, and as you do, see that frail man of God in chains, and a fat and sweating constable taking his personal revenge with Satanic glee." He put the paper back in his pocket.

"I stood helpless with the rest of the townsfolk and watched as the flesh was torn, piece by piece from his back. When the constable finally tired of his play, the preacher hung unconscious in his chains, with no fewer than seven ribs exposed to the elements. I'd never seen anything so heinous nor so cruel. As I rode out of Culpeper early this morning, I saw them dropping his blood-soaked body into an unmarked grave by the roadside. It was a shallow grave, so the dirt was over him in minutes. I stayed after the two men left and offered a prayer in the little preacher's behalf—that he had not died in vain."

Listen again to the man's last words. Mister Henry spoke this time from memory. "Is life so dear, or peace so sweet, as to be purchased at the price of chains and slavery? Forbid it, Almighty God! I know not what course others may take; but as for me, give me liberty or give me death!"

It took John several moments to absorb the truth of the preacher's words. Then he nodded and whispered. "Amen."

Both men sat with their emotions for several minutes before Patrick finally stood to leave. John followed to the street where Patrick hesitated again. "We both have important missions, Paul. Do what is right and God-honoring, regardless of the outcome! Compromise your convictions for no man!" Patrick took John's hand and squeezed it firmly. "May God go with you and your young friend."

"And you, Henry!"

Patrick had been gone only minutes when David entered the shop and laid his satchel across the cutting table. He looked about for his partner. "John?"

John stepped to his office door. He was smiling for the first time in several days.

David noticed the change of mood. "You wouldn't believe who I just saw riding through town."

John took a gold coin from his pocket and threw it onto the cutting table. "Throw a guinea on the table and you'll have yourself a wager."

"He was here, wasn't he?"

"Yes he was, and he brought some tremendous news."

"What?"

"He's arranged for us to meet with Mister Joseph Hewes, the newly appointed chairman of the Marine Commission. Hewes will be selecting the first naval officers."

David could hardly believe his ears. "When do we leave?"

"Pack your things, David. We depart for Edenton tomorrow at first light."

David pulled several pieces of paper from his satchel. "What about the shop? I have three orders from Woodbridge, five from Dumfries and two from Stafford. Somebody will have to—"

"Mister Peters is fully capable to run things while we're gone."

＊＊＊

Patrick Henry rode down to Sophia Street and walked into the public room of the Blue Grass Tavern.

A man beckoned from the shadows of a corner table. "Have a seat, Patrick. Did he accept the letter?"

"They'll be leaving at dawn tomorrow, just as you expected they would." Patrick sat down. "But tell me something, Nathaniel. Why did you ask me to approach him when you had made all the arrangements? Does this have anything to do with Dorothea?"

"That's my concern, not yours. I have a very good reason for everything I'm doing. You'll see it in the end—that it'll work to both our benefits." He could tell that Patrick was not convinced. "If you consider it, wouldn't a letter of introduction from Patrick Henry—the new and upcoming statesman—carry more weight than one from a retired naval officer with questionable loyalties?"

Patrick nodded. "I just hope those two find what they're looking for."

Nataniel gave a smile and took a sip of his ale. "Does it really matter?"

Patrick studied Nathaniel carefully. "I thought I understood your intentions, sir, but now—"

"Didn't you tell me you wanted to ask my daughter for her hand in marriage?"

"Yes I did, just as soon as I get back from my trip."

"Why wait? John Paul and his friend will be gone in the morning."

"I don't need him out of Virginia to propose to Dorothea."

"I agree, but considering Dorothea's feelings for the man, it couldn't hurt."

Patrick considered. "So...shall I assume this satisfies my debt?"

"Debt? What debt?"

"The money you lent me for my law studies. William Paul helped me somewhat, but yours was the bulk of the money I needed."

"You disappoint me, Patrick. To satisfy that debt—and I never intended to call it due—you'd have to pay back the entire sum, or do something..."

"Dishonorable?"

Nathaniel frowned. "That's a dangerous word, my friend."

Patrick leaned forward and lowered his voice. "Nathaniel, you know as well as I what their chances are of getting one of the first naval commissions."

"Very well." Nathaniel extended his hand to the younger man. "Your debt to me is satisfied."

"Thank you. And now, if there's nothing else you require of me, I've a long ride ahead."

"Oh? Where are you going?"

"To Richmond, to attend the Second Convention. And as you'll be riding back to your home tonight, would you deliver this letter to your daughter?"

"I'd be glad to. She'll be pleased to hear from you."

Patrick handed the letter to Nathaniel. "It's not from me."

"Then who is it from?"

"It's from Captain Paul."

"Do you know what he wrote?"

"He knows that there's the possibility he may be gone for a long time. I believe he just wanted her to know so she wouldn't worry."

"Yes, I'll deliver it."

The moment the statesman was out of the tavern, Nathaniel broke the wax seal and read the short note:

18 March 1775

My darling Dorothea,

Time did not allow me to tell you this in person, but as you read this note, David and I will be well on our way to Edenton, North Carolina. We are going there to request Naval Commissions from Mister Joseph Hewes and may not return to Virginia for some time.

I apologize for not meeting you at the park last week, but your father met me and forebade that we meet again, or even write. This hand delivered letter is the only way I could tell you I was leaving without your father finding out.

Dorothea, I know it is premature at this time to promise it, but if I obtain my commission, I'll return to your home at the earliest moment to ask your father for your hand in marriage. Please wait for me.

I remain, my dearest, eternally yours,

John Paul

Nathaniel Dandridge smiled to himself, refolded the note and placed it in his pocket. "It's too late, Captain Paul."

***

By the time the sun had begun to rise from behind the rolling hills of Fredericksburg to paint the chilly March morning a dark pink, John and David's carriage had taken them across the covered bridge at the Mattaponi River and into the low farmlands surrounding the town of Spotsylvania. The new housekeeper had packed them a basket of fried chicken, honeyed cornbread and dried fruit, enough for the first two days of their journey. Their chestnut mare trotted along the muddy roadway at an easy pace, with little clouds of moist breath blowing from her swollen nostrils.

David brushed the cornbread crumbs from the seat between them. "He must have told you more than that—something encouraging."

"The most I could get was that Mister Hewes will be at his shipping company in Edenton until the 22nd of March, and that our names were brought up at a planning meeting in Harrisonburg a few days ago. This letter of introduction from Mister Henry is all we have."

"Only an introduction?" David gave a shake of his head. "Surely he could have done—"

"That's the one thing he wouldn't do. He told me that it'll be up to us to convince Mister Hewes of our integrity and qualifications."

"Well, at least we've an open door, and that's better than nothing."
John only nodded.

The trip passed without incident through mile after mile of
beautiful countryside and quaint townships. On the first night, the two
weary travelers stopped at a roadhouse in Richmond. John pulled a
crown piece from his pocket and flipped it high into the air.

David called it in the air. "King's head!" The silver coin struck the
cobblestone apron in front of the inn, bounced once, and settled onto
the stones.

"Ah! Sorry, David. You get to stall and feed the horse, while I see
to our room."

David jumped from the carriage. "Let me see that coin."

"Well, David Noble." John's tone was both condescending and
sarcastic. "Do I detect a spark of mistrust in your voice? You wouldn't
be suggesting that I'd use a trick coin just to get out of doing your work,
would you?"

"For one thing, it's only my work if I lose the toss. And yes, I'd
suggest exactly that!" David inspecting the coin carefully.

"Satisfied?"

"Yes, but somehow you've managed to win every coin toss we've had
since I met you!"

Grabbing his bag, John hopped from the carriage and walked past
his young companion to the tavern door. He stopped and turned.
"When you're finished with your chores, you can meet me inside for
dinner and a drink."

"My chores? Ha!" David pocketed the coin and led their horse and
carriage to the back of the building. By the time he had finished and
made his way to the public room, John was involved in a lively
discussion with two Virginia militiamen.

John spotted him at the door. "David! Over here!" David walked to
the table and looked at the two men. "Take a seat and wash the Virginia
road from your throat." He pushed a large tankard of ale across the table
to the young Jamaican.

John turned to the two men. "David Noble, Gunnar Andersen and
his traveling companion, Thomas Matthews. They're both in the
Virginia Volunteers."

Gunnar, a man in his late twenties, reached out his hand. "Pleased
to meet you, Mister Noble. Captain Paul was telling us that you're from
King's Town."

"That's right. Born and raised there."

"Mister Andersen was just telling me about an incident here in Richmond, very similar to what Mister Henry described to me last week."

Thomas shook David's offered hand. "That wouldn't be Patrick Henry, would it?"

"Of course it's Patrick Henry." David was proud to be able to claim the acquaintance of so famous a man. "He lives only two miles from us, and we have him over for dinner often." The militiaman studied the two travelers carefully. "If you don't believe me, look at this." He reached into John's traveling bag and pulled out Patrick's letter. He showed them the wax seal with the statesman's signet ring impression, then returned the letter to its place. "So tell me, Mister Andersen, what is this incident you were telling John about?"

"Our preacher is sitting in the Richmond jailhouse as we speak." Gunnar leaned close and lowered his voice. "As I was telling your friend, he was arrested for tearing in half his license to preach the gospel.

"License to preach?" David looked at John. "In the carriage…that's what you were telling me, isn't it?"

Thomas continued. "He's been there for over two weeks."

Gunnar put a hand to Thomas's arm. "He wouldn't be there, except he did it in front of his congregation."

David was shocked. "One of his flock betrayed him?"

"No." Gunnar gave a slow shake of his head. "The constable was sitting in the back of the church, but we didn't know it until he left and returned a few minutes later with two of his soldiers. They took Pastor Allen off to jail right in the middle of his sermon."

John slammed his fist on the table. "Damn them!"

A hush fell over the tavern. Then, one at a time, each of the other fifteen or so men seated about them joined in the curse of their oppressors across the sea.

John touched Patrick's letter. "Can't his solicitor do something for him?"

"Solicitor?" It was Thomas. "His wife's tried to retain one, but nobody'll have the case." He pulled his own letter from his pocket. "That's why we're riding to Fredericksburg. We carry a letter signed by every faithful member of Pastor Allen's congregation asking your Mister Henry to come and defend him." He looked to Gunnar and back to John. "We would be in your debt if you would put an endorsement at the bottom of the letter? Tell him how desperately we need his help?"

"I'd be honored." John left and was back in a moment with a quill and ink from the innkeeper. He penned a short note of introduction below the other signatures and handed the letter back to Thomas. "Will that do?"

Thomas smiled and nodded. "Thank you, Captain Paul."

"You're welcome. But I'm about to do you an even greater service. You see, you needn't travel to Fredericksburg. Mister Henry is here in Richmond."

"He is?"

"He's attending the Second Virginia Convention."

Gunnar put a hand on Tomas's arm. "I should have remembered! They're convening here this time." He turned to John. "Thank you, Captain Paul. I'm sure he'll help when he sees your name on our letter." Thomas refolded the petition and put it away. After a quick sip of ale he continued. "Just before you joined us, we were discussing a desperate situation in the colonies."

"How desperate?"

"I told you they'd be concerned, Gunnar." The younger man was anxious to tell his story and moved his chair a little closer to John. "There are only a handful of foundries in all of America—six at the most. The few weapons they produce are truly dangerous to the men who have to use them—nothing like what they make over in Europe. Yet, even with the inferior workmanship and performance, a pair of locally produced naval cannons can cost as much as fifteen hundred pounds.

David brightened. "The colonies can't manufacture any good cannons?"

"Not yet. There are two new foundries being built in Massachusetts and Pennsylvania that will, but they won't begin production until September at the earliest. Couple that with the recent embargo on the importation of both cannons and gun powder, and you have the…desperate situation."

There was suddenly a commotion at the far end of the public room. Thomas leaned a little closer and continued at just above a whisper. "Most privateers go to sea with only two cannons, one at each gunwale. The rest of their ports are either kept closed or filled with Quakers."

"Quakers?" David had never heard the term. "What's a Quaker?"

"Not so loud." Thomas nodded toward the two soldiers who had stepped through the door and were searched the tavern. "A Quaker gun is a cannon made from wood and painted black. Half a privateer's success depends upon bluff, and if a ship's captain thinks the privateer is heavily armed, he'll strike his colors without a fight. Then, one at a time, the privateer captain will replace his Quakers with real cannons.

It's slow and risky, but for now, I'm afraid it's the only way the colonies can arm their ships."

John gave David an accusing look. "It's strange that I hadn't heard of this before tonight."

David looked away from his friend.

Thomas noticed, but misinterpreted the short encounter. "I'm not inventing this, Captain Paul, if that's what you're suggesting. My father and I operate one of those six foundries."

"I'm not saying that you are." John gave David another questioning look. "It's just surprising that something so important would be kept such a secret."

Gunnar knew something was wrong between David and John. "I find it difficult to believe that Mister Henry hasn't told you all of this, being such a close friend."

Suddenly, the level of conversation in the tavern increased. John looked around. The two soldiers left the tavern. He turned back to Gunnar. "Mister Henry and I are close, but he doesn't confide everything—"

The tavern door banged open again. The soldiers were back, and this time the constable was with them. A middle-aged man in buckskins bolted from a nearby table with a curse and ran through the kitchen and out into the night. The constable spoke quietly to the two uniformed soldiers. One of them pointed to John and the other three.

"Listen here!" The taller of the two soldiers pointed at the empty table. "There was a tall man in buckskins sitting at that table a moment ago. We've a writ for his arrest!"

All of the customers turned to their drinks.

"You, there!" The shorter soldier walking to John. "Where did the man go?"

John looked up at the man. "We all saw him leave."

"Are you going to tell me where he's got off to, or do I take you in his place?"

"He was out through the kitchen as you and your fellow soldier stepped in the front door." The soldier pushed his way past three tables and through the door to the kitchen. His partner and the constable followed close behind.

Gunnar was shocked. "Why'd you tell them?"

"You must not have seen what the soldier next to the door was doing." John pointed to where the other soldier had been standing. "He had his pistol drawn and cocked, and just like Boston in '70, he was ready to fire into the crowd. I've seen that mood before."

"I'm sorry. I didn't see that."

"Quite an example of Richmond's hospitality." David picked up a chair that had been upset by the soldiers. "Have you any idea what that man is wanted for?"

"There've been several of his cut picked up in the last three days." It was Thomas. "Last week, a soldier was set upon by a mountain man after the soldier made a lewd remark about the man's wife. He deserved the thrashing he got."

After another round of drinks, John and David excused themselves and climbed the stairs to their room. It was small, but clean. After they had unpacked and changed, John stepped to the window and looked out on the night.

"I've seen that look before, John. What's bothering you?"

"It's your father's cannons. If they were in the bilge of a merchantman, they were being smuggled into the colonies. I can't help wondering who they really belong to."

"Does it really matter? My father owns them now."

***

On the 21st of March, John and David arrived at the offices of Hewes and Smith Ships, in the port town of Edenton, North Carolina— a small but vital link between the colonies and the outside world. An unbroken chain of wagons snaked through the wide gate at the entrance to the yards, their cargos of tobacco and cotton spilling over their sides as they plowed through the soft mud toward the loading docks beyond the offices. To their larboard, not more than a stone's throw away, rolled the departing wagons stacked high with the finished goods that had arrived from England.

"What if Mister Hewes refuses our application?"

"I've already considered that." John stepped out of the street and up onto the boardwalk. "If we can't get the commissions, then we'll return to Fredericksburg as quickly as we can. And as we've already returned the carriage, we might find passage on one of Mister Hewes' merchantmen." He pulled Patrick Henry's letter from his coat. "Amusing, isn't it?"

"What's amusing?" David stepped onto the boardwalk.

"Now that we're so close, the object of this trip seems even further away than when we first discussed it in King's Town."

"Chin up, old man." David put a fist to John's face and gave a slight push. "Things'll work out. You'll see."

John gave David a long look, wondering how the lad could suddenly speak with such confidence.

The counting house stood just before the first warehouse, overlooking the Edenton River and the clutter of anchored ships that swung in the gentle current, waiting to get to the docks. The company sign over the door indicated that this was where they should find Joseph Hewes. A young clerk sat at a neat but crowded desk just inside the doorway. His back was to the window.

He turned and studied John and David for a moment. "May I help you?"

"Yes you may." John held Patrick's letter in his hand. "We would like to speak with your master, Mister Hewes."

"Do you have an appointment?"

John held up the letter. "No, but we carry a letter of introduction from Patrick Henry."

At the statesman's name the clerk's demeanor changed from detachment to urgency. "If you'll give me your letter, I'll announce you and your friend."

In less than a minute, the clerk had returned, followed by a short man in his late sixties. The older man wore a heavy hunting jacket, which carried the strong odor of pipe tobacco.

"Captain Paul. Mister Noble." He shook their hands. "I'm Joseph Hewes. Won't you come in?" He led them into a back office. "You'll have to excuse the mess, gentlemen, but as you can see, you've caught me at loading time."

While John and David looked about, the clerk brought two oak chairs and placed them before his master's desk. The large, cluttered office was richly decorated. A dozen certificates attesting to the man's importance hung on the dark oak paneling behind the massive mahogany desk. Models of ships and various nautical implements of navigation competed for the meager shelf space near the ceiling, and a small Franklin stove burned hotly, removing the morning's chill from the room. There was a lit briarwood smoking pipe setting in a small dish at the corner of the desk. The wisp of smoke climbing into the air gave the room the distinctive fragrance of Turkish tobacco.

Joseph stepped behind his desk and pointed to the chairs. "Please be seated, gentlemen, and tell me how I may be of service to you." He glanced at Patrick's letter and set it on the desk.

John spoke first. "Sir, we have just arrived from Fredericksburg. As you can see from that letter, my companion and I are here to apply for commissions in the Continental Navy."

There followed a very long and uncomfortable silence while Mister Hewes looked at the two young travelers and then read the letter of introduction a second time. He pulled at his lower lip, causing it to deform in a most unseemly manner, and revealing his tobacco-stained teeth. He brightened with the recollection. "Ah yes! Now I recall where I heard your names." The man lowered the letter and peered at the two over his spectacles. "It was Nathaniel Dandridge—our meeting a week ago up in Harrisonburg."

John was confused. "Captain Dandridge?"

"Yes, I'm certain of it. He named you both and then told me that you two would be coming to see me." He paused to collect his thoughts.

"Don't you mean Patrick Henry?"

The older man continued, ignoring John's question. "It is true that we'll be forming a navy soon, and you've been told correctly that I'll be heading the committee to select the first officers." He exhaled loudly through his nose with a distinct whistling sound, and then picked at the guilty nostril. "You have to understand that the selection process is a little more complicated than a letter of introduction and my merely giving you the nod."

"More complicated?" David gave John a sideways glance.

"Exactly." The old man studied the two young men again for several moments. "Have either of you been told what kind of men we're looking for?"

John put a silencing hand to David's arm. "If I were selecting men to fight the British navy, I would want men with experience as ship's captains and with a thorough knowledge of how the navy fights."

Without commenting on John's statement, Mister Hewes took a piece of paper from his top desk drawer, picked up the smouldering pipe and walked to the window.

After an awkward minute, David spoke. "Is there something the matter, sir?"

Joseph pulled a metal tool from his pocket, tamped the tobacco down, and drew several puffs. He turned back to the two. "There most assuredly is, young man." He puffed the pipe back to life and then held up the paper. "These are the requirements the Marine Commission has decided upon." He adjusted his wire-rimmed glasses and read. "First and foremost, an applicant must be able to prove he was born in the American colonies." Hewes gave the two an inquiring look. They made no move, so he continued.

"Second, he must be a privateer captain who has distinguished himself in combat against French or Spanish shipping." He gave the two another quick look. "Finally, he must present a personal letter of recommendation from the governor of his colony." After several more determined puffs on his pipe, he laid the paper on the desk and removed his glasses. "Do either of you meet these three prerequisites?"

John and David sat silent in their chairs while Joseph pulled a tall stack of letters from a tray on his desk. "I already have far too many qualified men to choose from, Captain Paul, and I've only been authorized to appoint sixty officers—twelve of whom will be chosen as ships captains."

There was a long and uncomfortable pause. Finally, John stood. "Sir, my friend and I have already taken too much of your time." He took a long breath while he thought. "We'll not trouble you any longer, except to ask one small favor."

"And what might that be, young man?"

"Is it possible that you have a couple of openings in your shipping company? We would make fine officers on one of your merchant vessels."

"I respect your enthusiasm and I truly sympathize with your difficult situation, but there's something you can't possibly know." He beckoned John to the window. "You undoubtedly observed the confusion at my docks when you arrived. Normally, such activity would indicate a surplus of jobs, but the opposite is true."

"Sir?"

He took a puff on the pipe and waved away the smoke. "You see, Captain Paul, I lost three ships to pirates last month, and all but a handful of the crewmen have returned, all of them expecting to be re-employed. Until I can replace those ships and put those three crews back at work, I simply can not hire any new seamen, much less two new officers. On top of that, before things get any better, I expect them to get worse."

"Then we'll trouble you no longer, sir." John hesitated. "But I have one question before we leave."

"Yes?"

"Why did you say that it was Captain Dandridge who told you about us?"

"Young man, your letter of introduction may have been signed by Patrick Henry, but it wasn't he who sent you to me."

David was already at the door, hoping to disengage himself and John from this fruitless and uncomfortable situation.

Joseph could feel David's discomfort, so he offered a scrap. "Gentlemen, I don't know what your plans for the coming days may be.

If you are still in Edenton in one week's time, come see me then. I may be able to find you some temporary work with one of our contractors. Failing that, I'm sure I can at least arrange working passage back to Fredericksburg for the both of you."

"We're not lacking for money, sir." John stepped toward David and turned back to the older man. "Thank you for the offer, but we came to Edenton for naval commissions, not employment as common seamen." The two young men turned and left.

Chapter 7

At the carriage, John stopped and looked down at the mud. After a long moment, he looked up at his young friend. "I want to apologize for bringing you all this way for nothing."

"You needn't say a thing, John. You were acting on the best information available at the time, and nobody could expect more." David put a comforting hand on John's shoulder. "Let's go back to our room and talk."

Their inn lay two leagues to the northwest—a small, out-of-the-way place on the banks of the Chowan River.

As they passed the last farmhouse and rode into the open countryside, David finally broke the silence. "What was that about Captain Dandridge? You told me it was Patrick Henry who recommended that we come to Edenton."

"He did. He wrote and signed the letter." John shook his head slowly. "You heard what Mister Hewes told us. It was Henry who came to the shop, but it was Nathaniel Dandridge who was behind the whole thing." He fell silent for a moment, pondering whether to tell David the rest.

"I had no idea Dorothea's father cared so much for you, John. But why send Patrick instead of coming himself?" David considered, and continued. "And another thing—a letter of introduction from Captain Dandridge would have been just as good as Mister Henry's, if not better."

"David, there's something I didn't tell you."

"Oh?"

"Mister Dandridge knew from the beginning that we could never qualify for those commissions."

"What?" David gave John a confused look. "Why would he do such a thing? I thought he liked you."

"It wasn't a matter of liking me or not. It was to get me out of Fredericksburg. He even had Henry tell me that Mr. Hewes was leaving Edenton tomorrow—in order to ensure that I left right away, I suppose." John tightened his grip on the reins. "It all makes sense now."

"What are you talking about? What makes sense?"

"Mister Dandridge knows Dorothea and I are in love, and he's sent me away on this fool's journey to get me out of her life. If he had his way, I'd never come back."

"But, I thought you and Dorothea—"

"A week before Henry wrote us the letter, Dandridge confronted me at a park near his home. He had a copy of the King's warrant for my arrest. That's why I've been—"

"Hiding in the shop?"

"The warrant was from the Admiralty offices in King's Town. Dandridge must still maintain correspondence with some of his Royal Navy acquaintances there."

David thought for a moment. "That explains Captain Dandridge's motive, but why would Henry be a party to such a cruel deed? He seemed to be a man of honor and integrity."

"I don't believe Mister Henry knew about the warrant or Captain Dandridge's intentions. He was probably under the impression that he was doing a favor for both Dandridge and me." John shook his head. "No, this was all Dandridge's doing."

"Will Dorothea wait for you?"

"Yes, unless…"

"Unless what?"

"Unless her father intercepted the letter I sent her the day before we left."

"And if he did?"

"One condition that he would not inform the King of my presence in Virginia was that I not see or write his daughter again. If he somehow intercepted that letter, then there's a good chance that the authorities in Fredericksburg are looking for me as we speak." John turned and looked at David. "He threatened to tell Dorothea about the warrant."

"If that's true, then what do we do now?"

"I don't know, David. You could always return to Jamaica, and I suppose I could sail back to Scotland." John took a long breath. "I don't know."

***

It was dinnertime when they reached their inn, but John was not hungry. Instead, he purchased a bottle of cheap rum.

John stopped at the public room door. "I'm going to our room. I'd like to be left alone for a while, if you don't mind."

"Are you all right, John?"

"I'm as right as I can be, considering what we've been through today." He pulled the stopper from the bottle and raised it to his lips.

"Before you drink yourself unconscious, I've something very important to tell you."

"I'm a grown man, David. I don't need you to tell me what I should do."

"Aye, but you're not going to help things a bit by drowning yourself in spirits."

"You're neither my Holy Spirit, nor my Father Confessor." John turned and walked down the hallway. He pushed the door to their room open with his foot and raised the bottle to his lips a second time. He noticed that David had followed. "Go eat, David. I need to be alone."

"Not until you hear me out."

John gave a long sigh and lowered the bottle. He walked into the small room and across to the bed. He turned and sat down. "All right, but make it quick."

"I've been thinking as we rode back here from the ship yards."

"And?"

"Well, with a little luck, we don't need Mister Hewes to get our commissions."

"What?"

"We have something better."

"What, our honor and integrity?" John held up the bottle. "This takes neither."

"I'm serious, John. We really do have something more valuable than Mister Hewes and his naval commissions—something so valuable that you could purchase a commission, or that plantation in Virginia that you want."

"Don't mock me, David. You heard Mister Hewes. We'd be lucky to get working passage home on one of his ships, much less a paying job."

David knelt down in front of John. "Have you ever heard of the Treasure of Dead Man's Chest?"

"'The Treasure of Dead Man's Chest'?" John repeated the words with a mocking tone. "Of course I have...many times. My crew sang the ballad when they hauled the lines."

"I don't mean the song, John. I mean the actual Treasure of Dead Man's Chest."

"Go on."

"Dead Man's Chest is a small island off the north coast of Saint Croix. That's not its real name, of course, but the one given to it by pirates."

"So there's a real island called Dead Man's Chest. Are you telling me there's a real treasure also?"

David was pleased that John still had a spark of interest in him. He pulled a chair close and straddled it. "In July of 1754, one of the last Spanish treasure galleons to put out from Porto Bello lost its cargo—the equivalent of one-and-a-half million pounds in gold, silver, jewels, and coin—to pirates. Part of that treasure—roughly seven hundred pounds pounds worth—was buried on John Flint's Island in the southern Bahamas and retrieved in '64 by an expedition out of Bristol. I know for a fact that the remaining half of the galleon's treasure was buried on another island—Dead Man's Chest—that same year."

"A million pounds in treasure? Why, that's as much as Henry Morgan took when he sacked Panama."

"It's actually a little less, John. More like nine hundred thousand."

John sat the bottle on the floor and gave David a piercing look. "What makes you think it's still there?"

David held up two fingers. "Two reasons. The man who buried it never drew a map, and they still sing the song."

"I miss your point, David." John was out of his depression, but was now turning to frustration and anger. "If there's no map, then how in the name of Providence are we supposed to find a treasure that was buried thirty years ago?"

"Twenty years."

"Twenty or five hundred years...it doesn't much matter if nobody knows where it's buried, does it?"

The moment John Silver had planned and hoped for had finally arrived. David savored the moment as if it were the best meal he'd ever eaten. He leaned forward and spoke his next five words slowly and just above a whisper. "I...know...who...buried...it."

"You know who buried nearly a million pounds in Spanish treasure and waited till now to tell me?"

David nodded.

"Good God, man! Why didn't you say something about this in King's Town? We wouldn't have had to go through all of this! Who is he?"

"He's a merchant in New York."

"Who is he? What's his name?"

"Wait...there's a problem."

"Large or small?"

"Well..." David pretended to wrestle with the facts for a moment. "For some reason that nobody quite understands, the man has no intention of ever going back to Dead Man's Chest. Several have tried to convince him to draw a map, but to no avail. I'm afraid that without a very convincing argument, we would meet with the same disappointment."

John was on the verge of hitting the younger man. "What would he consider a convincing argument?"

"That's the problem, John. I don't know."

"But you know who this man is?"

David nodded. "My father's done business with him for years."

John was up and pacing about the room in a frenzy. After several laps, he came to a sudden stop and spun to face David. "Nine hundred thousand pounds, you say?"

"Eight or nine." David nodded. "That was its value twenty years ago."

"New York is a Tory stronghold. Do you know where this man's sentiments lie?"

"I don't know where he stands, but I know his father was killed by soldiers during the massacre in Boston five years ago."

"What are your father's cannons worth?"

"My father's cannons?" David feigned confusion. "I suppose on the right market they'd go for a thousand pounds each, but..."

John calculated quickly. "There's more than enough!" He spun on David. "Do you remember our conversation with those two volunteers at that Richmond tavern the other evening?" David pursed his lips and tilted his head as if he were having difficulty recollecting the place. "They were telling us about the critical shortage of cannons and artillery pieces in the colonies!" David continued to wrestle with it, trying not to look too stupid. "I wrote an endorsement to Patrick Henry on their letter!"

"Oh, yes! Now I remember! Thomas Matthews and that Dane— Gunnar Andersen!" David's heart was pounding with anticipation and amazement at how accurately John Silver had predicted his friend's thoughts.

"Don't you see it yet?" John held up his hand and began counting on his fingers. "The colonies are sure to be at war soon with England, is that correct?"

David nodded. "It certainly looks that way."

"And they lack good naval and artillery cannons, is that correct?"

David nodded again, but feigned confusion.

"Your father has eight or nine hundred high-quality European cannons sitting in his warehouse, is that correct?"

"There are a thousand of them, John, give or take a few, along with all the—"

"Right!" John continued quickly. "And if we could somehow convince this New Yorker to help us get that treasure, with the understanding that it's to be used to purchase your father's cannons to fight for freedom, Mister Hewes would certainly grant us two of his sixty naval commissions!"

David pretended to finally get it. "As a reward for our service to the American colonies!" He gave John a questioning look. "But why do we need the commissions if we have the treasure?"

"Because I want Dorothea's hand in marriage, and her father considers me a commoner. He won't even talk to me unless I can achieve true respectability. A Continental Navy commission will give me that!"

"Then...you think Mister Hewes and the New Yorker—"

"Yes!"

Suddenly, as if struck by lightning, David leaped to his feet and began dancing around the room like a schoolboy dismissed for summer vacation.

"Calm down, David!"

"But it'll work!" David continued his wild dance. "I know it will!"

"There are still too many unknown factors remaining to begin celebrating just yet, David, but we've the rest of the day to figure the thing out."

David's thoughts returned to that night in King's Town when his father showed him the game of farthings. "All right, John, let's get to it!"

For the rest of the day, David was careful to let John think that all the important ideas were his, with David only suggesting possible solutions to a couple of minor problems. But all the time he was keeping his friend on John Silver's predetermined course.

***

Joseph Hewes was in his office early the next morning. His clerk stepped to the elderly man's door.

"Sir, the two gentlemen you spoke to yesterday afternoon are back. Did you ask them to return?"

"No, I did not. Not today, anyway." It had been a difficult and tiresome night for the elderly ship owner. He removed his spectacles and massaged his eyes for a long moment.

"Shall I show them out sir?"

"No, I'll see them. But pray give me a few minutes to freshen up first." While the bookkeeper returned to the outer office, Joseph washed and dried his face at the sideboard. He looked into the mirror and muttered. "Why would Nathaniel send these two on such a long and costly trip when he knew I had no positions open? It just isn't like him, especially after I made it so clear what had happened to my ships, unless..."

"Mister Hewes?" John stood at the half-opened door. "May we come in?"

The elderly man turned. "By all means, Captain Paul." He gestured at the stove. "I've some fresh tea if you're so inclined." His words were hospitable, but his tone was not. He finished wiping his hands dry and then bent painfully backwards at the waist to stretch his cramped and complaining muscles. "I've sugar, but I'm fast out of lemon."

"Thank you, sir!" John stepped to the stove, poured a cup and reached into the salt. "I'll take a dash of salt unmixed, to commemorate Sam Adams's tea party."

"You two are acting very strangely." The old man retreated to his desk and sat down. "I'm certain I did not invite you to return too soon. Why—"

"Before you say anything else, sir, perhaps I had best explain what we discovered yesterday evening." John leaned forward in his chair.

"What you discovered?"

"David and I may be able to earn those naval commissions."

"Earn them? I thought I made myself clear yesterday afternoon."

"Oh, you did, sir. You were perfectly clear. It's just that—"

"Then why do you insist on putting me—and yourselves—through any more discomfort? You don't qualify for naval commissions, and nothing you could do would possible change that. You'd stand a better chance of working your way into heaven."

"If you'll just hear me out, sir, I think—"

"Captain Paul, the only thing I might have for you is working passage back to where you came from." He was doing his best to contain himself, but the veins at his temples were beginning to swell.

"Sir, what John has to say is well worth the hearing. His plan might be just the—"

"I'll tell him, David."

"One of you had better tell me quickly while I still retain a small portion of my patience!"

John sat up and lowered his voice. "We know, Mister Hewes, that there is a critical shortage of quality naval and field artillery weapons in the colonies."

"That's absurd!" The old man's fingernails bit into the leather writing mat. "We have all the foundries we need, and they're turning out high quality weapons every day—especially the two up in Pennsylvania and Massachusetts."

David copied John's posture. "We know about the new foundries, sir, and that they won't begin production for at least six more months."

"Well, I'm a curious fellow." Mister Hewes relaxed his hands and sat back. "Let's say—just for the sake of this conversation—that your information is reliable. What could it possibly have to do with you two and those commissions for which you are grossly unqualified?"

"In the first place, sir, I am correct about the shortage of cannons, and you know that to be true." John's tone sounded slightly arrogant. "And what I'm about to propose may just change the future of this land you love so much."

Hewes forced himself to remain calm. "Go on."

"For some time now, not a single cannon or artillery piece has been allowed into the colonies. It's no secret the government wants your weapons limited to small arms and swords." John stopped for a sip of tea and a glance at his young companion. He set his cup on the sideboard and continued slowly.

"If David and I could lead an expedition that would provide the colonies with nearly a thousand of the latest naval and artillery cannons—weapons made at the foundries at Carron, Scotland—and at very little cost to the colonies, would you grant David and me two of your naval commissions in exchange?"

Joseph was stunned. He knew all too well how badly the colonies needed armaments. "Captain Paul, if you could accomplish what you are suggesting, I would not only see to it that you are commissioned, but that you'd both have your own commands the moment you put on the uniform." He leaned forward and stared intently at the two. "Can you do what you're suggesting? Can you bring me a thousand Scottish cannons?"

"I believe we can, sir. But before we reveal how we'll do it, I need to know whether you have the authority to deliver on your part of the bargain."

"I have that authority, Captain Paul, although there are several others I would like to consult with. Now, tell me how you two expect to accomplish such a miraculous feat?"

John did not want to give away too much yet. "By collecting some valuable items on a small Caribbean island, bring those items to a safe location where they can be exchanged for the cannons, and then bringing the cannons here to America."

David, of course, was anxious to tell all he knew. "You see, sir, there's a king's rans—"

"No, wait! You come recommended by Nathaniel Dandridge and Patrick Henry, so I trust this isn't a cloud-spun fantasy. You can explain it to me at the same time as the others I spoke of. They are occupied now, but I am expecting them here one week from today. Can you remain in Edenton that long?"

John smiled. "Yes, sir, we can. And we promise not to disturb you again in the coming week."

"That is the least of my concerns, Captain." He took up a quill and began writing on a slip of paper. "In fact, I hope you'll be my guests for the remainder of your stay." He handed his address to John. The man stood and led his two guests to the door. "And now, my friends, I have much to do today."

"Thank you, Mister Hewes." John gave the ship owner a curt salute.

Once out of the office and beyond earshot, David broke into his loudest war cry. "Ho-ho! We're on our way!"

***

John and David drove through the front gate of the Hewes estate amidst the exaggerated shadows that the setting sun threw across the roadway and through the oak trees. The quiet crunch of wet sand and mud under the wheels of their carriage fell silent when they turned onto the green carpet of well-swept grass that led to the front of the two-story home. A Negro servant met them at the front steps.

"Welcome back, sirs." He gave a slight bow. "Mister Hewes and his other guests are waiting for you in the library." He led them up the steps and across the wide porch to the front door.

"I told you!" David whispered as they stepped through the front door. "We stayed in town far too long. We should have started back a half-hour ago."

John wasn't listening. He had enjoyed his week's stay in the Hewes mansion, but he had never stopped thinking about the meeting he was finally about to enter.

Joseph was waiting in the vestibule. "You're right on time, Mister Noble." He gave a quick glance toward the library. "My other guests are anxious to meet you." With this, he turned to lead them through the large double doors.

"Mister Hewes?" John caught his host by the sleeve. "Before we meet with these other men, who are they, and how much have you told them?"

Joseph stopped in the hallway. "Relax, young man. These are the very people we need to make your plan work. I can assure you that your information will be safe with them."

"But…"

"Be patient, Captain Paul. You'll understand when I introduce you." He gave John a confident smile and a fatherly squeeze on the arm. "Shall we go in now?"

The library was a sacred place, a massive wood-and-velvet cathedral dedicated to the worship of the hunt and to man's battles against evil and tyranny. The walls were lined with the instruments of this high religious order—firearms and sharp-edged weapons of various sizes from two previous centuries and countless crusades. Between these hung at regular intervals the martyrs of the various missions, the stuffed heads of beasts from several continents. At a special place near the windows hung the uniforms of foreign soldiers taken after the many battles. An officer's sword, far more elegant than John's, hung over the fireplace, framed on either side by models of famous British ships of the line. And serving as pews, four massive chairs upholstered with roughly tanned leather were set about the fireplace. Finally, alone in a small alcove stood the patron saint of this worship of the masculine—a small bronze cannon that had been inscribed with a message of gratitude and presented to Joseph Hewes by the Royal Navy.

Women were not allowed in this hallowed hall, except to tidy up after the royal priests had conducted their rites and rituals. It must have been the housekeeper who had set the holy water—a yet-unopened bottle of brandy—and six glasses on the doilies.

David whispered. "Look, John!"

John whispered back. "That older man was at the tavern in Charles Town!"

"Gentlemen!" Joseph spread his arms "May I introduce Captain John Paul of Fredericksburg, Virginia and his companion, Master David Noble of King's Town, Jamaica!" He turned to John and David. "Gentlemen, please meet my distinguished guests and our partners in possibly the most important single venture in the fight for American independence!"

The glow of the fireplace cast an amber hue over the two remaining men. John and David knew both of them from the pictures that hung on the walls at the Paul residence in Fredericksburg.

Joseph picked up an out-of-place doily and stuffed it into his pocket as he walked towards a thin, bony man with broad, square shoulders. He was several inches over six feet tall, but his face was short. "This is Assemblyman Thomas Jefferson, one of the most enthusiastic supporters of our plan."

John accepted Jefferson's huge hand and gave a curt nod. "Very pleased to make your acquaintance, Mister Jefferson."

"Likewise, Captain Paul."

Following David's handshake, Joseph pulled them across the room to a man in his early 50s who was nearly as tall as Jefferson. He had a heavy brow over a pair of piercing, blue-gray eyes and a large, straight nose.

"This is George Washington, the favored nominee for the position of Commander in Chief of our Continental forces."

"This is a special privilege, sir."

"For me as well, Captain Paul. I look forward to hearing the details of your plan."

Now Joseph led John and David to the older man whom they had seen before in the tavern. He had white hair and stood with his hip at an awkward angle. "Our last distinguished colleague is Alexander Forrestal, the owner of perhaps the largest shipyard in South Carolina."

As the six men exchanged handshakes and introductory information, Joseph became aware of the maid standing in the doorway. "Gentlemen, I believe supper is served. If you'll follow me to the dining room, we can continue our discussion over some of the finest cooking this side of the Atlantic Ocean."

The enthusiasm for treasure quickly changed to a manly drive to satisfy a hearty appetite. The six men took their places about the massive cherrywood table. So as to allow for their continued discussion, all six were seated toward one end. While they conversed, the servants brought and then removed the six separate courses of the exquisite dinner.

Jefferson brought the discussion back to the topic at hand. "We're all anxious to hear the details of how you plan to acquire so many of these wonderful weapons. The Carron company has only been making them for a little under two years."

David wiped the peach cobbler from his lip and told them the story of his father's fortuitous trade with Joshua Smoot.

"Your father deals with pirates?" It was Washington, the most decorous of the four.

"My father's a businessman, sir, and makes deals with whomever he must."

Jefferson spoke next. "Can you tell us more about the cannons, Mister Noble?"

"Aye. There are 540 naval carronades, varying in bore from six to twelve inches, and 645 of the long range cannons that can serve equally well aboard ship or in the field. If you and my father agree to the purchase, he'll provide a detailed list of not only their bore sizes, but the dimensions of their mounting points, so you can plan to attach them to ships or carriages."

Joseph smiled at the others. "That will expedite their deployment throughout the colonies."

Jefferson turned to David. "I have an important question, and I trust it won't offend you."

"Sir?"

"If your father's such a good businessman, why hasn't he already begun selling these cannons, a few at a time?"

"Because he is a good businessman, sir. He knows that the value of a piece of merchandise is dictated by how badly it's needed at a given moment. He also knows of the trouble between the colonies and England, and he's simply been waiting for the right time to accept an offer." He looked around the table. "And to set your minds at ease: although Jamaica is a loyal British colony and my father is a British subject, I know that in your current dispute, he favors America over England."

"Oh?" Jefferson gave his customary raised brow. "And why is that?"

"Because he knows America will be a vast treasure of commerce, sir, and he desires to be a part of it. It's as simple as that."

Jefferson glanced at Washington and smiled. "A colleague of ours has been in London for some time, trying to make that exact point. He has calculated that within a hundred years, our population will be larger than England's, which means there will be more employees and more customers here than there. He believes that if he can convince the King that it is in England's economic interest to maintain good relations with us, then His Majesty will undo all of Parliament's and the Ministry's heinous acts toward us."

As usual, David spoke first. "I've heard that His Majesty has not seen fit to meet with or listen to Dr. Franklin."

Jefferson nodded. "Even if he were to do so, I'm afraid it's much too late. Dr. Franklin has been abroad for nearly ten years. He doesn't realize that here at home, nothing will appease us any longer except independence."

David took a sip of wine and continued. "I know how my father thinks. He'll sell his weapons to the colonies."

Washington sighed. "That's as may be, but I'm afraid the colonies will find it very difficult to raise the funds to meet your father's price."

John figured the next part of the tale would sound less outlandish if it came from him. "Mister Noble knows a man in New York whose sympathies also lie, we believe, with the colonies. If we're right, he can tell us where to find more than enough money to pay for the cannons."

"Where?"

"On an island near Saint Croix called Dead Man's Chest.

Joseph cleared his throat. "Mister Noble, would you tell us how the money got on Dead Man's Chest?

"It's a rather complex set of circumstances, gentlemen, but as best as I remember, it came from a Spanish treasure galleon called the Santissima Trinidad. She was one of the last to transport gold and silver from Porto Bello to Spain. This was an especially large treasure that turned out to be nearly a million and half pounds. It was captured by two pirates—Andrew Murray, who went by the name "Rip-Rap," and John Flint. They were partners and commanded two ships—the Royal James and the Walrus. Murray talked Flint into laying up at Spyglass Island for the better part of a year—from the early summer of '54 to around March of '55—to construct a fort and wait while Murray attacked the galleon."

"I've heard tales of John Flint." It was Alex Forrestal. "I find it difficult to believe such a rogue would agree to sit on an island while another pirate captured a Spanish galleon carrying so much treasure."

"That's how the gentleman in New York got involved."

Alex gave a nod. "Go on."

"Flint agreed to keep his unruly crew on Spyglass only if he was provided with a worthwhile hostage. The hostage was Murray's grandnephew, Robert Ormerod."

"Captain Murray would risk hiding eight hundred thousand pounds on Dead Man's Chest with his grandnephew held hostage?"

"Aye, Mister Washington. Even though Flint agreed to half of the treasure, Murray knew he'd kill for the other half. It was a desperate act that ended up costing Murray his life." David pointed to the southeast. "The treasure is still there, sir, right where Mister Ormerod buried it."

Washington shook his head. "I don't understand. If Ormerod was left with Flint as a hostage, then how could he also bury Murray's half of the treasure?"

"Things changed at the last minute."

"How so?"

"Well, Peter Colraer—that's the Indian fighter—insisted on staying on Spyglass with Ormerod. When they were locked down in the Walrus's lazarette, Colraer insisted that if they didn't escape and rejoin the Royal James, Flint or his men would kill them long before Captain Murray could return with Flint's share of the treasure."

"But—" Alex tried to interrupt, but there was no stopping David.

"Peter Colraer had the strength of four ordinary men and made quick work of the rotted planking that held them in the bowels of the Walrus. They had to kill two men on watch before they slipped into the lagoon, and then they had to swim as fast as they could to reach the departing Royal James. They climbed her rudder and let themselves into the ship through the master's cabin."

"Why didn't Captain Murray return them to Flint?"

"Ben Gunn hid them in Murray's lazarette for two days—enough time for the Royal James to put a hundred miles between them and the Walrus."

Alex shook his head. "Who is Ben Gunn? And why didn't Flint chase after Murray as soon as he realized his hostages were gone? And why hasn't Ormerod gone back to Dead Man's Chest himself? Surely he has the money to hire a crew. And considering the size of the treasure…well, it just doesn't make any sense."

David gave John a quick glance and continued. "As for why Flint didn't chase Murray—who's to say? You have to understand that when pirates sign articles, it's a blood oath. There were things between Murray and Flint that nobody ever fully understood."

John finally managed to speak. "Flint did kill Murray in the end. As to Mr. Ormerod's retrieving the treasure, it's not that simple, sir. As David explained to me last night, there are at least two very good reasons why he hasn't. In the first place, Dead Man's Chest lies no more than two miles off the north coast of Saint Croix, fully visible from Christiansted. Ormerod knows—as do all the pirates who sail those waters—that the moment a ship departs from Dead Man's Chest, it'll be boarded and searched from stem to stern and from its bilges to its crow's nest."

"And what is the other reason?"

"The other reason has to do with a promise he made to his bride at the altar."

Jefferson raised a hand. "Do you think his support of the colonies will outweigh his promise to his wife?"

"If you send David and me to New York with letters from each of you esteemed gentlemen stating why the colonies need the cannons, I believe he'll change his mind." John hoped that David would not give away the fact that he was bluffing.

Joseph stood. "Before we go any further, might I suggest we move this discussion back to the library where we started it? I've some very old and friendly brandy I'd like you all to try."

As promised by their host, the brandy was spectacular. After a sea story or two from Joseph, John made his way to Jefferson. "Do you agree with what I told you in the dining room—about David and me going to New York with your letters?"

"Yes and no."

"Sir?"

"You should go to New York alone."

"What about David?"

"At the same time you depart for New York with your letters, David will be sent with a similar packet of letters to his father in King's Town. By the time you each return to Mister Forrestal's yards at Charles Town—you with the map and David with his father's agreement—the twin frigates should be ready to sail."

"Twin frigates?"

"Yes, Captain Paul." Alex stepped up to the two. "It has to do with the exchange at sea. Joseph will explain later."

Jefferson turned to David. "It'll be up to you, Mister Noble, whether you go with Captain Paul to Dead Man's Chest or return to King's Town on the second ship."

"I'll go with John."

"We expected you would."

"Mister Jefferson? How soon will David and I leave with our letters?"

"You can leave on the morning tide. But there's one more matter we must settle."

"Sir?"

"It has to do with the King's warrant for the arrest of a certain Scottish captain named John Paul." The statesman pulled a folded piece of paper from his waist pocket and handed it to John.

John read the familiar King's Town warrant. It was identical to the one Nathaniel Dandridge had shown him in Virginia.

"Yes, Captain Paul, we know all about the man you killed at Tobago, and of your subsequent flight to King's Town and then Virginia."

"But how?"

"You've a room above your tailor shop. Do you know how it's used?"

"It's a storage room."

"What else is it used for?"

"I rent it out to the Masons. They meet there once a month."

Mister Washington stepped to them. "I am a member of the Masons, Captain Paul."

John suddenly realized the obvious. "How long have you been watching me?"

"Ever since last year when you and your friend arrived from Jamaica. I learned you were a ship's master from Captain Dandridge, and thought you might be valuable to our cause."

"Was it Captain Dandridge who told you about this warrant?"

"We have many friends in the government, Captain Paul. As far as I know, Dandridge knows nothing of your fugitive status."

"Yes he does." There was a note of shame in John's voice.

Washington gave a tilt of his head. "Oh? What makes you think so?"

"That's the reason David and I are here. I'm in love with his daughter."

Alex looked about at John. "Isn't she engaged to Patrick Henry?"

"He hasn't formally asked for her hand, but everybody assumes they will be married this summer." John handed the warrant back to

Jefferson. "Captain Dandridge had a copy of that warrant. He threatened to turn me over to the King's men if I had any further contact with his daughter, and then a week later, Mister Henry gave us his letter of introduction to Mister Hewes."

"So, your coming here to see me..."

"I thought that if I could get a naval commission, it might make a difference with Captain Dandridge." John thought for a moment and then pointed at the warrant. "Does that change things? Can you still trust me to lead this secret mission for you?"

"It makes you perfect for the mission."

"But..."

"You're a desperate man, Captain Paul." It was Alex. "As such, we are convinced that you'll go the extra league to make sure your mission is completed."

Jefferson held up the warrant. "I've just had a thought. We may be able to make this warrant work to our advantage. But only with your permission, Captain Paul."

"Sir?"

"I'd like to make it appear that you're hiding somewhere in the northern colonies.

"Oh?"

"Now that the King's warrant is about, it would be much better for all of us if the King's men were looking for the fugitive John Paul up north while the treasure hunter John Jones is in the West Indies."

"How would you accomplish that?"

"By having you carry on a weekly correspondence from the north with the people you know in Virginia

"But—"

"I already have someone in mind who'd write and receive letters in your name."

"Isn't that a bit dangerous?"

"Not if you provide me with enough information about those who might correspond with you."

John considered for a long moment and then nodded slowly. "Perhaps while your man is at it, he could write to my partners in Tobago. They owe me some money."

Jefferson nodded his agreement. "There is one other thing we'll need, and it's quite personal."

"Sir?"

"We'll need to know everything about your relationship with Miss Dandridge."

"But she has nothing to do with—"

"She has everything to do with it." Jefferson stepped closer. "Think carefully, Captain Paul. What better way to send the King's men searching in the opposite direction than on information provided by an angry father? That's why you'll have to provide me with those personal facts about yourself and this girl, and especially what you told her about this trip to Edenton."

"But my partners on Tobago could provide the authorities with my supposed location. I owe the lieutenant governor some money. They could deliver it, and I'm certain..."

"Of course that would work if we had the time for a postal packet to sail down and back, but we don't. It'll have to be Captain Dandridge who gives you up."

"Very well, but whoever writes for me must follow my instructions to the letter. Otherwise—"

"Don't worry, Captain Paul. Everything will be done exactly as it should, and with the utmost discretion."

"I hope I can trust you, sir, because I won't abide seeing our relationship damaged any more than it already is."

"Thomas, I think our two young friends should retire now. They have to be at my docks early, and Captain Paul has a lot of notes to write."

Jefferson looked at his pocket watch and then at the two young men. "Joseph is correct, gentlemen. If all goes as planned, we'll meet again in a few months to celebrate the success of this mission."

John and David stepped into the vestibule, then stopped and turned back to the statesmen. "I speak for both of us when I say thank you for placing this special trust in us. We'll do everything within our power to accomplish this mission for you and the colonies."

"We're certain you will, Captain Paul." Jefferson raised his glass in a salute to the two young seamen. "May our Father in heaven grant you fair winds and following seas." He hesitated at the look on John's face. "Is there something else, Captain Paul?

"Yes, there is, sir. What are David and I to be during this voyage?"

"I don't follow you."

"Are we to be merchants, privateers, or pirates?"

"Does it matter?"

"Not unless we get captured by the navy."

David turned to John. "Are you saying that we could be hanged?"

"Yes, unless we have a letter of marque from one of the colonial governors."

Jefferson stepped toward the two young men. "I'm not sure that would be enough. Our plan was that you and your men would pose as a Dutch crew trading with the islands. I suppose..."

"Sir?"

"Give us some time to consider the problem." Jefferson looked back to his friends. "Hopefully, we'll have an answer before you depart in the morning."

"Good enough, sir." John gave a nudge at David's ribs. They turned and headed toward the staircase.

Once he was certain the two were gone, Joseph put a hand on Jefferson's shoulder. "Well, Thomas, was I right?"

"About our cannons, or about your two young men?"

"Both."

"Well, it's no longer a mystery where our cannons went. What's important is that we get them back." Jefferson took a sip of his drink and continued. "If these two prove to be what they appear, I'd say we've made a very worthwhile investment. And even if they turn out to be thieves or incompetents, what have we lost?"

"Two very expensive ships! My ships!"

Jefferson put an assuring hand on Alex's shoulder. "You can trust us for the ships."

Washington stepped toward them. "And when the Continental Navy is formed, I'm certain the Continental Congress will authorize the reimbursement of the moneys we've taken from our pockets."

Alex wasn't convinced. "And what of my Dutch investors? What shall I tell them about their two ships?"

"Tell them the British navy commandeered them, and that you'll build them two more exactly like the first."

"I suppose you're correct."

"I am, Alex." Joseph took quills, paper and an inkwell from his desk. "We've some letters to write, gentlemen, to add to the ones we brought with us. And there are still several important matters left to discuss before we retire."

"Oh!" Jefferson grabbed his host's arm. "There's one thing you must tell Captain Paul before he sails in the morning."

"And that is?"

"He must not go anywhere other than New York and then back to Charles Town. To do otherwise would not only harm himself, but would surely jeopardize the security of this mission."

Joseph nodded. "I'll tell him in the morning."

Washington held up a hand. One by one, each of the men noticed and fell silent. "Gentlemen. It is clear to me—just as it must be clear to each of you—that the Lord God Almighty, in His Providence, has this day sent these two young patriots to us to undo the harm that the pirate, Joshua Smoot, inflicted upon us. That rogue's taking of our ship has delayed the fortification of Boston, New York and Charleston by nearly two years. In light of the paramount importance of this mission to our cause, I have a compelling need to bring a petition before the Lord." He looked at each of the others one at a time. "If you will bow your heads, I would ask that you join me in a short prayer."

The other three men set their glasses on the table and lowered their heads.

"Our most Gracious heavenly Father, please extend Your mighty hand of protection an extra span this day, so that the efforts of Captain Paul and David Noble may succeed. And grant our fervent prayer for the release from the grasp of England, every man, woman and child of these American colonies, whom You have given by your divine Providence into our stewardship. It is in the name of our sovereign Lord and Savior, Jesus Christ, that we ask these things of You. Amen."

The four men repeated the sacred word and then stood quietly for nearly a minute with their heads bowed.

It was Jefferson who raised his head first. He picked up his glass and lifted it toward the ceiling. "And here's to liberty!" The others took up their glasses. "May she reign forever!"

Chapter 8

Two hours before dawn, three silent figures stood at the upper end of the Hewes and Smith Shipping Company's dock, which extended a hundred and twenty feet into the Chowan River's frigid waters. Their knit caps were pulled sailor-fashion down over their ears, with their collars overlapping the lower edges, leaving only the minimum of skin exposed to the nip of the chilling breeze. Tied up at either side of the dock were two nearly identical Virginia privateers, the most beautiful vessels John and David had ever seen. Each carried fourteen cannons and combined the best features of both the sloop and the brigantine, with masts raked aft nearly ten degrees for the greatest advantage in stiff winds. As they watched in silence, a dozen men aboard each craft were making their final preparations for getting under way; their bodies silhouetted against the light of the lanthorns hanging from the taffrails. The complaints of the rigging against the timbers and the smells of fresh varnish and bare wood made John's pulse quicken. Joseph thrust a small leather packet toward the young captain.

"These are the letters you'll present to Mister Ormerod. Washington and Jefferson added theirs to the collection last night. I must insist that once Ormerod reads them, they be burned. This mission is much too important to be compromised by allowing them to fall into the wrong hands."

John took the leather case, but it fell to the dock with a deep thud. He bent down and picked up the packet. He turned it over in his hands. "Why's it so heavy?"

"I've had three pounds of lead sewn into the bottom so it'll sink. If you're boarded by a British scout ship, throw the packet into the sea." He handed David an identical leather pouch, weighted as the first.

"Mister Noble, you'll carry similar letters to your father in King's Town, but I doubt you'll have as much difficulty convincing your father to sell his weapons as Captain Paul will have convincing Mister Ormerod to reveal the location of the treasure."

John started to look into the packet but hesitated. "How do the letters refer to me?"

"Pardon?"

"I'm to be called John Paul Jones for this mission, aren't I?"

"You're quite right." The old man began walking down the ramp toward the waiting ships. The river's current dragged at the pilings, bringing a gurgling sound from beneath the dock. Joseph pointed to one of the ships.

"Mister Jones, you'll sail onboard the Eagle with Captain Alan Steele. He'll see to your every need. If you desire it, he'll even accompany you to Mister Ormerod's home." He pointed to the other ship. "The Swan will take you, Noble, to King's Town. I would enjoy speaking with both of you longer, but you must set sail now or you may not clear the sound before the tide changes."

"Thank you for trusting us with so much, sir." John shook the elderly man's hand, then he gave David a manly hug and a fist to the shoulder. "Give your father my best!"

"I will, John. And be extra careful in New York. I hear the women up there are hungry for husbands—especially sea captains."

"Ha!" John gave David a wink. "And I suppose those Jamaican women aren't?" Several of the seamen joined the two in a knowing chuckle.

"Oh!" Joseph touched his forehead as the memory returned. "I knew there was something else!"

"Sir?"

"It took us a while, but Mister Jefferson and I finally arrived at an answer to your question."

"My question?"

"You asked about your status while on your mission."

David offered the answer he wanted to hear. "We're to be privateers, aren't we?"

"Better still." The elderly man offered his hand to John. "You're to be commissioned officers in the Continental Navy."

"But there is no Continental Navy."

Joseph pulled two rolled parchments from his pocket. "These are only temporary, but they'll serve the purpose much better than privateer commissions. If you're arrested, we'll see to it that the necessary documents are prepared in order to convince them that our Navy was formed prior to your departure."

John and David studied their commissions and then looked at each other's. After taking solemn oaths to serve and protect the American colonies, the young adventurers stowed their precious packets in their bags and leaped aboard their ships. Moments later, the bow lines of both craft were released, and the crews piked away from the dock far enough to allow the long sweeps to be set for the pull into mid-river.

"Captain Paul!" Joseph remembered Jefferson's warning. "Go nowhere but New York and back!"

John could barely hear the old man's feeble voice over the clatter of the ship and his crew. "And may God bless you as well, sir!"

The strong current of the Chowan River carried the two craft eastward to the Currituck Sound by six bells, about the time the winds began to pick up. Until they were well past the anchored ships and into the easy current, the Swan and the Eagle held close formation, the Eagle leading the way by a hundred yards. The only sounds reaching back to the elderly shipowner were the faint calls of the watches and the orders of the first officers. As planned, both ships glided out through Oregon Inlet and into the open sea just after six bells—eleven o'clock in the morning.

With a dip of their colors and traded hand salutes, John and David exchanged their final farewells. It would be nearly a month before their paths would cross again at Charles Town.

The winds were strong and steady, and the Eagle was extremely fast, taking only three days to reach the northern colonies and round Sandy Hook for the predawn glide into New York Harbor. A thick and tiresome ground fog surrounded them from water line to mid-mast. It began at Gibbet Island and carried on far into the East River, obscuring the town completely. But if one looked straight up at the dark sky, most of the stars were still visible, with faint streaks of sunlight trailing in from the east.

The watch called down from his perch atop the mainmast. "Gibbet Island, three points off the larboard bow!"

Captain Steele turned aft. "At the tiller! Come starboard half a point!"

The tiller was brought over, and then recentered when the sleek privateer was on the new course. The only sounds breaking the death-like silence were the rhythmical dip of the long sweeps and the dripping water from their tips as they swung forward for their next stroke, mixed with the ever-present whisper of the icy water sliding past the oak planks of the Eagle's hull. The sun sent more of its illuminating rays across the harbor, allowing the watch aloft to begin to make out the tops of the higher structures along the town's approaching skyline.

"Battery and Crager's Wharf 400 yards and two points off the larboard bow!"

Steele called back. "Do you see any men-of-war?"

"There's two of 'em at Crager's, Captain Steele!"

"Bosun!" Captain Steele's graying beard glistened with water droplets. "Go below an' get Jones! Tell him to get his things together. Tell him we'll be at Peck's Dock within a glass."

Captain Steele had taken a quick dislike to the John. In only three short days, the younger man had managed to disrupt Steele's chain of command with his continual meddling and criticism of the older man's control over his crew. Steele would be glad to be rid of the man for a day or two. A few minutes later, John joined him on the quarterdeck.

John made a quick survey of the ship. "What's this about Peck's Dock?"

"That's where we're tying up."

"But you told me Pearl Street was next to the Battery. Why not land at Crager's, nearer to Mister Ormerod's home?"

"Because two men-o'-war are tied up there, Mister Jones. That's why!" Steele walked forward a few paces. "Mister Peck's a good friend of mine, and there should be less chance of questions being asked at his dock." He turned back to John with a wry smile. "And besides, the walk through the streets will be good for you." Steele relished the thought of John suffering through the two-and-a-half mile gantlet of hucksters and beggars. "It'll build you some character."

John moved to the larboard rail to get a glimpse of the town and the two British warships just becoming visible through the fog. Eight ruddy ducks that were busy diving for breakfast were startled by the dip and feather of the Eagle's two larboard sweeps. They scurried across the water toward the shore like flat stones thrown across a still pond. Once they'd settled back into the cold brine, the four hens scolded the Eagle while the drakes resumed their feeding. Another quarter mile up river, the Eagle emerged from the low fog, exposing the moisture-covered rigging to the new sun. The water droplets sparkled like diamonds about a countess's throat.

John looked at the passing flotsam. "We must be near a shipyard."

Steele barked back sarcastically. "Quite the astute observation!" The older captain spit a stream of tobacco juice over the rail at a scrap of freshly cut oak.

"You're still angry with me, aren't you, Steele?"

"It's 'Captain Steele' to you. And yes, I'm very angry at you!"

"Your problem is that you just can't take constructive criticism."

"Wrong!" He was in no mood for this. "You questioned my authority in front of my crew, and even though you know you were wrong to do it, you've never apologized!"

"But I was right! You had no cause..."

"Enough!" Steele glanced forward at his crew. They had stopped their work to listen to this often-played friction between the two captains. "I'll not speak to you of these matters in front of my crew again!" He turned and walked to the aft companionway, stopped and turned back to John. "I've business below. Do you think you can get the Eagle to Peck's dock without causing a mutiny?"

John turned to look where he was pointing. "Aye!"

"Then be about it, Mister Jones!"

New York City wasn't but twice the size of King's Town, although it was more elegant and at least as busy for this early hour. At a hundred yards from the slip, Captain Jones brought the tiller to starboard. "Stand by forward with the lines!" The sleek privateer closed on an anchored Dutch merchantman that was taking on dark barrels and fresh-cut oak planking from a barge.

John barked another order. "Ship your sweeps!" While the bow eased between the two docks, one of the crewmen leaped across to the weathered planking and threw several turns about a bollard. The Eagle gave a steady tug and came to a stop.

Two soldiers stood on the dock. "Ahoy there!" The taller of the two approached the ship. "State your business and present your papers!" John strode across the deck toward him and then turned back to see if Captain Steele had come on deck yet. To his astonishment, a naval lieutenant stood next to the tiller, with the Royal Navy's ensign hanging behind him at the half-staff.

"'Tis the HMS Eagle, on the King's business!" Steele's assumed aristocratic accent was perfect. He looked the two young men up and down for a moment. "By the looks of your uniforms, I'd say you've spent the night asleep yonder on that pile of fishing nets!" Steele jumped to the dock with his false papers in hand. "Who's in charge of you two sorry excuses for soldiers?"

"General Gage, sir, but he's up in Boston." The soldier on the dock was completely intimidated and gave the papers only a cursory inspection before returning them to the imposing 'officer.'

"It's a good thing for you that he is!" Steele refolded the papers and gave the two another inspection. "If he were here, you'd both be before him within an hour explaining your slovenly appearance! By all that's holy, those uniforms would embarrass an ape!" Steele pointed toward the town. "Now, be about your duties!"

"Yes, sir!" The soldier shouted back obediently and then marched smartly to where his bewildered companion stood.

John stepped next to Steele and whispered. "You did that well, Captain."

"I used to be one of 'em." He turned about to John and gave the young man a tilt of his head. "But now to your mission, Mister Jones. According to my employer's instructions, I'm to send two armed men to accompany you on your way."

"Mister Jefferson's orders?

"No, it was Mister Hewes who ordered it." Steele's tone had not thawed from the trouble at sea. "I'll expect you back before dark."

"Before nightfall." John gave the older man a curt but reluctant nod. "I'll be sending your two men back once I reach Mister Ormerod's home. Whatever the outcome of my meeting, I would expect my host will provide me a carriage for the ride back to the Eagle." John turned and began to walk away, but stopped. He turned and looked back at the disguised Steele.

He gave John a disgusted stare. "Was there something else?"

"Just a thought." John took a step back toward the captain.

"You never held your tongue since North Carolina whenever you thought to correct my command of the Eagle, so out with it!"

"I know you don't like me, so I'll make this easy for both of us. Given that David Noble won't return to Charles Town for at least a month, I may want to return there by land."

Steele knew the plan the young man was proposing violated his employer's instructions, but he also feared he would be provoked into killing John Paul Jones if they were to spend much more time at sea together. "And when will you know for sure?"

"I'll make my decision before I return tonight."

A slight smile worked at the corner of Steele's mouth. "You do that, Mister Jones."

With the packet of letters under his arm and his sword hanging from his belt, John and his two escorts marched off the dock and onto the wet cobblestones of Water Street. A morning fog had left a silver sheen on the cold stones and across the slate roofs of the closely huddled shops. The many peddlers driving their carts from the docks into town were silhouetted against the bright reflections. An equal number of vendors and runners from the various brothels along Queen Street jostled past the three men, racing to be first at the objects of their animal needs. John was surprised that so much activity was taking place at such an early hour on a Sunday.

The three marched to the south end of Water Street, past several dank smelling sail lofts and chandler's shops that huddled under the tangle of ship's bowsprits. Finally, they broke from the crowded narrows and into the little open courtyard at the head of Crager's Wharf. A knot of Royal Navy sailors stood at the foot of one of the great men-of-war's gangplanks, but they took only slight notice of the three men passing over to Great Dock Street. In a moment they were across Parade Street and to the edge of the shore battery. Here finally, was Pearl Street, containing only six large homes. The second on the right was number 86-90, the home of Robert and Moira Ormerod.

Robert Ormerod was a third generation New Yorker, and was one of the three wealthiest merchants in the town. He had become so by inheriting his father's well-established business in '70. His home reflected his affluence—a two-storied structure of red bricks laid in the rarely used Flemish cross bond pattern. The checkerboard of small windows covering its face was an artist's gallery of rolled glass and French lace curtains, attesting to the presence of a woman of taste and quality. It was Moira Ormerod who answered the heavy knock on the double oak doors.

"Good morning, sirs. May I help you?" She was an exceptionally fine woman, hardly the sort John would expect could help bury a treasure on some God-forsaken island in the Caribbean. Although she was clearly in her early forties, John was taken by her youthful beauty and her light Irish brogue. His thoughts went back to the girl he hoped was waiting for him in Virginia.

John gave her a curt salute. "Yes you may, ma'am. Is this Mister Robert Ormerod's house?"

Moira was confused for a moment. She looked to the two sailors. Robert had never met with business associates at their home, especially not ones with an armed escort. "My husband told me that he would stop at the docks on his way home from church. I expect him to return at any moment." Her hand came to her lips as she went pale. "Is that why you're here? Has something happened to Robert?"

"No, ma'am, not to our knowledge." John could sense her uneasiness and wished to cause her no further distress. "I'm Captain Jones from Edenton, North Carolina. I carry several very important dispatches for your husband." He touched the leather pouch hanging at his side. "Would you mind if we waited here on the porch?" Before she could answer, a highly polished black carriage turned into the drive and stopped adjacent to John and his two escorts.

Moira gave a relieved smile. "Oh, there he is now."

John and his two men stepped from the porch.

"Robert, these gentlemen are here to see you! They've some dispatches from North Carolina!"

John walked to the carriage with an extended hand. "I'm Captain John Paul Jones, sir. I carry letters from several men, including Thomas Jefferson and George Washington."

"Well, in that case, won't you and your friends join us for morning tea?" Robert stepped from the carriage and turned to his wife. "That's if we have the food and you're prepared for unannounced visitors, dear."

"Don't be silly, Robert." She gave John a demure smile and a laugh. "We have enough tea for an army."

"It would only be me, as my escorts will be returning to our ship."

"Very well, Captain Jones." Robert climbed the steps, stopped next to his wife and turned. "Won't you come inside?"

John turned to his two escorts. "You may return to the ship." With a salute, the two were gone.

Robert led John through the foyer and into the library. "They must be rather important letters to have a ship's captain hand-carry them all this way."

"They are, sir. Very important." John set the packet on a table where he could be sure Robert would see him break the wax seal over the single buckle. He laid back the flap and pushed the packet across to the older man. Inside the pouch were the five letters Joseph Hewes promised would be there. Robert took the first one and walked to the desk by the front window. Like the leather packet, each letter bore a wax seal—a different color and signet on each. He broke the seal and read quietly.

To Mister Robert Ormerod:

The purpose of this letter is twofold; first to introduce Captain John Paul Jones, and second, to request your assistance in a most important and strategic mission for these thirteen American Colonies.

As I'm certain you already know, the relationship between the Colonies and the current government in London has deteriorated to an intolerable level; a level most certain to foment open warfare in the very near future. The Colonies are ill-prepared at this time for such a conflict. We are dealing as best we can with most of the deficiencies, but I fear that in our present state, we have little chance of holding the invading forces back, much less of defeating them either on land or at sea. The four other letters Captain Jones carries will explain in detail how you may serve your fellow Americans.

Mister Ormerod, your people need your help, and I beseech you to assist Captain Jones with his mission. May God give you the wisdom to make the right decision in this most urgent matter.

G. Washington,

General, Virginia Militia

"Interesting." Robert looked up at the younger man. "I was expecting you a week ago."

"A week ago?" John was taken aback. Robert crossed to his desk and picked up an open letter. "How could you possibly know about me when we hadn't even..."

Robert held out a letter. "Here, read this before you tell me any lies."

John took the letter and read quickly.

To my old friend, Robert Ormerod:

I am writing to you anonymously regarding a matter of grave concern to these thirteen American Colonies. As you know, revolution is at our doorstep and is as certain as the rising of the sun. We find ourselves ill-prepared for a protracted battle and need your help to rectify that condition. The Colonies need cannons, and you have knowledge that will make it possible to purchase a thousand.

A man will be coming to you in a week or two. He will represent some of the most important men in the Colonies.

I know about your father's death at the hands of our common enemy. I also know about your daughter and the two men who tried to ransom her for a treasure map. If you want their deaths avenged, then come to the aid of your fellow Americans.

Anon

John looked up at Robert. "Who sent this to you?"

"Someone close. Somebody who knows far more about me and my personal affairs than he should."

"But—"

"Look at the penmanship." Robert stepped to John and took the letter. "This is a trained hand—the hand of a scholar. I suspect he's one of your five statesmen."

"No—that isn't possible."

"Whoever he is, his intention was clear. He was preparing me for your coming."

"This is impossible. Nobody could have known about any of this." John took back the letter and scanned the words quickly. He looked back up at Robert. "Nobody could know about me, the cannons, or the treasure."

"The treasure?"

"Yes—the treasure of Dead Man's Chest."

"Hmmm." Robert gave John a curious look.

"Where did this letter come from, Mister Ormerod?" John turned it over. "It has no return address."

"Look at the seal." Robert picked up the leather pouch. "It's the same imprint as on your leather pouch, which means that someone in the Committees of Correspondence wanted to predispose me in favor of your mission before you arrived. It had to be one of these five men."

John shook his head. "No. It couldn't be one of them."

"Then how would you explain the letter?"

"I can't, but I only approached them a week ago with my plan, and I boarded a privateer the very next morning for this place to solicit your assistance."

"Then the only explanation is that there is a puppet master, and he is pulling the strings of both you and the men who wrote these letters." Robert took back the letter. "I suspect that you know who the man is."

For the next ten minutes, the merchant sat at his desk reading and re-reading the lengthy letters, making several notes and underlined sections he found questionable. Finally he turned to the young captain. "You know of course, that they want me to accompany you to Dead Man's Chest?"

"Oh?" John shook his head. "My understanding was that you were only being asked to provide me with a map. May I read that letter?"

"No, you may not."

"But—"

"No arguments, Captain Jones." He got up, stepped to the fireplace, and dropped the five letters one by one into the flames. Once the last one was consumed, he turned on the young captain. "You have a personal stake in all of this, don't you?"

"A stake?"

"Come now, Captain Jones. Don't paint me the fool. They've promised you something if you succeed."

John nodded. "If they get their cannons back, then I will receive a commission in the Continental Navy."

"Aha!" Robert gave a laugh. "I had heard that a large cache of Scottish cannons were being smuggled into Charles Town two years ago, but my colleagues assured me that it was just a rumor."

"It's true. They would have arrived the summer of '73 but for a pirate and the Devil's luck."

"Regarding the map, your friends are correct." He nodded toward the fire. "I'd go with you before I'd ever consent to draw another."

"You would?"

"In an instant—but for a promise I made on my wedding day." He took the poker and stirred the burning letters until the last scrap turned to ash. A clay pipe with a half-smoked bowl lay on the mantle. Robert took a burning piece of kindling and puffed the pipe alive while he considered. He turned to John and blew a perfect smoke ring into the still air of the library.

"Moira was a passenger on that treasure ship we attacked twenty years ago. During the year we were in league with my granduncle, and finally the prisoners of John Flint, she and I witnessed more than a hundred fifty men lose their lives because of the treasure you and your supporters want so badly. She watched as my granduncle was killed by pirates, and she was standing next to her own father when a passing cannonball felled him. Every farthing of that treasure was paid for by the blood of good and bad men. On our wedding day, Moira asked me to promise her that no matter what happened, I would never go back to Dead Man's Chest, or aid another in retrieving that treasure."

Robert took another puff on the pipe and continued. "As much as I want to go with you, Captain Jones, I can't break my vow to Moira."

"But the coming war..."

"I know how badly the colonies need Charles Noble's thousand cannons, but I cannot break my vow to my wife. I'm sorry you had to travel so far for nothing."

"Is there no way I can change—"

Moira backed through the partially opened door with a tray. It contained a teapot, two cups and several covered dishes. "Please excuse the intrusion, Captain Jones, but the morning grows late, and my husband needs to eat breakfast." She set the tray on the sideboard and served up two bowls of oatmeal with raw sugar and butter. She turned, straightened her apron, and looked at the young captain. "I would assume you haven't eaten either, Captain Jones."

"No, I haven't." John smiled and picked up the bowl. "Thank you."

Moira leaned close to her husband and whispered. "Robert, may I speak to you alone for a moment?"

"Certainly, Dear." He looked at John. "Has it anything to do with Captain Jones?"

"It's something..." She hesitated while she gave the young man a long look. "It's actually something you both should hear." She handed Robert his cereal and then took a seat opposite the fireplace.

"First, I must apologize for eavesdropping on your conversation a moment ago."

Robert lowered the spoon from his mouth. "How much did you hear?"

"Enough." She looked from one man to the other. "Robert, I know I made you swear never to go back to that evil place. At the time, that vow was fully appropriate to everything we believed in. But there is now a need that outweighs my fear of further bloodshed. The colonies need those cannons, and you owe it to your father and the families of those four other people killed with him in Boston to do what Mister Washington, Mister Jefferson, and the others are asking of you." Moira stood and walked to her husband. "I want you to go with him, Robert."

"Then you release me from my oath?" He set down the bowl, took his wife by the shoulders, and looked deeply into her brown Irish eyes.

"Yes, I do, Robert. And I know the good Lord would have it that way also."

"Thank you, Moira." He took his wife's left hand and kissed the open palm gently, just where he had been forced to cut the cross twenty years before at Savannah. The scar had never disappeared completely, leaving a small white "X" over her heart line. It was a constant reminder of that fateful night on the pirate ship Walrus when he had cut Billy Bones, and John Silver had helped the young couple escape. The experience had been bloody and almost more than either of them could endure, but during idle moments—when his thoughts were allowed to wander—they always went back to the deck of the Royal James and the excitement of his short career as a pirate.

Robert released his wife with a kiss to her cheek. "Captain Jones, do you have transportation back to Charles Town?"

"Yes, I do. The privateer Eagle is waiting for me at Peck's Dock. But I was hoping to make other arrangements."

"Other arrangements?"

"I told the captain that I may go back to Charles Town by land. I'm to send him word as soon as I know your decision."

"Why would you go by land? It would be so much quicker by ship, provided the weather remains good."

"Well..." John hesitated, searching for the best way to put it. "There is...someone...living near Fredericksburg whom I wish to see."

"But you could see her much quicker if we went by sea, and you were dropped off in the Rappahannock. From there you could reach Fredericksburg in a day by horseback."

"I suppose you're right." John didn't want to see Captain Steele again, but neither did he want Robert to know of the trouble between them. "You're right, of course. We'll go at least that far on the Eagle."

Robert took a bite of his oatmeal. "Have you heard about any other part of the treasure—any part not on Dead Man's Chest?"

"If you're referring to the part that was buried on Flint's Island, yes, I know. It was recovered some years ago."

"Yes, that part." Robert paced across the room and returned to the hearth. "I have in my employ an elderly gentleman by the name of Benjamin Gunn. He was my granduncle's personal steward on the Royal James, and before that, he was the closest confidant of John Flint. The man's a little odd, but he has a heart of pure gold."

"Odd?"

My granduncle chose him because he's totally incapable of the most benign treachery. He operates my Boston warehouse, but he's as close to this treasure as anyone."

"But how—"

"After we buried our share on Dead Man's Chest, we took the remaining treasure to John Flint on Spyglass. No sooner did we have it ashore than there was a great battle that ended with my granduncle killed and Moira and me taken captive aboard the Walrus. As fate, or Providence would have it, one of the pirates—a fellow named Long John Silver—helped us escape one night at Savannah, along with three others. One of those others was Ben Gunn."

"And this is your employee in Boston?"

"The same. I offered him a job that night in Savannah, but he declined it for the first passage that would take him back to sea. There was a Barbados packet leaving Savannah the next day, so he stayed behind while we made our way north. I cautioned him to keep quiet about Flint's treasure, but as he tells it, he couldn't resist the temptation to brag to the small crew. He and his new mates searched Spyglass for nearly a fortnight before they finally marooned the poor soul for treachery. He was rescued a few years later by a group of men out of Bristol who had somehow come into possession of Flint's 1755 map. As you might guess, many of the pirates from the Walrus managed to get aboard that ship as crewmen, and once on the island, turned against their employers. Ben tells me the pirate's leader was that same man who freed us in Savannah."

"Long John Silver?"

"Yes." He took a sip of tea. "What I'm getting at is that there were, according to Mister Gunn, several hundred bars of silver and a chest of jewels left in a second cave on Flint's Island. If I can convince Ben to go back with us, he can lead us to that additional treasure." He paused for a spoonful of oatmeal. "Would there be anything to prevent us from stopping at Spyglass?"

"I'll be the master of the treasure ship. If I choose to stop at Spyglass, we'll stop. And as long as there's enough treasure to pay for the cannons, what should Mister Jefferson and the others care about splitting the extra swag with the crew?"

The two smiled at each other like two schoolboys preparing to steal apples.

"When can we contact this Mister Gunn?"

"He's on his way from Boston at this moment with some contracts. Would it pose a problem for you to wait here as my guest until he arrives?"

"I don't see why." John knew the delay would anger Captain Steele. "But something about Mister Gunn doesn't quite make sense."

"And that would be?"

"If he returned to Bristol with the bulk of the treasure, he should have been able to retire on his share. Why is he working for you?"

"That was his intention—to retire in ease. But you must realize that Ben is a rather simple man. Between the hatters, the tailors and the carriage makers, his money flowed like blood on the gundeck of a man-of-war. He purchased an estate, staffed it with too many servants, and entertained royalty several times a month. It wasn't two years and he was back here in New York asking if my offer of employment was still good."

John gave a shake of his head. "I feel bad for your old friend, but I understand it's a common malady with pirates."

"I don't think of Ben as a pirate. He's just a simple man who fell into...extraordinary circumstances. And for that reason, I would ask one thing of you, Captain Jones."

"Anything."

"The old man's suffered enough humiliation over his foolhardiness. Your discretion would be appreciated."

John gave a nod. "I'll never bring up the subject."

"Thank you."

Moira stepped forward and gave John a smile. "We'll try to make you comfortable while you're here, Captain Jones. You'll stay in the Pirate Room."

Both men looked around. "The Pirate Room?"

Moira laughed. "The family who sold us this house told me that Captain William Kidd once lived here, and that the room you'll be using was his. It's quite manly. You'll like it."

"Then it's settled." Robert clapped his hands together. "As soon as Ben arrives, we'll be off to Dead Man's Chest!"

Chapter 9

Long John Silver sat at his desk, quickly sorting through a stack of mail. A very wet and nervous man in the uniform of the Royal Navy stood nearby, peering through a peephole in the alleyway door.

The old pirate gave a growl. "Quit yer fidgetin', Jeffrey! Nobody followed you!"

"Sorry, Mister Bridger." The man took another look through the hole. "I just don't want to be caught lettin' ya look through the Admiralty mail like this."

"Is this all the mail to and from the Wasp?"

"Yes, sir. That's the only bag that came in on the packet."

"Then this shouldn't take long." The old pirate shuffled through a few letters that remained, finally coming upon one he recognized. Taking a sharp penknife, Silver carefully scraped the wax seal from the parchment. He blew away the broken wax particles, unfolded the paper, and smiled. "Perfect."

"Anything there, Mister Bridger?"

"The lad's been promoted again!" Silver took up a quill, and after a quick search for the perfect spot, he wrote his initials in the artwork atop the document. "There! Now we'll see if he's as clever as he used to be."

There was a soft knock at the hallway door. Both men jumped.

"John?" It was the voice of a woman.

"Yes, dear?" He gestured to the courier that there was no danger.

"That ship's boat you asked me to watch for has just docked, and your nephew was on board."

"Thank you, darling!" John Silver turned back to the man with the mailbags.

"I've seen enough, Jeffrey." Silver held three of the opened letters in his hand.

"Those three? Something you can use this time, Mister Bridger?"

"Very useful! You can bag those other letters while I take care of these."

While the courier went about his task, Silver skimmed over the letters and made several notes in his journal. Then, he selected the appropriate seal from a tray and dripped a fresh puddle of hot wax on the first of the two military dispatches. He pressed the counterfeit tool into the red wax and gave it a slight twist, making the false impression impossible to detect, even to the most careful eye. He did the same with the other letters.

"That should do it." He waved the last letter about in the air to cool the wax. Satisfied, he dropping the dispatches and the love letter into the bag with the rest. He reached into his pocket and pulled out a silver crown.

"Why, thank you, sir!" The surprised courier had never received so generous a reward from the old man.

"You're welcome, Jeffrey."

"Will you have anything to be sending out, sir?"

"Yes I will, but not today. The timing must be perfect."

After a careful check of the alleyway, the courier was out of the little office and on his way to the postal house on the other side of King's Town.

John Silver emerged from the office and threw on his coat. His wife, Betty, was coming from the galley. He buttoned the front of the coat and pulled the collar up. "I'll be going to see my brother."

"How long will you be gone, John?"

"No more than an hour or so." He stepped to the kitchen door, and hesitated. He crossed back to his gentle wife and took her face in his hands. "If I ever get myself another ship, it'll be your likeness beneath her bowsprit. And I'll name her after you too. The Bride O' King's Town, she'll be!" A kiss on her nose and a pinch to her backside brought a maiden's blush to the elderly woman's cheeks.

"You're still a pirate, John Silver, but I love you anyway. Be careful on that clicking leg of yours, you hear?"

"You worry too much about me, woman!" He grabbed at her breast and then ducked under her slap.

A moment later, Silver had taken to the cobblestones of the side streets and was en route to his brother's home as quickly as his uncertain gait would carry him. He arrived at the side entrance just as David and his party neared the front gate.

"It's just here." David stopped and turned to his escorts. "Reed, you and Samuels can go back to the Swan now. When you get there, tell Captain Johnson that I'll be spending the night with my father. You can call for me at noon tomorrow."

"By yer leave, sir." Reed was a giant of a seaman, but he stammered when he spoke. "Uh…Cap'n Johnson…told us not to leave ya…'til ya were inside, safe an' sound."

"Oh, very well!" David walked across the small courtyard and pushed open the front door of his father's home. He turned back to the men. "There! I'm home!"

"Orders, sir!" The two men gave David a salute, turned and left the way they had come.

"Is that you, David?" Charles Noble jumped up from his favorite chair and hurried to the hallway. "Well, I'll be flogged! It is you! Come in, boy, and tell me all about America!"

Outside, the two seamen walked to the corner and turned along the side fence of the Noble estate. Reed nodded as they walked. "Noon on the 'morrow, an' not to be late."

John Silver pressed himself flat against a whitewashed wall while the two seamen passed by. Then he stepped from the shadows and crossed the narrow street into his brother's garden and to the back door.

Charles saw the pirate first. "Ah, John!" He pulled the first letter from David's satchel. "Take a seat and listen.

The old sea dog gave a grumble and reached for the satchel. "I can read them myself."

Charles pulled it back. "These letters are addressed to me! You can read them after I do!"

Silver gave another growl and dropped into the chair, his wooden leg standing out before him like a bowsprit. He reached down and depressed a catch on the outside of the knee to release the lock, but the lower half of the leg dropped only an inch. With an oath, he gave the thing a kick with his right foot, driving it to the floor.

"Damned thing started making noises again, right when I was serving a brisket to the Admiral and several of his staff. Claimed it was a childhood accident."

"I told you it was overdue for attention before you went, if you'll remember. If you'll leave it with me for a couple of days, my carpenter will service the mechanism."

"Forget my leg!" Silver gestured at the letters. "What'd the Americans say?"

Charles read quickly and then looked over the top of the letter. "It's good. Very good! Everything's gone exactly as you planned that it would."

David cleared his throat. "With only a couple of exceptions."

"Exceptions?" Silver looked at the lad through squinted eyes. "What exceptions?"

"Listen to this!" Charles gave the second letter a shake. "Captain Jones is in New York with Robert Ormerod..." He waved the first letter. "...and the chairman of the colonies' Marine Commission—a Mister Joseph Hewes—has offered me eight hundred thousand pounds for my cannons!" He handed the letter to Silver.

"The treasure!" Silver raised his hands and gripped at something the others could not see. "It is the treasure, isn't it, Davey?"

David gave them a slow nod and a grin. "Aye, and when I return to Charles Town, I'll know whether or not Mister Ormerod has agreed to draw us a map."

"A map?" Charles held up the third letter. "Not according to Mister Jefferson."

Silver pushed himself up from the chair and reached for the letter. "What are you saying, little brother?"

Charles shook his head, reading further. "There won't be a map."

Silver grabbed David by the upper arm. "What went wrong this time, Davey?"

"Leave the lad alone, John. It was Jefferson's idea."

The old pirate released his grip and looked to his brother. "Jefferson? How does he expect to find the treasure without a map?"

"He says here that he has asked Robert Ormerod to go with Captain Jones and lead him to the treasure."

"Map or no map, we could still overpower Jones and his crew when they tie up at your dock."

"No!" Charles held up the remaining letters. "We'll not betray these men!"

"You're not going honest on me, are you, Charles?"

"It wouldn't matter if I were or not, John, because they're sending twin ships." He handed the third letter to his older brother. "One ship for the treasure and one for the cannons."

"Twin ships? Why would they—"

"Think about it." Charles held up his hands as if they were ships. "They know that if we get the treasure back to King's Town, they would have no way of forcing us to send them the cannons. They're statesmen, but they're also businessmen."

"So how's the exchange to take place, if they don't trust us?" Silver scanned the third letter and looked back up at his younger brother. It suddenly hit him. "They want us to exchange ships at sea!"

"It's right here!" Charles held up the fourth letter.

Silver rubbed his beard. "Well, that's not how I planned it, but if it gets me the gold, I guess I can agree to it."

"We can agree to it."

"Don't worry, Charles." Silver knew his brother never really trusted him. "You'll be compensated far beyond your expectations for both your trouble and the cannons."

"You can be sure of that, John Silver. I'll be well compensated, or there will be consequences."

There was an uncomfortable moment while the two stared at each other. Finally, the older man spoke. "Why don't you get us some of your fine brandy while Davey tells us what prompted our Little Captain to finally apply for his naval commission?"

"Yes, David." Charles stepped to the liquor cabinet and picked up the bottle and three glasses. "We were very upset when you wrote that he just wanted to get married and buy a farm."

"I was upset too, father. He's so in love with this Miss Dandridge that I think he'd have done most anything to win her hand in marriage."

Charles poured the first drink and handed it to David. "Even promising to never go back to sea?"

"Even that." David shook his head from side to side. "I was so convinced the plan was dead that I nearly..." He looked to his father and back to Silver. "You both read my letter."

Silver accepted his drink. "Then why didn't you come home, Davey?"

"It was the strangest thing, Uncle. John was making regular visits to the Dandridge estate and the girl's father seemed to like him." David took a sip of his brandy and gave a cough. "Then, about a month ago, he stopped going to see her and refused to even talk about her. I was worried, because all he wanted to do was hide away in the tailor shop. Next thing I knew, Patrick Henry gave us the letter of introduction to Joseph Hewes."

Silver gave Charles a wink.

"The next morning, we were on our way to Edenton."

"You have no idea, then, why Captain Jones changed his mind about the commission or why Mister Henry gave you that letter?"

"No." David shook his head and took another sip of the brandy. "And I didn't want to ask him for fear it might ruin the plan."

Silver pulled his knife from its scabbard and put it an inch from the lad's nose. "Sounds to me like you lost control of the situation."

Charles put a hand on Silver's wrist. "Don't do it, John, or you'll have me to reckon with."

Silver gave a chuckle and patted David's shoulder. "I was only playing with the lad. I wouldn't ever hurt Davey." He pulled a whetstone from his pocket and began to hone the knife.

David looked from one to the other. "One of you did something, didn't you?"

"I'll tell him." Charles held up a hand to Silver. "When you wrote us about this girl he had fallen in love with, your uncle sailed to Virginia and handed Nathaniel Dandridge a copy of the King's warrant. And just to make sure Captain Dandridge would choose the right option, your uncle also suggested that Dandridge send John away."

David's mouth dropped open. "So that's how..." David's mind raced, putting the pieces together. "John told me that Mister Dandridge had a copy of the warrant, and Mister Hewes told us that it was Dandridge, not Patrick Henry, who told him about John and me." He paused to consider further. "John must have figured the King's men were already looking for him in Virginia, when in reality that warrant may not have reached America at all!" He looked at each of the older man. "Ha!"

Silver chuckled. "That'll teach you to underestimate an old pirate's powers, Davey."

Charles raised his glass and took a sip. "So, what's next, David? How will we know whether Ormerod has agreed to go along and lead Captain Jones to the treasure?"

"As I understand it, you won't until one of the twin frigates arrives here in King's Town."

"Frigates?" Silver coughed half a mouthful of brandy onto his trousers. "They'd be daft to sail an American frigate into King's Town! If the government finds out that the colonies are starting up their own navy—"

Charles gave a laugh. "My God! These Americans are either very brave or very stupid!"

David pointed at the yet-unopened fifth letter. "It's supposed to be in Mister Forrestal's letter. As I understand it, he's been building two identical merchantmen for a Dutch company for the last year. As soon as he heard our plan, he ordered his carpenters to begin certain modifications."

Silver gave Davey a squint. "What kind of modifications?"

"When they're finished, those two merchantmen will be frigates. But even if the authorities send an inspection team aboard, they will still think they're Dutch merchantmen, including a full Dutch crew."

"And cannons?" It was Charles. "They can't be frigates without cannons."

"Only the one headed for Dead Man's Chest will be armed. They want you to fill your ship's gun positions with a standard mix of long cannons and carronades from the inventory, and store the rest in the bilges, instead of ballast."

"And tell us, Davey. How many escorts is this Mister Forrestal sending along to Dead Man's Chest?"

"Sending along?"

"Escorts!" Silver slapped his wooden leg. "These statesmen must know there are pirates in the Caribbean, for God's sake!"

"Well, I don't know." David tried to remember back to the night at Edenton. "Mister Jefferson did say something about sending the privateer Eagle ahead to clear the way, but it was never decided."

"A privateer, eh?" Silver groaned as he pulled his blade across the whetstone. He set the edge on his forearm and shaved away a one-inch square of hair. "One escort won't be enough."

***

It was Tuesday afternoon when Ben Gunn finally arrived in New York. Early the next morning, the Ormerod carriage rolled onto Peck's Dock. A short distance away, a ferry was getting ready for its morning run across the East River to the neighboring city of Brooklyn. Captain Steele was sitting in the dock house with William Peck, engrossed in a game of cribbage, when a crewman from the Eagle knocked at the door.

"Cap'n Steele, sir?"

Steele knew that tone. "Are they finally back, Martin?"

"That they are, sir, an' there's three of 'em."

"Three, you say?" He threw his cards on the table, took up his winnings, and stepped onto the dock with his hat and coat in hand. "Did Jones tell you who the others were?"

"I didn't talk to him, sir." Martin glanced to the Ormerod carriage. "Came straight to you when I seen 'em turn onto the dock."

"Don't worry about it." Steele pushed past the seaman. "I'll find out soon enough. I was hoping it would be a messenger to tell me he had decided to go back by land."

The angry captain marched toward the large Ormerod carriage as the three men stepped down onto the dock. The driver handed down several pieces of baggage, and as quickly as it had come, the carriage thundered away over the weathered planking and onto the street beyond.

"Ah!" John nodded toward Captain Steele. "Here he comes now. Just as I described him, is he not?" Ormerod and Gunn agreed quietly. They could sense the approaching man was in a bad mood.

"Captain Steele!" John's tone was forced. "I've two passengers returning with me to Charles Town!"

Steele strode up to the three, stopped abruptly and gave each of them an angry stare. "I'd love to have a friendly chat, gentlemen, but we've just enough time to get into the open sea before dark."

"Of course." John gave the other two an apologetic look. "We'll get to know one another once we're under way." John led the other two up the gangplank and aft to the cabin the three would share. Once inside, John touched the two bunks. "It'll be a bit cramped, but being the youngest, I'll sleep on the floor."

Robert set his bag down inside the door. "What was that I saw between you and Captain Steele?"

John stood for a long moment, not quite sure what to say.

Ben saw it too. "Is he always like that, sir?"

"To be honest, I've only known the man for a little over a week— the trip here from Edenton."

"It's more than obvious that he detests you."

"He's just being over-sensitive about—"

Robert put up a hand. "I don't need to know the details of your issue with him, Captain Jones. My only concern is that what ever it is, it will not hamper our mission."

"But—"

"If you don't mind, Mister Gunn and I would prefer to stay outside of your personal problems with Captain Steele."

John stood for a moment and then nodded. "Very well."

Up on the main deck, Captain Steele barked orders at his men, bringing the small ship alive. Within minutes, the lines were thrown from the dock and the Eagle was piked clear and into the steady current of the East River. A nor'easterly breeze added several knots to their downriver reach to the sea. By dusk, they had cleared the Narrows and were once again into the icy waters of the North Atlantic.

Robert took Ben Gunn aft so they could introduce themselves properly to the ship's master. After the obligatory handshakes, Captain Steele asked the obvious question. "So you're the object of this voyage?"

"Yes I am, sir." Robert leaned against the railing several yards from the captain and sipped his cup of coffee. "I'm sorry it took so long, but I needed to wait for Mister Gunn's arrival from Boston."

Steele gave Robert a cold stare. "Mister Jones could have had the decency to inform me of the delay."

"You didn't know he might be delayed?"

"No, Mister Ormerod, and he probably forgot to tell you my crew wasn't allowed to make liberty in New York."

"No...he didn't tell me. How long has it been?"

"We spent three days en route from Edenton, and they've had to sit for three more days watching the crowds come and go along the docks. That's no way to treat men."

"Well, that doesn't make any sense." Robert looked forward to where John was standing alone. "Was your crew told anything—why you've come to New York?"

"Mister Ormerod, I don't even know the nature of your mission, so my men certainly don't! Mister Hewes was adamant that except for Mister Jones and the two escorts I sent with him to your home, none of us were to go ashore for any reason." He spread his hands in frustration and raised his voice so John could hear. "If we weren't privy to his plans, then what possible harm could there have in going ashore?"

"Hmmm." Robert looked forward to where he had left John. "Did Mister Hewes give you any special instructions concerning the voyage back to Charles Town?"

"Only that I'm to get you and Mister Jones back as quickly as possible."

"I wish I could tell you what it is we're up to, Captain Steele, but—"

"Never mind, sir. It's probably best that I don't know."

For the next day and a half, the Eagle beat southwesterly along the rugged Atlantic coast. John kept to himself most of the time, avoiding Steele whenever possible.

On the second afternoon, the forward watch sighted Cape Charles, at the mouth of the Chesapeake Bay.

"Steele." It was apparent that John had been mulling over his thought for some time when he finally blurted it out. "I want you to take me to Fredericksburg."

"Is this something Mister Hewes has ordered you to do?"

"Does it matter?"

"You're damned right it matters!" Steele turned on the smaller man. "If Mister Hewes has given you some additional mission, and it's in writing—because this is the first I've heard of it—then I'll take you wherever he tells me. Otherwise, we're sailing straight through to Charles Town!"

"It's a personal matter."

Steele took on a sarcastic tome. "Of course it's a personal matter!"

"What difference does it make to you if it is? You're supposed to take me wherever I say."

"That's a damned lie, and you know it! My orders were to take you to New York and then back to Charles Town! My employer didn't authorize any side trips, especially not to Virginia!"

John began to burn with rage. "Especially not Virginia? If that's true, why didn't he tell me?"

"He did—as we were pulling away from the dock at Edenton!"

"Well, I didn't hear it!"

"You only hear what you want to hear!"

"That's not true!"

"Even if Mister Hewes had not forbidden my taking you to Virginia, I would still refuse!"

"You dislike me that much?"

"Oh, it's not for my sake I refuse, Mister Jones. I have a much better reason!"

"What?"

"It's because you have no common decency!"

"What are you talking about?"

"My men were confined to this ship for three days in New York while you were ashore! You didn't care!" Alan pointed to the west. "I'll not put in at Virginia and subject them to any more of that!"

"Confined to the ship? What in God's name for?"

"Because Mister Hewes ordered it, that's why!"

"And you assumed I knew?"

"You should have, just like you should know that your mission has to be kept a secret!"

"Are you implying that I'd let it slip to someone in Fredericksburg?"

"It doesn't matter what I'm implying, because I'm not taking you anywhere close to Virginia!"

"Steele, you're nothing but a dried up old prune!" By now, every man on the ship was watching and listening to the growing battle. "You've forgotten what it's like to love a woman!"

"The hell you say!"

"You went to sea with a sick wife at home and let her die, and I'd wager you haven't been with a woman since!"

Six seamen who were splicing and coiling ropes nearby began moving to the rail behind John, anticipating the argument's inevitable escalation. Ben Gunn and Robert came on deck to see what all the yelling was about.

Steele hissed through clenched teeth. "You bastard! You insolent, self-serving, egotistical bastard! I told you about my wife in confidence, only because you were so depressed about that girl in Virginia. And now, just because you want to go see her, you'd throw my dead wife in my face?" Steele's hand went for a belaying pin while John began to draw his sword. "Damn your selfish soul to hell, John Jones!" Steele pointed at the sword. "Before you pull that blade, consider where this crew's loyalties lie!"

Steele raised the wooden weapon to strike, and just as John had reacted when the mutineer attacked him at Scarborough a year and a half earlier, his sword flashed through the cold air with a demon's howl. The two weapons met just inches above Steele's forehead, the sword's razor edge cutting a third of the way into the grain of the oak belaying pin.

Steele wrenched his weapon free for a second swing at John's head, but before he could strike, the six crewmen grabbed John, threw him to the deck, and twisted his sword from his hand.

"I'll take that!" Steele grabbed the weapon and walked to the rail. He drew his arm back to throw it into the cold Atlantic waters. "If you were anybody else, I'd hang you for that!"

John reached out for the sword. "Wait!"

"For what?" He hesitated, the sword poised over his head.

"Don't throw it away! Please!"

"Are you suggesting I should give it back so you can use it on me a second time?" He raised his arm slightly.

"It was given to me by my father just before I left home! It has sentimental value!"

"Sentiment? There's no sentiment without love."

John nodded.

"Well, I love this ship and its crew. It's my world—my private little kingdom, if you will—and as you've noticed by the twelve hands holding you down, my men love this ship too. I may be rough, and my speech might offend a landlubber now and then, but I'm a God-fearing man who's learned to recognize and respect authority when I see it! You, on the other hand, lack that maturity." He paused to take a breath. As he did so, he brought the sword down and touched John's exposed abdomen with the tip. John took a large breath and clenched his teeth. "You like to quote Patrick Henry, don't you?"

John nodded, keeping his eyes on the sword.

"I know he's important to the colonies, but with all due respect for your friend, I find myself unimpressed with his effect on you. He evidently speaks volumes on liberty, but by your conduct, very little of loyalty. Take a lesson from real life, Mister Jones. There is no question as to whom my men obey. At my command, they'd kill you where you lie!"

John watched the tip of his sword as it hovered above his stomach.

"Very well!" Steele pulled the sword away and stepped back from his antagonist. "I'll not throw your sword away this time, but it goes into the armory under lock and key until you're off my ship! Now, get out of my sight!" With a nod to his men, John was released and allowed to get up.

Robert helped the young Scotsman to his feet, "Go to the bow and remain there!" The infuriated youth hesitated longer than Robert felt he should. "Now, Jones, while you still can!"

John backed slowly from the quarterdeck, and then after a long moment, turned away as ordered.

"Keep him away from me, Ormerod!" Steele dropped the belaying pin back into the pin rail. "One more confrontation like that and one of us is going to be killed!"

"Don't worry. I'll see to it that the two of you are not left alone again." Robert watched John until he had reached the bowsprit, and then turned back to Captain Steele. "I think it might be best if you reconsider his request."

"That was no request, Mister Ormerod. He ordered me to take him to Virginia. I'll be damned if I—"

"Calm down, Captain, and consider. It will give you and Captain Jones time to cool back down. And besides, you and your men can take a day of liberty at Dahlgren once he's gone."

"You can authorize that?"

"Of course I can." Robert spoke with an air of impunity. "I can do most anything I want until I provide the information Mister Jefferson needs."

"And that would be?"

Robert shook his head and smiled. "Good try, sir, but not good enough."

Steele considered the suggestion for a moment. He nodded. "Very well. I'll put him ashore, but not alone." He turned and strode to the fife rail where he placed his hand on the belaying pin so recently cut by John's blade. "He may be a bastard, but my employer says he's a valuable bastard."

"Well, I'll agree with you that he's valuable, Captain, but your differences are strictly your own. If you don't have anybody in mind to go with him, I'd welcome the visit to Fredericksburg. I've been meaning to go there for several years now anyway."

"Absolutely not!" He spun about. "If that man needs a companion, I'll send anybody before I send you! Mister Jefferson and the others haven't gone to all this trouble to have you and Mister Jones lost on the highway together, not that I'd miss him at all."

"Then what if my assistant, Mister Gunn, accompanies him?"

"That's fine by me, as long as Mister Gunn's life isn't essential to this mission." He considered for a moment. "Since our employer didn't expect your Mister Gunn to be coming along, the old man can't matter that much anyway—to the mission, that is."

"Shall we tell Captain Jones?"

"I'll leave that to you!" Steele looked forward at John. "I want nothing more to do with the man."

"You're not going to forgive him for his stupid remark about your wife, are you?"

"He cut me deep!" Steele paused in thought. "The Good Book says I have to forgive a man if he repents. But I'm fair sure it'll be a cold day in hell before John Jones admits he did wrong and asks for my forgiveness."

"Can I have your word you'll try to avoid any further confrontations?"

"You get Jones to promise that first. After he does, then ask me again."

Robert strode forward to John's side. "Captain Steele's agreed to set you ashore with Mister Gunn. You'll continue to Charles Town by carriage."

"What changed his mind?"

"He knows I'm essential to this mission, but he is not convinced that you are."

"That damned—"

"He wants you off his ship as much as you want to be off it. I offered to go with you, but he knows that I must be delivered safely to Charles Town."

"Very well! I'll go alone!"

"Mister Gunn will be accompanying you, John. He wouldn't be worth much in a fight, but he'll be a fine companion during your long ride."

John nodded. "Very well."

Robert returned to the quarterdeck.

Steele was waiting. "Well?"

"He's agreed to take a carriage all the way to Charles Town if you'll take him to Fredericksburg. Oh! He wants his sword back."

"Then we have a deal, Mister Ormerod! He'll get the sword as he leaves my ship, and good riddance to Mister Jones!"

***

Twelve hours later, and after the slow sail up the conjested Potomac River, the Eagle made port at Dahlgren—the intended landing of the Falmouth Packet the year before. With his sword returned to his side, John hired a horse and a small carriage from the town blacksmith, and by four bells, or ten o'clock in the morning, he and the ex-pirate Ben Gunn were out of the small riverfront hamlet and into the wooded countryside on their twenty-mile ride to Fredericksburg.

After a lengthy silence, John opened the conversation. "Your employer told me what he knew of your pirating years. How did you get associated with John Flint and that treasure?"

"Ah, John Flint!" Ben was thrilled that somebody was finally asking to hear his story. He crossed his fingers as he continued. "We was like this, we were. Met on the merchant ship Elizabeth, takin' indentured servants from England to the West Indies."

"You and he were crewmen on the Elizabeth?"

"No!" The old man shook his head. "We was indentured as bondsmen to Cuba!"

"You indentured yourselves?"

"Aye, sir, for seven years, me an' Flint did. And that bein' my first time at sea, I must 'a spent half the trip hangin' over the lee rail feedin' the fish. Ha!" Ben didn't mean to laugh quite so loudly, but a quick look to the captain assured him that it came to no harm. "When we got to the dock in Havana, they stood me an' Flint on the same block, together. They must'a figured we were a matched pair. Leastwise, they sent us to the same plantation."

"Was it your own idea to indenture yourself?"

"Had no choice." The carriage clattered through a covered bridge. Ben seemed to wake up when they broke out of the other end into the morning sun. "The whole family was put off the land when they brought in the sheep, so we followed everybody else to London."

"For work?"

"Aye. But there weren't no jobs to be had."

"How did you and your family live?"

"While my father and I looked for work, my sisters and Mum sold off our belongings for food." He fell silent.

John waited. "Ben?"

The old man jumped from his daydream. "It was a very bad time, Cap'n Jones. I watched my father work his teeth loose one at a time for worry, and pull them out'a his head with pliers. There was no work, so there was no food or shelter. My little sister needed our parents worse then me, so I went down to the docks and indentured myself. That's where I met John Flint."

"How old were you?"

"I was eleven." He scratching his cheek. "I think Flint was twelve or thirteen."

"So you spent seven years on a plantation?"

"Oh no, sir. Wouldn't have survived, an' that's for certain. Had to run off after six months."

"But you signed on for seven years. Why would you—"

"That's 'cause you weren't there, sir. They treat their blackbirds better 'n any bondsman." Ben gave John a questioning look, surprised the young man didn't know more about life on the plantations. "They pay good money fer them blackbirds, so they want 'em to last! Flint figured it out before me, an' we ran away the first chance we got."

"You must have bitter feelings for the Africans."

"Oh, not at all, sir. Them Africans had no choice 'bout being slaves, no more than the white slaves before them. We were the only ones with a choice."

"White slaves?" John slowed the gelding to ford a shallow stream. "What white slaves?"

"You don't know?" Ben gave the Scotsman another questioning look. "Fifty or sixty years before there was any blackbirds in the West

Indies, the Mohammedan slavers was stealin' whites from wherever they could find them an' wholesalin' them to the Spanish. At first it was the criminals and the prisoners o' war of course, but when them ran out, the slavers began kidnappin' children an' older folk. Nowadays, a full third of the respectable white folk up in New York and Boston can trace their lines back to the plantations in Jamaica and Cuba."

For years John had been shamed by his one experience transporting African slaves to the West Indies. "I know very little about the slave trade."

"But did ya know that the amount of slavin' the Brits an' Scots done was only a speck to what the Spaniards an' the Arabs were doin'? Figure the thing out, sir. Who owns most all the land in the new world? Not the Brits or the Scots. Why, every time one of our Massachusetts privateers comes on a slaver, they take over the ship an' sail it back to where it come from."

John wanted to leave the subject of slavery. "So you and Flint ran off because you were treated badly?"

"That's puttin' it mild." Ben scratched his right thigh, chased the itch up to his rib cage and around to his upper back. "There were no beds, the food weren't fit fer pigs, an' the water was so bad you'd drink it through yer beard to get the bugs and other floating stuff out—that's if you were old enough to have a beard." The itch became worse. "Me an' Flint were just lads, so we used each other's hair. It was Flint's idea to run off, all right. Took him five lashings an' watchin' half a dozen o' the other indentureds dyin' of their infections before he struck upon the truth of it."

"Where'd you go?"

"Into the hills at first, until our empty bellies finally drove us down to Havana. We jumped the first ship leavin' port an hid away in the chain locker. Then Flint got to thinkin' that we'd be worse off back in England—that's where the ship was headed—so when we were passin' Hispaniola close abeam, we pissed in the ship's water."

"You did what?"

"We…uhh…passed water into all three of the casks on the main deck." Gunn winked and snickered. "You never done that—pissed in somebody's water?"

John gave a laugh. "Can't say as I've had the pleasure."

"Had to get 'em to stop somehow before they left the Caribee."

"And?"

"Worked like a charm, it did! Next thing we knew, everybody's yellin' an' cursin' and then we're droppin' anchor on the north coast of

Hispaniola. Me an' Flint slipped over the side an' were ashore without them knowin' we was ever aboard."

"What did you do on Hispaniola?"

"Joined the buccaneers, we did!"

"You just came ashore and joined a pirate crew?"

"Not that kind o' buccaneer, sir. The kind what lives off the land, sleepin' in caves, an' huntin' wild cows an' hogs for food."

"Of course. I remember now. I've always wondered what kind of life that was."

"Hard, sir, damned hard!" The old man fell silent for a moment, and then brightened. "But at least you're free an' ya got all the meat ya want to eat."

"Freedom." John thought back to his conversation with Patrick Henry. "That's worth more than most of us realize."

"Aye! Six months me an' Flint spent as cutters an' smokers before they let us start huntin' with 'em. Had to earn yer musket, ya did."

"How'd you and Flint become pirates?"

"Same way all buccaneers do—we was forced into it."

"Oh?"

"It were them Spaniards what done it to us." John noticed that as Ben told his story, he sounded more and more like a pirate. "Once a year, regular as the seasons, they'd make a sweep o' the island lookin' fer us. Didn't want us shootin' their beef, yet it was their ships what bought most of the meat we smoked!" Ben scratched himself under the arm and then behind the right ear. The lice had been gone for over ten years, but the memory was there, and old habits die hard.

"So you joined a pirate crew after that?"

"Not directly. We was chased to the coast where some of the others had a boat. It was their idea to go to Tortuga, an' we were sorta swept along, as they say."

"Tortuga's where most of the French pirates holed up, wasn't it?"

"Aye, an' it was there we signed articles with Charles Vane, not two months before he was voted out in favor of John Rackham."

"Rackham? Calico Jack Rackham?"

"The same."

"But Rackham's crew was caught in their sleep and all hung in Jamaica."

The old man gave a laugh. "Not me an' Flint."

"How'd you escape, if the whole crew was captured?"

"Weren't a matter of escapin', 'cause me an' Flint was marooned before the rest of 'em was caught."

"Then you were marooned twice?"

The old man gave John a wide smile.

"But why? I heard Calico Jack was one of the easiest captains to pirate with."

"Flint an' Rackham got into a scrap when we found out he was hiding these two females out on the ship, disguised as men. Flint was a superstitious sort, twice what I was." Ben rubbed his nose till it was nearly raw. "Mind ya, when things get rough I'll plant my blade in the mainmast with the best of 'em, but the thing worked on Flint's soul somethin' fierce. He told Rackham the crew was double cursed, there bein' two o' them females aboard, an' all. One of 'em—no more than a child herself—got herself pregnant an' Rackham put her off at Havana in '20 to have the pup. That's how we found out they was women, an' that's when Flint 'n Rackham got into their fight. That's when we was marooned—while Jack was ashore at Cuba."

"They marooned you on Cuba?" John laughed. "Don't they usually maroon someone on a deserted island so you'll die?"

"Like I told ya, a real botch of a job, 'cause we were signin' articles within two weeks aboard the Walrus." Ben squirmed sideways in the seat to scratch his underside. "Wasn't but two or three months an' we heard a Brit man-o'-war took Jack and the rest of his crew an' hung 'em at Jamaica."

"Did the women hang also?"

Ben shook his head. "Not them two."

"Because they were women?"

"Not strictly speakin'." Ben gave the thing a moment of thought. "You see, when judgment was spoke on the whole bunch, them two seamen done a strange thing."

"The two seamen? You mean the two women, don't you?"

"Seamen! The court didn't know they was females till they stood up and shouted, 'We plead our bellies!'"

"They were both pregnant?"

"Both of 'em, sir, and both by John Rackham, hisself. It was just after the younger of the two returned from Cuba. The judge wouldn't hang them two 'cause of the law about not killing the innocent unborn child, regardless of the mother's crime."

"I know the law, Ben." The carriage clattered across a bridge. "So, what did the court do with them?"

"Put 'em in prison, sir, right there in King's Town. Mary Read—the older one—took sick an' died 'afore she had hers."

"And the other girl?"

"Anne Bonny's father sent the money from America an' ransomed her."

"What about her child?"

"Died during birth. Poor whelp never had a fightin' chance."

"Who told you all of this?"

"Why, Long John Silver, of course!" Ben spoke as if the story was common knowledge.

John reined the horse left into the open field to avoid a fallen tree. "And how does this Long John Silver know so much about Anne Bonny?"

"Why, he went along with Mister Taylor when they paid her ransom."

"Taylor?"

"You wouldn't know him neither." Ben's scalp began to itch again. "Mister Taylor bought John Silver as a lad—sorta like an adopted son— but he bought Flint to work him like a slave."

"Hmmm. Mister Ormerod mentioned John Silver that first evening in New York. He told me Silver was on Flint's Island with the group out of Bristol back in '64, and that you released him the night they anchored at Puerto Plata."

"Aye, an' if it weren' for me, Silver would have been hung fer sure!" Ben fell silent, thinking back to Flint's Island. "I owed John Silver. If he hadn't come fer the treasure when he did, I would 'ave died there fer cert's."

"How'd you meet Silver?"

"He signed articles with Captain Rip Rap in '50, an' then shortly thereafter, Flint—he were captain of the Walrus by now—he traded me to Rip Rap in exchange fer Silver. It were right after he marooned those fifteen mutineers on Dead Man's Chest with only a cask o' rum. Killed 'em dead, 'cause ya can't live on rum very long without water."

"I know."

"Captain Rip Rap saw that I was special, so he made me his personal steward right off. First time Flint an' me were apart since we was indentured, but lookin' back, it was best fer both us."

"Let's get back to John Silver. You say he went with this Mister Taylor when they ransomed Anne Bonny?"

"Aye! John Silver was an orphan—'nother one of several that Taylor bought and raised. King's Town has always been John Silver's real home."

"Any idea what happened to Silver after you released him at Porto Plata?"

"That were the only thing I could do, sir!" Gunn thought the young captain was accusing him of wrongdoing. "Like I told ya, I owed him."

"Calm down, Ben." He put a comforting hand to the old man's shoulder. "You did what your conscience told you to do." John rephrased the question. "Do you figure Silver might have made his way back to Jamaica?"

"Yer askin' things I don't rightly know, Cap'n. John Silver might be dead, or he might even be somewhere here in America. But if I had to wager on the thing, I'd bet he's over in France or Spain where the King's men aren't lookin' fer him, and if he's there, they can't likely find him."

"But how about King's Town? Is there any chance he might have gone back?"

Ben shook his head. "Not very likely."

"And why's that?"

"Haven't ya been listenin' to me, Cap'n?" Ben gave John a questioning look. "He had a King's warrant for his head. John Silver's smarter than t' be stickin' 'round right in the middle of a British colony."

"Did he ever contact you after that?"

Ben considered the question carefully for half a minute.

"If you'd rather not say, that's your right and very understandable."

"It's not that, sir. I was just tryin' to remember back."

"And?"

"Haven't heard a thing of him in New York or Boston, sir, but just after we got back to Bristol with Flint's treasure, there was a rumor 'bout someone with a missin' left leg runnin' a tavern on the waterfront at King's Town." Ben gave John a wink. "But you know how them rumors go."

***

By noon, John and Ben had reached the Rappahannock River, where they purchased a ferry ride across to Fredericksburg. After a quick stop at the Paul Tailor Shop for additional money and a fresh change of clothes, they were once again on the road toward the Dandridge estate.

"You're a man of few words, aren't you?"

Ben looked across at the young captain. "It's taken me a lifetime to learn when to speak and when to keep my mouth shut, Captain Jones. I've also learned to back away when people aren't getting along."

"Then that's why you were so quiet while we were on the Eagle."

Ben nodded. "My mouth got me marooned, and nearly killed several times. When Master Ormerod and I realized that there was trouble between you and Captain Steele, we determined to lay low."

John considered the old man's words for a quarter mile. "Speaking of marooning, Robert was telling me three of Silver's pirates were marooned on Spyglass in '64."

"Aye, an' it couldn't have been three worse men."

"Oh?"

"It was Tom Morgan, Dick Gaffney an' Morley Rowe. But they'd all be dead by now."

"But you spent three years there, and you survived?"

"Well, it was actually longer, now that I seen the dates an' such. An' as for them three livin' even one year on Spyglass, I think not."

"Why?"

"Well, with nobody lookin' over 'em, they'd be at each others throats in a day or two, 'specially since they knew about all that silver left in my secret cave."

The sun was nearing the western horizon when John reined the horse off the road and behind a small hill.

"Why are we stopping, sir?" Ben looked around the carriage. "I thought we were going to spend the night at the Dandridge estate."

"I didn't tell you the entire story, Mister Gunn." John climbed down from the carriage and tied the horse to a small tree. "I'm not supposed to visit Miss Dandridge."

"Oh? Trouble between you and her father?"

John nodded and strapped on his sword. "John Silver isn't the only one with a price on his head."

"Master Ormerod told me about your trouble in Tobago, sir." Ben hesitated, afraid he was going to overstep his bounds or say too much. "I don't wish to pry none, sir, but is that why he doesn't want you to see her?"

John nodded. "Yes, he knows about the warrant."

"If he's threatened you, what are we doing here?"

"I have to speak with Dorothea. I have to be sure she got my last letter."

"Has Mister Dandridge told her about the warrant?"

"I don't know." John took several steps back toward the roadway but stopped and turned back. "I just want to see her again, before we go to sea."

"How long do I wait before I come after you?"

"I shouldn't be long. If it gets dark and I haven't returned, bring the carriage to the estate. It's the first one you'll come to."

Ten minutes later, John stood behind the large oak tree he and Dorothea had sat under so many times that previous summer. John gathered up several small stones and began throwing them at Dorothea's window. After two successful hits, Dorothea stepped from the back door and walked across the lawn to his hiding place.

"Well, if it isn't John Paul Jones!"

John stepped to meet her but she held up a hand to stop him short. "What's the matter?"

"You don't know?"

"Dorothea, I've just come from New York—over two hundred miles to see you." He looked about, not sure what to do. "I have to explain some things."

"Things? Don't you mean lies?"

"What's the matter with you?" John reached out again, but she pushed his hand away. "What's happened?"

"You have a lot of nerve coming here."

"What do you mean by that? Didn't you get my letter?"

"Of course I did, and that's why I'm so surprised to see you in Virginia. Won't your new employers be angry when they find out you've come here?"

"You know about them?"

"I know everything." She pulled a letter from the pocket on her skirt. "Why didn't you tell me about the warrant and the man you killed in Tobago?"

"The warrant?"

"Father also told me that when you're not in Fredericksburg, you go by a different name! Is that true?"

"I...there was a good reason for that."

"But you kept it from me! How could you do such a thing and then pretend to love me?"

"But that's exactly why I did it." John was confused. "I didn't want you to worry." John looked down at the letter she had now crumpled in her hands. "Is that my letter?"

"Yes." She gripped it more tightly.

"Then you know part of what's going on—my trip to Edenton and why I had to leave without coming to see you." He stepped toward her, but she retreated from him. "I've been sworn to secrecy, but when my friend and I reach Charles Town—"

"Charles Town?"

"I know my letter only speaks of Edenton, but things have taken another, most unexpected course. David and I were hoping to be granted direct commissions in the Continental Navy, but..."

"What are you talking about?"

"Well, as it has turned out, what we're now involved in is far more important than—"

"Edenton?"

"Yes, Edenton. To see Joseph Hewes."

"John, I'm trying, with everything in me, to remain calm. Your letter says so little—just that your employers had sent you away. I want to understand what's happened between us, but you're making this very difficult for me."

"What's happened between us?"

"Don't do this, John. You're wanted by the King for killing a man in Tobago. You've changed your name. You tell me in your letter that you've taken employment with a company in Philadelphia and that you must leave for the Hudson Bay immediately, and then you show up here saying that you're en route from New York to Charles Town on some secret mission."

"The Hudson Bay?"

"Yes, the Hudson Bay." She remembered something else. "This letter's from Philadelphia, and you just told me you came from New York."

"But I did just come from New York. I've never been in..." John suddenly realized what had happened. Dorothea's father must have somehow intercepted the letter he had asked Patrick to hand deliver, and Mister Jefferson's agent in Philadelphia had already sent a letter in John's name telling Dorothea that he was headed in the opposite direction. More letters would follow at one week intervals, each from somewhere between Philadelphia and the Hudson Bay. "I..."

"What, John? Another lie on top of the first?"

"But it wasn't..." He let out a defeated breath. "I mean, it isn't a lie. If you'll just give me a chance to explain."

"My father was right after all. He told me you were no good for me."

John tried to protest, but she continued.

"Until yesterday when your letter arrived, I had hated my father for what he'd done to us. I suspected all along that he had something to do with you going away, but I didn't know why. Now that I understand everything, I never want to see you again!"

"Please, Dorothea..."

"No more!" She pointed at the road. "I'd appreciate it if you would leave now and never come back. That's unless you have no fear of my father and the King's men."

"The King's men?"

"Father showed me this after I got your letter." She pulled a second piece of paper from her skirt and thrust it in his face. "He told me about his warning to you that Saturday we were to meet at the park, and now I agree with him. You're a very stupid man, John Paul!"

John unfolded the warrant. It was the one her father had shown him several weeks before, the one with the stamp of the Admiralty at King's Town. While Dorothea stood with her arms crossed, John read the charges against him for the first time:

WARRANT

EXTRACT from the Register of the Magistrate of Scarborough on Tobago, 22 November 1773.

WHEREAS; an accusation being pursued at the instance of the KING'S Procurator-General against one John Paul, Master of the merchant vessel Betsy, who had taken upon himself to escape the Island of Tobago aboard the Postal Packet Falmouth, and,

WHEREAS; the Court, having declared this date that the aforesaid John Paul did on 20 November 1773, murder Jack Fry, an able bodied seaman and inhabitant of the King's possession of Tobago aboard said merchant vessel Betsy, does,

THEREFORE; in justice to the English Nation and Her Colonies, and according to the indications the Court hath received;

DECREE that an Accusation and Warrant be drawn against Captain John Paul, that he may be proceeded against, according to the utmost rigor of the Law. Given Thursday the 22nd of November, N.S., 1773.

(Signed) R. ANDERSON, Greffier of the Court.

"You never intended to tell me about killing that man, did you?" John considered his words carefully. "There was no reason..."

"That's exactly what Father told me you'd say." She backed away several steps. "What a fool I've been to think that somehow that none of this was true."

"But I can explain everything."

"What is there to explain?" She snatched the warrant from his hand and read the charges. "It says here that you killed one of your crewmen." She looked up at him. "Then you fled Tobago under an assumed name."

"Assumed name? The warrant didn't..."

"My father told me. Who was Jack Fry?"

"He was a mutineer. The man attacked me."

"And a jury wouldn't have believed you?"

"Not on Tobago, and besides..." John broke off with a defeated huff. "It's too long a story for now. You'll just have to trust me that I was justified in not only killing the man, but also in my subsequent actions."

"Don't waste your breath!"

"But when you understand why I've done all of this, you'll forgive me. And after you do, I plan to ask your father for your hand."

"You're truly insane, John Paul." She stepped close, drew back her right hand, and slapped his face as hard as she could. She turned and walked toward the house. Half-way, she stopped and turned back to her vanquished suitor. "As for marriage, that slap is the closest you will ever get to my hand. Or to my heart!"

She turned and continued to the house. Her father was waiting and watching. John could see them speak, but could not hear their words. Dorothea turned and pointed to where John was hiding behind the tree. Before John could retreat, Nathaniel Dandridge was striding across the lawn toward him.

"Well, if it isn't John Paul, fresh from Philadelphia. Or are we going by our other name today?"

"That's none of your concern." John grasped the handle of his sword.

"But it is my concern that you are on my property and that you have come to see my daughter!" Nathaniel spread his coat to show that he was unarmed. "I'll say one thing, young man. What you lack in intelligence, you make up for with bravado."

John pulled the sword halfway from its sheath. "I have no desire to fight you, sir."

"Then what do you desire, Captain Paul, seeing that I'm unarmed and my daughter will have nothing more to do with you?" John stood for a long moment, unable to answer. Nathaniel continued. "Are you going to draw that sword and attack me, or are you going to turn tail and run like the coward you are?"

"I..." John let the sword slide back into its sheath.

"Go away, John Paul. You're no longer welcome here." With that, Captain Dandridge turned and walked to the house where Dorothea waited. With one last look of defiance, Dorothea followed her father into the back porch and slammed the door closed.

Ben was waiting patiently at the carriage. John untied the horse, threw his sword and belt behind the seat, and climbed up beside the old man. Ben looked across at the red handprint on John's cheek.

"Looks like ya took a pretty hard slap, sir."

"I should have listened to Captain Steele. He told me that Mister Hewes didn't want me stopping anywhere. I was too proud and arrogant to obey his warning, and now everything's ruined."

"The way you were talkin' before we got here, it sounded like everything was set between you two. What happened?"

"It's a little complicated." John laid the whip to the horse's back and turned the carriage about toward the south. "Apparently my relationship with Miss Dandridge is ended."

"Well, sir, it pains me to see you hurt this way, but maybe it's best." Ben scratched his armpit nervously, gathering his courage. "John Flint used to tell me somethin' that I didn't understand at the time, but it makes a lot of sense now."

"What's that?"

"Well, they say he spawned at least one man-child—it was by a woman he took from a prize and brought back to Savannah—but he was happy that he never got married."

"Did he tell you why?"

"He used to tell me, 'Wings aren't much use to a nestin' bird.'"

"Wings? A nesting bird? What's that supposed to mean?"

"Like I told you, I didn't have a clue for many a year, but now it finally makes sense." Ben scratched again. "I've known many a female in my day Cap'n—and mind ya, this Miss Dandridge sounds to be a winsome lass—but it's just that its too early for marriage."

"What are you saying, man?" John was losing his patience. "What do you think is wrong with her?"

"It's not her, sir, it's you."

"Then what's wrong with me?"

Ben stopped and chose his words carefully. "Well, sir, Miss Dorothea Dandridge sounds to me like the serious nestin' type."

"You've never met her."

"Am I wrong?"

John thought a moment. "Go on."

"Well, sir, I'll put it as plain as I know how." Ben scratched his scalp once again. "No offense to the lass, sir, but she'd be pluckin' yer flight feathers to line her nest, and your wings still have to carry you too many places fer that."

John considered the old man's counsel for a moment. "I understand what you say, Mister Gunn. But I may not be as ill-suited to nesting as you think."

"Had to get it off my chest, sir."

Chapter 10

The Swan had been at sea for nine days when the forward watch spotted the Charles Town Harbor in the predawn light. The fingers of land to either side of the large bay looked like the pincers of a great crab. "Charles Town Harbor, two points to larboard!"

"Edwards!" The first officer pointed aft. "Go an' get the captain." The young seaman knuckled his forelock and ran barefoot across the deck to the master's ladder. "Tell him we'll be makin' the Forrestal yards by noon!"

"Aye, aye, sir!" Edwards dropped into the darkness. A moment later he was at the captain's cabin.

"Captain Johnson!" Edwards put an ear to the door and listened. He gave three more light taps. "Charles Town Harbor on the larboard bow, sir! Mister Peters says we be makin' Forrestal's yards by noon!"

The door pulled open. "Thank you, Edwards." The somewhat portly man turned to the young man sharing his cabin. "That's good news, Noble. This has been too long a voyage, what with no prizes to take and passing by so many ports o' call." He pushed the door closed and looked at the younger man for a long moment.

David swung his legs out of his bunk and sat up. "I'm truly sorry, sir, but just like you, I've been sworn to secrecy. All I can tell you is that you've done your part well. Very well." David liked Captain Johnson, but the man had complained about the strictness of his orders every day en route to King's Town and every day back.

The Swan passed Fort Sullivan and neared the large sand bar that stretched across the mouth of Charles Town Harbor making David somehow feel at home. It was here that he and John had put in for three days of repairs on the Falmouth Packet more than a year before.

By noon, just as the first officer had predicted, the Swan pulled up to the leeward side of the Forrestal outfitter's dock, where two beautiful Dutch merchantmen the size of frigates were undergoing their final work. They were stately creatures, with lines much like the Swan, but more than twice her size. The presence of various decorations and the total absence of gun ports left no doubt that these were indeed merchantmen. A slow-moving wagon carrying several tons of anchor chain pulled onto the dock between the waiting ships.

"I see our arrival hasn't gone unnoticed." The captain gestured with his bushy blond eyebrows toward the black carriage that followed along the dock. "If I'm not mistaken, that's Mister Forrestal's personal carriage. Whatever you and Captain Jones are up to, it has to be something very important."

"It is, sir. Very important."

Alex Forrestal's carriage was equally as impressive as the two great ships that flanked the fitter's dock. The gold leaf and rich, enamel paint decorating its lavish appointments would pay a duke's ransom. The coachman reined the matching coal-black stallions about in a lazy arc to the left and stopped at the end of the Swan's gangway. A footman riding on the rear step jumped to the ground and was already at the carriage door before the wheels had come to a complete stop.

David stepped from the sleek privateer onto the gangway and stopped. "Farewell, Captain Johnson. I've learned much from you these past weeks."

"It was my pleasure, lad." He nodded toward the carriage. "Now be off with ya before I receive a reprimand from our employer."

Alex called from the carriage window. "Welcome to Charles Town, Mister Noble! I trust you had a successful voyage!"

"Very much so, sir. Did John?"

"Captain Jones will tell you all about his successes at supper this evening. For now, though, will you join my wife and me for dinner? She's preparing you a meal fit for a king."

David threw his bag up to the coachman and climbed inside, next to his distinguished host. "I'd love to, sir. I'm famished."

Alex closed the door behind him. "So, tell me. What of the cannons? Has your father agreed to the terms and conditions of our offer?"

"He has, sir, just as I told you he would." David loved to be in the midst of such momentous goings-on. "By the way, where are the two frigates we're to use?"

The shipbuilder was amused. "Why, they stand right next to us, young man!" He pointed across the dock to right and left at the two Dutch traders.

"But I thought..."

"You thought you'd be able to see the gun ports—especially at such close range!"

David leaned across his host and peered carefully at the solid planking where the gun ports should have been. There wasn't the slightest evidence, not even a single vertical crack, to give the frigate's secret away.

"That's amazing!"

"Aye!" The old man sat back. "My wife described them best: At first they'll appear to be caterpillars, but when they must, they will turn into butterflies."

"Do we have time before dinner to stop and inspect them?"

"I'll bring you back afterwards for a closer look. We Americans can be quite clever when we put our minds to it." Forrestal pulled a sash cord next to him, and the driver laid his whip to the backs of the stallions, sweeping the carriage off the dock and through the yards to the town named for a King of England.

The Forrestal estate was by far the grandest home David had ever seen. Two masonry lions stood guard at either side of the entrance. The black iron gates that hung from the whitewashed stone walls provided the only opening between the Forrestal grounds and the outside world. The carriage slowed and passed through at a walk while the gates were pushed closed behind them by two Negroes.

The long drive was bordered on each side by red brick walls two feet high. Cypress trees as tall and as straight as ships' masts stood soldier-like in neat rows from the gate to the great parking circle before the porch steps. At the center of the circle stood a fountain of snow-white alabaster marble with three dolphins of black stone leaping skyward like startled birds. Around the fountain was a belt of well-manicured grass.

The great Forrestal mansion was pure white and seemed to stretch from horizon to horizon. Its roof was flat, yet measured nearly thirty feet from the rose beds about its base to the rain gutters at its majestic head. A narrow row of basement windows skirted the massive stairs to either side, with twelve steps leading up to the extended portico. Finally, at the top of the marble steps and just inboard of the six Corinthian pillars, stood two Negro servants dressed in red tailcoats and white gloves.

The servants trotted down the steps, arriving at the carriage just as it came to a stop. They stepped to their well-rehearsed positions to receive their master's guest in the proper Southern fashion.

The taller Negro opened the door and offered the aged man his hand. "Will you be needing help from the carriage, Master Forrestal?"

"Not this time, Abraham. My hip's much better today." The old man let out a muffled groan as he lowered himself to the ground. He turned to the second Negro. "Take Mister Noble's bag to the guest room and inform Mistress Forrestal that our guest has arrived."

"Very well, sir." The slave rushed off to comply.

Alex stood for a moment to let his hip get used to the change of posture. David stepped next to him and offered his arm. "You'll like the mistress of the house. She's a...well...let's just say she's quite a woman." He walked with the young Jamaican to the steps, continuing to refuse David's assistance until the pain finally forced him to take the lad's arm at the fifth step. Even so, he was determined not to complain in front of the young seafarer.

The foyer of the mansion was like another world to David, equally impressive as its exterior. The closest thing he had ever seen to its grandeur was the governor's mansion at King's Town—the very one Sir Henry Morgan had originally commissioned as his private residence following the sack of Panama in 1666. Except for the fresco ceiling depicting the founding of the colonies, along with their thirteen crests, the interior of the Forrestal mansion was made entirely of hand-carved mahogany and cedar. While David stood in awe, he failed to notice the stately woman in her early seventies approach from a room behind him.

She stopped just past the arched doorway and followed David's gaze up to the ceiling. "Alex, did you let in another mockingbird?"

Alex gave a start and turned. "No, dear. Our young guest is just admiring the artwork on our ceiling."

David turned to look at the elderly lady. Anne Forrestal stood to nearly David's height of five foot ten inches, with strong, almost manly features framed in a close arc of silver curls. She wore a high-necked gown of light blue brocade and carried a small book of poetry before her in cupped hands. As her gaze fixed on David, her face paled slightly, as if an arctic wind had touched her fair skin. The book of poems fell to the floor with a slap, and she brought her right hand to her mouth to cover her astonishment.

Mister Forrestal stepped toward her. "Dear, what is it?"

"I..." She reached out to Alex's offered hand.

"David, help me get my wife to the sofa!" With a man on each arm, Mrs. Forrestal was assisted to the parlor where a servant girl was cleaning. "Maggie, get your mistress a moist cloth and smelling salts! Quickly now!"

The servant rushed from the room while Alex tried to communicate with his wife, but her eyes were fixed on David as if she had seen death himself.

"What is it, dear? What's the matter?"

She turned her head slowly to gaze into her husband's eyes and began to blink. "Who is he? Where did you find the lad?"

"This is David Noble, the young man I've been telling you about for days. He's the one who'll be going with Captain Jones to bring the cannons from King's Town."

The indentured servant returned with the required items.

Alex took them and began to wipe her forehead. "Dear, are you all right?"

"Yes, I think so." Mrs. Forrestal looked once again into the young visitor's eyes and shuddered slightly. Some of the color had now returned to her cheeks. "When I first looked at you, Mister Noble, I mistook you for someone I knew as a young girl. It must have been the light—the way it was cast across your eyes and nose."

"I was here—in Charles Town—last year, but I don't believe we met, ma'am." David looked to Alex and back to her. "I'm told I have a strong resemblance to my father—Charles Noble. He's in shipping. Perhaps you met him once."

"Perhaps."

One of the servants stepped to the hallway and looked to the three. Alex saw him. "Thomas has already laid your things out in your room, David." He looked to the servant and received a confirming nod. "We've a few minutes before we eat, and I'm sure you'd like the opportunity to freshen up first."

"Yes, that would be most welcome."

Alex turned to the servant. "Thomas, show David to his room and the bath. He'll be staying with us for several days." He turned back to David. "We'll dine in twenty minutes."

"Thank you again, both of you." He stepped to the hallway and followed the servant to the second floor and his room.

***

Dinner was a simple but tasty affair consisting of roast beef and chicken with candied plums and tea. David ate like a starving man—taking several servings of everything.

Anne cleared her throat. "Alex and Captain Jones have told me all about this fantastic quest you are about to embark upon. I must assume everything went well in King's Town?"

David wiped his mouth with the fine linen napkin and nodded. "There isn't that much to tell, ma'am. My father read all the letters and was pleased. He'll begin loading the cannons just as soon as the ship arrives."

Alex smiled. "What about the rendezvous at sea? Did he have any difficulty with the dual ships and at that aspect of the agreement?"

"Yes, he was very surprised until he read Mister Hewes' letter. His first reaction was that you didn't trust him, but now he agrees that the transfer at King's Town would present an enormous security problem—with not only pirates, but with the King's men."

Anne had been studying his features again. "What do you know about your father's background?"

"Nothing much, except that he was an orphan. He was purchased and raised by a wealthy merchant who left the business to my father when he died."

"So you don't know where he was born, or to whom?"

"No." David shook his head. "We don't even know his real name."

Alex gave a chuckle. "Does it really matter who his father was, as long as he delivers those weapons?"

She gave her husband's hand a pat. "Of course it doesn't matter. I was only making conversation." She made an excuse to go to the kitchen.

David used her absence to change the subject to a topic he knew Alex would enjoy. "Sir, will there still be time to tour the two ships this afternoon?"

"Of course there will!" Alex wiped his mouth and pushed himself up from his chair with a groan. "Give me a minute to tell Anne that we're leaving, and then I'll be right with you."

In the kitchen, he found his wife moistening her face with a cloth. He put a comforting arm around her shoulders. "Dear, are you sure you're all right? You were getting pale again just before you left the table."

"I don't know what it is." She set down the towel. "Maybe I just need a little rest."

"Why don't you lie down while I take Noble down to the fitter's dock?"

"That would be good. Yes, a short nap would help." She gave Alex a kiss on the cheek, turned and walked to the sitting room. He followed to make certain she got to the sofa. She sat down and turned to him. "Don't fret yourself, Alex. I'm stronger than you think."

By the time the Forrestal carriage had arrived back at the dock, the fitters had hoisted the enormous foreyard and were securing it to the lower crosstrees of the foremast. A flock of local children scrambled about the remaining stack of hewn timbers, collecting firewood for their parents. Alex and David stepped from the carriage amidst the teams of sawyers and fitting gangs moving to and from the massive ships.

"Come here, Mister Noble." The old man limped toward the stern of the closest ship. "I want you to see a true artisan at work." High on the stern, like monkeys perched on the side of a Hindu temple, hung two half-naked carpenters. With each strike of their mallets against chisel, walnut-sized chips flew from the expensive wood. David stood for a moment marveling at the two young men and their craftsmanship.

David waited for a break in the pounding and called out. "You, there, with the red hair!"

The nearest of the two turned and looked at the Jamaican with a flash of emerald green eyes. He lowered his mallet. "You talkin' to me, Govn'r?"

"Yes, you! I was admiring your work! Where did you learn it?"

"Learnt it on Tortuga, I did! Innkeeper o' the Musket's Muzzle—he be the one what learned me the trade, Govn'r!"

"You're Henry Morgan, aren't you?"

"Aye, an' I be the great, great, great Grandson o' Sir Henry—the same what sacked Panama in '66 an' took the King's blade on 'is shoulder fer it!" The lad took another careful slice of mahogany from the side of a partially carved windmill and looked down at David. "Say, 'ow be it ya know me name, Govn'r? I don't 'member speakin' to yer likes 'afore."

"I heard a story about you in King's Town—how you killed the notorious Captain Claw with one swing of a mangrove root."

The orange-haired lad smacked his fellow carver on the toe with his mallet. "Did ya hear that?"

"Ow!" The other carver pulled back his foot and rubbed the injured tow.

"Tolt ya I were famous!" He turned and called down to David. "You tell 'im, Govn'r! He'll believe ya!" Henry tilted his head as he thought.

"Captain Claw? With a mangrove root? That were a long time ago, Govn'r!"

Forrestal touched David's arm. "I've hired only the best to prepare these two ships—only the best." While they continued to admire the ornate carvings, a large man with bushy blond eyebrows and an unkempt mustache thundered down the gangway and across the dock towards them. Over his bald crown lay a powdered wig, which looked like last year's robin's nest blown onto his head in a gale. His nose and cheeks were covered with a spider web of purple veins—mute testimony to the thousand hogsheads of brew he'd consumed over the years.

"Ahoy, Mister Forrestal!" The man's accent was thick and very Dutch. "You come to see how Captain Van Mourik hide der cannons, ya?"

The shipbuilder leaned close to David and whispered. "This is going to be an experience you'll not soon forget." He turned to greet the approaching Woodshoe. "Ah, Captain Van Mourik!"

"I take it this is our Dutch captain?"

"Yes, it is."

The Dutchman's ham hock of a right hand was already extended for the painful greeting as Forrestal whispered another warning. "Don't ever underestimate the man for his blubber. I've seen him break an oak belaying pin with his bare hands."

David's eyes began to flicker in anticipation of the painful handshake.

Alex stepped back and out of Van Mourik's path toward the Jamaican. "Jan Van Mourik, this is David Noble. You two will be spending a lot of time together in the next few months."

Like so many hefty people, the large Dutchman was loud and tended to get too close when he spoke. An intermittent shower of saliva descended onto David throughout the rough greeting.

"I been waiting a long time to meet der man mit' der cannons an' der treasure!" He paused for a labored breath. "You call me 'Dutch,' ja?"

"Damn it, Jan!" Forrestal spoke in a loud whisper, close to the Dutchman's ear. "I told you to keep quiet about the treasure! Do you want every pirate in the Atlantic on our heels the moment we leave Charles Town?"

"Oh, you forgive me please, Mister Forrestal?" The big man let go of David's hand. "I be more careful from now on. You see!"

"If you can keep your mouth shut, you can show Mister Noble what you've been up to on the gun deck."

"Ah, goot!" Dutch was relieved that forgiveness had been granted. "You follow mit me to der gun deck, an watch yer steps, ja?" They followed his stumbling gate up to the gangway, holding back so their combined weight would not break the straining planks.

The main deck was cluttered with workmen, each with his set of tools and specific job. Van Mourik led the two men aft to the companionway and down to the second deck where a large bale of cotton was secured to the hull by ropes. Next to the bales were several large chains laid in parallel rows.

"Morgan an' me been figurin' fer days mit der cannons, Mister Forrestal, an' we tink we got her figured goot dis time."

"Morgan?"

Van Mourik gave his employer a worried look. "Aye. He had some goot ideas on how we gonna hide dem."

"Well, since Morgan knows already, why don't we call him in while you explain your plan to us, Dutch?"

"Goot idea!" The Dutchman walked to the ladder and bellowed. "Morgan!"

David waited for the Dutchman to return. He swept his arm toward the cotton bales. "So, just what are we supposed to be looking at?"

"Them bales, Govn'r!" Henry Morgan dropped like a cat to the gun deck and strutted forward. "They ain't real!"

"Not real?" David stepped to one of the bales and touched it.

"Watch dis!" In a moment, Dutch and Henry released the ropes and lifted the large bale as if it weighed only a hundred pounds. Hidden underneath the shell was a large shipboard cannon. They turned the bale around and set it on the deck with the open end toward their employer and the Jamaican.

David walked around the bale and stopped at the cannon. "This is ingenious!"

Henry beamed with pride. "Aye, Govn'r!"

David turned to Alex. "When we return, what cargo will we carry?"

"Your father will have this deck filled with large barrels of molasses." Mister Forrestal turned to his two employees. "Which one of you came up with this?"

"It vas mostly young Morgan's idea."

Henry gave Van Mourik's arm a backhand slap. "Ah, Dutch, ya ain't doin' yerself 'alf fair."

"Well, I don't care who's more responsible." Forrestal pulled two shiny gold coins from his watch pocket and handing them to the pair.

"Go have yourselves a nice dinner on me. You've both earned it twice over."

The Dutchman put the coin between his oversized teeth to test its metal, but noticed Alex's disapproving stare and pulled it from his mouth.

"Just a habit, sir." Henry had found that it was a daily thing to apologize for the large man. "We know yer money's good, don't we, Dutch?"

"I know you do." Alex gave the pair a fatherly grin. "But if you'll excuse us, I've several more things to show my friend before tea time."

"It were a pleasure meetin' ya, Govn'r." Henry stuck the gold coin in his right eye like a gentleman's monacle and extended his hand.

"And you, Henry." David shook the lad's hand and then followed Alex to the ladder and up to the main deck. A moment later, the shipbuilder and the Jamaican stood on the dock studying the ship's planking just above her water line.

"Your men did an incredible job, Mister Forrestal. I'm no more than a single span away and I still can't see the gun ports."

"One of my other sawyers did it. He cut the planks to the precise length and butted the ends together, but with different lengths so you would not see a hard vertical line. A thick coat of paint will finish the job."

"But if we have to use the cannons..?"

"Your first volley will take care of opening the ports. Of course, that would end the deception."

David looked up into the rigging at the workers. "I've dreamed all my life of going to sea in a ship like this."

"Not this one. It won't be carrying any guns until they're loaded by your father at King's Town." He turned and pointed to the second Silver Cloud, across the dock. "There's your ship. An exact duplicate of this one, but she's going fully armed."

"How many cannons?"

"Twenty in all, collected from every source available. We've come up with an excellent mix of short and long range pieces, plus a half dozen swivel guns for the rails."

"Are they from our foundries or from Europe?"

"They're all from Europe. Some from Scotland, a few from England, and the rest from Spanish and French ships my privateers have taken. She's as big as a frigate, but since she's only a conversion, her design allowed for but twenty cannons. Even so, I believe Captain Jones will be pleased."

"I have a question, sir." David looked back at the special planking that hid the gun ports.

"Yes?"

"If our mission and these disguised frigates are supposed to be a secret, then what about all these carpenters and fitters? Won't they figure it out when they bring the cannons aboard?"

"When these men are paid and dismissed, another set of men—your crew for the voyage—will come up from Mister Hewes's shipping company at Edenton."

"Ah! Mister Hewes told us about all the men who were out of work because of his lost ships."

"Well, it's those very men who'll install the cannons and other special provisions. As I told you, other than Captain Van Mourik and Henry Morgan, these workmen here today and your crew will never meet."

"So they're both coming along?"

The old man nodded.

"It'll be good having Morgan along. My uncle tells me it's good luck to have at least one man aboard with red hair."

The two continued their tour of the ships for another hour and then returned to the mansion for tea, as they had promised Anne they would.

By four bells, or six o'clock, the spring sun had fallen so low toward the western hills that further work in the yards was impossible. The sawyers, painters and other shipfitters left the dock in small groups. Two of the last to depart were Henry Morgan and Jan Van Mourik.

"Me belly be cryin' fer a noggin o' grog, Dutch! What say we stop at the Patriot fer a drink?" Henry flipped his coin high into the evening sky and caught it behind his back.

Dutch, admiring the lad's trick, tried to imitate the feat, but failed. He scrambled around on the ground searching for his lost treasure. After a lengthy and unsuccessful search in the grass, Dutch looked up at the lad.

"Ja! Sounds goot to me. And maybe we get us some grub too, ja?" By now the captain's knees were wet with mud, but he wasn't going to get up until he found his reward.

"Why looky 'ere!" Henry lifted his foot. "There's yer bleedin' coin, right there under me foot!" He was pleased with his joke on the Dutchman, but the cruelty was wasted on the good-natured Woodshoe.

The Patriot's Rest was noisier than Forrestal's dock, what with all the sailors and tavern wenches calling obscenities at each other from across the public room and fighting for the silver that flowed so fast and free. The two men took a small table near the back of the tavern that became available when a woman of the night lured a rum-soaked sailor away to her nest. Henry ordered a bottle of the Patriot's best, the stuff that hadn't been diluted yet, along with two cups. Within a half hour, Dutch had consumed most of the bottle himself, and set to bragging.

"Related to Sir Henry Morgan, are ya?" Dutch struggled for a full breath. "Well back in der olt country—before I went to sea—I were a constable fer six years, ja?"

"Go on!" Henry pretended he was just as drunk as the old Woodshoe. "You? A bleedin' constable?"

"I was! An' a right goot one too!" The large man spilled half his glass on the table. He looked at the liquid for a moment, removed his wig and then mopped up what he could. He held it up to Henry. "Comes in handy, dis here vig, ya?"

Henry burst into laughter while Van Mourik twisted the hairpiece between his large hands, squeezing what he could back into his cup. Satisfied with the effort, he attempted to replace the tangled mess on his bald head.

Henry leaned close and tugged at Van Mourik's ear. "If you can keep a secret, Dutch, I'll tell ya 'bout a treasure what I know of on Tortuga."

"A treasure, you say?" Dutch looked about the tavern suspiciously, pulled a fat finger across his lips in a salute of silence, surged forward and turned an ear to the lad. "My lips are sealed, Henry!"

"I helped Joshua Smoot bury nearly a thousand pieces of eight behind the Musket's Muzzle four years ago." It was a lie, as bait often is.

"Dat's not'ing!" Dutch grabbed his young friend by the collar and pulled him nose-to-nose, forcing Henry to turn his head away from the foul breath. "The Silver Cloud with the cannons is sailin' fer Dead Man's Chest in a fortnight ta dig up nearly a million British pounds in golt!"

Henry set the hook. "No!"

"An' Henry, we're part of dat crew!" Dutch toppled backward into the upright position and wiped his itchy nose across his sleeve. When he finally opened his eyes, he made the proudest look he could. "How's dat fer a treasure story?"

"I've heard tell of that treasure, Dutch, but word is nobody's alive what knows where it's buried."

"Don't be so sure o' dat, my little friend!" Dutch's beady blue eyes flashed with pride. He looked about the tavern once again and tried to lower his voice. "I hear one of dem who buried it'll be goin' wit us, soon as we got da Silver Cloud ready fer sailin'." Dutch's attention was seized by the prominent bosoms of the barmaid standing next to his shoulder.

Her nasal twang could curdle milk. "You two done with them cups, or what?"

"Come here an' give Dutch a little kiss!" The fat man pulled the woman down into his lap. She let out a giggle and slipped her hand into his pocket while they traded kisses.

***

Alex and Anne Forrestal sat near the fireplace and listened as Robert, who had finally acceded to the requests they had been making since he'd arrived at their house, described the massacre of the Royal James crew at Flint's Island. Captain Steele had beaten David for the second time at chess, and had just begun his third attack on the younger man.

Alex scooted to the front edge of his chair. "Then the only reason you and your wife were spared by Flint was for your ransom value?"

"I was worth a ransom to my father, sir, and I also knew where my granduncle's half of the treasure was buried. Moira helped me bury it, but as far as the pirates were concerned, her only value was that she was a woman. With her father dead, there was nobody left to ransom her, and John Flint and several of the others wanted her for their deviant and perverted purposes."

"Dreadful!" Anne set her teacup on the tray and stood. "Gentlemen, if you'll excuse Alex and me, it's past our customary hour to retire." All of the men rose and watched her walk to the archway from the library. She stopped and looked back at her husband. He was still seated. "Alex?"

"I'll be along in a moment, dear." Alex looked to Robert and back to Anne. "I want to ask Mister Ormerod a few more questions. Do you mind?"

"It's after ten, Alex, and you know how crabby you get when you stay up too late."

Alex gave her a defiant, almost child-like look, and then turned back to Robert.

"How did you...ahh...keep your wife to yourself if it was just you and this Peter Coleaer pitted against the entire crew?"

"John Silver told me to put my mark on her." Robert traced a cross on his left palm. "It's the pirate's way to show his mates that a woman is his."

"A mark?"

"With my dirk. I had to cut an X in the palm of her hand or watch her be raped and killed."

"Well, well." Alex sat back against the pillows. "Since you and she are now happily married, it obviously worked."

"Not quite." Robert paused to remember that dark night. "I was thrown into a ring of the cutthroats anyway, and forced to fight Billy Bones for her."

Alex sat forward. "Go on!"

"I had a clear advantage over Bones, for two reasons. First, he was three sheets to the wind, as the pirates say, and second, I'd done some Indian fighting. I gave him a bad cut to the face, starting at his right eye, and running all the way down the cheek to the corner of his mouth." Robert traced the knife cut across his own face. "That pretty much ended the fight. Next thing we knew, John Silver ushered the four of us—Peter, Moira, Ben and me—aft to a waiting boat while he somehow set half the crew against the other half with knives."

"How wonderful!" Alex clapped his hands like a child on Christmas morning. "And here you are, some twenty years later, on your way to dig up that same treasure you buried! It's such a marvelous story!"

There was a knock at the front door. Alex and his four guests fell silent while the servant opened the door. There were muffled voices, and then a servant entered the room.

"It's Captain Jones and Mister Gunn."

Pleased, Alex pushed himself up and followed the others to the massive foyer. "We were beginning to worry about you two."

"My apologies, sir. Ben and I wanted to stop in as many of your local taverns as possible."

After the introductions and hand shakes, Ben gave John a nervous look. "Captain Jones said that he wanted to find out what the people of Charles Town had to say about the goings on here at your shipyard."

"And what did you hear about my twin ships?"

"No fewer than a dozen different stories. But not one of them mentioned the treasure or the cannons."

"That's exactly what we wanted to hear!" Alex turned back toward the parlor. "I don't know if I need to offer you two more drinks, but please come in and join us."

They all returned to the parlor, and everyone except Alex sat down. "Mister Ormerod has been telling us of his thrilling true-life adventures. He turned to Ben. "And if just half the stories that he and Mister Noble have been telling us about you are true, Mister Gunn, you're quite an interesting fellow."

Robert scowled. "I meant to ask, Mister Noble. How did you hear any stories about Mister Gunn?"

"I..."

"There are only a handful of men still living, apart from my wife and me, who know anything of Ben Gunn, especially his involvement with the treasure and the bloody events of two decades ago."

Before David could conjure a plausible explanation, Alex interrupted. "Gentlemen, we could tell sea stories all night, but my wife is correct. I really need my sleep. I'm sure Captain Jones and Mister Gunn would benefit from some sleep at this point, too. Please don't keep them up much longer."

Captain Steele was quick to join Alex as he limped from the foyer toward the stairs where a servant was waiting.

"Mister Forrestal."

"Yes, Captain, what is it?"

"May I speak with you for a moment before you go up?"

"You sound grim, Alan, as if you're carrying a heavy burden."

"I am, sir. If you still intend that the Eagle to escort the Silver Cloud, then you and Mister Hewes will have to find a new master for one of the ships."

"I've noticed the hard looks you've been giving Captain Jones since he stepped into my home. What's happened between you two?"

"We nearly killed each other after New York, just before he took his unauthorized side trip." Steele shook his head. "I'd not be a proper choice as the man's protector."

His words shook the older man. "Alan, there's nobody else to do the job." He put a hand on the captain's arm. "I've no choice but to send you."

"What about Captain Johnson? The Swan's just as capable a ship as the Eagle. And besides, Johnson was tellin' me a couple months back that he wanted to see some of this kind of action."

"The Swan has already set off for New Orleans. She won't be back until long after the two Silver Clouds have departed." The old man grew stern. "You have no idea how important this mission is, and how desperately I need you, Alan."

"Then why don't you tell me how important it is, sir? Everybody else around here seems to know."

The old man rubbed his eyes like a person waking from a long sleep. With a groan, he asked Captain Steele to join him in the kitchen where they could speak in private.

***

The smells of breakfast cooking in the Forrestal kitchen drew John and David down before the rest of the guests. To their surprise, Anne Forrestal stood at the pastry table in a white cotton dress, with flour to her elbows.

John sniffed the air and studied the little pile of white balls stacked on the pastry table. "Those look good. What are they?"

"They're sour milk biscuits." She flashed the two young men a broad smile. "Alex keeps telling me I'm famous all over the eastern seaboard for my baking." She continued to form the little rolls as Ben Gunn stepped to the kitchen door, drawn from his room by the same delicious smells.

"Am I missing something?" Ben looked about for something to eat.

Anne looked up. "Alex is having coffee on the back porch with Captain Van Mourik. Why don't you three join them until the servant calls you for breakfast?" She noticed the odd look on Ben's face. "Perhaps you two should go on. I think Mister Gunn wants to ask me something."

John gave a chuckle. "As long as you're sure you'll be safe with the old pirate,"

"I'll be quite all right, Captain Jones." She gave John and David a motherly smile. "Go along now, and tell Alex some more of those fascinating sea stories."

Ben was still studying her when she once again wiped the flour from her hands. "Pray forgive me for prying, Ma'am, but I've been thinking about this since we met. Have you ever been up in Boston?"

"Yes I have, Mister Gunn, but many years ago."

"Did we meet there once?"

"In Boston?" She shook her head. "No. We've never met in Boston."

"But you seem so familiar, ma'am." He studied her for several moments. "I'm almost certain..."

She turned her back and began cutting out another batch of biscuits, but stopped and turned back to the old man. "If you do happen to remember where we met, Mister Gunn..."

"Ma'am?"

"Nothing." Then she reconsidered. "Later." She turned back to her biscuits and began humming a familiar sea ballad.

***

After a large breakfast, Alex escorted his guests to the library for a late-morning brandy. He broke open a fresh box of Cuban cigars and offered them to those who had developed the habit. There was a large bundle of new charts lying on the desk, their seals yet unbroken.

"Gentlemen!" Alex raised his glass and looked across at David. "My wife tells me that Mister Martingale delivered these charts earlier this morning. If they're what I believe them to be, we'll all be anxious to see them."

David set his glass down and searched quickly through the rolled parchments until he came upon the two he wanted. Cutting the seals carefully with a letter opener, he spread them out before the others.

John stepped close and gave them a cursory inspection. "These are wonderful!"

"Mister Martingale and his sons draw all my charts. The older son spends half the year at sea updating their master charts."

David took a dry quill pen and pointed to Buck Island. "This line shows the channel—a narrow break in the coral—to the west beach." He looked at the small numbers surrounding the island. "If for any reason we needed to take the Silver Cloud to that beach, we could only do it for an hour either side of high tide."

Robert stepped to the table and spoke with a sarcastic tone. "The only thing your mapmaker's left out is the location of the treasure."

John gave him a narrow look. "What's the matter with you, Ormerod? We need these charts, especially for the anchorages they show."

"But now that mapmaker knows exactly where we're going." He turned to Alex. "With all respect, sir, you may have cost us the secrecy we've sought so diligently to preserve!"

Alex smiled. "You underestimate me, sir. I had Mister Martingale make charts of at least a dozen different small islands along the major shipping lanes. He has no reason to suspect that this one is more, or less important than the rest." Everyone in the room relaxed. "I told him I wanted to locate a small island where I could establish a warehousing and ship repair facility. If you'll look at the legend, you'll see that Mister Martingale suggests Buck Island is not a good choice for the facility because it lacks a fresh water supply, and because widening the channel through the coral reef would be prohibitively expensive."

Ben joined the others at the table. "Did he make similar notations for Spyglass?"

"I told him to do so." Alex selected the other chart and spread it over the first. He read through the several notes in the legend. "He says that Spyglass would make an excellent island for a repair facility, except that it's too far off the normal shipping lanes to be practical."

John turned the chart around so he and the former buccaneer could get a closer look. He pointed to Captain Kidd's Lagoon. "That's where we'll anchor, Ben." He gave the ex-pirate a gentle squeeze on his shoulder. "Provided we have time before we make the rendezvous." David raised an inquisitive brow at John.

Ben ran his hands over the chart, along the east and west coast lines, and finished at the lagoon. "That's where young Hawkins an' the rest of 'em dropped anchor back in '64." He touched the island with a bony finger. "Be kinda pleasant to look on my old manor again."

"And you will, Ben." John lay the chart of Dead Man's Chest on top again. "I'm almost certain of it."

John turned to Robert. "That's quite a reef, Ormerod. Exactly where did your granduncle put you and the others ashore?"

"We came in from the south in the long boats, using that same break in the coral to reach the beach. He put us off just here." Robert's penknife came to rest at the lower end of a strip measuring about a hundred yards from north to south and forming a thin crescent at the west end of the small island. "He picked us up again several days later at the same beach."

"Can you see the place where you buried the treasure?"

Robert gave John a grin. "Good try, Jones."

"I'd have been remiss not to try." The young captain gave Robert a squint. "Besides, you should let somebody else know where it's buried, just in case something happens to you."

"Sorry. If I die, the secret dies with me. That's the way Mister Jefferson and the others want it and that's the way it shall be."

"Well, I don't like it!"

Alex cleared his throat. "Not to change the subject, Captain Jones, but I've been going over this list of preparations you gave me. We've already taken care of the bulk of the items, but you'll have to deal with the ship's surgeon and cook yourself for some of this." Alex tilted his head forward to peer at John over his spectacles. "As far as the training and watch bills, I don't see how you're going to make any progress until you assign your friends here to their duties."

"I've been considering that." John looked about at the others. "I have all of the assignments covered except for Mister Ormerod and Ben."

"How about your cabin boy?" Robert grabbed a servant's towel from the back of Alex's chair and hung it over his left arm. "Might I be capable of that?"

John ignored him and turned to Alex. "After lunch, I'll make time to see the surgeon and the cook. Could you arrange those meetings for me?"

"Why not right now, John? Since you appear to need a little more time to think about the officer assignments, you could speak with the surgeon and be back before we eat."

"Yes...I'd like that."

"If my guess is right, we'll catch Doctor McKenzie aboard. He's been laying in his supplies since last night."

***

Alex led John aft through the gun deck. "Doctor McKenzie!" He called toward the small storeroom the surgeon had been assigned. "Are you there, Doctor?"

"Aye!" The man spoke with a Scottish brogue, much thicker than John's. "If your shoes are clean, you can enter. If not, I'd appreciate you speaking from the companionway."

"Our feet are clean, Doctor. You can put up your shillelagh." John stepped inside the small space. The doctor was bent in half, his head deep in a wooden box of oddly shaped and gaily colored bottles. His voice reverberated inside the chest. "Can you not tell the difference between Irish caterwauling and a fine Scottish brogue?"

John thickened his speech to match the doctor's. "Aye, sir, I ken the difference."

The doctor straightened up. He was a thin man of thirty, with sharp features and thick black hair brushed back over the ears. His eyes widened when he saw who his visitors were. "Mister Forrestal! Flog me sir, but I didn't recognize your voice. I thought you were one of the workmen."

"It's all right, Doctor. I've someone very important for you to meet."

The doctor's face beamed in anticipation of his employer's next words.

"Adam McKenzie, this is the master and commander of the Silver Cloud, Captain John Paul Jones."

"Very pleased to meet you, sir!" The Scotsman took John's hand and pumped it several times. "Very pleased!"

"And I'm equally pleased to meet you, Doctor." He pulled his hand free and turned back to Alex. "This should only take an hour or so. I'll still need that talk with the cook if you will arrange it."

"I'll have him at the house when you're finished here." With that he excused himself and returned to his waiting carriage.

"I'm sorry for my comment about the shoes, sir, but some of these workers forget to clean the mud from their feet before they bring me my medical supplies."

"No offense taken."

"How may I be of service?"

"I'd like to go over your list of medical supplies."

"Oh?" Adam gave John a concerned look. "That may be more difficult than—"

"You do have a list, I trust?"

"I've a dozen lists, and therein lies the problem. I've divided it up between all these crates so I can take my inventory as I open each one." He looked around the cluttered room for a moment. "If you can give me ten minutes, sir, I'll collect them for you."

"That'll be fine." John stepped to the companionway. "I'll be in my cabin when you're ready."

The master's cabin spanned the entire aft width of the ship and was nearly as long as it was wide. It smelled like a sawmill, with the subtle aroma of Cavendish pipe tobacco and wax mixed in. John's hand went to one of the massive waxed overhead beams. He relished the rich texture of the hand-rubbed grain.

Much better than pitch and turpentine. A man can feel a ship's soul better through wax.

A massive table was positioned near the rear hatches, with a large chair at its after side, facing forward. This table was as long as a tall man and four feet across, doubling as the navigation table when the officers were not gathered about it for a meeting or their mess. At the starboard side of the room was the master's bunk and toilet, while against the larboard side was a large oaken cabinet for the storage of his clothes, ship's charts and other essentials of life at sea. At David's suggestion, several sets of uniforms had been prepared and hung in the wardrobe, along with an equal number of new boots and shoes. John was busy trying on one of the coats when the doctor knocked.

"Come in, Doctor!" John lay the coat across his bunk.

"Shall I leave these on your table?"

"I'd prefer you stay while I read through them, if you don't mind." John gestured toward a chair. "Please, and take a seat." He picked up the stack of papers and walked to the row of windows for better light. "I'd want you here in case I have any questions."

"As you please." Adam eased himself into a chair and watched his new captain pace back and forth along the row of larboard windows, studying the lists. At the third sheet, John gave a low groan and looked across at the doctor.

"Anything amiss, sir?"

"Where'd you come up with the quantities on this list?"

"It's my standard kit, sir. I know what ten men need for one month and then I simply multiply in the size of the crew and the length of the voyage. Mister Forrestal has provided me with those missing numbers." He stood and approached John. "Why, is there something missing?"

"Did Mister Forrestal tell you what we'd be doing on this mission?"

"Just that we're headed for the Antilles chain. Nothing more."

"Did he mention anything about pirates?"

"Yes he did, sir, but that list provides more than enough supplies for any injuries we might expect."

"I'd agree with you, if this were only a merchant voyage."

Adam gave John a studied look. "It's not?"

"No." John scanned the remaining pages quickly and then took his chair at the table. "For now, I can't tell you where we're going or what we'll be doing when we get there. But you'll have to double the number of battle dressings you've listed." John selected another list. "And we'll need a full supply of apothecary chemicals and extra…"

"It sounds like you're taking the Silver Cloud into battle."

"I hope not, but it's a distinct possibility." John pushed the stack of papers across to the doctor. "Can you increase your supplies to a fighting ship's inventory?"

"Aye, sir, but it'll take me a few more days. I have my battle list at home."

"Order what you need, and as quickly as possible."

"Yes, sir." Adam stood and straightened the pieces of paper. "Will there be anything else?"

"Yes, one thing more. I'm a stickler for personal cleanliness. I want you to teach the men how to keep themselves clean."

"I'll order an extra supply of soap and rubbing alcohol, sir."

"Good." John stood and took a step toward the door. "You may—"

"How do you feel about swim calls, sir?"

"Swim calls?"

"If you let the men swim at least once a week, they'll be a cleaner and happier crew."

"Let them swim?" John considered the idea with a tilt of the head. "I'll go you one step further, Doctor. I'll make swimming mandatory."

"You can do that if you're so inclined, sir, but why not let the men think they're working for the weekly swim?"

"I don't take your meaning. The only issue here is that they maintain a certain level of personal hygiene. If I order them to swim and to keep themselves clean, it'll be done."

"Yes it will, sir, as it should be." The doctor took a breath and let it out slowly. "But think of the good morale you'll create by letting the men believe they've earned the right to swim? They'll work harder and keep the Silver Cloud twice as shipshape if it's for a reward, rather than to avoid a flogging."

John stared at the man for a moment and wondered why the doctor wasn't a ship's captain. Perhaps, John thought, if I'd treated the crew of the Falmouth Packet more like McKenzie's suggesting, they wouldn't have jumped ship.

"I like your recommendation, Doctor." He led the man to the cabin door, where he hesitated.

"Is there something else, sir?"

"Just one thing. If you ever see me doing anything you believe to be detrimental to our crew's morale, tell me. I don't want officers who agree with me just because I'm their captain."

"If you're serious, sir, then you can count on it."

***

John sat in the library with Alex Forrestal, going over what seemed to be an endless series of questions. It had been a long and tiresome morning.

Alex gave a huff of frustration while he pushed aside the stack of lists and heaved himself up from his chair. "Captain Jones, most of what you ask has already been taken care of by my fitters and ship's company. If you'll give me the benefit of the—" He was interrupted by a lean man in his mid-thirties, standing in the doorway. The man fidgeted like Ben Gunn.

"Ah!" Alex was thankful for the chance to disengage from the young Scotsman. "Seamus Barragan, the ship's cook. And ten minutes early, besides."

"I were told you wanted to see me, Mister Forrestal." Seamus's tone was apologetic, even though he had not yet spoken or done anything offensive. "What ever it is, sir, I didn't do it, an' it ain't my fault neither." It was a tired joke—one the Irishman had used often. John rose from his chair and turned to face his former crewman.

"Cap'n Jones!"

John spread his arms and smiled. "In the flesh, Seamus."

"Are you comin' on this 'ere 'venture with us, too?"

"Yes I am."

"Ha! I'm to be ship's cook!" Seamus took a step forward, but checked himself with a sideways glance at Alex. "You hirin' on as one o' the officers?"

"You might say that." John flashed a smirk at the old man. "So, Mister Barragan, have you told the crew yet that they'll have to hold their bread up to the sun before they eat it?"

"That's not fair, sir. There was weevils in that flour from King's Town, an' they only hatched out cause o' the warm weather."

"Relax…I'm only jesting with you." He walked to Seamus with an extended hand. "It's good to have you on the crew."

Seamus took John's hand. "Yeah, you an' me again, just like when we sunk the Tiburon!"

"David Noble's coming along also, and concerning the Tiburon, we only disabled her."

"I been tellin' the rest of the crew we sunk her, sir." The Irishman gave John a searching look and pulled away his hand. "You don't mind, do ya?"

"The officers already know the truth, but I'll let you tell the rest of the crew whatever you wish."

"Thank you, sir."

Alex stepped to the door and stopped. "Well, Captain Jones, it's obvious you know Barragan much better than I do, so I'll leave you two to discuss your business. When you need me again, I'll be with Anne in the kitchen."

The shipbuilder limped from the room with a wince of pain each time his leg brought its complaint against him. By habit, he had learned to inhale every time he put his weight on the painful hip, just in case he needed to curse.

"How'd you get a spot on this cruise, Cap'n Jones? I thought ya had to be somebody special to sign on."

"You could say I knew the right people. But let's talk about me later. Last I saw of you was when I went off watch the night before you and the others drove us onto that mud bank and jumped ship." John gestured for the man to take a seat across the table from him.

"I was hopin' you'd forgotten. I feel bad 'bout that, Cap'n, an' I'd rather not talk 'bout it, if ya don't mind."

"But I do mind." John took his seat. "We'll be at sea for the better part of two months, and I don't want to set any part of the crew against me, as I apparently did you three after Charles Town." John leaned forward. "Why couldn't you and the others wait a few more hours to reach Dahlgren?""

"Well..." The Irishman squirmed, searching for the words. "It were yer treatment o' the crew after Charles Town, sir. Especially Clark."

"Go on."

"Well, it didn't lay well with us what ya did to him. Carini was 'is best friend. It just weren't fair."

"Fair had nothing to do with it!" John was suddenly angry. He stood and walked to the window. After a moment of thought, he turned. "Clark disobeyed a direct order to man the mains'l sheet. When he did that, he put the rest of us in jeopardy! I couldn't allow his act to go unpunished and then expect to maintain discipline for the rest of the trip." He took a moment to calm himself. "Is there more?"

"Aye."

"Go on, Seamus. Get it off your chest, here and now."

"Well, it's like this, sir! You can have strict articles, but when ya make a judgment, ya need to stick to the thing, right or wrong. An' when ya do decide to punish a man, do it quick an' get it over with." When John did not reply, he continued. "Before Charles Town, you seemed to understand why Clark disobeyed yer order. You had him an' the rest o' us believin' he was off yer hook. Then once we're back to sea and thinkin' the incident was forgotten, ya flogs him out o' the blue anyway, like he'd just broke another rule." He stopped to catch his breath. "Ya lost our loyalty that day, Cap'n Jones. We four just couldn't trust ya no more."

"Four?" John turned on the man. "Mister Noble, also?"

"Aye, sir, but he wouldn't agree ta jump ship with us."

"He knew of your plans?" John looked away to think. "Did he say why he stayed behind?"

"Something 'bout a mission you two had..." The Irishman's eyes brightened. "He was talking about this 'ere secret voyage of ours, weren't he?"

"Now that you mention it, I believe he was." John looked out the window at the spring morning and considered the implications of this new revelation. "It wouldn't surprise me if Mister Noble's known about this secret voyage since the day I met him in King's Town."

"When did he tell you 'bout it, sir?"

John didn't answer, but returned to their former subject. "Your advice about giving orders and disciplining the men is well taken, Seamus. If you see me getting out of hand once we're at sea, I'd be obliged if you'd come to me about it."

"I'll do that, sir."

John sat down, and Seamus relaxed a little. "Tell me something else. What happened to you three after Matchotic Creek, and how'd you get hired as our ship's cook?"

"Not that much to tell, sir." He rubbed his nose from side to side. "Clark an' Etinger headed south toward Richmond to find their families, while I went north, up to a place called Alexandria. Couldn't find my people there, so I took a job in the Truman shipyards. After a month in the sawpits, I got word about a planker's job at a small yard back down in Dahlgren, so I packed up the tools I'd collected and went. When the ship we was makin' was finished, I was out o' work. Word come up that they was hirin' a sailin' crew on these here two Dutch ships in Mister Forrestal's yards, so I made it down the coast quick as I could."

"And how, pray tell, did a carpenter's mate become a cook?"

"It were the other men, sir. The company put us—the sailin' crew—in a camp on the north of the town and kept us there 'til yesterday." He stopped and gave John a questioning look. "Why'd they do that, Cap'n Jones? Why didn't they have us help with the last work on the ship?"

"I'll explain that later...once we're at sea."

"Well anyway, the food at the camp was God-awful bad, an' I bore up to the other men's complainin' as long as I could. I finally told 'em I'd done some cookin'. Well, before I knew it, word got to the foreman, an' next thing, I'm the camp cook. Then when it were time to move us down here to the shipyard, everybody told about my cookin', an' here I am. The privateer's cook on a secret mission."

"Who told you the Silver Cloud is a privateer? Who told you we're going on a secret mission?"

"Well, nobody an' everybody." He leaned forward. "Consider it, sir. Why else would they keep the sailin' crew up in that camp, away from everybody and everything happenin' down here at the dock? An' now that we're finally here, they won't let any of us leave the yards to go into town?" He held up a finger. "An' why would they be hidin' all them cannons behind that fake plankin', 'cept to fool other merchantmen?"

John was taken back at the Irishman's grasp of the thing. He leaned back—pretending that it was only of slight importance—pulled a short stack of pepers in front of him and leafed through them. "The reason I called you here was to ask a few questions about our provisions."

"Then you are one of our officers!" Seamus waited for John's nod and continued. "Anything you want to know, you just ask me."

The two talked for more than an hour and a half, until Alex reappeared to announce that coffee was being served in the parlor.

"Thank you, sir." John stood and rubbed his backside. "The cook and I have finished what we needed to discuss, so I'll be with you in a moment."

Seamus welcomed the opportunity to get back to his chores, especially the changes John had suggested. "Then I'll be seein' ya when we set sail, Cap'n Jones?"

"Yes, Mister Barragan. You will."

"An' if anybody asks fer me mark next to yer name for anything, you can count on Seamus Barragan."

"Thank you. I may need that endorsement before this mission is concluded."

Chapter 11

One hundred miles to the south of Charles Town and fifteen miles inland from the Atlantic Ocean lay the small village of Savannah, Georgia. In 1732, this harsh piece of ground—then a wilderness—was granted to James Oglethorpe by King George II for the purpose of creating a settlement for England's poor and those who had been imprisoned for debt. Although its growth was slow, its morals were unusually high—one of its first regulations was the absolute prohibition against the importation of slaves and rum. In 1743, after nearly nine years of rule as their first governor, James Oglethorpe left the colony of Georgia and returned to England. His absence created a political and moral vacuum that was quickly filled by the pirate captain John Flint.

Captain Flint's reputation for cruelty had infected the entire eastern seaboard. Disobedient children were kept in check by the words, "John Flint will eat your heart!" It was common knowledge that in the spring of '39, Flint sailed the Walrus into Salem Harbor with the body of one of his crew killed in action. The rotting thing was sewn up tight in sail canvas and thrown down in the town square. All the townsfolk were rounded up to witness the funeral and interment. With muskets at the full cock and cutlasses drawn, Flint's crew forced the hundred and ten citizens to sing hymns, throw flowers into the grave and even weep for the heathen. When the whole thing was over and the dirt was finally stomped hard over the unholy grave, John Flint was slightly displeased with the performance. To punish the town, he set fire to the church and forced the townsfolk to watch it burn to the ground. Years after the cruel incident had taken place, there was much talk of removing the dead pirate from the sacred graveyard, but none of the townsfolk could muster the courage.

For over a decade, Flint and the merchants of Savannah enjoyed a prosperous, secret and sinful relationship. Flint provided the merchants with high-quality goods at pennies on the dollar, while the merchants provided the pirate and his crew with a safe port and total immunity from the law. A thousand yards to the east of the town's bluff was a seasonal stream that provided irrigation through a system of dikes and gates. John Flint owned the stream and charged the rice plantation owners a fee for opening and closing the gates.

In '65, Captain John Flint died of liver sickness. Captain Billy Bones assumed the position of captain and took the Walrus to sea on several raids. But in the late summer of that same year, while the Walrus was hauled down for repairs in the Bahamas, Bones boarded another ship and ran off to England with Flint's treasure map. Sixteen months later, most of the Walrus's crew had followed Long John Silver to Bristol where they were hired on by Captain Smollet for the expedition to Spyglass Island to retrieve Flint's half of the treasure.

A full decade later, a young and aggressive pirate by the name of Joshua Smoot was approached by the merchants of Savannah and offered the same unholy alliance they had enjoyed with John Flint. The young pirate captain accepted their offer. Although Smoot's true origins were uncertain, several of the older inhabitants of Savannah believed him to be the bastard son of Captain Flint.

To show their gratitude, the town fathers granted title to the Oglethorpe estate to Captain Smoot, much to the consternation of the colony's new governor, James Wright.

High Tortuga, as Smoot had named the mansion, was situated on Abercorn Street overlooking Oglethorpe Square. It was a three-story mansion of red brick, with white trim and four massive columns across the porch. Although built for Oglethorpe, the governor never occupied it, having returned to England before its completion.

Fishbone Smoot, as he was called for his habit of picking his teeth with the rib bone of a barracuda, was in his mid-forties, and looked like he'd been thrown out of hell for meanness. But for a thick mustache that hung two inches below the corners of his mouth, he was clean-shaven, with tar-black hair cut shoulder-length and pulled back in a tight braid at the back of his neck. He had a hawkish nose, deep-set eyes, and a mouth full of crooked teeth, all but hidden beneath his great bushy mustache. A deep scar ran from the corner of his mouth to just above his right ear, where it became lost in the forest of hair at his temple. When he sailed, he wore a flame red coat all cobwebbed over with gold filigree.

At the moment, though, he was more conservatively dressed, and he held a letter in one hand and his dirk in the other. He was ready to kill. "Damn you, Wright! Why the hell do ya keep pretendin' it'd be such a bloody crime to take my money and give me what I deserve?"

"Because you're a pirate, that's why!"

"Aye, but once ya sign the letter o' marque, I'll be just as respectable as any o' yer other pirates! An' ya know I'd be bringin' ya twice the swag as the rest put together!"

"My signature wouldn't change you a farthing, Smoot, and you know it better than I do." The governor looked out onto Oglethorpe Square and the raging storm that tore at the live oak trees. "Unlike you, none of my other captains kill for the pure joy of it." He turned about and scowled at Smoot. "You're nothing but a heartless cutthroat, and that you'll be until your Maker sends you to hell."

"Aye, a pirate through an' through, but 'tis only yer signature on this piece o' parchment what keeps me that way." Smoot laid down the letter with the dirk on top, held up the document, and ten thousand pounds in crisp notes. "Here's yer price, Governor Wright. Take it. The letter's ready fer yer mark."

"Keep your blood money, Smoot. I don't care what you offer. You'll never see my signature on any document that contains your name, except to order your execution." He took up his hat and satchel and walked from the library and into the halway.

Smoot followed. "Where are you going?"

"Back to Atlanta." The Governor pulled open the front door to the rain that blew across the square. "My business here is finished, and you can count yourself fortunate that I even came. Now that I've repaid the debts I owed to those money-hungry merchants who protect you, I hope to never see your evil face again, except with the hangman's rope pulled tight against your throat."

"I'll get that letter o' marque, one way or another, Governor Wright. You can lay to that."

"One way or another?" He stopped and turned in the open doorway. "You aren't so presumptuous or so stupid as to think you can threaten the governor of Georgia, are you, Smoot?"

"Oh, it's much more than a threat. I can promise that you'll sign my letter, and you'll do it without the ten thousand dollars, too."

"And you, Jushua Smoot, can expect a visit from the local constable for that promise!"

"Send yer constable, an' see what good it does. Seems like I remember Constable Gilmore bein' one o' my closest friends and wealthiest accomplices in Savannah. Ha! Ha! Ha!" Smoot slammed the door behind the departing man.

Halfway down the walk toward his waiting carriage, the governor brushed past a youth with carrot-orange hair and green eyes. The two stopped for a moment while their eyes met, and then the governor was gone.

The rain that had fallen most of the morning had soaked the lad to the bone. His unshod and half-frozen feet carried him up the stairway to the protection of the porch. He shook like a dog and then watched the fancy coach clatter away down the cobblestone street. Without knocking, the lad pushed through the front door and stepped into the foyer. One hand held a small, brown satchel. His other hand was in his pocket and wrapped around a small pistol.

"Well! Well!" Smoot stepped in front of the startled young man. "If it isn't my former cabin boy, Henry Morgan! I didn't think I'd ever see the likes of you!"

"Me neither, Gov'n."

"How long's it been since New York—since I tried to kill ya?"

Henry tightened his grip on the pistol, not certain whether the older man still coveted his life.

Smoot clapped a hand onto Henry's shoulder and pointed at the library. "Come in an' have a seat, lad, an' fill yer scupper with a noggin' o' fine Jamaican rum!" He stepped to a sideboard and fetched a clean glass, filled it to the brim, and thrust it at the young man.

"Thank ya, Cap'n." Henry blew the weather from his nose and gave another canine shake of his head. Water droplets rained about him for several seconds before he took a large mouthful of rum. "Ah!" The warming liquor reached his stomach. "In the words o' Darby McGraw, rum'll do a man's innards good every time!"

"So tell me, Henry, where have you been all this time?"

"First, tell me yer not out to kill me no more, Govn'r."

Smoot gave a dismissive wave of his hand. "That was long ago...much too long ago for a regular grudge."

"But the little girl. She died because of me."

"Aye, but I got what I wanted from John Silver, so ye're off me hook, Henry." Smoot poured himself a glass and turned back Henry. "Back to my question. Where have ya been since New York?"

"Here and there. But my latest job was as a carpenter at the Forrestal shipyard up in Charles Town." Henry laid his satchel aside, took the seat across from his former captain, and pointed back toward the front door. "Who was that fancy gentleman what almost put me on me backside?"

"That, my young friend, is the man who'll make Fishbone Smoot a respectable privateer."

"That was the Govn'r of Georgia?"

"Aye, an' I've a plan what'll twist his arm more 'n it's ever been twisted 'afore." Smoot reached across and refilled Henry's cup.

"What kind of plan?"

Smoot stood and walked behind his desk where he had left his dirk on top of the letter. He raised the letter to his nose. He closed his eyes and inhaled deeply. "This kind of plan!"

Before Smoot could open his eyes, Henry circled the desk and snatched the letter from the pirate's hand. He ran across to the far side of the room.

"Got a girlfriend, Govn'r?" Henry mocked while sniffing at the light perfume that escaped from the folded parchment.

"Damn you, Henry!" Smoot palmed his dirk. "Give me that letter!"

The lad began unfolding the paper. "An' if I don't, what ya gonna do 'bout it?"

Before Henry could recoil, Smoot had leaped over the desk and pinned the lad's right hand to the floor with his knife. The boy's scream was like the first scream of a lost soul thrown into hell. "I should take off yer hand here an' now, Henry. It's the least you should pay for killin' that little girl."

"Belay!" Henry watched the blood begin to run from under his hand onto the floor. "I be needin' that hand fer diggin' up the treasure!"

"What treasure?" Smoot snatched back his letter and wrenched his blade loose.

"That's what I'm here fer, Govn'r!" Henry clutched his injured hand to his chest and wrapped his rain-soaked shirttail around it. "I'm here to strike a bargain with ya 'bout a treasure!"

Smoot studied the young man through narrow eyes. He stood and laid the letter on his desk. "I'll ask ya only one more time, Morgan. What treasure?"

Henry scuttled to the corner and pulled his knees up in front of his chest. He pulled the pistol from his pocket with his good hand and leveled it at the older man. "I'll not say nothing', Cap'n...not till we strike our bargain first."

"What sort of a bargain did ya have in mind?"

"I want five shares o' whatever we bring back...treasure and booty put together."

"That's captain's pay!" Smoot shook his head slowly from side to side. "I only get five shares meself!"

"That may be, Govn'r, but my share's gonna be the same as yers, or you an' yer crew can find yer own treasure."

"And how much money will these five shares bring you, Henry?" Smoot was a rogue, but he was a clever rogue. He knew Henry was figuring on a split with over a hundred and fifty men, and he knew enough of his sums to calculate the size of the treasure by Henry's part of it.

Henry smiled. "Not till ya agree to me price."

"I'll have to speak to my crew, but you gotta give me some kinda hint first. They'll be wantin' to know if the work's worth their blood."

Sensing a momentary advantage, the youth gathered his feet beneath himself and pushed up. He stepped to a chair and sat down. "Let's say that its so big that neither of us would ever hafta work again fer the rest our natur'l lives, if we didn't want to."

"Hmmm..." Smoot was interested, and would say anything to get more information. He could always kill the young man when the time was right. "Tell ya what, Henry. If me crew agrees, and mind ya they're not likely—"

"Don't give me that bilge water!" Henry leaned forward and let some of his blood drip onto the desk. He dipped a finger into it and started to draw an island. He stopped and looked up at Smoot. "Your crew does exactly what you tell them to!"

"If I agree—"

"It's aye or nay—nothin' in betwixt!"

Smoot studied the outline in blood. "All right, you can have yer shares, but—"

"All five?" Henry interrupted, reaching across the table for the bottle.

"Aye, all five of everything, just like me." Smoot leaned forward and spoke slowly. "But, if we set sail and this turns out to be another of yer lies, I'll have yer heart fer supper!"

"It's no lie, Govn'r." Henry dipped his finger in the blood again and finished the outline. "You an' me—we be goin' to get—"

Smoot suddenly recognized the shape. "It's the Treasure of Dead Man's Chest...the other half from the Santissima Trinidad!"

Henry sat back and took a large drink of his rum. "Aye, an' what's more, the treasure's to be used to buy your thousand cannons for the Continental forces."

Smoot grabbed Henry by the collar and pulled him close. "Show me yer chart!"

"I don't have none, Govn'r." Henry tapped the bloody outline. "There's only one man what knows that, an' he's settin' sail from the Forrestal shipyards in a fortnight."

Smoot sat back and rubbed the afternoon stubble on his chin. "A fortnight ya say?"

"Aye, a fortnight."

"Besides you an' me, how many know about this?"

"It's a well-kept secret, Govn'r. Only the four or five of 'em what hatched the plan knows."

"And just how, pray tell, did Henry Morgan find out about it, if it's such a big secret?"

"One o' the crew—a big Dutchman with the pride of a dozen men—tolt me." Henry smiled. "Took me a half crown o' rum to loosen his tongue, but he told me enough. All we have to do is beat the Silver Cloud to Dead Man's Chest and watch when they start diggin'."

"And will this Silver Cloud be sailin' alone?"

"I'm not sure of that, Govn'r. There's a rumor that the Eagle, a fourteen-gun privateer, is supposed to be waiting for them at Christiansted—to make certain the way's clear."

"And ye're certain the "Yorkman" will be with them?"

"I seen Mister Ormerod at the shipyard." Henry nodded. "He's goin' with them, Govn'r."

Smoot leaned forward. "Did he see you?"

Henry shook his head. "I turned away before he had a chance, and then I left the place that very day to come here."

Smoot fell into deep contemplation.

After several minutes, Henry broke the silence. "What's the matter, Cap'n?"

Smoot picked up a barracuda bone and picked at a piece of meat wedged between his front teeth. "I was just thinkin'. If we could beat the Eagle to Saint Croix..." He stopped and gave the lad a poke with the sharp bone. "Ya know, Henry, it sure would be a help if you could get yerself on the crew of this Silver Cloud. What da'ya think?"

"It's not possible."

"Why not?"

"Robert Ormerod for starters. It's impossible fer a redhair lad to hide hi'self anywhere—'specially on a ship. An' then there's Cap'n Van Mourik—the one what leaked the whole thing to me. Won't take him long to start askin' me where I've been this last month, an' then he's sure to remember tellin' me 'bout the treasure."

"Then I'll just have to arrange fer a couple of me best men to get on that crew."

"But I tolt ya that the crew's already full up. Been full from before I left the place."

"I have a man what knows how to create the openin' he needs." Smoot gave a chuckle, picked up the letter and ran it under his nose. "An' this, my young friend, an' a short side trip on our way to Dead Man's Chest, will get me that privateer commission I've been wanting for so long."

Henry studied the letter. "Who's the woman? Anybody I would know?"

"We've never met, but we will."

"So ya stole it?"

"Aye, from a postal packet. Ye can get a lot o' information that way."

"Hope it were worth more'n a new rudder this time."

Smoot planted the tip of the dirk in the center of the bloody outline of Dead Man's Chest. "Watch yerself, Morgan. Ya already had yer hand pierced. My next cut will be that insolent tongue." Smoot left the dirk standing while he leaned back to reminisce. "You should have been there—the day we attacked David Noble's postal packet—rather than hiding away from me after New York."

"Missed me, did ya?"

"No, not at all." Smoot put his finger tips together and smiled. "I just think your blood, bones and inards would'a looked better than Danny Hunter's on the spanker, that's all."

Henry gave his captain a dark look.

∗∗∗

It was a morning of excitement at the fitter's docks. The two Dutch merchantmen stood tall and proud in the warm morning sun with their virgin canvas and fresh paint playing games with the crew's nostrils. For those who had come aboard secretly at four in the morning and now sat impatiently below decks, the pungent linseed oil fumes had an almost anesthetic effect. To the uninformed—if such a thing were possible in the small town named for one of England's kings—this was just another launching, not unlike the hundreds the townsfolk had witnessed during the preceding eighteen years. The only remarkable thing about these two magnificent vessels was that they were identical, from their fittings

to the black paint that concealed their gun ports. And even more
unusual were their names. They were both called Silver Cloud. That
was Jefferson's idea. He told the others that it was the only way Captain
Jones could make it back through the blockade.

The crew of the treasure ship was busy making ready to get
underway while John and his officers stood next to the Forrestal
carriage.

Alexander Forrestal leaned his weight against one of his footmen.
"Gentlemen, you'll find your orders and license to trade in the
Caribbean in this sealed packet. I would request—for security reasons—
that you refrain from opening it until you're well underway and beyond
that man-of-war." He handed John the leather case and nodded at the
ship.

John turned and studied the man-of-war at anchor between the
island and the great sand bank that stretched across the harbor to Fort
Sullivan.

"Be on your way, Captain Jones, and remember this. You're doing
God's work! May He be with you and your crew!"

"Thank you, Mister Forrestal." John lifted his hat in salutation and
began to move toward the gangway with the others.

"John!" Alex stepped away from his footman. "One last word, if I
may."

John stepped back to the elderly man. "Sir?"

"I know I raised my voice last night, but I want to assure you that
I'm not angry with you."

"I know that, sir."

"You've a legitimate concern. You'll simply have to trust me that
you'll receive the rendezvous instructions in plenty of time. I can't tell
you who will get them to you, or how, but Mister Jefferson and the
others have made ample provision for any eventuality."

"Even the man's death?" John spoke the words very slowly and with
all the force he dared—just short of angering his superior.

"Yes, John, even his death."

"Well, I certainly hope so, for all of our sakes."

"The Good Lord's in charge, young man. If He sees fit to bring
those cannons to our shores, then no power in this world will thwart
His will. But if He chooses otherwise..."

"I share your faith in God's purposes, but I wish I could share your
optimism, sir." John pulled his sword several inches from its sheath.
"Sometimes a man must put his trust in his own hands." He let the
sword slide back with a ring of brass against steel. "When you remember

us in your prayers, sir, ask that our aim be true and that our hands not waiver when we hold our weapons in battle." He looked across the pier to the second Silver Cloud. "When the second Silver Cloud sails to Jamaica, who will be at her helm?"

"We haven't decided yet, except we know it'll be a skeleton crew. Charles Noble will have to provide the additional men after he loads the cannons."

"For the other officers and myself, I thank you and your lovely wife for everything, Mister Forrestal. Please convey that to her."

"That I will, John. That I will." Alex reached forth and gave his young agent a fatherly handshake of farewell. "Go now, and if you'll allow me to twist the words of your lawyer friend from Virginia, may the good Lord give you and the American colonies liberty, and not death."

With brisk salute, John turned and marched aboard his new ship. The bosun was waiting and piped the crew to attention. David stepped forward, saluted and asked for his captain's instructions.

"Pipe the men to their stations for getting underway, Mister Noble."

"Don't you want to talk to them first?"

John shook his head. "It's more important that we get into blue water as quickly as possible. After we clear the harbor and that British man-of-war, I'll assemble the men."

"Aye, aye, sir!" David gave his captain a curt salute and turned about. "All hands to stations for getting underway!" The bosun echoed the command and added the details to the various line hauling crews and topmen. For several minutes the deck of the Silver Cloud resembled a street riot, with men running in every direction. Several men dropped down the various companionways while most climbed, cat-like, into the rigging. Suddenly everything was quiet and all eyes were trained toward the quarter deck and Captain John Paul Jones.

David turned back to John. "The men are at their stations, Captain."

"Very well, Mister Noble." John gave a glance seaward. "Cast off and set a starboard reach for Hadrell's Point."

Before David could relay the command, the bosun barked out. "Set the gallants and royal tops!" With a cheer, the topmen jerked the slip knots loose from the appropriate yards, allowing the Silver Cloud's virgin sails to unfurl and capture the rising wind like enormous wings. "Cast off all lines!" The taut canvas strained at the rigging, pulling the disguised warship gently from its dock to leeward. The tide was good, and within an hour the Silver Cloud had passed Hadrell's Point.

John called his officers to his cabin. There were five of them—all standing just inside the door. Captain Van Mourik stood to the left, with Robert Ormerod and the ship's surgeon at his right shoulder. Behind them and slightly to the right stood the young Jamaican, David Noble, and his new companion, the ancient pirate-turned-businessman, Ben Gunn. The leather packet lay open on the desk behind John.

"Captain Van Mourik, you'll be in charge of the watch schedule and seeing to it that the men are kept busy with their training and shipboard duties." The Dutchman nodded. "If we encounter any of the King's ships, it'll be your special duty—along with your thirty crewmen—to assume temporary command of the Silver Cloud. I'll expect you and your men to put on a convincing show for the inspectors while the rest of us hide below."

"Aye, Captain Jones! Dat what we be here for, ja?"

"David, as I told you the other day, you'll be my first officer. And if you're willing, I'd like you to assume the responsibilities of ship's navigator."

The young Jamaican nodded his approval and acceptance of the assignment.

John continued. "I'll work with you for the first week or so, until you feel secure in your duties." The older men gave David their congratulations and then returned their attention to the captain.

"Adam, as ship's surgeon, you'll be in charge of not only the men's physical health, but indirectly, their morale. Get close to the men. Learn their names and as much personal information as you can."

"I'll not be your spy, Captain, if that's what you're suggesting."

John shook his head. "What I'm asking from you is not spying. I need to get the 'feel' of the crew, all of whom are unknown to me. Find out as quickly as you can who are the natural leaders. Get to know these men well. While you're at it, identify the potential troublemakers. Listen to the rumors and complaints and advise me before we have a problem." John shot a stern look at David. "I've had some bad experiences in the past and can't afford anything like that on this mission."

The doctor spoke. "I've been tending to the men for several days while they've been waiting for our departure, sir. They already trust me."

"Good. I don't want you to betray any confidences, Adam. I just want to know the climate below decks at all times."

"Understood, sir."

"Robert, since you're the only one on board who's ever been on Dead Man's Chest, I'll make you my tactician. And since you and Ben are the only ones who know the location of the treasures, I'll expect both of you to keep out of harm's way as much as is humanly possible. We can't afford to lose either of you, until we retrieve the treasures."

John noticed Robert's questioning look. "Is something bothering you?"

"Ben and I must be worth more than that."

"I know how it sounds, Robert, and I apologize. Please realize that the treasure is our only mission, and the two of you are only special until we know where the treasures lie." John turned to Ben. "Mister Gunn, I'd appreciate it if you would assist Adam with morale, and identifying the good and bad elements among the crew. I believe you have a God-given talent with men."

The old man touched his forehead with a knuckle—man-of-war style. "Thank you, sir."

"Your other duties, Mister Gunn, will be to oversee the food preparation and to teach the landlubbers the courtesies they must render to myself and the other officers."

Ben's nerves were agitated by the weight of these new responsibilities, causing him to itch in several places at once. "We have landlubbers aboard?"

"We have forty Indian fighters with us who have never been aboard a ship before. That can present several unique problems unless the men are trained when and when not to get in the way."

Ben nodded. "So...you want me to make seamen of them."

John nodded and then turned to the others. "We have several very capable ship handlers aboard, both in the officers and the crew." John scanned the five men before him for a moment. "Captain Van Mourik, even though I've chosen David as my first officer, it does not mean that I think any less of you or your many years at sea. Our mission will call for the combined knowledge and skills of every one of you." John looked to each of the others in turn. "For that reason, I'm placing a special burden upon Jan and asking that he train each of you to be capable first officers." He turned to Dutch. "Can you do that for me?"

"Ja, Captain Jones." The Dutchman looked at the others. "I do like Mister Gunn. I make dem right fine sailors. You see!"

John snapped the latch on the leather case and then looked up at his officers. "I'm sure all of you have many questions for me, but they'll have to wait until supper. David, I'll expect to be called when the crew is assembled on the main deck."

***

The morning sun was high in the sky when the Silver Cloud finally reached the open sea and cut through the murky waters south of Charles Town Harbor. The Royal Navy seemed to have no interest in the disguised frigate, or if they did, they never made any attempt to close with her. A fifteen-knot southwesterly fit well with the course John had selected. In accordance with his sealed orders, he set a course of 155 degrees, which would take the Cloud along the eastern edge of the Bahamas and into their first port at Puerto Plata. There, if all went according to plan, all of the cargo would be unloaded, except for that which hid the cannons. From Puerto Plata, the Silver Cloud would make no other ports until it had reached Dead Man's Chest.

The bosun stepped to the great wheel and called forward into the cluster of men. "On deck! Attention!" John and his first officer came topside and took their position on the raised quarterdeck.

Within seconds, the little knots of conversation about the deck were untied and one hundred fifty sets of eyes were turned to gaze for the first time on this unknown Scottish captain. The only sounds were the groaning and snorting of the new timbers under the driving force of the wind.

It wasn't difficult to recognize the three classes of men who made up the crew of this new fighting ship. The thirty Dutchmen wore the brown attire of their fatherland and stood behind Captain Van Mourik. The second group was the largest—the American sailors. They numbered eighty and wore loose-fitting, blue-and-white striped shirts and light canvas breeches suited to the arduous work at sea. The final group was the mountain men, all of them in buckskin and numbering forty.

The bosun looked about at the sailors and Indian fighters. "This is Captain John Paul Jones, an' he's got some words to tell us 'bout this secret mission we be on!"

A rumble of excited conversation ran the length of the deck.

John stepped forward. "After a short stop at Puerto Plata, we're headed for a small island off the north coast of Saint Croix to recover possibly the largest treasure ever taken from a single Spanish galleon."

A voice cried from high above in the crosstrees. "Is it the treasure of Dead Man's Chest?"

John flashed a questioning look at David and got the usual "not me" gesture in return. John shaded his eyes and looked up at the man. "You have heard correctly, but—"

A cheer rose from the men, and then another one of the crewmen called out. "An' how we gonna divy it up, Captain? The usual way?"

John was becoming angry, but realized that in the absence of the truth, men will fabricate any story to fill in the gaps. It was obvious that the crew knew nothing about the cannons and the final use of the treasure. "You've assumed wrongly about the treasure's purpose. You're a hired crew, not pirates or privateers. Each of you has agreed to a certain wage, and nothing more. Neither I nor my fellow officers will receive any portion of the treasure either. The treasure is not to be shared in the usual manner, unless we—"

Another wave of grumbling passed over the deck. Captain Jones raised his voice. "Unless we find extra treasure, that is, above the eight hundred thousand pounds needed by the American colonies."

Another man called out. "Extra treasure? How can there be any extra unless it were planted there at the first?" Several others joined with similar questions.

John turned to the bosun.

"Shut yer gaps if ya want'a hear the captain out!" After a long moment, the men fell silent again.

"I have standing at my side one of the four who buried the treasure twenty years ago. He tells me that its estimated value was just over eight hundred thousand pounds sterling at that time. He'll count the treasure after we get it aboard, and appraise it at today's value. If after purchasing the needed materials there's any left, that portion will be split square and even without the officers taking a greater portion. I feel certain that there will be extra."

The crew cheered.

John gave a look to Ben Gunn. "And if our schedule allows it, we'll attempt to retrieve the rest of the treasure from Flint's Island—that portion the group out of Bristol failed to take ten years ago."

"And what about pirates?" It was the man in the rigging again.

"Mister Forrestal has sent the privateer Eagle ahead of us to ensure our path is clear. Captain Steele will hold up at Christiansted and then be standing off Dead Man's Chest when we arrive."

Another man called from the main deck. "What about liberty at Puerto Plata?"

"My first officer will answer your questions later below decks." John signaled Von Mourik to take charge and then descended the companionway toward his cabin.

David followed at John's heels. "Captain Steele's still on the Eagle?"

"Of course he is." John stopped on the ladder and looked back up at David. "Why would you think otherwise?"

"Because Mister Forrestal told me that he refused to sail with you again. Something about trouble in New York."

John dropped to the companionway and waited for David to join him. "There was trouble during that trip, but I didn't know he tried to beg out of this mission. The man's being paid very well."

"Then...are you and he on speaking terms?"

"No, and I have no intention of being so unless circumstances require it." John turned to walk aft toward his cabin, but stopped and turned back to the younger man. "If we need his assistance for something, I'll send you or one of the other officers to the Eagle in my stead."

David followed John into the main cabin. He held the list of rules the bosun had read before they had gone above deck.

John noticed. "You seem troubled by something. Is it my rules?"

"Can I speak frankly, John?"

"Yes, you may, but you will address me as 'Captain'."

"Yes, Captain, I have trouble with your rules."

John answered with a guarded tone. "You may be my friend, but you're also in my chain of command. Be advised that I'll not tolerate insubordination, especially from you."

David gave John a long look. He raised the list. "All you have here are crimes and punishments." David pushed the door closed. "A dozen lashes for being late to watch. Two dozen lashes for fighting, and a half dozen lashes for whistling?"

"Yes?"

David paused for a moment and stepped toward his new captain. "Do you honestly intend that if the men are in a good mood—good enough to whistle—that they be punished?"

"I didn't want to involve you with this, but since you brought it up, I'll explain a few things." John stepped behind the great table with measured strides. "First, any set of rules is, by its very nature, a negative document. That much you'll simply have to accept. As to the rule against whistling—you've never sailed on a ship this large, have you?"

"No, but I don't see—"

"I welcome good cheer from my crew, as much as any other captain would. I've gone to great lengths and made several compromises with Captain Van Mourik and Doctor McKenzie for that very purpose. But because of the ship's great size, many of the orders must be given by bosun's whistle, and none of us can afford the confusion the occasional good-natured whistling might create." David nodded his understanding. "As for the rest of my rules—and there are few compared to most ships—each one is there for an important purpose."

"But this crew. They're—"

"Very special—I know." John didn't like finishing David's sentences, but he was losing his patience. "Every man on this crew—be he Dutch or American—was handpicked by Joseph Hewes. Each was chosen for talents that go far beyond their ability to fire a weapon or sail a ship. They were chosen because they're brave men—proven in battle several times over."

"And that's exactly my point. You don't need to tell men of such high calibre not to cheat or fight with each other."

"You're omitting one thing. These high-calibre men are to be confined to a very small and restricted world for six to eight weeks, without female contact or any of the other outlets for venting their built-up anger and frustrations. We've already had one minor fight over berthing, and we've only been underway for part of one day. Since there are very few rewards to keep the men in line, I am forced to resort to the threat of punishment. Without that threat, their petty bickering would surely turn into anarchy and even mutiny in a matter of days."

"But what about the treasure?"

"You put too much weight upon that. The promise of treasure has never ensured proper discipline on a ship—actually quite the opposite. If I were to relax my discipline and withhold the lash—which you obviously find so repugnant—you'd see our special crew at each other's throats long before we reach Dead Man's Chest—especially those forty Indian fighters."

"Well, I think you're wrong."

"You can think what you please, David. Your lofty appeal to reason and man's good nature wears very thin aboard a warship."

"But—"

"Have you ever seen what happens to a young man or woman who were raised by permissive parents?"

"Yes, but—"

"You'd be surprised at the good a few well-administered lashings would do for most landlubbers."

"But it seems so cruel."

"It's not a matter of cruelty! If a little blood doesn't flow from a deserving back now and then, I can assure you that a whole lot of blood will flow from those same men's veins when they perish in an undisciplined battle. Your complaint should not be against the just punishment of a disobedient subordinate, but rather against the faulty judgment used in the administration of that punishment."

"These men were selected for their courage, and—"

John slammed his hand on the table. "Enough! You don't understand the meaning of the word!"

"Courage?"

"Yes!" John stopped to gather his thoughts. "Courage isn't some inborn quality of man. It's a trait we learn through hours and hours of training and discipline." John walked to the windows and gazed back toward Charles Town. He turned back to the younger man. "It's the dominion of the will over the natural instinct of fear and panic. It's the ability of men to reload and fire their weapons even when being rushed upon by a screaming enemy, or with iron and lead balls flying amongst them. That's courage!"

"But where's the respect and compassion? These sailors share our hatred for the government in London."

"You are not mature enough to balance the respect and friendship you feel for this crew with the necessary discipline and justice they require." John realized he was making very little headway with his stubborn and immature friend. "David, I don't have time to argue the point further. Suffice it to say that this mission is much too important for me to experiment with this crew, simply to satisfy the unproven whims of my first officer. Our benefactors have provided these men with as much comfort as possible, including a share in the excess treasure. But even with that, there are always a few men who wouldn't be happy in heaven, and it's for those we have these barbaric rules, as you perceive them." John stepped close to the young man. "Trust me when I tell you that I know how to keep this crew working as one body and with a singleness of purpose. If at any time you disagree with my methods, keep them to yourself and speak to me in private. By the time we make it back to Charles Town, you'll see that I was right."

"I know I'm young, and but for the Falmouth Packet, I lack sea experience. Yet..."

"The Falmouth Packet!" John knew David would raise that subject. "I made a great mistake during that trip."

"Aye. Joshua Smoot nearly sank us that day."

"But do you realize why?"

"Isn't that obvious? They were bigger and faster than us." David could see his captain wasn't going to endorse his estimation of the event. "You're talking about what Carini did, aren't you?"

"Yes I am, and I won't allow it to happen on the Silver Cloud. I experimented with that crew—precisely what you are proposing I do with this one."

"Experimented? I thought everything went well until..."

"My mistake was that I treated the crewmen like friends, rather than as the sailors they signed on to be. It didn't cause a problem until that lucky shot took off Carini's arm and Clark ran to his aid, rather than obey my order to man the sheets. We all could have been killed for Clark's refusal to obey my order."

"But his friend—his best friend—was dying! You can't expect men to ignore an injured or dying mate, no matter how well they're trained!"

"But that's where you're wrong, David, fatally wrong! And that's exactly why I had to flog Clark."

David spoke the words slowly. "Nearly two weeks after his offence?"

"I'll be the first to admit my error. But therein lies a second lesson. Never lose control of your men in the first place, because in the act of recapturing that control, you may very well create a mutiny."

"You really believe you lost control on the Falmouth Packet?"

"I'm certain of it. The men were quick to obey an order they agreed with, or for which they could see a personal benefit. But when it came to the blind obedience required during battle, my control ended. Had the situation been slightly different that day, you and I would not be speaking thusly in the master's cabin of this fine man-of-war." John had been wrestling with something since his talk with Barragan, and figured this was the most appropriate time to broach it.

"David, when you refer to the Falmouth Packet, it's always the crew against me."

There was an uncomfortable silence while David considered his words. "I was always on your side."

"And that's why you stayed with me at Machotick Creek?"

David gave his captain a questioning look. "What are you implying, John?"

"I had a very interesting talk with our cook."

"Barragan?"

"Aye. He believes you would have jumped ship with the rest of them, except that you told him that we were on some sort of mission."

"And you think he was talking about the treasure and the cannons?"

"That's what I'm asking you. Did you know about all of this before we left King's Town?"

"We both knew about the cannons, John, and as for the treasure, there's not a seaman in the Atlantic who hasn't heard of the treasure of Dead Man's Chest."

"You're avoiding my question, David." John rephrased it. "Did your father select me for this mission?"

David shook his head. "Think about it, Captain. Why would I follow you all the way to Virginia and work in that sweaty tailor shop for over a year? Believe me—if I had known about all of this, I'd have told you in Jamaica."

John sat down across the table and considered the puzzle. "Then you didn't know about the shortage of cannons?"

"Neither of us knew that before we talked to those two fellows in Richmond."

"Then you stayed with me on the Falmouth Packet because…"

"Because I wanted a naval commission, and you assured me that we could have one for the asking." David sensed a momentary upper hand. "Were you lying to me about the commissions?"

There was an urgent knock on the cabin door. John held a hand up to David. "Come!" One of the powder monkeys entered. "What is it?"

"The watch just spotted two ships off the port bow at several leagues, Captain. He says one is a British man-o'-war. Mister Ormerod would like you on deck."

"Tell him I'll be there presently." The boy left. John turned back to David. "Find Van Mourik and have him round up his men."

By the time the Silver Cloud had reached Andros Island, the fourth rate man-o'-war had broken off with the English merchantman and had set sail to intercept the disguised frigate.

Robert lowered the spyglass as John joined him at the rail. "Do we stop or do we make them chase us down?"

"We don't need any trouble with the authorities yet, so I'm going to cooperate." John turned to David. "Give the order to shorten sail to only what we need for steerage."

"Aye, Captain."

Twenty minutes later, the ship's boat from HMS Wasp had tied up alongside, and a young lieutenant had stepped through the rail. The entire American crew was hidden far below with the water casks, leaving the thirty-one Dutch seamen to meet the inspector.

Captain Van Mourik held out his shipping papers to the officer. "Velcome aboard der Silver Cloud. Come to see my cargo, ja?"

The officer took the papers and scanned them quickly. "I'm James Hawkins; Lieutenant, Royal Navy." He looked about the deck and into the rigging. "It says here that you're carrying cotton from South Carolina to the Antillies."

"Ja! Dat's what we got below, sure enough, Mister Harkers."

"It's Hawkins."

"Ja!" Dutch turned and pointed to the aft companionway. "I show you da cotton now, ja?"

The young officer followed the heavy-set Dutchman down to the gun deck. Dutch stopped in the middle of the ladder and pointed at the bales of cotton. The lieutenant read how many bales there were supposed to be and gave the cargo a quick scan.

"It says on your manifest that you will be picking up molasses and returning to South Carolina. When do you expect to return this way?"

"Oh, a month, maybe quicker."

Just then, one of the marines called down from the main deck. "Lieutenant!"

Hawkins turned and looked up. "What is it?"

"Semaphore from the Wasp, sir. There's another ship coming up from the south and the captain wants us back aboard."

"Very well." Lieutenant Hawkins handed the manifest back to Van Mourik and scaled the ladder. At the deck, he called to another man who was holding a large mallet. "Everything's good! Stamp them!"

The man nodded, took careful aim and swung the stamping mallet down onto the rail, leaving the King's inspection seal deep in the oak.

Jan Van Mourik caught up with Lieutenant Hawkins. "I have some goot Scotch whiskey in my cabin. You got time to share a drink, ya?"

Lieutenant Hawkins stepped through the opening in the rail and stopped to look back at the Dutchman. As he did, a sliver that had been raised when the mallet struck the wood jammed under his right thumbnail. "Damn!" He jerked his hand back. The splinter was almost an inch long and had buried itself to the quick. The young officer grabbed it and gave a painful jerk. Blood quickly filled the void when the wood was removed.

"Dat looks bad, Lieutenant Hawkers. I have a man who would dress dat for you. We can have dat whiskey too, while he works dat thumb, ya?"

The young officer turned about and started to descend the ladder. Half way down stopped and looked up at the Dutchman. "Yes, when I inspect you on your return trip."

Hawkins was in no mood for the Woodshoe's hospitality and dropped quickly to his waiting boat. A moment later, he was gone.

Chapter 12

On the 24th of May, 1775, the privateer Eagle nosed into Christiansted Harbor, a quiet port on the north shore of Saint Croix. Since '71, the small port had lost much of its share of the thriving slave, sugar and rum commerce that followed the trade winds between England and the new world.

With her cleaner lines and earlier departure from Charles Town, the Eagle was well ahead of her ward, the Silver Cloud. There was only one other vessel in the harbor large enough to be worthy of the title "ship," and this black-and-red monster with gold trim was flying a French flag. Captain Steele surveyed her lines carefully for a clue to her identity, but the cut of her stern and the low angle of the afternoon sun made it impossible to read her name.

"Cap'n Smoot! She's 'ere Govn'r, just like I tolt ya she'd be!" Henry Morgan gave a series of urgent raps to the heavy oak door with the butt of his cutlass. "That means the Cloud'll be here shortly!" The youth sprang away and up the companionway to the top deck where he took two vicious cuts at the heavy Caribbean air with his blade and yelled once more down the companionway.

"Cap'n Smoot!" The lad dropped again to the dark passageway and pressed his ear to the cool oak door. "Are you up, Govn'r?"

"Aye!" Smoot pulled the door open, and Henry fell headlong into the master's cabin. Smoot stepped over the prostrate lad and walked out into the passageway. "Is it the Eagle?"

"Aye!" Henry struggled to his feet and scurried after the older man.

The two climbed the ladder into the bright morning sunlight. Once on deck, Henry brandished his cutlass toward the Virginia privateer that was tacking into the bay. "She's the escort I been tellin' ya 'bout."

"Well, well." Smoot laced up his shirt. "Looks like ye'll be earnin' them five shares after all."

While they watched, the Eagle luffed her main and jib and dropped her larboard anchor, putting her approximately three hundred yards seaward of the Tiburon. An hour later, when two-thirds of the crew would normally have gone ashore for liberty, a lone ship's boat with but three men aboard pulled slowly past the stern of the pirate ship and then turned toward the cargo docks.

Henry whispered from his hiding place while the boat passed within earshot. "They're checkin' us out, Govn'r."

Smoot called out something in French and got the appropriate answer from Captain Steele.

"Did it work, Govn'r? Do they think we're frogs?"

"Aye, Henry." Smoot gave the lad a confident nod. "That they do."

"Aren't ya forgettin' somethin', Govn'r?" He gave his captain a squint and an outstretched hand. "We had a bet, ya know."

Smoot gave the young man an angry stare for three seconds and then pulled the agreed prize from his pocket.

"It's only fittin', Govn'r, since ya made me pay ya the ten quid back in Savannah." Henry's eyes were fixed on the shiny gold coin that promised another night of good grog and female companionship.

"That was a fair bet, Morgan, and you lost." Smoot flipped the coin high into the air toward the mizzenmast, sending Henry down the deck in a mad scramble toward a waiting scupper.

When the boy returned with his prize, Smoot was deep in thought. "Somethin' wrong, Govn'r?"

"I was just countin' on most of the Eagle's crew bein' ashore tonight in them taverns, that's all. We'll just have to change our plans a little to make up fer it."

"Well, they gotta go ashore some time." Henry bit his newly won prize to test its metal. "And when they do, we'll make our move."

*** * ***

After three days, not a soul besides Captain Steele and the other two men had gone ashore. Every morning at four bells they would pull to shore in the ship's boat and return two hours later with supplies. Then again at eight bells—four o'clock in the afternoon—the same three men would make their second trip, returning after the same amount of time ashore. Try as they might, Smoot's spies couldn't find out a thing from the seamen who stayed at Drake's Dock while their captain was about his business. Only that Captain Steele was buying supplies and negotiating for the sale of his cargo.

By the afternoon of the third day at anchor, the Eagle's crew was clearly ready for any diversion. As her captain's boat passed abeam of the Tiburon for its afternoon run to the town, Smoot turned to a group of women sitting in a launch next to the dock. "Go!"

The Eagle's watch saw the launch first. "Mister Todd, sir!"

"What is it?"

"We've a boat full o' ladies approachin' from the larboard beam!" The first officer closed the logbook and walked quickly toward the rail where the agitated young seaman stood pointing. "There, sir!"

"They're still so far out." Todd shaded his eyes against the afternoon sun. "What makes you think its ladies?"

"Look how they're pullin' them oars an' meanderin' about the bay, sir. That's gotta be ladies or children, an' they're much too big fer children!"

Most of the other crewmen were quicker on their feet than the first officer, and were already crowding and shoving for a spot along the port rail.

"Back away there!" Todd moved toward the bow and pressed himself between two of his crew. It was just as the watch had reported. "Well, I'll be!"

The liberty-starved sailors barely heard his orders for their hooting and hollering at the approaching women. The shifting breeze brought the full impact of the lady's sweet fragrances across the water, up over the bow and along the ship to the thirty-five waiting noses. The perfumes were mostly cheap, but the sailors were more interested in where the lotions had been applied than with their value. Todd was a man of similar desires, but duty to Captain Steele and their mission prevailed.

"You there!" Todd called out in a stern voice while the crew watched the boat circle around to the east side of the Eagle. "In the boat! Stand off and state your business!"

A bovine blond stood carefully to her feet and shaded her eyes with a woven cane fan. It wasn't that she was actually better endowed than her companions, but rather that she had paid her dressmaker better than the rest. She called back to Todd in a bubbly voice. "Captain Steele sent us!"

There arose a cheer from the crew for their absent captain. When the yelling finally subsided and two sailors had been fished from the warm water, Todd continued his interrogation of the visitors.

"And what evidence of that do you offer us, young lady?"

"This, sir!" The young lady reached between her generous breasts and searched for something. The entire crew sucked in its breath as one man. She extracted a small, rolled parchment tied with a crimson ribbon. The eleven other ladies giggled as thirty-five lusty sailors exhaled together and let out a second cheer.

The sailor next to Todd began to climb over the rail.

"Not so fast, MacPherson!" He reached out and caught the eager seaman by the rope that held up his britches.

"By yer leave, sir! I were just goin' fer the note!" There was another round of laughter and catcalls from both vessels.

"Well, go ahead then." Todd released the rope, and the youth, cheered on by his mates, leaped to the bottom rung of the ship's ladder with the agility of a spider. "But mind you MacPherson, touch nothing more than our captain's note!"

Todd knew that if he wasn't extremely careful, he could lose the entire crew on the spot. MacPherson was back in a moment with the note between his teeth. He held it up to the crew and twirled about with the prize. Todd held out his hand. "MacPherson! May I?"

Todd read it to himself:

Mister Todd:

I have reconsidered the present situation and have decided the men deserve some female companionship. Since they cannot come ashore, I've decided to send several women to the ship. Please take these ladies aboard for the evening, along with the refreshments they convey. I may be detained ashore with Mister Lewis longer than usual, but I expect to be back before the ladies are gone. If not, have them escorted to the dock no later than midnight.

A. Steele
Captain: Privateer Eagle

Todd studied the signature for a moment. There was something different about it, but his baser nature prevailed. He turned and looked down at the ladies. Any suspicion was forced aside by the temptation awaiting him at the water line.

"Bosun! Bring the ladies aboard!"

The crew exploded in cheers and praises for their captain and first officer. Within minutes, the ladies were on deck with their six casks of rum, and both quickly disappeared below decks. The first two mugs of rum were brought to Todd and the bosun. The men cast lots, and those who would have to wait on deck for their turns with the women made a sport of outdoing one another in toasting their absent captain and throwing their dirks at the mainmast.

Todd sat on one of the cat's heads with his rum and called aft at his crew. "I'm sure our captain would appreciate your enthusiasm, but the women are to be put ashore no later than midnight. And mind you, I'll see to it personally that any man of you caught fighting will find himself in irons. Nobody heard him.

Within an hour, the strong drink had done its job. Every sailor, to a man, was fast asleep long before the women were to be returned to Christiansted. The ladies, who knew nothing of the sleeping potion Joshua Smoot had put in the rum, were returned unconcious to their brothels.

Without a single inhabitant of the small port town noticing, the senseless crew of the Eagle was taken to an empty sugar warehouse at the west end of the wharf and put into irons. As the sun rose the next morning above the quiet Caribbean, a new crew was being selected to man the now-empty privateer Eagle.

***

Joshua Smoot and Henry Morgan walked about the deck of the privateer Eagle, surveying their new prize. Henry was unhappy about something.

"Are ya sure that Privy's the best choice fer the Tiburon? I'd be more than—"

"Watch yer tongue, Henry." Smoot ran his hands along the newly varnished tiller. "I've cut tongues from men's mouths fer questioning my decisions. Pritchard'll do the same if he catches wind of you callin' him that."

Henry gave a gulp and touched his mouth. "Sorry, Govn'r, but if I heard rightly, it were Privy at the helm when that little postal packet took off yer rudder."

"Aye, it was Pritchard, all right." Smoot gave the lad a quick glance, wondering at his intent. "You got a complaint about him?"

"Well, maybe I be missin' somethin' 'ere, Govn'r, but I 'ear tell he's not so good in battle." The youth ran a calloused finger across his wet nose and dried it through his shoulder-length orange hair. "What if he gets the Tiburon sunk or somethin'?"

"What's that to us?"

"But the crew? They'd miss out on their share..." The lad turned to look at his captain and was met with a toothy grin. "Ya don't care if they die, do ya?"

"As I see it, Henry, if Pritchard an' his men can get the treasure, then we all split it up, just like normal. But if they get themselves sunk in the try, that's just bigger shares fer you an' me, and our thirty men." Smoot's teeth flashed while his bushy black brows danced on his forehead. "Now that we got this fine Virginia privateer with her rows of new guns, we can take your Silver Cloud all by ourselves."

"But..." Henry began to protest, and then checked himself.

"The Cloud's gonna' think we're their protectors, Henry, and we'll play our part, just as they expect. We need the fighters from the Tiburon to help get the treasure, but after that, I'd be willin' to help the Cloud sink Pritchard an' the rest of them fishbait troublemakers."

"Troublemakers?"

"Aye." Smoot turned about and rested his backside against the rail. "I heard tales about how Captain Rip Rap was always tradin' crewmen between him an' John Flint. I know what he was up to."

"Oh?"

"Well, my quick mind sprung on the thing right off. Rip Rap would send all the scoundrels and cutthroats over to Flint in exchange for the good followers—most o' the ones impressed into service. Ended up, the Walrus was havin' a mutiny 'most every day while the Royal James ran like one o' the King's own men-o'-war." He gave the boy a knowing wink and held up the paper. "That, my boy, is how I chose the twenty-nine men we're takin' with us on the Eagle."

"Well, I guess ya gotta have a little of the troublemaker in ya, or ya don't make as good a captain as you been, Govn'r." Henry looked about at the Tiburon. "When are we splittin' the crew?"

"I'll be readin' the list to the men as soon as we return. Soon as they get settled aboard, we'll be takin' the Eagle for a cruise 'round Dead Man's Chest. Give us a chance to see how she feels on the wind, an' scout the lay o' the land at the same time."

***

The Eagle was a splendid craft. She was quick at the helm and had the latest "sharp" hull design, much like the Tiburon and the faster French corvettes. Her two masts were raked aft to improve her upwind abilities, and she carried half again the sail of most other ships of equal tonnage. She was a warship from stem to stern, but built along the lines of the agile racing sloops at Oxford. Her thirty crewmen had no difficulty adjusting to her special needs.

"She's better than the Tiburon, Henry!" Smoot ordered her tiller to lee for the tack back to the windward side of Dead Man's Chest.

"Aye, Cap'n. She's a real fine lady all right."

"As sweet a lady as Governor Wright's daughter." Smoot and Henry walked to the bow and leaned against the windward rail. The Eagle's sails filled for the larboard reach back toward Christiansted. Passing the western tip of the island, Smoot studied the line of coral and the thin band of white sand called Rip Rap beach.

"Have ya ever been on the Chest, Henry?"

"No, Govn'r, only heard tales 'bout it from the old crews what stopped at Tortuga when I were a pup."

"Then you know nothin' o' the reef, other 'n what our chart showed?"

"You got me there, Govn'r. You figgerin' the Silver Cloud'll be puttin' in on the south side?"

"That's what I'd do if I were them, and I'd reckon that's where Captain Murray put his grandnephew ashore with the treasure."

"Does Privy know how many men to put ashore tonight?"

"It's all been arranged." Something caught Smoot's eye. At three leagues was a large merchantman with gleaming new sails on a starboard tack and paralleling Saint Croix. "Morgan!" Smoot pointed. "What do you make of that?

"It's the Silver Cloud! She's 'ere, sir!"

"Look carefully, Henry. Are you certain?"

"Aye, Govn'r. There's no mistakin' 'er. I carved most o' her decorations an' painted 'alf her colors."

"Well then, we'd best get to playin' our part. Tell the men to break out those colonial outfits and tell the helm to set a course to join with the Silver Cloud." Smoot studied the Silver Cloud for a moment through his spyglass. "We'll also need our prisoner on deck."

***

Two leagues to the northwest and driven by the steady afternoon trade winds, sailed the majestic Silver Cloud. She was half a day ahead of schedule.

"Captain Jones!" Robert stepped close to the young captain. "I must insist you reconsider. Just because we haven't seen any pirates yet doesn't mean they aren't waiting for us on the island."

"You're being an old lady again, Robert. If our secret were out, don't you think we'd know it by now?" John strode to the rail and spun on a heel with spread arms. "Where are they? Do you see any other ships?"

No sooner were the words out of his mouth than the foretop watch called out the familiar words. "Ship on the larboard bow!"

John shaded his eyes and searched the horizon. "It looks like the Eagle." John stepped to the binnacle and took up the spyglass.

David joined the two older men. "Is it they?"

"We'll know in a moment." John raised his spyglass and studied the ship. "I can't make out anybody on deck yet, but there's no doubt that it's the Eagle." John spun about. "Do you see, Robert? I told you our secret was safe."

"Just the same, I'll not lead anybody to the treasure until I'm certain."

"Damn it, man!" John strode to the center of the deck and pointed into the rigging. "We have lookouts in the crosstrees! Nobody can get near us without being spotted, and we have enough armament to sink a ship twice our size. If we send everybody but the gun crews, we can have the treasure dug up and back aboard within five or six hours." He waited for Robert to answer. "Nobody is going to attack us until we start digging."

"Just the same, it'll be my way or none."

John looked about the quarterdeck at the other officers and men on watch. Each was curious as to how this little drama would play out.

John stepped close and lowered his voice. "We had best finish this discussion in my cabin." He turned to David. "Find Mister Gunn and meet us there."

David had not seen John this upset since their heated discussion about crew discipline the day they had departed Charles Town. He found Ben in the galley helping with the noon meal. As the two made their way aft, David informed Ben of the argument between the captain and the New Yorker, and cautioned him to mind his tongue.

David and Ben entered the master's cabin. John held up a glass to the old man. "Ah, Mister Gunn." John and Robert were already sharing a glass of scotch over one of the charts Alex Forrestal had provided. "Take a seat and pour yourselves some of Scotland's finest." The air was thick with tension.

John began, as if nothing were wrong. "Gentlemen, we've had a long voyage and we're very close to our goal." He reached his right hand across the green felt. "Robert, I'd like to apologize for my outburst a few moments ago. You're right to be cautious concerning the treasure."

"Thank you, John." Robert was surprised with John's change of mood and accepted the offered hand. "I'm acutely aware that you three, and the whole crew for that matter, are anxious to bring the treasure aboard and be on our way as quickly as possible. But I've seen how pirates work. They may not use a whole lot of intelligence in their way of life, but when it comes to treachery, there's none to match them."

Ben nodded. "I can vouch for that, Master Ormerod."

John gave the old man a paternal smile and turned to Robert. "You claim that you had a plan, Robert. Now's the time to tell us, before we get to our anchorage."

"As I was saying on deck, we can't be too careful. If there are pirates about, they will most likely have a contingent on the island waiting for us. The moment they see the treasure, they'll attack."

While Robert explained the details of his plan, Ben Gunn turned the chart about on the table. "Beggin' yer pardon, Captain Jones, but where do you plan on leavin' the ship while we're ashore?"

"We'll drop anchor at this opening in the reef." John pointed with his dagger and looked to Robert for confirmation. "Isn't that where you told us your granduncle put the Royal James when he put you ashore?"

Robert nodded. "Yes, right there."

David wanted to go ashore in the worst way. "While we're ashore, Captain, who's to watch the ship?"

"We'll be leaving Captain Van Mourik and a third of the crew. The winds'll swing the ship about to expose her starboard cannons to seaward. Between our long guns and the Eagle patrolling the deep waters outside the reef, no ship would risk an approach."

By dusk, the Silver Cloud had come within three hundred yards of their protector and traded both semaphore and hand waves with the Eagle. Captain Jones and Captain Steele studied each other through their spyglasses for nearly a minute before the larger ship finally dropped anchor just outside the island's protective reef. As expected, the winds pushed the camouflaged frigate about its anchor into the perfect position to give any approaching vessel a full broadside. As the sun set beyond the port of Christiansted five miles to the southwest, final preparations were underway for the morning's assault on Dead Man's Chest.

***

It was early, and the sun was still far below the eastern horizon when the last of the Cloud's boats skidded onto Rip Rap Beach. These final twelve men marched across the sand toward the rest of the shore party, each man carrying an assortment of cutlasses, pistols and shovels.

The beach had been named Rip Rap by Andrew Murray's crew—for that was the pirate captain's favorite brand of snuff. Although the small beach was shunned by most sea-going brigands, Captain Rip Rap found the privacy of this particular stretch of coral sand to his liking. It was here that Robert Ormerod and his fiancée, Moira, along with her father and the Indian fighter Peter Corlaer, had been set ashore with the treasure twenty years before.

With the pinking of the eastern sky, John stepped out of the boat and onto the sand. "Let's get to it, Robert. Where's our treasure?"

Robert looked to the hillside. "We're not moving off this beach until both of the lookouts are in position and have given their signal."

"Damn!" John gave a frustrated huff, pulled his sword and began hacking at an obnoxious looking cactus at the upper edge of the beach.

"What was that?" Ben Gunn had his hand cupped to his good ear.

"Did you hear something?" Robert turned and looked to the old man and then to the hill that was now silhouetted against the rising sun.

"I thought I heard a man scream, sir, Master Robert." Several of the mountain men also heard the man's cries and had instinctively moved to the tree line for cover.

John ran back to Ben and Robert. "What's going on?"

"Up there!" Robert pointed to the spine of the island. "It came from one of our men. I told you there'd be trouble."

The screams of a man in full flight could now be heard by all hands, leaving no doubt that they weren't alone on the Chest. With a wave of his sword, John deployed the men to positions of defense—most of the sailors to the tree line with the mountain men, and the three gunners to man the single swivel gun they had brought ashore.

David saw the man first and pointed to the disturbance in the bushes. "There he is!" It was clear the poor soul was not following the path he and his comrade had used to ascend the hill. A moment later, he crashed onto the beach and spun loose from the tangle of vines. The man stumbled about for a moment and then took off running to the water.

Robert tried to stop the man but was unable. "What in God's name?"

David looked to the others, just as confused. "I didn't see any wounds or blood!"

"The other one must already be dead." John watched the man thrash about in the water for a moment. He turned to Robert. "I owe you another apology."

Robert turned about to watch for the watchman's attackers. "Save it until we see how many there are."

By now, the sailor had finished in the water and had walked back up behind his captain. "Sorry 'bout that, sir, but I never felt nothin' hurt that bad before."

John turned, surprised at how calm the man was. "How many were there?"

"Just one, sir." The seaman looked about the beach at his armed and ready mates. "There weren't but me an' O'Toole."

"Then what in God's name were you running from?"

"I wasn't runnin' from nothin', Cap'n." The man shook the seawater from his hair. "Just before we reached the top, I tripped against some sort o' tree with white ooze runnin' down its bark. Stung the hell out'a my skin wherever it touched."

"Then the other watchman's all right?"

"Far as I know, he is." With that, the dripping seaman walked across the beach and headed up the trail to resume his duties. As he entered the bushes, the "all clear" signal rang out from high above the beach. The man stepped back down onto the sand and called out. "See? There's nobody up there but O'Toole!"

"It seems my apology was a bit premature." John spoke the words with an air of contempt. "Do you still believe we're going to be attacked?"

"We're still going to do it my way, attack or not." Robert walked away to the north end of the beach and climbed to the top of a rock. From his vantage point, he could see both sides of the island for a distance of half a mile.

Finally satisfied, he turned back to the hundred-odd men gathered below him. "It's there!" He called out, pointing to the north coast of the island. "Near Dorsal Rock!"

***

The northern two-thirds of Dead Man's Chest was dominated by a flat plain covered with waist-high grass and an occasional bush that reached to a man's shoulders. A half-mile from Rip Rap Beach stood Dorsal Rock, a hump of black volcanic stone fifty feet long, twenty feet wide and a dozen feet high. It was so named because it resembled the back of a dolphin breaking the surface for a breath of air. It was an excellent spot to bury a treasure. Ten minutes at a quick pace brought the shore party to its western end.

John turned about to survey the surrounding land. "This is it?"

"There's none better." Robert pointed at the hill to the south. "There were only four of us, and we had to find a place close to the beach to carry the bags and boxes, and far enough from cover that we couldn't be watched and attacked. A compromise to be sure, but weighing all the elements, the logical choice."

John pointed back the way they'd come. "But your granduncle put you ashore back on the west beach." He turned and pointed to the nearby north shore. "Why didn't he set you ashore here, closer to this spot?"

"He was already gone when I decided this was the best place."

"But—"

"He left us a single ship's boat, so we used it to float the treasure around the coastline."

John spread his arms. "Well, Robert, you're on foredeck, and this is your moment. Please."

With a nod, Robert walked away to the eastern end of the mound. After what seemed to be an endless contemplation, he strode off to the south for ten paces, stopped and turned ninety degrees to the right. At the fourth step, he stopped and drove his sword into the fertile topsoil. He turned and called back. "Here! This is where we dig!"

***

The Indian fighters smelled it first—that unmistakable acrid odor of unclean men. By ones and twos they turned toward the hill.

David noticed the men's concern and whispered to John. "Something's wrong, John. Look at our fighters." Now more of them had dropped their tools and had taken defensive positions.

"Robert!" John pointed south. "Look there—to the tree line!"

There was a flash of reflected sunlight, followed by several others.

"I knew it." Robert stepped to John and pulled his pistols from his sash. "It seems we have company after all."

John climbed up the side of the mound. "Listen here!" He pointed south. "We've a large group of men hiding at the tree line several hundred yards to the south! Now that the treasure's location has been revealed..."

It was too late for making plans, for out of the trees and through the tall grass came fifty hairy sea dogs, running at top speed and screaming like men just released from hell. Each carried a cutlass and a brace of pistols slung about his shoulder. A hundred yards from the mound, the pirates broke into four separate groups—two diverting laterally into flanking positions while the remaining two groups charged directly toward Robert's sword.

When the pirates were at fifty yards, John barked his command. "Fire!"

***

The Silver Cloud had been left with a skeleton crew—just enough men to man the long chase guns should another ship approach. She was anchored three hundred yards beyond the reef, giving her plenty of room to swing about her chain. If all went as planned ashore, she would be back to the safety of deep water by late afternoon of that same day, and the treasure would be safe within her lazareete.

The sun was still low on the morning horizon when the battle began on the north shore. From the Silver Cloud, the sound of the musket fire could easily have been mistaken for the popping of green wood in the galley stove, but the cook was ashore and his fires were cold. Jan Van Mourik and most of the gunners lay peacefully asleep in their hammocks about the deck. Only two of their mates remained awake, pacing quietly about the quarterdeck and forecastle.

It was the forward watch who heard the musket fire first. Within minutes of his call, all hands except the old Dutchman were climbing into the rigging. If they were lucky, they hoped to catch a glimpse of the action from the upper yards.

Seamen are a hard lot—they always were and they always shall be. After months or even several weeks at sea—as these men had been—a man thirsts for the solid earth under his feet and a chance to find himself any diversion from his shipboard duties. It is unheard of for a man to knowingly trade away his chance to go ashore.

But the Savannah carpenter's mate who signed on to replace the man killed in an accident had done just that. He had no explanation for trading it away, and the young seaman who benefited, and who was now engaged in the battle ashore, hadn't given it a second thought. If the rest of the crew had been sharp, they would have noticed that while they climbed as high as possible into the rigging, this particular young carpenter climbed only a short way up—not nearly high enough to see over the island's low ridge to the grassy flats of the north shore.

With their attention thus engaged, they failed to notice when he dropped to the deck and made his way forward to the anchor chain.

None had missed him, not even the gunner's mate who had offered him a hand to one of the yards. And likewise, no one saw him lower the bucket into the jade-green waters, retrieving it full a moment later.

A quick glance into the rigging assured him that his absence and strange actions had gone unnoticed. With the swiftness of a cat, the traitor wet the deck from gunwale to anchor cable in an irregular pattern of splashes and footprints. He dried his feet and replaced the bucket and rags at their station.

With a quick glance upward, he pulled loose the cable's wraps about the bitt and then cut the stopper. Nothing moved. He had calculated correctly, that everything was still and the morning's first breeze had not yet begun to pull at the mighty ship. It wouldn't take much—perhaps as little as the negligible swells that crept around Cottengarden Point—to set the great ship in motion. And then, once the cable began its run across the deck, nothing could stop it.

Before the ship gave its first lurch, the traitor was high in the rigging again, balanced atop the main t'gallant yard next to the same gunner's mate who had given him a hand up earlier.

***

David studied the apparent confusion among the approaching pirates. "What on earth are they doing?"

What had appeared at first to be a well-planned flanking maneuver in support of their main attack was quickly losing all headway.

John noticed and called back to his first officer. "It's as if they forgot what they were up to, or they've lost their leader."

"If my guess is right, it's quite the opposite." Robert had seen the Walrus's old crew in action many times, and these men were acting in much the same way.

"The opposite?" David took aim and felled a man.

"Yes, David, the opposite." Robert gave John a quick glance. "I believe John will agree with me, that their problem is that they've too many leaders." He looked to John and received the expected nod.

Each group, consisting of ten to fifteen men, seemed confused about which way to go, or which tactic to use next. Visible infighting broke out in the pirate's right flank, first with shouts and then with a discharged musket. Within minutes, their main force had moved forward far enough that the little group of bickering pirates was now completely isolated from the rest. Before they could figure out what had gone wrong, two of their number were cut down by musket balls, leaving nine. Six of these dropped their weapons and fled for the trees behind them. One of the remaining three ran toward the main body of pirates and the other two turned and ran toward the water in a desperate attempt to avoid the thick musket fire from John's complement of Indian fighters. These two fell dead on the sand just short of the water.

John and Robert climbed to the top of the mound for a better view of the battlefield. Following their hand signals, David and the bosun led two separate flanking forces about the pirates, keeping low and out of sight in the tall grass. At every ten paces, David and the bosun turned to watch for John's signal, but before they were in position, one of the fleeing pirates from the aborted flanking maneuver ran headlong into David, knocking the young Jamaican flat on his back.

Surrounded by twenty men, the poor pirate, a young man of no more than twenty, was too startled to do anything but let out a faint cry while David's sword passed upward through his naked stomach and into his heart.

Another of the pirates called out in panic. "They be all about us, mates!" He jumped up and fired both of his pistols at David's men. The rest of the pirates stood and began firing in panic before breaking and running back for the tree line. When the last musket was fired and the final sword was wiped clean of dishonest blood, eighteen pirates lay dead or dying on the north plain of Dead Man's Chest.

"Bosun!" Captain Jones returned his sword to its sheath. "Sound the order to reassemble!"

"Aye, aye, Cap'n!"

Within ten minutes, all the bodies had been found and dragged to the beach for viewing. Of the six survivors, only three were in any condition to talk, and only one seemed at all willing. Leaving David in charge of the other prisoners, Robert motioned for John to follow him to where he had planted his sword.

John followed. "What now?"

Robert leaned close and whispered. "Before we begin questioning that cutthroat, there's something I must tell you."

"What now?"

Robert pulled his sword from the earth and wiped the blade clean. "The treasure isn't here."

"What?" Everyone within earshot turned and looked at the two. "What do you mean, the treasure isn't here?"

"It's on the island, John, but not here, where I planted my sword."

"You risked the lives of my crew for..." John paused, suddenly realizing what Robert had done. He whispered. "You knew we'd be attacked, didn't you?"

"I was almost certain of it, and I didn't want the treasure's location revealed to those scoundrels—whomever they are."

"Couldn't you have told me?"

Robert nodded. "Of course I could have, but if the men knew they were defending empty dirt instead of the treasure, do you suppose for a moment they would have fought quite so gallantly?"

John turned and looked at the dead and dying. Only one of the Silver Cloud's crew had been killed. "No, I suppose not."

"May I assume then, that you're not angry with me?"

"No, I'm not angry with you, Robert. I would ask, however, that from now on, you be honest with me."

"As you wish, John." He turned back toward the captive pirate. "Shall we see what our prisoner has to tell us?"

***

The breeze from the southeast had freshened to five knots—plenty to pull the great anchor chain from the ship. Several of the men in the uppermost rigging noticed the movement, but none—save the traitor—realized what had happened until it was too late. As her keel ground to a stop on the line of submerged coral, the great vessel shuddered, throwing one of the seamen from a yardarm to the shallow sea below.

The gunner's mate standing on the yard next to the traitor looked about and cried out. "What was that?"

"Look!" The traitor pointed down at the bow with feigned dismay. "The anchor chain's gone and we're on the reef!"

As quickly as they could, all thirty-one of the sailors slid the sheets to the deck, as if this effort could undo the harm already done.

"Vat is dat?" Captain Van Mourik jumped up from his slumber, stumbled about the deck for a moment and rubbing his swollen face. He gazed about the deck, trying to remember where he was.

"We're in trouble, Dutch!" McCoy was the senior gunner and didn't respect the overweight Dutchman enough to address him by his proper title.

"Trouble? What trouble?"

McCoy ran forward to the wet footprints and then looked into the sea. "Someone's come aboard and released our anchor chain, and we've drifted onto the coral!"

Without waiting for Van Mourik to remember his instructions from Captain Jones, McCoy gave the order to fire three cannons.

***

David, who had never seen a man tortured before, walked to the far end of Dorsal Rock and put his hands over his ears. While the others watched and waited for the man to tell what he knew, David noticed a ship silhouetted in the sun. He turned and ran toward the rest of the crew. "Captain Jones! The Eagle—" Before he could get the words out, the three cannon reports reached the north shore.

John turned to look at David. "Something's happened!"

David stopped several yards from John and pointed to the north again. "The Eagle! It isn't supposed to be on this side of the island!"

"I told Van Mourik to fire three cannons if there was trouble on the Cloud." He looked north to their protector. "As for the Eagle, I must assume Captain Steele heard the musket fire and figured we needed help." John made a quick survey of his men and turned to Robert. "I want you to remain here with six of the Indian fighters to protect our wounded and guard those prisoners." He looked about at the others. "There's some sort of trouble on the Silver Cloud. The rest of you will come with me!"

"Do you think they're under attack?"

"They can't be under attack, David, or there'd be more cannon fire."

John spun and looked to the Eagle once more. "The man may hate me, but Alan Steele would never abandon the Silver Cloud if there were an enemy within sight."

After ten minutes of running, John and his men rounded the last row of trees, giving him a clear view of his ship.

David ran at John's side. "Can you tell what's wrong?"

"It's hard to say for certain, but I believe the ship's listing slightly." A moment later John came to a stop on Rip Rap Beach. What met his gaze confused him greatly. There was now no doubt that the Silver Cloud was on the reef, but he was more puzzled by the strange activity at her waterline.

"This is all I need!" John pulled his sword from the sheath. "Another mutiny!"

***

The sky was clear the morning the Silver Cloud had been set aground. By the time her shore detachment had run the mile back to Rip Rap Beach, the sun had risen high enough to cast its rays across the mighty ship's upper rigging. There was no doubt about it. She was beginning to list to larboard, exposing her starboard underbelly to the air.

Smoot's plan had worked perfectly, although much of its success was simply due to dumb luck. While the musket fire from the north shore had been the signal for the traitor to release the anchor chain and for Smoot to sail away to the north side of the island, the three cannon shots were the signal for a third ship—the Tiburon—to set sail from the south end of Saint Croix.

Smoot tried to take credit for the tide being just right when the anchor chain was released, and if Henry Morgan were a speck more gullible, he'd have convinced the lad that the Cloud leaned larboard by his doing also. This was Smoot's greatest stroke of luck, for had she leaned toward the open sea, then her seaward-facing cannons could still be brought to bear against any would-be attacker.

John had no reason to suspect that the Eagle's abandonment of the Silver Cloud was for any reason other than to assist with their battle on the shore. It was exactly what he would have done had he been the protector rather than the protected.

McCoy was beginning to lower the first of two cannons over the side and into the bow of a waiting ship's boat when the shore party arrived back at Rip Rap Beach. The small craft sank nearly to her gunwales as the heavy cannon settled amongst the powder kegs, tools, and various shot loads.

While McCoy shoved off toward shore, John and his first officer stopped at the waters edge, with Ben Gunn tottering far behind.

John spoke first. "What on earth?"

David studied the strange doings at the ship. "Is that even our crew?"

"Oh, there's no doubt about that!" John could point out the various men by name. "That's McCoy at the first boat's helm!" John studied the ship carefully. "The question you should be asking is why they've turned traitors against us."

Ben finally reached the rest of the crew. "What's happening, Cap'n?"

"See for yourself, Ben!" John pointed to the slow-moving boats at the Cloud's water line. "While we were gone, it seems our loyal gunners decided to put the Silver Cloud on the reef and steal our cannons."

"Steal our cannons?" Ben struggled for his breath. "That doesn't make no sense, Cap'n. That isn't how you steal cannons."

The old maroon didn't get an answer, for his captain and first officer were now busy launching one of the larger boats with a crew of eight armed men.

John pulled his two pistols and turned back to Ben. "Are you coming with us?"

"No, Cap'n! I'll wait here with the others. There's sure to be gunfire, an' I'd just be in the way."

Midway between the crippled Silver Cloud and Rip Rap Beach, eight flintlock muskets leveled on the five gunners who were pulling toward the beach in the first boat.

"Heave to, Mister McCoy, and explain your traitorous folly!"

"Traitors, you call us?" The startled gunner ordered his men to ship oars and then threw the tiller to starboard to stop his boat. "Are you daft, Captain Jones?"

"No, I'm not! Unless you have a good explanation for these bizarre actions, your life will be forfeited here and now!"

"Captain, you mistake us!" It was one of the other gunners. "We're not traitors!"

"Then why's my ship laying on the reef with a dozen of my gunners stealing two of my cannons?" John swung his pistol arm about and pointed toward the beach. "Were you planning on cutting us down with grapeshot as we returned with the treasure?"

"Captain Jones!" McCoy stood and bellowed at the younger man. "Before ya make a complete arse o' yerself, ye'd best hear what happened aboard the Cloud!"

"I'm listening!"

"Someone came aboard from the sea during all that shootin' across the island and released our anchor chain. None of us saw him because we were watching your battle."

David called to the man. "And how do you know it wasn't one of your own men?"

"The deck was still wet where he came over the rail, sir. By the time the chain finally began slipping from the hawspipe, the man was back in the sea and long gone."

John lowered his pistols and gesture for his men to do the same. "What about these two cannons and all that ammunition?" Four casks of powder and a score of balls lay in each boat's bottom, along with the other equipment necessary to carry on a protracted land battle.

"That's how I explain it, Captain Jones!" McCoy stood and pointed seaward, past the Silver Cloud, to the ship approaching from the southeast. "By the time that ship gets here, our ship will have listed too far larboard to use her seaward guns!" McCoy pointed to the northwest. "Without the Eagle to protect us..." McCoy gritted his teeth and looked back at the fat Dutchman watching from the ship. He turned back to his captain. "I had to make a decision, Captain!"

A chill ran from the base of John's spine to his neck while he surveyed the approaching ship. It was far more than coincidence that had brought this third ship to Dead Man's Chest. John strained his eyes to make out any markings on the large French corvette that was crossing quickly toward his stricken ship.

"Take a look at her, David, and see if she reminds you of another ship we've encountered."

David pulled his spyglass from its pouch and raised it to his eye. "Good God! That's Joshua Smoot's ship! It's the Tiburon!"

"I'm afraid so, David."

"What are you talking about, Captain?" McCoy had directed his men to start pulling toward the shore. "Do you know her?"

John turned back to his gunner. "Winter of last year, Mister Noble and I were attacked by that ship several leagues south of Savannah. Before her crew could board us, a stroke of luck allowed us to tear her rudder clean away with one shot of barstock." John suddenly realized why McCoy was taking the two cannons ashore. He glanced quickly at the island and at the approaching pirate ship. He pointed.

"McCoy, get those cannons ashore and up to that cliff! We're in for a battle!"

David pushed the rudder over to turn their boat around. "They must think we already have the treasure."

John gave a nod and reached out for David's spyglass. "No doubt about it. Our gunfire on the north shore was obviously the signal to release our anchor, and the Cloud's three cannons signaled Smoot to begin his attack." John thought for a moment and continued. "I wish there was some way for them to find out we haven't dug up the treasure yet."

David straightened the tiller and paralleled the two boats with the cannons. "Why don't we release the prisoners?"

"Why should I do that?"

"Because they know, and they might signal Smoot to break off his attack."

"You're right!" John turned toward the beach and called out. "Mister Gunn!"

The old man called back. "I was right, wasn't I? They weren't stealin' 'em after all!"

"Send one of the men back to the north shore to tell Mister Ormerod to release the uninjured prisoners!"

"Aye, aye, Cap'n!"

"Make sure he tells the prisoners that the treasure wasn't at Dorsal Rock!" He turned back to David. "I should have thought of that myself."

David pointed to the northeast, back past Rip Rap Beach. "Look! It's the Eagle, and they've come about! Maybe they can get back around the reef before the Tiburon gets close enough to fire on the Silver Cloud!"

"Not likely with these winds. I'm afraid our only real hope is to get these cannons into position before they get within range." John looked back toward the Silver Cloud and called to McCoy. "I trust the remaining gunners know enough to move all the swivel guns to the starboard gunwale."

McCoy called back. "Aye, Captain! My boys know their jobs!"

Pulling the 800-pound cannons through the sand and up the hill to the cliff took just over an hour and all of the available men. The small wooden wheels were designed for the hard planking of a ship's deck, not the soft sands of the island. But using a combination of dead heads buried along the way and the blocks and tackle the gunners had brought along, they made steady progress. They finally twisted the second cannon about to face down toward their stricken ship just as the Tiburon set up for her first attack run.

David watched the pirate ship through his spyglass. "The Tiburon is within range of the Cloud, Captain Jones. What are they waiting for?"

"With the cannons hidden as they are, Smoot must think she's unarmed. He's going to get close before he fires on her."

The words had no more left his mouth when two of the Tiburon's cannons fired, their balls falling short of the stricken ship. John put a hand on McCoy's shoulder. "Steady now, McCoy, and make this count."

Aye, Captain." The gunner sighted down his barrel at the approaching ship. "On yer command, sir."

"Fire!"

Chapter 13

The three reports of the Silver Cloud's distress call rolled like thunder across the sea in all directions, bringing Henry Morgan down the Eagle's companionway to his captain's door. He gave three taps with the hilt of his sword and stepped back. "Cap'n Smoot! Did ya hear it?"

The middle-aged pirate had just begun a breakfast of biscuits and gravy with his two prisoners. He excused himself, wiped his face clean with a fine French napkin and pulled open the cabin door. "Of course I heard it, Henry. That's exactly why we're here on the north side of the island."

"But they're firin' on each other!"

Smoot paused to listen for additional cannon shots. "You're wrong! Those three shots were a warning signal, not a battle. I'd say they just now lost their anchor and went up on the reef."

"But—"

Smoot placed a large hand on the boy's face and pushed him backwards toward the ladder. "Get above deck an' come about for the south shore! We've been gone long enough!" Smoot turned to rejoin his breakfast guests, but stopped and took a threatening step toward the carrot-topped lad. "And I swear, Morgan. You bang on my door one more time with that damn cutlass an' I'll have yer heart for supper!"

***

Before the Eagle had reached the western tip of Dead Man's Chest, the Tiburon was positioning herself for her first broadside, seemingly unconcerned by the occasional small iron balls flying through her rigging. At one hundred yards abeam, she backed all but her fore t'gallant for steerage, and coasted to a near halt in the calm sea. Expecting little if any opposition, Captain Pritchard brought his forty-gun ship as close to the coral as was safe, putting it well within the range of the yet-unseen shore battery atop the hill.

"Gunners!" Pritchard was still reveling in his new-found authority. "They be unarmed, mates, so take yer time strippin' off her plankin'!!" At Pritchard's order, two cannons threw their twenty-pound balls at the Silver Cloud's exposed underbelly. Neither shot found its mark, and before the deafening roar of the Tiburon's cannons spent itself to the horizon, there were two similar explosions on the cliff above and to the right of Rip Rap Beach.

Pritchard and half his crew saw the white puffs of smoke. "What the—" Before he could finish his oath, the first of McCoy's two rounds smashed into the bulwarks just above the Tiburon's number-three starboard cannon, killing two men instantly and sending their nearby mates into a temporary panic. The second ball followed the first by five seconds, hitting the mizzen topmast a glancing blow, tearing away several inches of wood just above the crosstrees. It continued through the luffed mizzen royal in a shower of splinters.

"What the hell?" Pritchard looked back at the shore.

"There!" One of his gunners pointing. "They got cannons on the cliff!"

By the time Pritchard had located the cliff battery with his spyglass, McCoy and his gun crews had reloaded and sent two more shot at the Tiburon. This third shot struck the pirate ship's hull just above the waterline amidships, punching a three-foot hole in the planking. Shocked, Pritchard turned to his helmsman.

"Come about!" As the great ship began its turn to larboard, Pritchard turned back to the gun crews. "Fire as you bear!" One by one, and then in twos and threes, the twenty cannons began firing on the Silver Cloud. But since the ship was well into her turn, only the first three cannons came close to their marks. While the shore battery reloaded for their next volley, the gunners aboard the crippled ship continued peppering the Tiburon with small balls from their muskets and larger balls from the eight swivel guns. Two of the one-inch balls found their mark, killing one pirate and wounding a second man.

Smoot watched the whole affair through his spyglass. "Morgan! Trim yer sails for more speed and begin firing at the Tiburon!"

"At the Tiburon?" Henry was confused. "Don't you mean the Silver Cloud?"

"No!" Smoot lowered his spyglass. "Not 'til we know for sure where that treasure is!"

"But we do!" Henry pointed back toward the north shore. "It's next to that black mound!"

"Not necessarily." Smoot continued to study the site of the short-lived battle on the north side of the island. He lowered the glass and looked at Henry. "When I see the chests of gold and silver with my own eyes, then I'll be convinced. Until then, we've no choice but to play the Silver Cloud's protector, just like they expect us to do."

"Do ya think Privy'll know to set sail and run when we start firin' on 'im?"

"Take a look!" Smoot handed Henry the glass. "They've already hauled the wind to get away from those cannons on the cliff. Our attack'll only be for show."

By the time the Tiburon had sailed beyond range, she had put three holes in the Cloud while taking seven hits herself from the shore battery. She had a small fire burning in the forecastle, and nearly a dozen of her crew lay dead or injured. By the time the Eagle began throwing balls from the other side of the western reef, the Tiburon had finished her turn and was running toward the safety of Cottongarden Point at the eastern end of Saint Croix.

"McCoy!" John stood on the ledge thirty feet above the cannons. "I want you and the other six gunners to remain here while I go down to assess the damage to the ship. If you see the Tiburon turn back for another attack, fire a warning shot." He trotted down the dusty path to the beach. David and Ben Gunn had just climbed down from the crippled ship's deck into one of the ship's boats and were now pulling toward the beach.

As soon as they were within earshot, John called out. "Did they hit her?"

David called back. "Three hits, Captain!"

"How bad is it?"

"Two of their three shots penetrated the hull, Cap'n!" The boat skidded onto the sand and David leaped out. "One close to the bow and the second one amidships!"

"What kind of repairs do you—"

"Temporary patches won't do, Captain."

"How long do you think it'll take for repairs?"

"The one at the bow is high enough that we can leave it alone." David stopped and looked back at their badly listing ship. "The other is just below the waterline and is pretty large. I'd say repairs will take at

least two days, provided the pirates leave us alone long enough to get
her off the reef, moved to the beach and hauled down."

"I think they'll be more than busy with their own repairs." John
looked out to the fleeing pirates. "They're on fire and I believe we hit
their mizzen mast."

"Good!" David pointed at the Eagle as it continued to pursue the
Tiburon. "I'm glad Mister Forrestal sent the Eagle along. Between our
shore battery and Captain Steele, we should be well protected."

John watched the Eagle for several moments. "I misjudged Captain
Steele. If it weren't for him and those shots they took at the Tiburon,
we'd have likely lost the Cloud altogether."

"Does this mean the water between you two will be calmer now?"

"To a point, yes. But if you're asking whether it heals all the
wounds—no, Ben, it doesn't."

"I'm sorry to hear that, Cap'n. It does us no good for you two to be
at odds like this."

***

As the tide receded, John, David, and Ben stood watching their
injured ship list further and further toward shore. Robert trotted onto
the north end of the beach with the six Indian fighters.

He spotted the other officers. "Is it bad?"

John turned about. "Bad enough! David and Ben tell me that
there's a large hole amidships at the waterline." John took several steps
toward Robert and stopped. "How'd it go with the prisoners? Did you
get my message?"

"It's done, just as you ordered."

"Did they believe you—that the treasure wasn't there?"

Robert nodded. "I made them dig a hole four spans deep and twice
that across where I had stuck my sword. They promised to signal their
captain if we'd let them go."

"Good." John stepped into the boat. "I'm going out to see the
damage myself. While I'm gone, David, make sure the gun crews on the
cliff are provided with food, water, and some shelter from the sun. It's
going to be a long day." He turned to Robert. "Would you and Mister
Gunn accompany me?"

Within a half-hour, John, Robert, Ben, and Captain Van Mourik
were inside the crippled ship's lower decks inspecting the damage. It was
now low tide, and the ship was listing nearly fifteen degrees from the
upright. The hole in her side was at least two spans above the sea.

"That looks bad." John pulled away several loose pieces of oak from the large hole in the ship's side.

"As I tolt Master Noble, we took three rounds to de hull, Cap'n, an' there's some damage to her innards besides." Van Mourik spread a sheet of parchment on the deck and pointed to the areas of greatest damage.

"Damage to the innards?" John looked at the drawing. "How much? Where?"

"Here and here." Van Mourik pointed to a lower-deck beam and stanchion. "I tolt David we can leave der hole in the bow alone, but we'll have to move her to Rip Rap Beach at de next tide ta fix dis one, ja?"

"Can you have your temporary patches in place that quickly?"

"That'd be about six bells, just before sunset, Cap'n." The Dutchman nodded. "Aye, she be ready to float clear of da reef by den."

***

By late afternoon, the hole at the Silver Cloud's waterline was covered with a temporary patch of canvas and tar, and by sunset, just as the Dutchman had predicted, the sea had returned far enough that three of the ship's boats were able to pull the great ship free from the coral and into the deeper waters. By dark the Silver Cloud was secured near the high-water mark of Rip Rap Beach. The heaving-down post had been buried deep in the sand and a winching system put in place long before the ship had reached the shore. A heavy line was attached to the mainmast crosstree and run several times through a block and tackle system attached to the post. While the heavy ship was hauled down to expose its damaged hull to the carpenters, John met with his officers.

"The carpenter tells me that if there are no more attacks by the pirates, the permanent repairs could be completed in two days." He poured himself a cup of tea and looked back at his crippled ship. Lanthorns were being set up and lighted to give the carpenters the light they needed to begin the removal of the damaged sections of planking.

"We figured as much." Robert mixed a spoon of sugar in his cup. "Was that the 'something important' you wanted to tell us?"

"No, it wasn't." John gave the older man a raise of his brows. "Today's encounter with pirates—both on the north shore and from the sea—has put this mission into a completely different light and forced an important and essential decision upon us."

Robert was suddenly suspicious. "What kind of decision?"

"You could have been killed this morning."

Robert looked at the others. "Any one of us could have been killed."

"But you're still the only one who knows where the treasure's buried. If you're killed, we won't get the treasure, and the colonies won't get their cannons."

"I'm aware of that risk, John, but Mister Jefferson gave me explicit orders to tell nobody, including you, until we have our shovels in hand."

"He didn't even trust me?"

"That's why he didn't ask me for a map." Robert took a sip of his tea and continued. "Once it was put to paper, anybody who managed to get their hands on it could get the treasure."

Ben stepped close. "Beggin' yer pardon, sir, but Captain Jones is right. It doesn't matter any more what Mister Jefferson told you. You have to tell the rest of us."

Robert considered the old man's admonition.

David knew he was the youngest among them, but he felt compelled to be a part of the debate. "You shouldn't have to ponder this, Mister Ormerod. You know they're right. You have to tell us where it's buried."

Robert considered for a long moment. He gave a huff. "You're right, all of you." Robert stepped to the table where the map tubes lay. "Which one of these contains the chart of the island?"

"Here it is." John pulled the chart from the tube and spread it across the table, weighing it down with a lamp at each end.

The chart showed the outline of the island with the reef and beach at the west end, but none of the island's interior detail. Robert dipped a quill in John's ink well and drew a heavy meandering line across the island from west to east. Then, near the center of this first line, he drew a second one, perpendicular to the first and running halfway toward the northern shore.

"It's here." Robert touched the spot with his finger rather than make a mark with the quill. "Right at the head of this valley. We figured the trees and bushes would grow the best there."

John looked at the spot. "Can you be more specific?"

"Yes I can. As you're climbing the hill, you'll come to the point where this valley disappears into the ridgeline. Twenty paces back down into the valley and you'll come to a manchineel tree—probably the one our lookout encountered this morning." Robert looked up at his three friends. "The treasure lies under its roots."

David touched John's arm. "When do we go, Captain?"

John looked across at his ship. "If we bring the treasure down before the ship's ready to sail, we'll have pirates on us like lice on a maroon." Everyone looked at Ben.

The old man stifled an itch while he answered. "They'll be all over us no matter when we dig it up, Cap'n. Why wait?"

"Aye." John held up a hand and looked at Robert. "Since we already know they'll be watching our every move, why not turn it to our advantage?"

"What kind of advantage, John?"

"You've all heard the fable about the little boy who cried 'wolf.'" He looked about at the men one at a time. They each nodded. "Why did the townsfolk stop coming to the boy's aid?"

David spoke. "Because he called for help three or four times when there was no wolf. The people stopped believing him."

"We're going to cry 'wolf' to the pirates?"

"Yes, Robert, we are."

"How?"

John lifted one of the lamps and let the map roll closed. "I intend to send out two or three digging parties a day with empty wooden boxes. The men will be instructed to select an obvious spot in the trees or along the coast and dig a large hole. Then, after they bury their boxes, they'll return to Rip Rap Beach. Another team of a dozen or so men will go out and dig those same boxes up and bring them back to the beach."

Ben scratched his throat and squinted in his confusion. "I may be a little slow, Cap'n, but where's the sense in that?"

"I understand." Robert turned to his employee. "After a dozen or so false holes, the pirates will tire of watching. When we finally send out the real treasure hunters, the pirates won't be able to tell them from the others."

"Exactly." John was pleased that he didn't have to explain the plan. "Another benefit is that it will keep those who aren't repairing the ship busy."

Robert raised a hand. "You told us that there was something else we should do."

"One of us can pay a visit to Captain Steele to let him know what's going on." John turned to David. "That will be your job."

"But shouldn't you go? You're the captain."

"Aye, but I doubt the man would allow me aboard."

David considered. "When do you want me to go?"

"Tomorrow morning, just after breakfast. We can send out a couple of shovel crews before dark, and more early in the morning while you're at the Eagle. I'd like to hear Captain Steele's reaction to it."

"And what if I run into trouble aboard the Eagle? What signal should I give you?"

"Trouble?" John raised his hands. "What kind of trouble could you get into?"

"There's pirates afoot, Captain. They could be anywhere."

John laughed and looked at the others. "Fine. If you get to the Eagle and discover that the whole crew has been replaced by pirates, wave your handkerchief in the air."

The others joined John in a hearty laugh.

David looked about at the other three. "My kerchief is bright yellow."

***

Perhaps it was the Silver Cloud, crippled as she was and hauled down on her larboard side. Or perhaps it was the knowledge that their every move was being watched from the hills. Whatever it was, a burdensome heaviness of spirit hung over Rip Rap Beach. But the digging parties provided a perfect diversion, so much so that most of the men were volunteering for extra trips into the island's interior.

At Captain Van Mourik's request, a dozen sleeping tents had been erected along a single line running north to south, just above the high-water mark. Armed watches with battle rattles stood near the end tents, and two others stood watch aboard the hauled-down ship, one at the bow and the other at the stern. Further up the beach, almost to the tree line, an extra sail was held aloft by upright oars and stretched taut so as to create a shaded work pavilion for the officers. Similar pavilions were erected next to the ship and circled with oil lamps so the carpenters could work twenty-four hours a day at fitting the fresh planking to the Silver Cloud's hull.

It was six bells between midnight and dawn, and neither John nor Robert had been able to sleep. Somewhere aboard the Silver Cloud, a lone sailor sang a familiar verse from a sea ballad to the accompaniment of his concertina.

"A curse on the jewels, the pearls an' the gold,
A curse on the pirates what's honor was sold.
A curse on the Yorkman what refuses to tell,

Of the treasure laid by — may he rot in hell."

Robert swung his legs out of his cot, stood and walked across to the small cast iron stove. He picked up the teapot and shook it to judge its contents. He poured himself a cup and took a sip of the strong brew.

John looked across the pavilion at Robert. "He's singing about you, isn't he?"

"Yes, I am the 'Yorkman' of song and fable." Robert looked about the camp. Everything was quiet except for the sounds of work from the far side of the ship. "But the way things have gone so far, I've a bad feeling the whole crew may taste of that curse before we get off this island."

John got up and poured himself a cup. "You made the right decision to tell us."

Robert didn't answer. His mind was on the treasure. The secret had been his for over twenty years, and it had given him a sort of power. A large secret will do that, especially when it concerns money. It also gave him a tremendous sense of security, knowing that any time he needed it, he could sail to this—his private island bank—and take away what he needed.

"What is it, Robert? You look a hundred leagues away."

"Oh, I was just thinking." He downed his tea and threw the last quarter inch of liquid and wilted leaves onto the dark sand. "Remember the other day when I asked you how you learned about me and the treasure?"

"Yes?"

"I don't mean anything personal against the lad, but doesn't it strike you as a little odd that it was David who told you?"

"Who else, if not David?"

"Look at it, John. His father owns the cannons, and David knew all about me and the treasure?"

John stroked his chin and considered the chain of events between King's Town and Edenton. "The only part that bothers me is that he kept it from me until I was desperate."

"Exactly."

"Do you think David had the whole thing planned from the beginning?"

Robert nodded. "David, or his father. What do you know about Charles Noble?"

"Not very much." John looked across the pavilion to where David was sleeping. "I only met the man a week before David and I sailed for

Virginia. The few times that we spoke, it was about my ship and its provisions." He paused as a new thought struck him.

"What?"

John shook his head. "Mister Noble begged me several times to not take David to Fredericksburg."

"Even so, I'd like a talk with David, provided you have no objections. I have a distinct feeling he's not telling—"

Robert fell silent in answer to John's raised hand. The young captain sat up from his cot and bristled like a threatened dog.

"What is it?"

"Listen!" He looked about at the ship. "Something's wrong." John stood and looked across the camp to the north. A group of men had assembled and were speaking in agitated tones. He could only make out a word or two, but it was enough. "Somebody's been kidnapped!"

"There!" Robert pointed. "Someone's running this way!"

While they watched, a powder monkey named Gilcrest ran down the line of tents, under the Cloud's masts and haul-down tackle and then straight for the pavilion.

John called to the boy. "What's wrong, Gilcrest? What's happened?"

The lad was still thirty yards out when he started crying something about men missing. But then, just before reaching them, the boy fell face down into the sand.

Robert ran out and jerked the boy up. "Who's been taken, lad?"

"The pirates got 'em, sir!" The excited youth thrust a piece of parchment at John.

"Who'd they take?" Robert gave the boy a shake. David heard the commotion and leaped up from his cot.

John took the paper and pushed past them to the table. He adjusted the lamp. The message was crude and most of the words were misspelled, but there was no mistaking what it said.

Gilcrest pointed back toward the north. "They took the old man—Ben Gunn—and our carpenter!"

"What do they want?" Robert read the message over John's shoulder.

"Isn't it obvious?" John handed him the paper. "They want the treasure."

"Damn it! How in God's name..." Robert reread the message while a group of two dozen armed men began to assemble nearby.

David ran from that group back to the pavilion. "On the beach, north of the mound! One of the men heard screams and went out to look. He reported that there were three campfires at water's edge."

"Three fires..." John was buttoning up his breeches. "That means there's at least fifteen of them." He strapped on his sword and jammed two pistols in his belt.

David ran back to the pavilion and grabbed his pistols and sword. "Are you going with us?"

"Of course I am. Those are my men out there!"

After a few words with Robert, John and his first officer led the rescue party northward, out of camp. With their lanthorns trimmed to a flicker, the darkness quickly swallowed them from sight.

As they neared the mound and the campfires, David whispered to John. "I know this is probably stupid of me, but aren't they going to be waiting for us?"

John nodded. "They've probably dug up every inch of earth about the mound and didn't find anything. I'm hoping they want to strike some sort of bargain for those two."

"But what if you're wrong and they just want to kill as many of us as they can?"

"If the battle goes the wrong way, then we'll fight until we have to swim for it."

"Swim for it? Swim for what?"

John had been scanning the horizon to their left for the last several minutes. "Take a look out there, just inside the reef."

David turned and looked where John was pointing. He couldn't see anything at first. John opened and closed the shutter on his lanthorn to give three flashes. A moment later, a similar signal returned from a hundred yards to sea.

"Who's that?"

"It's Robert with three of our boats. I hope you're wrong about the ambush David, but if not, at least we'll have a second way of escape."

***

As a man grows older, more things change than the color of his hair and the number of creases on his face. Out of necessity, he becomes wiser and more cautious about nearly everything. This aging process, and the desire that things come a little slower and easier than they did when he was young, happens to landlubber and seaman alike. So it is with ship's masters, and the art of driving a vessel at night in strange waters. Although the brightness of a full moon will reveal his position to an enemy sooner, it is much more comfortable to have it than not.

Old ship commanders especially like it. Thus the full moon came to be called the "commander's moon."

It was one of those special moons that rose from the eastern tip of Dead Man's Chest the night Ben Gunn and the ship's carpenter were kidnapped. John and his rescue party crouched in the shadows of the mound, a hundred and fifty yards from the three campfires. Nothing moved for ten minutes.

"This is a trap, isn't it?"

John glanced seaward. "Of course it is, David." Robert's three boats were approaching their rescue position.

"Shall I pass the word for the others to move up?"

"Aye, but I want them going—" Before he could finish the sentence, there was a cough and a cry of pain from the smoldering campfires. The rescue party bristled to a man while a flurry of angry whispers swept through their ranks.

John rose slightly. "Damn their souls! If they've killed either of our men..."

"At least we know one's still alive, Captain."

"Don't count on it, David. Anybody can scream out as if he's being tortured."

Captain Jones ordered the lanthorns trimmed and left at the mound. As the moon emerged from behind a cloud, Robert's three boats were suddenly silhouetted against the horizon.

John turned to the nearest crewmen and whipered. "Pass this along. We're going to be totally exposed from the moment we leave these rocks until we return to their cover. Pair up with a mate and follow Mister Noble and me by twos. Until I give the order, I don't want any of you to break ranks, regardless of what you see or hear. Is that understood?"

There was a muffled response and nodding heads. John continued. "If we're attacked from the treeline as we were this morning, I want you to return to the mound and use your muskets to best advantage, being sure to watch your flanks." John pointed to sea. "If we're pushed to the sea, those three boats are our salvation."

The nearest crewman nodded and began passing the word.

"Then let's get to it!"

Like a flood of ants at a picnic lunch, the rescue party poured over the rocks toward the sea. At the high-water line, they turned eastward toward the darkened campfires and their two kidnapped shipmates. Two of the fires had died completely. The light north breeze fanned a flurry of orange sparks from the third up into the night air, and for a just a moment it took the shape of a human. From fifty feet away the camp appeared to have been abandoned for some time, but one man's moanings continued to come from its general direction. The rescue party's pace quickened to a trot as they passed the end of the mound.

"Do you think that's Ben, Captain?"

"I hope so, David."

With only a hundred feet between them and the pirate's camp, there came a blood chilling cry from their right—from the tall grass where several of the pirates had fallen the previous morning.

"Save me, mates! They're cuttin' off me legs!" Another long scream followed and trailed off as if it were the poor man's last. Before Captain Jones could stop them, two of his men had broken ranks and were running in the tortured man's direction, intent upon his rescue. But no sooner had they entered the tall grass than a dozen muskets fired, cutting the would-be rescuers down in their tracks.

John recognized the tactic. He stood and pointed. "To the water line!"

"Help me, Captain Jones!" The mocking cries continued from the south and the tree line. "Help me, Mister Noble!" Another called. "Help us, shipmates!" And then the calls were replaced by a barrage of mocking laughter.

David and several others dropped to the sand next to John. "They've tricked us!"

"Aye, and we've paid dearly for it, too!"

The rescue party lay for half an hour at the high-water mark, watching and waiting for the inevitable attack. The taunting calls for help and the cruel laughter continued for a short interval, and then trailed off.

David looked about. "What now, Captain?"

"Get me two volunteers. We'll give the camp a quick check before we go."

"I'll go!" It was Gilcrest, the powder monkey. Neither John or David had known he was among their number.

David put a hand on the boy's shoulder. "And I'll go with him."

"Very well, but go with caution. They'll be watching your every move."

"Don't worry." David gave the lad a nod and they crawled forward.

While David and Gilcrest moved off across the sand toward the campsite, there was a clatter of oars being shipped and of boats skidding onto the sand a hundred feet to the west, announcing the arrival of Robert Ormerod and the extra men.

After a moment, the Yorkman dropped onto the sand next to John. "What's happening, John? I heard the gunfire and the screams for help, and figured the rescue had been accomplished by now. What are you watching for?"

"David and one of the powder monkeys are checking the pirate's camp. I'm certain they've already killed Ben and Sanders."

"You haven't found them yet?"

John shook his head. "We're not even certain they're in the camp."

"Then what was all that gunfire?"

"Unfortunately, some of the pirates lured a couple of the mountain men away and killed them."

Robert studied the flickering campfire. "They knew exactly who to kidnap."

"How do you figure?"

"Think about it! They know why Mister Gunn's with us. They needed him to find out where he hid the silver bars on Flint's Island."

"I figured that much, but why our carpenter?"

"They don't intend that we ever leave this island."

"Oh?"

"How better to accomplish that than to kill off the men who know how to make the repairs?"

"If you're correct, then Sanders is done for."

As they spoke, Gilcrest ran across the sand to them. "Mister Noble says it's all clear and to bring the men up."

John and Robert stood. "What about our two men?"

Gilcrest pointed. "They're both at the fires, and there's at least a dozen dead pirates laying about."

John turned to the nearest crewman. "I want four of you with Mister Ormerod and me. Tell the rest of your men to take up defensive positions back at the mound." The man nodded, and a moment later, John and Robert stood and followed the lad. "Are either of our men alive?"

"Aye, but they're both senseless."

The smell of burnt flesh hung heavy over the two injured men. They were laying together amidst the three fires. Ben was naked to the waist and lay on his face, with a small puddle of blood in the sand where it had run from his mouth and nose.

Robert dropped to his knees. "Ben!" He turned his old friend onto his back. "Ben, can you hear me?"

"Oh God...I hurt so..." The old maroon whispered through bloody teeth. "I didn't...oh, Master Orm...they tried..."

"Save your strength, Ben." Robert cradled his friend's head in his hands. The old man closed his eyes and swooned back into oblivion. "I'm just thankful to God that you're still alive." Robert looked to John and David. "How's Sanders doing?"

"He's alive, but just barely." David held up the lanthorn. The back of the carpenter's shirt was split open from waist to collar, and his torn flesh was caked in a mixture of blood, sand, and ashes. "They must have laid the cat to his back for most of the night."

John stood and pointed back where Robert had come ashore. "Robert, put these two in your boat and return to our camp as quickly as you can. They need the doctor's care, and I'm afraid they wouldn't survive being carried that far."

"You're not coming with us?"

"Not just yet—not until we have a good look about this camp."

Robert looked about at the dead. "Those bodies—very strange that they would lay their dead out like that."

John nodded and stood with David in silence until Robert and the wounded were gone. Then he stepped back and circled the line of dead men. Something was odd about the five bodies at the center of the line. While the arms of the outboard seven were at their sides, the center five were spaced apart further than the others, and their arms stretched out in various positions, like the hands of so many clocks.

John kicked at one of their feet. "Take a look at this, David."

David stepped to his captain and raised his lanthorn. "What?"

"Do you know semaphore?"

"A little. Why?"

"These five in the center…look at their arms." John pointed. "If I didn't know better, I'd say these five were signalling the letters C-O-L-J-S."

David knelt down next to one of the bodies. "Is that supposed to mean something?"

"I assume it must."

"I don't believe these are the men we killed yesterday morning, John."

"Oh?"

David brought his lanthorn close to one of the dead men's faces. With his free hand, he wiped the man's bloody throat with a finger. The blood was fresh and the body was still warm. "This man's been fresh killed! They must have got into a fight before we got here, and their mates laid out the dead ones to confuse us."

John touched another of the bodies. It was the same. "Either that, or Captain Steele was over here earlier."

"I don't think he had anything to do with this." David checked three more of the dead. "He couldn't have known our men were kidnapped. And besides, he'd have brought Gunn and Sanders back to us rather than leave them here." David looked to John and shook his head. "No, this was done by somebody who hates Smoot and his men as much as we do."

"But who?"

"My guess is that we've another ship of pirates out there somewhere. After all, every pirate in the Caribbean wants to get their hands on that treasure."

John stood and searched the sea for ships. "If that's the case, then Captain Steele needs to know about this as quickly as possible."

***

The ship's doctor had been tending to the two injured men for a half hour when John and David rounded the last outcropping and stepped onto the north end of Rip Rap Beach. Robert was waiting for them.

John spotted him and called out. "How's Ben faring?"

"He's some nasty burns, but that seems the extent of his sufferings." He turned and matched strides with the younger men. "The poor soul was unconscious most of the trip back. He's lucid now, but in the boat he kept raving about Long John Silver."

"Long John Silver? What did he say?"

"Nothing I could put together. Ben's carried a heavy burden these past eleven years."

"But his wounds—he'll be all right, won't he?"

"McKenzie says he'll be up and about within a week."

"What about Sanders?"

"Died in the boat before we could get him back. The surgeon figured he lost far too much blood for his size." Robert stopped and turned to John. "You were wrong about his back."

"Oh?" John looked to the surgeon's tent. "Then it wasn't the cat after all?"

"No." Robert leaned close. "They cut something in his flesh—something I've told the surgeon to show to no one but you."

"A message?"

"Much worse." Robert pushed into the tent, leaned close and whispered. "It's the map."

The pungent odor of fresh blood nearly made the three men retch. The body of the ship's carpenter lay under the piece of sailcloth he had been carried upon, with the dark red blood and caked sand scattered about the surgeon's table.

Doctor McKenzie was tending to the burns on Ben's legs. "Captain Jones, Mister Noble." He stood and stepped to the other table. "Mister Ormerod told me that you'd want to see this."

"Yes, I would." John stepped to Ben's side and put a gentle hand on the old man's shoulder. "But first, how is our old friend?"

Ben began to answer, but the surgeon spoke for him. "They burned his lower legs pretty bad with their irons, sir, but he'll recover."

"Good." John turned and lifted the corner of the sailcloth that covered Sanders's back. The blood and sand had been washed away, revealing a very accurate outline of the small island. It was cut into skin with the man's own chisel. The ridgeline and the two small valleys that radiated toward the north were there also, cut just to the left of his spine.

"There!" Robert pointed to the crescent shaped puncture wound between the seventh and eighth ribs. "That's what I wanted you to see."

McKenzie touched his own chest. "I believe the chisel damaged his heart, sir. He'd have died anyway, even if he'd got here sooner."

John turned to the doctor. "Is Mister Gunn well enough to speak with us for a few minutes?"

"I'd rather he didn't, Captain. He has several deep burns to dress yet, and I'm afraid of the strain the affair has had on his heart."

"I can talk with you, Captain Jones." The old maroon raised himself onto an elbow. "These burns aren't nothin' anyway." He took the edge of the temporary dressing and raised it from his right leg, revealing three rows of iron burns from his ankle to his upper calf. "Look at that. Straight as tattoos from my ankles all the way to my knees."

"I'll give you ten minutes with him, Captain, but please no longer." With that, Adam excused himself and walked from the tent.

Robert began. "It's obvious they tortured you, Ben. Can you remember whether you told them anything?"

Ben shook his head a little too enthusiastically. "I didn't tell them nothin', sir. Every time they burned me, I'd pass out stone cold."

John lifted the canvas from Sanders's back. "Then how do you explain this map and the spot where they stabbed him?"

Robert looked at the puncture mark with John. "If you didn't tell them anything, then how'd they manage to get so close?"

"That was just a lucky stick, sir. They cut the map first, an' then tried to make me finger the treasure. When they could see that I wasn't gonna tell them nothin', one of them grabbed the chisel, hauled back and plunged it into his back. Then, after he was senseless, they took to torturin' me again with their cauterizing irons." Ben was in great pain, but the thought that his employer and his captain didn't believe him hurt worse than the fresh burns.

Robert pointed back to the north shore. "Do you know anything about all those dead pirates at the edge of the camp?"

Ben shook his head. "Last thing I remember before wakin' up here is my legs bein' burned. I never saw any dead pirates."

"Robert told me you kept talking about Long John Silver."

"I always dream 'bout Long John Silver—ever since I freed him from the Hispaniola—but I don't remember talking about him this morning."

"Thank you, Ben." John gave the old man a pat on his shoulder. "We'll leave you to Doctor McKenzie's care for now. Do what he says so we don't lose you also."

"Aye, Cap'n Jones." The old man lay back on the cot with a groan.

The doctor and David were waiting outside. Without a word to them, John and Robert turned and walked quickly to their pavilion.

"What do you think, John?"

"We'll just have to wait and watch. He might have told them, but considering..."

"Considering what?"

"Think about it, Robert. It's obvious they never intended to kill Ben."

"Agreed. Go on."

"How'd they know to take Ben in the first place, unless someone told them about the remaining treasure on Flint's Island?"

"You think there's a spy on the Cloud, don't you?"

"It's a possibility, but we've very little to go on at this point. It may simply be a case of loose talk."

"Do you think Van Mourik's in league with Smoot?"

"I don't believe he's a spy, Robert, but he is a chronic braggart. There's no telling how many people he boasted to at Charles Town."

"Hmm." Robert looked across at the ship where Seamus Barragan was cooking breakfast. Captain Van Mourik was elbow deep in flour.

"That's why he's conspicuously absent from most of our staff meetings, right?"

"Right. It's best for all concerned that we control what Van Mourik knows and doesn't know."

"But I heard you telling him our departure will be delayed for at least another week. Why would you confide something like that when you know he'll tell everybody?"

"For exactly that reason. Consider it, Robert. Our secrets are reaching the pirates. If Van Mourik is the cause—and I hope he's not—he becomes the perfect conduit for relaying false information."

David approached from the surgeon's tent and called out. "When do you want me to go out to meet with Captain Steele?" David reached the pavilion. "What do you want me to ask and tell him?"

"I want to know if he killed those twelve pirates last night, and I'm certain he'll want to know about the digging parties."

"Should I tell him when we expect to load the treasure and depart?"

John thought for a moment while he searched the sea to the south. The Eagle was tacking slowly from the east to the west. "Only if he asks, and tell him we've lost our carpenter so it may take four or five more days."

"Do you really think it will take us that much longer, Captain?"

John shook his head. "There's evidence that we have a traitor on the Silver Cloud. If it's true, then we must keep our knots tighter than normal."

John looked up to the shore battery. "Send someone up there and have them fire one shot to call the Eagle to anchorage."

Chapter 14

"Henry!" Captain Smoot stepped from his stateroom door to the ladder. "Henry Morgan!"

"Aye, Govn'r!" The orange-haired youth slid down one of the mainmast stays and made a light-footed landing on the deck next to his captain. "The cannon! You heard it too?"

"Of course I heard it!" Smoot shaded his eyes against the morning sun. "Fetch Captain Steele!"

"Aye, aye, Govn'r!" Henry was down the hatch and past his captain in a flash, his trusty cutlass slicing the dark air ahead of him while he traversed the passageway toward the middle hold. The prisoner sat on the deck. The single whale oil lamp hanging from the overhead had run out of oil the day before.

Alan Steele looked up and raised his chains. "Finally come to kill me, or does Smoot need me at another one of his tea parties?" His water had run out hours before, and he was already feeling the effects of dehydration.

"T' kill ya!" Henry raised the cutlass and leaped toward the prisoner. "Smoot's sick o' feedin' ya, an' sent me to do ya in!" He put the tip of his blade to Steele's throat and pressed it into the flesh. "But first he wants you in his cabin to answer a question."

Minutes later, Steele was pushed through the door of the master's cabin and forced to his knees. Smoot sat tilted back in the imprisoned captain's chair with his boots resting on the fine cherry table. The vulgar cutthroat pried at his teeth with a very large barracuda bone to extract the final remains of his breakfast.

"Ah, if it isn't the pride of the colonial privateers 'imself!" He flipped the bone into the air and flashed a toothy grin at Steele. The bone dropped into his empty water cup. "Me an' the crew was wonderin' what that single cannon shot might mean. You wouldn't happen to know now, would ya?"

Steele scowled at his captor. "You're going to have a visitor."

"That were me very guess." Smoot eased the chair down onto all four legs and looked to Henry. "Wasn't it, Henry?"

The lad nodded. "Aye—yer 'xact words, Cap'n Smoot."

Smoot stood and pushed past Henry to the starboard windows. The careened Silver Cloud was just coming into view. "A visitor, an' so much to talk about." He turned and looked down at Steele while he pulled his dirk.

Steele noticed the movement and feared that his next words might be his last. "And I suppose you want my help?"

No sooner had his words left his parched throat than the old pirate's dagger pierced the decking between his knees. "Not 'specially." Smoot raised his right eyebrow. "It seemed to me more appropriate to present yer head to 'em on a platter, since they'll find out we've taken your ship now anyhow."

Captain Steele spoke just above a whisper. "But they don't have to find out."

"They don't?" Smoot walked across the deck and stood over his prisoner for several seconds. "Might ya be volunteerin' yer services to me?"

"I might be willing to help you, if you'll agree to release your other prisoner."

"We're making bargains now, are we?" Smoot gave a laugh. "And just who do you suggest I release her to?"

"See here, Smoot. They all know what I look like. You need me to convince them the Eagle's still their protector, especially if it's Captain Jones or that man from New York."

"Oh, Captain Steele." Smoot gave his best frown. "You disappoint me somethin' fierce. If it's either o' them two, they'd make a much better hostage than you. If it's anybody else, then with all the things I learned from you these last five days, I should have no trouble foolin' 'em into thinkin' I'm you. If I can't fool 'em, then I'll just kill 'em." He threw back his head and laughed.

"Then why have you kept me alive this long? I must have some purpose."

"Some purpose?" The pirate thought while he sucked at his teeth. "Aye, ya both do. Actually, the girl's worth more to me than you at this point."

"Then what advantage do I win by helping you?"

"Why don't we wait to see how well you play your part. Then—"

"Cap'n Smoot." Henry was looking out the starboard window. "Ya better come see this."

"What is it, Henry?"

"Look there, Govn'r, just below where they set up their shore battery."

Smoot stepped to the window and studied the activity at water's edge. "Why I'll be! They've gone an' dug up the treasure in broad daylight!"

"Aye!" Henry pulled his cutlass and began moving toward the shackled prisoner. "An' now there's no reason ta keep this one alive no more, is there?" He stepped beside Steele and raised his blade.

"Belay that!" Smoot caught Henry's hand. "You can kill him, but not before we hear what our visitor has to say."

"But—"

"Lower yer weapon, boy, or by the powers, I'll parcel you into fours!" Smoot gave Henry a shove and then looked down at his prisoner. "Now, regarding our other special guest, I'll consider your proposition. Play your part well and maybe both of you will survive this affair."

Henry scrambled to his feet. "But you told me—"

"I don't care what I told you. Remove Captain Steele's chains and see to it that he's washed and dressed in his finest clothes."

After several tacks, the Eagle dropped anchor at the break in the reef, near where the Silver Cloud lay the previous morning. It was taking far too long for Steele to get prepared, and Captain Smoot was becoming impatient.

"Morgan!" Smoot bellowed from the quarterdeck.

A mass of orange hair popped from the forward ladder. "Did you call me, Govn'r?"

"I wasn't calling yer sister! Where is Captain Steele? The Cloud's boat is halfway here!"

"He's comin' now, Govn'r!" He leaped to the deck and stood with his cutlass drawn. Steele climbed slowly up behind him, blinded momentarily by the bright sunlight. When he hesitated in order to gain his bearings, Henry began kicking at the backs of his legs.

There was a flurry of arms and a flash of steel. Before the youngster could counter the attack, Steele had twisted the cutlass from his hand, thrown him to the deck and pressed the blade to his throat.

"Kick me one more time, you worthless urchin, and you'll go into hell without your head. I'm a dead man anyway, and I'd love to take you with me."

Smoot called out. "Morgan! Yield!"

Steele released his grip of the lad's hair and threw the cutlass over the rail. Henry jumped up and watched his favorite toy spin through the water and come to rest between two coral heads. He gave his attacker a dark scowl.

"Well, Captain Steele!" Smoot beckoned for the captain to come aft. "Are we ready for some playacting?"

"I'll play my part well enough!"

Smoot was now in colonial seamen's dress. "If they ask where your first officer is, you tell 'em that you had to put him ashore someplace with a bad fever."

Steele gave Smoot a defiant glare.

"Careful man! You can rough up my good luck charm, but cross me once and not only will you die, but the good lady in chains will as well. And mind you, hers won't be a quick death. My men can make killin' her downright fun."

Smoot leveled his spyglass at the approaching boat and studied the young man at the helm. Something about the young officer tickled a memory.

"Morgan!"

"Aye, Govn'r?"

"Take a look at that man at the tiller."

Henry adjusted the instrument to one eye, and then the other. "Why, that's the one what knew 'bout me killin' Captain Claw back on Tortuga!" He lowered the glass. "Do you know 'im?"

"Aye, its young David Noble—Charlie Noble's pup."

"Charlie Noble what traded you the Tiburon?"

"The same." Smoot took back the spyglass and gave the small boat another close inspection. "That boy was there in '71, too, when that innkeeper—Jack Bridger—made that covenant with us for John Flint's bones."

Smoot turned about to Steele and grabbed him by the beard. "Looks like you'll be on yer own. Think you can handle it, without putting yourself and your cellmate in jeopardy?"

Steele pulled Smoot's hand from his face. "I can do anything I set my mind to."

"Of course you can!" He gave Steele's back a slap, as if they were mates. "But just to make sure you keep yer word, there'll be a dozen cocked pistols about the deck."

"Ahoy, Eagle!" It was David Noble at two hundred feet. "Permission to come aboard?"

Captain Steele stepped to the rail. "Permission granted, Silver Cloud!"

Henry dropped down the forward hatch and Smoot stepped behind the mainmast.

Steele called out. "How go the repairs on the Silver Cloud?"

"Going well, sir!" The man in the boat's bow threw his line aboard the privateer and they were hauled along side. David started up the ladder. "If nothing else goes wrong, we could refloat her in four or five days."

"That long?" Steele extending a hand of welcome, and pulled the young Jamaican aboard.

"Our carpenter was killed last night on the north shore. That's the delay." David flashed a look at the crew. "Mister Forrestal told me all about you and your fine ship, and I'm sorry now that I didn't take the time to come aboard when you were still at his docks."

"I hope Mister Forrestal's report on me wasn't all bad."

"On the contrary, sir. He tells me Mister Jefferson hand-picked you and your entire crew for this mission." David looked about at the crew for the first time and was struck with how rough they appeared.

Steele gave David a raise of his brow. "So…why did you summon us?"

"For several reasons, sir." David collected his thoughts to be sure he wouldn't miss anything. "Captain Jones wants to know what happened to the Tiburon."

"Last we saw of her, she was on fire and headed around the eastern tip of the big island. Like the Silver Cloud, she's probably hauled down on a beach somewhere for repairs."

"We figured as much." David gave a chuckle. "We put several good ones through her hull and our gunner says he took away half of her mizzenmast."

Steele gave a quick glance to where Smoot was hiding. "What else did Captain Jones need to know?"

"Last night, two of our men were taken from our camp to the north shore and tortured. When we found them, there were a dozen freshly killed pirates laid out in a line like cordwood. We wondered who killed them."

"Does Captain Jones think I did it?"

"He was hoping so."

Steele shook his head. "Could it have been a mutiny among the Tiburon's crew?"

"We thought of that, but it doesn't figure they'd lay them out that way. It's almost as if whoever did it was trying to tell us something." David paused. "We think there's another ship out here someplace."

Steele raised his brow. "Another pirate ship?"

"No telling until we spot her. Captain Jones wants you to make a circuit of the island as soon as you can, and report back to him."

"We'll do it as soon as you go back." Steele noticed the trail of men carrying boxes and shovels below the cliff.

David gave a knowing laugh. "I see you've noticed our digging party."

Steele wanted to question David, but knew it would work to Smoot's advantage.

"We started yesterday after we got back from the north shore. You had to have seen the two we sent out in the afternoon."

"Sorry, I missed them. Have you dug up the treasure yet?"

David shook his head. "No, not yet."

"Then what's in the boxes those men are carrying?"

"Nothing. They're empty."

"Empty? Then why—"

"That's Captain Jones' idea to fool the pirates."

"Fool the pirates?" Steele gave another quick glance toward where Smoot was hiding.

"Aye! He's sending out three or four of those crews daily to bury and dig up empty boxes. One of them will be carrying back the real treasure, but not even I will know which one."

Smoot heard every word from his hiding place. He stifled a curse.

"I suppose Captain Jones will want us to keep the Tiburon occupied when you dig up the real treasure?"

"Well...yes, provided he knew when that would be. And mind you, I'd tell you if I knew. It all depends on how soon the Cloud's planking is repaired." David looked to the island as he considered. "There might be a way you could know."

"Oh?"

David pointed to the crest of the hill. "As you know, we've two cannons on that cliff yonder. Captain Jones won't leave without taking them with us."

"I don't see why not, seeing as how..." Steele fell silent, realizing what he was about to disclose to Smoot.

But David had no idea Smoot was listening. "The cannons we'll purchase from my father are all going to the defense of the colonies. The Silver Cloud will need those two for her next mission, whatever it may be." He turned back to Steele. "I'd say that when you see those two cannons moved down the hill, then you can be pretty certain the treasure's already on the Cloud and she's ready to float. That's when you want to begin watching for the Tiburon."

While David was explaining about the cannons, one of Smoot's crewmen had stepped behind him. The pirate's eyes were fixed on the brightly colored kerchief hanging from David's back pocket. With a quick but indelicate jerk, the yellow square of cloth was out of David's pocket and behind the pirate's back.

Noticing the tug at his trousers, David's hand went to the now-empty pocket. "Hey!" David spun on the man and held out his hand. "Give that back!"

"No!" The pirate spoke with a schoolboy's impudence. At that, the man began tying the kerchief about his unkempt hair, pirate fashion.

David made a lunge at the bandana, but the pirate twisted away and hid behind two of his mates. David turned to man he thought was in charge. "Captain Steele!"

"Give it back!"

The pirate gave a quick glance toward the mainmast and back to Steele.

"Now, or I'll have you flogged!"

The pirate's face contorted with frustration. "But it's so purdy!"

"Now!"

The pirate looked at the mainmast. This time, Smoot's pistol was leveled at the man's chest. He pulled the cloth from his head and held it out to David. "Here then, an' a curse on the thing!"

The argument on deck was more than Henry Morgan's curiosity could stand. As carefully as he could, the young pirate poked his head from the forward hatch for a quick look at their visitor. But a quick look was all it took, for in that split second before Henry could duck away, David's eyes caught sight of the red hair and green eyes of the Charles Town carpenter.

A flash of heat raced up David's back. "Captain Steele...is anything wrong?"

"Wrong?" Steele looked about to see what his young visitor had seen. "I don't believe so. Why do you ask?"

"Captain Jones..." David pulled the yellow kerchief from his pocket and began wiping his face and neck. He fumbled for some words to say. "If you're short of any supplies...he wanted me to offer you whatever you might need. That is, if you're low on anything."

"You can tell my good friend that we have everything we need, unless he'd consent to sending across some rum."

"Rum?" David knew these two captains hated each other. Steele talking this way confirmed his suspicions about the situation on board the Eagle. "I'm sure he'd do that for a good friend like you."

"Then rum it is!" Steele took a step toward David. "Was there anything else Captain Jones wanted to tell me?"

"No, that was all. He just wanted you to know about the digging parties and ask about those dead pirates."

"Then convey my respects to your fine young captain, Mister Noble, and tell him I look forward to our reunion at Charles Town."

"Thank you, sir. I will."

As quickly as he could go, David was over the rail and into his waiting boat. As the oars took their first bite at the sea, Steele found Smoot's hawkish nose in his face.

"So his father's trading my cannons for the treasure, is he? This is better than I ever hoped for."

Henry trotted down the deck and stopped next to the two. "How so, Govn'r?"

"Don't you see it, Morgan? I was planning on sending Pritchard and the Tiburon against the Cloud if they escaped from the Chest, but..." Smoot paused to consider the implications of the new revelation. "Fate has finally smiled on Fishbone Smoot! We won't have to risk sinking the Silver Cloud in deep water because the treasure's destined for the Noble warehouses in King's Town!"

"When do we tell Privy?"

"Not just yet." Smoot turned to watch the retreating longboat. "Matter of fact, I don't believe it's in our best interest that Pritchard ever knows."

"What?"

"If things go sour and the Silver Cloud escapes the Chest before the Tiburon returns, we'll simply beat her to King's Town and wait."

Steele couldn't resist making a comment. "You think you have it all figured out, don't you?"

"Ah, Captain Steele!" Smoot gave the man a toothy grin. "I forgot all about you for a minute there, what with all this wonderful news about the treasure and my cannons." Smoot gave a squint. "What was all that chummy talk between you and David Noble?"

"What chummy talk?"

"All of that...'best friend' bilge! Sounded like you an' this Captain Jones were best brothers or somethin'."

"He and I nearly came to blows about putting in at Virginia last month so he could visit a woman friend of his. I just wanted him to know for sure we'd made up properly."

"If I find out you and Noble been tradin' signals—"

"And what if we were? You're planning on killing me now anyway, aren't you?"

Smoot toyed with the thought. "No, not just yet." Turning, Smoot ordered Steele returned to the empty storage room and the sails set for the trip about the island.

***

Atop the hill, five gunners watched with mild interest the arrival of their first officer's boat at the privateer Eagle. They had heard the jokes about the yellow kerchief and had contributed their share of sarcastic comments about the young Jamaican's paranoia.

One of the half-naked gunners' mates straddled the larboard cannon with the spyglass at his eye. "Well, what's your guess?"

"My guess?" It was McCoy—the senior gunner. "Noble's either gone to reprimand Captain Steele for allowing the Tiburon to attack the Cloud, or he's asking about all those dead pirates on the north shore last night."

The young gunner handed the spyglass to his superior. "Steele's sure to ask about that digging party down below us too." He gave a laugh and threw a small stone down the slope at his shipmates. "I thought this was bad duty manning these cannons, but digging holes an' carryin' empty boxes all day's a far cry worse. I just hope the effort isn't wasted on them pirates that be watchin' us from these hills."

McCoy studied the Eagle. "Baker, I don't think we could break wind without the pirates knowing about it." The three others on watch burst into laughter, and one of them bared his backside toward the hill above them. "And you, Cooper, are gonna take a lead ball in the butt if you keep that up."

Baker took the spyglass from McCoy and stretched himself prone on his cannon to watch the Eagle. For some time David Noble simply stood amongst the others on deck and talked. But then, something changed.

"McCoy!" Baker thrust the spyglass back at the senior gunner. "Take a look at that!"

"Damn! Do you suppose he just forgot and pulled it out by mistake?"

"It's hard to tell, Gunny. But I do know that Mister Noble was serious about his kerchief being the signal for trouble. What's he doing now?"

"He's still got it out and he's looking straight at us." McCoy lowered the glass. "Let's light our linstocks and take aim, just in case." A moment later, both the cannons were sighted at the Eagle's mainmast.

"He's leaving!" Baker turned and gave the senior gunner a questioning look.

"Could be a false alarm, but we've our orders."

"We could send Easton down the hill to find out."

"Good idea!" McCoy turned to the lad. "Easton! You heard Baker! On the double, lad!"

The barefoot and half-naked powder monkey took off down the path at a gallop. John and Robert were already waiting on the beach for David's returning boat.

Easton hit the hot sand and ran for the two officers. "Captain Jones! Captain Jones!"

"What is it, lad?"

"McCoy wanted me to tell ya that Mister Noble pulled out his yellow kerchief. It might be nothin', sir, but—"

"We saw it too, Easton." John focused his spyglass on the Eagle. By now, the sleek privateer had set sail for her circuit about the island.

Robert studied the Eagle from under a shading hand. "Can you see anything amiss?"

John was still watching David's approaching boat. "Nothing on the Eagle, but David still has the kerchief out."

A few minutes later, David's boat pulled within earshot of the beach. But mindful of the way sound travels over water, David waited until he was nearly to shore. Then he stood and cupped his hands about his mouth. "John! Robert! Something's terribly wrong on the Eagle!"

"What did you see?"

"I talked with Captain Steele, but everybody else on board is a pirate!" David ordered the oars shipped and then leaped into the knee-deep water before the boat skidded onto the sand.

"Calm down, David. What happened out there?"

"We've got to get Dutch and ask him about one of the men at Mister Forrestal's shipyard." David began walking toward their hauled-down ship.

"A moment, David!" John grabbed the younger man by the arm. "I need to know what happened out there!"

"There was a carpenter with orange hair working on the Silver Cloud the day I arrived from King's Town. He was supposed to be part of the crew, but he disappeared. His name is Henry Morgan, and that young man is now a crewman on the Eagle!"

John looked out at the departing privateer. "Why does that concern us?"

David was surprised his captain didn't see it. "Think it through, John! He had nothing to do with Captain Steele's crew. How would he get on the Eagle, unless—"

"Unless what?"

"Unless they're all pirates!"

"That's absurd! What did Captain Steele say about the boy?"

"He couldn't say anything! He was their prisoner!" David turned and pointed at the privateer. "I'll wager my share of the treasure that Captain Steele is the only Eagle crewman left aboard."

"That's ill news, if you're correct." John looked around at their ship. "Where's Van Mourik?"

Robert pointed across to where the breakfast line was just trailing off. "Last time I saw him, he was taking a nap in the shade of the Cloud."

"That worthless piece of Holland!" John looked about for the powder monkey. "Easton! Go fetch Van Mourik! Tell him to report to my pavilion at once!"

"Aye, aye, Cap'n!" The lad galloped off toward their crippled ship.

John turned and began walking. "David, how much do you know about Jan Van Mourik?"

"Only as much as you, John. Why?"

"I have a very bad feeling about the man."

The three officers stood in the shade of their canvas pavilion and watched Dutch lumber across the hot sand toward them. In the heat of Dead Man's Chest he was a revolting human, and had acquired the disgusting habit of tying a small towel to a rope about his waist to wipe the sweat from his belly. The towel smelled worse than he did.

Van Mourik bellowed from twenty yards away. "You want me, Cap'n Jones?"

"Mister Noble just got back from the Eagle and tells me he saw one of the carpenters you were working with at Charles Town."

"Who dat be?" Van Mourik stepped under the pavilion and wiped the sweat from his bare belly.

David gave the fat man a nod. "He was the one with the green eyes and orange hair."

"Ja!" Van Mourik took another swipe at his dripping belly with the towel. "Dat be Henry Morgan! A right fine woodcarver, dat boy."

"What happened to him after that first day we met?"

The big man gave David a confused look. He was a good enough ship's master, but he lacked a quick mind.

David gave the man a prod. "Dutch, it was the day Mister Forrestal gave you and Morgan the gold sovereigns."

"I 'member now! Me an' Morgan, we go out dat night to celebrate. Met me a woman with..." Van Mourik held his cupped hands in front of his sweaty chest and winked.

"Forget that part, Dutch. What happened to Morgan? I don't remember seeing him again after that day."

"Went off to Savannah, he did. Tolt me der sea vas callin' to him again an' he knew a ship's captain down der who'd sign him on, ja?" Van Mourik tilted his head slightly. "What? Didn't he tell nobody he was goin', Mister Noble?"

John interrupted. "Why would he tell David?"

"Why, Mister Noble an' Henry go way back." The Dutchman gave David a questioning look. "They knew each other on Tortuga."

"I didn't know him, Dutch." He gave John and Robert a nervous glance. "Not before that day I met you."

John held up a hand to quiet the two. "Slow down a bit. Why do you think David knew this woodcarver?"

"Well, sure he knew Morgan! Master Noble tolt Mister Forrestal and me stuff 'bout Morgan neither of us knew before. Somethin' 'bout the lad killin' a crab with a mangrove root when he vas just a pup on Tortuga."

"Oh that!" David gave a dismissive laugh. He couldn't tell them he'd heard the tale from his uncle. "It's just a story I heard from a seaman in King's Town. I only guessed it was Morgan because of his looks."

John held up a hand to quiet the two. "We aren't concerned about the stories, Jan. We just want to know what happened to Morgan after Charles Town."

"I already tolt ya, Cap'n. He went down to Savannah."

"Did he say who the Savannah captain was?"

"No. Only dat dey went way back."

John pulled Robert and David off to one side. "Do you suppose the braggart got drunk and told Morgan about the treasure?"

"That's got to be it, Captain." David gave the Dutchman a quick look. "Dutch let it out on the dock in front of Morgan, Forrestal and me, and a half dozen others. He called me the man who knew where a treasure was buried. Morgan must have got the rest out of him that night when he was drunk."

Robert touched John's arm. "There's something else."

"Yes?"

"If Morgan wanted to go to sea so badly, why didn't he stay and sail with us? He already had a place on the crew."

"So!" John turned and looked across the hot beach to his injured ship. "Our ship's got a hole in it that a man can crawl through, and it's hauled down on an island that's crawling with pirates! We've lost our carpenter, and now we find out that the only ship sent to protect us is manned by pirates!" Another thought struck him. "And they know about our hidden cannons. What else can go wrong?"

"I know it looks bad, John, but—"

"There is something else, Captain."

Both John and Robert looked at David. "What?"

"Captain Steele asked about the digging parties."

"And I suppose you told him?"

"It was before I saw Morgan—"

"Then you did!" John paced out into the hot sun and mumbled something vile toward the Eagle.

Robert called after him. "It doesn't matter, John! David didn't know when we'd be digging up the real treasure, so neither does the Eagle."

David shrugged. "There is one more thing, Captain."

"Damn!" He looked back to his first officer. "What is it, David? Did you tell him where the treasure's buried also?" All the men within earshot stopped what they were doing and turned to stare at their captain.

David shook his head. "But I did tell him that when we leave, we'll take the two cannons off the hill first."

John looked up, spread his arms, and cried into the sky. "Oh, Lord! All they have to do is watch for the cannons to come down the hill!"

David stepped to him. "We could fool them with Quakers."

"We don't have any Quakers!"

"I know, Captain, but some of the extra men—the ones not repairing the Cloud—could build a couple. They could be carried up the hill the same night we're ready to leave."

John shook his head in frustration. "Well, at this point, I'm willing to try most anything!"

"Shall I assign some men to the project?"

"No David, not just any men." John turned and looked across to where they had left the Dutchman. "This would be a perfect job for Captain Van Mourik and some of his Woodshoes. Doesn't take much talent to carve a square beam round and paint it black, does it?"

***

Everything had been done that could be, but an uneasiness still gnawed at John's insides. It was the type of gnawing that tells a man more trouble is waiting on the next tide. He sat for nearly ten minutes staring at the words he had just penned in the log, wondering how many more obstacles would be thrown in his path. Could Captain Steele be rescued, and was the man even worth the effort? Was there another pirate ship out there somewhere? Could the Silver Cloud be floated and escape the island without detection? The odds of the mission being completed seemed to diminish with each passing hour. Out of the corner of his eye, John caught a shadow on the sand.

Without turning, he reached across and placed his hand on his sword. "Yes?"

"Cap'n Jones?" It was the cook, Seamus Barragan. "Beggin' yer pardon, sir, but I gotta talk with ya 'bout somethin' important."

"What is it, Barragan?" John twisted about in his chair. "Need some help in the galley?"

"Oh no, sir." The Irishman gave a nervous glance back at the ship. "I got all the help I need, what with not much for the crew to do." Seamus was a talented cook, but he was possessed by a double portion of nervous energy and a huge need for approval. The small towel in his hands began to feel the effects of his nervousness, being twisted first to the right and then to the left. "I were just tellin' Strocco 'bout it, an' he told me I should come right over an'—"

"Get to your point!" John always felt bad when he had to cut Seamus off in the middle of one of his lengthy explanations, but if he didn't, the Irishman would go on half the day before he hit his mark.

"It's the new carpenter, sir." Seamus twisted the towel until it broke into a set of spirals.

"Jamison?"

"Yes, Cap'n." He hesitated, not knowing whether he should have brought the subject up.

"What about him?"

"Well, sir...I been down watchin' the plankin', an'..." He looked about at the ship again.

"Damn it, man, will you get to it?"

Seamus jumped. "He's botchin' the job, Cap'n, an' the man should know better."

John stood from his small desk and walked toward the edge of the shade where he could get a better look at the ship. "The work looked good to me."

"But it won't hold the oakum, sir."

"Why not?"

"The spaces between the planks—they're too wide an' there's no taper to 'em." He took a step closer to his captain and looked about for eavesdroppers. "I may be wrong 'bout him, sir, but it's almost like he's doin' it on purpose."

"That's a serious accusation."

"I know, Cap'n, but I can't figure it no other way." The cook stopped twisting his towel and stood a little straighter. "I asked him about it an' he got downright angry that I'd question his work." Seamus gave the ship another quick glance. "I just came from there, sir, an' it's 'xactly like I say."

"Let's go take a look." He set off at a fast march, leaving the cook several paces behind. "If what you say is true, then we're in more serious trouble than I thought. Especially if they've used all our spare lumber."

"There's enough lumber to redo the job, sir, but with the water supply like it is..."

"You needn't remind me of the water supply." The cook finally caught up with John. "I'm fully aware of our dilemma."

Seamus whispered as they neared the carpenter's benches. "Cap'n Jones, please don't get me in trouble with the carpenters!"

"It doesn't much matter what they think of you, Seamus. If the Silver Cloud isn't seaworthy, then we sink, hurt feelings or not."

"When ya put it that way, sir, I guess..."

The two were met by Jamison, the new ship's carpenter. He had been lounging in the shade of the bow with several of the others, but jumped up and ran across the sand to meet his captain.

"Good day, Captain Jones!" Jamison knuckled his forelock. "Can I be of service?"

"No, Jamison. You and the others finish your break. I just want to take a look at your work."

"Aye, Captain, but if there's anything you need, give me a call."

"I will." John followed Seamus aft. It was a short climb up the scaffolding to the patch.

"Here, sir, take a look at how they done these spaces."

It was exactly as he had described. The spaces were at least a half-inch wide, twice what they should be. Seamus pulled a twist of oakum from his pocket and pushed it between the planks.

"See there?" Just as he had claimed, the fibers pushed all the way through and into the space beyond.

John ran his finger along one of the seams. The edges of the plank were neatly rounded and sanded smooth, but as nice as they felt, they were still wrong, just as Seamus had reported. "What will it take to fix this?"

"It'll make Jamison angry, sir, but he's either gotta lay extra planks inside, over each seam, or do the whole job over again. There's just no other way to hold out the sea."

"Is there anybody else who can take over your cooking duties till we get off this island?"

"My cooking duties?" Seamus gave his captain a tilt of his head. "You want me to take over the Cloud's repairs?"

"Can you do it?"

Seamus nodded slowly. "Aye, Cap'n."

"And if I give you all the men you need, how long until we can refloat her?"

Seamus studied the side of the ship carefully. "I'd have to pull these new planks off back down to the ribs, and have the new planks shaved to fit." He looked forward to the second hole, the one above the waterline.

"Don't worry about that one, Seamus. Just this one. How long?"

"Give me enough men to work around the clock, sir, an' she'll be ready to float tomorrow night."

"A lot depends on this, so be absolutely sure before you make me that promise."

"Tomorrow before sunset." Seamus gave a confirming nod. "She'll be ready, Cap'n Jones."

Across the beach, one of the young gunner's mates was searching about camp. Finally, in desperation, the lad walked to the captain's pavilion and yelled. "Captain Jones!"

"Over here!" The Scotsman called back from atop the work platform. "What's the matter, lad?"

It was Easton. He ran over to the ship, stopped and pointed to the north. "There's another privateer holding several leagues off the north coast, sir!"

"Oh no!" John climbed upward over the Cloud's planking and onto the tilted deck.

"Barragan!" John pointed aft. "See if you can make it across to the binnacle for my other spyglass."

"Aye, aye, Cap'n." The cook slid across the tilted deck. He was back in a minute with the device. John raised it to his eye and studied the intruder for several moments.

"Who is she, Cap'n?"

"I can't make out her name yet, but she's a Virginia privateer all right. She's a little older than the Eagle, but equal in sail and firepower. And except for her red sails..." John fell silent when the ship's stern finally came into view.

"What is it, Cap'n?"

"Have you ever heard of the Remora?"

"Once or twice in King's Town. If you hadn't come along when you did, me an' Etinger were thinkin' of signin' on with her crew."

John lowered the glass and gave the cook a long look. "Did David Noble or his father ever mention the Remora?"

"Mister Charles Noble was the one, sir. He was sayin' somethin' 'bout expectin' her in port soon an' not wantin' to give you as much flour an' salted beef as he finally did."

"Interesting." John continued to study the Remora. "I wonder..."

***

The treasure of Dead Man's Chest had begun to live more in the realm of legends and myths than in the world of reality. Each time the story was served up, the teller would add another helping of gold and an extra spoonful of blood and treachery, until even the oldest of seamen began to doubt its veracity. It was only the ballad that maintained the accurate tale. And what a tale it was! There was hardly a man on the seven seas who hadn't sung its words while he hauled on the sheets, buntlines and halyards. Every man jack of them wondered after the treasure, hoping to somehow win a share of it. As each year passed, the chances of it ever being dug up diminished. But today, the first day of April, 1775, Captain John Paul Jones led the digging party that would unearth the legend.

The repairs to the Silver Cloud had gone just as Seamus had predicted. The faulty planking was removed and replaced with wider pieces, and this time with the proper fit and taper necessary to hold the oakum. The shrill ring of mallets against the hawsing irons that rammed the oakum between the planks testified to everyone on and about Dead Man's Chest that the Silver Cloud was nearly ready to float. Since the Remora's unannounced arrival the previous day, she had maintained a position about the island exactly opposite from the Eagle, a tactic that puzzled John and his officers.

After the midday meal, the captain raised his glass in a toast. "To the Silver Cloud and her successful launching."

The other officers raised their glasses.

John laid an unsealed letter on the table before the others. "This was left in my logbook."

Robert reached for it. "What is it?"

"It's our rendezvous instructions. We're to meet the second Silver Cloud near Tortuga, and by my calculations, there won't be enough time to stop at Flint's Island for Ben's silver bars."

David didn't like what he was hearing. "But the crew's counting on it, Captain. It was to be their bonus."

"I know that, but there simply isn't enough time, and the additional risk is more than I'm willing to take."

"But Mister Forrestal told us that there would be several rendezvous locations and times. Couldn't we delay at Spyglass and meet the other ship later?"

John shook his head. He took the letter from Robert and handed it to David. "Read it, David. It says that after Tortuga there may not be another rendezvous for several weeks."

Robert looked up. "Do you believe that?"

"I have to until I receive something that makes me believe otherwise. We have a time limitation on us, Robert. For all we know, the colonies may have already begun fighting."

David took the letter and read quickly. "It shouldn't take that long to sail back to Flint's Island after we trade ships. A day or two at most."

John shook his head. "We could be at war as we speak. If so, the colonies need this ship more than they need a few silver bars."

David gave a shrug. "Then there's no use arguing about it."

"I'm sorry, David, but that's just the way it is. Our immediate goal is to load the treasure and get the Silver Cloud away from this accursed island without detection." He paused and scanned a list of duties he had penned on the back of the rendezvous letter. "We'll be splitting the crew in thirds, with one group staying here at Rip Rap to make preparations to float the ship. The other two groups will climb the hill to dig up the treasure."

"What about Ben?" Robert pointed up to the east where the treasure waited. "If he can't take us to the treasure at Flint's Island, then he at least deserves to be there when we dig up this one."

"Of course he does." John turned about to the doctor. "Is he well enough to go up the hill with us?"

The doctor shook his head. "I'd be worried his heart couldn't take the climb. But if we can find a couple of the men to carry him on a litter, then he'll do just fine."

John looked about at the others, spread his arms, and gave a broad smile. "Then let's be about it!"

Within half an hour, forty-five men stood in a great circle amongst the waist-high brush and cactus, looking at a twenty-five foot high manchineel tree. When last seen by Robert and his then-fiancée, the tree was a mere sapling, three feet tall and no thicker than a man's wrist. Twenty years and the torment of hundreds of storms had taken their toll on the once-straight tree. Its trunk was now nearly two feet thick and resembled a twisted collection of slimy sea creatures, oozing their caustic sap downward into the earth to mingle with the treasure.

"Listen here!" John looked about at the forty men while their conversations died into silence. "You're about to unearth the largest treasure ever buried in one location. It's going to be difficult work, but I can assure you that it'll be worth every drop of sweat and every ounce of blood it demands of you. The weapons this treasure will purchase may be the one thing that frees the colonies and your loved ones from the death grip of Mother England!" He turned to his right. "Robert?"

The Yorkman stepped forward and pointed at the tree. "That manchineel tree—the very one that burned the watchman's face and arms the day we came ashore—is the center of the treasure. We need to clear the brush away for a distance of five paces in all directions from its trunk. Once all the gold is exposed, you'll switch places with the men with muskets and they'll carry it down the hill."

John stepped to Robert's side. "Let the work begin!"

A cheer rose from the seamen as they attacked the brush. Within ten minutes, the large tree stood naked in the center of a thirty-foot circle of bare red dirt.

"Sir?" It was the bosun. "Do you want we should cut down the tree?"

John looked to Robert.

Robert shook his head. "Only if we have to. Somehow, I don't feel it would be fair to kill the old soldier, especially after guarding my treasure for all these years. I'm sure it'll have to lose a few of its roots, but let's go easily on it for now."

When Robert and his friends buried the treasure, they had laid earth a cubit deep atop it. Nothing had changed, except that the tree had sent out its tentacles in search of the scarce water. At the end of the predicted two hours, all the treasure lay exposed to the late afternoon sun. Here and there—where a workman had torn a canvas bag—fifty and seventy pound gold ingots reflected the sunlight as brightly as the day they were cast by the Spaniards in the smelters near the Aztec mines.

"I had no idea there was so much, Robert." John surveyed the spectacle before them. "Fate is a fickle mistress. If I could entice her to ensure the success of this mission, I'd be willing to offer most anything she wanted."

"Careful, John. She may be fickle, but she has an insatiable appetite for human pain. You may not be able to bear the price she requires of you."

As Robert spoke his words of warning, two of the seamen placed a large chest before him and the other officers.

Ben Gunn reached out to one of the seamen. "Help me stand, lad." With an oath, Ben stood and hobbled to the chest. He looked at Robert. "May I open it, Master Robert?"

Robert nodded and struck the lock away with the point of a shovel. He stepped back to give the old man room. "Be my guest, Ben."

Ben pulled the last rusted fragments of the lock loose from the hasp and raised the lid. There was a collective gasp from those who could see the contents.

"This is all surplus, Master Ormerod!" Ben reached deep within the jewels and wiggled his fingers, just as a child will run his hands through a tub of beans.

"What are you saying, Ben?" John picked up several brightly colored jewels. "What do you mean that these are surplus?

"He's right, John." Robert looked upon the jewels. "I had no idea what was inside this chest until now." He looked back up at John. "This is all extraordinary—above the eight hundred thousand we'd counted on."

The sun was now two hours above the western horizon, a perfect angle for its rays to set the jewels afire in an aurora of radiant splendor. Even Robert—who had buried the treasure twenty years before—gasped at the sight. There were diamonds the size of walnuts and rubies that would choke a cow. Saphires, aquamarines, emeralds and topaz lay about as single gems mixed with sundry gold coins. And then there were the gems set in broaches, in necklaces, in bracelets, in crucifixes, in medallions, in rings both large and small, in cups and plates of silver and gold—every design and use the human mind could contrive. Several leather pouches of black and white pearls lay about the edges of the open chest, spilling their precious contents between the larger gems. At its center, nearly hidden by the free stones, was a circle of gold discs, each standing upright in the sea of glitter.

Ben reached into the gems and pulled the object from the chest. "It's the King's crown!" Ben lifted the large ring of gold high into the air and turned about so all the men could see it. He stopped facing his employer. "It's just like the one on Spyglass!"

John looked up from the chest. "There's another crown like that on Flint's Island?"

"There is, Cap'n Jones!" Ben lowered it toward his head. "But that other one is the queen's crown—nowhere as big as this one."

The crown was oval in shape, with the head band nearly a quarter-inch thick and solid gold. Atop the two-inch band were alternating crosses and sun-shaped discs—eight in all. At the center of each disc was set a ruby or an emerald, and around each of these was a circle of smaller prescious stones.

Ben tried to set the king's crown on his head, but it was so large that it dropped past his ears and rested on his shoulders.

"Ha!" Robert burst into laughter. "You're a royal sight, indeed!"

Ben blushed and returned the crown to the chest. As he did, he noticed a folded piece of paper among the jewels. The old man picked it up and unfolded it while the other three officers watched.

"What have you there?"

"It's—" The old man began to shake and dropped the note as if it was on fire. "Oh Lordy! It's a death curse!"

"A death curse?" John picked it up the paper and read the cryptic words out loud. "Beware the fires of Hell! He who first touches this treasure shall die within a fortnight and burn forever in the Lake of Fire!"

Ben stumbled backwards and fell to the ground. "I'll never live to see America!"

"Calm down, old friend." Robert took the note from John. "You're not going to die."

"But it's a death curse, Master Ormerod!" Ben stayed on the ground and struggled backwards to the line of brush. "I touched the jewels first, so the curse is on me!"

"It's only words, Ben." Robert held up the note. "There's no power in words written on a scrap of paper, except for what you allow them to have."

"That's easy for you to say, sir, 'cause the curse isn't on you!"

"But I can remove them, as simple as this." Robert tore the paper in eight pieces and threw them into the wind.

Ben ducked away from the fluttering scraps that were carried upward into the sky. "They're still on me, Master Ormerod!"

"No they aren't, Ben, and I'll tell you why."

"Then pray tell me quick! I can feel my heart startin' to falter as we speak!"

"I wrote those words myself, twenty years ago!"

Ben's mouth was frozen in a gasp of terror while he watched his death sentence flutter away over the ridge to the north.

Robert pointed into the sky. "The curse is gone, Ben! I'm afraid I'll be stuck with you for at least another decade."

"Enough of this!" John turned to the diggers. "I want each of you to lay down his shovel, go find your partner and take his rifle. We've a treasure to move and we're running out of daylight!"

Shortly after sunset, a stream of treasure-laden seamen began to flow like leaf-cutter ants down the easy slope toward Rip Rap Beach. They kept close to one another in order to avoid the need for lanthorns that would alert the Eagle and Remora that the treasure was finally moving.

It became quickly apparent to all but a few of the men that the cannon attack on the Silver Cloud had actually worked to their advantage. With the great ship hauled down on the dry sand, it cut the loading time to a fraction of what it would have been had the ship remained at anchor outside the reef.

By midnight, the entire treasure was secured in the ship's lazarette, behind a massive oak door and a special lock.

John called to the portly Hollander. "Jan! Is everything ready?"

"Ja, Captain Jones!" The Dutchman wiped himself dry with his little towel. "Another half hour at most, Captain Jones, an' we'll have da tide fer easin' her down into the sea."

"And the cannons?"

"Aboard and secured just like you ordered me." Van Mourik pointed to the cliffs where two lanthorns burned brightly. "An' them two Quakers is in der place on the cliff, ja?"

John looked around at his ship and crew. "Then we're ready."

While the tide lifted the twenty-gun frigate from the white sands of Rip Rap Beach, thirty-six of the crew's strongest oarsmen put their backs to the task of pulling her hull clear of the shore toward the break in the reef. At John's order, the beach crew began to let out on their blocks and tackle, being careful to keep the ship from righting herself too quickly. An accidental slip during this delicate operation would not only allow the massive hull to bury its keel in the sandy bottom, but the whipping action could actually break one or more of the masts. A ship aground at high tide is a ship lost forever.

Before the tide had begun to drop again, and before the full moon had come up to expose their activities, the great ship was pulled beyond the reef and northward, away from the anchored Eagle. Just as John had ordered, several men continued to strike caulking irons with their mallets, even though the job had been finished for several hours.

Before the eastern sky had begun to pink, the boat crews had pulled the Silver Cloud four leagues to the west—nearly beyond sight of Dead Man's Chest.

***

Henry Morgan was on watch, but had sat back against the mainmast and dozed off. One of the other men slapped him on the face and pointed at the island.

Henry jumped up and doubled up his fists for retaliation. "What the—"

"Somethin's missin', Morgan!" The man was pointing at Rip Rap Beach. "An' guess what? She got away on yer watch!"

Henry ran to the rail. Sure enough, the Silver Cloud was gone. He looked to the cliff where the two cannons still stood. "He'll have me heart fer this!" He turned and ran for the aft ladder, then dropped into the companionway. He was about to strike the door with the butt of his cutlass, but seeing the marks from the last time he had done so, he lowered the weapon. "Cap'n Smoot!"

"What is it, Morgan?"

"They're gone, Govn'r! The Cloud's got away durin' the night!"

Something crashed down inside the cabin and then the door swung open. "Damn yer eyes, Morgan!" Smoot stepped into the companionway half-naked. "You knew they were ready to sail! We all heard the caulking mallets!"

"But it were dark, Govn'r, an' they weren't gonna float her until after they had the seams filled!" Henry stepped aside and then followed his captain to the main deck. "And you tolt me to keep a weather eye fer 'em to move them two cannons off the hill 'cause you were so sure they wouldn't leave without them!" He pointed at the cliff. "Look! They're both still there!"

Smoot turned west and strained his eyes to locate his fleeing prize. The sails of the Silver Cloud and the Remora were still visible above the horizon. Smoot spun on Henry. "You were sleepin' on watch, weren't you!"

"No I weren't, Govn'r!" He tried to sound indignant as his mind raced. "They fooled us on two accounts."

"Two accounts?"

"Aye, Cap'n." Henry thought hard. "The cannons are still there, an' they were floatin' her off the beach while they was still caulkin' them seams!"

"An' I don't suppose you noticed their camp fires dyin' out to hide the launching, either."

"I didn't think—"

"Maybe I should'a let you skipper the Tiburon after all." Smoot looked about toward the far end of the larger island. "Which reminds me—where is Pritchard and the Tiburon? If the Cloud can be repaired in three days, then so can my ship!"

"But they took a hit to their mizzen, Govn'r, not countin' all them shot holes to her hull an' the fire in her hold." Henry kept his distance from his irate captain. "And they'd also hafta pick up their men from off the Chest 'afore they could begin to take up the chase anyway, so there's that besides."

Smoot didn't hear the lad's last excuse, for out of the corner of his eye he caught sight of something astern. The first rays of the sun streaked across the glassy sea to splash against the sails of a large American "clipper" just emerging from behind the eastern tip of Saint Croix.

Henry spotted her and pointed with relief. "There she is, Govn'r! Right on time, just like I tolt ya she'd be!"

"And it's a good thing for you she is!" Smoot knew the lad wasn't responsible for the Tiburon's timely appearance. "Make ready to set sail, Henry!"

The lad began barking orders to the waking crew, his favorite pastime. "Think we'll be able to catch the Silver Cloud before sunset, Govn'r?"

"Of course we will, but it really doesn't matter."

The lad paused from his duties and looked back at his captain. "Pardon?"

"You forget, Henry, that I've still got my spy aboard the Silver Cloud."

***

"Sail Ho!" The cry came from high in the Silver Cloud's upper rigging. "Two more sails on the stern at five leagues!"

John grabbed his spyglass and scanned the sea about Dead Man's Chest. "Well, well. It took them long enough to finally notice."

David shaded his eyes and searched. "Well, at least we got back to sea without a fight."

"Aye." John continued to study the two ships. The Remora was under full sail and the Tiburon had come about near Rip Rap Beach. "The Tiburon has stopped to pick up their men from the island."

With every inch of sail the frigate could hoist, the Silver Cloud gained valuable distance between herself and the two known ships. But the Remora, which had watched her midnight escape, dogged her at every inch of headway. By midmorning the wind had shifted to larboard, giving all three of their pursuers an advantage; the Eagle and the Remora with their staysails, and the Tiburon, with her greater waterline and resulting speed. By noon, it was clear the enemy was closing the gap.

John paced nervously about the quarterdeck, but stopped when he noticed the doctor standing at the aft ladder, shading his eyes against the sun.

"What is it, Adam? You look like a bear just ate your best fowling dog."

The doctor stepped close and whispered. "May I speak with you alone for a moment, sir?" Doctor McKenzie was by nature a soft-spoken man, having been born to an aristocratic southern family and trained at the School of Surgeons in Boston.

John sensed something was very wrong and tried to assure the young man. "There's nothing Robert or David can't hear, Adam. What's troubling you?"

"Something's wrong with those men from the boats—the ones who were pulling us away from the island this morning."

"Go on."

"Well, at first I thought it was just the heat and their fatigue, but they've not gotten any better, no matter how much water they drink or how much they rest." He wiped the sweat from his face with a sleeve. "It could just be a coincidence, sir, but it's like they all caught falling sickness at the same time."

Robert stepped to them. "How many of them are affected?"

"All of them. Every last man."

"Is anybody else sick?"

"A few, Captain—maybe half a dozen." He was ashamed that he couldn't be more certain what was happening. "It might be the remitting fever, Captain, but then..."

"What do your books say?"

"That's what's so confusing, Mister Ormerod. It's a lot like the fever, but then there's too much belly pain."

David gave a tilt of his head. "Did they come aboard sick, or did it start after they got below to rest?"

"They seemed fine when they came aboard, sir, except for being tired and thirsty."

"Find out what you can, Adam, and get back to me."

"Aye, Captain Jones."

The surgeon turned to leave, but John called after him. "Make sure they are given all the water they need. If it's the remitting fever, they'll need a lot more than normal."

"The water!" Adam spun about. "It could be the water!"

"Damn!" John cursed loudly, bringing a chill to all within earshot. "David, go with the doctor and inspect the casks." He turned to the bosun. "Pipe the men to assembly!"

Within three minutes, all but the sick crewmen were assembled on the main deck. A rumble of muffled conversation ran through their ranks.

"Pipe down there!" The bosun gave his captain a glance to make sure he was ready. "Cap'n Jones has some words for ya!"

"I assume you all know by now that a large portion of the crew is sick. Doctor McKenzie suspects that somebody has poisoned our water."

Another murmur ran across the deck and up the mizzenmast to one of the top men. He called down. "I told 'em we have a traitor aboard, Captain Jones!"

John looked up and called back. "We don't know that for sure! Doctor McKenzie will be reporting back to me as soon as he inspects the casks. Until we know for sure, I don't want you to drink any water."

322 Roger L. Johnson

"What about water taken from the main supply before we sailed, John?" It was Robert. "If someone poisoned the main casks this morning, the water up here on deck shouldn't be contaminated yet."

"You might be right." John turned back to the assembled crew. "Mister Ormerod has suggested that there may be some good water aboard. If any of you drew water prior to our sailing this morning, I want it turned over to Doctor McKenzie for testing."

Robert stepped to John's side. "I want to see those water casks too."

A few minutes later, John and Robert found David and Adam in the bilge. The younger of the doctor's two assistants sat atop one of the massive casks.

John touched Adam on the arm. "Have you found anything?"

"We've a traitor all right!" The assistant held up a hand with white powder on his fingers. "And from the looks of it, he's done a thorough job."

"Come down and show me that!"

The young man jumped to the deck. "Look at this." He held out a moist handful of freshly cut wood shavings to his Captain. "Our saboteur has drilled a hole in the top of every cask and dumped in some sort of poison."

John turned to Adam. "How long before you know what it is?"

"Ten to fifteen minutes if it's common. Longer if it's something more complicated." Adam gave the powder a close look. "I won't know for sure until run my tests, but I'd wager it's strychnine—rat poison."

"Damn him!" John turned and stared aft between the casks while he pondered their situation. "I've ordered all hands to turn over their personal water supplies to you. Is there a way to test it?"

"Once I know what he used, yes." Adam scraped together a small sample of white powder and placed it in a folded piece of paper. "With any luck, I'll have an antidote in my supplies."

By noon, fully half the crew had been stricken with stomach cramps and burning throats. Activity aboard the Cloud had been reduced to the bare minimum in order to reduce the need for water.

Adam stepped through John's open door. John was writing in his logbook. He looked up. "Well?"

Adam nodded. "It's strychnine."

"Is there an antidote?"

"My medical books call for emptying the stomach, and then drinking charcoal and permanganate of potassium—"

"I don't need to know all the details, Adam. Do you have what you need to make them well?" The doctor didn't answer. "Well?"

"The saboteur knew exactly what he was doing, Captain."

"Which means?"

"He knew it would take a lot of water to save these men's lives, and that would force us to make landfall to find a fresh water supply."

"How much good water do we have?"

"Fifty, maybe sixty gallons at most, sir. That's only going to last through tomorrow morning."

"I was afraid of that." John unrolled a chart of the Caribbean. "Would you do me a favor and ask David and Robert to join us? We've several important decisions to make."

"As you please, sir." Adam turned to leave but hesitated. "Might I have a half-hour to check something first?"

"A half-hour?"

"I just remembered something I heard at school about rat poison. That should give me enough time to test my theory on a couple of the sick men."

At four bells in the early afternoon, Adam was followed into the master's cabin by David and Robert.

"Have a seat, gentlemen." John gave the doctor an inquiring look. "Well, Adam, did your theory prove well?"

"Yes it did, sir. It's a crude poison, just as I suspected. My theory was that sugar-based alcohol might counteract its effects, or at least give some relief."

"And?"

"I was right. The three men I tested are improving as we speak."

"Then, you're telling me that we aren't going to lose any men?"

"Not a man, provided we can get to a supply of fresh water before noon tomorrow." The doctor pulled a note from his pocket. "But we did lose two pigs and a half dozen chickens."

"Hmmm." John paused and then looked back at Adam. "Do you think the poison had time to get into the animals' flesh?"

"Probably not. Why do you ask?"

"Well, since the cook has to slaughter three or four pigs every day anyway, we haven't really lost anything."

"We can't eat them, Captain." It was David. He had an apologetic tone.

"Oh? And why not?"

"Because I had them thrown over the side."

"You what?" John jumped to his feet.

"They died of the poison, sir. I figured they weren't safe to eat, and we couldn't have them rotting on the ship.

"You fool!" John turned and looked aft into the ship's wake. "Don't you realize what you've done?"

"It's water we're short of, Captain, not food."

John spun on the younger man. "You've just told Joshua Smoot and those other two ships that their plan has worked!"

"What?"

"He's right, David." Robert stepped beside John and looked back at the other three ships. "You gave the best possible signal to Smoot and the others that he's succeeded in poisoning our water. Now they know we'll be forced to find an island large enough to have a river."

"I'm sorry, Captain. Is there anything I can do about it?"

"No! It's too late to go back for them. It's more important that the crew gets fresh water than worrying whether the pirates know about our dilemma." John stared into the wake for a minute before turning about.

Robert finally broke the silence. "John, you know my position on the cannons, so I may as well not mince words. The pirates are frustrated. They lost us once, and they won't be so stupid the next time. If they can force us to pull close to a river mouth, then they'll try to sink us in the shallows where they can retrieve the treasure at their leisure. I say we sail on. The loss of a few men's lives is just part of the price the colonies must pay for the cannons and the freedom we're hoping they may bring."

"That's no choice!" It was the doctor. "That's murder! I say to hell with your treasure and the cannons! Sink or float, without a new supply of water, and a lot of it, half the crew will be dead by noon tomorrow, and the rest in two days."

"But you told me that alcohol will counteract—"

"Aye, Captain, but not without several gallons of fresh water per man! We've no choice but to find a river!"

Before Robert could answer the doctor's objection, there was a knock at the door.

John welcomed the momentary diversion. "Come!"

One of the bosun's mates stepped through the door and stood at attention. Several others remained in the passageway, one of them wearing shackles and chains.

"We caught him, sir, and it's just like we all figured. Captain Smoot sent him to kill one of the other carpenters so he could replace him. He's the one who cut our anchor loose."

"How'd you find him?"

"He kept a supply of clean water for himself. It was in his sea chest, under a false bottom. Wouldn't o' found it but for the wetness around the chest. We also found this." The man held up an empty leather pouch with white powder coating its inside.

The doctor reached out. "I'll take that."

"Bring him here."

The large bosun's mate pulled the door open and grabbed the prisoner by his chains. Jamison was pushed to the center of the cabin where he scanned the officers defiantly. He had been beaten badly, but none of the officers objected, not even the doctor.

John stepped in front of the man and traded stares with him. "Did you ask him about the Remora?"

"We did, but he refuses to talk."

"Well, perhaps a few days in irons up in the hot sun will loosen his lips. Chain him to the mainmast and give him all the water he needs."

The doctor protested. "But, Captain Jones—"

"We have six casks in the hold, Adam. Surely we can afford a few gallons for our prisoner."

Jamison dropped to his knees and a weak cry escaped his mouth. It sounded more animal than human.

"Do you want to say something, Jamison?" John bent and put his ear near the man's mouth.

"I've seen the Remora workin' around Jamaica and Cuba, takin' their share of ships."

John stood and looked at David. "Then they are pirates!"

"Aye, sir, as best as I know. But they're not workin' with Captain Smoot."

"You know that for certain?"

"Aye. Smoot's never worked with the Remora."

"And what about Captain Steele? What's Smoot planning to do with him?"

Robert shook his head. "He couldn't know that, John. He hasn't had any contact with Smoot since before we left Charles Town."

"Robert's right." John looked to the bosun's mate. "Take him up and nail his chain to the mainmast."

"And the water, sir?"

"All he wants, as long as it's from the main cask." John bent down and whispered to the traitor. "How's the Bible put it? An eye for an eye?"

The sailors dragged Jamison from the cabin. John looked down the companionway until the traitor's cries died away. He finally turned to the doctor. "Adam, when Jamison finally begs for the poisoned water, give him one ration of our good water."

"But why, John?" It was Robert who spoke, but all of the others agreed. "He intended that we drink the bad water."

"It's because we're better than he is, Robert." John walked to his table and looked at the chart again. "I'd like to return to our former conversation, gentlemen. Are there any more suggestions?"

Adam stepped to the map and stared at the islands near their intended route. "We don't have the luxury of a choice. If we can't get to a supply of fresh water, then we must trade the treasure for our lives."

Robert slapped the table. "We can't give up the treasure! Even if we did, they'd kill us after they got it!"

The doctor studied the Yorkman. "What possible advantage would there be in harming us after they've achieved their aim?"

"You really don't understand pirates, do you, Adam?"

"All I understand, Mister Ormerod, is that the lives of these men is our most immediate concern. If we don't get fresh water, and very quickly, most of the crew will be dead or dying in two days. Those who linger for another day will be so weak that they won't be able to fend off the lightest attack. Smoot's going to get the treasure either way. It's our choice whether we come through it alive or dead!"

"Horse feathers! They've no choice but to kill us! They know that as soon as we turn over the treasure to them and get the water we need, we'll come after them."

John tapped the edge of the map with his finger. "Then what do you suggest?"

Robert stepped to the table and turned the map about. "There must be a river with a deep anchorage on one of the islands along our route."

"The doctor's right, Robert. The moment we drop our anchor, we become sitting ducks! Why in the world would we do that?"

"Because the poison in our water has forced it upon us!" John began to protest, but Robert held up a hand. "Hear me out, John. Smoot's too smart to sink us in deep water where the treasure would be lost forever, but the moment we reach the shallows, as the good doctor points out, he'll put us on the bottom and kill every last one of us. Our only refuge lies in a deep water anchorage near a river mouth."

"But why not drive the Silver Cloud into a river?" asked Adam. "We could throw buckets over the side and have all the water we need while the gunners hold off the Tiburon."

John looked about at the windows and then turned back to the doctor. "We could put two, maybe three cannons in this cabin, but that's not enough to hold off an attack. It doesn't matter to the pirates if we're sunk in a river or at a shallow anchorage."

Robert studied the map while John walked to the window and looked aft at the three ships that trailed them.

"Here!" Robert put the point of his knife on the spot. "Pillsbury Sound!"

John returned to the table.

"It'll still be very risky, John, but the water there is deep! We can make a series of slow passes to load and offload the boats, and still have the ability to maneuver for a fight!"

"I like it!" John turned to his first officer. "David, set a course for Pillsbury Sound." He turned back to the doctor. "Adam, your job will be to distribute the uncontaminated water in the most beneficent manner until we get a fresh supply."

"Thank you, Captain Jones." The doctor looked to Robert. "Mister Ormerod, permit me to apologize for my harsh words. I don't really believe you have no concern for the crew."

"Your apology is accepted." He looked about at the others. "Getting the treasure to the rendezvous point and then to our military is my primary concern, but I fully realize that a healthy crew is essential to that end."

John waited a moment and turned to the doctor. "How's Ben?"

"Much better, sir. I've done everything I can for the burns, but his age is now his worst enemy."

"He didn't drink any of the poisoned water, did he?"

"Fortunately not, but I'm afraid that with the infection and the lack of water, he may not survive."

David and Adam stepped to the door while John turned to Robert. "You and he are so close."

"He's like a father to me in some ways, John, and like a son in others." Robert waited until David and the doctor had left, and then turned back to the young captain. "When this war finally starts, thousands of men will die painful and sometimes obscure deaths. If I should lose Ben Gunn to his age and his burns, his will be one of those obscure deaths. Nevertheless, I'll consider his loss one of the most courageous of all."

"Aye." John picked up his glass and pitcher of water. "I believe I'll pay Ben a visit."

Chapter 15

By the time the course change for Pillsbury Sound was passed to the helm, John had reached Ben Gunn's cabin with the water. He tapped gently at the half-opened door. There was no answer, so he pushed it open with his shoulder and stepped inside.

"Ben?"

"Come in, Cap'n Jones." The elderly man answered weakly—just above a whisper. "Maybe you'll give me a straight answer."

"A straight answer?"

"Aye." The old man pushed himself up onto an elbow with a groan of pain. "Jan Van Mourik was just here. I asked him about the ship's course change, but he pretended not to know. I hate secrets, Cap'n Jones."

"He didn't know, and probably didn't want to admit it." John set the cup and pitcher on a sideboard. "I'm surprised you could feel it. We only changed course ten degrees."

"Meanin' no disrespect, sir, but I've been at sea more years than you been suckin' the good Lord's air." Ben gripped the rail of the bunk and swung his legs over the side with another groan. "Can't ya feel a course change yet?"

"Yes, I can." John filled the tin cup with the precious water. "That's what I wanted to speak to you about." John pulled a stool close to the bunk and handed the old man the cup. "We've had a meeting, and decided our only option is to make for a river mouth on Saint John where we can refill our water casks."

"Which river were ya lookin' to use, sir?"

"From my charts, it looks like Pillsbury Sound is the best choice."

"Van Mourik told me about the poison." Ben drank the cup empty. He lowered his hand and gave his captain a tilt of the head.

"You look perplexed, Ben. What's bothering you?"

"Well, not to suggest you don't know what ye're doin', sir, but won't we be sittin' ducks at Pillsbury Sound?"

"Yes we will, but we've no choice. It's either Saint John for water, or we lose everything."

"But we do have a choice, Cap'n." Ben lowered his feet to the floor and pushed himself upright. "If you'll help me to yer cabin, there's something you need to see."

A few minutes later, Ben sat in one of the padded chairs in the master's cabin. The chart of the Antilles was still on the table. Taking a set of dividers in his hand, he pointed to a river near the eastern tip of one of the larger islands. He looked up at his captain. "There's your choice, Captain Jones."

"I don't follow you, Ben."

The old man gave John a wink. "And neither will the Tiburon or the Eagle."

John looked where Ben was pointing. "Explain."

"The map doesn't show it, Cap'n, but a quarter mile up this river, there's a deep, freshwater lagoon plenty big to take the Silver Cloud."

"But we'll be trapped, Ben. We won't be able to get back to the open sea."

The old man smiled and nodded. "If the tide's right, we will."

"Just a moment, Ben." John took a closer look at the chart. The island was several leagues more distant than Saint John. "I've already been through this discussion with the other officers. Half the crew has been poisoned, and if we don't get them a fresh supply of water, we could lose them." John sat back and shook his head. "It makes no sense."

"It makes all the sense in the world, Captain, fer them what knows the secret, that is." Ben was enjoying his moment of intrigue. "That's why they call it Deception Lagoon."

While Ben explained his plan to John, the block and tackle was being lowered into the hold to raise the first of the large water casks so that the contaminated water could be poured out through the scuppers. Doctor McKenzie started rationing the few gallons of good water that remained.

John rubbed his stubbly chin in thought. "So you figure the tide's our only real concern?"

"Aye, an a prayer to the good Lord that our friends on the Tiburon don't know the secret too."

"Excuse me, sir." It was Doctor McKenzie. He pushed the door open several degrees, but not enough to see John's elderly guest.

"What is it, Adam?"

"I'm afraid I have some bad news, Captain."

"Oh?"

"We've lost one man, and two others are doing very badly." The doctor began to back out into the companionway when he noticed Ben sitting at the table. He stepped into the cabin. "Is that you, Mister Gunn?"

Ben twisted about in his chair. "Aye, 'tis me, sir."

"I didn't expect to see you up and about this quickly."

"Come in, Adam. Ben was just showing me something very interesting on the chart."

Adam turned to close the door. "Oh?"

"He assures me that if we bypass Saint John by about twelve hours, we can get fresh water and escape the pirates without the risks we'll take at Pillsbury Sound."

"Twelve hours?" Adam turned and strode to the table. "Pardon my language, sir, but that's too damned long!" He stared at John for a long moment. "I just told you we've already lost one man! The other two could make it to Pillsbury Sound, but no further!"

"I've made my decision!"

"Then I'm making mine!"

"And what is that supposed to mean?"

"It means, Captain Jones, that I'm making an official protest of your conduct to our employers when we reach Charles Town! You asked if we'd lose any men, and I assured you we wouldn't. But that was based upon your assurance that we'd sail directly for Pillsbury Sound! Every man who dies from now on will be on your head!"

John jumped to his feet. "The health of the crew is your concern. Their lives are mine. I agree with Robert. The loss of a few men is a small price for the colonies to pay in exchange for liberty."

Adam stood eye to eye with John, too angry to speak. He wanted to swear at this heartless man, but restrained himself and moved for the door. He pulled it open, but hesitated.

"Was there something else, Doctor McKenzie?"

"If it comes to it, Captain, which of the officers will you let die first?"

"What did you say?"

"You heard me, and you know exactly what I mean."

"So that there's no question, Doctor, why don't you tell me...exactly what you mean?"

"Obviously you and I get enough water to live, because we're important!" He pushed the door closed and walked toward the far end of the table, next to Ben. "But what about Mister Ormerod and your young Jamaican friend? If it's only the mission that matters, then I don't see why we need those two any longer." Adam stepped behind Ben and placed his hands on the old man's shoulders. "And what about our old friend here? Is he expendable also, or does he get to live until he shows you where his silver bars are hidden on Spyglass?"

John couldn't answer. As painful as the words were to hear, the doctor was correct. After several moments, he walked to the door. "Unless you intend to lead a mutiny against me, Doctor McKenzie, I would appreciate you leaving my quarters this instant."

"I'll leave, sir, but I don't understand how you can sleep at night."

"That's my concern, not yours!"

Adam paused at the door.

If John's angry stare could kill, the doctor would be the first casualty among the officers. "Was there something else?"

As the doctor opened his mouth to speak, Ben Gunn began shouting.

"Salvation!" John and Adam turned to see what the old maroon was yelling about. Ben stood and hobbled toward the larboard windows. "The Lord's delivered us from death!"

"What is it, Ben?" John looked out to the sea. "What do you see?"

"Look there! On our windward bow!" The old man pointed. "My prayers have been answered!"

John took a step toward the old man, but just then cabin door burst open. The three men turned.

It was David Noble. He was out of breath and clearly agitated. "Captain Jones!"

"What is it, David?"

David took several breaths. "You didn't see it yet, Captain?"

Ben was still pointing. "It's the Lord! He's sent us His salvation!"

David stepped to Ben's side and pointed. "We've a rain squall a half mile on the larboard bow, Captain! I've ordered the spare sails spread on the deck! If we adjust our course a bit and set up catch-alls, we might be able to fill most of the small barrels."

John moved to the larboard side of his cabin and peered into the setting sun. "If your God did this, then I might be obliged to convert."

It took little maneuvering to intercept the squall, and by the skillful employment of all able-bodied hands and most of the extra sail cloth spread between the standing rigging, all of the on-deck water casks were filled, plus half those on the gun deck. The water tasted of old canvas and dust, but it was wet and safe, and everyone got their fill.

Doctor McKenzie made a quick survey of the poisoned men and reported to John. "It's still not enough to get us out of trouble, Captain Jones, but it will get us to your other island."

John gave Adam a guarded smile. "I'll take that as your assent, Adam. Seems the Lord intends that we succeed on this mission after all."

The doctor gave his captain a stern look. "You were very lucky this time, Captain Jones. Very lucky."

***

The hour was late, and the gray cliffs at the eastern tip of Ben Gunn's secret island stood out of the dark waters of the Caribbean like a row of bank buildings in downtown London. The Silver Cloud approached the craggy rocks bow-on, and then turned to parallel its face. At the same time, the Eagle turned larboard to keep herself between the treasure ship and the Tiburon.

"Morgan!" Captain Smoot searched the rigging for the monkey of a lad. Frustrated, he turned and searched the main deck. "Where is that son of a sea hag?"

From the trail of dead animals in her wake, Smoot knew the Silver Cloud was in trouble, and he'd expected the stricken ship to put in at Pillsbury sound. He studied Ben Gunn's cliffs, but to the best of his recollections there were no rivers at this end of the island.

Henry slid one of the buntline sheets, then dropped his calloused feet lightly to one of the lower spars where he could answer his captain without shouting. "I'm here, Govn'r! Up here on the gaff spar."

While Henry waited for a reply, the Eagle edged forward by a hundred yards, far enough to make out a narrow crevice in the cliff face just beyond the Silver Cloud's bowsprit.

"Take a gander at that, Morgan! What do ya know 'bout that crack in the cliff up yonder?"

"Nothin', Govn'r, 'cept the color of the water's different outside it." Henry gave a quizzical tilt of his head. "It looks to me like some sort o' river mouth."

From their oblique angle, the opening didn't look large enough to take a ship, especially not one of the Silver Cloud's tonnage and girth.

"Don't figure, does it, Henry?"

"What's that, Govn'r?"

"That they'd choose this place for water, unless..."

"Unless?" Henry looked down at his captain. "Beggin' yer pardon, Govn'r, but do you know somethin' 'bout this place?"

Smoot gave a slow shake of his head. "They must be figurin' we wouldn't risk sinkin' them in this deep water—like we would if they were next to a shallow beach."

As they watched, the Silver Cloud's running lights disappeared one by one into the darkness of the narrow crevice.

Smoot leaned forward. "Would ya look at that?"

"They're goin' into that crack! What are they up to, Govn'r?"

"It's a river, lad! They must think they'll find refuge up that narrow river."

"This doesn't make no sense, Govn'r. They'll have to come back out the same way, and they know the Tiburon will be right here waitin' for them."

"Must be somethin' damn important in there."

Henry looked north to find the Remora. "Cap'n Smoot! Look there!"

Smoot looked up at him. "What now?"

"The Remora! They've broken off and are sailing around the point to the north."

"Now that don't figure neither, unless they decided we got the Cloud fer sure this time."

"This time we do, Govn'r!" He slid another line and landed beside his captain. Henry had learned long ago that it went better for him if he agreed with anything Smoot told him. "You tolt me that we lost our edge back at Dead Man's Chest, Govn'r, but I knew all along you had another plan what was even better."

"Tell me about that river mouth, Henry. How far in could ya see from up there?"

"Hundred yards at best, Govn'r. It be too dark now to make out much."

The two pirate ships dropped their anchors and began to swing about their chains in the easy current while the Silver Cloud disappeared into the darkness of the narrow passage. Within ten minutes, she had disappeared behind the second bend, leaving the faint reflection of her stern lanthorn as the only evidence that the dark river waters had ever been disturbed by man.

Henry watched as long as he felt he should, and then turned to his captain. "So, what's yer plan, Govn'r?"

"My plan?"

"Aye! We gonna follow 'em in, or what?"

"I'm thinkin', Henry, I'm thinkin'." Smoot surveyed the cliffs. "One thing's certain. We got 'em trapped fer as long as we want."

"Aye, but they know they're trapped, too."

"What's that s'posed to mean?"

"Well, the way I figger it, if I were trapped with that same treasure in me hold an' two ships was standin' guard at my only way back to the sea, I'd be lookin' to bury all that gold before I was attacked. That way, I'd have somethin' fer dealin' me release later—if the battle went the wrong way, that is."

"Hmm." Smoot didn't like to admit it, but the lad was right. "I was thinkin' them same thoughts, Henry." Smoot looked seaward at the Tiburon and back to the cliffs. "We'll have to attack them tonight, before they get a chance to unload the treasure."

Henry pulled his new cutlass from his belt. The thought of finally getting to cut a man excited him. "By land or by water?"

"Both!" Smoot looked to a short strip of sand to the port side of the river mouth. Next, he looked to the top of the cliffs. "But first—before we attack them—we'll need to take the high ground."

"You thinkin' o' puttin' a few men up on top of those cliffs, Govn'r?"

"Aye, and then we'll send as many of our men as we can up the river behind the Silver Cloud." Smoot turned and looked to the Tiburon. "Order my boat over the side. I need a war counsel with Captain Pritchard."

"Did you say up the river, Govn'r?"

"Aye, that I did."

"We'll be leadin' the raid—you an' me—right?"

"Wrong! We'll be stayin' right here on the Eagle."

"But—"

"Somebody's gotta be here to meet the Cloud if she tries to make it back to sea."

Clearly disappointed, Henry shoved his cutlass back into his belt with a curse.

Smoot turned and strode toward the aft ladder. "I've somethin' to get from my cabin. Have that boat ready when I get back on deck."

"Does that mean you're leavin' me in charge o' the Eagle, Govn'r?"

"Aye, if ya think ye're up to commandin' a ship at anchor! Ha! Ha!"

"That I be, Govn'r! That I be!" The lad recognized the insult, but didn't mind it much, since he'd get to play captain for a while.

Two of the ship's crewmen waited at the waterline in the boat. Smoot backed down the ladder with a new bottle of brandy slung from his belt and ordered them to pull toward the other anchored ship.

"Ahoy, Tiburon! I'll be needin' a counsel with Ezra Pritchard!"

The older man had been watching Smoot's approach and called back. "I'm here!"

Smoot pulled himself up the ladder onto the main deck and was quickly swallowed up by the hundred-odd cutthroats who infested the dark ship. His crew was glad to see their real captain, and reached out to touch him like orphans crowded about prospective parents. Pritchard pushed his way through the press of bodies with a string of profanity that made the others fall aside.

Smoot looked about at the crew. "Where's the rest of the men?"

"There ain't no more! We lost 'bout a third of 'em on the Chest."

"Damn! I was countin' on more than this!"

"What'cha got in mind, Captain? You plannin' on followin' the Cloud up that river?"

"Aye, an' the sooner the better."

"I seen yer crew puttin' yer other boats over the side before ya came across. Yer not plannin' on doin' it all by yerself, are ya?"

Smoot gave a shake of his head. "My men will go to the top of those cliffs to give you musket cover. As soon as they're in place, they'll give us a signal. Then you'll send as many of your men—your best fighters—up the river for the attack. You need to get to the Silver Cloud before they have a chance to unload and bury the treasure."

"That's kind'a risky, isn't it?"

"Hell yes it's risky! But we got no choice!"

"But you don't like fightin' at night."

"You don't need to remind me of that, Ezra." Smoot looked out at the cliffs. "If we wait, they'll have time to set up their defenses and bury the treasure, and we can't risk that."

Pritchard turned to the nearest men. "You heard Captain Smoot. Get to the boats!"

Smoot held up the bottle. "It'll take my men 'bout 'alf an hour to gain the heights. That'll give us time to go below an' and kill this bottle of brandy I brung along fer good luck."

Before they could take their second drink, a very disturbed seaman was pounding on the cabin door. "Beggin' yer pardon, Cap'n Smoot, but Morgan's callin' fer ya from the Eagle. Says it's mighty important, sir."

"Damn that boy! Probably wants to know which direction to coil a rope or somethin' foolish like that!" He gave Pritchard a disgusted look and rose to follow the seaman. At the door, he paused and pointed back at the bottle. "Don't you be touchin' no more o' that brandy till I come back, Ezra! I know its waterline!"

The deck of the Tiburon was busy with battle preparations. Every conceivable weapon was stacked at the rail for loading into the four boats that had been lowered to the water. There were cutlasses, battle axes, flintlock pistols and rifles—most of them Spanish-made. The men were in high spirits, for this promised to be a decisive battle with enough spoils that every man could retire permanently from the Brotherhood.

Smoot made his way to the starboard bow. "Ahoy, Eagle! Is Henry Morgan there?"

"Aye, Govn'r!" It was Henry. "Look to the cliffs!"

Smoot turned about and looked up to where there was the glow of at least two fires. He turned and called back to Henry. "How'd you get them up there so quick?"

"Them ain't our men, Govn'r! The bonfires belong to the Silver Cloud's men!"

"The hell you say!" Smoot threw back his head and shouted a string of curses that brought every man on both ships to see what had happened.

Pritchard climbed the ladder and looked to his captain. "What's happened now?"

"Look there, Ezra!" Smoot pointed. "The Cloud's beat us to the cliffs!"

"And the raiding party?" He walked to the rail and looked down on his four boats, then turned back to Smoot. "What do you want I should tell my men?"

"They're my men, not yours!" Smoot stormed across the deck and stopped at the ladder. "I'm goin' back to the Eagle. In case we don't talk again, I've two orders for you. I want those four boats of men up that river at first light. If you can't defeat the Cloud inside, on the river, then I want her boarded when she returns to sea! Under no circumstances is the Silver Cloud to be sunk in deep water! Understood?"

"But—"

He pulled his sword. "You heard my orders, Privy!"

***

While Smoot was dropping anchor and considering his options, John was preparing to take the Silver Cloud from the open sea into the narrow river. He called to his first officer. "Mister Noble! Order the sails furled and the long boats over the side!" As David hurried to comply, John walked forward to where Ben Gunn stood at the windward rail, just aft of the cathead.

"There it is, Cap'n, just like I told you."

"And you're sure the Cloud will make it through?"

"Flint told me the old Walrus made it through, and she was at least a span or two wider than this ship."

John studied the narrow opening. "Well, I hope that John Flint was telling you the truth, because I don't like this at all."

"Don't worry, Captain. We'll be in an' back out again by dawn tomorrow."

"There's something else I don't like, Ben."

"The Remora?"

"You noticed."

Ben looked back to where they had last seen the mysterious privateer. "Doesn't make any sense they'd give up the chase like that, unless..." The old man fell silent.

"If you know something, Mister Gunn, please tell me before we are enmeshed too deeply to get out again."

Ben turned and looked at his captain for several moments. "I don't know who is on the Remora, Captain Jones. The secret of Deception Lagoon was known by the whole crew of the Walrus, but I may be the only one left."

"Do you think one of them might be on the Remora?

Ben gave his captain a worried look. "I hope not, sir."

The Silver Cloud's boat crews had attached themselves to her dolphin striker and had their massive ship moving smoothly into the narrows. The rock walls were a mixture of gray and black slate, with long shadows falling downward from each outcropping like the torn fringe of a witch's skirt. Every sound—from the jabbing and scraping of the pikes against rocks to the creaking of oars in their locks—echoed back at the officers and men from the cold, wet stone. A deep despair crept across the deck and into every man's soul while the sea was choked from view by the tomb-like narrows that had swallowed them and their great ship.

While Captain Jones and the old maroon considered the situation, Robert approached from aft. "May I join you, Captain Jones?"

"Of course!"

Robert stepped to the two and gave a raise of his shoulders. "I don't like this."

John gave one of his rare laughs. "Sort of like being lowered into a grave, isn't it?"

Robert returned the laugh. "May I make a suggestion?"

"Please."

"Shouldn't we be doing something about protecting our backsides?"

"I was just discussing that with Ben." John put a comforting hand on the old man's arm. "Ben suggested we trail one longboat with sharpshooters, but..."

"If they follow us in, I'd agree, John. But I don't think they know Ben's secret."

"Might I suggest something, sir?" John and Robert turned their attention to the old man. "If I remember anything about Joshua Smoot, it's that he's a cautious and calculating man." Ben pointed up at the cliffs. "He'll put sharpshooters on the high ground before he sends his boats up the river."

John looked up. "Then we'll just have to put a few of our own up there first."

Ben considered. "To make it worthwhile, Captain, it'll take at least six, or maybe eight men on each cliff. With so many men sick from the poison, and the rest needed to refill the water supply, that's gonna hurt us bad."

"I know." John walked away to the larboard rail. After a minute, he returned. "If everything was in place, one man on each side would be able to keep a couple of fires and half a dozen lanthorns burning."

"One man on each side?" Robert gave John a questioning look. "What could two men do against a full attack?"

"Have you ever watched a magician closely, Robert?"

"Yes."

"It's deception—just like the name of this lagoon. While they have you watching one hand, they are doing the trick with the other."

"Go on."

"If Joshua Smoot and his men see several fires atop the cliffs, they will assume we've put those eight sharpshooters on each side."

Robert smiled. "One man—even a sick one—could tend several fires by himself. We just have to get enough wood up on the cliffs for him to tend."

Ben saw the plan. "Those wooden boxes that look like bales of cotton. We don't need them hiding the cannons any more, Captain Jones."

"Ben's right, John. If we break them up and send half a dozen men up each side with the wood and lanthorns, then one of the weaker men could maintain the fires while the rest return to the ship."

Ben pointed back to the pirate ships. "If the deception works, we might not have to contend with an attack at all!"

"Would you put the contingents together for me, Robert? We'll hold the ship up just ahead where the cliffs begin to drop away."

"Consider it done, John." He grabbed a nearby bosun's mate by the sleeve and the two disappeared below.

Ten minutes later, two large piles of scrap lumber had been heaped on the deck, along with lanthorns and extra containers of whale oil. The boat crews sat quietly with their oars propped against the rocks, holding the Cloud against the river's easy current.

With their last-minute instructions delivered, the two groups of men were set ashore—half to the starboard and the rest to larboard. The two men who would remain and tend the fires and lamthorns carried only their personal weapons and enough food and water to get them through the night.

By John's estimation, the boat crews had pulled the Silver Cloud a quarter-mile up the river before it finally opened out into a lagoon sixty yards across. Like the narrows, the lagoon was very deep, with a thirty-foot waterfall dumping several thousand gallons every minute into its depths. While the boat crews loosed their lines, David ordered the anchor dropped. At the same time, two of the large water casks were hoisted over the side with all their bungholcs uncapped.

John studied the east shore of the lagoon. A thick underbrush had crept from the nearby tree line to the water's edge, where it sucked at the life-giving liquid. "You told me that there'd be a way out of here, Ben. I don't see it."

"Captain Flint swore to me that it was here, Captain Jones." The old man searched the same shoreline. "He swore!"

***

The night in Deception Lagoon was as dark as the ink on the King's warrant that had driven John Paul Jones from Fredericksburg. Lacking an explanation from their captain, the crew's fear and mistrust had grown with each bend in the narrow river. Captain Jones had gotten them through some desperate situations in the previous week, but for all the gods, nobody could figure how he'd get them out of this one. They were obviously trapped—landlocked in a small, freshwater lagoon. Every man knew it was only a matter of time before the pirates would send their raiding parties up the channel and over the hills to take the treasure—and as many lives as they pleased.

Before first light, an impatient Captain Jones stood outside Ben Gunn's cabin, listening for the old man to stir. There was no sound. "Ben!" John whispered and tapped lightly on the door. "Ben, are you there?"

"No, Cap'n Jones, I'm not."

John turned about to find the old man standing behind him, fully dressed. "You're already up!"

"Couldn't sleep, sir. After tellin' ya there was a way out'a the lagoon last night an' me not bein' able to show ya, well, I figured I'd have her spotted before you came for me."

"Well? Did you find it yet?"

"Not yet, sir, but the sun's comin' up and there's just now enough light to see the shore." Ben turned and climbed back to the main deck, with John at his heels.

The old man's dressings had been removed, exposing the results of his recent torture on Dead Man's Chest. A neat row of diamond-shaped burns ran up the inside of each calf from ankle to knee.

Ben noticed his captain looking at his calves. Ben twisted his right leg outward toward the younger man. "Sorta fashionable, in't it?"

"Fashionable?"

"The perfect scars fer a storyteller, says I." Ben gave a laugh and strode aft to the taffrail. After a long moment, he pointed to the eastern shore. "There it is, sir!"

John followed. "I don't see anything. What am I looking for?"

"Look there, at the moving water."

"What moving water?"

"Don't ya see it?" He continued to point. "Right there, just this side of the white rock."

John squinted.

"Look how the water's bein' sucked under them vines." Ben was right. Even though the sun hadn't crested the hills, there was just enough light in the sky to see the unmistakable swirl of a strong current pulling angrily from under the mass of vegetation. This was their escape route—the one John Flint had told Ben about more than two decades before.

David called from amidships. "Captain Jones! Ben! I was on my way to wake you." He noticed them looking toward the shore and stepped to the rail. "What have you seen?"

"We've found the second river, David. How long would it take to put the hand crews ashore to begin cutting our way out of here?"

David looked to where John was pointing, but couldn't see anything. "The last three casks will be aboard in a half-hour, and that's taking all of the men who weren't poisoned." He looked to the shore again. "What do you want them cutting?"

"That's the second channel—our way out of this lagoon—and those plants need to be removed before we can enter it."

David looked to the men working with the water casks. "Another half-hour, Captain—maybe sooner."

"Make it quick, David. Ben is convinced that Smoot will attack us at any time."

In fact, it was just a half-hour later that they heard a volley of musket fire from the river.

"David, get Doctor McKenzie up here on the double. I need to know how many able-bodied men we can deploy."

"Aye, aye, Captain!" David bounded away to the ladder and passed Robert on his way below.

Robert ran to John and Ben. "They're attacking! We need more men on the cliffs, John!"

"Our men are coming, Robert, but we'll have to split them between our defense and our escape."

"Escape?" Robert looked where Ben was pointing. "Where?"

"There, sir!"

As a dozen of the Indian fighters rowed toward the head of the first river to lay in wait for the approaching pirates, two boats of men rowed to the opposite side of the lagoon. Most of the vines were a very soft kind of water plant that yielded quickly to the persistent tugging of the pike poles and cutting blows of the sharp cutlasses. Within an hour, the work parties had replaced the water casks in the hold and opened the head of the escape channel to the north side of the island.

John turned to his first officer. "It's time to recall the men from the river and the cliffs."

"Aye, Captain."

"And once you've done that, order the anchor weighed and have the Cloud pulled into the river." The young Jamaican saluted and sped away to comply.

Robert stepped to his captain. "You're not going to wait until it's cleared to the sea?"

"It will be, Robert. By the time David can get the Indian fighters back and our boat crews have maneuvered the ship into the current, the cutting crews should be nearing the beach. With any luck, we'll be at sea and under sail again well before noon."

The second river was slightly wider than the first, but without the hundred-foot cliffs to either side. The Silver Cloud was piked between the two shores at a walking speed, with hand crews on both shores to man the hauling and restraint lines. The morale of the crew had been resurrected, especially as the unmistakable sound of the nearby surf became louder and louder with each step. David had joined the starboard shore crew, but he dropped his line and ran up the bank to meet a sailor hurrying back from seaward.

John saw the excited man and called to David. "What's the matter? What did he see?"

David pointed down river. "We've some shallows about two hundred yards ahead, Captain! We may have some trouble getting through unless we can wait for high tide."

"We can't wait, David! I don't want the Silver Cloud stopped for anything!"

John watched from the forward rail as the mighty ship inched forward toward the shallows. He and the other officers had been able to see the river's bottom all along, but now the boulders were even closer to the surface, almost as if someone had rolled them there to form a barrier to their escape. Then, as if his ship had been seized by the hand of an angry god, the Silver Cloud came to a sudden and frightening stop. The shore crews paused to look up at their captain.

Before he could think what to do next, the river had made its own decision. There came a terrible rolling and scraping sound from below, followed by an uncomfortable lurch forward. The river's waters had backed up behind the Cloud's stern until it finally pushing her up and over the boulders and on toward the waiting sea.

The good Lord was on their side that morning, for within minutes, the mighty treasure ship had coasted into the low surf and had spun about on her hauling lines to face the beach. And none too quickly, for no sooner had the Indian fighters and the work crews been taken aboard and the order given to set sails, than three boats full of Smoot's men emerged, accompanied by curses and musket fire, from around a last bend in the river and into the open sea.

The gunner stepped to the quarterdeck. "Shall I order up a broadside, Captain Jones?"

"I'm tempted, but I don't want to waste the time. Seeing us escaping like this is punishment enough."

The Silver Cloud's great sails dropped from the yards like a bride's petticoats on her wedding night, each one filling with the gentle southerly breeze that rolled over the low hills of the island. Within minutes, the ship gained steerage and pulled through the surf into the open waters of the Caribbean.

John watched the pirates storm about the beach and fire their muskets in frustration. "By the time those boats get back to Smoot, we'll be well out of sight."

Ben clapped his hands in triumph. "And we'll be done with pirates for good!"

The rest of the officers joined in their captain's elation, but it was short lived.

"Sail astern!" It was the top watch. "It's the Remora, sir, and she's under full sail!"

"Damn!" John searched the deck for his gunner. "McCoy! Man the guns!"

Chapter 16

There was no sense in running from the Remora. It was common knowledge that a Virginia privateer could easily outmaneuver a square-masted brig. Within minutes she would easily close with the Silver Cloud and maneuver into a position to attack the larger ship from either the stem or stern.

John studied the activity aboard the Remora for several minutes.

"John?" It was Robert.

John lowered the spyglass and turned to the other officers. "Gentlemen, we've a golden opportunity before us which we simply can't afford to pass up. I don't expect we'll ever find our three pursuers separated like this again, so I intend to engage the Remora."

John looked to David. "Pipe the crew to general quarters and clear the decks for action. I told McCoy to keep the siding in place, but I think it's finally time to show our guns."

"But—" David began, and then checked himself. "Aye, aye, Captain."

The deck came alive. Whereas half a dozen teams of men had been pulling at the sheets, there were now over sixty men running for the ladders that led to the gun deck and their battle stations. Many of the men who had been suffering the ill-effects of the strychnine poisoning took their places with the rest of the crew. John stood with his hands on the starboard rail as his ship cut smoothly seaward into the deeper water that she would need for maneuvering. Predictively, the Remora continued on its course to intercept the treasure ship, but her captain had not ordered her gun ports opened.

"I can't figure her, Robert."

The older man studied the smaller ship. "She obviously knew about this second way out of the lagoon, yet didn't tell the Tiburon or the Eagle."

John rubbed his chin and realized that he had forgotten to shave. "There's something else."

Oh?"

"Why didn't she attack while we were still in shallow waters—when the men from the Tiburon were at our backs?"

David stood several feet behind the two older men. "Maybe she's not who we..." He checked himself when the two turned to look at him.

John took a threatening step toward his young friend. "You talk as if you know something about the Remora." He looked back at the fast approaching ship and then continued his interrogation. "Do you?"

"It's just that there's something strange about her." David looked to Robert and back to John. "You sense it too, don't you?"

"We all do, but until we know better, she'll be treated exactly like the others." John looked forward to where McCoy was standing by. "You've an order to give, David."

The first officer looked to the Remora, and then forward to where McCoy waited. "Gunner!"

"Aye! At your command!"

"You can raise the planking and run out the guns! As soon as the Remora is in range, I want one warning round put across her bow!"

"Should I take off a foot or two of her bowsprit, Mister Noble?" Laughter and cheers reverberated up from below.

"No!" David gave his captain a nervous look.

"Make it close, David."

"But we don't want to provoke them into firing on us, do we?"

"Give the order, Mister Noble. I wouldn't ask for the round unless I wanted to provoke them."

David turned and shouted the order forward. "Make it close, McCoy, but don't hit them!"

The gunner gave a quick salute and dropped from sight. He was met by another muffled cheer from the bowels of the ship. Ten seconds later, there was the roar of a six-inch cannon. Then, as all hands watched with certain expectation, a column of water leaped into the morning sky from under the Remora's bowsprit, showering her foredeck with brine.

"Well done, David!" John raised his spyglass at the Remora. "Now we'll see what she intends to do!"

"They won't fight us, Captain."

"Won't fight us, you say?"

David pointed. "Look!"

A white flag climbed its rope, and the captain of the Remora called out. "Ahoy there, Silver Cloud!" The voice was strong and deep, with an unmistakable Scottish brogue similar to the one that John had been working so diligently for the past year to lose. "Daniel Archer here! Have I permission to come across?"

John gave David another questioning look. He turned, raised his speaking trumpet and called back. "Aye, but be warned that we've another ten cannons trained on your vessel!"

"Thank you, sir! Let me assure you that you'll not be needin' any armament against us!"

While the two called back and forth, a six-man boat was already lifting from the deck of the Remora to transport Captain Archer across. "I've a gift for you, Captain Jones—a gift that'd tempt a Papist out'a his hassock."

"You know my name! Have we met?"

"No, we haven't, sir, but we do have a mutual friend!"

"I'm anxious to learn who this mutual friend is, Captain Archer!" John moved closer to David's side as he continued to exchange shouts with the Remora. "Make haste, Captain Archer, for we must be underway!"

John turned to David. "You have some explaining to do." David remained silent, so John continued. "You've known about the Remora all along, haven't you?"

"No I haven't, Captain. I didn't suspect anything until just now, just like you."

"That's a lie! You knew something when I ordered you to put one across her bow!" John pointed across at the smaller ship. "I have a strong feeling Captain Archer already knew about the false sides on our ship. He couldn't have known that without being told."

David fidgeted with his sword while he searched for the right words. "I thought it possible that my father sent them to protect his investment, but—"

"Your father, you say?" John set his jaw and faced David squarely. "I have tremendous difficulty believing that! If he had, you'd have told me long before they arrived so mysteriously at Dead Man's Chest!" John took a long breath. "What did you tell your father about our mission?"

"I told him about Mister Jefferson sending the Eagle, that's all. He must have figured to protect his interests by sending his own ship."

"Damn you, David!" John's outburst caught the attention of all hands on the main deck, including that of Robert Ormerod.

"'Damn you, David'?" Robert stepped across to the two. "What's the lad done now?"

"We may have another traitor in our midst, Robert!"

"You don't mean young Noble here, do you?"

"Yes, I do!" He looked back at David. "That's unless he can do some quick explaining."

"What is it? What is John talking about?"

"David's known about the Remora from the first—even before she joined us at Dead Man's Chest!"

"Is that true?" Robert backed away from the young man. "Did you know?"

"Not for sure, sir."

"Not for sure, my eye!" John gripped the hilt of his sword. "You knew enough to tell me they wouldn't fight back!"

"Well, yes...sort of, Captain, but—"

Robert joined the grilling, but spoke with cold and determined tone. "If you knew they were coming, then you know who sent them."

"Out with it, David! Tell us before I throw you in irons with our other other traitor."

"I really..." David looked back and forth at the two. "I don't know for sure. As I was telling John—Captain Jones—they...I mean, my father didn't discuss it with me."

"They?" Robert touched the knife at his belt. "Who else is in on this?"

David looked down at John's half-drawn sword. "Captain, do you remember the old innkeeper when we first met?"

"The white-haired man with the articulated wooden leg?"

Robert gasped. "Articulated wooden leg?"

John gave Robert a glance. "He's David's uncle."

Robert pulled his knife from the scabbard and held it at David's face. "Is it his left leg?"

David nodded. "Yes, it is."

John had heard enough. "Gentlemen, I think we can stop playing games." With his sword now fully drawn, John touched his first officer on the boot with its point. "What's your uncle's real name?"

Before David could answer, there came a lusty greeting from forward where Captain Archer climbed onto the main deck of the Silver Cloud with a velvet bag the size of a woman's purse. "Greetings, gentlemen! Greetings from my employer and your protector, Long John Silver!"

David backed away from Robert's knife. "I didn't know he sent them! I only guessed it from how the Remora's been acting!"

"He's telling ya the gospel, Captain Jones!" Archer strode aft, holding out a sealed letter. "Neither Silver nor Davey's father told him a thing about me or my ship."

John took the letter, broke the seal, and read aloud.

To my predictable and most cooperative friend, Captain Jones:

First, allow me to congratulate you for accomplishing what hundreds have tried and failed. You are about to hand over to me the legendary Treasure of Dead Man's Chest.

That may stick in your craw, good sir, but we're all winners in this exploit. The Colonies will have their cannons, you and David will get your naval commissions, and Charles and I shall have our long awaited rewards. Please don't feel badly that you've been manipulated and oft deceived. There was no other way to accomplish what you and your comrades have done.

Until we meet again—and that shall be sooner than you think—I am your true friend, humble servant, and greatest admirer.

Long John Silver

Robert reached for the letter. "Let me read that!"

John handed him the letter and returned his sword to its sheath. "So that sweet old innkeeper, Jack Bridger, is the infamous pirate, Long John Silver?"

Archer nodded. "You didn't know?"

John shook his head. "I expected someone much more..." John searched for the words.

"A bloodthirsty cutthroat?" Archer finished John's thought and gave a hearty laugh.

"Well, at least somebody who looked like a pirate!"

Archer held out the velvet bag to John.

"What's this?"

"It's Captain Silver's special way of saying thank you, Captain Jones. He told me he promised it to you when you were in King's Town the winter of '73."

John untied the knot and pulled a bottle of Scotch whiskey from the pouch.

"It took him until now to locate just the right bottle—one from the distillery near your birthplace in Scotland."

"Yes it is." John turned the bottle around and read the label. He looked up at Archer. "I assume I will be able to thank Mister Silver personally in a few days."

Robert turned to John. "The only way you'll meet John Silver is by looking down at his dead body! He sent the men who killed my daughter!" He turned to Archer. "What can we expect from John Silver when we reach the rendezvous? Are we to be killed?"

"For the treasure? Why no, sir!" Archer had hoped the bottle of spirits and his good humor would relax his hosts. "Silver may be a pirate, but when he gives his word on a thing, he'll never go back on it. Pirates can be some of the most honorable men afloat. You'll get your cannons, as long as he gets his treasure."

"No tricks then?"

"None, sir!" Archer gave a slow shake of his head. "There'd be no point to it."

There was a moment of uneasy quiet as the two captains studied each other. Finally Archer spoke. "I'd think my saving your two men on the north coast of the Chest would have convinced you of my good intentions, Captain Jones."

"So that was the Remora?"

"Aye, that was us."

"It would have helped if you had left us a message on one of the bodies."

"I did!"

"Oh?"

"Didn't you see the semaphore?" Archer was sure someone in the Silver Cloud's crew would have picked it up.

"The dead pirate's arms?"

"Aye!"

John looked to David. "What were they?"

"There were five of them, Captain. I believe they were O-C-J-L-S."

"No!" Archer turned to John. "They were C-O-L-J-S." Nobody ventured a guess, so Archer continued. "They stood for 'Compliments of...'" He paused when he saw Robert's expression change.

"Compliments of Long John Silver!"

"Ah! I knew there was a clever one amongst ya!"

John pointed east, toward Dead Man's Chest. "If you wanted us to know you were responsible, then why didn't you just spell out your ship's name? There were more than enough bodies!"

"And tell Smoot's men too?"

John considered for a moment. "No, I suppose you did all you could."

"And that's the only way John Silver would have it."

Robert suddenly realized something. He looked aft to where Archer had left his boat. "I have the sense that the old pirate is among us."

"I am, Robert!" John Silver stood on the ladder just high enough to see onto the deck. "If ya promise not to shoot me or run me through, I'll come aboard and we can discuss our business like gentlemen."

"My God!" Robert pushed past David, pulled his pistol and fired it at the old man. It missed to the left. He continued forward with his knife drawn.

John called to the nearby seamen. "Restrain Mister Ormerod!"

"Not yer God, Robert." Silver chuckled while he pulled his bulk up and onto the deck. "But I'm certainly your benefactor."

"If these men weren't holding me back, I'd choke you to death with my bare hands!"

"Well then, I certainly thank God for their restraining hands!"

Captain Archer stepped to John Silver's side. "Gentlemen, may I introduce the unofficial Mayor of King's Town, and my employer, Long John Silver?"

Robert gave a jerk at the men on each arm. "Your mayor is a murderer!"

To Captain Jones, John Silver was the crude but friendly innkeeper from Silver Jack's Tavern on the wharf at King's Town. But to Robert, who had watched the man kill at least seven of Captain Murray's men during that final battle on Spyglass, he was the vilest of cutthroats.

Silver gave his articulated leg a slap and then walked about in a circle. "Aren't I a vision o' heaven in my new waistcoat and fancy articulated leg?"

"More like a vision from hell, you thieving cutthroat!"

"'Thieving cutthroat'?" Silver echoed with feigned disappointment. "You wound me, Robert."

"But that's exactly what you are! A thief and a cutthroat!"

"And I suppose you and my little brother are respectable merchants?"

"Of course we are!"

"Wrong!" Silver leaned close to the Yorkman. "We're all cut from the same cloth—you, Charlie and me. The only difference is that your lines follow a slightly different pattern."

"Never!"

"We both deal in valuable goods and we both ask the highest price the market will bear. As I see it, the only place we truly differ is that I take a slightly higher percentage of the swag than you."

"But there is a difference!" Robert struggled again to get loose. "You and your kind kill for the goods you take!"

"And what if I were to purchase a letter of marque like those colonial pirates you deal with?"

"Nothing would make you..."

"Or what if I were a Spaniard? Would you still hate me as much?"

"A Spaniard?"

"Aye, a Spaniard! Ten years ago when we were at war with them, I heard you blew up at the mere mention of the race!" Silver took a long breath and waited for Robert's answer. "At a loss for words, Robert?"

"Calm down, you two!" John stepped between them. "We've more important things to accomplish than settling old scores."

"It cuts my soul in half to know you're finally going to get the treasure."

"And did you ever doubt I would, Robert?"

"Yes! I figured you'd be shoveling coal in hell by now, provided the Devil would allow you into the place!"

The thought of tangling with Satan, one-on-one, amused the old pirate. His lips curled back in a wry smile, revealing the row of large white teeth.

"Enough!" John turned to Silver. "I need to know several things from you, Mister Silver."

"Such as?"

"Why are you on the Remora rather than the Silver Cloud that is carrying the cannons. And what are we going to do about the Tiburon and the Eagle?"

"I'm on the Remora because of the treasure."

"But that wasn't your mission! You were supposed to meet us at the rendezvous!"

"I have men whom I trust to do what I've told them to do, Captain Jones, unlike your Mister Jefferson."

Robert was still restrained. "What do you know about Jefferson?"

"Nothing directly, but from what I've seen, he isn't a very good judge of character."

"What do you mean by that?"

"Didn't he choose the captain of the Eagle?"

"Go on."

"Well, I'd say it was a poor assignment by the way Captain Steele allowed the Tiburon to get close enough to disable the Silver Cloud like that?"

"Smoot's not on the Tiburon, Uncle."

"Oh?"

"He and Henry Morgan are on the Eagle, or at least they were when we departed the Chest."

Silver looked at his nephew. "A lad with green eyes and flame-red hair?" David nodded. "Well, I'll be a maroon's armpit!"

John gave Silver a tilt of his head. "You know Smoot and Morgan?"

Robert twisted loose from one of the men, but was grabbed by another. "Of course he knows them! They're the two he sent to get the treasure map. I brought it, but they killed my little girl anyway!"

"That was a stupid accident, Robert. As I heard it, Morgan was left with the girl but wondered off long enough that she kicked over the lanthorn. When he saw the flames and got back, it was too late."

"But you sent them, and my little girl died! In my book, that means you killed her!" Robert tried to pull loose again.

John turned to the bosun. "Take Mister Ormerod to his cabin and place two guards at his door. Keep him there until Captain Silver is gone." A moment later, Robert was gone.

Silver gave a shrug. "Thank you, Captain Jones. Now where was I?"

"Smoot and Morgan."

"Ah, yes! I met Morgan briefly ten years ago on Tortuga. The two of them came to King's Town together several years later. Smoot wanted to know where his father—John Flint—was buried. Our deal was Flint's grave for the map to the treasure." Silver looked back toward the south and the rocky cliffs that hid the anchored pirate ships from view. "So Joshua Smoot's been playing your protector?"

"Aye."

"You know of course, that he'll sacrifice the Tiburon and most of his men if he has to in order to take your ship?"

"That's why I want to get under way as quickly as possible. Would you and Captain Archer please return to your ship?"

Silver stroked his beard in thought. "Smoot doesn't know about the second Silver Cloud, does he?"

"Not unless Morgan figured the thing out before he ran off from Charles Town to join him."

"Good! That means there's a chance he'll wait until we unload the treasure at King's Town."

David shook his head. "I believe he'll order the Tiburon to attack us before King's Town."

"How do you figure, Davey?"

"You know the man better than I do." David pointed to the retreating pirates back on the beach. "Unless he's among those men, he figures we're still trapped in Deception Lagoon. When his men return with word of our escape, he won't take it very well."

"I think David's right. But he won't attack us in deep water."

Silver held up a cautioning hand. "He could order the Tiburon to attempt a boarding, after he's raked your rigging with shot. He only needs to disable the Silver Cloud, not sink it."

"One more question, Captain Silver."

"Yes?"

"When I delivered the letters to Mister Ormerod in New York, he showed me a letter that he received a week before my arrival. It told that I was on my way. Did you send him that letter?"

"Aye, that was mine, and I was at the Dandridge estate the day you and Dorothea planned your little picnic."

John's mouth dropped open. "That was you? Why?"

"To deliver a copy of the King's warrant to the girl's father and make a suggestion how he might get rid of you." The old pirate pulled a piece of parchment from his waistcoat and opened it. It was another copy of the warrant. "Didn't ya suspect anything when ya saw the King's Town Admiralty stamp on it?"

"You bastard! How dare you?"

"How dare I?" Silver retreated a step. "Would the Americans be getting their cannons if I hadn't arranged for you to be sent to Edenton?"

"No, but—"

"And would you and David be getting your naval commissions if I hadn't?"

"The only reason you did any of it was to get the treasure! Only God knows how many lives you've affected by your greed!"

"And there's a lot more to come, my friends." The old pirate turned to the opening in the rail. "A whole lot more!"

Before anyone could react, Robert had climbed from the aft ladder, run forward to the retreating pirate, raised another pistol, and squeezed the trigger. Everyone gasped together, expecting the point-blank shot to fell the old man. But in his haste, Robert had only pulled the hammer to the half-cock position.

"Damn your soul to hell!" Robert stepped back toward David and pulled back on his pistol's lock. There was a moment of confusion. David reached at the pistol as it fired. John Silver cried out and fell to the deck. Before the smoke had cleared, David was at his uncle's side, and several crewmen had pulled Robert away.

"Uncle Silver!" Certain that he was dead, David turned and looked up at Robert. "Damn you, Ormerod! You shot him! You've killed my uncle!"

Robert pointed down at the fallen pirate. "He killed my daughter!"

"He never meant for her to be hurt!" David shielded Silver with his own body. "He explained about the fire! It was an accident! When he found out what his two agents did, he ordered that they be shot!"

"Well, his remorse doesn't bring back my daughter!"

David broke into a storm of tears and sobs. "How will I tell my father?"

The old pirate's eyes flickered while he whispered to David. "Tell him I died in a fight with Joshua Smoot."

David sat up with a start. "Uncle?" David gave a nudge to the old man's ribs. "I thought you were dead?"

"Not quite, Davey." Silver blinked up at the men standing over him. "I think it's just my wooden leg he's killed."

"You'll die this day, you black-hearted snake!" Robert tried to pull loose and grab one of the men's cutlasses. "My little girl's death will be avenged today!"

John pointed aft. "You men! Escort Mister Ormerod to the quarterdeck and hold him better this time!"

"Thank you, Captain Jones." Silver pushed himself up into a sitting position. "I'm truly in your debt."

"You're not in my debt yet, Mister Silver."

John pointed back at Robert. "You're in his debt, and he's a determined man. After you get your treasure, I would suggest you find a hole someplace and pull a rock over yourself."

"Such hatred!"

John pointed at the Remora. "Leave my ship, before I release Robert and supply him with a fresh pistol!"

Archer pulled Silver upright and put a shoulder under his left arm for support. The articulated leg was shattered. Silver stopped at the rail. "What about the treasure on Flint's Island?"

"I didn't think we had time."

Silver nodded. "The cannon ship is at the rendezvous as we speak, Captain Jones. My men will wait, no matter how long it takes you."

"Very well. We'll go to Spyglass. Signal us when you're ready to get underway."

"Before I go, any special instructions for when the Tiburon catches up with you?"

"Just keep the Eagle out of cannon range. I can handle the Tiburon."

As John Silver turned about to descend the ship's ladder, he noticed the crewmen who had been gathering on the main deck to get a look at the famous pirate.

Archer noticed their gaunt and tired look. "Your men don't look well, Captain Jones."

"They aren't. We had a traitor on board since we departed Charles Town. He not only released our anchor to put us on the coral, but when we put back to sea from the Chest, he poisoned our water supply."

"Could you use a few of my men until your crew's stronger?"

"Yes, I could. I'd take a dozen topmen, if you could spare them."

"I'll order the exchange. If you'd like, I can take your weakest men aboard the Remora until we reach Spyglass."

Within a half-hour the Silver Cloud had taken on the Remora's crewmen and the two ships were underway. At John's request, David and Robert were waiting in his cabin.

"Well, well!" John closed the door and walked to the table. "As John Silver wrote in his letter, I've certainly been manipulated."

David shook his head. "We've all been manipulated, Captain, from the very start."

"From when you went back to King's Town to deliver the five letters, you mean?"

"Oh no, Captain. He used us from the afternoon you arrived at Silver Jack's Tavern in '73."

"Silver Jack's?" Robert closed his eyes and exhaled in frustration. "My God, John. The name of the place should have warned you!"

"You forget that I'd never heard of Long John Silver before I met you and Ben. I suspected something when Ben told me about Silver on our way to Fredericksburg, but...well, I guess I chose to ignore it."

"He had to ignore it, Robert, just as I had to deceive him." David turned back to his captain. "John, be honest with us. Would you have thrown in with me if you knew a pirate was using us like this?"

John shook his head.

David turned to Robert. "And would you have agreed to lead John and me to the treasure if you knew my uncle was involved?"

"Never!"

"Answer me one more thing. Do the colonies need those cannons?" Neither of them could argue with his logic. "Now that you know it was Long John Silver all along, does it really change anything?"

John shook his head. "Not really."

"Speak for yourself, John. The moment we arrive at Charles Town, I'm issuing a warrant for John Silver's head. I'll not rest until he's punished for his crime against my family."

***

The Silver Cloud plowed through an endless parade of rolling swells, spawned in some far off storm toward the equatorial coast of Guatamala or Panama. A steady quartering wind from the south filled her canvas, pushing the great frigate ahead of the following sea and encouraging a school of sleek, black-and-white dolphins to play like a group of graceful school children upon the ship's bow wave, leaping to take a fresh breath of air or to capture one of the many flying fish startled into flight by the ship's onrushing stem. The deep, pounding sound of faraway surf breaking over an unseen reef, mixed with the complaining of rope and leather against mast and yard, created a symphony most pleasing to the nautical ear.

By dusk of that first day out of Deception Lagoon, there was still no sign of their two pursuers—the Tiburon and the Eagle. The Remora, by request of Captain Jones, had stationed herself a league to windward— the best position for a quick rendezvous should her assistance be necessary.

John looked into the wake in quiet contemplation as David joined him at the taffrail. "It feels good doesn't it, David?"

"Aye, but I was truly doubtful we'd ever see open water again."

"Oh?" John glanced aloft to check the trim of the sails.

"You have to admit that Ben's escape route was a bit risky, even for a gambler like you."

"It was a gamble I had to take, and I apologize for making the decision without conferring with you and the others. If it hadn't worked out the way it did, well…" John paused for a moment to think while he rubbed the accumulation of salt crystals from his eyebrows.

"You're the captain, and it was your decision to make." David turned about and studied the sea behind them. "How long do you figure before they'll catch us?"

"I'm surprised we haven't spotted them already." John looked about at the setting sun. "It's nearly dark, but I'll wager ten crowns the watch reports two sails astern by first light."

The evening was uneventful aboard the disguised frigate, except that a rumor had escaped from the quarterdeck and had run through the ship like a fox with its tail afire. Scuttlebutt was what they called it, and this rumor predicted a deep water battle with the Tiburon the next day.

John had insisted from their departure at Charles Town that all personal weapons be kept battle-ready at all times. There was no need for a reminder this night.

The young Scotsman sat down at his table to consult his charts and bring his logbook up to date. It might be his last chance to record the happenings of the last several days.

At first light there came an impatient hammering at John's door, along with the excited calls of one of the young gunner's mates. It was clear that his prediction of the previous evening had come true.

John pulled the door open. "How far astern are they?"

"Five to six leagues, sir, and Mister Noble says they'll be on us before noon!"

"Tell Mister Noble I'll join him presently."

"Aye, aye, Captain!"

By the time John had gained his position on the quarterdeck, the other four officers were assembled and awaiting his orders.

David asked the question they all wanted to ask. "Shall I sound general quarters?"

"Not yet, Mister Noble. I'm still convinced they'll not attack us in deep water."

"You're wrong, John." Robert spoke softly so as not to be heard by the crew. "As much as I hate to agree with John Silver, I feel he and David are correct."

"I can't run a ship on feelings, Robert."

"You forget, John, that I lived and served with some of those beasts. I know how a pirate thinks."

"And how do they think, Robert?"

"They're angry, and frustrated. They've failed in four separate attempts to take the treasure from us, and they think our next stop is King's Town."

"But a deep-water attack?"

"They don't have to sink us to take this ship, John." Robert pointed aloft. "If they can't take down our sails, then they'll aim for our rudder. Once we flounder, they'll board us."

"Well, I'm still certain you're wrong." John looked to each of the other officers.

Ben Gunn called from the taffrail. "Cap'n Jones!"

"What is it, Ben?"

"I think you'll change yer mind when you see this."

"See what?" John took his spyglass from Robert and joined Ben aft. Ben pointed. "Take a look at her flag, sir. It's red."

"Damn!" John lowered the glass and turned back to the others. "They've hoisted their 'no quarter' flag. Seems our Yorkman has predicted correctly once again."

The crew of the Silver Cloud had been in a state of readiness since they had departed Dead Man's Chest, so it took them only moments to begin transforming the hybrid ship into the man-of-war she truly was. The barrels of sand by each of the great masts were spilled onto the main and gun decks in preparation for the blood that might shortly flow over the planking. Doctor McKenzie and his two surgeon's mates descended to the interior of the ship where they began to lay out their medical tools and set two dozen cauterizing irons in a small stove prepared for that purpose. The bilge pumps were primed, and a continual procession of seamen brought an assortment of ball, grape shot, bar stock, and neatly tied flannel bags of black powder from the ship's bowels to the gun deck. It was no small task to roll away the casks of molasses and swing away and secure the interior facades that had hidden the twenty cannons from the inspector's eye. Within an hour the Silver Cloud had completed its transformation.

With the Tiburon and the Eagle at half a league, the ship's gunner approached the quarterdeck to report. "The guns are loaded an' manned, sir. An' the men asked me to thank ya."

"Thank me for what?"

"Why, fer orderin' the attack against the pirates, sir."

"It's not for their benefit, McCoy, but you can tell them I've accepted their gratitude anyway."

"An' will ya be wantin' ta make yer inspection now, sir?"

"Aye." John gestured for the man to proceed him.

A large smile broke across the gunner's face. He turned about and ran quickly down the aft ladder to the gun deck and marched amongst the cannons and their half-naked gunners. The hatch aft had been removed, and a group of crewmen were crowded in the narrow passageway. John gave McCoy a questioning look.

"That'll be the two cannons I ordered set up in your cabin, sir. I apologize fer disturbin' yer furnishin's, but we'll be needin' the aft firing position if the Tiburon positions herself to attack our rudder."

"No apology necessary, McCoy."

The gun deck had changed. Where there had been hundreds of barrels of molasses, there were now eighteen fine black cannons already loaded for action. The rammers, sponges and worming irons were laid in neat rows between the guns, with small arms enough for every man stacked neatly against the masts. A cask of seawater stood next to each cannon in case of fire, and the racks of cannon shot looked like so many strings of expensive black pearls.

"You've done a good job, McCoy. If Mister Noble's done as well above deck, I'd say we're ready for anything they can throw at us."

"Aye, Captain. Those pirates don't have a chance against these fine lads o' mine—not a chance."

John turned about toward the forward ladder, but hesitated. "While I'm down here, McCoy, would you show me where the doctor's set up his treatment station?"

"Aye, sir." The gunner turned aft. "Accordin' to one of my mates, he's on the deck below us, just aft of the mizzenmast step."

"In the tiller room?" John spun about and marched off toward the companionway, with McCoy at his heels.

"Did ya not want him there, Captain?"

"Not unless it's the only place left on the ship!" At the base of the ladder he swung about the great mast and stepped through a small hatchway. Several pairs of taut rope lines stretched down through the overhead and about pulleys to the great tiller. The doctor was giving his men a drill in amputations.

"Captain Jones!" Doctor McKenzie stepped away from the surgeon's mates. "You startled me. We didn't expect you to pay us a visit this early."

"Why'd you set up here, Adam?"

"It looked like a good spot, sir. I figured we'd be out of the way, yet close enough to the gun deck and one of the ladders for quick access to both fighting decks."

John turned to the gunner. "McCoy, is there an open space forward where we could move the Doctor and his men—maybe the forcastle?"

"Aye, sir, but—"

"Adam, pick up your wares and move forward at once, away from the tiller area."

"But why, Captain?"

"I'll explain later when we assemble the crew on deck. As for now, move your men and equipment forward as quickly as possible." John turned back to the gunner. "I can find my own way above deck, McCoy. Pass the word to the gunners that the doctor has moved forward."

"Aye, aye, sir!"

John scaled the ladder to the main deck. By now the sun was well into its slow arc skyward, bathing the ship in a sparkle of reflected morning light. Waiting for John on the quarterdeck were his four officers; Ben Gunn, Robert Ormerod, David Noble, and Jan Van Mourik.

"David!" John trotted aft. "Order the men piped to muster!"

Moments later, the shrill tune of the bosun's pipe rang out over the ship, bringing the hundred and forty men to the main deck.

"Attention on deck!" The bosun waited for the chatter to stop. "The Captain has a word for you before we go into battle!"

Doctor McKenzie joined the others as John stepped forward. "As I'm sure you all know by now, we'll be engaging the Tiburon, and possibly the Eagle, in approximately one hour. Since we carry an enormous treasure, I don't expect either of our enemies to fire at our hull—at least not below the water line. Their strategy will be to disable the Cloud by taking off her masts or by hitting her rudder." He looked to the doctor, to see that he understood about the tiller room. Adam nodded that he did. John was satisfied, so he continued.

"Whether or not they're successful in either of these tactics, they'll then attempt to board us. We can expect to lose several men to their cannons and musket fire, but I've fought the Tiburon before and I believe with a little providential help, we'll prevail."

A man called out. "Will we attack both of 'em at once, sir?"

"The Eagle's been playing the part of our protector thus far, and I'm hoping they'll stand off and watch how the Tiburon fares."

"And if we sink the Tiburon?" It was another man—one of the Indian fighters. "What then, Captain?"

"Then it's off to Spyglass for the rest of John Flint's treasure!"

The crew broke into three cheers. "Hooray for Captain Jones!"

"And now my fellow Americans—to your battle stations! We've a pirate ship to sink!"

***

The watch had just struck four bells, or two o'clock, when the Tiburon began her attack maneuver. She approached from slightly windward of the Silver Cloud's wake, thereby avoiding the nine waist cannons. Just as John had predicted, the Eagle made a faint show of repulsing the Tiburon by sending several balls through and around the attacker's sails, but broke off when the Tiburon returned her fire.

"I was hoping for that." John watched the Eagle break away to the south. "It confirms that Smoot still believes we're still fooled. Unless

I've measured him wrong, he won't interfere again until he sees we're either disabled or taken."

"And the Remora?" David looked about to the fourth ship. "Do you think Captain Archer will do his part?"

"That's what John Silver's paying him for."

At two hundred yards astern, the Tiburon altered course slightly to starboard to cross the Cloud's wake to lee. John turned and called. "Robert! Go to my cabin and supervise those two aft gun crews. I want the Tiburon kept out of range of our rudder as long as possible!"

Shortly after Robert had dropped from sight, the first of the two stern cannons sent a round of barstock twirling through the Tiburon's rigging, leaving a bone-shaped tear in the flying jib and splintering a lower yard as it continued aft through the forest of masts, spars and ropes. The second cannon fired a round shot through the pirate's bow planking and gun deck. But on she came, apparently unconcerned with the damage Robert's two cannons were inflicting upon her.

Robert climbed the ladder enough to report to John. "She didn't return my fire!"

"I noticed! My guess is that Smoot has ordered the Tiburon's captain not to sink us, and the fool's probably taken that to mean he can't use his cannons at all!"

"They've moved forward, out of my two cannon's range! Do you want me to remain with these two cannons or come above deck?"

"Come up, but leave word with the two crews to protect the rudder!"

Two minutes later, Robert joined his captain near the aft rail. John was still studying his attacker. By his count there were more than fifty pirates along the rail, and they were all armed with flintlocks, daggers and cutlasses.

"They're preparing to board us, aren't they?"

John nodded. "The fools want the treasure so bad that they'll commit suicide to get it." He looked to the Tiburon's rigging. "They'll attempt a boarding from our lee, if I allow it!"

"If you allow it?"

"Aye." John pointed at the Tiburon's rigging. "Their canvas is set for speed, and they'll have to spill half of it to slow for a boarding maneuver."

"And?"

"They'll try to do it, but they won't be able to touch a single line." John turned and pointed into his own sails. "Look! All of our best marksmen are up there and will rain down lead on the first man who tries."

"I'm not sure I follow you, John. What are you planning to do?"

"Once they've moved far enough forward, we'll cut behind their stern to leeward where we can bring our windward guns to bear on their hull. With any luck, we can sink her before she can reposition."

As the Tiburon neared their abeam position, the façade that covered the gun ports were raised and the eight cannons fired into the Tiburon's hull at nearly point-blank range. At the same time, a steady barrage of small arms fire rained from the Silver Cloud's rigging, keeping most of the pirates off the deck and away from the sheets. Just as John had planned, the Tiburon's greater speed quickly drove her past her prey and into the open water beyond.

The Cloud's helmsman watched his captain.

"When I give the signal, I'll want you to bring the ship hard starboard."

"Behind her, sir?"

"Aye! She can't board from windward, and we need a little more time."

"On yer signal, sir!"

John looked into the rigging. "Mister Noble! Have your sharpshooters take a last shot at them and then have them come down to join the gun crews to larboard! We'll be moving to her lee and I'll want your best broadside into her stern and up her starboard side!"

"By your order, Captain Jones!" David slung his rifle about his shoulder and slid a sheet to the deck.

John watched for the exact moment and turned to the stearsman. "Now, Poynter! Hard to starboard!" The Silver Cloud seemed to bury its bow in the waves for a moment as her forward movement was cut in half and her massive bowsprit swung within twenty yards of the Tiburon's taffrail. For a brief moment, the eyes of the two captains— Pritchard on the Tiburon and Jones on the Silver Cloud—met in a defiant stare.

"I'll have that treasure or die tryin', Captain Jones!" Pritchard drew and fired his pistol at the Scotsman. The ball hit the young helmsman in the left thigh, dropping him to the deck.

Captain Jones grabbed the spinning wheel and yelled back a cryptic reply. "Since you know me by name, then you'll remember the Falmouth Packet also, and how she took off your rudder near Charles Town winter of '73!"

"That was you?"

"Aye, and I'll do worse today!" A new helmsman relieved John at the wheel and the injured man was taken below. John turned to his first officer. "Raise your veneer, David! We'll serve the Tiburon her broadside now!"

A moment later, the afternoon sky was filled with white smoke as a wall of iron crashed into and through the Tiburon's hull. The two massive ships stood no more than a hundred feet apart, making every shot point-blank. But still the pirates sent their cannon shot upward through the Cloud's rigging, to no effect.

"They'll be moving to our lee again, Robert, just like before. But this time I've a little surprise for them!" John picked up his speaking trumpet and called forward. "All sheet crews, take up grappling hooks and small arms to larboard, for we've a hand fight before us! And since the cutthroats offered us no quarter, there'll be none returned!"

As the critical moment approached, John studied the Tiburon's deck crew for the slightest sign of movement. It began with a signal from the pirate captain to his first mate, and then the first mate calling to the several groups of half-naked men at the sheets. A moment later, the Tiburon's sails began to slack to slow the ship for her turn behind the treasure ship.

Rather than risk having his helmsman misunderstand his order and turn the wrong way, John took the helm once more. At just the right moment, he threw the Silver Cloud hard to larboard, driving her directly into the path of the turning ship. A panic broke out on both ships as the bowsprit of the Tiburon rammed over the Silver Cloud's larboard bulwarks amidships.

There was a tremendous shudder aboard both ships as the figurehead on the Tiburon's bow shattered against the Cloud's rail. Nearly every man was thrown to the deck as the two entangled ships began to twist counterclockwise in the blue swells. A dozen grappling hooks flew through the air and bit deeply into the Tiburon wherever they could, solidly coupling the two together.

"My God!" Robert was certain John had gone mad. "What on earth have you done? Do you want us to go down with them?"

Robert recoiled from the mass of pirates who scrambled through their jib stays toward the Silver Cloud, and a thunder of small arms fire erupted from the Cloud's deck and crosstrees. Those pirates not killed by the first volley, or by the jabbing pikes, quickly retreated to their own deck.

There was no point in John or the new helmsman staying at the wheel, nor for any of the crew to remain at their sailing stations, for the two ships were locked together like lovers on the dance floor. The Tiburon was fastened amidships and perpendicular to the Cloud, forming the top of a large "T." With his sword drawn and flashing in the afternoon sun, John rushed forward to join the attack.

"McCoy!" He called behind him. "Open their hull with bar stock until you've a hole large enough for a dose of hot loads and grape shot! I want her set afire, and her planking stripped from her ribs!"

One by one the great frigate's cannons belched out their fire and brimstone into the bow and flanks of the helpless pirate ship. Helpless, because none of the Tiburon's main cannons could be trained forward more than ten degrees beyond the perpendicular. The only firepower she could return was small arms and the three swivel guns mounted on her forward rails.

It was a short and one-sided battle. While the Cloud's center guns punched holes in the Tiburon's bow and sent a hail of destruction through the length of her gun deck, guns one though three and the three aft cannons raked the pirate ship at her waterline. While the two great ships twisted in their grisly dance of death, the breeze began to carry away the accumulation of sulphurous smoke, revealing to the Silver Cloud's crew the destruction they had wrought on their enemy.

Like the executioner who tore the flesh from the old Baptist preacher's spine and ribs in Culpeper, the Silver Cloud's gunners peeled the Tiburon's planking away piece by piece. Between each explosion of cannon and shattering of wood, the screams of pirates could be heard as they were either thrown or leaped from the holes opened along her waterline. Just as John had ordered, cannons four through seven were loaded with a combination of barstock and what McCoy called a hot load—pieces of burning oak and coal. Two of the loads hit their mark, causing several secondary explosions within the great hull.

Only the more seasoned sailors aboard the Silver Cloud had ever witnessed such human carnage. One of the Tiburon's powder monkeys—a lad no more than ten or twelve years old—jumped from the inferno that his ship's gun deck had become. It was to quench his burning clothes that he leaped, completely unaware that his left arm and part of his shoulder had been ripped away in the battle. Another pirate stood in one of the yawning holes on the windward side, holding his face. The way his hands wrapped about his mouth, it appeared as if he was going to call out to someone on the Silver Cloud. But then he dropped his hands to his sides, revealing that his jaw was missing. He stood for a moment longer, then toppled forward into the sea.

The dark waters now began to spill into the Tiburon's stern, pulling her several yards lower in the water. As her bow began to rise and she backed away, the grappling lines began to tear loose from the Silver Cloud. Now, nearly free from her tormentor, the pirate ship wallowed and turned about in the surge of oncoming swells, exposing her main deck to the Cloud's cannons. These gunners reloaded with grape shot and methodically cut down every pirate who had run topside from the fires below.

"John!" Robert grabbed him by his sword arm. "Haven't they had enough?"

"Not until they're sunk and every last one of them is dead!" John pried the hand from his arm.

"But have you no mercy?"

"It's justice, Robert, not mercy they've earned! If the tables were turned, do you suppose for an instant they'd treat us otherwise?"

Robert opened his mouth to speak, but it was drowned out by two more of the Silver Cloud's cannons ripping men from the Tiburon's deck in a spray of blood, splinters, and pieces of bone.

The two ships had been coupled in battle for no more than six or seven minutes when the Tiburon's taffrail sank into the cooling waters, extinguishing the fire that had ventured to her stern.

"Noble!" John thrust his sword through one last man and then started for the quarterdeck. "Give the order to cut her free!"

***

The warm waters of the Caribbean are teeming with sharks. At feeding time, these mindless wolves of the sea are drawn to their prey by not only the smell of blood, but by low-frequency sound waves pulsating for long distances through the water. While the one-sided battle raged between the two great ships, each crash of ball into and through the inner members of the Tiburon's hull, and each thud and bump of her stores colliding with her bulkheads, sent out that unmistakable call to assemble for dinner. And long before the last grappling hook had been severed and the great bowsprit had ripped itself loose from the Silver Cloud's lower rigging, the sea churned with the frenzied, gray beasts.

The cannon fire had finished its ugly work, turning over the task of sinking the Tiburon to her own ballast—the tons of stones placed years before in her bilges for lateral stability. She was sinking rapidly now, slipping backwards below the swells more quickly with each passing moment. The thick smoke that had been pouring from her hatches and lee side ceased abruptly with a hiss and cloud of white steam, indicating that the sea had reached the seat of flames. She was a dying beast, crying out her agony in tremendous groans and heaving sighs as one after another compartment flooded and filled from stern to bow. As her ballast continued to pull her down, she pitched backwards until her mainmast lay back flat in the water and the bowsprit pointed skyward in a final salute to her defeat and a fruitless grasping for redemption from her fate.

And then, with a final burst of air and smoke through the churning water, it was over. The bone-chilling sounds of sucking and blowing, rather like the sound of a drowning cow, had finally stopped, and her shattered figurehead and bowsprit descended from view, leaving only the tangle of rope and torn canvas as mute testimony that a ship had once been there. But there were also the survivors—seven pirates clinging to the splintered planking and broken pieces of rail and yardarm.

David pointed at the men crying for mercy. "What about them, John? Shall I order the boats out?"

John shook his head. "There won't be time!" While the two watched, the sharks circled closer to their prey. "But I guess decency demands that we do something for them."

"Time?" David couldn't believe his ears. "I don't understand!" David fell silent when he realized that the survivor's calls for help had changed to screams of terror. Up until the Tiburon had sunk, the sharks had remained at a distance, as if the great ship were a competitor for the meal they had come to take. But with its descent into the depths, the sharks closed in. The first three to venture close to the men were small, only six to eight feet long. The fourth shark was a giant—a great white. Its slate-gray pectoral fin stood two feet out of the water as it cruised straight for the three men clinging to a length of top rail.

Before the great shark had made its attack, one of the dead pirates, who had been cut in half and thrown into the sea by an explosion, suddenly popped to the surface, twitching and jerking about as if it had regained life and was back to cast a final curse upon its enemy. As the pale face turned about for a lifeless gaze at the Silver Cloud, three large barracudas thrashed about at the surface while they played a tug-of-war at the flesh of the pirate's arms and ribs.

"Help us, mates!" It was one of the pirates. "Don't let us die like this! Don't let the sharks..." He fell silent to watch the large fin pass close abeam and then twist about toward him and his mate. There was a flash of white underbelly as the monster rolled onto its back.

It's claimed by some that what's in a man's heart will come out just before he goes to meet his Maker. If that's true, then this pirate was a Godly man, for his last words—the words spoken just before the great shark pulled him below the waves—came directly from the pulpit.

"Oh sweet Jesus! Save this poor sinner!" Then he was gone.

A deathly quiet fell over the Silver Cloud and the six remaining pirates while they stared at the spot on the splintered yard where the man had clung a moment before.

David pointed at one of the ship's boats. "The boat, John? Shall I order it lowered?"

"There's no point." Two more of the pirates were pulled from the flotsam amidst screams and boiling water that suddenly turned crimson with their blood. "Even if they deserved the least mercy, those sharks will have finished their task long before we could begin ours."

"Our captain is right, David." Robert was as shocked by the spectacle as David, but this was not the first time he had seen such carnage. He turned to John. "But David's right, too. We can't let them die that way."

"No, I suppose we can't." John turned. "David, I want four of our best marksmen to the rail with their muskets."

"But there are too many of them!"

"They won't be shooting at the sharks."

It suddenly struck David what was about to happen. "You're going to shoot the men, rather than try to save them?"

"I have no choice, David, unless you want those poor souls to die like their mates."

The four riflemen stepped to the rail as ordered, and at their captain's signal, fired at the four pirates. David turned away in horror when the four balls struck their marks.

The battle was over, with only two of the Silver Cloud's crew dead and three others injured. While the seabirds were fast at work cleaning up after their larger cousins' furious lunch, John walked to the starboard rail where his friend from Jamaica was retching.

"I'm sorry I had to do that, David. The sharks gave me no choice."

"Don't you think I know that?" David wiped his sleeve across his mouth and turned. "It's just that...to shoot the men for the sharks..."

Robert stepped to the two. "This is exactly why I made that vow at my wedding ceremony. Moira and I witnessed tenfold what we saw here today. All we can do is put it behind us and continue with our mission."

Within twenty minutes the damaged rigging had been cut away and the salvageable lines and sailcloth stowed, while the rest was cast over the side. Following a quick look at his chart, John reset the course for Flint's Island, with the Eagle a half-mile on their stern and the Remora another quarter mile further aft.

The closer the Silver Cloud got to Spyglass, the more the old maroon, Ben Gunn, changed. He grew quieter by the hour, and the scratching became more furious as he drifted back to that other world— the solitary life of guarding John Flint's share of the treasure. The transformation bothered John deeply, but there was nothing to be done for the old soul.

Chapter 17

Spyglass Island sits in the vicinity of the Turks and Caicos island group. It measures nine miles from north to south and four miles from east to west. It is roughly the shape of a man's tongue and is cut from its upper right edge to nearly the center by the North Inlet. Foremast Hill stands above the inlet, forming one of the three mountains that run down the spine of the island. A mile south of the headwaters of the inlet stands Spyglass Hill, also known as Mainmast Hill, the highest point on the island. At the southern end of the island is Mizzenmast Hill. In the afternoon, it casts its shadow across Captain Kid's Anchorage and Skeleton Island.

In 1764—when the brig Hispaniola departed Spyglass with the bulk of John Flint's share of the treasure—three of Long John Silver's crewmen marooned themselves when they ran inland to escaped capture. Without provisions beyond the meager tools that had been left for them, survival for these unruly pirates was difficult at best—the three subsisting mostly on roots, coconuts, and the sea creatures they could pull from the tide pools along the eastern shoreline. There were plenty of goats roaming the hills, but once their supply of powder and balls had been spent, they were forced to live hand to mouth—no better than the animals they sought to capture.

It was during their fourth month on the island that "Morely the Demented," as the other two had named their slow-witted mate, was off on one of his wanderings about Mizzenmast Hill. He noticed several goats scaling a steep cliff face. This puzzled the man, so he followed and discovered a narrow pathway—no more than a foot wide—that led up to a flat meadow approximately five paced wide and six long. While surveying the area he spied a narrow opening in the rocks that was turned in such a way that only the most discerning would detect it. He knew right off what he had found. It was Ben Gunn's secret cave, where the old maroon had hidden the silver bars and chest of jewels left in haste by Captain Smollet.

Despite his slower wit, Morley Rowe was a cut above his mates, always looking for a nicer place to claim for his own. Even though there was a fresh spring, the old stockade had long since begun to smell like the bilge of a slave ship, and Morley wanted to be out and away from his mates.

He stood just inside the cave entrance and looked about while his eyes adjusted to the darkness. On first examination, the cave was empty, except for a low bed frame with rope woven to make a mattress. He sniffed the air. There was a slight sulphur smell that drew the man to the back of the cave. By the reflected light of the afternoon sun, Morley spotted Ben Gunn's treasure. The pile of silver bars—each weighing seventy pounds—stood eight feet across and as high as Morley's torso. On top sat a small chest. Morley climbed the silver bars and pulled the chest down and toward the cave entrance for better light.

Amongst the gold coins, pearls, emeralds and rubies sat a gold crown, the companion to the one now lying in the lazarette of the Silver Cloud. It was this crown that Morley foolishly brought back to Flint's stockade.

Dick Walpole and Tom Morgan lay on their makeshift cots in the smelly stockade, scratching the body lice that Ben Gunn had so graciously left for them.

Morley stepped into the doorway. "Rise and pay homage to your king!"

Dick and Tom sat up and shaded their eyes against the bright morning sun that shined past Morley—blinding them.

Dick raised himself on an elbow and chucked a stone toward the light. "Ye're daft, Morley! Go back and talk to yer goats. Ha, ha, ha!" Tom and Dick could only make out Morley's silhouette and missed the object that adorned his head.

"Daft, am I?" Morley strode across the room and stood proudly between them. "If I be daft, then what do ye call this bauble on me head?"

Dick sprang to his feet and grabbing for the thing. "Where'd ya get that?"

"Yeah!" Tom joined his mate. "Where'd that come from?"

"Why, it's the other part o' John Flint's treasure, it is!" Morley dodged them and strutted about the dark room with his new toy. "Ben

Gunn must'a forgot 'bout this part when he and the rest of them ran away."

Tom Morgan—the meaner of the two—had his cutlass drawn. "We're still under John Silver's articles, an' that means we share and share alike."

"Not so fast, Tom!" Morley pulled his own cutlass and backed away toward the door. "Kill me and ye'll never find the rest of it."

Tom stepped forward. "Oh, I won't be killin' ya, Morley. I were only fixin' to torture ya just enough to get ya to share the treasure with yer two mates, as is only proper." Tom continued his press forward, but noticed Dick wasn't following. "If ye want yer share, Dick, then take up yer weapon an' join me!"

"But this isn't right, Tom. Ye're both me mates—not just you, Tom!" Dick Walpole had never been a man of decision. He was strong, and he was a faithful follower—the perfect mix for a pirate—but when faced with an important decision, his timid nature took over and held him back as surely as irons hold their prisoner.

Tom slapped the man's cot with the flat of his blade. "Choose quickly, man!"

By now, Morley had backed out into the bright sunlight. Since he had just been out in the light, his eyes adjusted quickly, giving him a temporary advantage over the other two.

Tom followed but was temporarily blinded. He turned back to his mate. "Pull that cutlass now, Walpole, and stand by one of us!"

While the two argued over their loyalties, Morley seized his chance to flee. By the time Tom and Dick had realized he was gone, Morley was down the hill and across the swamp, halfway to Captain Kidd's Lagoon. It was a simple matter to follow their prey, for rather than choose the rocks and dry ground where his tracks would be concealed, Morley plodded through the mud and knee-high grass, laving a trail even he himself could follow. While his two pursuers neared the short stretch of beach, Morley's voice pealed out at them in panic.

"Ye've ganged up on me again, an' that's not fair! An' besides, it's my treasure by all rights!"

Tom called from a hundred yards. "By what rights?"

Morley had backed himself to the water's edge, right where the first boat from the Hispaniola had landed several months earlier. He held his cutlass in one hand and the crown in the other. His pursuers skidded to a halt thirty feet up the beach.

"By the right of me findin' it, that's what right I be claimin'!"

Tom put an assuring hand on Dick's back. "You go first, on account as he trusts you the most. Besides, I'll be right here at yer shoulder."

With a push from his mate, Dick stumbled several steps closer, then stopped. He held up his cutlass. "Don't make me hafta cut ya, Morley." The timid man flashed Tom a glance over his shoulder to make sure he wasn't alone. "You know I'm the best with a cutlass, an' besides, we should share the treasure three ways, shouldn't we?"

"Of course we should!" Tom gave his timid mate another shove and called over Dick's shoulder. "Tis better it be shared by all three of us than fer us to hafta kill ya and split it in twain!"

Morley circled crab-style up the sand to the high-water mark, while the other two continued to advanced. At six paces, he replaced the crown on his head and switched his cutlass to his left hand. With his right, he drew his cocked pistol, aimed it at Dick's head and hissed. "That'll be far enough, Walpole!"

His two pursuers stopped, frozen in their tracks, with Dick leaning backward against Tom's pushing hands.

Tom whispered in Dick's ear. "That pistol's empty! He ran outta powder a full month ago, 'bout the same time we did."

Bolstered by Tom's words of assurance, Dick ventured one more step forward.

Morley raised the pistol and pointed it at Dick's forehead. "I'll give ya that one step, Walpole, but yer next'll be yer last."

"It be a bluff, Dick. Don't believe him!" Tom gave the timid man another shove, which was followed by an explosion of white smoke and two screams, one from a dying man and the other from a greedy pirate.

Out of the sulphurous cloud came Tom Morgan, swinging his cutlass like a madman. Morley stumbled several paces backwards into the water, threw the spent pistol aside and met his second attacker with the cry of a cornered animal. The rusty blades clattered together for several confusing moments amidst a tangle of grunts, growls and profanity. When the brief battle was over, the three pirates lay senseless on the beach, each with blood pumping from his wounds.

***

The King of Spyglass lay atop a pile of rotting seaweed for three days, while a herd of small crabs competed for the delicious meal that the right side of his wounded head had provided. The cutlass blow hadn't killed Morley, but it had taken his right ear completely off and cut deeply into the bone of his skull. When he finally regained consciousness, it was to a world entirely different from the one he had left. Whereas the problems of his past were hunger and itching from the body lice, this new world was filled with pain and double images—a confusing carnival that spun about him with every movement of his body.

When he lifted himself from the seaweed—slowly, so as not to retch—a searing pain shot through the right side of his head. It felt as if Tom's blade were still embedded in his skull, when actually it was only the gentle afternoon breeze, which happened to blow into the gaping hole the crabs had made of his right ear canal.

"Damn you!" Morley raised the cutlass for the next attack, but dropped it into the sand, causing the hungry crabs to scatter. He searched the sand, hoping to see the ear, but lost his balance and plunged face first into Tom's body.

"Ye've opened me head to the elements, ye have!" The small herd of glutted crabs backed away a few feet to wait patiently for the pirate to lie down again so they could resume their feast of blood and inner ear. Morley saw them approaching. He grabbed Tom's cutlass and slapped the sand amongst them.

"Damn you crabs too!" Morley struggled upright again for a brief moment before falling senseless back into the shallow water.

***

Ten years later, nearly to the day, the pirates Morley Rowe and Dick Walpole stood on Mizzenmast Hill, watching as three ships glided toward Captain Kidd's anchorage a quarter-mile below. Morley gave Walpole a rough shake.

"There! That were me!" Morley pointed at the man in the Silver Cloud's fore chains. "I were the one what threw the lead line fer John Flint, I was! Ya can't be too careful comin' in through them mud flats, ya know. Only measured four fathoms at high tide, it did."

The Silver Cloud edged past Skeleton Island with only her t'gallants and spanker catching the light evening breeze. The water depths were relayed aft by three of the crew, while a man standing on the lower foremast yard signaled the helm when to turn.

When the massive anchor finally dropped into the black waters, Morley poked his mate once more in the ribs. "I tolt ya, didn't I, Dick? This should teach ya once an' fer all, ya bilge-lickin' swab!" He gave his mate another short shake for emphasis, and then the two stood watching, using each other for support. The same wind that pushed the ships to their anchorage whistled into Morley's enlarged right ear canal, bringing with it the same pain he had felt nearly a decade before when he awoke on the rotting seaweed. While his mate watched the ships with his typical hollow stare, Morley drooled slightly.

A large blowfly that had orbited Morley's head three times finally decided the gaping hole would make a fine place to rest a spell and perhaps lay a few eggs. Morley took a swing at the insect just before it landed, sending it off for a moment. The six-tiered gold crown the others had voted to let him wear fell into the dirt between them.

Morley blurted. "What's that ye say?" He set the crown back on its rightful spot. "How'd I know they was comin'? Don't ya remember what I tolt ya last night? I can smell a ship at ten leagues, I can."

He pulled Dick close and looked about just in case someone might be eavesdropping on their conversation. "It be John Silver an' Jimmy Hawkins, comin' back to rescue us. I knowed they wouldn't be maroonin' us here fer good." He took another swing at the blowfly and adjusted the crown once more while he studied the largest of the three ships.

Morely was by nature a very suspicious fellow. He never brought but one of his mates across the swamp with him at a time when he foraged for food. To do so was to risk an open mutiny and the loss of his crown. And likewise, he never left them alone together in his cave on Mizzenmast Hill, for he knew they would plot against him in a minute if he should. He seldom got a full night's sleep for all their whispering and bickering, and there was no way around it except by sleeping between them.

"Ye best be thankful I brought ya out here with me to see our rescuers, rather than Morgan." Morley gave Dick a serious look. "Tom's a nice enough fellow when we're all together, but when you ain't around, ya oughta hear him talk about ya. If it weren't fer me, you'd have no friends at all, an' ya know that to be true, right?"

Dick spoke not a word, but his toothy grin signaled his agreement.

"There!" Morley pointed at the ships. "Didn't I tell ya they'd drop anchor right there? Why, that be 'xactly the spot where Cap'n Flint an' me put the Walrus." Morley looked Dick in the eyes, suspecting the other didn't believe his story. "John Flint trusted me, Dick Walpole, an' don't you let Tom tell you otherwise."

By now the Silver Cloud had swung about her anchor chain, the Eagle stood at the mouth of the lagoon and the Remora was another two hundred yards beyond in open water. The sounds of the captain's orders and the men going about their duties stirred a hunger inside Morley that he hadn't felt for years.

He tilted his head and closed his eyes as if he sat in a symphony hall. "Aye, listen to the bosun's commands! 'Tis music to me ears, it is." Dick seemed to whisper something, so Morley pulled him around to his good ear.

"Them other two?" Morley looked to the smaller ships. "Why, that's simple enough. They be rescue ships fer you an' Morgan. John Silver knows us three never got along very well, so he had to send one fer each of us."

Morley turned his head a bit too quickly to look back down at the three ships, and he had another of his frequent dizzy spells. He fell sideways to the ground, and Dick Walpole fell full-length on top of him.

Morley's dagger flashed in the afternoon sun. "I warned you 'bout that, damn you! This time ye've gone an' done it, and with yer rescue so close at hand, too!" Morley pressed the blade against Dick's windpipe, just above the Adam's apple. The two faced each other nose-to-nose and Dick's eyes seemed to plead for mercy.

"Oh sure!" Morley pressed the knife against Dick's throat. "Go on, won't ya, usin' that same line on me! Fer all I know, ya never did have a wife or no four spawn ta feed back in Savannah! Ya think old Morley Rowe's a long-gone fool, don't ya? My brains didn't slip out through no scupper!" Morley glanced behind them, sure to find Tom skulking about in the shadows somewhere, just waiting for the opportunity to jump him while he was down.

"You an' Tom think it's right funny to make old Morley fall in the dirt, don't ya?" Dick's head shook slowly from side to side.

"No?" Morley sensed that his mate was beginning to show true repentance for tripping him. "Well, since our rescue's so close, I might let ya off this one last time. But don't try nothin' tonight, ya hear?" Morley threw Dick backwards against the cliff. "An' if I see ya talkin' with Tom 'bout me fallin' down, you'll have hell to pay."

While the two maroons replayed this oft-acted scene, the orange orb of the sun dropped quietly into the dark Caribbean waters to the west. Old seamen used to say that if you listened very carefully, you could almost hear the hiss when it was extinguished for the night.

With the sun's last pink rays reflecting off the high clouds, the three ships folded their wings for the long-awaited sleep they so well deserved. Nightfall was also the signal for Morley and his mate to return to the protection of their cave on Mizzenmast Hill.

"Ye'll see!" Morley jerked Dick to his feet. "They'll come fer us at first light, so we'd best be about gettin' our things together."

While the two edged their way along the narrow ledge toward Ben Gunn's cave, Morley turned for one last look at his rescuers. But as always, the movement was just enough to confuse what remained of his mutilated right inner ear, throwing the two against the cliff wall and provoking a string of curses. The words wove an especially disgusting tapestry that floated like a magic carpet downward across the beach and over the glassy waters of Captain Kidd's Lagoon.

***

"Cap'n Jones!" It was the stern watchman. He pointed at the silhouetted hill. "There it is again, sir!"

"You still think you hear the cursing, Clark?"

"Aye, sir, I'm certain of it!"

John pointed. "And you're sure it's coming from that hill?"

"Aye, an' it be as plain as you speakin' to me, it be."

John walked to the rail and listened carefully, but the maroons had retired to their cave for the night. "Interesting." John walked toward the aft ladder, stopped, and turned back to the seaman. "Inform Mister Noble that I've retired to my stateroom."

"Aye, aye, sir, and by yer leave, sir?"

"Yes?"

"I were just thinkin', sir. If ya be needin' volunteers to go ashore in the mornin', I'd be in yer debt if I could be in one of the first boats."

"You're a good man, Clark. I'll have a word with the other officers."

"Thank you, sir." John turned to leave, but the lad remembered something else. "Oh! An' you'll still be wantin' a call tonight at four bells?"

"Yes, I will." He looked across the hundred yards of still water to where the Eagle pulled gently at her anchor chain. "It's a perfect night for a swim."

***

Shortly after ten o'clock that night, twelve men clad only in their britches slipped over the starboard rail of the Silver Cloud and into the warm waters of Captain Kidd's Lagoon. Each man was armed with a cutlass and several daggers, which hung from sashes about their shoulders.

Silence was the order, but with the raucous singing and laughter coming from the Eagle, their detection was next to impossible, even for the single watchman who sat alone on the privateer's bow. Strains of a familiar line-hauling song filled the sultry air:

"Buckets o' blood spilt in the hold,
Flint accused Rip Rap, The treasure ye've stolt.
Ye took it to the Isle called Dead Man's Chest,
Where ye laid it by fer half a score's rest.

"Fifteen men on the Dead Man's Chest,
Yo ho ho and a bottle of rum.
Drink and the devil has done for the rest,
Yo ho ho and a bottle of rum.

By the time the drunken pirates had finished the song and repeated it for a third time, John and his eleven men clung to the Eagle's planking. The singing continued, but the rum had slurred the words so badly that it sounded like most any other late-night tavern song. Several men had begun to argue, and three or four others slept. From the thumping and yelling, it was plain that at least two men were engaged in a fight somewhere on the main deck.

David pulled himself up next to John. "I don't think anybody's on watch."

John nodded. "From the sound of it, they're all forward, near the fo'c'sle." He wiped the salt water from his eyes and made a quick head count. Everybody was there and anxious to make their attack.

"David, take half the men to the larboard side and climb to the gunwale. Hold there until you see me come over this side." Turning to the rest of the men, he gave a final note of caution. "Remember, our primary objective is to rescue Captain Steele. If we can do that, and take the pirates alive—especially Captain Smoot and that boy with the orange hair—then well enough. But if some of them die, then that's the price they'll just have to pay." He paused and looked about his small raiding party. "Any questions?"

There were none, so John continued. "We've the advantage of surprise on our side, and what's more, their only lanthorn is that one at the bow. It'll be nearly impossible for them to see us until we're upon them." He turned to David. "Go now, David! I'll give you a count of one hundred before we move."

Several minutes later, twelve pairs of eyes peered over the rails. Just as John had predicted, all the topside crew was gathered forward about a single lanthorn and two men who were in a heated knife fight.

As David and his five men reached the far side of the ship and John finished his count, a voice bellowed from aft. It was Captain Smoot. "Damn you two! Why don't you kill each other, and be done with it?"

The cutthroats burst into laughter and catcalls while they egged on the two combatants.

"Now!" John and his five men slid over the rail and began to creep forward, meeting David and his team just aft of the mainmast.

David studied the two pirates while they circled and slashed at each other's faces. "Why are they fighting that way? Why don't they let go and back away?"

"Because they can't." It was Robert. "Look closely at their left arms."

"My God! They're strapped together at the forearms! Why...?"

"They did the same thing on the Walrus twenty years ago. It was Flint's way of settling disputes and providing a show for the rest of the crew."

John looked about at his men. "Then there are only twenty-six to contend with. Let's take them now, while their attention's drawn toward those two."

As they watched, the two men sank to their knees in their own blood. Their cries of pain and curses had become feeble, almost inaudible whimpers when John and his men descended upon the others. A confused moment later, eight of the pirates lay dead or dying. Of the remaining eighteen cutthroats, only eleven had the presence of mind to surrender without further bloodshed. The other seven leaped over the side and swam for shore, with the two non-swimmers among them drowning within seconds. But the sounds of the short battle were just loud enough to bring Captain Smoot from his cabin in a rage.

He stepped out onto the deck with his fighting sword. "Damn you! Do I have to kill ya meself?" Before him stood twelve men with cutlasses and daggers at the ready, clad in britches and silhouetted by the forward lanthorn.

"So it's a mutiny, is it?" Smoot waved the sword in their faces. When they didn't retreat, he slashed at the two nearest men. "You fools! I told you we'd wait an' take the treasure after it reaches King's Town!" He waited for one of the men to answer, but none did. "If ye've had a fo'c'sl council, then be men enough to tell me!" There was still no answer. "Very well. If ya intend to cut me down, then do me the decency o' lettin' me choose who I fight first, like is fittin' fer pirates." His eyes darted back and forth at the dozen men. "Where are ya, Morgan? Step forward, lad, and be the first to taste my steel! You owe me that much!"

Henry called from the bow. "I'm up here, Govn'r, tied up with the others!"

"Tied up! Then who...?" Smoot raised his sword hand to shade his eyes from the light behind John. "Who are you?"

"I'm John Paul Jones, captain of the Silver Cloud!"

Smoot's eyes flashed fear and hatred as he retreated a step.

"And while your men sang and drank to their own damnation, I've taken your ship!" The Scotsman took a step forward with an outstretched hand. "Your sword, Captain Smoot!"

Robert stepped forward, next to John. He studied the pirate. "That's not Joshua Smoot! That's John Manley!"

Smoot looked at the Yorkman. "Well, well! If this isn't a homecoming, then what is?"

"John Manley?" John gave Robert a quick look. "That's Joshua Smoot."

Robert lunged at the pirate with his sword, but John pulled him back. "He's the one I told you about—one of the men John Silver sent for a map to Dead Man's Chest. Let me kill him!"

John pushed him back. "We're civilized men, Robert. Joshua Smoot will be tried and hung by the courts." John reached out again to the pirate captain and repeated his demand. "Your sword or your life!"

Expecting what followed, John was quick to pull back his hand when Smoot slashed downward through the sultry night air. The pirate's descending blade cut deeply into the oak decking between the two captains. John signaled his men to back away and give the two combatants a clear deck. Then, as he and Smoot circled each other like two wolves fighting for dominion over the pack, he called out more orders. "David, take several men and find Captain Steele!"

"Aye, aye, Captain!"

John hissed at Smoot. "That's unless you've killed him, like the rest of his men!"

"Ha!" Smoot's sword glanced off the younger man's blade with a clatter. "If cuttin' sugar cane on Saint Croix means they be dead, then indeed, dead they be!"

"So you're not a complete barbarian after all?" John fended off several more wild cuts from the pirate. In a moment of carelessness, Smoot's neck was exposed—a perfect opportunity to decapitate the pirate. But rather than kill the scoundrel, John cracked Smoot upon the left side of his throat with the flat of his sword.

"Ahhhh!" Smoot grabbed at his throat and looked at the fingers. There was no blood. "You bastard! Why didn't you kill me?"

"I'm not sure. Something tells me I should keep you alive."

Smoot backed away a step and lowered his sword in a gesture of surrender.

John relaxed his fighting arm and reached out his other hand. "I'll ask you just one last time, Captain Smoot. Will you surrender now, or must I kill you?"

"Since you put it that way, sir, I've no choice but to..." Smoot turned his sword flat, as if to lay it in John's open hand, and then lunged forward with a vicious slash, just as he had done before. As before, John was expecting the action and pulled his hand back to safety. But this time he had positioned his hand over the mainmast pin rail, so that Smoot's downward blow cut away two buntline sheets.

With a resounding slap, the starboard half of the spencer unfurled directly above the two combatants. Smoot, expecting rigging to come clattering down about their ears, ducked and made a quarter turn to his left, bringing his sword hand across in front of John. There was a flash of polished steel and a high-pitched whistle as John's sword arced downward through flesh and bone. Captain Smoot had surrendered his sword after all, but with his hand still gripping its hilt.

"My hand! My hand!" He fell backwards against one of the waist cannons and then dropped forward to his knees, watching wide-eyed at the fountain of bright red blood squirting from the severed limb. "You've killed me! I'm losin' me life's blood all over the deck!"

"Captain Jones!" It was David. "Look what I found!" David walked forward toward the light with Captain Steele at his left side. Behind him and to his right stood a young girl about fifteen or sixteen years old. She was a little shorter than David, five foot four at the most. Her dress was of a light cotton fabric, torn in several places at the hemline. Her shoulder-length blonde hair showed the last traces of curls at the ends. She looked down in shame at her condition.

John studied the girl. "Well!" He turned to Smoot. "Who might this be?"

David took her hand and urged her forward. "It looks as if our little rescue party's netted us two prizes rather than just the one we'd hoped for!"

John took a lanthorn from one of his men and brought it near the girl. "Who is she, Smoot?"

"What about my hand?" By now, the pain had driven the pirate forward so that all his weight was divided between his knees and forehead. "Look at it!" He gripped the wrist with his other hand. "My blood's leakin' down through the scuppers!"

John ignored the man's cries and raised the lanthorn to the girl's face. "If Captain Smoot won't tell us, then perhaps you will, young lady?"

The girl just stared at the young captain.

"Smoot knows!" Captain Steele stepped forward and gave Smoot a kick in the side. "She was aboard before he took me prisoner at Christiansted."

"I'll ask you one last time, Smoot. Who is she, and where'd you get her?"

"She's nobody!" Smoot raised his head and looked up at the girl. "She's just a plaything we took from a prize."

John turned to the girl. "Did they...er...I mean...were you...uhh..."

She shook her head.

"I can attest to that, Captain Jones." It was Steele. "As far as I know, nobody's laid a hand on her since they brought me aboard."

John gave Smoot a sword prick to the shoulder. "If that's true, then she must be somebody special. You must have expected a large ransom for her, or else you and your men would have—"

"John!" Robert leaned close to whispered. "She shouldn't hear what you're about to say."

John pulled the light away and turned to Steele. "Did she tell you anything?"

"She couldn't. Smoot kept us separated except for the occasional meal he'd force us to eat with him. Neither of us spoke a word at the meals, and he kept her locked in the cabin next to his own. I heard her threaten Smoot several times that her father would take revenge, but that's all I heard from her."

John looked back to the girl. "Well, the sooner we can get her back to the Silver Cloud, the sooner she can begin to recover." He turned back to David, who was still holding the girl's hand. "Since you found her, David, I'll trust you to see that she's taken care of."

David gave a nod. "I'll send back the boat as soon as I get her and Captain Steele across."

John nodded. "That'll give us a chance to deal with Captain Smoot properly."

Smoot didn't like being ignored. "Is anybody going to do anything about my hand?"

"Perhaps if you'll tell us who she is." John waited until David and the young girl were far enough away, and pressed the tip of his sword against the raw flesh.

Smoot jerked the bloody stump away with a scream. "I told you! She's nobody special!"

"Hold his arm down!" Once again, John moved the tip of his sword toward the bleeding flesh. "May I remind you that my sword feels no pain."

"Ahhh!" Smoot shrunk back. "I'll tell you! I'll tell!"

"Well?"

"She's the governor's daughter!"

"Which colony?"

"Georgia! She's Governor Wright's daughter!"

"Governor Wright's daughter?" John looked around at the girl. "That's Jane Wright?"

"Yes, for God's sake!" Smoot raised the bloody stump. "Now will you do something about my arm? I need a tourniquet!"

"And you figured he'd have paid dearly for her return, right?"

"I wasn't after money! I was gonna trade her for a letter of marque."

Steele stepped back to Smoot. "And what if the governor hadn't agreed? What then?" He bent down, grabbed a handful of the pirate's tarred hair and twisted the man's head sideways. "You'd have eaten her heart, wouldn't you?"

"Eaten her heart?" John held the lanthorn close to Steele's face. "What do you mean by that?"

Steele released the pirate and stood up. "Smoot's a cannibal. I heard his men brag about it. They say he cooked and ate a man's heart."

"Is that true?" John raised his sword above the kneeling pirate. "Did you allow your crew to eat a human being?"

Smoot stopped moaning. "It was only to scare her and Captain Steele!" He looked up at Captain Jones. "It was only talk!"

David stepped to his captain and put a restraining hand to his arm. "Don't, Captain!"

The sword hung in the night air above the decadent pirate's neck, with only a speck of human compassion holding it back. It quivered with each of John's heartbeats, poised for the downward slash that would take the animal's head off.

John was so angry that he could hardly get the words out. "He doesn't deserve one more breath of God's good air! Not another breath!"

"But we're civilized men, Captain. We're not animals like him. We're men of law, not of passion! He'll surely hang from the gibbet, but he deserves a fair trial first."

John held the sword in the air for another moment and then drove it downward with all his might into the planking next to the pirate's bleeding wrist. "Burn his wound shut, and burn it well!"

Within an hour, Smoot's unconscious body was trussed up in leg irons alongside Henry Morgan and the other pirates who had survived the battle.

***

The next morning was clear and bright. A single shot hole in the planking of the Eagle allowed the morning sunlight to stream in upon Smoot, Morgan and the others. Henry pressed his face to the hole, intent on something.

"What ya be lookin' upon, Morgan?" A shudder of pain coursed through Smoot's bandaged right wrist.

Henry answered without looking around. "The boats, Govn'r. They're goin' fer the rest of Flint's treasure."

***

"Miss Wright?" David spoke the words quietly after giving three gentle taps on her cabin door. "Are you awake?" There was no answer, so he tapped a second time. He waited several more moments, then called through the closed door. "I brought you some breakfast! I thought you might be hungry!" There was a sound from within the cabin, followed by the slide bolt retracting from its keeper. The heavy door swung open a few inches.

"Miss Wright?" She still didn't answer—she had not spoken a word since her arrival on the Cloud the night before. David pushed the door with the side of his foot and looked inside. The girl stood at her porthole with tears running down her cheeks. She held a bar of lye soap in her hand.

David set the tray on the desk. "Our cook has prepared something special for you." She turned and looked at him and then turned back to the activity outside her porthole.

"They're going ashore for provisions and to get the last of John Flint's treasure. I'd be going along also, but I told Captain Jones that I'd rather stay on the ship with you."

She spoke without turning. "I want to go ashore. I want a freshwater bath and clean clothes."

"I don't know if that's possible."

"It has to be possible! I won't come out of this room except to take a bath in fresh water."

"Captain Jones ordered that you remain aboard, but I might be able to..."

The girl turned and wiped the tears from her cheeks. "You'll ask him for me, won't you?"

"Couldn't you bathe in salt water, like we do?"

"No. My soap won't work in salt water." She held up the white bar just as Ben Gunn stepped from the stateroom across the passageway.

"Good morning, Master Noble!"

"Good morning, yourself, Mister Gunn! You're doing quite well."

"Aye!" Ben turned a pirouette and then looked into the young lady's cabin. "Will you an' the lass be comin' ashore with us?"

David stepped back into the passageway and pulled the girl's door closed behind him. "The captain gave me explicit orders that she remain aboard."

"But you'll miss all the fun, lad."

"That doesn't bother me as much as..." David glanced toward her door.

"What's the matter, sir? Something wrong with Miss Wright?"

"Ben, you know this island, right?"

"I should! I spent more time on it than any man should have to!"

"Is there someplace where a body can take a freshwater bath—a place with a sandy bottom and plenty of rocks for privacy?"

Ben considered. "Aye!" He gave David a nudge to the ribs. "Were ya plannin' on makin' yourself clean for the little lass?"

"It's Miss Wright who wants the bath, not me. Her soap's made from lye."

"I see." Ben gave his scalp a scratch to bring out the memory.

"I told her it was impossible, but perhaps—"

"It isn't impossible, Mister Noble."

"Oh?"

"There's a stream that runs from the spring up at Flint's stockade. There's not a lot of water, but there's a large pool that's always full. I expect the trail would be grown over by now, but if you skirt the swamp, you'll come upon it in due time."

"Thank you, Ben." He turned aft toward the master's cabin.

Ben called after him. "If he gives his permission, I'd take along a couple o' weapons, just in case. Captain Jones tells me some of Smoot's men made it to shore last night during the raid."

Within a half-hour of talking with the captain, David, and Jane were ashore with one of the last groups of seamen. Following Ben's instructions, they found where the stream cascaded down the hill from the stockade and onto the flats before the swamp. The pool was just as Ben had described it: two rods wide and three long, and just under a rod deep.

David made a quick circuit of the area and returned. "It looks safe enough."

Without a word, Jane laid her change of clothing across a rock and began unbuttoning her bodice. She stopped and pointed to a large rock.

David looking about. "I'll sit on the other side of that rock until you're finished."

Jane watched until he was out of sight, and then finished undressing. A moment later, she lowered her tired body into the cool clear water. As the soap began to cleanse her skin, the young girl started humming a familiar ballad.

David leaned his back against the rock, imagining what she looked like. "With all that commotion on the Eagle last night, I didn't get a chance to tell you about myself."

"No, you didn't." She rubbed the soap into her hair. "I did hear your captain say something about Jamaica, however. Are you from there?"

"Born and raised in the place. My father's a merchant there, and if I do well, I suppose he'll turn the business over to me some day."

"If you do well?"

David faltered, not knowing quite what to say. "What I meant was that if I get the naval commission I'm hoping for, then Father will probably give me a partnership in his business."

"And how could a young man your age get a naval commission?"

"It's this mission. I can't—"

The air about David seemed to come alive in a high-pitched scream that pierced his ears like a knife. He leaped up and over the rock while Jane ducked down and refilled her lungs for a second scream, this one louder than the first.

Across the pool, on a flat rock at water's edge, stood five sailors.

David ran to the water's edge and yelled at them. "What are you doing here! Why aren't you helping with the provisions?"

The five began cavorting about like they were carrying burdens and then one pretended to whip the others with a twig. Jane waiting for the men to obey David. When it became obvious they had no intention of leaving, Jane cast a look back at her protector.

"That's it!" David pointed one of his pistols above their heads and fired. By the time the smoke had cleared, the five were gone, leaving the two young people alone once more. David watched the trees for another minute, and then sat down on the shore to reload his pistol.

"Ahem!" Jane scowled at David while she remained crouched in the water.

David looked up from his work. "What?"

"Would you please?" She pointed back at his rock. "I'm not quite finished."

"Oops! I'm sorry!" He scrambled to his feet and walked beyond the rock.

Once he was hidden, Jane called. "Do you know which five they were?"

"No. There are nearly a hundred and fifty of us on board. Those five are probably on another watch."

"Will they be punished?"

"Aye, at least a dozen stripes each. They know better than to do that."

"Twelve stripes? Isn't that a trifle severe? After all, they've been at sea for a long time and they were only curious."

"They should have been working rather than watching you bathe. Besides, I I was assigned to watch you bathe."

She giggled. "Oh?"

"I didn't mean it that way, Miss Wright."

"Oh? How did you mean it?"

"I'm your protector, not a voyeur."

As David rammed a fresh lead ball down the barrel of his musket, a man cried out from the direction of the stockade and pointed at David and Jane.

"There they are! They're at the stream to the north of the stockade!" A moment later, Jane had ducked into the water and twenty men stood about the pool with pulled weapons.

John stepped through the crowd. "What was that shooting?"

"Five of our men were watching Jane bathe. I had to fire one of my pistols to drive them off."

John looked about the nearby forest. "Those had to be Smoot's men—the ones who got away last night. I didn't expect them to show themselves this soon, if at all."

David held up his pistol. "Well, they won't be back again, because I put a ball right over their heads."

"You underestimate them, David."

"Robert's right, David." John looked to the girl hiding in the water and back to David. "See that she's taken back to the Cloud as quickly as possible and kept there. She's too big a temptation to be off the ship."

"Do I have a say in this?"

John answered her. "No!"

"But this is the first time I've been on solid ground in nearly a month! I insist you allow me to remain ashore!" She paused and looked about at the two dozen men watching her. She ducked a little deeper in the water. "If you please!"

John turned to the men. "You men, return to your duties."

The men snickered and ambled away.

"Thank you, Captain Jones. Now, concerning my remaining ashore, I'm certain I'll be quite safe if I restrict my movements to the beach—where, by the way, I'll be watched by everybody in your crew—and then I'll return to the ship before dark. Mister Noble has two pistols, and he'll be with me at all times."

John looked to the tangle of vines and undergrowth beyond the stream.

Robert gave a slow shake of his head. "I wouldn't advise it, John."

"Captain Jones! Need I remind you that my father is the governor of Georgia?"

John considered for a moment. "Very well, but only on the beach, and you must be back aboard the ship before dark."

She smiled. "You're very kind, sir. I'll be sure to tell my father all about you."

"I pray my kindness isn't tested, young lady."

"It won't be, Captain, not again." David pushed his pistols into the webbing that hung across his chest. "I won't let her out of my sight."

As they turned to leave, Ben tugged at John's sleeve. "When can I take you up to my cave, Cap'n Jones?"

"First things first, Ben. I want all the provisions aboard and the rigging repaired. There'll be plenty of time once those things are done."

When the last of the crew had left the pool, David took up his position of defense once more, unaware that the maroon, Morley Rowe, was watching their every movement from the cover of the bushes.

***

Despite the heat and humidity, the work went quickly that day on John Flint's Island. When the sun finally began to drop toward the western horizon, David escorted Jane to one of the campfires. They stood for a moment staring into the dancing flames.

She touched his hand. "Do you suppose your captain would mind if we took a short walk along the beach?"

"No, so long as we stay in the open." David looked at the sun to estimate how much more daylight remained to them. "Besides, those five would never try anything so close to the rest of the men."

John spoke to them as they passed. "Mind yourselves. You can predict most of what a pirate will do, but—"

"Don't worry, Captain Jones." Jane took David's hand and pulled him toward the setting sun. "I'll keep your first officer out of trouble."

John flashed a stern look at David.

She gave a giggle and pulled David away. "Your captain seems to spend a lot of time worrying."

"He's our captain. Every man, and woman, onboard is his responsibility. He has to worry when so much is depending on him."

"So much?"

"Didn't Captain Steele tell you about our mission?"

"He never had the opportunity. We were kept apart except when Smoot brought us together two times to dine." She gave him a bewitching look. "Captain Steele and I were never allowed to talk in private."

"I don't know whether I should say anything—"

"Of course you can tell me! I'm Governor Wright's daughter. I hear all the secrets eventually anyway."

David stopped walking while he considered. Jane stepped in front of him and looked up into his eyes. Her innocent beauty overwhelmed him.

"Mister Noble?"

"Yes?"

"You were going to tell me about your mission. What did you come here to get?"

"All right, but you have to promise that you'll not let anybody else know I told you, especially Captain Jones."

"I promise." She kissed her finger and drew a cross on her heart.

"There's over 800,000 pounds worth of Spanish treasure in the Silver Cloud's lazarette, and we've stopped here to pick up another chest of jewels and over three hundred fifty silver bars. From here, we sail to a secret rendezvous with a twin ship filled with a thousand cannons for the American colonies."

"Oh, my Lord!" She looked back at the Silver Cloud. "Will you get a reward for doing this?"

"Thomas Jefferson has promised Captain Jones and me commissions in the Continental Navy."

"Is that all?"

"And a share of the treasure—whatever's left after we purchase the cannons."

"A share?"

"Adding in this new treasure, my part is roughly fifteen thousand pounds."

"How delicious." She brushed her fingers against his left arm, then urged him forward toward the rocks at the end of the beach. Stopping under a rock ledge, they watched the sun drop, degree by degree, toward the sparkling sea. "Would you like to know what kind of a man I'll marry someday?"

"Excuse me?"

"First, he'd have to be a God-fearing man like you, with..." She flashed a glance at his face. "...with hazel eyes, black hair, and he'd be exactly..." She reached up and put her hand on top of his head as she spoke, "...this tall."

"Are you saying...?"

"Do you like me, David?"

"Yes. Very much."

"Enough to kiss me as the sun sets?"

David took a quick glance at the sun and then down into her face. The reflection of the sea set her eyes ablaze. "We've only known each other for—"

She giggled teasingly. "They say it's good luck to kiss at sunset—especially a first kiss."

"Uh, I've never..."

She continued toying with him. "You've never kissed a girl before?"

"Oh, I've kissed lots of girls. I've just never kissed one... at sunset."

As David melted into Jane's eyes, a black form dropped from the rocks above them like a panther, knocking them both down. David felt a whack on the back of his head. When he regained his senses a few minutes later, it was dark and Jane was gone. The only hint she had been on the beach was the single shoe left next to him.

Somebody called out. "There he is!"

John was the first to reach the young Jamaican. "What happened, David? Where's Miss Wright?"

"I don't know. We were talking about...uhh...heading back up the beach, when someone hit me."

"Damn!" John looked about for Robert. "Why must he always be right?"

Robert knelt next to David. "Was it those same five?"

David rubbed the lump on his head. "I didn't see anybody, but it had to be them." He stumbled to his feet and pulled his pistols.

"Not tonight, David." John pushed down the two pistols. "I know you want to go after her, but there's no way to follow those men in the dark."

"Captain Jones!" It was Ben. He was pointing down at the sand. "Come here!"

The three officers approached the old man. "What is it, Ben?"

"I don't think it was Smoot's men. Look at this!"

David was still shaking and dizzy from the injury to his head. "What did you find?"

"There was only one of them, Mister Noble, and he was barefooted." Ben pulled off his shoe and stepped next to one of the prints in the sand. "Look how deep his prints are. He carried her off on a shoulder."

John compared Ben's footprint to the abductor's. "But who is he?"

"It's one of the three we left here ten years ago. I'm certain of it."

"You honestly believe a man could survive here for ten years?"

"Aye, Captain. I did it for five."

"I don't care who it is or how long they've been here!" David raised his pistols again. "Let's go find her before he has a chance to molest her!"

"If that's his aim, David, then we're already too late."

"But we can't just stand here and do nothing, Captain!"

"Back your sails, David." It was Robert. "Other than a search at Flint's stockade, we can't do a thing until first light."

Ben shook his head. "I was up there shortly after we came ashore, Captain. Nobody's lived there in years—so long that there aren't even any lice in the place." He pointed at the silhouetted hill to the west. "My guess is that if it's the three we left ten years ago, they'll have taken Miss Wright to my cave."

"Then we'll be climbing the hill at first light."

***

Before Captain Archer had barked the orders to raise the mains'l and weigh anchor to turn the Remora about toward the open sea, Captain Jones and his twenty armed men were already halfway along the narrow ledge up Mizzenmast Hill—the only access to Ben's cave. At one point where the ledge was only six inches wide and required both hands to navigate, John turned back to Ben. "How did you manage to carry all of those silver bars up this path? They must have weighed fifty pounds each."

"Seventy pounds, Captain." Ben welcomed the moment to catch his breath. "I made me a chest sling and carried one bar at a time. Took the better part of five months, with the weather and all." He took a couple more breaths. "By the Powers, I'd never do it that way again."

"Wasn't there another place you could have hidden it? Somewhere a little easier to get to?"

"There were several, Cap'n, but none as good." Ben gave a quick shake of his head. "I'd still use the same cave, but I wouldn't carry them bars up by hand."

"You had another option?"

"I'll show you after we find out if the girl's up here."

While John helped Ben across the narrow section, David reached the plateau and ran ahead to the cave entrance. The eastern sky was alive with fire, but the sun had not yet broken the horizon. Stepping inside, David felt about the chamber with his sword. A rock fell from the wall and landed with a loud thump next to his foot, followed by a string of screams from the terrified girl, who was certain her abductor had returned for her.

David called back to the others. "She's here!" One of the seamen entered with a lanthorn that illuminated the cave.

Jane continued to scream and jerk at the manacles that held her to the table—so much that her wrists were wet with blood. The skeleton of a man became visible across the table from her. "Let me go! Oh, dear God! Please let me go!" The frantic girl continued to scream and twist in her rusty bindings until she was nearly breathless.

"Miss Wright! It's me, David Noble!" He rushed to her side. "You're safe now."

"Oh, David! It was terrible!"

David's eyes quickly adjusted to the darkness. "What happened?"

"It was awful!" She stopped pulling at the manacles. "He was hairy and naked, except for a belt and his cutlass! He gagged me and tied my hands and feet and carried me up his trail! He smelled of a dead animal!

I must have swooned, because when I finally woke up, I found myself here, in these irons!"

There was a call from outside. "David!"

"In here, Captain! She's in here!" David unbolted the manacles and took the sobbing girl into his arms. "You're safe now."

The others entered the cave—first John, then Robert, and finally Ben. Robert took a lanthorn from one of the sailors and held it up. "Is she all right?"

David looked to the older man. "I think so, Robert, except for the wounds at her wrists."

Seated at the table was the entire skeleton of Tom Morgan, knit together with fine roots and palm fronds. Ben held his lanthorn close to the bones. "He must have the other one with him."

John studied the skeleton. "Do you think two of them are still alive?"

"No, Cap'n." Ben pointed at the empty set of manacles—the ones with Jane's blood. "Look at the fragments of bone on the table. He has two skeletons."

"That poor soul. He must believe they're still alive." Robert lifted Tom's chains from the table and inspected the manacles. They were so oversized that the skeleton's left hand slid loose and fell onto the table with a clatter.

John led David and Jane out of the cave. "David, take a couple of men and escort Miss Wright back to the ship."

Jane tried to get down from David's arms but he held her tight. "I'll be all right, Captain Jones." She gave up the fruitless struggle and clung to David's neck. "I'm safe now. Why can't I stay up here with the rest of you?"

David ignored her protest. "We'll go back to the ship, Captain. I'll take four men with us in case we run into the escaped pirates." After dressing her wounds, David and the others left the small meadow and began their climb down the narrow path.

John watched until they passed out of sight around a bend. Then he turned to Ben. "It's gone, isn't it? The treasure isn't in your cave any more."

Ben shook his head. "It's right where I left it, Cap'n Jones, but not quite the same way."

"But we were inside the cave, Ben. It isn't there."

"Follow me." The old man led John and Robert back into the cave.

"The second chamber, Cap'n!" Ben pointed to the dark corner of the cave where a rock protruded from the wall. "It's all there. Every bit of it."

Ben squeezed around the protruding rock and into the narrow opening. He looked back at John. "It's a wee bit tight, Cap'n, but I think you'll both fit."

Before they had squeezed halfway through the narrow passageway, there was shouting behind them in the first chamber. They backed out and looked to see what had happened. What met their gaze was incredible. Morley Rowe, in all his shabby hair and nakedness stood at the table yelling at the the four sailors who remained. In one hand was his rusty cutlass, and in the other was the skeleton of Dick Walpole.

"Stand back or I'll cut ya down where ya stand!" As they all watched in disbelief, the naked maroon scuttled past them and placed the second skeleton in the spot where Jane had been sitting a moment earlier. With the dexterity of a turnkey, Morley slid the bony hands into the bloody manacles. Then, noticing that Tom's left hand was free, he gave the sailors a furtive glance and let out a guttural growl at the bones.

"I told you not to talk to them!" He replaced the boney hand in the iron bracelet and gave Tom a backhand slap that nearly knocked the skull from the backbone. "And look what they got you to do! That's gonna cost you dearly, friend Tom." With his jailkeeper duties complete, Morley laid the cutlass on the table between the two men of bones. Satisfied, he dashed to the back of the chamber and slipped through the crevice like a wisp of smoke.

The three officers followed the naked maroon to the second chamber and stood with lanthorns held high. Everything was exactly as Ben had described it, except that the silver bars were no longer in a loose pile. Instead, they had been stacked to create a massive throne that now stood in the center of the chamber. In that throne sat Morley Rowe. There was a small chest at his right side on the floor.

Morley's backside was seemingly numb to the chill of the silver bars. He reached down and opened a small treasure chest and pulled something from its center.

Ben gasped. "That's it, Cap'n Jones!"

Morley turned the thing about in his hands and then placed it on his head.

"That's the mate to the crown we dug up at Dead Man's Chest! And that small chest he pulled it from holds the queen's ransom I told you about!"

Morley surveyed the three new members of his imaginary court. "I am Morley Rowe—the King of Treasure Island!" He pointed down at the chest. "This is my treasure! Touch it and my two subjects will kill ya 'afore ya can take yer next breath!"

While the three stood in stunned silence at the strange spectacle before them, the maroon leaped down from his throne and ran past them through the crevice. They looked at each other and followed. When they reached the outer chamber, Morley was at the table with a hand over Dick Walpole's mouth.

"Don't you listen to 'im!" Morley looked about at the sailors and gave the bones a shake. "I never done them things to these two!" And then it was the other skeleton the demented man attacked with a backhand across its jaw. "They're lying, just so you'll rescue them before me!"

John stepped to the seamen and whispered. "Bind him and then take him down to the beach." The sailor gave his captain a curt salute.

The four sailors stripped Morley of his cutlass and crown, and then dragged him kicking and swearing from the cave. John, Robert and Ben followed out of curiosity. It was one thing to watch a sane man wrestled to the ground, but it was a completely different thing for the young sailors to do it to a naked crazy man. After five minutes, Morley was bound and dragged across the meadow to the trail head.

Once they were gone, John spoke. "Robert, there was more than enough treasure on Dead Man's Chest to pay for the cannons. With what's in that second chamber, I estimate that we'll have nearly a half a million sterling to split with the crews."

"The crews?"

"Aye. The Eagle as well as the Silver Cloud. Captain Steele and his men deserve a fair share."

Robert looked down at the two ships. "What about the Remora?"

John shook his head. "Captain Archer and his crew will get their pay, but it'll have to come from John Silver once they reach King's Town."

John looked back to the cave and then to Ben. "You said there was another way you could have carried the silver bars up here. Where is it?"

Ben stepped toward the pine grove and stopped. "Follow me." When he was sure they were behind him, he hurried off through the trees at the edge of the meadow. When they emerged from the trees, John found Ben looking over a hundred-foot cliff.

A single banyan tree stretched its massive branches in all directions. One thrust out over the cliff directly toward Captain Kidd's Lagoon and the waiting ships.

"There!" Ben pointing up at the branch. "If I were to ever come back here alone, I would set up a hauling rig to that branch and lower several bars at a time." He looked around at John and Robert. "With a team up here loading a sling and a team down below, we could have all three hundred and fifty bars down and aboard the Silver Cloud in a couple of hours."

John looked up at the branch. It was four feet above his head. "We'd have to throw a rope over it and have someone climb up to attach the rig." Then he peered over the cliff at the jungle below. "We'll have to put a dozen men to work chopping a trail to the lagoon, but I believe they could do it more quickly than we could get the hauling system set up. We should be able to lower a half-dozen bars at a time."

It took even less time than John had hoped. Within three hours after the block and tackle had been secured to the banyan tree, the entire treasure had been lowered to the base of the cliff. Like cutter ants, a continuous line of men carried a bar apiece down to the beach for transport to the Silver Cloud. Then, at John's order, the hauling system was cut down and the four ship's boats began ferrying the silver bars out to the Silver Cloud.

Throughout that first day, Alan Steele had avoided John, confining himself to the Silver Cloud. John finally spotted him on a boat headed for the beach, and waited at the tree line for his arrival.

The older man climbed from the boat and walked up the beach. John met him half way. "Welcome ashore, Captain Steele. I was beginning to worry about you."

"I need to speak with you, Mister Jones."

"By all means. How is Miss Wright?"

"I just spoke with her before coming ashore. She seems much stronger than I'd expected, considering her encounter with that dreadful naked man." He shook his head. "From the way she's acting, I believe the whole affair's actually done her good."

John gave the older man a wink. "It's my first officer who's done her the most good."

Steele looked about at the departing Remora. "Why did Captains Archer and Silver leave without coming ashore for fresh water and provisions?"

"There were two reasons. First, John Silver wants to get to the cannon ship at least a day before the rendezvous. Second, he knows better than to get anywhere near Robert Ormerod."

"Oh?"

John told him of Robert's hatred of the pirate and the tragedy that spawned it. "He tried to kill Silver several days ago—the day we came out of that lagoon—and he'll succeed if given a second chance. I don't wish to provide that opportunity."

"Good thinking." Steele took several steps southward along the beach, stopped and turned back. "Will you walk with me?" John nodded and followed.

"I'm..." He hesitated while he searched for the words. "I'm not really sure how to put this, but..."

"Just say it."

Captain Steele stopped. "Do you know what our Savior taught about forgiveness?"

"He taught many things, but you seem to have one verse in mind."

"Jesus taught that if someone offends me, I'm to rebuke him. If that person repents, then I'm bound as a Christian to forgive him. I believe it's in Luke, chapter seventeen."

John stopped walking. He knew Alan was speaking of the rebuke he had given John at the Rappahannock River. After an uncomfortable moment, John spoke. "I was a problem for you and your crew during that entire trip to New York, wasn't I?"

"To say the least."

"It's bothered me ever since. I..." John fell silent, hoping his gesture was enough. Alan remained quiet, so John was compelled to continue. "As much as it hurts my pride to admit it, you were right about me from that first morning at Edenton. I was wrong for undermining the orders you gave your crew, and for taking that side trip to see Miss Dandridge. I had my priorities mixed, and I'll be the first to admit so. Can you find it in yourself to forgive me for my insolence, and for what I said about your wife?"

Alan smiled and nodded. "Of course I can, Captain." It was the first time he had addressed John by his proper title.

John took Alan's offered hand. "John."

"You're a good man, John." They resumed walking. After a moment, Alan spoke. "Do you know about what Smoot did with my crew?"

John remembered the pirate's boast the night before. "You'll want to return to Saint Croix for your men, won't you?"

Alan nodded. "Yes, I will."

"How many of my men will you need?"

"I could do with ten, but twenty would be better. And since we may have to fight for my crew's release—"

"Then I'll make it twenty, and half of them should be the Indian fighters. They wouldn't be much use sailing the Eagle, but they'd come in very handy after you get ashore at Saint Croix."

John looked back up the beach to where the landing parties were working. "The provisions will be aboard in another hour or so. If nothing else goes wrong, I'll want to weigh anchor by the noon tide." He looked back at the other captain. "I'll need a list of the crewmen and supplies you want, as quickly as you can put it together."

"I've already made them up. There are more than enough men who've told me they want to help. All I needed was your approval." He pulled a folded paper from his pocket and handed it to the younger man. "These are the names of the ten seamen I was hoping for, along with the provisions we'll need. I'll trust you to select the fighters." He looked back to the Eagle. "I'll be ready to leave shortly after you."

"You can see Robert about the provisions, and I'll pass the word for the men to transfer their gear."

"There's one other thing, John."

"Yes?"

Alan reached into his pocket and pulled out a gold ring. "One of your men gave me this. I thought you'd want it."

John took it and spent some time studying the crest. "Whose is it?"

"It belongs to Joshua Smoot. It was on his right index finger, and your crewman thought it should be returned to the pirate."

"Hmmm." John thought for a moment, then dropped it into his pocket.

The two turned about and started back up the beach toward the boats.

The ship's cook and Gilcrest the powder monkey were waiting for them. "By yer leave, sirs?"

John liked the Irishman. "What can I do for you, Barragan?"

"Well, sir, a couple of the men was complainin' 'bout them two skeletons up in Morley's cave."

"What about them?"

"The crew and me think we shouldn't leave the island without givin' 'em a proper Christian burial."

John looked at Alan and then up at the cliff. "You honestly believe those two were Christians?"

"Probably not, sir, but the rest of the men still feel uneasy leavin' them bound to that table."

"We're going to sail on the noon tide. How long would it take you?"

Seamus looked about at the hill and back to his captain. He raised a canvas bag with shoulder straps attached "We're both pretty quick on our feet, sir, so it shouldn't be more than an hour 'til we'd be back with the two bags of bones."

"Go ahead, then, but go armed. Those five pirates are still out there somewhere."

"Thank you, Captain Jones." The two ran off toward Mizzenmast Hill with their bags.

"I don't want to interfere, John, but Mister Noble told me of the narrow path along the cliff face. I hope those two aren't planning on carrying the bones back that way."

"You're right." John looked once more to the cliff. "We cut off the hauling rig just before you came ashore."

"Where's the rope?"

"It should still be at the base of the cliff with the rest of the silver." He held up a hand to the older man. "I'll be back in a few minutes."

"Where are you going?"

"To take the rope up to the cave!"

It took John twenty minutes to coil the rope and to climb the narrow ledge to the cliff. Seamus and Gilcrest had just finished tearing apart the two skeletons and had stuffed them into the separate bags for transporting back down the hill.

"Captain Jones! What are you doing up here?"

John dropped the coiled rope beneath the banyan tree. He motioned for the two to approach. "It's too dangerous to take the bones back down that way. I brought a rope so we can lower them the same way we lowered the silver."

Seamus stepped to the edge. "If ya think about it, Cap'n, these two aren't feelin' any pain." Before John could object, he threw his bag over the edge. He gave John a broad smile, then grabbed Gilcrest's bag and heaved it over, too. "There!"

John stared at him, slackjawed. "Why didn't we just do that with the silver bars?"

"I couldn't say, Cap'n."

Gilcrest looked up at the branch. The cut end of the hauling rope was dangling out over the precipice, just out of reach. "You know, Captain, if we could bind your rope to that one on the tree, we could slide down and be back to the beach in five minutes."

"Good idea." John looked about for a stick. There were none in sight.

"What ya lookin' for, Cap'n?"

"We'll need a pole to hook the line so we can pull it over to us." John looked out at the hanging line again. "Take a look in Ben's cave. There might be something that would work."

Seamus pointed to the trees to the right. "I'll take the cave, lad. You look up by those trees."

As the two ran off on their quest, John remembered his sword. He pulled it from the scabbard and reached out. The tip extended three inches past the hanging rope. He couldn't hook it with a straight sword, but gave it a push to make it start swinging. This is going to work! On the fifth swing, the tip of the rope was within reach. He caught the line and pulled it as close as it would come, but as it arced toward him, it pulled from his fingers. He gave a defeated huff. Before he could try again, there was a scream from the cave.

"Barragan?" John drew his sword and ran through the trees. On the other side, he ran into the five pirates. One of them held Gilcrest by the shoulder. Seamus was on the ground in front of them with blood flowing from his throat.

"They killed him, Captain Jones!" The lad struggled against the strong grip. "They was waitin' for him in the back of the cave!"

"Well, well!" Their leader waved a hand toward the boy. "Let the lad go, Deuce. Lady Luck's given us a bigger prize!"

"Are you all right, Gilcrest?" John made a quick survey of the five pirates. Only two of them had cutlasses, but two of the others held the pistols Seamus and Gilcrest had brought with them. John stood his ground and watched the boy run along the path toward safety.

At twenty yards, Gilcrest stopped and called back. "I'm fine, Cap'n, but I can't leave you here like this!"

"Keep going, lad!" The five pirates advanced on John. "Tell Captain Steele and the rest what's happened. Maybe they're planning on trading me for something—maybe a boat and provisions so they can sail away from this God-forsaken place!"

The pirate's leader stopped and seemed to brighten at the suggestion. "Them's exactly my thoughts! We'll trade this fine captain for a boat and provisions!"

John had held his ground and watched until he was certain Gilcrest was beyond harm. Then he pulled and fired his pistol at the closest pirate. The man fell to the ground clutching his face. Before the smoke had cleared, John turned and ran back through the trees toward the cliff.

The other pirate with the cutlass began running after him. "He's gettin' away!"

The leader caught the man by the shirt. "No he isn't, you sod! There's no way off this hill but the path, and it's behind us. He's got nowhere to go."

As John burst out of the trees and on to the top of the cliff, he realized the pirate was right. His way to the footpath was blocked, and his captors were advancing, slowly but steadily, through the trees. The rope could be his path to safety, but it dangled just out of his reach.

Then he had a thought. It might work! He tied a loose slipping noose in the end of the rope and made one last calculation. Setting his feet at the edge, he gave the stack of coils a kick, sending it over the cliff toward the workmen a hundred feet below. Then, with all the strength he could muster, John leaped into open space.

As he flew toward the length of hanging rope, he twisted smoothly to his back and slipped the noose up and over the end. Then, with a quick jerk on both ends of the noose, the hoisting rope was trapped, forming a sheet bend, just as the old tailor had done with his shoe lace. Before the pirates realized what John had done, he had slid halfway to the jungle floor.

"What the...!" The two pirates with pistols fired down at him, while the other two sliced at the rope, but it was beyond their cutlasses by two inches.

"Take me other hand an' belay me!" The others grabbed the man so he could lean further out. After three vicious swings with the rusty blade, the pirate finally managed to cut the rope, dropping John the last fifteen feet to the ground.

One of the work crew cried out. "Captain Jones! Where the hell did you come from?"

"Never mind that for now!" He threw off the tangled coils of rope and retrieved his sword. "Grab those last bars of silver and let's get away from here!" As he spoke, a storm of large rocks began falling about them, hitting one of the crew a solid blow to the shoulder.

A voice called from the shore. "John!"

"Over here, Alan! Help me with this man!"

"What happened up there?" Alan hoisted the injured sailor to his shoulder. "Where are the others?"

"Barragan's dead, and Gilcrest is—"

"Dead? Who...?"

"Smoot's men—the five who escaped from the Eagle last night." He pointed up at the cliff. "As soon as we reach the beach, I want a dozen armed men. I'm going back up there."

Robert called from twenty yards away. "They're already on their way!"

"Who are on their way?"

"David and McCoy. They took ten of the Indian fighters up the trail as soon as we heard the first pistol report. Don't worry. They'll catch all of them."

"Unless..." It was Ben.

John looked to him. "Unless what?"

"I never had cause to do it myself, but a desperate man might risk scaling the cliff face above my cave. It's about thirty feet—mostly straight up—but once over the top, then it's just an easy slope and lots of jungle for them to hide in."

John looked up again. "I don't care how long it takes. They'll pay for killing my cook!"

Robert put a hand to John's arm. "But we've a rendezvous with John Silver. If we're to reach him before dusk as planned, we'll have to depart by noon."

"I want those pirates in irons or dead! Only then will we leave!"

"But if they make it over the ridge, we'll never find 'em, Cap'n."

John continued to watch Mizzenmast Hill, trying to see David and the fighters. He wanted revenge, but he knew Ben was right. "Then we'll maroon them if we have to."

By six bells, an hour before noon, the last of the silver and provisions had been loaded aboard the two ships. Both crews watched the trees from the decks of their ships, listening for gunfire. There wasn't a sound.

"There they are!" It was the top watch calling from high atop the Silver Cloud's main mast. "They're on the trail near the cave!"

John called back "How many can you see?"

"It's just Mister Noble, McCoy and the ten others! They're carrying a body!"

"What about the pirates?"

"I don't see none of 'em, Captain! It's just the dozen who went up!"

John turned to Ben and Robert. "They must have made it over the ridge after all, Ben."

Robert hated to be so persistent, but the mission was and always been his highest priority. "Then we can get underway as scheduled?"

John nodded. "Aye. The moment David and the others are aboard."

Within the hour, the disguised frigate and her escort weighed anchor. As they cleared the last line of coral, the four newly marooned pirates burst onto the beach, along with Morley Rowe.

John pointed aft. "Look there!"

Robert joined him at the rail. "You told us that you killed one of them."

"I did." John handed Robert the spyglass. "The fifth one is the lunatic."

While the four officers watched, Morley yelled something at the group of pirates, and then stormed off toward the pile of tools that John had ordered left for them at the stockade. A few minutes later, he was back with a shovel and searching about the beach for something. There was more yelling and shoving.

Robert continued to watch. "He's trying to dig up his skeletons."

Ben gave a rueful snort. "The poor, demented man believes they're suffocating under the sand."

While most of the crew of the Silver Cloud watched, Morley threw dirt into the air by the shovelful. As he did, one of the pirates rushed him from behind and grabbed the tool from his hands. There was more yelling, followed by the shovel being thrown to the water's edge. This infuriated Morley. He broke loose from his captor, stumbled after it and fell headlong into the water from another dizzy spell. A moment later he was back up the beach and once again digging between two of the pirates who had taken up their position atop the graves.

Robert handed the spyglass to John. "He's certainly a persistent dog."

Ben gave a laugh, but it had a touch of sympathy in it. "And I don't expect those others will take much more of it."

"That's his concern, not ours."

Ben turned to his captain. "Is it too late to go back an' get Morley?"

"Why?"

"Well, Cap'n, ten years is a long time to be marooned."

"Look at him. He'd never adjust to our civilzed world."

"Captain Jones is right, Ben. The fine people of New York Town would put the poor wretch in a cage and display him like an animal."

The last that the crew of the Silver Cloud saw of the five maroons was the bizarre sight of Morley Rowe tied against a palm tree with his eyes covered. While he was thus constrained, the others dug up the graves and moved the two skeletons to a new location. It was the only thing they could do, short of killing the King of Treasure Island.

Chapter 18

Lieutenant James Hawkins had been away from England and his fiancée, Christiana Osbourne, for over fourteen months when the accident occurred and the midshipman lost his life. Nobody understood why the captain insisted upon the court martial at sea, rather than making for King's Town or one of the ports in the American colonies. But but at the well-intended advice of the executive officer, none of the junior officers questioned the action until it was too late. Mutiny is a hanging offense, and for the crew to object openly to an execution, no matter how much they disagreed with their captain, would be to face the same fate. Lieutenant Hawkins had wanted to get off the HMS Wasp from long before the incident, but it would be bad for his career to ask for a transfer at this sensitive time.

Jim sat at his desk with pen, inkwell and paper. He was trying to reread his still-unfinished letter to Christiana, but his thoughts kept intruding. Perhaps her father can arrange my transfer, so I can get off when we reach New Orleans. He touched the pen to his chin. And if my orders come directly from the Admiralty, Captain Stevens would have no reason to take any action against me.

"Mister Hawkins!" It was one of the midshipmen. "Are you there, sir?"

"Yes! What is it?"

"It's me, sir! Presley!" The young man pushed open the cabin door. "You asked me to tell you the moment I spotted the next postal packet."

"Thank you, Presley!" The midshipman saluted and left. Jim looked down at the letter. There's sure to be a letter from Christiana, and figuring how long it takes for my letters to reach England, I might be off this ship by July or August! He quickly finished the paragraph he was writing and slipped the four pages under his desk pad.

The young officer emerged onto the main deck, still buttoning his tunic. Out of habit, he squinted up into the rigging to check the winds and then turned toward the quarterdeck. He saluted first, then called out. "Permission to come aft, sir?"

Lieutenant Commander Foster leaned against the rail and looked down at the lieutenant. The executive officer was thirty-eight years old, and had been in the Royal Navy since he was seventeen, working his way up through the ranks with comparitive ease. He was more fair and even-handed than any officer Jim had ever served under, and he respected him like a father. He smiled down at Jim. "Not until you're properly dressed, young man."

Jim looked down at his misaligned buttons. "Excuse me, sir." The embarrassed youth turned away for a moment to straightened his clothing. "I understand we've a postal packet inbound."

"Yes we do, lieutenant. The officer pointed to the small ship to lee. One of the Wasp's boats was already returning with several large bags. While they watched, the mailbags were hoisted hand over hand to the main deck, where Captain Stevens waited. His was a special bundle of dispatches and letters, packaged separately from the rest.

"You seem anxious, Lieutenant Hawkins." Commander Foster gave a fatherly chuckle. "Hoping to hear from that young woman you left in Edinburgh?"

"Aye, sir." Jim climbed to the quarterdeck. "We're to be married when I return to England."

"I saw her, James. She's a right handsome young woman. I'm sure she'll make you a wonderful wife."

Jim only half-heard his superior, so intently was he watching the letters flowing to the waiting hands of the crew on the deck below them.

"If you're waiting to hear your name called, Jim, you'll be waiting all day. By Captain Steven's order, the officer's mail is being segregated and will be handed out in his cabin in a half-hour.

Jim turned to the commander. "In his cabin? What kind of—"

The commander held up a restraining hand. "I know exactly how you feel, Jim, but my advice is that you keep your thoughts to yourself."

"But, why?"

"It's his new policy. He told me that since he calls all the officers to his cabin to hear the new dispatches anyway, he might as well hand out our mail at the same time." As the commander spoke, several of the other officers began drifting toward the aft companionway.

"Do you think it has anything to do with this recent trouble, sir?"

"I'm certain of it." The older man's used a guarded tone. "But if we cherish our careers, we'll keep our mouths shut and pretend full agreement with the captain." He put a fatherly hand on the young officer's shoulder. "Shall we go below?"

A half-hour later, the mail had been delivered, but the door to the master's cabin was still closed. It was another ten minutes before the captain unlocked the door and hooked it back against the bulkhead. "Enter and stand at ease, gentlemen." One of the midshipmen set the personal letters out in alphabetical order across the table.

Jim pushed his way to the front and searched quickly for any letters that bore his name. There were none yet.

The captain looked over his reading glasses at his officers. "As usual, we've received several important dispatches. None of them concerns the junior officers except this one from the Admiralty in King's Town. It seems we're not relieving the Queen Anne at New Orleans after all." He looked over his glasses to catch Jim reaching out toward the mail. He slapped the stack of letters with his ever-present riding crop. "Are you with us, Mister Hawkins?"

Jim jumped and pulled back his hand. "Sorry, sir! I was just—"

Several of the other junior officers snickered and traded looks.

After another disapproving look at Jim, the captain continued. "As I was saying, we'll not be going to New Orleans next month as previously ordered." He scanned down the first page saying half-words and mumbling phrases here and there while he read. "Ah! "Here it is." He stopped to adjust his glasses. "As of your receipt of this dispatch, trade between America and the West Indian colonies shall be restricted to consumable and dry goods only. So as to insure that no weapons or..." He skipped down the page to another short passage. "...only those vessels which have been previously inspected and are returning to the American colonies from ports in the West Indies shall be allowed passage. Should one of these ships be found to carry any arms, ammunition, or gun powder, the captain and all officers will be arrested, and the ship will be sailed to the nearest British port."

He looked up at his officers and removed his glasses. "It seems that an anonymous source in King's Town has informed the Admiralty that a very large number of cannons and quantities of gun powder are being shipped from somewhere in the West Indies, and will pass Andros Island on its way to America. The Wasp...I have been tasked with the interception and commandeering of those weapons."

Jim looked about at the others. Nobody was going to speak. "Why us, sir?"

"The dispatch didn't say. I would assume, however, that we are the best qualified, since we probably inspected the same ships when they were en route to the islands." The Captain looked about his junior officers. "Are there any other questions?"

Jim nodded. "Just one, sir."

"Yes?"

"Well, a little over a month ago, I inspected a Dutch merchantman by the name of Silver Cloud near Abaco Island. They were transporting cotton to mill in Saint Croix, and should have returned by now with molasses for our distilleries in New York. Must we inspect that one again?"

"Of course we must, and she'll be allowed to pass only if she has the proper papers and your seal in her gunwale. Is there a problem with that?"

"No sir, except that..."

"Then I'll assume you believe there is a problem, Lieutenant."

"Well, I was wondering if maybe another officer might inspect her when she returns."

The captain laid the dispatch down and studied the young officer. "Get to your point, young man. Is there something about the Silver Cloud you failed to put in your report?"

"My report?"

"It was, as you reported, a Dutch crew, wasn't it?"

"Oh, they were Woodshoes all right!" Jim shivered at the memory. "You should have seen their captain! Disgusting man! Got so close when he talked that he spat all over my face!" There were snickers from about the cabin, which encouraged the young officer. "It was like sitting under my old minister back in Bristol. The front two pews got baptized with spittle every time..." The other officers burst into raucous laughter before Jim could finish. He enjoyed the attention. "And his smell! I've known swine that smell better."

"That will be enough, Mister Hawkins." The captain's voice was firm, but a smirk danced across his lips while he spoke. "I don't care what your personal problems are with this Dutchman. Since you inspected her the first time, you'll be the inspecting officer when the Silver Cloud returns."

The captain took off his glasses and looked about at his officers, one at a time. "Before Midshipman Beasley distributes your personal letters, I have a grave matter to discuss with you." He paused to let the officers ponder the words. "I have information that one of you has been talking of a mutiny against me."

A chill fell over the room as the young officers looked about at one another. Each knew it was true, because all but the executive officer had spoken against the captain and the recent execution.

"I felt the same way when I first learned of this treachery, and have been forced by this individual to take extraordinary and drastic measures. Those of you who are innocent of this seditious behavior will agree with me that my new policy is fair and necessary. I expect that the mutineer will give himself away by his protest of that policy."

"And what might that new policy be, Captain Stevens?" Commander Foster's voice was cold and direct.

"Effective this date, I will open and read all of your personal mail as it comes aboard, and before your outgoing mail leaves the ship, I will likewise read and censor it."

An almost audible wave of anger swept across the officers, while nostrils flared and jaws tightened. The captain waited for a full minute for his imagined mutineer to expose himself.

"I will take your lack of objections as a vote of confidence, gentlemen, and as full agreement with the new policy." He scanned each man's face as before, and then continued. "If there are no further questions, I expect you to return to your duties. You'll be notified when I've finished reading your mail."

***

The distance between Flint's Island and the rendezvous point was no more than a half-day's sail. Morale was higher than it had ever been since they left Charles Town. The excitement that their mission was nearly completed, and that they were no longer threatened by pirates, could be felt radiating from the very timbers and planks of the great frigate.

The top watch called out. "Land Ho! Land Ho!"

John strode quickly to the starboard rail and leaned far outboard for a look. Beyond the Remora, which was leading them by a half-league, all that was visible of their destination was the windswept cloud of moist afternoon air that had been pushed aloft by the updrafts at the island.

David handed John the spyglass. "Do you still think we can make the strait before dusk?" The spyglass was a bulky thing—the size of a man's arm and wrapped in the distinctive coach whipping of the bosun's mate's trade, with large Turk's heads adorning either end. John took a long look at the area below the cloud, hoping to see the masts of their twin ship.

John lowered the spyglass. "Aye, and with two hours of light besides."

"Mast Ho! Mast in the straits!" It was the top watch again.

"They're here!" John turned to his first officer. "David, see to it that the crew's ready. I want to put as many miles between ourselves and John Silver as possible after we trade ships."

"The men were ready when we left Spyglass, Captain." David paused while as a thought came to mind. "What part of the treasure are we keeping?"

"What part?" John gave David a questioning look.

"I would suggest we leave the silver bars for my uncle and take the more valuable parts of the treasure with us—the excess, that is." David hesitated. He could see by John's concerned look that he had just realized the logistical problem involved.

"We stacked the silver on top of the gold, didn't we?"

David nodded. "Yes, we did."

"I didn't even consider that." John was disappointed in himself for the error. "I was planning on taking the silver with us, since we'd already calculated the eight hundred thousand from what we got off Dead Man's Chest. We're going to have to recalculate and then adjust what we bring above deck for transfer."

"If you'll give me the key to the vault, I'll find Robert and Ben, and begin the work. At the same time, we can begin loading the more valuable parts of the treasure into canvas and cloth bags for the transfer."

"Why?"

"To make it look like personal gear, Captain. My uncle is a pirate, remember? No use tempting him any more than necessary."

"Good idea." John pulled the chain from around his neck and handed the key to his capable young friend. "See to it."

At seven bells—mid-afternoon—the treasure ship's massive anchor splashed into the turquoise waters between Little and Great Inagua Islands. As the bubbles spread out on the surface and then cleared away in a circle of light foam, the enormous iron and oak hook struck a coral head and settled into the white sand. The chain was allowed to slack another twenty-five yards before it was stopped and the shackle was driven through the enormous link. The great anchor rose on its side for a moment while one of the large flukes drove itself deep into the sandy bottom. The second Silver Cloud lay anchored two hundred yards to the south and was already lowering a boat. According to John Silver's order, the Remora remained under full sail a league to windward, just in case any other ships tried to approach. John ordered all boats lowered and the crew to make ready to begin moving across upon his signal.

John watched the activity at the other Silver Cloud. "It appears they're more anxious than we are to trade ships and get underway."

David held a piece of paper. "We've finished our calculations and loaded all the jewels and a large part of the gold into the bags. Do you want the men to take it across in the first boats?"

"Not until we inspect and count the cannons." John looked at the paper. "I assume that's the manifest of the treasure to give to Captain Silver when he arrives."

"It is, Captain, and Robert will be waiting at the lazarette."

John shook his head. "That won't do."

"What?"

"We can't risk allowing those two together again. Robert will kill him this time for certain."

"We can't arrest Robert again as we did the other time my uncle came aboard."

"We'll wait until John Silver comes across. If you can go through the inventory with your uncle, I'll take Robert with me." As they spoke, the gunship's boat pulled within earshot.

"David!" The voice had a Jamaican accent. "Is that you?"

David ran to the rail and looked down. "Father! What are you doing here?"

"I'm here to count the treasure!" A moment later, Charles Noble's boat was secured to the ladder, and he was climbing to the main deck. He carried a package wrapped in oilcloth and tied up with a leather thong.

"Welcome aboard, Mister Noble!" John extended a hand of greeting. "This is a pleasant surprise, especially for your son! We expected John Silver to be coming across again."

Charles looked back at the cannon ship. "Again?"

"He didn't tell you about our meeting before we arrived at Flint's Island?"

"No, but my brother keeps a lot from me." Charles gave his son a hug and handshake. "He did tell me about Mister Ormerod trying to kill him, but didn't say when it happened. I just assumed it was at Flint's Island."

"We'd assumed he would want to count the treasure personally."

"He's tired. When his articulated leg was destroyed in that gun battle with the pirates, he had to switch to the peg leg. He gets a sore back when he wears it."

"Then he sent you across in his place?"

Charles nodded. "He told me that before you gave up the treasure, you'd insist on counting the cannons." Charles looked about the main deck. "Shall we be at it?"

John nodded. "Your son assures me that everything's ready for you, Mister Noble."

David held up the manifest.

"Will David be helping me?"

"Robert Ormerod and Ben Gunn were going to do it, but..." John noticed the begging look David was giving him. "But then, I suppose David could help you with the count just as well."

"Could I?" David held up the manifest. "I'm sure Robert or Ben would be more than willing to go count the cannons with you."

"I'll not take Robert to the ship John Silver is on. When you get to the lazarette, send Ben up on deck."

"Thank you, Captain Jones!" David grabbed his father's arm and began escorting him to the ladder. "This is wonderful, Father! We'll have time to talk before you have to leave again."

John called after them. "Watch for my signal before you start sending the crew across."

With a curt salute from David, John climbed down into the waiting boat. David led the way down to the officer's companionway, but stopped and turned to his father.

"I've missed you so much, Father. I wish there were a way you could continue with us to Charles Town."

Charles gave his son a broad smile. "Well, David, the Good Lord has indeed smiled on both of us this day."

"Oh?"

"I am continuing with you to Charles Town."

David stopped. "You're coming with us?"

"You're pleased, aren't you?"

"Of course I'm pleased, but I thought you'd be returning to oversee the unloading of the treasure at Jamaica. What if he—"

"I've already discussed that with your uncle. I think after all these years I can trust my own brother."

"Which reminds me, Father. After we inventory the treasure, there's someone very special I want you to meet."

"Is he someone you've written about?"

"It isn't a he, Father."

***

The eighty-man crew of the gunship was a mix of slaves, indentured servants and pirates. The slaves were the easiest to pick out, because their skin was black. The indentured servants looked more like the lighter-skinned sailors, but their clothes were hardly better than rags when compared to the regular crew's finer dress. As John and Ben stepped through the opening in the larboard gunwale, Captain Silver stumped forward with outspread arms.

"Well, well!" The old pirate stood in his finest seagoing attire, the light breeze blowing through his white hair. Protruding from his left trouser leg was the new wooden rod that had replaced the articulated wooden leg Robert had shattered the week before with his pistol shot. "If it isn't my old mate, Ben Gunn!"

"Top o' the day to ya, Captain Silver!" Ben flashed John a nervous look while he received the old pirate's embrace.

"Ye're lookin' a far sight better than when they was burnin' yer legs on Dead Man's Chest." Silver stepped back and eyed Ben's legs. "Are they healing well?"

"They still sting a bit when I sweat, Captain Silver, but other than that, I'm doing fine." The old man remembered something. "You were there that night, weren't you? It wasn't just a dream."

"Aye, that were me alright, an' I killed two of those blackhearts."

"He and his men killed all the pirates, Ben—all twelve of them."

"There were only nine of them torturing Ben and that other poor soul, Captain Jones. Three of the dead were mine."

"Ben and I appreciate what you did for him, Captain Silver, but could we get to the business at hand?"

"What's the rush? Ben an' I haven't seen each other for over ten years—not since he saved my life at Puerto Plata. That deserves a minute or two, doesn't it?"

"Yes, but you and he can reminisce while I count the cannons, can't you?"

"Aye, that we can!" The old pirate pushed himself away from the pin rail and pointed to the ladder. "After you, Captain Jones."

As they navigated the ladders, John and Ben stopped at each deck to allow the old pirate to keep up. Silver stopped for a breath at the gun deck, and then stumped through the barrels of molasses and bags of sugar to the mizzenmast. He stopped and turned about. The false piles of sugar bags had been pulled away from the gun stations, revealing the twenty new cannons lined up at the ports. They were a mix of long barreled twenty-five pounders and the shorter-ranged carronades of various muzzle sizes.

Silver spread his arms as if introducing his grandchildren. "Ain't that a pretty sight now?" He turned about and admired the bronze and iron beauties. "Like Papists lined up to torture a Baptist, they be. But you be wantin' a look at the bilges, what? Nine-hundred and eighty Scottish cannons make a fine ballast fer a frigate this size, Captain Jones!"

"I was told by Mister Forrestal that to help us pass inspection, there would not be any cannons on the gun deck."

"He told me that same thing, good sir, but then I figured it wouldn't hurt none to have a little fire power, just in case. I hear tell that a dispatch went out from King's Town to watch for these cannons."

John gave Silver a long look as the pirate continued.

"That was some pretty piece of work the other night at Spyglass, Captain Jones."

"Our attack on the Eagle?"

"Aye. We heard the yelling and saw several men jump overboard. What happened to Joshua Smoot? Did he die or did you leave him on the island?"

"He's alive, but not very happy with life right now."

Silver stopped at the head of the ladder and turned. "Oh?"

"He and the red-haired lad who calls himself Henry Morgan lie in chains in our brig with ten others from his crew. The rest of his men, the ones we didn't kill, escaped onto Spyglass. We killed one and the others remained there with Morley Rowe."

"You took Smoot alive?"

"He surrendered his sword to me on the deck of the Eagle."

Silver descended two rungs and stopped. "Never! Joshua Smoot'd never surrender his sword! Gentlemen do a fool thing like that—not men of Smoot's cut!"

"Well, he didn't exactly surrender it, Cap'n Silver." Ben gave John a wink. "He was sorta forced to give it up."

"Ha! I knew you had to take it from him! Smoot's a true pirate, he is!"

"I had to take his right hand off to get it."

"Argh!" Silver rubbed his right wrist in sympathy. "An' ya say ya got the lad—Henry Morgan—too?" It had been several years since he'd seen the curious orphan.

John nodded. "We do—chained up right next to Smoot."

"An' what might ye be plannin' fer the lad, Captain Jones? Is he to dance at the gallows with Smoot an' the others? "

"They'll all stand trial in Charles Town, for piracy and cannibalism."

"Cannibalism, ya say? Well, I can't say the passin' of Smoot'll be a loss to this 'ere world none. He were a curse on himself and his crew, an' by yer measure o' him, he don't sound to 'ave changed a single spot since he were hatched."

Ben gave a nod. "I spoke with him last night, and I can assure you he hasn't."

Silver gave a clap of his large hands and a laugh. "But hell, we've more important business at hand than blowin' wind about them two." He stumped down the rest of the rungs and stood on the flat deck, then turned to the two. "Say, where's Robert Ormerod?"

"He's counting the treasure with David and his father. To keep you two from crossing paths, he'll come across when you go across." John looked about the bilges. "No use throwing oil on the flames, is there?"

The old pirate gave a smile and gestured for John to proceed him forward.

John shook his head. "This is your ship, at least until I've accepted the cargo."

"I get the feelin' I'm not trusted, Captain Jones."

Ben stepped next to John and gave Silver the most serious look he could muster up. "You're not!"

"Now you've really gone an' hurt me, Ben Gunn, an' after all I done fer ya at Savannah."

John held up a hand. "Please, gentlemen. We all have enough hurts and offences so as to flog each other for days. Can we rise above them long enough to count the colonies' cannons?"

The three men finally stopping just above where the planking met the keel. There lay the nine hundred eighty other heavy cannons—the arsenal that had slept for nearly two years in Charles Noble's warehouse at King's Town—rows upon rows of sleek, metal cylinders.

"We threw out all them ballast stones, we did!" Silver pointed down the long rows of bronze cannons. "And there be no shot or tools with 'em either. Just the cannons and the powder like yer Mister Jefferson ordered."

John busied himself counting the cannons he could see and estimating the volume of the bilge.

Ben stood with each foot on a cannon and looked about. "There's no way that we can unstack them to make a full count, Captain."

John spoke over his shoulder. "The number is certainly close to correct, Ben. Assuming this isn't a layer or two of cannons stacked on rocks or lumber or some such."

Ben gave the pirate a suspicious look. "Can Captain Jones trust you that they're all here?"

"Well, by the powers! If ya can't trust old Long John Silver when he gives his word, then ye can't trust Charlie Noble, neither!"

John gave Ben a nod. "We can trust David's father, Ben. If Charles says all the cannons are here, that's good enough for me."

"Ben, ya pain me to me marrow, ya do. Weren't it me what fixed it so's you an' the others could 'scape from the Walrus in Savannah? Billy Bones was gonna have you all killed, except for me steppin' in."

John had heard quite enough of the old pirate's protests. "Don't waste your breath, John Silver. We know your allegiance lies with the greatest advantage, just as a whore lies with the man with the largest purse. If it weren't for Robert and his wife knowing where the treasure was buried, you'd have joined the rest in killing them, and you know it!"

Silver lowered his head like a scolded child. "Do ya really believe I'd stoop so low, Captain Jones?"

"Massa Silver!" One of Silver's Negroes called from the ladder above them. "Massa Charles' be comin' back in the boat."

"Well, mates, what say we go up an' hear what Charlie has to report?"

When the three finally reached the main deck, Charles and David Noble's boat was tying up to the side.

John Silver walked across the deck and looked down at his brother. "Is it all there, Charles?"

"Every farthing, just as you told me it would be."

"And the chest of jewels from Spyglass?" Silver licked his lips and gave Ben a questioning look. "It it there too?"

"I can answer that, Captain Silver."

Silver looked about at John. He didn't like the young man's tone.

"Our bargain was the thousand cannons for eight hundred thousand pounds sterling in treasure. That's exactly what we're leaving for you on the treasure ship—that and the twenty cannons that came with her from Charles Town. As far as the jewels from Spyglass are concerned, they're excess and we're keeping them to split with the crew."

"Like hell you are!" Silver's eyes burned with fire, and he dropped the pretended accent. "One word from me and my men will scuttle this ship where she stands! We're anchored over a canyon that's forty fathoms deep! Your precious cannons and the future of the American colonies will be beyond salvage!"

"No you won't!" It was Charles. "We made an agreement with them, and they've fulfilled their part of it, to the letter!" Charles had placed himself between the two captains. "They've delivered the agreed amount, and I'm satisfied!" He turned to John. "When can we begin exchanging crews?"

"Wait!" Silver's tone had softened. "I'll agree to hold to the bargain, but there's one minor concession I'd ask of you, Captain Jones, just to sweeten the pot a bit, as they say."

"And what might that be?"

"It's something without value to you, but with great value to me."

"What is it, Mister Silver?"

"I want Smoot and the lad Henry Morgan."

"I already told you that they're to be tried and hanged."

Silver nodded. "There's no question those two have earned a date with the hangman, but Fishbone Smoot earned an obligation from me in King's Town three years ago when the King's men were coming for my head. You'll have to pardon the sentiments of an old man, but since he saved my head, I'm obliged to save his."

"Yes, but Joshua Smoot deserves to die for his piracies...for the death of my men. I'll not release him to satisfy an old man's sentimentalities. You've fulfilled your side of the agreement and I have fulfilled mine. Joshua Smoot has earned himself the gallows."

John Pual Jones stood in front of Long John Silver with a defiant stare. It was the classic case of an unstoppable force meeting an immovable object. Neither man intended to give.

Finally, Charles intervened. "Is it so important that Smoot and Morgan be hanged, Captain Jones? Isn't your mission to bring the cannons to the colonies?"

Silver looked at John for a long moment. Then he lowered his voice and spoke in perfect English. "Please. Give me Joshua Smoot and Henry Morgan."

"Very well. Smoot, Morgan and the rest will remain in the brig."

The old pirate smiled and clapped his hands. "Then it's settled!"

John finally nodded. "As much as I hate to admit it, Mister Noble is right."

John began to turn but remembered something. He reached into the pocket on his waistcoat and pulled out the gold ring. "This belongs to Captain Smoot. One of my crew retrieved it before his hand was thrown overboard. It's only fitting he have it."

Captain Silver closed his hand around the ring. "Aye, if ye're certain that's what you want done with the thing."

"I'm certain." John turned to his first officer. "Give the signal to begin the transfer, David. I want to be under sail before dark."

***

Within an hour, the gunship weighed anchor and set sail for the American colonies. It was John's plan to utilize the shallows as much as possible until they reached the relative safety of the coast of Spanish Florida. This would give him the option, if they were attacked and the ship were sinking, of running her aground or letting her slip to the bottom at a depth at which the cannons could be retrieved. Their loss might mean the loss of the war to the Americans, but to the Royal Navy, which had as many cannons as it needed, their value was not as great as the time and money it would cost to salvage them.

The trade winds blew fair through the Bahamas, driving the cannon ship forward nearly two hundred miles each day. From the rendezvous, John steered a course directly for the southwestern tip of Acklin's Island, passing close abeam its lush but rocky coastline. By late afternoon of the second day, they had crossed Crooked Island Passage and were nearing Deadman's Cay, two miles west of Long Island.

At David's request, John had assigned Doctor McKenzie to Ben Gunn's cabin. It was only right that David and his father be able to share a room for the remainder of the voyage.

David knelt and pushed the drawer under his bunk closed. "Father, you never explained why you aren't returning to King's Town with the treasure."

"It's a matter of business." Charles threw his son one of the fresh blankets the cabin boy had brought them. "We're making an offer to Mister Forrestal. An offer that my brother assures me, has the potential of creating the greatest shipping company in the Western Hemisphere."

"Then I must assume this package contains the details of that offer?" It still lay on the desk where Charles had set it the day before. David picked it up and turned it about. "Do you know what it says?"

Charles shook his head. "I don't know anything more than you. And nobody will until we open it in front of Mister Forrestal and his wife."

"Uncle Silver wouldn't tell you?"

"You know your uncle and how much he loves surprises. The only thing he'd say was that when the Forrestals open it, we're all going to be thrilled at what it contains. And for us to be thrilled—and those were John Silver's exact words—it must be something very important."

"Hmmm." David laid the mysterious package down and ran his hands across the tightly bound oilcloth. "You're certain we can't open it before we get there?"

"I'm tempted, David, just as much as you. But I gave your uncle my word, and my word is my bond."

David shook his head. "The man has so many of us under his spell. Why do—"

There was a knock at the door. "Mister Noble, sir?" It was the voice of one of the powder monkeys.

"Yes?" David opened the door.

"It's nearly time to relieve Captain Jones at the watch."

"Thank you, Billy. You can tell the captain I'll be up in a few minutes."

"Aye, aye, sir." The boy turned and ran off.

"You've turned into a true ship's officer, David. I'm proud of you."

"Thank you, Father."

"Captain Jones tells me that you and this girl—Governor Wright's daughter—are getting along quite well."

"I'm in love with her, father. If she'll have me, I plan to ask for her hand tonight."

"Well, congratulations! I might be a grandfather some day after all."

"Not so fast. I still have to get married."

"I'd like to know more about her."

"I'll be off watch at eight bells. I might be able to tell you for certain then."

"I'm supposed to have dinner with Captain Jones at five o'clock—which, as I remember, is 'two bells.' When we're finished, I'll come back up to see."

A few minutes later, David bounded up the ladder to the quarterdeck. Captain Jones was at the taffrail, watching as one of the seamen checked the ship's speed and leeway. He couldn't miss the young man's noisy approach.

"David. Your young lady's already on deck for her evening stroll."
He gave his friend a broad smile. "Are you ready to assume the watch,
or do you need a couple minutes alone with Miss Wright?"

"I'm ready to take the watch, sir. Do you have anything to pass on?"

"Yes, two things. First, we'll be changing course once we pass abeam
Deadman's Cay. I want to head for the southern tip of Andros Island
and then skirt its western coastline as far north as possible. The second
thing has to do with the man-of-war that inspected us on our outward
sail. We've some preparations to make just in case they're still there and
decide to stop us. I'm meeting with all the officers in my cabin at eight
bells. I'll need you there."

"Very well, sir." David gave his captain a crisp salute.

The older man had been gone for no more than three minutes when
Jane wandered aft, waiting for her usual invitation to the quarterdeck.
Neither she nor David had realized that he seemed to always get the
afternoon watch. It was perfect for them because they got to enjoy every
sunset together. John had planned it that way, more to divert Miss
Wright's thoughts from the atrocities she had witnessed than to foster
romance.

"Good evening, Miss Wright!" David tried to appear as mature as
possible. "Have you noticed how beautiful the sunset is tonight?"

"Good evening yourself, Mister Noble. And yes, it is a most
beautiful sunset."

"Mister Noble?" David gave her a frown. "Why are you being so
formal?"

"It's you who's being formal, David. You have been calling me by
my Christian name, but suddenly I'm 'Miss Wright' again?"

"I'm sorry. I'm a little nervous this evening."

"Oh? Is Captain Jones after you about something?"

"No, it's just that..."

"Yes?" Her voice sounded like a kitten purring.

"Why don't you join me up on the quarterdeck?" David offered his
hand.

"Well thank you, kind sir. I'd love to."

David was fascinated with the way she moved. Whereas a man
walked from one place to another with no other purpose than to get
there, Jane somehow made an art of it. It was almost as if she were
stepping to a minuet, the way she glided along. Even her hands grasped
the rail differently from a man's. Before he realized it, she was standing
with her back against his chest, watching the western sky change from

a deep blue to pink as the sun approached the horizon. The sweet smell of her freshly washed hair was overpowering.

"Are you sure you won't get into trouble for having me on the quarterdeck?"

"What?" He was confused. He knew she had just asked him something, but his mind had somehow missed everything but the musical lilt of her voice.

"Won't Captain Jones be angry at you for having me up here while you're on watch?"

"Oh that!" His tone was dismissive. "Don't worry about John. He may be my captain, but he's still my friend."

Satisfied, she reached down and grasped his hand in hers. The sun was now poised at the horizon, ready to make its nightly plunge into the sea. Its lower edge began to distort as it became one with the dark waters, but David missed it all together. He was only concerned with her scent and the closeness of her warm body to his own. They stood like that for several minutes while David gained his courage. Finally, he leaned down and gave her a gentle kiss upon her right temple.

As he opened his eyes, he noticed a reflection from her cheek. "Jane, you're crying."

She wiped the tear away and sniffed.

"Does it still bother you—the things you saw when you were on the Eagle?"

"Of course all of that bothers me, but I'm not crying over that anymore."

"What is it then? Something obviously has you disturbed."

She turned about and placed her hands on his shoulders. More tears had welled in her eyes and began to spill more quickly down her cheeks.

"I'm just so happy I met you, David, and that I'm safe, and that I'm finally going home to Atlanta."

"We're going home to Atlanta, Jane."

She gave him a questioning look. He bent down and kissed her lightly on the lips. He straightened himself and spoke with all the conviction he possessed. "I'm going with you to Atlanta to ask your father for your hand in marriage."

"Oh, David, do you mean it?" She pushed him out to arms length and studied his face carefully. "Do you really mean that?"

"Of course I do. Ask Captain Jones."

"Ask me what?" It was John. David and Jane hadn't noticed that John, joined now by Robert, had tarried on the deck just forward of the mizzen.

"I asked Miss Wright to come up to the quarterdeck. It won't happen again."

"You have the authority to invite anyone up there you please." John walked aft with Robert. They stopped and looked up at the young lovers. "What was it you wanted Miss Wright to ask me?"

"Oh!" He collected himself. "She didn't believe I was serious about wanting to marry her." Jane pinched David's arm, making him jump.

John looked at Jane. "I'd say he's as serious as a man can be, Miss Wright. Why, just this morning he was asking me if I had the authority to perform a marriage at sea."

"Do you?"

David couldn't believe she would be so bold.

"I told him that was a legend, nothing more. I also suggested that it would go much better for both of you if he asked your father's permission first."

"Thank you, Captain Jones." She turned back to David. "Then it is true. You really do love me."

"I wouldn't joke about a thing like that." David gave her another kiss on the lips, not caring that the two older men were watching.

***

Joshua Smoot, Henry Morgan and the ten others had been in the brig for three days and nights when Silver finally ordered their release. The bright sunlight nearly blinded them as their weak legs carried them onto the main deck. They stood for a long moment shading their eyes while they gained their bearings.

"Welcome back from the gates of hell, mates!" John Silver walked aft and stopped face to face with Smoot. "Do you remember me?"

"Aye." Smoot studied the old man from under a shading hand. "You're Jack Bridger, the King's Town tavern-keeper." He looked about the deck. "I was told that Long John Silver was the man who negotiated for Morgan's and my lives. Where is the old devil?"

John Silver spread his arms. "Ya don't see 'im, Joshua?"

Smoot searched the deck. Every crewmember was looking their way. He looked back at the old innkeeper. "I would if I knew what he looked like."

John Silver continued to smile at the two.

Joshua finally realized the obvious. "It's you! You're Long John Silver!"

Henry Morgan stepped forward and pointed at the old man. "I knew that was you in King's Town when we made that deal!"

Silver turned on the lad. "You did not, Henry, no more than Joshua did."

"But—"

Smoot pointed down at Silver's left leg. "Ormerod asked us about John Silver—if he sent us. He asked about a wooden leg. You didn't have that when we met you in King's Town."

Silver raised the peg leg and brought it down hard on the deck. "I had on my articulated leg when we met before. I couldn't let you know it was me because Ormerod would never be in league with the likes of Long John Silver."

Smoot studied the old pirate for a long moment.

"Don't feel bad, Joshua. I've been Jack Bridger for ten years—ever since the King put a price on my head. If the King's men didn't know who I was, how could you expect to see through the disguise?"

"Then—"

"That map you brought back from New York was a nasty trick, so by all rights I shouldn't be givin' ya this." Silver reached into his pocket and pulled out the ring.

"My ring!" Smoot reached for it but Silver pulled his hand back. "How did you get it?"

"Captain Jones gave it to me to give back to you. He told me it was only fitting that you have it." Silver held it up to the sun. "That set me to thinkin'. Just what is it about this stolen ring that's so important to Joshua Smoot?" He turned and looked at Joshua. "Well?"

"I told you in King's Town. I didn't steal it!"

"Do you know what this crest is?"

"All I know is that it was my mother's stick pin, and I had it made into a ring at Porto Bello." Smoot reached out his hand. "It's mine."

Silver handed him the ring, and watched as the younger pirate put it in his teeth and then pushed it onto his left index finger. "She died when I was born. When I sacked Porto Bello, I forced an old Jew to make it into a ring for me. Besides her journal, it's all I have to remember her."

"Are you certain it was your mother's stick pin?"

"Aye!" Joshua gave Silver a questioning look. "Why so much concern for my ring?"

"Oh, nothing." Silver gave a dismissive wave of his hand. "Just my curious nature."

Chapter 19

"Mister Hawkins! Mister Hawkins!" The young midshipman knocked frantically at the junior officer's stateroom. "Lieutenant Hawkins! Captain Stevens wants you on the quarterdeck!"

The young officer laid his pen aside with a huff and slipped on one of his freshly polished boots. He could finish the letter to Christiana later. There probably won't be another packet by for a fortnight anyway.

"Are you there, sir?"

"I'm coming, Walker!" I'm coming!" He opened the door to see that the midshipman was red-faced and sweating. "Good Lord, lad, you really shouldn't run so in this weather. You're asking for a case of heat prostration."

"But, sir, the captain—"

"The captain's always in a rush. Go tell him I'll be along smartly. It's probably a question about my inventory of the weapons locker, or something else of an equally mundane nature. God, but I'm tired of that."

The executive officer stepped into the passageway behind the midshipman. "Lieutenant Hawkins!"

"Yes, sir!" Jim jumped to attention. A stack of novels fell from the desk onto his second boot.

"You've a poor attitude, Mister Hawkins!" The executive officer paused at the ladder. "Yours is not to question the order, but to obey it in a timely manner."

"Sorry for the delay, sir!" Jim reached down and pulled on the second boot. "On my way, sir!" He grabbed his coat and hat and followed the commander up to the main deck. As he squeezed past the executive officer, the older man seized him roughly by the shoulder.

"Look there, Mister Hawkins!" He pointed to the south. "The Silver Cloud's returning! That's why the captain has summoned you, not your weapons report! Go now, and let this be a lesson to you!"

"Aye, aye, sir!" Jim gave a salute and ran aft.

"Up here, lieutenant, and stand at ease!" Captain Stevens strode up and down the quarterdeck, his hands under the skirts of his coat. He stopped and pointed at the approaching ship. "It appears your Dutch friend is returning from Saint Croix with his molasses and sugar." He scanned through the report Hawkins had filed regarding his first inspection of the approaching ship.

"Is there anything wrong with my report, sir?"

"Nothing at all." He handed the report to an aide. "I needn't remind you of the importance of this inspection, do I, Mister Hawkins?"

"No, sir!"

"Good!" The captain turned again to the approaching merchantman. "According to my dispatches, the cannons have not yet been found. If they're aboard the Silver Cloud..."

"I understand, sir. May I assume then, that I'm still to be—"

"Yes you may." He gave a huff. "As I told you and the other junior officers, you'll be able to detect a deception better than someone who's never been aboard that ship. Look for anything different. Anything."

"Yes, sir." The young lieutenant tried to sound as obedient as he could. "I'll go over her like a ferret. If she has the cannons aboard—even one—you can be assured I'll find them."

"The Admiralty is counting on us, Mister Hawkins! Take as many men as you need." Jim saluted and excused himself.

***

As the Silver Cloud approached Andros Island, the HMS Wasp rotated her luffed sails to catch the southwesterly breeze and set a course to intercept the disguised frigate. Within an hour, the two great ships stood to at a hundred yards. Jim had taken four armed marines to assist with the inspection—the standard number for such an assignment. As his boat neared the merchantman, he and the others could hear the sounds of a man being flogged somewhere on the main deck.

"Damn!" The boat bumped against the Cloud's planking, and one of the marines stood to climb the ladder. The young officer caught the man by the sleeve.

"Hold here until they've finished with that poor soul." He looked down at the bottom of his boat. "God, but I hate this ship."

The young British officer and every one of the four marines cringed
with every cry from the man's parched throat. They had been required
to witness the two recent hangings and many similar floggings aboard
the Wasp, but none so prolonged. Finally the screams stopped, but not
the lashes.

"I can't abide it any longer!" Jim stood, grabbed the ladder and put
a foot to a rung. Before he could shift his weight, the fat and sweaty face
of Captain Jan Van Mourik poked rudely over the rail.

"Goot day, sir!" There was a moment of recognition. "Hey, isn't dat
Letenent Harkers down der?"

Jim looked up at the man in anger and disgust.

"Why…it is! It is!"

The young officer hesitated halfway up the ladder, fearing to get too
close to the hideous thing that reached down at him.

"I still got some a' dat goot Scotch whiskey left, an' dis time you
gotta have dat drink with me, ya?" The Dutchman always shouted, even
though Jim was within arms reach.

Jim retreated a rung.

"Hey! Are ya comin' 'board or not, Letenant Harkers?"

"Not until you put an end to that lashing! My God, the man's
unconscious!"

The captain turned away and barked something in Dutch. The
whine of the angry cat stopped.

What happened next was the Woodshoe's own idea for keeping the
young Britisher out of the bilge. With the dexterity of a beached sea
elephant, Dutch sucked a mouthful of bread from a moldy loaf he held.
By the time he had leaned over the rail a second time, the bread was
well saturated with saliva. Taking careful aim, he opened his mouth as
if to speak. The chunk of wet bread glanced off Jim's right shoulder and
landed with a plop amongst the disgusted marines.

"Is done!" Dutch smiled and wiped his mouth with the back of his
sleeve. "You come up now, ja?"

Jim hesitated and looked to the marines for moral support. They sat
with wide eyes and closed mouths.

"Here, take my handt, Mister Harkers!" He switched the bread to
his left hand and extended his right.

"No thank you. I can make it up myself."

Dutch acted crushed for a moment while Jim gained the deck and
made a quick survey of the filthy ship. At Charles Noble's
recommendation, several cages of pigs, goats and chickens had been left
in the warm sun and none of the animal's droppings had been picked

up. The dung and urine had been walked into the decking and tracked fore and aft to each companionway. This, combined with the appearance and smell of the dozen Dutch crewmen topside, made the Englishman want to turn and flee to the safety of his boat.

The young lieutenant forced himself to regain his composure. He placed his left hand on the rail just above the ladder. "How was Saint Croix?"

"Ah...Saint Croix!" While the fat man recollected his supposed escapades at the island, the senseless body of the prisoner was cut loose and allowed to slump to the deck with a thud. "Dat first night—dat's when we soldt all dat cotton—I had three women undt three plates o' ham! Ha! Saint Croix is a goot place to play!"

More by instinct than intent, Jim ran his finger into the dirt-filled grooves of the King's seal he had stamped in the rail on his previous inspection. He glanced down at the deep impression, wondering why it seemed different.

It was different, but only slightly. When it had first been placed in the rail of the other Silver Cloud, Captain Jones had ordered his smith to copy the seal, knowing that this second Silver Cloud—the one carrying the cannons—would have to receive the same inspection marking. True to John's instructions, Dutch did not allow the Englishman to inspect the impression closely.

"I not see ya fer der longest time, ja?" He closed in on the young officer, reaching for the hand at the counterfeit seal. Jim jerked his hand away and stepped sideways past two of his marines, moving beyond the Dutchman's saliva range.

"I don't have any time for visiting, Captain, so if you don't mind, I'd like to get right to your cargo."

"If ye're sure of dat, den here!" Dutch put on his best tone of disappointment. He shoved the cargo manifest and King's order for three hundred tons of molasses and raw sugar at the young officer. Thomas Jefferson and the others had done their work well, even down to the wax seals on the forged documents.

Jim took the documents and pointed to the ladder. "Yes, I'm sure of that! Would you lead the way, please?"

"Oh, poop!" The pouting Dutchman threw the remainder of his bread at the pigs and marched off to the forward companionway. Stopping for a moment at the ladder, he begged his visitor a second time to have just one drink with him. Jim refused.

The gun deck had been carefully prepared for this inspection, just as thoroughly as the main deck. The stacks of muscovado sugar bags covered the cannons, and the molasses casks had been arranged to create two aisles, one to either side of the mainmast. In order to prevent the inspector from leaving either aisle toward the rows of hidden cannons, the casks were pressed close together and stacked two deep with additional bags of sugar on top. While Jim walked quickly through the deck, he occasionally kicked a cask or stuck a sugar bag with his penknife, making sure none of them contained gunpowder. Dutch continued to beg the young officer to stay for a visit, but he steadfastly ignored the invitation.

"I'll see your bilge now, if you please, Captain Van Mourik." Hawkins stopped to read the manifest. As he looked up for the Woodshoe's response, a noise from below caught his attention.

"What was that?" Hawkins took a lanthorn from one of his marines and leaned over the ladder. Something in the darkness below them had moved.

It was one of the remaining Indian fighters, dressed as a Woodshoe and being helped up the ladder by a mate. The man stumbled up the ladder with one arm across his mate's shoulder and the other across his stomach, as if he were sick.

Jim looked at Dutch, then back down at the two men. A stench worse than the animals on the main deck blew upward past the two while they hesitated on the third step below the young officer.

"That man doesn't look very well, Captain Van..." Before Jim could finish, the man vomited directly onto his newly shined boots. Some of the mess ran down onto the ladder and dropped into the bilge far below.

The other crewman shook his fist at his captain and yelled something in Dutch. Hawkins and his four marines beat a quick retreat up the ladder to the main deck and the open air, ignoring the rest of their inspection.

"My God!" Hawkins stamped the vomit from his boots and retreated toward the ladder. "What are you feeding your men?"

"Den you won't be eatin' no lunch wid Cap'n Jan?"

"No, I won't!" The disgusted officer climbed down the ladder as quickly as he could and threw the manifest and sugar order back up to the deck at Dutch's feet. He had intended to impress a second King's seal into the railing next to the first, but decided nobody would ever miss it.

Dutch could barely hold back the laughter. "Oh, please tell Cap'n Jan you don't go now?"

"I'm sorry!" Jim pointed to the Wasp, and his marines shoved away from the disgusting Dutch merchantman. "We do indeed go now!"

As soon as he was back aboard the Wasp, Jim reported to his captain.

"Well, Lieutenant Hawkins? Anything unusual to report?"

"She's exactly what she appears to be, sir. A Dutch merchantman with three hundred tons of molasses and raw sugar destined for the King's distilleries in Charles Town—the same ship I inspected last month. The only cannons she carries are her four swivel guns on her deck."

Captain Stevens gave Jim a squint. "No large cannons at all?"

"None, sir. She wasn't even fitted with gun ports. We laid at her waterline for several minutes before going aboard. I made a close inspection of her planking. It was solid oak from rail to waterline."

"Hmmm." The captain tapped the Admiralty dispatch with his letter opener. "They've probably smuggled them around the other end of Cuba and up the west coast of Florida—maybe into New Orleans. If so, HMS Windsor will most likely intercept them." He looked up at the young officer and realized he was muttering.

"I think you're correct, sir. Yes...I'm certain of it! They must have gone for New Orleans." Jim was relieved that his commanding officer hadn't asked for any further details of the inspection.

"Have a boat take across our outgoing mail for America and tell your Dutch Captain he has my permission to continue."

"Aye, aye, sir!" Hawkins was glad to leave the cauldron, as the other junior officers called the master's cabin. He rushed to his own room and sealed up the partially written letter to his fiancée, along with the four others he had been saving from the captain's scrutiny. He met the mail orderly as the last mailbag was being lowered to the waiting boat and pushed the letters inside. Within half an hour, the mail was aboard the Silver Cloud, and the precious cargo of cannons was once again en route to America.

"Well done!" It was Jim's roommate, Lieutenant Montgomery Mason. At shortly before eight bells, the young officer was dressing for his watch.

"What?" Jim closed the door and stamped his feet.

"The mail! You managed to get your letter off the ship without the Old Man's censorship."

"It was a risk I had to take."

"What were you risking?"

"Christiana's father knows several important men at the Admiralty. I've asked her to see if he can arrange for my transfer."

Montgomery's interest was piqued. "Do you think her father would do that for me if I asked?"

"It's too late, Monty. The letter is already on its way." Jim stepped across to his desk and looked back at the other officer. "Have you ever inspected a Dutch merchantman?"

"No. Can't say as I've had the honor. Why?"

"If you're ever given the option to, refuse. Refuse!" He threw his coat and hat across the room at his bunk, and then sat down at his desk to remove his boots. "Filthy people. I think I'd rather be on a slaver than on a ship like that again!"

"That bad?"

"Monty, you wouldn't believe it!" Jim threw one of his boots, still dripping with seawater, at the other officer. "Look at that! I kicked my foot about in the water all the way back, but there's still vomit along the sole line! Ate the finish right off the leather, it did!" Monty held the boot with his fingertips and then let it fall to the floor. "One of the sailors retched on the deck in front of me, and the others stank so badly of sweat and urine..." He shook his head again and continued. "And that captain! He has to get this close when he talks to you!" Monty backed away from his roommate's face.

"If they're so disgusting, why do we employ them?"

"Politics." Jim pulled on a clean boot. "Politics and greed."

"Well...on that sour note, I'll be leaving you for my watch."

"Filthy people!"

"Too bad you didn't remember the Old Man when you were over there."

"Remember the Old Man?" He gave his roommate a quizzical look.

"Aye. He's always telling us to keep a weather eye for men we can impress into service of the Crown."

A broad smile broke across Jim's face. "Ha! It'd serve the Old Man right to get vomited on now and then."

Monty gave a measured chuckle. "A dose of his own medicine!"

As his roommate departed, Jim sat down to write up his inspection report. He was careful to expound upon the thoroughness with which he had inspected every deck, including the bilge. When the report was finally complete and delivered to the captain, Jim descended the companionway to his stateroom. He prayed silently. Dear Lord, please don't think me selfish for this, but if there's any way, please get me off this ship. I ask this in the name of our Lord and Savior, Jesus Christ. Amen

Three hours later, there was a frantic knocking at the young officer's door.

"Enter!"

It was the same midshipman who had called earlier that day. "You'd best get to the captain's cabin on the double, sir! I've never seen the Skipper and Commander Foster so agitated."

"Both of them?"

The boy nodded.

"What now?" Jim pulled on his other boot and grabbed his coat as several of the other junior officers ran past his door. By the time he had made his way aft, all ten of the others had assembled outside the captain's cabin, speculating about the reason for this latest of so many panic situations.

Jim asked a nearby officer. "Does anybody know what's going on?"

The man gave a shrug. "If you ask me, I'd say the captain's gone mad." Before the lad could finish, Stevens and Foster burst through the door and marched past the startled officers, almost knocking several to the deck.

Captain Stevens stopped halfway up the ladder. "Lieutenant Hawkins! Up here!"

"Sir?" Jim and the others followed up to onto the main deck.

The captain walked to the starboard rail and turned back to the cluster of young officers. "Mister Hawkins, would you tell me and the other officers what that is?" He was pointing to the departing Silver Cloud, now at least two leagues to the northwest and under full sail.

"Why, it's the Silver Cloud, sir! I just inspected her and then sent her on her way, as you ordered."

"Well, then, what's that?" The captain swept his arm in a great arc toward the southeast and stopped on an approaching ship.

Less than ten miles away was what appeared to be an exact duplicate of the ship he had just inspected, and following the same route toward the HMS Wasp.

"She looks like the Silver Cloud, sir." Jim spun about to the departing ship to make sure. He looked back to the approaching ship again. "But that can't be."

"And what do you propose we do about her, Mister Hawkins?"

Jim was confused, and sensed that Captain Stevens was setting him up for something.

Monty answered for Jim. "Shouldn't we detain and inspect her, sir, just as we did…that first one?"

The captain held his arms up as if signaling in semaphore. "Thank you, Mister Mason, for that inspired suggestion!" He turned and stepped to within six inches of Monty's nose. "And since you seem to know exactly what to do, why don't you accompany your roommate to find out what the hell's going on here, unless that's too taxing for your young brain?"

"No it isn't, sir!"

Commander Foster leaned close. "I'll have the gunners man their cannons."

"We're a man-of-war, aren't we?" The captain made the question as sarcastic as he could. "Unless you'd like to meet them unarmed."

Commander Foster gave his captain a questioning look.

"Select a dozen marines to go with you, Lieutenant Hawkins, and if there's anything amiss, even a sick crewman, fire a warning shot."

"Aye, aye, sir!" Jim took his roommate by the arm and descended to the main deck.

As the treasure ship approached within cannon range and began spilling her sails, the inspection boat shoved away from the windward side of the HMS Wasp.

***

"What a day!" Monty released the tiller of the ship's boat long enough to wrap and buckle his sword belt about his waist. "Up until a few minutes ago, the captain seemed to like me."

"Don't blame me. As I see it, you got yourself into this one without anybody else's help."

The twelve marines acted as if they didn't hear the conversation between the two young officers.

Monty shook his head in disgust. "I've two more reports due before I turn in tonight, and I'll no sooner get back from this stupid inspection and I'll have to take the forward watch." He adjusted the sword and straightened his coat. "There. How do I look?"

Jim was studying this second Silver Cloud, but he flashed a glance at his fellow officer. "You look fine, Monty. If this is anything like my first inspection, your concerns for your uniform will be as the Good Book says—casting pearls before swine."

"You expect another Dutch crew?"

"I don't know what to expect." Jim looked back at Monty and shrugged. "Something very strange is going on here, and—"

"You think there'll be trouble, don't you?"

"Something was different about that first ship, but for the life of me, I can't put my finger on it."

"Well, you'll get no argument from me, Jim." Monty pulled his musket and checked that it was loaded and primed. "Why are there two of them? Why has this second one driven straight for the Wasp and then furled her sails and heaved to, almost as if she were asking to be inspected?"

They had covered only a quarter of the distance from their ship when the strange merchantman's upper rigging began to throw shadows across the small boat. As they neared the lee waterline and the waiting ladder, Jim turned to the marines. "I want every man of you to be especially alert once we get aboard. I'm sure each of you realizes that we're not here to simply inspect this ship's cargo, but her captain and crew as well." The marines nodded their understanding.

Jim climbed the ladder cautiously and was assisted over the bulwarks by two large Negro seamen. One by one, the marines began to follow, but much too slowly for Jim's liking. As he waited for the others, his hand went instinctively to the King's inspection seal in the rail. It had been impressed from the deck side of the bulwark, as was proper. Jim suddenly realized what was different about the seal on the other Silver Cloud. It had been impressed backwards, as if the man holding the iron were standing in mid-air, outside the rail. And then there was the small groove where a sliver of wood had been torn from the seal.

"What's the matter, Jim?" Monty was still in the back of the boat far below. He was the last in line for the ladder, and there were still seven marines in the boat ahead of him.

"Do you remember the infection I got last month from the splinter under my thumb nail?"

"How could I forget? You whined about it for a full week."

Jim tapped the rail. "Here's the spot that splinter came from."

"But that can't..." Monty suddenly realized what his friend had discovered. It was clear that this was the ship Jim had inspected a month earlier. The one he had inspected earlier in the day was its twin, yet the crew from this ship was now sailing away to the north on that twin, toward the American colonies.

Jim scanned the fifty-odd crewmen who had been collecting on the deck. None of them were Woodshoes, but rather Englishmen and Negro slaves—and far too many for a merchant vessel. Then he spotted the major damage to the far bulwarks. The gunwale was destroyed for a twelve-foot span amidships, with a nasty gouge in the decking at the center of the broken rail. He had seen this type of damage only once before. It had been caused by a collision at sea with another ship of equal size—one ship had been sailed directly into the other. While he wondered after the damage, a very tall Englishman dressed in some sort of officer's uniform approached him.

"Greetings, Mister Hawkins!" The tall man offered his right hand. Being a gentleman himself, Jim accepted it without hesitation, an act he would soon regret.

"Greetings, sir." He gave a quick glance to the rail where only two of the marines had gained the deck. He wished Monty had followed immediately behind him and that more of the marines were aboard.

The tall Englishman's tone was disarming—almost hypnotic. "You'll be wanting to inspect our cargo of course, but first, my captain desires your presence in his cabin." Jim struggled slightly to free his right hand—his sword and pistol hand—but the other man held him firmly and led him aft through the other white-skinned sailors and black Jamaicans who infested this strange ship.

Jim called back. "Monty! If I'm not back in ten minutes, come after me!" He wasn't sure whether his fellow officer had heard his cry for help, but he knew the marines had. While he being pulled down the ladder and into the companionway toward the master's cabin, he realized a second anomaly.

"How do you know my name?"

His captor ignored the question as he pushed open the master's door.

"Come in, Lieutenant Hawkins!" The voice was strangely familiar.

Jim's hand was released and he was pushed roughly through the door. He searched the cabin from starboard to larboard, finding only one other man. He was bent over the great table, pushing a line of farthings across a chart of the Caribbean toward a gold pocket watch. The chart had a course drawn in red from the Bahamas to the southern tip of Florida, and then straight to the Mississippi delta.

Jim stooped over slightly to get a look at the man's face, but to no avail. He was an older man, judging by the color of his hair, with large, leathery features and skin burned as dark as mahogany by too many days in the sun.

A single shove to the back by the tall officer sent Jim stumbling forward, into the table. He spun about and grabbed at where his pistol should hang in its holster. It was gone. He turned to the man at the table.

"I'm Lieutenant James Hawkins of His Majesty's Ship Wasp. I demand to know the meaning of this treatment."

Without looking up, the man held up his left hand in a gesture of "Wait!", and then gave the coins a final push. Pleased that the last coin had touched the pocket watch, he brought his hands together at the center of the chart, fingertips to fingertips. There was something familiar in the way he interlaced his fingers one by one. Without saying a word, the old man raised his head and gave the lad a wink.

At first there was no recognition. The ten years since their last meeting had changed the old pirate as much as it had changed the young British officer. Jim stood not six feet away, but it might as well have been a hundred, for he still did not know who he was looking at. And then the old man spoke.

"Well scuttle me if it be none other'n me old ship mate, Jimmy Hawkins! Har! Har! Har!"

"Long John Silver?" Jim whispered in amazement and shock. In a strange way he was thrilled to see his old friend again. Even so, he drew a small pistol from his right boot, pulled back the flint and aimed it at the old pirate.

John Silver was using his best scupper talk on the lad, for old times' sake. "Aye, Jimmy, 'tis a sweet reunion, it is, exceptin' ye're 'bout to put a ball betwixt yer old shipmate's eyes." Silver leaned back and laced his fingers behind his head. "Are ya certain, lad, that ya wants to do such a thing to yer old shipmate?"

Jim looked down at his hand. Sure to the old man's words, the pistol was cocked and pointed between the snow-white eyebrows. For a moment he had forgotten why he was aboard this strange ship, but then it came back to him. He turned and yelled. "Marines! Arrest this man!"

The three men waited for nearly a minute before the cabin door pushed open. Without lowering his pistol, Jim turned his head for a quick look, hoping to see several of his uniformed men. Instead, the tall officer stepped out and was replaced by two other pirates. One was a young man about Jim's age, with carrot-red hair and emerald-green eyes. The other was in his late thirties, with his right wrist bandaged tightly.

"Lower yer pistol, Jimmy." John Silver spoke in a fatherly tone. "It'll do ya no good ta resist. An' besides, a fine lad what's life's been saved so many times shouldn't go shootin' the one what did all the savin' now, should he?" Silver's soothing tone had an almost hypnotic effect on the young officer. Against his best judgment and all his military training, he allowed the old pirate to reach across the table and remove the pistol from his hand. While Silver did so, the red-haired lad removed Jim's dirk and sword from their sheaths.

"There now, that's better fer us all." Silver studied the small pistol carefully while he lowered the flint to the half-cocked notch. "Ye've taken' good care of it, Jimmy, just like old Long John learned ya."

"How'd you know it was me?"

"Why, Jimmy, I seen ya through me spyglass as ye were pullin' across to us."

"But how did you know I was even on the Wasp?"

Silver leaned forward. "By yer letters."

"My letters?"

"Haven't ya never heard of the Admiralty mail?" Silver pulled three envelopes from the same drawer and then pushed it closed. "Which reminds me. I believe these are yours."

"Mine?" Jim took the letters. "These are from Christiana! How...?" He looked up at the pirate.

"I figured we'd be seein' each other sooner'n you could get 'em by postal packet, so I brought 'em along from King's Town. Why, most of what makes its way out to the Kings men-o'-war passes through John Silver's hands first. Didn't it seem a little unlikely yer ship'd get assigned back to the Bahamas so soon after it were ordered moved to New Orleans?"

Jim pointed at John Silver. "You sent those dispatches to Captain Stevens!"

"Aye, an' the one about the cannons, also. A pretty piece o' forgery now, wasn't it?" Silver brightened. "Oh! My congratulations on your recent promotion. I couldn't be prouder if you was me own son!"

By now, the young officer was near a rage. "I was right! Those were your initials on my commission!"

Silver gave the lad a toothy grin and a nod.

"And you've got the cannons and powder we're supposed to stop!"

"Wrong, lad, by about six hours!" Silver gave a chuckle. "I've got the treasure that Robert Ormerod hid twenty years ago on Dead Man's Chest! That other Silver Cloud had the cannons—the one your officers inspected and passed through earlier today."

"Oh, my God." Jim looked out the rear windows toward the departing ship. "I was the inspecting officer."

"Then ya disappoint me, lad."

"I'll take the responsibility for my error, but why would you send a dispatch out to the British about the shipment of cannons? I don't understand."

"I only told the Wasp, Jimmy."

"Did you intend that we discover them?"

"Didn't matter one way or the other."

"But why not just let them get through to the colonies?"

"Because it added the authenticity I needed to fool yer captain." Silver pushed himself up from his chair and stumped his way to the starboard windows. Leaning his hip against the sideboard, he studied the British frigate as the two ships drifted closer. He turned back to his young friend.

Silver looked down and patted his left thigh. "What do ya think of me stump, Jimmy?"

"I don't care about your peg leg."

"But you always told me I should have one."

"I told you that I don't care about it!"

"You should see the one my carpenter's repairin' fer me, Jimmy. It looks like a real leg, and the knee even bends."

"The dispatch to Captain Stevens. I don't understand. How was it supposed to fool my captain?"

"Your Captain Stevens would be so excited over the prospect of capturing a thousand cannons bound for the American colonies that he wouldn't think twice 'bout bein' ordered back to Andros Island, now would he?"

"But why the Wasp?"

"I wanted to see you again, Jimmy."

"You're mad, John Silver!" The others burst into laughter. Jim turned about. "And who are these two?"

"Why that's none other'n Captain Fishbone Smoot, now missin' his right flipper, he is." Silver made a hook of his index finger and wiggled it at Smoot. "True to his oath, he lost his hand rather than surrender his sword in a fight." Silver threw his dirk across the room. It stuck in the deck between Morgan's feet. "An' that's Henry Morgan from Tortuga. He helped me with my sea chest a few days after Ben Gunn released me from the Hispaniola."

Jim eyed the two suspiciously while they joined John Silver at the starboard windows.

Silver watched the Wasp with fixed attention. "Answer me somethin', Jimmy."

"What?"

"What ya doin' in uniform aboard a man-o'-war? Seems I 'member you sayin' that once ya reached Bristol, ye'd never set foot 'board a ship again."

"I never intended to, but when all this trouble with the colonies—
"

He was cut off by a series of ten explosions to starboard that rocked the great vessel.

"What was that?" Jim ran to the windows. Nothing could be seen for the white smoke that hung between the ships. "Why would they attack before my men and I could get off your ship?"

"Har! Har! That were the sound I been waitin' fer, Jimmy." Silver pointed. "Take a look at yer fine little man-o'-war now."

The Wasp hadn't fired upon the Silver Cloud, but rather the other way around. It was this supposedly unarmed merchantman that had leveled a perfect ten-gun broadside at His Majesty's Ship Wasp. When the smoke cleared enough to see the British ship, men were already abandoning it by the tens. Both the main and mizzenmasts, and all their yards and tackle, had crashed to the deck and into the water on the near side of the ship. There was no use for the panicked crew to try cutting the debris clear from the guns, because thick black smoke and flames were already billowing from all but the two of the forward gun ports.

While the four watched from the safety of John Silver's cabin, three more explosions sent a shower of chain plates and pieces of oak into the air about the two great ships. And as if the fate of the Wasp weren't already obvious to all hands, the ship's drummer began to beat out the abandon ship order.

"You devil!" Jim screamed and spun about on John Silver. He grabbed at his empty sword sheath. "What have you done?"

Silver spoke as if he had accomplished a great act of charity. "Why, I just paid back a long-owed debt to me good friend, Jimmy Hawkins, I did."

"Paid back a debt?"

Jim looked back to his ill-fated ship to watch more of his shipmates leap into the churning sea. "What are you talking about?" Jim pointed at his burning ship. "I never did anything like that to you!"

"Oh, Jimmy." Silver held a hand to his chest in mock pain. "Ye wound me to the marrow, ya do. I'm not payin' ya back fer some hurt ya did me, 'cause ye're right. Ya never did any such thing." Silver stepped to Jim's side and laid a large hand on the lad's shoulder.

Jim pulled away in revulsion.

"This is fer tellin' Cap'n Smollet he could trust old John Silver to the care o' Ben Gunn while you four went ashore at Puerto Plata to arrange me hangin'." He gave a laugh. "If ya hadn't done that bit o' fast talkin' fer yer old shipmate, he'd 'a been crab food ten years ago!"

"But you've attacked my ship! You've killed all those men!"

"Aye!" Silver looked across the water, admiring the wonderful job his gunners had done. "But I've saved yer life, Jimmy, an' that makes us square again, don't it?"

"You're insane!" Jim searched the cabin for another weapon. "I demand to be released, this instant!"

Henry pointed at the Wasp. "He wants ta swim fer it with the rest of 'im, Govn'r. Why don't ya let 'im?"

"Because the lad comes with me, that's why!" Silver advanced on the red-headed lad. "If anybody swims, it'll be you, Morgan!" The young pirate backed a step away as John Silver turned back to his young friend.

"Ya might as well get used to these two, Jimmy, 'cause ye'll be seein' plenty of 'em for the next week."

"'The next week'?"

"Aye, lad." John Silver walked to the map and gave it a tap. "At least until we reach New Orleans."

***

Following John Silver's chart, the treasure ship sailed due west for the passage between Long Key and Grassy Key, and then turned northwest to hug close along the western coast of Spanish Florida. At first, Jim refused to speak at all to Joshua Smoot or his young mate, Henry Morgan. But on the third day following the attack on the HMS Wasp, he was drawn into Silver's discussion with the two concerning what had happened at Dead Man's Chest and Flint's Island. It was a fascinating tale, and impossible to believe except for Smoot's freshly severed right hand and the treasure in the ship's specially built vault.

Jim was a privileged prisoner, with free run of the ship. John Silver tried to convince his young friend several times to take a turn at the helm, but Jim had refused, saying it would amount to treason against the Crown to cooperate in any way with the pirates.

When the Silver Cloud, paralleling the coast, passed from the waters off West Florida to those of East Florida, the crew began to notice the first hints of an approaching storm. The weather front came upon their ship gradually, beginning with a darkening sky and a light rain. It was spawned somewhere in the Pacific Ocean near the equator, and had crossed land at the Yucatan Peninsula, gaining both moisture and power while it moved northeast through the Gulf of Mexico.

John Silver stepped next to the young officer. "She looks like a bad one, Jimmy, and I predict we'll be taking in the canvas to a storm reef by noon. I hope you feel different about helping us out, especially if this breeze takes the course I expect her to."

Jim acted as if he hadn't heard the old pirate, for he was adamant about not assisting the crew. He pulled the collar of the borrowed jacket high around his ears and continued to study the nearby coastline and the roughening waters ahead.

"Tell me when you change yer mind, Jimmy." The old man clapped a hand to the lad's shoulder. "When you do, you know where to find me." The old pirate turned and began to stump aft across the main deck.

Jim turned and called out to him. "Tell me what you did with Lieutenant Montgomery and my marines, and I might consider it."

The old man stopped and turned. "Ye'd blackmail yer old shipmate? Ye'd give him an ultimatum after he's done so much for ya?"

Jim shook his head. "It's not blackmail or an ultimatum. It's give and take. You tell me what I want to know and I'll help you sail your ship."

Silver stumped back to his young friend. "After things settled down, their weapons were taken and they were set adrift in their boat."

"If I find out that you—"

"Don't worry, Jim!" A heavy gust of wind nearly knocked the two to the deck. They clung to each other for a moment. "Your marines were pullin' their fellow crewmen from the ocean as we sailed away." Silver gave him a smile. "Let's go, Jimmy. We've a ship to sail."

It was a little before noon when the order was given to lower the yards for furling the massive square sails. Jim watched the sailors scramble aloft by teams, taking on one great sail after another.

Silver stepped away from the helmsman and called to Jim, spreading his arms in a gesture of invitation. "Come on, Jimmy! Come up on the quarterdeck with yer old shipmate!"

"If you need one more crewman so badly, why don't you ask Captain Smoot to take the helm?"

"I would lad, but that missing hand's got his whole body afflicted with the chills."

"What about Morgan? He knows how to sail, doesn't he?"

"He does, but I wouldn't trust nothin' more valuable than a bilge rat to the boy." Silver paused to yell an order to several of the sailors who'd begun to secure the aft hatch. "I need ya, Jimmy, an' you promised you'd help me!"

Jim stood for several minutes watching John Silver struggle to hold his position on the slippery deck. The sawyer who had fabricated the peg leg had covered its end with leather, which lacked the traction he needed against the wet deck.

Jim still didn't believe John Silver's claim about his friend and the marines. "I'll be below in my cabin!" He turned and dropped down the ladder to the main deck and entered the officer's companionway. Several crewmen stood in the passage, as if hiding from the weather. The men gave the young officer a queer look as he stepped past them.

Jim stopped. "What are you men doing here? Why aren't you at your sailing stations?"

"We were ordered below to secure a loose cannon, sir."

The ship lurched, throwing Jim against the bulkhead. "Then be about it or I'll report you to your captain."

The worst part of the storm was now upon John Silver's treasure ship. Jim had felt only one other storm this severe, and that time they were well to sea, rather than near a coastline. The water on the main deck had built to a point that the sea flowed in a steady torrent down the ladder and into the passageway where Jim and the three sailors stood. As he steadied himself against the aft mast, there was a tremendous cracking and ripping sound above. Something large had broken loose and crashed to the deck. While Jim turned to climb the ladder, but something cracked him on the head, dropping him to the deck unconscious. That was the last thing Jim Hawkins remembered of the Silver Cloud before he was found adrift on the piece of broken ship's decking.

Chapter 20

The cannon ship had put a dozen leagues between itself and the Wasp. John and his officers stood about the quarterdeck with glasses of rum to toast their success.

John walked up to Charles. "Well, Mister Noble, what do you think of our Dutch captain's performance back there?"

Charles and the real crew of the Silver Cloud, hidden as they were, had seen some and heard all of Dutch's charade. "If I were that young lieutentant, I'd have been off the ship in half the time!" He laughed and shook his head. "And that man who vomited on his boots! A talent like that could be worth a lot of money under the proper circumstances."

"These were the proper circumstances." John chuckled. "It's a good thing your brother didn't meet up with that man-of-war—vomiting crewman or none."

"Ease up, Captain Jones. I know you're offended by the way my brother and I used you. But you'll have to admit that he's probably done more for the Americans than any other single man."

"If he'd have just approached me honestly, I'm certain we could have reached an agreement."

"I doubt that."

"Oh?"

"Even I was against his fantastic plan at first."

"Most anybody would be against it."

"But even if you had been told, and you had agreed to be a part of it—do you honestly believe Robert Ormerod and your group of statesmen would have joined forces with a pirate?"

John could see that the merchant was correct, but didn't want to give in yet. "Not even for the sake of the colonies?"

"No, Captain Jones, not even for that. The times and circumstances were right, but the people were not. John Silver did it the only way it could have been done."

"I suppose you're right." John walked to the aft rail and peered at the shrinking war ship. "If that Lieutenant Harkers only knew how close he came—"

Charles corrected him. "His name is Lieutenant James Hawkins, and according to my brother, he's the very lad who was with John Silver on the expedition to Flint's Island ten years ago."

"Oh?" John smiled, continuing watching the man-of-war. "Wouldn't that have been ironic if it were the other Silver Cloud, rather than us, that was stopped by the Wasp? John Silver and Jim Hawkins back together again after a full decade."

"It's an amusing thought, sir, but hardly possible. John Silver's smarter than to get within twenty miles of a British warship, especially with that treasure in his lazarette. If his winds blow fair, I'd expect him to be unloading our treasure in King's Town by tomorrow afternoon."

"You actually trust that old pirate to split the booty with you?"

"Of course I do. He's my brother."

"Brother or not, I've seen men closer than you two turn on each other over a hundredth part of that treasure."

"Well, that's my concern, isn't it?"

"That it is, sir. That it is."

Nearly six hours after the Silver Cloud had been inspected by Lieutenant Hawkins, the top watch reported a column of black smoke astern—from the area of Andros Island.

John called back to the man. "Can you see what's burning?"

"It's too dark to make it out, sir, but my guess is that it's just a brush fire on the island!"

John gave a short look through his spyglass. "Well, it's none of our concern."

***

By dusk the next day, the Silver Cloud had reached Biscayne Bay and turned to a close parallel of the coastline, just as they had done during their passage through the Bahamas. Further north, as they passed the occasional river mouth, the muddy waters that spilled into the Atlantic testified to a very large storm somewhere inland—the same storm that had crossed paths with John Silver and Jim Hawkins on the opposite side of Spanish Florida. Four days later, the familiar coastline of South Carolina began to pass abeam.

The Cloud was still several leagues short of her destination when two merchantmen flying British colors took up an intercept course. Maneuver as he did, John could not avoid an encounter.

He turned to his young friend. "I know they are only merchantmen, but their persistence bothers me, David. Order the guns manned."

"But, shouldn't we—" Before David could make his suggestion, the lead ship hoisted a string of banners identifying itself as belonging to Alexander Forrestal.

John gave a laugh of relief. "Well, I'll be. It looks as though our benefactor has arranged a welcoming party for us."

Two glasses later, a long boat pulled across to the Silver Cloud with a written message.

Dear Captain Jones:
Given that you are reading this letter, you have returned with the prize. These two merchantmen will provide the distraction you may need to get past the blockade at the mouth of our fine harbor. I look forward to your present arrival.
With sincere and humble appreciation, I remain
A. Forrestal

The top watch called down to the helm. "Charles Town, one point off the larboard bow!" By now, every man aboard—including the officers—was suffering from what sailors call channel fever—that restlessness that always sets in during the last few days before a long journey's end. They all had pooled their money to bet on the day and hour they would first spot their destination. The one hundred forty pounds went to one of the surgeon's mates, but nobody really cared who won—their greatest reward was to finally reach home. It was as if the Lord Himself had reached down and touched the crew the moment the familiar coastline and Fort Sullivan was first spotted, for every man's spirit seemed to come alive at the same moment. Within six hours, their feet would once again touch America and their arms would hold their loved ones.

Shortly after noon on the 16th of June, 1775, the Silver Cloud rounded close abeam Hadrell's point, and trimmed for the larboard reach to the Forrestal yards on the north shore of Charles Town. The two British naval ships protecting the harbor were completely engaged by Forrestal's decoys, allowing the disguised frigate to slip past, unmolested. Several small fishing boats returning from the open sea joined the Silver Cloud on her larboard reach across the harbor toward her berth, creating a small parade for the returning ship.

Alexander Forrestal's carriage waited at the dock while the frigate backed her sails and threw across her first hawser.

John was the first on the gangway. "Good afternoon, Mister Forrestal!" He held Alex's letter in his raised hand. "Thank you for the reception at sea!"

"You're welcome, Captain Jones! That was my lovely wife's idea!" The elderly shipbuilder brushed away the helping hands of his footman and limped forward from his carriage.

"Then I'll thank Mistress Forrestal myself!" John trotted down the gangway to the steady planking of the dock, followed closely by his other officers. "Ah, it's good to be home!"

Alex gave John a handshake and a fatherly hug, followed by similar greetings to Robert, Ben and David. He turned and looked at Charles and the young girl. "Who are these two?"

David took Jane's hand and stepped forward to the old man. "Jane, this is our benefactor, Alexander Forrestal. Mister Forrestal, this is my— I mean, our...uhh...passenger, Jane Wright." David's feelings for Jane were written across his face.

Alex took Jane's hand and kissed it. "I'm very pleased to meet you, Miss Wright." He continued to hold her hand as he addressed David. "How did you manage to acquire a passenger in your travels, especially such a lovely one?"

"It's a long story, sir." David turned and gestured toward his father. "Mister Forrestal, this is my father, Charles Noble."

"Charles Noble?" Alex gave the middle-aged man a perplexed look.

Charles accepted the aged man's hand. "You're wondering why I'm here, rather than back in King's Town dividing the treasure?"

"Yes I am, sir. I am quite delighted to meet you, but this is very unexpected."

"My brother—who is also my business associate—insisted I come to meet with you. I'll return to King's Town as soon as my business here is concluded."

"Your business?"

Charles held out the package to Alex.

"Is that for me?"

"Yes it is, sir, but my instructions were explicit that I present it to you and your wife together."

Alex had already started to open the package. "If it has waited this long to be opened, I suppose a few minutes longer won't hurt." He turned to John. "General Gage has taken Boston hostage, and with his superior sea power, the situation has become desperate. Several colonies have sent troops to besiege the city. I dare say your cannons have never been needed more." He gave a raise of his grey brows. "Shall I assume that you have them?"

John nodded. "Yes, and for the sake of Boston, I pray we're in time." "Wonderful!"

John gave the old man a toothy grin. "And they're the most beautiful weapons I've ever seen."

"And do the carronades fire as well as we had hoped?"

John nodded. "Aye! We fired several rounds at a shore target a dozen leagues south of here, and my gunners couldn't believe how accurate they are. Hitting your mark is no longer a matter of luck."

Robert gave John a nudge. "So it shouldn't be necessary to lash your enemy to your rail with grappling hooks."

"Lashed to your rail?" Alex looked to the Silver Cloud.

"Aye, but it was the other Silver Cloud that was damaged that way."

"How? Where?" The old man hungered for a new sea story.

"We sank the Tiburon and captured the pirate captain Joshua Smoot."

"How delightful!" Alex searched the deck for the prisoner. "And what about the treasure?" He turned and searched the bay for another ship. "Where's the Eagle?"

"Captain Steele went back to Saint Croix with part of my crew, sir."

"What on earth for?"

"To rescue his men from a sugar plantation where they were made slaves."

"Slaves?" Alex was too excited to comprehend anything at the moment.

"That's where we found Miss Wright."

"You found this lovely girl at a sugar plantation?"

"We found her on the Eagle, sir, but..." John paused. "As David told you, sir, it's a long and complicated story, best told over some good Scotch whiskey, after dinner." He noticed a large group of men approaching along the dock. "Who are they, sir, and why are they looking at us so strangely?"

"Oh." The shipbuilder released Jane's hand and turned about. "Those are my men. They're going to move the Silver Cloud up the river to one of my older yards to unload the cannons. I've several warehouses where we'll store them until they can be distributed." The old man considered John's second question and continued. "Their odd look is because none of them expected you to get through the blockade."

"Without your two decoys, I don't believe we would have."

Alex smiled. "Yes...but I want to know about this pirate captain. Is he still aboard or did you already hang him?"

"No, sir. He isn't."

"He hasn't been hung, or he's not aboard?"

"Neither."

"But I was hoping—"

"We had to give him away with the treasure."

"To whom? Why would you give him away?"

John laughed. "We'll tell you all about it after dinner, along with the rest of our adventures." He looked about at the Silver Cloud. "But before I leave the ship, sir, I've a crew to see to." John pulled the lanyard with the key to the ship's lazarette from his shirt and turned back to Alex. "There was extra treasure...enough to split with the crews of the Eagle and Silver Cloud."

"Wonderful!" He stepped to John and caught his sleeve. "Please, Captain Jones. My men will take charge of the ship and see to it that everything is properly taken care of. We've set up one of my warehouses for your crew, and you'll have all day tomorrow to deal with them." He pointed to the carriage. "I promised my wife that I would bring all of you to the house the moment you were off the ship."

John hesitated.

"Trust me, Captain Jones. Everything will be taken care of."

Ten minutes later, the carriage rolled to an easy stop at the front steps of the Forrestal mansion. Anne Forrestal had watched their approach and waited patiently at the top of the stairs.

"I was right, wasn't I, Alex?" She called to her husband. "It is the Silver Cloud!"

"Yes it is, dear!" The footman helped the aged man to the ground ahead of the others. "We'll be having six guests for dinner."

"Splendid!" She studied each man as he stepped from the carriage. The last out of the carriage were Ben Gunn and Charles Noble. Anne descended the steps to Alex and nodded toward Charles. "Alex. Who is that man?"

Charles stopped several steps below the porch, and she walked forward to meet him. There was something about his face. It was the same peculiar cut of his nose and the way his mouth curled up slightly at the corners that had caught her attention several months earlier when she first met his son, David.

"This is Charles Noble of Noble Shipping in King's Town. He's David's father." Alex turned back to Charles. Mister Noble, this is my wife and best friend, the first lady of Charles Town—Anne Forrestal."

"I'm very pleased to meet you, ma'am." He took her hand. "David's told me so much about you and your husband and the splendid time he spent with you in April that I feel as if I already know you."

"Thank you, Mister Noble." She studied his face. "We enjoyed David more than either of you could know."

"Oh!" Charles remembered the package under his arm. "This is for you and your husband. My brother gave strict instructions that you open it together."

"For us?" She looked at Alex and back to Charles. "What is it?"

"I wasn't told." He handed the package to her. "I've an idea it has something to do with our shipping companies, but I wouldn't want to be presumptive."

She turned the package over several times. "Your brother? Who is he? What's his name?"

"He goes by Jack Bridger, but that's not his real name, ma'am. He asked that I not disclose his true identity until after you've opened the package."

She began to pull at the knot, and then looked back at the four men waiting near the front door. Someone was missing. She looked about. "Where's David?" She searched the porch and looked to Charles. "Did he go back to King's Town already?"

"No." Charles pointed back at the carriage. "He's with us, but pre-occupied." He took several steps back toward the carriage and called. "David!"

"Coming, Father!" The youth stepped down onto the cobblestone driveway. He turned back and reached inside the carriage. "I was just speaking with Jane." Taking David's hand, the young girl stepped to the ground.

"Who's the young woman, Captain Jones?" Anne handed the package to Alex and stepped toward the approaching couple.

John followed. "This is Jane Wright, the daughter—"

"You're Governor Wright's daughter! My Lord, girl...we'd given you up for dead when word reached us that you'd been kidnapped! How—"

David smiled. "We rescued her, ma'am. You should have seen it! It was—"

"You need a bath and new clothes, you poor dear!" Anne quickly gauged the girl's dress size, then turned back to David. "I apologize for cutting you off, but there will be plenty of time later to tell us all about it." She called to a servant near the front door. "Nelly! Warm a bath for Miss Wright and set out one of my dresses in the second guest room! Make it that light blue one with the lace…the one I wore to the Andersons' last month!"

Jane gave a nervous laugh. "I appreciate your kind offer, Mistress Forrestal, but have spent more than a week with these gentlemen and I insist on being present while they tell their stories, and especially when you open the package from Long John Silver."

"Long John Silver?" Anne looked back at Charles. "Oh my!"

Alex clapped his hands. "Well, there's no point in standing about out here. Shall we adjourn to the library and pour that Scotch?"

"Aye!" It was Robert. "And I would enjoy a glass of Madeira, if you have any, sir."

"That's a woman's drink, Robert! You want a man's drink like Scotch or Irish whiskey."

Minutes later, everyone was in the library with a serving of his favorite beverage.

"Gentlemen!" Alex stepped to the fireplace and raised his glass. "To the Colonies! To Liberty! To no king but King Jesus!"

The others repeated the toast and downed their drinks.

Alex ushered John to an overstuffed chair next to the fireplace and pulled another up close beside it. "Sit here, John. While Edward refills our glasses, you can begin telling me your story. I've never met a real pirate, except once in New York at a dinner party when I was just a lad. Now, tell me all about this Joshua Smoot!" He reconsidered. "No! Start at the beginning—when you left Charles Town in the Silver Cloud."

"Well, as you know, we left your docks in early April and set course for…"

"I know all of that!" Alex patted John's arm like an impatient child. "Get to the exciting parts!"

Robert and the others burst into laughter. "Tell him about arriving at Dead Man's Chest, John. That's when things really—" But Anne cut him off.

"Excuse my interruption, Mister Ormerod, but Miss Wright will never get to her bath and clean clothes unless we open John Silver's package." She scanned the room and spotted the package on the end table next to David. "Alex?"

"But Captain Jones was just about to tell me..." He stopped and gave the other men a look of husbandly despair. "We do have all evening for that, I suppose." Alex stood with a wince of pain. "Oh, there is one matter I must address before I attend to my wife's request, Captain Jones."

"Sir?"

The old man pulled two rolled and sealed parchments from his desk drawer and handed one to John and the other one to David.

"What's this?" John broke the wax seal.

"It's what you went on your adventure for, young man." Alex gave John a broad smile. "It's our offer of a permanent commission as a lieutenant in the Continental Navy."

David held up his parchment. "Then he's formed the navy?"

Alex shook his head. "There are a lot of details to be worked out yet, especially the necessary funding for ships. Personally, I believe it will be late in the summer or early fall. I'm not privy, mind you, to everything that Mister Jefferson is doing, but I do know about the ships."

"What's to happen to the Silver Cloud, sir?"

"She'll be fitted with two dozen cannons on her main deck and be renamed the Raleigh, provided we get the necessary funding."

John touched the old man's arm. "What about all the privateers? Couldn't they be commissioned right now?"

"They're already fighting, Captain Jones. But Mister Jefferson assures me that he'll find the necessary capital for real frigates."

"Alex?" It was Anne. "John Silver's package!"

"Yes, Dear." He pushed himself up with a groan and took a step toward the hallway. He stopped and looked back at his guest, trying to remember. "Oh, yes! Mister Jefferson is on his way to Philadelphia. He has asked that as soon as you and David can manage it, you meet with him there. He wants a full report of the expedition, and he needs help in forming the navy."

John looked to David and back to Alex. "We can leave tomorrow, sir, just as soon as we finish dividing the treasure with the crew."

"Let's not be too hasty, Captain Jones. I want to hear your story before you tell it to Mister Jefferson."

"As you please, sir. I will be delayed along the way to Philadelphia anyway, as I've an important appointment in Virginia."

Anne stepped to the fireplace mantle and picked up a delicate letter. "If your delay happens to be at the Dandgridge home, I'm sorry to say that you're too late, Captain Jones." She held the letter out to him. "This came while you were gone." Before John could open it, she continued. "Miss Dandridge accepted Patrick Henry's proposal of marriage not two weeks after you had set sail. That's Alex's and my invitation to their engagement party."

John read the invitation silently. A tear began to fill his right eye, but the wounded Scotsman blinked it away before anyone had noticed. He regained his composure and looked up.

"I'm…disappointed, but not surprised." John glancing down once more at the document that testified to his lost love.

Anne studied the young captain. "We were sure you'd—"

"I don't deserve her hand, ma'am. Perhaps I never did."

"You underestimate yourself, Captain Jones."

"It's all my fault." John handed the invitation back to Mrs. Forrestal.

"Oh?"

"You see, even though Dorothea's father forbade that I write her, I sent a letter the day before David and I left to go see Mister Hewes."

"But nobody could blame you for that, John."

"But there's more." John took a large breath and let it out slowly. "Mister Jefferson warned me against going to see her during that trip to New York." He shook his head. "Even Captain Steele tried to stop me, but I was too bull-headed and in love to heed their warnings." John fell silent for a moment and then continued. "Nevertheless, I still have a moral obligation to pay a visit to Dorothea and her father to explain what they must perceive as very bizarre behavior on my part during these last few months."

Anne cleared her throat, causing Alex to jump.

Alex gave the others a shrug. "If you'll excuse me, my good friends, my presence is required elsewhere." He picked up Silver's mysterious package and and followed his wife down the hallway and into the drawing room.

David held up the commission to John. "Captain Jones?"

John gave his friend a smile. "Now that we're back, and no longer on the Silver Cloud, I'm just 'John.' What is it?"

"I won't be going with you to Philadelphia. Not right away, at least."

"But it's an order, David. We're to be officers in the Continental Navy."

"I'll have to follow you later." David laid his commission on the table and took Jane's hand. "I've decided to go with Jane to Georgia as you recommended."

"But that advice was given only because you were insisting I marry you and Jane aboard the Silver Cloud. You're both young. You have plenty of time for a proper courtship and marriage."

Jane gave John a plaintive look. "Please, Captain Jones. Can't you tell Mister Jefferson that David will follow you in a month or two? I'm certain David will accept the commission, but first, I want him to meet my father."

While Jane spoke, John noticed the others were staring past the young couple toward the main hallway. John turned about. Anne Forrestal was standing in the doorway with a letter in her hand. Tears were streaming down her face.

"What is it, Mrs. Forrestal?" John stood and stepped to her. "Are you all right?"

"I'm fine, Captain Jones, better than I've been in many years." Without taking her eyes off David, she walked across and placed her arms about his shoulders. After a long embrace, she kissed his cheek. "Welcome home, David." Then, without an explanation for her strange actions, she turned and walked to Charles and stood for several moments in admiration. After Charles and the others were thoroughly perplexed, she wrapped her arms about Charles' shoulders and gave him a long kiss on the cheek, just as she had done to David.

"Oh, Charles, my wonderful Charles!" After a moment, she stepped back and placed the letter in his open hand.

"This letter is addressed to you."

"I don't understand..."

Anne put a gentle hand to his lips. "Shhh. The letter will explain everything. Please, read it aloud. It's important that the others hear it also."

Charles unfolded the letter and scanned quickly through the pages while Anne, Alex and the others took their seats. "This is the letter from..." He looked up at the elderly lady. "Do you know my brother?"

"I did for a brief time, when I was very young." She looked about at the others and back to her son. "Please read it, Charles." Charles gave her a questioning glance and began:

My dear Brother Charles:
By the time you read this letter, my wife and I will be well on our way toward our destination—a place of which I have never spoken. Yes, as you've suspected I would, I've taken the entire treasure. But in so doing, I have not violated my word to you. My promise, if you will

remember back to that first night I met Captain Jones, was that you would receive compensation far beyond your dreams.

Your treasure is the most wonderful and fitting I could possible give to you, my beloved Brother, and it is infinitely greater than the gold and silver which now lies in the lazarette of the Silver Cloud.

I had never told you the story of your youth, always waiting for that perfect moment that never seemed to come. It wasn't until I saw the name of Alexander Forrestal on one of the five letters David brought to you in April that I realized it was finally the right time.

Like you, I was purchased by James Taylor when I was just a pup. My mother, bless her soul, was a tavern maid and couldn't keep me. But unlike you, I had a double portion of the wanderlust running through my veins, and ran off to sea when I was nine. As I've told you often, that's how I lost my leg and ended up a cripple at ten years old. You'd have thought such a thing would have cured me of ever wanting to go back to sea, but at fifteen, I ran off to England on a merchantman. But before I left, our adopted father made several trips to Old Greystone prison, as we called the place, to purchase the release of a girl who'd been a pirate in Calico Jack Rackham's crew. The girl spent several weeks in our home trading sea stories with me until her father, William Cormac, came from South Carolina to collect her. I shipped out with them to Charles Town, and then continued on this same merchantman across the sea to Bristol.

It was during this voyage that I was befriended by the professor from Oxford University. He offered to educate me in exchange for my stories about Blackbeard, John Flint, and the other pirates I'd sailed with. As you already know, that's where I learned my cooking skills and the King's English. It was during this time that pour father purchased you, and when I returned from England eight years later, I met you for the first time. Soon after, I began to notice that a letter came from Charles Town every two months, as regular as the rising of the sun. Being the nosey fellow I was, I found and read several of those letters. I kept my ability to read a secret from Father, so it was very easy to keep abreast of all his affairs, as he often left the letters about his desk. They were all about you and the girl Mister Taylor had helped free from Greystone. One of the older letters explained the whole thing—how you were born in Cuba and were then sold to Mister Taylor in '20 for one hundred pounds, all at your grandfather's direction. Every subsequent letter contained ten pounds. I can only assume it was to keep our father quiet about your nativity.

I began to look more deeply into the matter and succeeded in collecting the documents you have just now turned over to Alex and Anne Forrestal. Do you remember the trip I took to Havana in '38? You pleaded with me to let you come along, but I wouldn't allow it. That's when I acquired the guest register and bill of sale for the infant child named Charles Noble.

You were born to Anne Bonny and Jack Rackham in late August 1719. They left you in the care of an Innkeeper and took to sea again. It was he who named you Charles Noble. As you probably know, Calico Jack and his crew were captured in 1720. Jack was hanged, but Anne Bonney and Mary Read were spared because they were both with child. When William Cormac—Anne's father—arranged for your sale to Mister Taylor, he paid the Innkeeper fifty pounds to tell your mother you had died in infancy, should she ever come back searching for you.

When old man Taylor died and left the shipping company to you, there was no longer the need for Cormac to send any more money. I lost contact with your mother, but not before finding out that she had married a wealthy shipbuilder's son by the name of Alexander Forrestal in 1725. Unfortunately, she was unable to have any more children after giving birth to your younger brother in Greystone prison. Sadly, that little soul died.

So, brother Charles, except for the part Captain Jones kept to split with his crew, I have the Treasure of Dead Man's Chest, and you have your family. And wouldn't you agree that you're the richer for it? Our paths may never cross again until we meet on the other side—wherever that may be. Until then, dear Brother, may the Lord grant you and your new family fair winds and following seas for the rest of your given days.

Long John Silver
Gentleman of fortune to the death

Ben Gunn leaned close to Anne. "That's why you asked if I remembered you."

Anne gave the old man a loving look, stood and walked to David. "Do you remember that first time we met, David?"

He nodded. "You nearly fainted. I must look a lot like my grandfather."

Anne gave David another kiss on his cheek.

"Is this true, Mistress Forrestal?" Charles lowered the letter. "Are you—my mother?"

"Yes I am, Charles, and every word of John Silver's letter is true." She walked to where she had laid the guest register, opened it to the seventh of August, 1719, and pointed to an entry signed by the innkeeper and herself, followed by Calico Jack's mark of a skull and crossed cutlasses. It was an agreement that Anne, who was heavy with child, would be kept at the inn until her child was born and she could return to the sea.

"Do you see, Charles?" She pointed to one of the entries. "Jack paid thirty-five pounds for my room and board, and the midwife. And look here." She turned a dozen pages. "The twentieth of August, 1719. It's the record of your birth."

In the open page lay a half-dozen letters and documents John Silver had collected over the years, each one verifying a portion of the story.

"There's more!" Anne continued. "This is your certificate of baptism, and here's the agreement and fifty pound receipt between Jack and the innkeeper that they keep and raise you as a God-fearing lad." She continued to leaf through the letters.

"You sold me?" Charles spoke slowly, with a tone of betrayal in his voice.

Anne stopped turning the pages and looked up at her son. A new flood of tears welled in her eyes and spilled down her cheeks as her joy turned back into the guilt she had carried for so many years.

"I was just a girl—young and full of the devil. Jack and I returned to the sea and...well, we were caught within six months. After a short trial, the entire crew was sentenced to hang. I wanted to return for you, but..." She wiped the tears from her eyes and gave him a pleading look. "You can see it, can't you? My father did what he thought was best for me. It was best that I didn't keep you."

"Answer my question. Did you sell me?"

"I..." She shook her head while trying to choke out the words.

Alex put his arm around Anne's shoulders. "No, Charles." He helped her to a chair. "Jack Rackham paid the innkeeper and his wife to care for you until he and Anne could return. It was Anne's father who sold you."

"My grandfather sold me?"

"Don't be too condemning, Charles. He didn't want the scandal of having a bastard for a grandson, but he also didn't want to lose you completely. That's why he arranged for you to be purchased by James Taylor. He was not a bad man."

"Was?"

Anne looked up at her son. "He died eight years ago, and took his secret, and my last hope of finding you, to his grave."

Charles looked at Alex. "Did you know any of this before today?"

"Yes, I did. We had been married twenty years without a child. When we finally consigned ourselves to the fact that Anne was barren, she told me the whole story."

Anne gave Alex a loving touch. "I took Alex back to Cuba to look for you, but the innkeeper told us you had died shortly after Jack and I went back to sea. He even..." She lowered her head.

"It's all right, dear." Alex put his arm around her and looked up at Charles. "The innkeeper took Anne and me to what he said was your grave. We stopped looking after that."

"Why didn't you come looking for me earlier?"

Anne looked up at her son. "Oh Charles, I'm so sorry about that. You were a part of my life I wanted to forget. I never wanted Alex to know that his young bride had been a pirate or that she'd had two children out of wedlock." The tears were once again pouring down her cheeks in unbroken streams. "I know I should have come for you sooner, but..." She broke into deep and convulsive sobs. "Please forgive me."

The guest register was still open, so Charles leafed through the remaining papers. Everything was there, even the letter from William Cormac confirming Anne's marriage to Alex Forrestal and the letter in which Taylor promised to keep the whole affair to himself.

"Mother?" Charles sat down next to her and put an arm about her shoulder. It was the first time he had called any woman by that title.

She looked up into his face. "Yes, Charles?"

"What's my real name?"

"Well..." She sat up straight and wiped away the tears. "My name was Bonny when you were born, but Jack Rackham was your father." She paused for a moment. "I suppose..."

Alex held up his glass in a toast. "It'll be Charles and David Forrestal! We—all four of us—finally have a real family."

John took a sip of his drink, then turned to David. "I suppose this means that with your new family, you won't need that naval commission after all."

Charles shook his head. "No, Captain Jones, he won't. My son and I will be too busy serving the American colonies through our shipping company."

Alex raised his glass again. "And between Jamaica and Charles Town, there'll be none greater in the Western Hemisphere!"

Epilogue

The Admiralty investigation of the near-sinking of HMS Wasp had gone on for two days and filled nearly seventy pages of testimony. It was late in the afternoon and the officers were tired.

Fairchild: I still don't understand how Captain Stevens could have been so unprepared—to be taken by surprise like that.

Hawkins: But he was prepared, sir. Every cannon was manned. Furthermore, he was so concerned by this second Silver Cloud's appearance that he doubled my inspection party.

Reynolds: Then why didn't the Wasp fire on the Cloud when she raised her gun ports?

Hawkins: At first I thought they had.

Reynolds: But surely you saw the Silver Cloud's gun ports when you rowed across from your ship. That should have...

Hawkins: They were too well camouflaged, sir, and they fired without raising the veneer that hid their guns.

Fairchild: They what?

Hawkins: Captain Silver explained it to me later. There were no covers, only a thin oak veneer that hid the guns from even the closest inspection. It tore away like paper in the first volley. Captain Stevens had no reason to suspect he was up against an armed ship.

Fairchild: There will be a ten-minute recess while the Board considers its closing questions.

(The hearing reconvened at 1640 hours)

Fairchild: We have only two or three questions to ask before we conclude this hearing, Lieutenant Hawkins. Mister Stewart will begin.

Stewart: How did this Captain Silver know you'd be the inspecting officer, Lieutenant Hawkins?

Hawkins: I asked him the same thing, sir, with the thought that if I hadn't gone aboard the treasure ship, the Wasp might not have been sunk.

Stewart: And?

Hawkins: He knew that I had inspected the first Silver Cloud when it was en route from Charles Town to Dead Man's Chest. He also knew that it's the Royal Navy's practice that the same officer conduct the inspection upon a ship's return passage to the Colonies.

Stewart: He knew you inspected the Silver Cloud before? How?

Hawkins: The mail, sir. He looked at nearly everything that passed through King's Town. Once he discovered I was on the Wasp and that we had been ordered to the gulf, he sent a false dispatch to Captain Stevens, ordering us back to Andros Island.

Stewart: Hmmm. My last question has to do with your capture. Would you sum up your testimony by recounting the events following the storm?

Hawkins: Well, sir, as I told the Board yesterday, the last thing I remembered before finding myself in the water was when part of the rigging fell to the deck above me and I turned to assess the damage. If you'll allow me to digress for a moment, that's one of the reasons I'm convinced the Silver Cloud sank.

Stewart: Very well. Please explain.

Hawkins: Consider it, sir. How could I have gotten from the inside of the ship to afloat in the water while I was senseless, unless the ship broke up?

Stewart: True, unless Captain Silver wanted you to believe that.

Hawkins: Sir?

Stewart: Did he ever tell you why he kidnapped you from the HMS Wasp?

Hawkins: He claimed that it was to pay back an old debt to me, and so that he could give me my share of the new treasure.

Stewart: And what did you do to earn a share of this new treasure?

Hawkins: He didn't say I earned it, sir. He said it was was because, in Puerto Plata ten years earlier, I had convinced our captain to leave him essentially unguarded.

Stewart: Had you done so?

Hawkins: No, sir.

Stewart: Interesting. Let's get back to your shipwreck, Lieutenant Hawkins.

Hawkins: After waking up, I spent two and one-half days on my piece of wreckage without food or water. When the storm had finally passed, there was no sign of the Silver Cloud. I was picked up by a fishing yawl at the latitude and longitude I told the Board yesterday, and was then delivered to a private residence near Saint Marks in East Florida, where a family by the name of Mendoza nursed me back to health. The Mendozas were, obviously, one of the few remaining Spanish families in the Floridas, and as kind as they were, the Spanish are no friends to the British. After I had been three weeks with them, two men came to their home. They spoke with Mister Mendoza for most of the morning, and then took me overland to the Georgia colony, where I was kept for the next thirteen months with another family named Clayton. Like the Mendoza family, the Claytons were also very kind to me. It wasn't long before I had convinced them that I wouldn't try to escape; that I didn't want to return to England and the war. I was given pretty much free run of the plantation. On occasion, I even went to the nearby town for supplies with Mister Clayton and his two older sons. In late August of '76 while on one of these trips, I managed to elude my keepers. I made my way to the British garrison at Saint Augustine, and eventually joined the crew of the HMS Expedition under Captain Alistair Eastman. I managed to return to England several months later. The rest you know.

Fairchild: That's a very interesting story, Lieutenant Hawkins, but I still have difficulty with the sinking of the treasure ship. Apparently, the thousand cannons did arrive in Charles Town, and it is true that a certain American Naval Officer; a Captain John Paul Jones, has given the British fleet fits for two years. But...

Hawkins: The treasure ship did sink, sir. She went down approximately five miles west, southwest of Saint Joseph Bay, just as I told you.

Stewart: How can you be so certain of that, Lieutenant Hawkins?

Hawkins: The piece of wreckage upon which I was found was twelve feet of the main deck and railing. I've thought it through many times and I'm convinced that the Silver Cloud couldn't have survived the forces necessary to tear its decking apart that way. Captain Silver couldn't have contrived such a large piece of wreckage, just for my benefit.

Fairchild: That's exactly what Long John Silver was, Lieutenant Hawkins; a master of contrivance. From what you've told this panel, and from the other information we have been able to glean from the Admiralty records, he's capable of anything, even such a piece of wreckage. But you stated in earlier testimony that it seemed strange that there was no other wreckage or survivors.

Hawkins: That's true, sir, and it did bother me at first. Then I figured the thing out. Isn't it possible that I could have been thrown overboard early in the storm, and at some distance from where the Silver Cloud finally broke up and went down?

Stewart: Yes, that's possible.

Hawkins: (to Fairchild) And you, sir…can't you also agree that it's possible?

Fairchild: (The Commodore shook his head to signify, "No".)

Stewart: I have one last question for you, Lieutenant Hawkins.

Hawkins: Sir?

Stewart: If you were unconscious, how do you explain not slipping from your piece of wreckage, especially in the storm?

Hawkins: I was tied to it, sir.

Fairchild: Tied to it? You were tied to piece of wreckage and you still believe Long John Silver could not have contrived the whole thing?

Hawkins: No, sir. He simply was not that powerful a man.

Stewart: Consider this, Lieutenant Hawkins. If you were tied, then someone had to tie you there. I know you're only a Lieutenant, but even you must be able to see that someone wanted to be sure you survived to tell your story.

Hawkins: I wasn't alone on that flotsam, sir.

Stewart: You weren't?

Hawkins: One of the other crewmen made it to the same piece of wreckage and must have tied me on until I regained my senses.

Stewart: That does make a difference. Who is this other man and how may we find him?

Hawkins: You can't, sir, because he's dead.

Stewart: Dead?

Hawkins: We were still in the storm when I regained consciousness. He lay at my side, still clutching the end of the rope that bound me. The side of his head was stove in from a heavy blow. He must have had the presence of mind to tie one of his own arms to the wreckage before he lost his senses.

Stewart: Can the people who found you corroborate your story?

Hawkins: No, sir, because he slipped into the sea that first night.

Stewart: Very convenient.

Hawkins: Sir?

Stewart: Nothing.

Fairchild: We appreciate your candor, Lieutenant Hawkins, and the cooperation you have given myself and the other members of this Board these two days. The Admiralty will publish its official findings in due time. Officially, I expect the record to show that the ship that attacked His Majesty's Ship Wasp was sunk in a hurricane off the coast of the British territory of East Florida. My personal, and unofficial opinion, however, is that your only purpose for being taken aboard the Silver Cloud was to provide this Captain Silver with the witness he needed so as to escape detection and pursuit by the Crown.

Hawkins: Sir?

Fairchild: From everything else you've claimed he's accomplished, it's certain that he could have made you believe anything he desired, even the sinking of his disguised frigate. As for the dead crewman on your piece of wreckage, it's possible he was already dead when he was placed there; killed when the Silver Cloud was hit by that same storm.

Hawkins: With all due respect, sir, I must insist that Long John Silver died at sea. He simply could not have…

Fairchild: Arranged for the storm?

Hawkins: Exactly! I can understand your interpretations of his other actions, but how would he create a storm?

Fairchild: My guess is that he had some other way of providing for your separation from the treasure ship. That storm was pure luck.

Hawkins: But you can't possibly know that for certain, sir. It's just as likely that he actually went down with his ship. With all due respect, sir, your line of questioning…well, it implies…

Fairchild: That I know something more? (Fairchild pulls folded letter from his file) I shouldn't be showing you this, but in October 1775, approximately four months after you were rescued, I received a most interesting letter from my cousin in Philadelphia where he's one of the principal stockholders in a very large bank. When I first read it, I knew it was important, but didn't know why until yesterday when you described Captain Silver and his treasure. Listen to this section of the letter and see if you don't come to the same conclusion as I have: "Something strange occurred last Thursday evening that I thought you might want to know. Benjamin Franklin, Thomas Jefferson, and three other gentlemen made an after-hours visit to our bank and spoke with Mister Harding for nearly an hour. The three unknown men made quite a spectacle. The oldest of the three was wearing a mechanical left leg that made a snapping sound every time he took a step. The second, a man in his forties, was missing his right hand, and the youngest had flaming red hair and radiant green eyes. After they left, Mister Harding told me that they would return at midnight with thirty-eight oaken barrels. It was a King's ransom in gold and silver; approximately 800,000 pounds. The entire sum was deposited in one of Mister Jefferson's personal accounts. I asked Mister Harding who the other gentlemen were and he told me that Mister Jefferson would not say." (Fairchild to Lieutenant Hawkins) Well, Lieutenant Hawkins?

Hawkins: I don't know what to say, sir.

Fairchild: Lieutenant, if and when Captain Silver contacts you next...

Hawkins: Sir?

Fairchild: Nothing, Lieutenant Hawkins. (to the board) Unless further evidence comes to light, I declare this hearing and the matters of the attack on His Majesty's Ship Wasp, the pirate, Long John Silver, and the Treasure of Dead Man's Chest officially closed.

THE END

Thank you for buying our book.

For sales, editorial information, subsidiary rights information
or a catalog, please write or phone or e-mail

iPicturebooks
1230 Park Avenue, 9a
New York, New York 10128, US
Sales: 1-800-68-BRICK
Tel: 212-427-7139 Fax: 212-860-8852
www.BrickTowerPress.com
email: bricktower@aol.com.

For sales in the UK and Europe please contact our distributor,
Gazelle Book Services
Falcon House, Queens Square
Lancaster, LA1 1RN, UK
Tel: (01524) 68765 Fax: (01524) 63232
email: gazelle4go@aol.com.

For Australian and New Zealand sales please contact
Bookwise International
174 Cormack Road, Wingfield, 5013, South Australia
Tel: 61 (0) 419 340056 Fax: 61 (0)8 8268 1010
email: karen.emmerson@bookwise.com.au